THE ANATOLIAN

THE ANATOLIAN

Elia Kazan

ALFRED A. KNOPF NEW YORK 1982

THIS IS A BORZOI BOOK
PUBLISHED BY ALFRED A. KNOPF, INC.

*Characters, events, and business establishments in this work are purely fictional. Any
resemblance to persons living or dead, or to localities present or past, is totally coincidental.*

Library of Congress Cataloging in Publication Data

Kazan, Elia.
The Anatolian.

I. Title.
PS3561.A93A82   1982   813'.52   81-48611
ISBN 0-394-52560-4   AACR2

Manufactured in the United States of America
FIRST EDITION

To the Unredeemed

THE ANATOLIAN

JANUARY 1909

Stavros Topouzoglou, the Anatolian, first son of Isaac Topouzoglou, lay in state, his arms folded across his chest, his head supported by an old-country bolster, his face open to the ceiling, not a dead king but the prince of a divided family, their hope on earth.

He was asleep, but his breath pumped hard, his brows squeezed into the frown which, at thirty-two, had become his face. Stavros was dreaming of his father, as he had so often since the day twelve years before when Isaac, the patriarch of a terrified family, had sent his eldest son west, down the road to Ankara, driving a donkey on whose back had been piled the entire wealth of the family. Stavros's mission: their salvation.

Over Stavros's bed, at its head, was a small framed photograph, a likeness of his father, Isaac. Its face was turned to the wall.

On the floor, within reach, were the young man's hook-and-eye black shoes and, in one of them, an unsheathed knife. Its end was square but its edge honed sharp, the blade weavers use to trim the wool knots of the rugs they work. Stavros had carried it ever since his days as a hamal on the Constantinople waterfront.

On the floor, at the foot of the bed, lay a woman. The Anatolian slept alone. If you were a female on the island of Manhattan in the year 1909 and Stavros Topouzoglou brought you home, what sleeping you did you would do on the floor. There he'd spread a hard-knot kilim and in the course of the night's shuffling his guest would move, or be moved, from the bed to the humbler place.

It was a bitter January in New York after a mild December and it was a small cold room they occupied. The single window onto the tenement's air shaft was curtained with grime and old frost. There was a bedroom that would have been more comfortable; in fact, it had a coal stove, since it was back to back with the kitchen. But Stavros kept that room inviolate; no one entered it except his sister, who cleaned it daily. The arrival in Weehawken of his father, herding the members of the Topouzoglou farmily from the Anatolian port of Smyrna, an event for which Stavros had labored seven full years and more, was now only thirty-six hours off; this other room was for the head of the family.

Stavros had furnished it as he knew Isaac would wish. A plate shelf was ready for the icons which would be coming. There also would be placed the lamps of holy oil; one small flame already burned by day and by night.

Until a few months ago no woman "from outside" had ever passed the night in the apartment. Stavros had made it a policy not to have intercourse more than once a week, on Saturday night, and that with only one spending. Repeated *gamo* drained his energy and for a man of his purposes, maximum energy at all times had been essential.

But four months ago there had come a change in his behavior. From the time he'd accumulated the last of the money necessary to bring his family to New York City, from the day he had, through the agencies of the Greek Orthodox Church, dispatched those final dollars to Smyrna, the harbor city on that distant shore where his family waited, the resolve which had been the core of his life for so many years had relaxed.

Until then he had done what his sister called his "dirty business" discreetly; he would bring each Saturday's woman into the apartment without Fofo seeing her, entering alone, ordering his sister with a quick shift of his eyes into the kitchen, closing the kitchen door, then leading his choice for the evening into his small, dark bedroom.

But while previously his sister could be sure that when she woke on Sunday whatever had taken place was finished and whoever it had been with had left, in the last few months Fofo had come across a number of her brother's prostitutes on the morning of the day of the Lord. This development dismayed her. "I think Father's coming right in time," she said, speaking to herself in Greek, which gave her moral judgment greater weight.

There were other changes, which Fofo could only guess at. Another side of the young man was emerging, one that would dominate later periods of his life. An indication: He'd begun to prolong his pleasures— Stavros learned with astonishment the extent of his sexual capacity—and what used to take place in discreet silence was now clearly audible to Fofo, sleeping on her mat on the floor of the front room; on Saturday nights she stuffed cotton in her ears.

Having money to spend at last, Stavros, known in the New York rug market as Joe Arness, now allowed himself certain Western indulgences: a phonograph for instance, "His Master's Voice," and a stack of records, among them many *amanees*, the Turkish songs Anatolian Greeks prefer, but also Caruso; Stavros found that the Italian tenor expressed his own newfound yearnings and he played "The Pearl Fishers" when he came home from work.

And further: There was always a supply of ouzo at hand, and the nargileh, new at his bedside, was in frequent use, its smoke bubbling through water to scent the apartment. Stavros's appearance had changed too. He combed and brushed his hair more carefully, often shaved his bluish beard twice a day. It even appeared that for the first time he was able to enjoy a friend of the opposite sex who was not a prostitute. He brought visitors home even on week nights, jolly new friends, who called him "Joe." Fofo could hear her brother's voice mixing with theirs, sometimes shouting about politics, other times laughing over stories and jokes. There were songs too, and, as the level in the bottle dropped, dancing.

For these new pleasures Stavros was enjoying, the Turks have a word: *kef.* Stavros had discovered *kef.* Having paid his debt to his tradition and to the father who had trusted him in a time of crisis, having fulfilled his duty to his family, he was now free to please himself.

Well, not quite. Stavros's days were as active as he could make them, but night brought mysterious and disturbing dreams. It was as if a flagstone had been lifted off a sepulcher. Events which had troubled him twelve years earlier and should have been forgotten, were still demanding expiation. Why don't they lie still, Stavros wondered, why aren't they silent? Again and again in these private visions, he would beg his father's approval for what he had done or his pardon for what he had not, and always, in these old scenes relived, he was precisely at the age he'd been when he last saw Isaac—a boy of twenty, obedient to the weight of his father's authority.

There was this oddity: Stavros felt that if he treated the prostitutes he brought home badly enough, he might not be losing his father's favor. This was entirely imaginary, of course; his father couldn't have had the slightest suspicion of what his son was doing.

But, for instance, now: His room on the air shaft was cold, but not for him. The largest bundle in Fofo's baggage when she'd arrived in this country three years before, dispatched by Isaac to keep house for his eldest son while he was accumulating the other passage moneys, had contained a heavy quilt as well as the country bolster which presently supported the dreaming prince's head. This quilt, thickly padded, adequately protected Stavros from the cold. But the woman on the floor had no such protection. Lying on the unyielding flat-weave carpet, she was clenched under her overcoat. Her face was unnaturally pale, drained of color as of blood, her hair not golden but lemon, and under her eyes, the smudge of exhaustion. Now the rattling of her teeth woke her. She needed more sleep and could not hope to get it while exposed to the freeze of that dawn-still-dark, so she reached, without opening her eyes, for more cover. When she pulled at the quilt which covered Stavros Topouzoglou, she made a mistake.

"Fofo!" he called, summoning his sister who was always within the range of his voice. Having so commanded, he pulled up the quilt and returned to his dream—confident that Fofo would know what he expected of her. After all, why had she been sent him except to keep things "correct" and to see that the precious prince did not sicken from a diet of American cooking.

Fofo was a doughty little warrior with square shoulders and an unaccented figure. She still wore the heavy black stockings and high laced shoes she'd brought with her from Anatolia three years before. The fact that her brother's "mousetraps" wore light-colored stockings confirmed the impression she'd formed the day she landed in Hoboken—that most American women were, or had recently been, prostitutes.

Now she minced into the doorway of the bedroom—what a show of courtesy!—then waggled her hand at the visitor, at the same time arching her eyebrows seductively and cocking her head to one side. Despite the eloquence of this little performance, the woman on the floor did not understand what was being asked. So Fofo, overcoming her revulsion for the visitor's undergarments, scuffed to a corner of the room, picked up everything the woman had been wearing when she arrived the previous evening, walked out of the bedroom, all affability, turned down the hall with a smile and a sweep of her head—follow me please!—and entered the bathroom. The woman had no choice but to follow. Shortly thereafter she was dressed and out of the apartment. The family heir, perfectly protected, took no notice.

Fofo tiptoed to her brother. "Stavros," she whispered, "Father Rondiris is coming. Soon. Now. When you said."

"*Ghet burdan!*" erupted the young prince in Turkish, a language spoken by men of uncertain patience to deal brutally with animals and absolutely with women.

Fofo backed off, but still hesitated; it was Stavros who'd asked the priest to come Sunday after mass and bless the apartment, cleaning it they hoped, before the big day, of what Fofo with her broom and mop could not: the invisible stains of sin. Then, from where she lingered in the doorway, Fofo heard a softer sound, that of a plea: "*Baba, yapma, yapma, Baba.*"

Turkish: "Father, don't, don't, Father."

It was not a moment to intrude on. Fofo retreated down the hall in her bedroom slippers.

He was seeing his father at the window of the great stone government house where the Wali, the governor of their province, had escorted him so that the petty bureau workers, those sycophants who filled the other corners of the room with their murmuring and conniving, and the soldier guards who stood in rigid silence across the entrance would not notice, even though they all knew what transpired whenever the Wali led anyone to that far corner and to that particular window.

The Wali, his back to the room, lifted his arm and held out his hand, tilting his head so that his eyes would be averted from what was about to happen. The dreaming prince, now again a boy, could smell the heavy perfume he wore and the perspiration that it covered.

Then he saw his father, the object of his deference and devotion ever since he had known deference and devotion, bend over, clasp the hand of the man who had the power, and kiss it. Stavros knew that in that clasp a transfer of money had taken place.

Outside the government house, he saw himself marching under guard, up out of the pit in the ground which was the jail for the political prisoners of the province, then along the path toward the window of the Wali's office. He remembered that he was about to be released from detention by the action that was happening at the window, and again he pleaded with his father not to do it.

"*Yapma, Baba, Baba, yapma!*"

No one heard. Except Fofo in the front room, sewing up the frazzled border of one of the rugs on which she and her brother worked every spare moment.

Stavros could smell the clean, sour smell of his father as it mixed with the heavy perfume the Wali wore. "He's only a boy," his father said to the Wali. "He found the wrong friends. Armenians! But he's a good boy." And his father took the fat of his son's cheek between the knuckles of his first and second fingers and squeezed till the blood stung. "Come, Stavros, tell His Honor you're ashamed."

And the boy saw his father's eyes, moist and anxious. "I'm ashamed," he murmured.

But the Wali was behind his desk, doing other business. They were alone in a corner, and the father saw his son's mortification. "It's nothing," he said, as he had so many times before. "If you don't allow yourself to feel it, the shame does not exist."

"What choice have you?" asked the Wali, prancing toward them—he was on hooves now. "Accept what we drop." He turned his back and they came tumbling out, firm little apples as from a donkey, splurts of loose grapes as from a rabbit.

"Gather them up," said the Wali in his kindly voice. "Burn them for incense in your fires; they will remind you that you are in this country only by our generosity."

"It's our country, you took it from us," challenged the boy before he knew he had spoken.

He heard the sound of his father's blackthorn cane, his *bastooni*, as it hit the floor sharply. "*Zhoo-hut!*" his father commanded.

And he was silent as his father wished him to be.

The Wali looked quickly to identify the coin again before pocketing it. The flies, wild with the heat, bounced off and on and off the ceiling.

"It is our country. You took it from us," insisted the boy despite himself to the room full of Turks.

His father's *bastooni* hit the floor sharply again.

But in the corners they were murmuring to each other and didn't hear him. The guards didn't move. The Wali didn't hear. Isaac turned away, ignoring his son publicly.

Only Fofo, needle and coarse waxed thread in hand, heard. She marveled that her brother could have the same dreams night after night.

"It's nothing," his father was whispering urgently. "Remember— when you don't notice, you don't feel."

But his son saw the wounds in his corpus, like those in Christ's own body, saw the blood, thick, sanctified, seeping through his clothing and splattering the dust at his feet. "It's nothing," Isaac said as his life's blood fell to the ground.

The room was full of soldiers standing at attention. The boy in his dream could smell their sweat-soaked uniforms, the heavy khaki wool they wore winter and summer. They stood at attention, their eyes not even flickering as the boy sprang at the Wali, pulling back his hair to arch the head and open the neck for the knife, then slicing it through with his weaver's blade, cleanly, easily, as with the tender neck of a festival lamb. The soldiers stood at attention, still not moving, as the Wali went to his forelegs, his knees hitting the tiles, his head cracking down, splitting like a gourd, spilling its contents, white stuff, while the blood-red gravy flowed from his nose and mouth and the gap in his neck.

The boy turned to his father, wanting his praise.

But Isaac accepted this event as he accepted the others. "Yes, yes," he said, "but it's not time yet. A better day will come for us, but now, no, not now and not this way." All this with the blood flowing from his own corpus, like the sanctified blood of Christ, splattering the dust at his feet. "Now it's better not to notice," he said, smiling. "That's how we survived, because we were silent, we didn't bring attention, that's why we're still here to greet the better day when it comes."

The petty bureau workers haggled in the corners of the room, murmuring, the soldier guards stood at attention, trained to notice nothing and act only in response to orders. The Wali floundered over the floor, his back feet twitching, like those of a festival lamb, the blood thickening in his nostrils, filling them. He coughed and sneezed it out in clots as he died.

Then came the miracle. As the Wali died, the blood stopped flowing from his father's body. Isaac was intact again.

Now Stavros paid his father true honor. They came to Santa Sophia, together, entered the huge quadridomed clover of stone, taking off their footgear at the door, Isaac his soft dusty pantofles, Stavros his heavy field boots, he the acclaimed hero, the conqueror of the Turk—at last! The huge medallions of Islam were crashing down, cut loose at his orders from where the Turks had hung them five centuries before. They fell at this moment of change, the calligraphed wisdom of their holy book smashing to fragmented nonsense, clattering over the floor like the counters of an insane game.

The boy led his father to where the sun fell through the west arch onto the body of the marbleized king, to where King Constantine in white stone lay waiting for this very day, the day of his liberation. There they knelt and at last the boy had a sign from his father; Isaac put his arm over his son's shoulders and together they said the prayers that Isaac had learned long, long ago when he'd sung them—a boy deacon, Isaac had been—singing them now in a man's voice, rising and falling to praise the displaced God of the Greek world.

Now, as it had been foretold, the marbleized king found his flesh again; as it had been promised long ago, he came back to his life, and to his proper destiny. He was king again because of this boy's act. Constantine lived again in Constantinople.

"You were right," said his father. "You were right."

Stavros wept with happiness.

Others now came forward and the boy watched his father marvel as attendants brought forward the precious stiffened robes, five centuries unused. And having dressed the regal person, they escorted him to his throne. The great circular plaques of Islam fell again, the letters proclaiming Allah's wonder and majesty and power smashed to the floor like the sugar candy of Bayram, as Constantine mounted the three hundred steps.

The boy was looking at his father's eyes where they shone.

Now the moment had come to lead Isaac across the threshold of the apartment he had prepared for him. What had taken seven years to ready was now about to be tested.

The sea voyage, he could see, had brought the color back to his father's cheeks. His mother who had stayed below for the entire journey west—his sisters and brothers were still giggling about that—watched anxiously to see what her husband's verdict would be.

The entrance hall was dark, much darker than Stavros remembered it, and it was dirty. Why hadn't Fofo cleaned it? They passed now from room to room, Isaac not speaking, hardly looking, dark they were and cold, room after empty room. "The apartment isn't this big," said the boy to himself. "Perhaps I brought him to the wrong place, no wonder he doesn't like it. The one I have ready for him has only two bedrooms, mine and the big one for him. And there's the room in front where the others will sleep and where we work the rugs. When he sees the work I been doing, he'll be pleased and speak."

Isaac now passed into the front room and walked on the rugs that were being worked. He flipped over the corner of a carpet with the end of his cane and looked carefully at the spot the boy and his sister Fofo had been reweaving. Still he said nothing. Now, with an upward sweep of his arm, he turned over the whole end of a large carpet and inspected the border as it had been combed out and trimmed, hemmed and bound by his son. Then he sat on the ground, knees folded in front of him, and began to pull out the stitches that Stavros had made to bind that border. Isaac's hand moved with the speed of a sewing machine.

There was a sound from the hall. The girl from last night, half-dressed, was still making clumsy preparations to leave. Stavros indicated to Fofo with a furious jerk of his head that she should get that damned whore with her lemon-colored hair out. It was fortunate that father Isaac hadn't looked into the bathroom on his way through the apartment!

Now the father, satisfied with the border—he had sewed it up with the same incredible speed—stood up, *bastooni* in hand. Stavros took his elbow and turned him with his back to that damned whore whose huge, slack breasts were still unbound, and pointed him toward the big bedroom, the one he had prepared for him. The glowing icons were being put up, the open lamps fed with flame. All the family, the girls and the boys and his mother too, were there, trimming the lamps, arranging those other re-minders of divinity, the portraits of the saints in red and bronze and gold, lifting them to their places as they had been placed in their first, their original home in Kayseri.

The father looked at the room. *He doesn't like it,* thought the boy, when the man didn't speak. *I've failed.*

But then he saw the marks of hurt on Isaac's face, of pain and of lifelong humiliation.

"What is it?" said the boy.

"It's nothing," said Isaac, as the blood flowed again from his body. "There's nothing you can do."

With a spring Stavros was on the Wali again, driving his knife's blade home, this time into the coiled intestines, turning it, slicing, shredding, ripping, finally feeling the whole mass give and fall, the warm salt of the man's blood smarting on his knife hand. He saw it flood out, not only along his knife's blade, but everywhere, out of his mouth and nostrils in clots, choking him as it filled those passages, till he fell to his knees on the tiles and keeled over, his hind feet twitching out their last foolish strength.

He looked at Isaac, who gave no sign. "See where the marbleized king comes to life," Stavros cried. "Constantine lives again. See where he mounts the three hundred steps!"

Isaac gave no sign.

Suddenly he knew why his father couldn't speak the word of approval for which he was waiting. Now he understood the look of longing on his father's face.

"I promise you," he said—and Fofo heard him from where she sat before a rug in the front room, reweaving the hole a dock hook had ripped in its corner—"I promise I will take you back. We will go together as conquerors. We will wash that whole country clean with their blood and our water. All Greece will be all Greece again."

Isaac looked at his son and saw that he understood.

"I know this place can never be home for you," said the boy. "But listen, Baba, this America is a powerful country. When we go back we will have with us the money which is their power. With that strength we will take again what has always been ours. Then we will go to Santa Sophia together and kneel before the marbleized king and pray; we shall be witnesses when he finds his flesh again."

They could hear the other children, his brothers and sisters, where they sat on the carpets that were being worked in the big front room, singing of their lost fatherland across the Aegean, *"Hameneemou Patridah!"*

"How could I expect him to like it here," said the boy to himself, "so far from his own land?" Then he turned to his father. "Remember I am a patriot, and always will be. I will never forget our home which has been taken from us."

Now, at last, Isaac smiled at his son and he went to the door and closed it and they were alone in the room with the icons of the family and the little oil lamps. And Isaac sat back into the chair his son had prepared for him, not looking out the window at the new country, as the boy had planned, but turning the chair so that his back was to the window. In the silence they could hear the wheels of the heavy beer wagons from the brewery stables on the street below and the cries of the dying Wali as his back legs twitched their last. And they heard the singing from the front room and Vasso, the mother, and Fofo, her eldest, from the kitchen, Vasso inspecting the yogurt Fofo had prepared. "What kind of yogurt is this?" she complained.

Isaac and his son smiled. And finally Isaac spoke. "I can only wait and hope," he said. "If God wishes that Greece be great again, it will come to be. But it is not for us to say or to do, not for you with your knife and their money, but for God to do it in his own time. In his own way!" And Isaac pounded the floor again with his *bastooni* and on the plate shelf the saints shook, reflecting little tongues of quivering flame. Then Isaac kissed his eldest son on the side of the mouth.

And Fofo, who had come into the doorway again, silently on her slippers, and was watching her brother and wondering if she dared wake him now, saw him reach up and wipe the moisture from the place where his father had kissed him.

"I promise," the boy said to his father, "that the story is not yet written. I will take you back myself, take you to Santa Sophia in Constantinople and from there to Smyrna, miscalled Izmir by the Turk, and from Smyrna, the Christian queen of that inland sea, now martyred but waiting, we will turn inland to Ushak and Karahissar and Konya, to Eskisehir and old Ankara and so to Kayseri, to the side of the great white mountain, Aergius, where I was born and from which the water flows everywhere through Greater Greece."

"I ask only," said his father, "that my body lie there when I'm dead."

"You will live there, I promise, and when your time comes, I will bury you there."

"May it be as you say," Isaac said.

"It will be as you say," the son answered.

Then someone was shaking him. Stavros opened his eyes and he was looking at his sister. Still coming out of sleep, he said, "Damn fool! I just bring him here, already he wants to go back."

"Who? Who you talking?"

"Your father. Who! Nothing. I had a bad dream. What's the matter now? What?"

"For God's sake, get up," Fofo said. "Father Rondiris is here."

After a few minutes' talk, Stavros showed the old priest the apartment, especially the room he'd kept aside for Isaac.

"He will be very happy when he sees it," the priest affirmed. "He is fortunate to have a son like you."

"I have worked seven years to bring him here."

"Seven is the number in the Bible. God blessed him in you."

"I had a bad dream about it. Just now. Before you came."

"Don't believe! Dreams, they're the mischief of the devil. He will be very happy here."

Still the young man was shaken. Was his father speaking to him through the mystery of a dream? Why would his father want to go back? Why that now?

"Bless the place for his use," Stavros demanded. "Clean it of all past sins. Do all you can for me."

When the priest had done his work, Stavros bent over the hand he extended. It smelled of dried perspiration and the incense of the Byzantine liturgy. Stavros kissed it, at the same time slipping a half dollar into the curled fingers. "For the church," the priest said as he palmed the coin. And he was gone.

Then Stavros went into his bedroom, reached up over the bed and turned the photograph of his father face out.

Now Stavros Topouzoglou, known in America as Joe Arness, and his sister Fofo were alone for the last time. He ate a little of the food as she watched, sampled the *plaki*, the dry white beans sautéed in olive oil and garlic, without disturbing the appearance of the platter she had prepared with carrot curls and parsley garnish. He tasted the yogurt and with a nod of his head pronounced it good. He pinched the seeded flat bread that Fofo had baked, found it fresh and soft. He watched as she wrapped it again in moist cloths. He was satisfied.

Then he stood over her as she cleaned every room, making sure she was doing it perfectly. He made her do the hall, where the coal grit blew, twice. Each time it needed it.

"My God," Fofo said, "where will they all sleep?"

"Father will decide that."

"The three girls in your room, I suppose."

"Father will decide."

"And all the boys in the front? Is that what you . . . ?"

"If that's how he wishes."

Stavros had installed a wide banquette across one side of the front room, decided that two of his brothers could sleep there and two on rugs piled on the other side of the room. As for himself, what he didn't tell Fofo was that he had plans not to live in the apartment; he had already found himself a furnished room some distance away, close to the river, where he could hear the boats. There he would lead his other life, the one he'd discovered during those last months, the life of *kef*. After all, he'd done his duty. The true head of the family was coming to release him from obligation. That was as it should be. Stavros was mortal. Isaac was a god. Isaac was perfect. Stavros didn't want to be.

He decided not to go out that evening but to rest so that he would be fresh in the morning. As Fofo washed his best white shirt and collar and put an iron to his black suit, he lay in bed, face open to the ceiling. Tomorrow he would be free. And in this promise, he stretched out and was asleep.

It was a day when everything is the same color, gray. On a dock in Weehawken, two figures in black waited at the bottom of a gangplank. The freighter had carried passengers as well as a general cargo of rugs, figs and hides. Its scarred red sides, long unpainted, were peeling.

"Why you jumping up and down?" Fofo said.

"That's a cold river from where the wind is blowing," Stavros said. "Also because my father's on that boat."

"You look very bad today," Fofo said.

"My best shirt and tie."

"I am speaking of your face. Today it's worse than usual. You don't live clean life. Why couldn't you stop with those street women of yours sooner, so you'd be clean for your father."

"Shshsh! Quiet! They weren't all—what you said."

"I forgot. Of course! A rabbi's wife you brought home one night, like a stray cat. You think Father won't know that when he sees your face? Thanks to God he will be here now. Oh, look! They're coming." Disembarking passengers had appeared carrying their bundles and bags. "There, see—Michaelis!" She waved her arm and called, "Michaelis!"

"He can't hear you. Where? I don't see him."

"The first one. Carrying father's bag."

Stavros recognized the valise; it was of the heaviest cowhide and its great brass buckles caught the last of the light. But he didn't recognize his brother. Michaelis was wearing dark blue trousers, a black sweater and on his head, pulled low, a black knitted cap.

"That's one of the sailors," Stavros said. "Isn't it? Those clothes? Is Michaelis so thin? He looks sick."

"He wrote he was working on a fishing boat, don't you remember what he wrote? Yes, he's too thin, but—isn't he handsome? Look at his eyes."

"Yes, yes, it's him!" Stavros had begun to recognize the boy Michaelis in the gaunt man with the piercing eyes and the defiant set of head. "Allah gave him those eyes!" he said in Turkish.

His brother Seraphim he knew immediately, the well-ordered one among the boys. His hair, as always, was neatly parted and he had a small "businessman's" mustache. Wearing a faded gray overcoat and a fedora, he hesitated at the top of the gangplank, then reached back and pulled their mother, Vasso, up a pair of steps to the top of the steep, ribbed incline of planks. The old woman was wrapped in a blanket, head to foot. Vasso's favorite, Vacilli, followed immediately, taking the old lady's arm to support her as she began to descend, inches at a time, to the pier.

"Seraphim's carrying father's cane," Fofo said. "See in his hand."

Someone flashed by the slow-moving couple, Eleftheria, head down in a rush, dodging and slipping past the other disembarking passengers.

"Crazy!" Fofo said. "Your dear little sister, just like before, crazy!"

"Vacilli," Stavros said, "he has such good clothes. That overcoat! And that hat, like new!"

"He was serving at the table of a wealthy Syrian," Fofo said, "Seraphim wrote us. The clothes the man discarded, Vacilli took and fitted for himself. When he had what he wanted, he gave up the position. Immediately! He is so lazy, Vacilliki!" She spoke affectionately.

"I think he met a wealthy widow, those clothes," Stavros said.

"Your ideas, Stavros, are not right," Fofo said.

"Look at Mother. I think she's shivering," Stavros said. "Where's Father?"

"Making sure everyone's off. He would get off last. A rabbi's wife you bring home. I would think that just for your father's respect you would—"

"That's enough from you! Your mouth is like a camel's bell, clang, clang, clang!"

"As soon as he sees your face, he will know everything, how you been living. Then Christ Risen save you."

"One more word from you and I will throw you in the river with the ice and the dead dogs. Look—Eleni!"

Eleni, the middle sister, had appeared at the top of the gangplank. She looked around, then stopped as if she didn't want to go farther.

Behind her was Demosthenes. He'd been a child the last time Stavros had seen him, a butterball. Now he was a confident young man of eighteen, saying goodbye to some of the ship's crew, sharing a joke with them, it seemed. He was the only happy one.

Stavros had imagined it all differently: They would descend joyously, rushing to embrace him and thank him. "Eleni is crying," he said. "She's a beautiful woman. Why's she crying?"

"She didn't want to come," Fofo answered. "Seraphim wrote that too. But you don't read your brother's letters."

"They're too long. She grew up a beauty. What are you doing?"

"There's a woman's hair on your coat. Hold still. She's not so beautiful now, Eleni. She doesn't look good when she's unhappy. Only my silly baby brother, Demo, he's happy. What's the matter with them all?"

"It's cold here," Stavros said. Then he moved forward, stood on tiptoe and waved to his mother. "Mommah! Mommah!" he called. Apparently she didn't see him. Vacilli, who was supporting her, didn't wave back. Only Seraphim acknowledged Stavros's call with a quick wave of his hand.

Eleftheria reappeared from behind Michaelis, pushing him out of her path, leaping off the bottom of the gangplank, running toward them, almost tripping, then tripping, falling, leaping to her feet again, rushing at Stavros, throwing her arms around his neck, kissing him, kissing him again, then saying, "Oh, Stavros! Father's dead!"

Stavros had borrowed a wagon from a fellow Greek in the sweets business. It was a lumbersome conveyance, a large blind box on high wheels and creaking springs, drawn by two broad-back grays. Although the owner had seemed happy to lend Stavros transportation, Stavros made sure it would be waiting at the ferry station on the Manhattan side ("Again a boat!" Vasso groaned) by promising the man a lovely blue Hamadan, five by three.

Riding in the dark body of the sweet-smelling wagon, the members of the Topouzoglou family travelled east from the river to Cornelia Street, near the tracks of the elevated railroad, without seeing the sights. The middle daughter, Eleni, cried bitterly all the way. Vasso, the mother, rode up front with the driver and Stavros but when he tried to tell her something about the city, she didn't respond. Nor did she look around when they arrived at the apartment building. Stavros led her from the curb to the entrance, and up the four flights of stairs, stopping for a rest at each landing.

He could see how she'd aged.

He showed her to the bedroom he'd prepared for Isaac and for her. She walked to the bed, sat down, still wearing her overcoat and a kerchief over her head. There she waited. Seraphim brought in her baggage, most of it in bundles tied in printed cloth. Then Michaelis, hollow-eyed and weary, brought in Isaac's huge cowhide bag with its brass buckles as well as his overcoat and his hat. Vasso didn't tell them where they should put anything, though they looked to her for instruction. After they'd gone, she got up and closed the door. Later she refused food. All she said was: "It's cold, this country."

The children drifted to the front room, carrying baggage and blankets. They found places on the carpets that Fofo and Stavros had been working, scattered about the floor like refugees from a disaster. One by one, they keeled over and slept. Their new surroundings were of no interest, their new circumstances didn't excite them. They were too bewildered and too tired.

In the middle of the night Stavros heard the old woman in her room. She seemed to be singing—though it could hardly be called a song, more a metered recitation of grief, a recrimination against life itself and against her fate. Sometimes she seemed to be scolding her husband for bringing her to this place and abandoning her there. Other times she was heard praising him again and again for the same virtues. Finally her keening subsided. When Stavros tiptoed to her door, he could hear her breath pulsing. Twice more in the night her voice broke out like the howling of an animal; then she was still.

Early the next morning, Stavros pushed Seraphim, the eldest of his brothers, into the bathroom and locked the door.

"Now tell me what happened," he said.

"We told you—" Seraphim stopped. "Don't yell at me anymore," he said. "Ever since I got here, you've been yelling at me as if I was a hamal. I had enough."

"I'm the hamal. For twelve years I've been working worse than a donkey to bring you here. All right, I won't yell. Here. Sit." Stavros sat on the rim of the tub. "Tell me now, everything!"

"In the morning he told me to take the baggage to the dock. When I came home, he was dead. Michaelis was holding him. Dead. Mother told us his wish at the end: that we should go without him. We buried him the same day. Our last money. We arrived here with nothing—"

"What did he die from?"

"Nobody knows."

"What did the doctor say?"

"He didn't know. That doctor! A French Jew from Syria."

"How could he not know something? What did the man die from? Come on!" On his feet now, he was shaking his brother. "I've got to leave for the job. Tell me!"

"Stop that. That hurts. He was bleeding, that's all we knew. It was running all the time."

"From where?"

Seraphim got up and turned. "From here, behind. The doctor said he should lie still and it would stop. He said the sea air would do him good. 'Give him plenty of water to drink!' he said. Then he never came back. But it didn't stop. Bleeding night and day. Not much, but steady. Ask Michaelis. At the end he was the only one Father would talk to."

Stavros went to the door and shouted for Michaelis.

"Yes, I was holding him when he died," Michaelis said. "My clothes still have his blood."

"You talk to the doctor?"

"He didn't know more than we did."

"He knew we couldn't pay him," Seraphim said.

"He said something must have broken inside. He tried putting some cloth in the hole, but the blood still came. Father got weaker and weaker, like an animal bleeding to death. Then the night before we left, he told me to call Mommah—he knew what was going to happen—and he told her we should go without him."

"What did she say?"

"What could she say?"

The three brothers, thirty-two, twenty-eight, and twenty-five, sat looking at the floor.

"We didn't bury him like good sons," Michaelis said. "He was still bleeding when we put him in—" He stopped to control his voice. "We buried him at the edge of the old cemetery in the Armenian section, where they have Egyptians, Syrians, Arabs, even Jews. The grave was shallow and near the edge where the land crumbles when there's no rain, and falls off. There's a gulley there and I saw dogs running in a pack. I still think of the dogs running in that gulley."

Stavros left the bathroom, put on his tie and his coat, combed and brushed his hair. Then he talked to his brother Vacilli, standing by his mother's door which was still closed.

"She's still in there," Vacilli said. "She didn't eat since we got here. Go in and make her eat. Also it's cold here."

"When she's ready, she'll eat," Stavros said. Then he found his sister Eleni. "I'm going to the job now," he said. "I'll be back to eat, noontime. When I come home, I don't want to hear any more crying from you. Father wouldn't like more crying here."

Eleftheria, the youngest of the girls, kissed him. She was surprisingly jolly.

As he went down the hall, Stavros stopped by the door to his mother's bedroom and called through, saying he'd be back at midday to eat.

No answer.

Seraphim walked down the stairs with Stavros and told him why Eleni was grieving. "She found a sweetheart in Smyrna, a schoolteacher, good family. He wanted to marry her and—"

"I don't want to hear more complaints. You all looking at me as if I've done something bad."

"Everybody is afraid of you," Seraphim said. "You've changed."

"I've had a bad life," Stavros said. He looked at Seraphim rather scornfully. "You all had it easy," he said, "waiting for my money."

"We had it easy? What do you know?" Seraphim said.

Then he ran up the stairs and Stavros went to his job at Sarrafian Brothers, Oriental Rugs and Carpets.

His patience had been rubbed raw. "I don't eat any more of those looks," he said to himself. "I'm not their father."

At lunch he rushed into the subway and came home to make sure everything was in order. When he got to the apartment, the two youngest —the girl Eleftheria and the boy Demosthenes—were sitting at the window where he'd left them, watching a commotion at the entrance to the brewery below.

"Stavros, look!" Demosthenes said. "Those men with the horses. Cowboys, they call them. I read that in school. Stavros, come look!"

Stavros looked but not out the window. Scattered about their two front rooms were five figures in attitudes of despondency, like refugees, temporary assignees to a hostile territory. They angered Stavros.

Michaelis, disheveled in his merchant marine blues, was curled on the floor, knees to chest, reading a Greek language newspaper. He didn't look up.

That pimp knows I came home, Stavros thought. *Why doesn't he lift his head and speak to me?* The words of his anger were Turkish.

On the banquette, legs folded à la Turka, Seraphim, the neat one, had his suit coat off and was making repairs with needle and thread to the lining. Biting off the thread, he looked at Stavros and said, "It's too cold in this country."

At the side of the dining room table Fofo sat, slumped toward the kitchen where the dinner she'd prepared was cooking. She was cracking sunflower seeds and spitting out the shells.

Vacilli, the handsome one, sat at the air shaft window at the far side of the dining room, chin in palm, like an exiled nobleman waiting in a cheap hotel for a letter with good news—and for the maid to bring his breakfast.

Eleni in her faded blue blouse, her complexion a pale rose, was sitting in the darkest corner, looking so sad that Stavros went to her, wishing to bring her cheer. She was the beauty of the family, but tears had stained her face. Stavros couldn't think of a good word to say to her.

Was this why he'd given up more than ten years of his life—to bring these people here? They weren't as he remembered them, boys and girls, lively and curious, but lumpish adults, sitting slumped like exhausted animals.

"Don't worry about me, Stavros," Eleni said. She'd guessed his thoughts. "I won't be a stone here. He's going to send for me. He's going to send money and—"

"How can that mouse send money?" Demosthenes said from the front window. "He has no money. He'll send kisses, paper kisses, written on paper."

"Shshsh!" Eleftheria said, taking a swipe at her youngest brother; but she was giggling too. The liveliest of the girls, at seventeen she was ready to marry. As Stavros sat in the armchair by the front window, he pulled her into his lap. She came cuddling, put her arms around his neck and kissed him.

Fofo stormed into the entrance from the dining room. "All morning," she said, "I'm weaving the Sarouk where the dock hook ripped it, cooking same time. You believe that little dog on your lap came to help? Or any of them?"

"Patience! They just got here," Stavros said, waving her off. "Go on now—something's boiling over in the kitchen."

"The spaghetti!" Fofo said as she ran out of the room.

"Listen, all of you," Stavros said. "Fofo said the truth. You want to sleep here and eat, you have to work! Fofo is not your servant."

"There's no room in this place," Vacilli said. "We should get a bigger place."

"Count Vacilli, if you don't like it here, go live somewhere else."

"Now you're yelling at him," Seraphim said.

"You have a bed. Mother has a bed." Vacilli waved his hand at the floor. "Why for us there, where it's hard?"

"You're not lying on the floor. On rugs, nice and soft. You, Michaelis, you listening?"

"Don't worry about me," Michaelis said without looking up. "I have no complaints." He went on reading his newspaper.

"You, Vacilli." Stavros made the effort to speak quietly. "Suddenly in America you need a bed?"

"He means, Vacilli," Seraphim said, "that when we bring money, we will have beds."

"Money here comes by working not complaining," Stavros said.

"That's right." Demosthenes jumped up. "They're complaining all morning while you were gone, Stavros, complaining, complaining—"

"Close your mouth, puppy dog," Stavros said. "What you said is for me to say, not you."

Eleftheria kissed her big brother. "With you here," she said, "I am satisfied."

Now Stavros spoke to all of them. "I brought you here, as I promised your father," he said. "Now my duty is finished. I go my way, you do what you want."

Down the hall, a door opened.

Vacilli jumped to his feet. "She's coming out!" he said. He trotted down the hall, running on his heels.

The old woman was calling, "Stavros! Stavros! Come!"

Stavros went to her. She was brusque with Vacilli, telling him to stay out. But she called Fofo to her and gave her what looked like a bundle of rags. "To start the yogurt," she said.

"We don't need this, Mommah," Fofo said. "I make it every day fresh. Also, after all these days, this won't be—"

"I kept it wet," Vasso said. "Inside, you will see, it's still good. We were at sea, remember; the air itself was wet. Go, make it. This is from the old country—better!"

She pulled Stavros into the room and closed the door.

"Sit here, Stavros," she said, indicating the big armchair, the closest thing he'd been able to find to the one his father had favored in Kayseri. When Stavros sat next to her on the bed, she pushed him off. "I told you in his chair," she said.

Stavros had done some figures in his head that morning and found he'd sent his family exactly twice the money necessary for passage. He meant to find out what had happened to the rest. He saw how gray his mother looked, how hollow under the cheeks, and he spoke gently. "Mommah, so I won't worry more, give me idea, the money I sent you, where it all disappeared?"

"The money came to the bureau of the cathedral in Smyrna," she said. "Your father went to the office of the archbishop and they gave it to him. I learned from my uncle who used to sell candles to the church that you must watch a priest like anyone else, so I asked your father how much the priest gave him in Turkish pounds for your dollars."

"What did he say?"

" 'Go cook dinner.' "

"I know about priests," Stavros said. "When they give you their hand to kiss, it's curled so you can put coin in there. Then they say, 'For the church.' "

"For the church!" Vasso laughed. "Come, sit down," she said, clearing Isaac's coat and his cane from the chair.

"You didn't eat," he said.

"Maybe after I talk to you," she said. "First about the money. Your father had one good friend, a Turk. Every day they were walking up and down the Corso along the edge of the sea, their hands behind their backs, Osman Hassapoglou, his name, like this, walking up and down, together." She got up and showed her son how his father and his friend had walked. "You know, like business partners, talking important matters and so on. He was very friendly, always smiling, this Hassapoglou Effendi—your father gave him that honorary way of speaking, Effendi! 'Why do you talk to that Turk all the time,' I used to say, 'telling him our news?' 'He is helping me with the emigration people,' your father would say. 'Be quiet, woman!'

"So I was quiet. Then I noticed that when we had a letter from you that money was coming, we would also have a visit from certain government officials—"

"What did they want?"

"There were certain new requirements for the infidel *giavour*—always expressed with regret—certain papers to sign before we could leave the country, regulations unfortunately overlooked—all spoken in friendship, you understand. Then they would leave and your father's friend, Hassapoglou Effendi, would come and smile and say, 'Rest easy, I'll take care of everything, leave it to me.' Then they'd go, your father and his friend, side by side, their hands behind their backs like I showed you, walking up and down the Corso. Your father would come back and say, 'Nothing to worry. Hassapoglou is going to help us.' "

"How?"

"When I was so foolish as to ask that question or even 'Exactly what's the difficulty?' Isaac would say, 'Quiet, woman! Are you a commissioner now?' But within myself I was puzzled. For instance, how did those people and Hassapoglou know exactly when to come to take our money?"

"How much was he taking each time?"

"Enough so when there was a boat leaving we didn't have money left for eight tickets. Which is why all those delays, months and months."

"Years!"

"Yes, years. We also needed money to eat. Then we'd write you—we had to be careful; I had the idea they read our letters in and out—asking you to send more dollars. As soon as we heard from the church office that the money had come, we would have the same visits, followed by Hassapoglou Effendi with his sweet smile, saying, 'Leave everything to me.' So it went. Until one day I found my courage and I asked your father was it possible that his friend Hassapoglou Effendi was not his friend? Of course your father got mad. The only person he wasn't afraid to get mad at was me! 'Hassapoglou has problems too,' he said. 'There been threats against us, he is paying people to hold them back. What do you know of these affairs, a woman who never goes out of the house?' 'Nothing,' I'd

say, which was the truth. But I said, 'Maybe next time the boy'—you—
'sends money, don't inform Hassapoglou. Then perhaps you won't have
visits from the Turks. Therefore you will not need Hassapoglou to help
you.' But your father paid no attention to my ideas. Besides, he was right:
they knew everything. They even had a spy in the office of the cathedral
where you sent the money."

"Did he have a black robe and wear a cross of gold, this spy?"

"Don't talk like that, Stavros. So it happened the same way again and
again: When there was a boat for us, we didn't have money for eight
tickets. 'Let me sew your pants,' I said to your father. 'It seems your
pockets have holes.' "

"What did he say to that?"

"He gave me one of his from-on-high looks. But it must have been clear
to him by then, even though he said nothing, that the Turk was going to
keep us there until they had taken everything they could get. Because
without telling me, he went to the cathedral, and begged for a meeting
with the archbishop. He was always impressed by heights, your father.
The archbishop of Smyrna! This man all the Greeks loved, and there is
no doubt he loves God, because when your father, out of breath, fell on
his knees before him, he said, 'Get up! On your knees only for God!' I
don't know what more he said—your father didn't discuss important
matters with me—but the next time the Turk smelled money and they
came with another tax for the infidel *giavour*, another regulation overlooked, your father told them they could go to the devil for the money
because they weren't going to get any more from him."

"The mouse showed his teeth!"

"Still Hassapoglou came, this time without the smile. 'They are very
angry,' he said, 'but perhaps I can still fix things.' Then they went walking
together, side by side, down the Corso along the edge of the sea, and your
father told him the same thing."

"Still best friends?"

"But less! When they came back I went to the door to overhear.
Hassapoglou saw me and said—first time he spoke to me—'Our sweet
Isaac, he's making a very bad mistake!' and he shook his head and made
'tst-tst-tst!' with his tongue. 'But I am still his friend,' he said. 'I will still
worry about you all.' And Father said, 'You worry. I can't anymore.' For
the first time in months, there was color in his cheeks. That's good for the
health, to lose your temper once in a while. The next day he went to tell
the archbishop what he'd done, our little rooster, and there was a lightness
to his step, he looked like he looked when we married, the end of his cane
came up again when he walked, pointing ahead instead of dragging in the
dust under his feet—remember how he used to drag the end of that black
stick in the dirt?"

"Oh, I do, I do remember that."

"And it was natural that the archbishop took a liking to your father, the way he was at that time, and they had many conversations. 'That man,' your father used to say, 'he could have been a generalissimo in the army. He's not afraid of the Turk!' "

"I read about him in the *Atlantis,*" Stavros said. "They printed his message to the faithful at Easter. Wherever there are more Greeks than any other people, as in Smyrna—he said—it must be Greece again."

"That's what he was telling your father. He hasn't got a gun, this priest, not a cannon, not a single warship, but he talks like he has a great army. He wants to beat the Turk with words."

"But Father never mixed up in politics!"

"This priest made him a different man. He went here and there, boasting about the No he'd given the Turk. He would walk along the Corso declaring that they weren't going to get another *droosh* out of him. In other words, considering where he was and what he was, he went insane. All his life, he learned what was necessary to keep his family alive in the land of the Osmanli, and we survived. So last thing before we leave forever, he needs to boast in the bazaar like he's an evzone, or play back-gammon in the kaffenion, slamming his pieces down like a *strategos,* throwing the dice like a *palikari*—which he was not. Michaelis used to go with him, he told me this. 'Isaac,' I said, 'a priest can talk that way: He is protected by his beard and that long black dress he wears. But tell me, where's your beard?' "

"I would like to have seen him like that. Once!"

"Here! But not there. The Turks have ears too. Well, I got mad because there I was with six children, waiting and he's waving his hands and defying the Turk. 'The day will come,' I said, 'when his long black dress and his beard won't protect your dear archbishop either. Meantime he's got you crazy!' "

"You spoke to him with that tone?"

"What else could I do, sitting there with six children. And your brother Michaelis, when he began to talk in the streets the same way, I got frightened."

She was weeping now.

" 'Look at your children's faces next time before you are so brave in the bazaar,' I said to him, 'then go kiss the Turk's feet like always before. You know how to do that very well—I've seen you many times—so do it now and keep quiet.' And much more. I'm ashamed of the things I said to your father."

"Don't cry anymore," Stavros said. "It's not necessary to tell me more."

" 'God made you a coward,' I said, 'so don't try, at the last minute, to be somebody God didn't intend you to be. He didn't give you that strength!' "

"I would have hit you!"

"He did. And I was silent again. Then, after some months, we had a letter from you that you were sending money to take the place of the other money. Remember how you were angry when you wrote—that was the only time you complained, remember?"

"I was complaining more than I wrote."

"So I was waiting to see what would happen. He hadn't talked to me since he hit me, he didn't even ask for his dinner. He sat there, what I put in front of him he ate. So one day his dear friend Hassapoglou Effendi came by again. 'Tell him I'm not here,' he said to Eleni, a whisper. So Eleni went to the door and she told Hassapoglou, who smiled and said, 'When he comes home at last, tell him they're talking about taking his three oldest sons for the army. They're fine boys; the authorities have noticed them.'"

"They don't put Greeks in the Turkish army."

"They don't give them weapons, but to dig holes in the ground for the Turk's *cahcah*, yes. So what could he do? The next day when Hassapoglou Effendi came around saying he was sorry to disturb us, but as our friend and so forth, your father came out and they went walking again, side by side along the edge of the sea. And it started all over again. He played your father like a fish and every day he was finding new ways to get money: This one had to be paid or he would be angry and that one or he would not sign a certain paper and a little more everywhere just to keep them all quiet. Soon we were begging on the streets. Michaelis found work, thanks to God, with fishermen. I used to go meet his boat when it came in at sunrise and take the fish they threw away. We ate some strange fish. I used to go to the market when it closed and see what I could find, half rotten, under the pushcarts when they left for the day; we'd eat the good parts. The girls were busy reweaving rugs. Who do you think found them the work? Our effendi, of course! He'd collect their pay for them, too, from the rug merchant; but when he'd pay the girls, some of the money stuck on his fingers like honey. Even those few piasters our friend was taking. To have his shoes polished. But the girls never stopped. 'A little money is better than no money, Mommah,' they'd say."

"Eleni has someone who wants to marry with her?"

"Oh, yes, a man, like your father, who learned to smile the bazaar smile, say 'effendi' and bow and all the rest of what a *giavour* needs to survive among the Turks. He walks in the streets like someone is chasing him, slipping by like a shadow, close to the buildings. That kind of man we Greeks don't need anymore. I don't want Eleni to go back to that."

"So that's when you wrote me the letter?"

"Yes. Isaac was doing what I had made him do, eating shame. When he came home his face was white and I could see how he hated me."

"What did he say?"

" 'It's arranged,' he said, not looking at me. 'They're going to let us go. This is the last we have to pay. Hassapoglou promised.' 'You believe that?' I said. 'I have no choice,' he said. 'He told me stories how the authorities were threatening his family too. He says he doesn't like to do the things he's done to me, a good friend. But he has no choice.' 'You believe him?' I said. 'I have no choice,' he said. And that is when I wrote you to buy the tickets here, send the tickets instead of money, so take it out of his hands."

"I should have thought of it before."

"You think of those things only in the end. So the tickets came and I told Isaac what I'd done. I thought he would thank me. But the next day he started to bleed."

"From behind?"

"Yes. It would bleed for a few days, then stop, then start again. Your father went to bed and he stayed there. During the day too, like he was hiding from everybody, like he was ashamed. At the last, the only one he would talk to was Michaelis. Still it bled. I had to change the sheets every morning and every night. And the day the boat sailed, we buried your father in the afternoon. As we left the dock, he was there, Osman Hassapoglou Effendi, waving goodbye. Michaelis went down to the lower deck, close to him, and spit in his face. Hassapoglou smiled."

"Don't cry anymore," Stavros said, walking to the window. "You're here now, with me."

"Your father was a good man. He was also a coward. He knew one rule in life: If you don't let yourself feel, it doesn't hurt. Remember that?"

"How many times he told me that!"

"After he spoke with the archbishop, he began to feel, and that is what killed him. I knew where it was coming from, the blood. He kept putting his hand here." She touched the middle of her belly. "Everytime I talked to him and anytime he saw Hassapoglou on the street, he would touch himself here and sometimes he would push in and twist, as if there was a knot he was trying to untie. You see, the worry and the shame ate a hole in his stomach, and that killed him. Every day I could see from his face that the hole was getting bigger. You sent tickets, which meant to him that you didn't trust him with money. And that I was not his friend anymore. I saw his shame and I didn't give him any sympathy."

She began to weep bitterly, tears of self-accusation. "I said a terrible thing to him when he was bleeding. 'It's your fault,' I said, 'that we are still here. So now eat it.' Of course I didn't know, then, that he was going to die. No, that's not true. I saw it coming. But I had the children and all I could think of was getting out of that place. I had begun to believe we would never leave there. Well—we're here."

She stopped. The story was over. She had her head down between her knees and her body shook. Then it started again, the song, expressing her grief and her anger. But now it was not at her husband, the anger, but at herself. She'd killed the man just as he had killed himself.

And her eldest son pitied her, but he didn't try to comfort her.

After a time she got up and went into some bundles, searched there and brought out what she was looking for, a heavy ring of the oldest gold. "He told me to give this to you," she said. "Also this." She reached to where she'd put the *bastooni.* "You know what it is," she said, "and what it means when you take it."

She watched her son frown as he examined the ring—one would think he'd never seen it before. He tossed it in his hand as if he was weighing it, looked at her, then back at the ring.

Finally he thrust it on his finger. He took the black thornwood cane too, and put it down to the floor between his legs and rested his chin on its gnarled nob, a condemned man.

That was it. She was satisfied. "Your father told me, 'Tell Stavros it's for him now to say what everyone should do. We're fortunate to have raised such a boy,' he said. 'Tell the children they must pay him the respect they would pay me. And you'—he said this to me—'you pay him the same respect you would pay a husband.' He didn't say 'the respect you would pay me,' because he knew I didn't respect him by then."

That was all Vasso had to say. She left the room and Stavros could hear the voices in the front of the apartment grow quiet for they all wanted to hear what she had to say after her silence. Perhaps she was talking about the yogurt culture she'd brought, because Stavros heard Vasso say, "It lived through the journey, don't worry."

Stavros sat alone, until he heard them in the front; they'd begun to complain again and to quarrel among themselves. Where a few minutes before it wouldn't have mattered to him, it was now his concern.

His dreams of pleasure, of *kef?* Finished!

When he walked into the front room, they all saw the ring on his finger and their father's stick in his hand and they all saw the change in him, and when he spoke they were still.

"I say what happens here now," he said, and his voice had an angry edge. "You will do what I say, all of you."

Then he looked at them in some new way and he was not satisfied.

"This is New York, the new center of the universe," he said. "Everybody in the world wants to come here. You're lucky to have a brother crazy enough to work twelve years to bring you here. So now don't push your vinegar faces against the window glass and say 'tst-tst-tst.' Yes, Vacilli, you, I saw you, no more complaints why you don't have a bed too. One more unhappy remark out of any of you, my dear brothers and sisters, and I will show you a few games I learned when I was a hamal for your sakes. I hurt many people to bring you here, and with this knife"—he'd taken out his square-end blade—"I killed a man so you could come here. I put a heavy load on my soul for you. Remember that."

"I haven't complained," Demosthenes, the youngest, said. "I'm glad I'm here."

Stavros ignored him. "Another thing," he said. "Everybody has a duty here. This is a bad year in this land, 1909, but by the time you learn to speak the language, there will be work for you, sure, plenty! Meantime you're lucky I'm working and bringing in the—Michaelis! Don't read when I'm talking!"

Michaelis had been reading, or pretending to, all the time his brother had been speaking. Now he looked up. "We can't leave him buried as he is," he said.

"I know, Michaelis. Your clothes are soaked in your father's blood. You told me. You wish it were your own? You, Mommah, you were wishing you were in the grave with him so you could explain why you talked to him that way in Smyrna. But in a few days you will find your bed here more comfortable. Vacilli, it's too cold for you and Seraphim, you don't like my loud voice. You like the Turk's better? When they yelled? Forgive me, Eleni, but I don't want to see your nose in the air again or hear you crying. What I say to all of you is what you're going to do and what you are going to do is what I say. Because in America the story is work. Work is the life here. Because of that there is hope that one day we will be rich. When you have money here, it's stronger than guns and powder. Michaelis, you hearing me? Money is their cannon here. We will earn it and it will protect us. But I tell you this straight: If any one of you doesn't accept what I say, pay me back the money I spent to bring you here and go."

No one spoke.

"And now, Michaelis," Stavros said, "I think I understand you best. Put that damned newspaper down. I am talking to you about the Turk who killed our father by slow torture."

"I'm listening," Michaelis said.

"It will be the purpose of my soul to find this man, Hassapoglou, and end his life. I will cut out his eyes with my knife and the smile off his face, both lips. I will let the blood out of his throat and drain it from the bottom of his belly. And where he put my money, in the little sack between his legs, I will slice that off and offer his stones to the cats in the alley. I will cut his heart out, too, and throw it to the dogs that run in the gulley by the cemetery where Father is buried, and I will throw what's left in the slaughterhouse for the pigs to fatten on. Then, only then, will I be satisfied."

No one spoke. They saw the man their brother had become and they were satisfied that he wore the ring now and held their father's *bastooni* between his legs.

That evening, Stavros took them for their first walk in the new country. They passed many blocks and came to an elevated railroad where an engine without steam was pulling cars on tracks far above the ground. They marveled at this. Then Stavros took them to the Oasis where he thanked the owner again for the loan of his wagon and grays and, speaking Greek, introduced the members of his family. The owner gave each of them an ice cream cone, despite the cold weather. They watched how Stavros consumed it and followed his way. It was the first time any of them had tasted ice cream and they marveled at it. Even Vasso had a cone, not because she wanted it but because the head of the house put it in her hand. She turned it this way and that, shaking her head in wonder.

After which they walked home together, Stavros leading the way.

SEPTEMBER 1911

Stavros Topouzoglou, young king of a transplanted family, woke with his face clenched in a frown. The instinct he'd developed on the docks of Constantinople was speaking to him, a warning with no names, no particulars—only to beware. There were two things Stavros had learned as a hamal: to suspect everyone, and that it was necessary to display strength at regular intervals. Humans, like animals, he believed, respect only what they fear. But here? In the family? There was only one problem he knew of: his youngest brother, Demosthenes. The others had stopped their complaining, seemed contented. But Demo was a worry; for instance, there he was, asleep on his cot near the door, when he should have been on his way to school, and once again Fofo had to come charging down the hall to wake him.

"Get up, lazy boy!" She pushed the door open. "Up, good-for-nothing!" She kicked the end of the cot.

The boy bolted out of cover like a rabbit and ran from the room, covering his groin with his two hands.

"You put that boy to sleep in your room," Fofo said, "you ruin him, puffing up his pride that way."

"Only problem Demo," Stavros said. "He's with American boys in that school and he get few wrong ideas. I fix him up, don't worry."

"You should listen to me," Fofo said.

"I'm thinking here," Stavros barked. "Get out!"

As she did, there was the sound of knocking on the pipes which ran up through a corner of the room. This brought Stavros out of bed. He was naked because the heat was heavy that week and the single window of his bedroom opened onto the yard back of the apartment building, a space filled with drying laundry which added humidity to the heat. Stavros picked up the knife that he left in a shoe at the side of his bed every night and banged the pipe with the butt of its handle. Then he knelt on the floor, an unseemly posture for royalty, lowered his head to the metal sleeve which fitted over the pipe at the floor and called down, "Ladies, you want trouble with me, you get trouble. Coming right down. Eh? What you say?"

Three months before, Stavros had moved the family to this larger apartment on 136th Street between Broadway and Amsterdam, and now everyone had a bed.

As he put on his bathrobe, Stavros heard Fofo outside his door. "Downstairs those women, they complain to Schimmel, the janitor, again," she said.

Stavros took a swift look at himself in the mirror before striding out the door. "For what?" he said. He decided to shave his mustache; he'd look more American without it.

"Water coming through the ceiling again," Fofo said to Stavros as he passed her.

"I told the boys put newspaper under rugs when they wash," Stavros said. "They don't listen." When he tried the bathroom door, it was locked.

"Demo!" Stavros shouted. "I have to go on job."

"You trying make that boy hurry?" Fofo asked. "Won't happen. Also, like I told you, he don't work, that boy."

"He work in school! I want one man this family with education, commercial school. Also speaking American proper way."

"You making bum out of him," Fofo said.

"You take care house, Fofo, I watch Demo. He's my hope maybe we'll have one American in this family. Why I'm sending him to school every day." He banged on the bathroom door. "Hey, you useless, good-for-nothing bum—one minute more I give you, then I break door."

Stavros strode down the hall, past the French doors which provided an entrance to the dining room and so into the large front room. The new apartment smelled heavily of what Vasso called *ilatch*—medicine, that is —for the cockroaches, a nostril-shrinking, eye-smarting fluid, deadly to the little brown warriors. Add to that the smell of perspiring bodies, blended with garlic and olive oil cookery!

The large front room of the new place was full of rugs and carpets in various stages of reconstruction, repair and touch-up. Rugs were also laundered here. One end of the room had been covered with newspapers and there were pails and scrub brushes there.

The apartment had twin windows over 136th Street, and sitting in an armchair beside one of the windows, dressed in black, was Vasso, the mother of the family, nibbling with half a mouthful of teeth at an edge of dry toast. From her dominant position, she policed the work of her children. For recreation, she would lift her head and look across the street at the children playing in the orphanage yard there.

Michaelis was on the banquette placed across one end of the room. He was reweaving a destroyed place in a nine-by-twelve Sarouk carpet, framing the damaged area in slats across which he'd strung new web cords. At Michaelis's side was a Greek language newspaper. He'd glance at it between tying the knots of brightly colored wool.

In the strong north light from the windows, Vacilli was working over the medallion of a powder-blue Kerman carpet, touching it here and there with a fine brush dipped in dye and twirled to a point. With the delicacy and care of an artist, he was correcting damage done by a spill of acid.

On his hands and knees, Seraphim, the manager of this minifactory, was carefully trimming the fringe of a Hamadan runner. Stavros watched him work the heavy scissors in a true line, then sweep away the bits of white webbing twine.

No one looked up at Stavros until he said, "Who fixed the border this five-by-three?"

"I did." Demo had appeared, combing his hair. "What's the matter with it?"

"What's the matter with it," Seraphim said, "is the girl in the window across the air shaft. That's where you were looking when you cut this."

"Demo, Demo," Stavros said in a tone reserved for the boy he was so fond of. "Why don't you try to make your father proud of you where he sits in heaven at the right hand of Jesus?"

"I'll fix it," Demo said. "Don't worry. It's done."

"No, I'll do it," Seraphim said. "You better go to school because you learn nothing here."

"No school today," Demosthenes said.

"Seraphim give him job, something," Stavros said. "He will learn here, don't worry. Tell me boys, why so hot here today?"

"Air not moving," Michaelis said, wiping his chest and armpits with a cloth. At his side the Greek language newspaper's headline denounced the peace terms the Bulgarians were prepared to accept from the victorious Greek army. "You see this, Stavros?" Michaelis slapped the *Atlantis* with his open palm.

"Why so hot I tell you," Seraphim said. He was rolling up the runner and had two lengths of cord over one ear with which to tie the bundle. "When we sleeping, this old lady here, she come in and close every window. Then in the morning when we wake up, it's like oven." He indicated his mother. "Look at her!"

Because of the intense heat, Vasso wore no stockings, but above her pantofles could be seen the cuffs of the long, coarse-weave underwear she'd brought from Anatolia two and a half years before.

"She thinks Turks outside," Demosthenes said, laughing. "Like we're still in Kayseri, she believes that."

Stavros raised one of the windows and leaned out, turning his face up to the sky, which was as flat and white as a piece of blank paper. The heat seemed permanent and the cloud cover lowering to suffocate the inhabitants of the earth. "Hey, you, Mister, up there, dear Sir. How about some rain today?"

"No Turks on streets here, Mommah," Demosthenes said, still laughing as he took off the shirt he'd just put on. "This is America here, Mommah."

Stavros called into the dining room. "Eleni, put my breakfast on the table." He turned to Seraphim and said, "Those old ladies from downstairs complaining again. Coupla days don't wash rugs."

"We have to make living," Seraphim said.

"And, boys, please," Stavros said, "remember put newspaper under when you wash them. You forget that sometime, no?"

"Yes. No." Demosthenes laughed.

Stavros strode down the hall and into the bathroom. From there, they heard him yelling, "Fofo, look at this tub here. For God's sake, it's for a pig."

Fofo came up, scuffing and sliding in her slippers. "Your little brother Demo, so dear—make your complaints to him please." She knelt at the side of the tub and sloshed water around with a rag.

There was a knocking on the door of the apartment and the voice of the janitor.

"They sent Schimmel," Fofo said, getting to her feet. "The old sisters downstairs complaining."

"Tell him come back when I finish shave." Stavros hated to rush his morning shave and he performed that ceremony now with the greatest care. Clean-shaven, he closed the door and took off his robe. Squatting in the tub, he soaked a rag, soaped it and rubbed the suds over his body.

There was a knocking on the bathroom door. "Mr. Schimmel say he can't come back later," Fofo called. "He has much work."

"Tell him come get in bath with me, we talk," Stavros said.

The janitor spoke. "Here is Schimmel, Arness. I told you many time, you breaking law. This is not factory building here."

"You speaking to me, Schimmel?" Stavros said, projecting his voice. "Because I can't hear what you say. Fofo, take Mr. Schimmel, give him nice coffee. We have coffee together, Schimmel, for God's sake. Fofo, go on."

"*Mein Gott,*" Schimmel called, "you don't want understand nothing. If it wasn't for me, owner, Mr. Wolkenstein, put you out on street already, whole family."

"So how much you want this time, Schimmel?"

"You don't 'preciate what I do for you, Arness."

"I 'preciate you want money from me again. Second place, next time tell Mr. Wolkenstein no hot water coming here, and when she comes, same color his shit. Tell him that if he complain."

"That apartment from Miss Lawler sisters, they have marks on ceiling from your water here, different colors. If I show Mr. Wolkenstein, he call police. All right, all right, miss—sure, sure, I take coffee."

"Give him egg too, Fofo. Schimmel, have egg before Wolkenstein drive you crazy. I come out quick, coupla minutes."

Stavros didn't hurry. He rubbed his body with a towel still wet from his brother Demo's use, then combed his hair, trying three different parts before deciding on the one he thought best. In his bedroom, he found the pile of linen Eleni had washed and ironed the day before. He put on B.V.D.'s, then pulled his trousers out from under the mattress, where he'd put them the night before to reinforce their press. Now he held up the coat of his suit, inspecting it with affection. It was a garment his brother Vacilli had urged on him, a flamboyant cut featuring a pinched waist and a flared skirt.

"Remember this is America," Vacilli, the touch-up artist, had said. "Clothes here is big liar, make thief look honest, weak man strong, beggar man rich. Salesman must look like he need nothing from nobody. When you put this coat on, you will make impression like what you will soon be, please God—famous importer high-class goods, plenty capital, so forth, so on. Big!"

It was time now to inspect the shirt to which Eleni had attached a starched collar. "Eleni!" he shouted. "Why you give me this collar, Eleni? Where are you? Fofo! Where the hell she disappearing all the time, that girl Eleni?"

Fofo came running. "She's writing letter again," Fofo said, "to Smyrna. Also Mr. Schimmel waiting at table for you."

"Why she sends me on Fifth Avenue with this collar?" he said just as Eleni hustled in. He unfastened the collar from the studs which attached it to the shirt, then ripped it down the fold where the fray was and handed both halves to Eleni. "Look!" he said. "Close examination not necessary."

Eleni ran for a fresh collar.

Again Stavros looked in the mirror. Vacilli's influence had developed in him a concern for the impression his clothes made, and he'd taken to studying other men on the street and comparing his own image reflected in store windows. It was a contest he needed to win.

Eleni was back, followed by Eleftheria with a necktie. "I pressed it," she said.

Stavros put the shirt on, fastened the collar to the shirt, and tied the tie. He looked at himself in the mirror as his three sisters watched anxiously. He was a handsome man of a certain style.

Now he was ready for Schimmel. Striding into the dining room, he sat in his place at the head of the table. "How's coffee, Schimmel?" he asked.

"Coffee is coffee," Schimmel said. "We must talk about this serious situation here, Arness. Your apartment must not be used for factory."

"You hurt my sister's feelings when you make such a remark, coffee is coffee. Fofo, where is Mr. Schimmel his egg? Here, Schimmel—meantime, some cheese? Olives? And my coffee—where's my coffee? Eleni! Eleni, Mr. Schimmel don't like your coffee."

"About your water leaking down all the time," Schimmel said. "You've been washing rugs on the floor here, right? You make me much trouble that way. But so far I told Mr. Wolkenstein nothing. This problem between you and me, Arness. Friends. My only wish to help you."

"So tell me, so friendly," Stavros said, "how much you want from me this time? When my family come here, I give you five dollar, last month, again five. You remember?"

"Yes, but every day I hear complaints, every day I have to protect you. Big trouble for me, keep those old ladies quiet."

"So I go down, make them quiet. Permanent!" He made a vulgar gesture.

From her chair by the window, the old lady, Vasso, snickered.

Fofo rushed in with coffee for Stavros. She watched anxiously.

"You know, Mr. Schimmel," Stavros said, "everybody has some kind trouble. You have lazy wife. When she don't give you breakfast, you come with complaints because you know coffee waiting here."

"Oppa!" Michaelis muttered in the other room. "Now you said something!"

"You changing subject again, Arness," the janitor said. "You wash rugs here, right?"

"Couple times, sure, maybe. Always with newspaper under—right, boys?"

"Absolutely!" Seraphim said. There was a murmur of concurrence from the others.

"Why not little water?" Fofo said. "What's the matter with that?"

"I told you, it goes through the ceiling." Schimmel stamped his foot on the floor impatiently. "Lawler sisters underneath, they—"

"Tell 'em next time I be more careful," Stavros said. "O.K.? Finish! Eat your egg, for God's sake, it's getting cold. Where's his egg, Fofo?"

"Look out on fire escape, Arness," Schimmel said as Eleftheria rushed in with a fried egg on a plate and put it before the janitor. "Thank you, little lady." Schimmel smiled at her. *"Schön,"* he said. Then he turned severe again with Stavros. "Always five, six rugs drying there."

"Not always. Once in while, coupla pieces, maybe," Stavros said. "One, two."

"No, no, many pieces!" Mr. Schimmel said. "But I tell Mr. Wolkenstein nothing. You know how those Jew people are when they are boss. He hears about it, first thing he raises your rent."

"What's the difference, I pay him, I pay you?" Stavros said.

"The difference?" Schimmel said. "You pay me less."

At that instant a face appeared in the window that opened onto the fire escape, the face of their neighbor Mitrovic, a city fireman. "Arness, I hear you hollering those one, two pieces lies to Schimmel," he said, raising the window sash and putting his head in. "This fire escape half and half—right? Schimmel, he put his goddamn wet rugs here not once in a while—every day! On my side too. And they smell from acid and paint and God knows what kind poison stink, Schimmel!"

The young king was beginning to lose his patience. "Get out your head, Mitrovic," he yelled. "Don't show your ugly face to me. You bother my little sister again yesterday, Mitrovic. One more time, I kill you."

"How I bother your sister?"

"You smile at me with that pig's smile, that's how you bother me," Eleftheria said.

"With the smile of a hog," Stavros added, "you Serbian garbage!"

From the front room, Vasso hissed.

"How you going kill me, you little Greek cockroach? I am hundred pounds more than you."

Stavros pulled his square-end knife from under his coat. "You see this knife?" he said. "Next time you don't see it, because it will be inside your body. If you make one more complaint how our rugs smell, I throw your half-wit son off this fire escape!"

The brothers on the floor of the front room nodded and chuckled.

"Then I do you big favor, Mitrovic. I throw your fat cow wife off too."

The Topouzoglou family burst out, a roar of laughter. The old lady trembled with pleasure. Michaelis crowed like a rooster.

"Now put down that window quick and get out from there." Stavros made a sudden move toward the fire escape, knife in hand, and Mitrovic disappeared, cursing in an unknown tongue and calling on the police.

"You too, Schimmel," Stavros said. "Finish my egg and get the hell out— Where is he? Where he went? Schimmel?"

Schimmel had slipped into the dark hall. Fofo pointed.

"Oh, there, eh? Come on—you too, out!" Stavros said. "You bother me too much. Every week coming here for money. No more. Finish! Tell those two Irish cows downstairs, Miss Lawler number one, next time I hear complaints from her, I throw boiling water on her canary birds, tweet tweet." The family murmured sounds of admiration. "She put those damn birds under our window to bother me. And tell Miss Lawler number two, stop her poodle dog shitting on the stairs where I step. Also she is losing her hair, tell her, from too much worry. And your dear wife, Schimmel, tell her you're fucking Mitrovic's dear wife, that's why you hide in dark when you see him. You think we don't know those things here, what's happening when Mitrovic goes to fire station?"

"All right," Schimmel said. "I get idea you be happier dealing with Jew boss on this problem."

"I have no money for you, Schimmel," Stavros said. "Goodbye."

Stavros walked into the front room. "Vacilli," he said, "you finished already that Kerman carpet, blue medallion?"

Vacilli was sitting cross-legged across from his mother at the front window, cleaning the paint from his nails. "I finish," he said.

"So there's no other job? Come on, Vacilliki—time is money."

Michaelis turned over the page of his newspaper. "War coming," he said.

Schimmel had followed into the front room. Stavros suddenly wheeled on him. "I told you I have no money for you, Schimmel. Now get out. You giving me headache!"

Stavros walked to where Michaelis was repairing the corner of the Sarouk and leaned over to inspect the new weave.

Again Schimmel followed him. "Arness, I'm talking last time for your good," he said. "You have beautiful family, don't need trouble."

"Michaelis, you getting through this Sarouk?" Stavros said.

"Tomorrow, maybe."

"If he don't read newspaper day and night, sooner," Seraphim said. "All night he talk politics in Kaffenion Cappodocia, what you expect?"

"You look tired, Michaelis, my heart," Eleni said.

Michaelis made a low growling sound in his throat and looked at Schimmel.

The janitor was inspecting a large framed photograph on the wall. "Who's that funny old clown from circus there?" he said, bobbing his head from side to side.

Michaelis jumped off the banquette. Stavros hooked his right arm around his brother's neck, holding him back.

Apparently Schimmel hadn't understood Michaelis's intention because he went right on looking at the photograph and chuckling. "Hey, Arness, what's that, a piss pot on his head?"

"That is not funny, what you call his hat, you son of bitch," Stavros said, facing the beefy German and poking him in the belly with a stiff forefinger. "That's my worshiped father, who is in heaven now, and when you speak of him, you animal, use your human voice, if you got one, because he is one of the saints now, he's honored there, he's not where your father is, frying in hellfire like a fat heinie sausage in its own grease and where ten devils with long horns are fucking your cow mother and a large black bird eating your brother's liver, the brother you drove crazy here, like you want to drive me crazy, you walking salami. Take your beer-bucket belly out of my place. Quick! Don't say one word more! What? You said what?"

Vacilli unfolded his legs and ran out of the room.

Stavros had taken the big janitor by the hair and in his other hand the square-end knife flashed. He pushed the janitor against the wall, put the blade to his throat and was banging his head against the wall, again and

again, while his sisters screamed, half in fear, half in delight, and Michaelis
shouted war cries: *"Embros! Embros!"* Only Seraphim urged, "Enough,
Stavros, enough!"

"Let go," Schimmel shouted. "For God's sake, let go."

But Stavros was past hearing anybody now. "Get down on your knees,
you piece of dead dog meat, and beg pardon from my father for what you
insulted him." He pulled the big German forward, down on his knees.
"Say the words!"

"What words?"

"Say, 'Pardon me I speak that way about you, Sir Isaac.' "

"Pardon me I speak that way, Sir—what?"

"Isaac, you pig." Michaelis had come up. "Isaac is his name, you piece
of shit."

"Isaac, Isaac, Isaac! Let me up."

Stavros released him. "Next time you come in here," Stavros shouted,
"I cut your ears off. Who you think you are to make tyrant with my
family? I kill a man with this knife once and I can kill you. Ten seconds,
no more, it take me, and it will run out, the blood, and leak on Miss Lawler
sisters and they will have big complaint then. But nobody else complain,
because you taking money from all of them too. But not from us again,
never again from us!"

Schimmel had run out of the apartment. Michaelis went to his brother
and kissed his hand.

Eleftheria brought Stavros his hat and cane. He kissed her, then he said,
"I notice lamp not burning Father's room, needs oil there. That job I gave
to you, Eleftheria. Lamp is for father's soul. When lamp go out, they say,
a hope die. So tell me, what you do all day?"

"Nothing," Eleftheria said. "Go for walk. Nothing."

"Streets no good for young girl. All kinda bums there." He kissed her
tenderly. "Be good girl," he said.

Seraphim walked him down the stairs. "I'm hearing complaints too,"
he said.

"Maybe now they be quiet coupla weeks," Stavros said.

"Not from those people," Seraphim said. "From inside."

"From who?" Stavros asked.

"I know nothing."

"Complaints? Why they don't tell to me?"

"They're afraid of you."

"Who's afraid from me?"

"Everybody."

"Why? I don't do nothing to them."

"Your face. On account your face."

"What's the matter my face?"

"It looks like—"

"Like what?"

"Like you could do something terrible."

"Who's complaining here my goddamn face?"

"I know nothing."

"What they complaining? Tell me that much."

"They say they work, they work, they don't see money. You keep it all."

"I tol' them hundred times, one day, soon, we will have our own store, Isaac Topouzoglou Sons. Money belong to everybody. I keep it for them. I tol' them that hundred times!"

"I know. I know. Don't get mad."

"What's the matter—they don't believe me?"

"What they asking is when?"

"Vacilli want to know that? Michaelis? Who?"

"I know nothing. But they think maybe they can make more other places. They have offers."

"Tell them talk to me. I'm not wild animal. Am I?"

"No, not exactly." Seraphim laughed nervously. "I mean no."

"So goodbye. Go 'head. I'm late."

Seraphim started up the stairs.

"Hey, you, Seraphim!" Stavros called after him. Seraphim stopped. "Tell me," Stavros asked, "you 'fraid me too?"

"Yes," Seraphim said from the landing.

"No reason. Because you're the one I'm trusting here."

But Stavros's instinct, the one he'd developed on the docks of Constantinople, now spoke a name he didn't expect. Not Michaelis, not Vacilli. Seraphim! Seraphim was ambitious enough to want more and to want more soon. And he was clever enough to pretend it was someone else's question. Well, let them be afraid of his face or whatever it was; he didn't mind. One thing Stavros was sure of: Fear makes order.

Walking down the hill to Broadway, he crossed to the traffic island, then forded the great macadam river to its west bank. His walk was slow and stately, his head tilted up and at an angle toward the left. He rarely looked to the right, the direction from which the traffic was coming. It took an exhaust explosion to make him turn that way.

The effect was excess of pride. This man, with rarely more than a few crumpled dollars in his pocket, gave the impression of total arrogance. He summoned the double-decker bus by raising his father's cane. Mounting the curved interior stairs, he moved to the front row, sat with his cane between the spread of his knees, palms on the gnarled knob. He oversaw his dominion, Riverside Drive, as it passed beneath him.

A few minutes later, as his vehicle passed the Claremont Inn, he was heard to mutter, "They will crawl!" The man seated at his side looked around. "Talking to me?" he asked. Stavros studied him, decided he didn't merit an answer.

He released the bus at Twenty-sixth Street. In the lobby of 1115 Broadway he encountered the elevator starter and flicked the lid of his straw hat with a fingernail, a patronizing gesture.

Sarrafian Brothers, Oriental Rugs and Carpets, occupied the entire sixth floor, 21,000 square feet holding well over $900,000 worth of stock.

By an accident of timing, someone swung the half-glass door of the showroom open for Stavros. It was Garabet Kelekian, the repairman, on the way to the garbage bin with that morning's sweepings of green dust and wool clippings. Stavros entered, closed the door, and turned to face the store's manager and number one salesman, Mr. Morgan Perry.

"Where's my racing form, Joe?" Morgan Perry demanded.

Stavros seemed stunned; turning away as if he'd been struck across the face, he dropped his head and stood absolutely still.

"Didn't I tell you yesterday to bring me a racing form, Joe?" Morgan Perry demanded, "which they do not sell in Mount Ivy, New Jersey? Did I ask you that or not, stupid?"

Still Stavros didn't answer, didn't give a sign of what he was feeling.

"What the hell's going on?" Mr. Perry said.

"I get it for you," Stavros said with a flip of the hand. It sounded like a condescension. "Why not?" He still hadn't looked at the store manager.

"What do you mean, why not?" Perry said. "Why not is because you're paid here to do what I order you to do."

He stopped. Without a word Stavros had left the store. Morgan Perry could see him through the half-glass door, walking toward the elevator, unhurried, swinging his elbow, his head tilted up and to the left.

The way Stavros walked infuriated Morgan Perry. He'd never been able to make the Anatolian hurry. "Who the hell does he think he is?" he demanded of Miss Emily Barton, Mr. Ara Sarrafian's plump secretary, who was just coming to work.

"Good morning, Morgan—Mr. Perry," she said as she walked past him toward the office enclosure at the rear of the floor.

Perry followed her. "I'm going to give myself the pleasure of firing that bowlegged Greek goat one of these days, God willing," he said, taking off the straw hat which he wore indoors and out all summer and wiping its moist headband with his handkerchief.

"Joe's a hard worker, Mr. Perry," Miss Barton said. She was thinking: *Morgan's nervous because the boss is coming back today.*

It was a day Stavros had been waiting for; his ideal was coming to town.

Each year on the Tuesday after the first Monday of September, Mr. Ara Sarrafian, after a few days in Constantinople, looking at the new acquisitions of stock with his younger brother, Oscar, indulged himself for a month in the company of his older brother, the fabled Fernand Sarrafian, at the watering places and casinos of Central Europe, renewing old friendships and resavoring old pleasures, after which it was the custom of the pair to return to New York City by steamer—they favored the *Mauretania,* the "Greyhound of the Sea"—and after a long night's sleep, join company to enter the lower Broadway headquarters of Sarrafian Brothers, Oriental Rugs and Carpets, arm in arm. Their arrival signaled the opening of the new business year.

The one Stavros waited for was not Ara, the "boss," but his older brother, the mysterious one, Fernand, the "big boss." Fernand was the man Stavros most admired in the world and most envied. One reason for this was the old man's cool *savoir:* he always seemed unimpressed and unconcerned—in fact, scarcely aware of where he was and who else was there. His manner was at once polite and completely indifferent, a style which Stavros intended to imitate as soon as he had the money—and the position—to make it possible.

During the previous week Morgan Perry, a bulky man in his mid-fifties, had returned from his own vacation spent in a less glamorous setting, the summer home of his wife's family in Southampton, Long Island. Perry's only son, known as "Young Morgan," also worked on the floor of Sarrafian Brothers, but he'd taken his vacation earlier so there would always be a member of the Perry family at service in the store.

Stavros had not even considered going away to escape the summer's heat; he wanted the double pay for those two weeks. All summer long he had checked in the great burlap bales as they arrived in New York harbor by slow freight. Some had bills of lading marked BANDAR EL ABBAS, goods that had come down the Persian Gulf, through the Strait of Hormuz, across the Gulf of Oman, around Cape al Hadd—Stavros had charted the course, he knew it well—then up through the Gulf of Aden into the Red Sea to use the Suez Canal as door to the Mediterranean, crossing those warm waters in seven days to go out, past the Rock, and do the belly of the Atlantic at nine knots. Other shipments had come over land by camel, by donkey and cart, to Smyrna, traveling across the kind of terrain Stavros knew well—he'd been raised with the dust of it in his nostrils. From Smyrna the goods had a shorter sea voyage but on equally slow bottoms. All bales were marked NO HOOKS on each of their six sides.

During those weeks when the Sarrafian brothers were in Carlsbad and Baden-Baden and Monte Carlo, the bales of new goods were opened in New York and their contents swept clean of the powdered refuse which still smelled of the animals of that other civilization. Then the rugs and carpets had been piled by size, type, and grade, flat out, as high as the men who worked on the floor could throw them, making islands of fragrant wool across the store, awaiting the inspection and disposition of the Sarrafians.

What the role or the proprietary interest of Mr. Fernand was, Stavros could not confidently say. It was rumored that he wasn't really a member of the firm, that he had other, more important financial interests, on a level of income far above that of his two younger brothers. Old Condit, the bookkeeper, had told Stavros in an indiscreet moment that Fernand had, years ago, set up his brothers in the trade of importing Oriental rugs and carpets to the United States and that he had performed this as a family duty. True or not, it was evident to all that on his frequent visits to the United States and the store, Fernand Sarrafian showed little interest in what was going on and no anxiety about the financial well-being of the family enterprise. He did receive mail there; it was—Stavros had riffled through the envelopes—from all over the world.

No one could say where and how he had made the fortune of which people both here and on the Continent spoke with awe.

By eleven-fifteen on this particular Tuesday morning, everything in the store had been put in perfect order. Big Morgan Perry was at the door when the Sarrafian brothers entered. Behind him stood the staff of the establishment in their work clothes—aprons for those who worked in the touch-up and repair sections, rolled sleeves for the porters who opened the rugs for customers and baled them for shipment, cuffed sleeves with links and elbow garters for the sales assistants who worked under Mr. Perry. The chief of these was his son, Young Morgan; another was the man Morgan Perry had referred to as "that bowlegged Greek goat."

Ara Sarrafian dressed to efface himself: business suits in gradations of gray—silver in summer, steel in the fall, oxford in winter. By contrast, his older brother, Fernand, dressed in a "continental" style that evoked wonder from all: for instance now, an "ice cream" suit of a white cloth graced with black pin stripes and, beneath its coat, a pongee shirt in a blush of pink made for him by Sulka in the high choker-collar style he counted on to conceal the infirmities of his neck. His very small feet were in black-and-white shoes. Tilted on his head was the softest and lightest Panama hat, which Stavros jumped to take and carefully put away. Everyone knew from Mr. Fernand's costume that he was going to the races that afternoon, as he did every afternoon of every meet when he was in New York, and that the chauffeur-driven Pierce-Arrow which had picked up his brother Ara in New Rochelle and then called for Fernand himself at his West Sixty-eighth Street town house was now waiting at the curb below.

The older brother walked quickly down the lineup of employees, nodding pleasantly but vaguely to each, a movement much like running a finger down a piano's keys, lingering on none. Then he disappeared, passing through a door concealed by a beaded curtain into his private office at the rear of the store.

Ara's reunion with his employees, on the other hand, was neither mysterious nor impersonal. He walked the line greeting each man by name, noting whose hair was a little grayer, who had put on weight, who'd shaved his mustache in the summer's heat. If the man had cause for congratulation or grief, Mr. Ara seemed to know about it. Of Stavros he inquired how the family was getting along and seemed happy to hear that they were in good health. Mr. Ara was the only person outside his immediate family who, on occasion, called Joe "Stavros."

Despite all this, Stavros preferred the colder brother. His mind had followed Mr. Fernand back into his private office. Since the door to this sanctuary was unlocked only when Mr. Fernand was in town, Stavros had never been inside, only on the threshold, to deliver a newspaper or a package of Melachrino cigarettes. These glimpses had brought back another world. While Mr. Ara's office was a model of 1911 efficiency, well lit and ventilated by a large ceiling fan, the chairs stiff-backed and arranged for a conference, the desk well designed and neat, Mr. Fernand's private office was a memory of the Near East. The walls were entirely covered with kilims, tightly woven textiles in small jagged designs, the kind used to line the tents of sheiks. There was no desk. One wall was spanned by a long, low, and unusually wide banquette, and in front of it, supported on a stand, was a large tray of pierced copper holding an earthenware dish of pistachios dyed a sandy pink, the old man's favorite nibbles.

Somewhere behind the wall coverings were windows, but there was no way of telling where they were and whether they were open or shut. The fact was that they were never open, especially in summer. Near Easterners know that a room stays cooler in the heat when there is no opening to where the sun is bearing down. However, there was no staleness in the air because of an unseen, uncapped bottle of attar of roses scenting the room.

There was only one decoration on the walls—Stavros had noticed this —a tinted photograph, full length, of the male parent of the three Sarrafian boys, a patriarch long gone to his reward. Here he was recalled in the classic pose, seated in an armchair before a backdrop of a garden scene, his cane upright between his legs. It reminded Stavros of his own father, Isaac.

Now Stavros saw Miss Emily Barton dash into this private place bearing a bottle of Apollinaris water. He had often wondered but never asked what that long green drink Mr. Fernand favored was. From the depths a phonograph could be heard, an *amanee*, a song of longing. Turkish. Was there an added voice? Was it Mr. Fernand's?

Meantime Ara Sarrafian, having greeted his staff, began his inspection of the new acquisitions of stock. Of course he'd seen most of the goods that summer or the one before in Smyrna or in Teheran where the firm had branch offices. His few words about them now were delivered in a low voice that reached Morgan Perry standing beside him but not to where

Stavros was straining to hear. Then Mr. Ara would speak to Garabet Kelekian, who was responsible for touch-up and repairs, speak in Armenian, then say, *"Oh-beer-eee-see,"* Turkish for "the next one," and with that, the rug he'd just looked at was flipped over or folded away.

Stavros suddenly noticed that Mr. Fernand was seated at the side of the floor—when had he come out?—just beyond the cloud of fragrant but invisible dye powder and cotton bits which rose from the rugs as they were flung open for viewing, flipped over to be put away. The old man was holding a tall glass containing a green liquid, and smoking a Melachrino which he had twisted into a cigarette holder of yellowing ivory. He seemed not to be looking at the parade of stock at all. There was a certain dreaminess in his manner, an aloofness, that was the source of the mystery which enfolded him and which enthralled Stavros. Mr. Fernand sipped his long cool green drink and glanced out of the side of his eyes at the pile of goods that were being laid out for his brother's consideration. Once he crooked his forefinger, calling Morgan Perry to his side and whispering; but all he wanted—Stavros had sidled close—was to give him a "good horse" in that afternoon's fifth race.

Meantime dispositions were being made by Mr. Ara. He designated some especially fine goods to be laid aside for certain especially valued customers. A few antique Bokharas he asked to be rolled and placed behind his desk in a corner of his office. One piece in particular he believed might be sold to a museum; a nod from his older brother confirmed this judgment. It was Mr. Fernand who suggested that a small mat, whose design was a warlike eagle holding the stars and stripes, be hung on a pillar facing the entrance to the store. A pink Isfahan also caught the older man's eye; it was what he needed for the bay window area of the upstairs sitting room he was refurnishing in his town house. He insisted on paying the company full price for this eight-by-ten carpet, and Stavros was impressed by this lesson in rectitude.

Once Mr. Ara had finished with his inspection, he moved to the open office enclosure at the back of the store, where American Beauty roses had been placed on his desk. There old Mr. Condit and Miss Barton showed him the company's "books" to quickly acquaint him with the financial history of the summer. While he was bent over the daybook and the ledger, Mr. Fernand came by, pinching a rosebud from the vase on his brother's desk and sliding its slim stem through his buttonhole as he went back into his inner office. As he passed, he hummed a tune, as he often did, moving to its rhythm; he seemed to be lost in thoughts which had nothing to do with the rug business.

Everything with the books must have been in order; everyone looked happy because Ara Sarrafian seemed to be satisfied with what he'd found after his two months' absence. Stavros was asked to jump out and purchase a bottle of Bristol Cream Sherry, a choice made in deference to Miss

Barton. He did it gladly. When he came back, Big Morgan Perry, Young Morgan, Garabet Kelekian, old Mr. Condit and Miss Barton joined Mr. Ara in a welcome-home drink, which was also a toast of hope to the new season. Stavros, bottle in hand, attended from a corner, ready to serve refills and wondering why Mr. Fernand had not emerged from his inner office to join the celebrants. He made a mental note in three parts: Don't be too friendly! Remain aloof! Cultivate a mystery!

Precisely at noon, Miss Barton delivered an order from Mr. Fernand to Stavros: He was to hurry downstairs and make sure that the Pierce-Arrow was there, with its chauffeur ready to drive to the track. Stavros came back and reported to Miss Barton that all was in readiness; she entered the private office carrying the news. Now Mr. Fernand emerged and called for his Panama. Stavros rushed to be the one to bring the hat —a marvel, he thought it, woven of a material as soft as silk. As he gave the hat to Mr. Fernand he didn't allow the opportunity to slip by. There was a quick exchange, unnoticed by the others.

"Can I talk to you alone, Mr. Fernand?" Stavros said. "Sir? Please? For a single minute only? Less!"

"Talk to my brother," Mr. Fernand said. He took the hat and—again humming and walking delicately in rhythm—found the mirror above Miss Emily Barton's desk and consulted it to make sure the hat was on his head at the correct tilt.

Stavros did the unforgivable, he followed the old man. How could he help it? Fernand Sarrafian was the man in the world he most wanted to be.

"You looking very good today, sir, thanks to God," he whispered from behind the old man's stooped back.

"No raises!" Mr. Fernand Sarrafian said in the friendliest possible manner as he lifted the ends of his Kaiser Wilhelm mustache with the tips of his thumb and fourth finger.

Stavros quickly turned his face away. He couldn't afford to let his anger be seen, above all by Mr. Fernand Sarrafian. When he turned back, Joe again, he was smiling.

Without waiting for his brother, the "big boss" had started for the door, humming to himself and waving the silver tip of his cane as he passed the length of the floor. Everyone stopped whatever he was doing to watch the fabled one's progress. He was happy! And why shouldn't he be? Ahead was lunch at Delmonico's and an afternoon on the clubhouse lawn of beautiful Belmont Park.

Stavros raced to open the door for the old man. So did Garabet Kelekian. They flanked the exit, bowing their heads as Mr. Fernand passed. Mr. Ara hustled to catch up with his brother who wasn't slowing his pace. Then they were through the door and gone; the store was empty.

Now everyone had work; the summer was over. For the rest of that day Stavros and Young Morgan, Garabet and all the others, hustled to Morgan Perry's orders. The store manager was too busy to needle Stavros and Stavros too busy to notice it if he had.

By six, the end of the workday, Stavros was exhausted. On the bus north, he was a less impressive figure than he'd been that morning; he dozed. But when he got off at 135th Street, walked the single block north, then up the hill to home, the tone and the posture of his body had altered. The anxious-to-please young man who'd spent the day eagerly running errands for the Messrs. Sarrafian, jumping to the orders of their store manager while suffering his jibes, had, by the time he arrived at the bottom of 136th Street, again become the redoubtable head of an embattled household, an embodiment of power not safe to challenge.

OCTOBER 1912

There comes a time in the life of a man as ambitious as Stavros Topouzoglou when he must realize that his career is not progressing at the pace he'd hoped for, that he is still precisely where he was a year before and that, quite possibly, a year hence he will still be working on the floor at Sarrafian Brothers, kept back from the important customers and given errands that should have been thrown to common porters.

Despite the firm's profits—because of the onrushing war, every piece had been marked up twenty percent—his salary had remained the same. His family's hope fund had hardly been enriched.

There was, above all, the problem of Young Morgan. While Stavros had always liked this affable young man, he now found himself unbearably envious of him. Perry's son, it was obvious to all, was being prepared to take his father's place as the number-one salesman for American buyers. That was the position Stavros had hoped for himself. He'd several times had dreams that Young Morgan was dead. These dreams did not shock him.

For the first time in his life, Stavros lost faith in the year that was coming, that it would bring better days. With some men this realization would have resulted in melancholia; with Stavros it sharpened the edge of his rancor and quickened his habitual impatience. What this ambitious Anatolian needed was movement, a triumph or a disaster, a breakup or a breakdown, a change, a release, a quarrel. Stavros was a man who would rather be set back than stand in place. Defeat was a stimulus for him. To be where he'd been a year before was killing his spirit.

Now that he was constantly on edge, his health suffered. He lost weight, his eyes were frequently bloodshot, he developed a tic. At night, he ground his teeth. Nightmares were frequent.

He even lost interest in women, cut off both his "regulars."

As for America, he saw it as a locked room to which he didn't have the key.

On this gusty October afternoon he came home late, as the twilight was ending. Morgan Perry and his son had left early to catch the most convenient suburban train for Mount Ivy. Mr. Ara had had one of his headaches at the end of the day and had gone home to New Rochelle, where he could go on with his drinking—that was the rumor—without being observed. Stavros had remained behind with the task of putting the store back in order after a very big and highly profitable sale which had left the floor in a mess.

At normal quitting time, Stavros had asked for overtime pay. Mr. Ara had said, "Talk to Mr. Perry," and Morgan Perry had said, "I know stiffs who'd beat you to death to get your job. If you don't like it here, you know where the door is; we'll have somebody better in your place first thing in the morning. Let me know!"

As he neared the entrance to the apartment house, black clouds were moving in and there was thunder from over the Palisades. Stavros came on his sister Eleftheria, sitting on the stoop just down the hill from their own. She was in conversation—no more than listening and laughing, since her English was still uncertain—with a boy on the block. The slap Stavros put across her cheek lasted for many months. The young man scurried like a thief into the hall of his building. Stavros led his sister by the lobe of the ear up the hill and into the entrance of their own building.

"When time comes for you to marry," he said to her as he pushed her up the stairs, "I find you high-class Greek man, merchant with good business and a few dollars." Unlocking the door, he said, "Also older man, maybe you pay him respect. Now go 'head, let me see you work!"

She dashed past him into the bedroom she shared with Eleni and slammed the door.

Vasso, who was staring out the window over 136th Street at the coming storm, said, "Too late!" but no one knew what she meant. Vacilli sat idly at the window opposite his mother, chin cupped in his hand, watching the day dying on the walls of the orphanage and the lights coming on inside the long brick buildings. "Ach, ach, ach," he said, a sigh.

He looked up at Stavros, read his expression. "Nothing ready for paint yet," he said. When Stavros's expression remained the same, he added, "When Michaelis finish that piece, I paint."

"Where's Michaelis?" Stavros said.

"Kaffenion," Vacilli said.

Stavros was looking at three carpets, rolled and ready for delivery. "Seraphim!" he called. "These pieces suppose to be deliver Mrs. Bernstein this morning. Seraphim!"

"Seraphim out." Vacilli's voice was untroubled, muted.

"What the hell he didn't deliver these three pieces all finished here?" Stavros turned to the dining room.

At the window, Vacilli sighed, "Ach, ach, ach!"

The dining room table was bare, not even a tablecloth.

"Fofo," Stavros called out, "I'm hungry!"

"She gone out," Vacilli said in his calming voice. He got up, moved to the floor in front of the chair where his mother was sitting, and proceeded to unwind a soiled bandage from the old woman's wrinkled calf. There was a black ulcer there, the size of a nickel. When he noticed Stavros watching, he said, "See. They don't go away. Other leg too, same thing."

"Best thing for that salt water," Stavros said. "We take her Asbury Park next summer. Why those goods not gone? I told Mrs. Bernstein sure today. Where's Seraphim, make me liar?"

"Went play cards," Vacilli said.

"Where he get money play cards every night?" Stavros said.

"Where getting money playing cards is playing cards," Vacilli said. "He always win; his pockets heavy all the time."

"Everybody here has money except me," Stavros said. "Fofo," he shouted. "Who's going to give me food here!"

"I told you she gone out," Vacilli said. He was patting a preparation known as Aseptinol on the ulcer, a salve which had a penetrating astringent odor as well as a mythic reputation in that house for healing. It was applied to every cut and bruise, used for chest colds too. "Much better," Vacilli said to his mother, calming her. "Aseptinol!"

She shrugged. "I hope so," she said. "Who knows?"

"Where Fofo go?" Stavros said. "I'm hungry."

"She went to his sister's house with Mr. Pandelis," Vasso said. "Let her go. Please God, we marry her soon; she's getting old." She bent over to look at her leg. "Put more, Vacilli," she said. "Aseptinol!"

"Please God, she marry," Vacilli said, patting on more of the salve.

"Nobody good enough for Fofo," Stavros said.

"Or rich enough, maybe," Vacilli said. Pat, pat.

"Men don't like her," Vasso said. "They can see she will never bring milk."

"Men want her," Vacilli said. "She doesn't want the men. Mr. Nassibian, he wanted her. He's pretty rich too."

"He's Armenian," Vasso said. "Also maybe seventy years old."

"Better," Vacilli said. "He die soon. Leave us money."

"Fofo pass thirty," Stavros said. "We have to sell her to some man before it's too late. Who's going to give me eat here? My belly is complaining."

"I'm here," Eleni said. She was standing in the doorway, a piece of notepaper in her hand.

"You finish corner Kerman carpet today?" Stavros said.

"Tomorrow, I promise. First thing."

"What you doing all day?"

"Writing letters," Vasso said. She was looking out the window again. "Big wind starting, bring rain," she said. "Leaves falling down."

"Weaving," Eleni said. "That piece sixty knots to inch. My eyes hurt. What you want to eat?" She put the letter in her dress pocket.

"I don't want anything," Stavros said. "I lose my appetite. Everybody doing me favor here, look like. I pay everything, get nothing."

"Go sit down," Vasso said. "Stop the complaints."

Stavros went to where Vacilli had covered the ulcer with Aseptinol. "Looks better," he lied. "Where Michaelis?"

"I told you. He went to Kaffenion Cappodocia," Vacilli said. "Big celebration tonight. Greece making war with Bulgaria and Serbia against Turkey."

"First we fighting Bulgars, now friends Bulgars," Vasso said. "I understand nothing."

"Some kind drill practice with guns there," Vacilli said, "then getting drunk, talking how they going to win war."

"Where the hell Michaelis getting money buy drinks Kaffenion?" Stavros demanded. "Ouzo, brandy, cost plenty."

"Ask him," Vacilli said, as he slowly and gently wrapped a fresh bandage around his mother's calf. "We need more Aseptinol," he said, holding up the flattened tube.

"He didn't finish his work, either, Michaelis," Stavros said. "I can see."

"Since he read paper this morning, war declaration, he don't work," Vacilli said.

"I'm fixing beans we had for lunch," Eleni said. "Come sit down, stop complaining. Michaelis good boy."

"I had lamb and beans my lunch. Give me couple pieces cheese, few olives, corner piece bread, what the hell." He turned on his mother. "Something wrong here," he said. "In the morning, I see they working hard. When I come down hall get coffee, maybe they hear my shoes squeaking, they work, O.K. I eat breakfast, I'm watching, everybody working. When I say goodbye, they don't lift their heads. But when I come home, work is same as in morning. What they doing all day? Eat? Talk? Play cards? Backgammon? What? Fofo tell me they fight among themselves. She tell me Michaelis sleep all day, worn out from being patriot all night. I say to her, 'Fofo,' I say, 'push 'im.' "

"They not 'fraid from her," Vasso said. "Only you."

"Also she say 'Those boys not workers.' 'What the hell are they?' I ask. 'Thinkers,' she say."

"That's the way he wanted them, your father," Vasso said. Then to Vacilli at her feet, she said, "Now other leg."

"I need more Aseptinol, Stavros," Vacilli said.

"Get from your brothers," Stavros said, reaching into his pocket. "They have plenty money looks like." He counted his paper money which he always did before paying any of it out, then cursed in Turkish, put it back, produced change from another pocket and gave Vacilli a fifty-cent piece.

"He used to say to them, your father," Vasso said—she was again looking out the window into the driving rain and the black night— " 'Greek man work with brains, Turk with body.' He filled them with those ideas."

"But tell me, Mommah," Stavros said, "what brains you talking? I don't realize any genius here. Only Demo, maybe, I hope."

"Their ideas come from your father, a man who left blood from his trouser bottom as he walked up and down the Corso of Smyrna with his arm over the shoulder of the man who was killing him. Is that smart? You waiting for his sons to show brains?"

"Don't talk against Father," Stavros said. "He was good man."

"Good people die quick this world. You tasted hardship in your life, it made you a man. How other one look, Vacilli?"

"Same," Vacilli said. "Better."

"What you do all day, Vacilli?" Stavros asked.

"I touch up red Bokhara prayer rug, six by three."

"How long that take?"

"This morning, I did it."

"Hours? Maybe hour?"

"Maybe more."

"Maybe less. What you do rest of day?"

Gently Vacilli wiped off the old salve and lifted the old wrinkled calf so it would catch the light. "I'm waiting them finish, Eleni, Michaelis," he said.

"Meantime you sit at window, making 'ach, ach, ach' all day?" Stavros said.

Vasso snickered. "Ach, ach, ach," she said.

"What the hell you laughing, Mommah, excuse the expression? I am getting idea, old woman, I'm only one working here. Well, now situation going change. I straighten everybody out here. I want cooperation. Vacilli, you know what that means, cooperation?"

"No." He squeezed the last of the Aseptinol out of the tube.

"So I'm going to give you lesson cooperation," Stavros said. "I got job for you. Garabet Kelekian, Sarrafian Brothers repairman, he say he need one other man for touch-up. I been speaking to him about you."

"I don't want that job there," Vacilli said.

"What you mean, you don't want job?"

"I deliver some pieces there, this Mr. Morgan Perry, patron, he don't like me."

"How you know that?"

"I see his face."

"What's the difference, like, don't like. That man, he don't like his wife, how he can like you?"

"I'm satisfy here," Vacilli said. "You bring job from there home. I fix 'im here. O.K.?"

"No! I work ten hours, you work one here. You eat good, sleep nice bed, same as me. Three home women here, they can fix Mommah's leg—"

"I like how Vacilli fix it," Vasso said. "He has soft hands."

"You telling me Eleni can't do that?" Stavros said. "Eleni!"

She appeared in the doorway, notepaper in hand. She'd been writing again at the dining room table. "Cheese, olives on table, beans on stove," she said. "What more you want?"

"I want now on, daytime, you fix Mommah's leg, Aseptinol. Watch how Vacilli does it. She like that, very soft. Also what the hell you're writing all the time, every day?"

"I don't go downtown work," Vacilli said. "I don't want to go among strangers."

"I know what you want, Mr. Soft Hands: Sit at window all day, complaining on me, 'ach, ach, ach.' What the hell everybody complaining, Mommah? Tell me so I can understand. Because in a minute, I go crazy here, Mommah. Then somebody getting hurt sure."

"You know what they say," Vasso answered.

"Let me hear before I kick everybody out."

" 'We work, we work,' they say. 'We don't see the money.' "

"It's in the bank for them, for the family."

"That's what I tell them," Vasso said. "Look how the rain coming now," she said.

"So what they complaining here?" Stavros said.

" 'Where's piece of paper saying it's ours too?' they say."

"Who say that?"

"Seraphim. Smart boy, Seraphim."

"He's so smart, he needs paper from his brother?"

"It would make him happier," Vasso said.

"Meantime he's downtown, Hotel Bristol, losing money pinochle."

"Seraphim always wins," Eleni said from the doorway.

"So let him win his living," Stavros said. "Let them all leave. Or I leave, Mommah; you and I, we go—"

"Be patient," Vasso said. "They're good boys."

"Patient! I put food in their mouths four years already. Clothes on their backs! Work all day while Mr. Morgan Perry, son of a bitch, hollering on

me, holler, holler! Come home late, no food waiting. Nobody give damn.
Let them be patient, not me."

"Sit down at the table, eat," Vasso said. "You feel better. Eleni put
yogurt, mix in some honey. Sweeten his mouth."

"I don't hear one word thanks from them. Four years, not one word!"

"They don't learn that word 'thanks' yet. Don't wait for that."

"I'm not waiting. I'm going to teach them." He made a fist and the fist
held a stick and he waved it, then brought it down through the air sharply.
"On their fat parts!"

Vacilli had finished, got up, holding the soiled bandages and the exhausted tube of salve.

Stavros stepped across his path. "You going tomorrow, that job?"

"If you say go, I go," Vacilli said and slid by his brother.

"Goddamn! I go crazy here!" Stavros said. "I give him job, this man
doing me favor work. Doing me favor! Goddamn *küpül kopek!*"

"Don't call your brother that dirty Turk name," Vasso said. Then she
snickered.

"I'm going out, get some spaghetti, something, before I—"

"Stavros," Vasso said, "come here first. Eleni, make Stavros spaghetti
quick, he wants spaghetti."

"Never mind. Beans O.K." Stavros stood before his mother like a child
expecting to be reprimanded. "I don't get help here, Mommah," he said,
speaking softly to her. "I don't know what to do."

Vasso reached out, took his hand, lifted it to her lips and kissed it. "For
everything you did, my family, my children, me, I thank you," she said.

He made a gruff noise, then spoke quietly. "I'm so mad tonight," he
said. "I could kill somebody tonight."

"You need a woman," she said.

"Every week, I have," he said, "one."

"I mean nice clean *copella* for wife," she said. "Look after you. Listen
to old woman on this subject."

"But where I find? I'm angry all the time. What woman wants that?"

"Food on table." Eleni spoke softly. "Stavros, come."

"They're good boys, your brothers, but without you here they fly out
the window like birds, everyone different directions, north, south. Then
my family finish."

"Why they so lazy?"

"Because you don't talk," Vasso said. "You had a big idea once,
the future, what it would be for this family. You never said it to them,
that idea, only to me. They think like it is now, it will be rest of their
time."

"They should trust me by now. Twelve years I worked—"

"I know. But man is not a grateful animal. Also this is not a country where people stay together. I see them on the street down there, nobody talk to nobody. Pass by, pass by. I watch. I see what's going on here, this country. No one is friends here."

"I see same thing," Stavros said.

"Sometimes I'm remembering the little girl across the road—"

"What little girl?"

"The people across the street, those Turks, they had a little *kore*. Did she grow up and marry? What happen there? They were good people, never mind what Greek newspaper say. Only Turk soldiers, they teach to be animals. But the people across the street and in the bazaar? Same like us. I tell this to Michaelis, but he don't listen. He wants to hate."

"He saw Father die."

"He wants to go back and fight there in the war. You see you have to give them reason to stay here. Something that's for them. For instance: How much money we have in bank, the family, now? Tell me that."

"I don't tell that."

"But they work hard for that money."

"This much I tell you, so you tell them, if you want—that in two years, I will start it."

"Start what? I don't know what you're talking, they don't know."

"Isaac Topouzoglou Sons. Our store. That was my idea. Then I will give them proper papers, their share, and they will have their names on the door in gold letters."

"But they don't know any of this. And there was more. You said—"

"I will open up office in many countries," he broke in. "Those boys, my brothers, they don't realize possibilities. I will have buyers in Teheran, in Damascus and Constantinople, and everyone in this family will be rich."

"Yes. And there was something else."

"Then we will be Americans! Nobody will be better than us. Topouzoglou Sons stores will be in Germany, in London, in Paris, taking their money, as much as here. Eh? Eh? Big idea, eh? What you say to that, old woman?"

"I say yes. And there was something more."

"This! Each of my brothers, if they trust me and work hard, will be king of one part and their names will be known. They will be famous."

"That's what they want to hear!"

"But first I have to see ambition from them. Three and half years they're here and their English is still monkey talk! Only Demo, he go to school, thank God, learn to speak proper way. He's my investment, Demo, my smart one. Like an American already! Even his nose. Notice? It's short, not like Anatolian nose. He will be boss our corporation when I'm old. He's my heart's hope!"

Vasso cracked one of the sunflower seeds she kept in her apron. "There was something else you promised me. That when a certain time came, you would take me back where I was born. Remember that?"

Stavros bent over and kissed her. "I promise that again," he said. "Now I'm hungry. Where the hell's Demo tonight?"

"Went to a show again," Eleni said. "Come on, the food is on the table."

"How the hell he go to show every night?" Stavros said.

"He pay, he go."

"How he get money?"

"He works," Eleni said.

"Works where?"

"He doesn't say. Every morning he go to job."

"When he goes to school?"

There was no answer until Vasso said, "He quit school."

"When?"

"Month before," Eleni said.

"Two months," Vasso said. "Maybe three."

"Why nobody tell me this?"

"Everybody 'fraid to tell you anything," Eleni said.

Stavros stood where he was, under the burning fixture, light pouring on his head, unmoving. His face had tensed, his eyebrows bowed up, his dark eyes fixed in the glare that always frightened everyone in the family.

Even Vasso was afraid to talk.

They waited.

"I don't eat," he said and left the room. The two women heard a door close down the hall.

"Ach, ach, ach," Vacilli said.

Stavros was up before the sun, but not before his mother. Walking slowly and gravely, he entered the front room and sat in the armchair opposite hers at the twin windows over 136th Street. Not a sound was exchanged. Together they watched the children of the orphanage across the way come out for a look at the morning. "They good boys," Vasso said and when he didn't answer, she pointed to the orphans. "I'm talking your brothers, not those!"

Stavros got up and looked at Michaelis, who had come home very late, begun to weave, then fallen over, and was now snoring gently.

"Normal," Vasso said. "How many times a war like this happen?"

Stavros turned away, walked slowly down the hall to the room he shared with Demosthenes. For a long time he looked at the young man curled in his blanket. Then he kicked him.

Demo groaned and cringed.

"Get up!" Stavros pulled the blanket off. Demosthenes slept in his underwear and his hands were between his thighs. "Don't play with that now!" Stavros said. "Get up! I want you to go with me."

Now Demosthenes realized who it was. He sat up straight. "Me?" he said. "You want me?"

"Put your pants, we're leaving."

They went down into the subway. The trains that hour were crowded to suffocation.

"Where we going?" Demo shouted to make himself heard.

"Don't speak Greek here!" Stavros yelled in his ear. "You learning English that school? Speak English!"

Stavros waited for Demo to admit to him that he'd left school. Demo didn't.

They got off at Wall Street. Demo had been many places on the island of Manhattan, but he'd never seen such high buildings fencing streets so narrow. He walked slowly, looking this way and that, stopped, turned to say something to his brother. Stavros wasn't there. Demo realized suddenly that he didn't know where Stavros had gone. Frantic, he began to move one way then another, searching for his brother through the crowds rushing to work. "Stavros!" he called, then louder: "Stavros!" Finally he gave up, lost, a child again.

Stavros stepped out from behind a doorway. Instead of sympathetic, he looked scornful. "I told you don't speak Greek, didn't I?" Stavros took long strides so Demo had to run to keep up with him.

"I only said your name," his brother said.

"Joe," Stavros said. "My name, when you speaking English, Joe."

"Where we going," Demosthenes said, "Joe?"

"Where I'm taking you," Stavros said. "I going to find out if you have brain."

"The teachers in Smyrna, they think so. I got good marks. In English too."

"Anybody can fool those teachers in Smyrna. What about teachers here? What they say, huh?"

Demo stopped. "I'm getting tired," he said.

"O.K., then, how about here? O.K.?"

"O.K. for what?"

"Where we are, financial center this country, maybe whole world, place where everybody talk money business. So let's talk money business, you and me."

"What business we have to talk about?"

"I understand you making plenty money, yes? So give me!"

"Give what?"

"The money!"

Demo hesitated.

Suddenly Stavros smacked him across the face, so hard that he almost knocked his head out of joint.

Then he held out his hand. "The money!" he said.

Demo reached into his pocket and pulled out a thin but neatly folded pack of bills. He gave them to Stavros.

Stavros counted. "Eighteen dollars," he said. "This is all?"

"Yes," Demo said.

"You have more, I think."

"That's all."

Again Stavros struck him hard across the face. "You become liar too," he said. "Where you learn lie so good, *pezeven?* Give me the rest so I go to show at night too."

"That's all I have," Demo said.

"You donkey-fucking bandit!" Stavros said in Turkish. "Where's the rest?" he said in English.

"I don't want to be your brother if you hit me again."

"Good! Leave, go 'head. Pay me fare from boat, the money I send family in Kayseri, in Smyrna, what I spend, apartment, food, your commercial course school, pay me for the years I work, the time and strength I gave to bring you here, then go, go 'head. But first—" Stavros held out his hand.

"I don't have any more money."

Stavros hit him with the full force of his anger, leaving the ground as he swung his arm. When Demo fell back off balance, Stavros followed, pushing him against the side of the New York Guarantee and Trust Building.

People passing slowed, stopped.

He went through his brother's pockets, first those in his coat, then his trousers, patting him other places where he might have hung a purse. "Fofo right," he said. "I make it too easy you people. Where you put the money? Come on. You want me hit you again?"

"No, no. Please." Demo rubbed his cheek. "That is terrible thing you do to your brother!"

"What about what you do your family, all your brothers, all working, taking no money so you can go to school, and you— Where is it, where's the rest? Come on! Come on!"

A small crowd had gathered to watch.

"What the hell you looking?" Stavros turned on a plump middle-aged man. "Get out, go watch your wife fuck the iceman!"

He made a sudden move at the man who hustled off.

At that instant, Demo turned and ran down the street.

As Stavros chased him, he noticed his brother had a slight limp, one he'd not noticed before.

The traffic helped him. He caught Demo in the center of the street, pushed him to the curb and up against another building.

"Help, help!" Demo called.

Passersby avoided the quarrel, hurried past.

"You hollering help against me?" Stavros said. "Your brother? Learn lesson: In this city nobody help." Suddenly he struck him again. Demo yelled. "Be quiet," Stavros said. "Now give me rest your money. Quick!"

The boy dropped his head. He was in tears.

"Your shoe," Stavros said. "Take it off."

Demo, leaning against the building, took one shoe off and pulled out a pad of bills, pressed flat. He gave them to Stavros, who counted them.

"One hundred seventy dollar?"

"That's all I have."

"I take chance, I believe you. Now you listen what I'm saying. Everything you make in this country until we have different idea, you give to me. I hold for the family."

"What about Seraphim, what he make card games?"

"Gambling, that is different. Go 'head gamble, I don't care. But when you leave school—" At this Stavros lost control and began speaking Turkish. "You goat-fucker!" he screamed. "You pimp-would-be-pimp! You small animal like a rat! I work hard ten hours every day to give you room, bed, food and everything else including soap in the bathroom, and you quit school. Why you do that?"

"It was too hard for me," the boy whined.

"For chrissake, Demo, you were instead of me! I had no school. So I send you. You I hope will speak American like American. Now it seems you are tricky criminal character. How I can trust you again? I should have left you other side. Maybe you get job on docks there and those hamals teach you what is life. You know what hamal does when somebody cheats him like you do me? They find that man's body garbage pile next morning. You been living like *agha*'s son! I had hope you be boss our company future time. Yes! You! So what you do to me? Tell me, tell! Come on, say it!"

"I quit the school."

"What else?"

"I got job outside."

"What else?"

"I kept the money."

"You know what I do if you try that again?"

"I don't want to hear it. I won't do it again."

"How can I be sure on that?"

"I give you my word."

"Your word is shit, your word. I gave you chance be only educated man in the family. You were reason I worked so hard. You were my hope, boy, my best hope." Stavros had tears in his eyes. "What's the matter with me," he said, "I didn't see what you were? What damn fool I was! Stupid?

Yes, goddamn fool, let you cheat your own family. Shame! Shame!"

"Don't; don't talk like that. I will do whatever you want."

"Damn right you do what I want. I be there make sure."

"Where we going now?"

"Follow me."

Demo had to run. "You can trust me now, Stavros," he said.

"I will find that out myself. It is my experience—come on, come on, I can't talk behind my back—my experience, after a certain age men learn nothing. You were youngest, which is why I pick only you go to school. So, *kaput!* Now can you learn to be honest man? I don't know. What's your answer?"

"What's your question?"

"Can I trust you? Tell the truth."

"I'm not sure."

Stavros laughed. He liked that answer.

"I hope so," Demosthenes said.

"Well, that's honest answer. Remember, if you do anything bad against me or the family again, I have no pity."

Suddenly he stopped. Demo saw they were in front of a tiny shoeshine establishment which hadn't yet opened for that day's business.

"What is this?" Demosthenes said.

"See up there."

Demosthenes looked at the sign: JOE'S SHOESHINE PARLOR.

"You own it?" Demosthenes asked.

"Lease. I own the boys who work here, those donkey droppings, still sleeping."

He'd found the key to the place and went to the door.

"When I first got here this country long ago," Stavros said, "this is place where I worked. I lived like a monk those first years, slept where I will show you, saved every penny. All for you, you pimp! The owner, he was a fine, fat Greek who was happy only when he was gambling. Every day the horses, every night card games. One day I catch him when he need money quick, so he sell me cheap."

Stavros turned the key, opened the door and walked into a dark interior.

When Demosthenes got used to the half light, he saw three elevated armchairs for customers and before them metal stands for their shoes.

Stavros had gone to a small door at the back and started down a narrow flight of stairs. Demosthenes rushed to catch up with him.

"Why you keep this secret?" Demosthenes said.

"It brings money. I don't like people know my money business."

"Even your family?"

"Especially my family. I'm taking big chance again with you. So watch you self."

They'd come to a sort of half-cellar lit by two narrow panes of glass set at sidewalk level and protected by an iron grille.

"Get up, you, turd Manolis," Stavros shouted. "Andoni, up, up. Customers waiting."

Again it took a moment for Demosthenes's eyes to get used to the murky light. When they did, he saw, curled on the floor, three human forms, whose first reactions to Stavros's sudden entrance was to cover their heads with blankets.

"They come from Bulgaria but Greek," he said. "That's how they sleep those villages there, the Greeks, with heads covered. They think that way they're safe." He pulled the blankets off, revealing boys of eighteen or nineteen years. "I paid their passage which they working here to pay back. Their work pay your passage, you can thank them you're here. Get up, boys! Hey, you, *vlax*, stupid Greeks from *Vul-vul-Vulgari.* Up!" He started up the stairs again. "These turds," he said, smiling, "like animals!"

"They're young boys!" Demosthenes said.

"Like I was when I came," Stavros said, throwing up a wide green roller shade that covered the street window. Then, with a shout, he opened the place for business. "Get your shoes shined here!" he called into the street.

Stavros took off his suit coat and turned up his sleeves. As he shined the first customer's shoes, he talked to his brother in Greek.

"So you left other school, O.K. Finished. Now you go to my school. Here you learn many things, maybe more useful. First how to add numbers."

"I know that."

"And keep books. And how to speak English like American. Not like me. Good! Hey, mister." He'd switched to English, speaking to his customer. "Look this damn Greek boy here—how he expect get along without speaking American, tell me that much?"

"Same way you get along," the man said, continuing to read his morning paper.

"The only way," Stavros continued to his brother in Greek, "is to speak nothing else. You can always insult a donkey like this customer in Greek. Look, he's got yellow from piss on his fly. Hey stupid, I'm insulting you. What you have to learn, main thing, Demosthenes, is the tough life. These boys here, they're the ones you have to boss—look at them! *Vlax!*"

The boys were coming up one by one.

"Where's Manolis?" Stavros shouted at the first boy.

"He's making coffee. We have to eat something, no?"

"No," Stavros said. Then speaking in Greek, openly in front of the boys, he said, "These boys here, they think I don't know they stealing. See this short fellow here, Andoni—yes, you. He has big smile but he's worst thief of all. I get the tips here, that's the contract, till their passage is paid off. You think they remember that? Look at him smiling, my dear Andoni. There's a lesson for you. Don't trust them when they're smiling. Understand?"

"So you want me to be . . . ?"

"Manager here. I want you to learn what life in this United States is. America, America, it's not what I thought. You see I still have maybe a little hope on you. Maybe you will become what is necessary to succeed here."

"What is that?"

"Wolf coming down from the mountains."

He snapped his cloth twice. "O.K., mister," he said. "How you like that shine? Huh? Huh?"

The man looked at his shoes while Stavros sidled to block the exit to the door. He smiled at the man. "Like a mirror, beautiful!" he said.

The man tipped him, had to.

"See that?" Stavros said to his brother, throwing the nickel in the air. "I learned here life, what it is, in this country." He showed his brother a fist. "To learn how to make this from your soft hand."

Demosthenes looked anxious. The boys were smiling at him.

"First thing, you must make these boys afraid of you. That is only reason for honesty in this country. Fear. America, America. Power and fear. The money from here, you bring it to me, every cent, every night, secret. Honest calculation. I am your capitalist! I will pay you three dollars week. Lots of money, three dollars. You'll find that out. I'm also paying your home, remember that and food—right? This way I will educate you in my school. Maybe it's too late for you. Or maybe I can make a man from you. You been listening me?"

Demosthenes had been examining the three young Greeks from Bulgaria who had suddenly been put in his charge.

"Everything you say," he lied.

"I'm putting you to watch these young thieves, you understand that?"

"You want this job secret? Even from Fofo?"

"Especially from Fofo. She'll get idea I'm rich man and begin to spend more money on the house. I learned when I was a hamal not to trust anyone on money. I'm going now. You stay here today. Learn the business. When I'm through work, I come show you how to lock up every night. Then we go home. Well, what you say?"

The shoeshine boys all smiled at their newly appointed overseer.

Demosthenes couldn't help smiling back at the boys.

"When they smile at you like that," Stavros said, "don't smile back. Friendly, so forth, no good. Come outside with me."

When they were on the street Stavros said, "First, here's a dime for your lunch, sandwich, glass of milk. Milk gives strength. Now listen good. They will try to make you cheat me. They will say, We take a little, you take a little, that way we all be happy. I'm warning you, that's what they will do. You understand?"

"Really, they will?"

"Of course. Everybody cheat everybody in this country. Same like Turkey. You will see. But be careful. If you take one nickel, they got you. Then they can threaten you."

"It's very complicated," Demosthenes said, "life in the United States."

"Now you learn something!" Stavros said. "Remember this: You will never fool me. Sooner, later, I find out. Because I learn on the docks to expect the worst from everybody. Now come here."

Demosthenes advanced cautiously. He thought Stavros might hit him again.

Stavros kissed him on both cheeks. "You're a good boy," he said. "I hope so. Goodbye."

"Goodbye, Joe," Demosthenes said.

NOVEMBER 1913

For almost a year, Vacilli worked at Sarrafian Brothers and worked well. But he was generally disliked. For one thing, he wouldn't talk. Spoken to, he'd nod his head or shake it, given an assignment, he did it skillfully, but when he was praised, he'd shrug his shoulders and pout.

Another thing: He had a strange body odor. Mrs. Morgan Perry, on one of her visits to the store, noted it. "Is that terrible smell coming from that man?" she asked, pointing. Mrs. Morgan Perry was a woman who insisted on good manners from those around her while claiming the privilege of behaving as she herself pleased.

One of the young porters, for the hell of it, told Vacilli what she'd said. That did it. Continuously depressed, he began to hint that he was going to leave.

Big Morgan Perry, give him credit, made an effort to be cordial. Vacilli wouldn't respond. He was afraid of Morgan Perry. Then Young Morgan tried, at his father's urging—for Vacilli was a conscientious worker, they all had to admit that, and good touch-up men were rare. Vacilli wouldn't yield to Young Morgan either.

Finally he did agree to a lunch, and it was at this lunch that Young Morgan was stricken for the first time.

Big Morgan connected Vacilli with his son's sudden illness. Vacilli noticed that the store manager kept looking at him in a threatening manner. He prepared for the worst. Not dismissal. Worse.

One day Big Morgan said to Vacilli, "Young Morgan is going into the hospital tomorrow."

There was something accusatory, it seemed to Vacilli, about the way Perry said this.

Vacilli muttered something inaudible. In another language.

"What was that?" Big Morgan said.

"He said, 'May Allah make his years green!' " Stavros had walked up to defend his brother.

"I mean, what language was he speaking?"

"That was Turkish," Stavros said.

"But we're Americans here, Christians," Morgan Perry protested.

"All the same," Vacilli said.

"It's not all the same," Big Morgan said. "It's all different."

"All one God, no?" Vacilli said, sure of his ground on this.

"It's not all one God. Don't call your God down on my boy." Big Morgan turned to Stavros. "Is that what he's been doing?"

"Only for health," Vacilli said. "Best wishes good health." He just managed to get this in before his brother waved him away.

When he was out of earshot, Morgan Perry asked Stavros, "Joe, why does your brother smell that way?"

"I don't smell anything," Stavros said.

"Because you smell the same way. Sort of a goat smell." Big Morgan laughed at his own joke and went to share the laugh with Miss Emily Barton. But his good humor didn't last. The news from the hospital was worrying, and later in the day, he cornered Vacilli again.

"What did you do at that lunch?" he asked. "Did you do something to Young Morgan there?"

"What lunch? Oh that? Do something? What?"

"That's what I'm asking. Where did you eat?"

"Armenian please. I mean, Armenian place."

"How come his stomach bleeding started that afternoon and hasn't stopped since?"

"Same thing happen my father," Vacilli said, "when he die."

It was then that Vacilli saw a light in the big Welshman's eyes that frightened him.

"He wants to kill me," he told Stavros that night. "He blames me for his son's death."

"What are you talking?" Stavros said. "Young Morgan did not die. What's the matter with you? There is something about you . . ."

Stavros didn't say what, but even he began to watch Vacilli in a different way. He always remembered the next thing Vacilli said. "He's going to die, and after he does, his father will blame me and he will kill me. I don't go back to that store, my Stavros."

Stavros couldn't budge him. As it happened, they had plenty of work for Vacilli at home so he never went back to Sarrafian Brothers, not even to collect the half-week's salary due him.

His sudden and unexplained disappearance confirmed Morgan Perry's suspicions. When Young Morgan died, his father blamed Vacilli and did forever after.

Although Stavros had no reason to dislike Young Morgan, and in fact liked him as a person better than anyone else at Sarrafian Brothers, he had feelings about his death which he wouldn't admit even to himself. It created the opening he had been waiting for.

On the thirteenth of November, peace was affirmed between Greece and Turkey. The draft treaty ceded to Greece the great island of Crete, where many Turkish people lived, as well as those Aegean islands not previously slipped across a green felt tabletop to the Italians by secret treaties.

After Michaelis had read the conditions of the peace to his brothers, Stavros said, "So at last, Michaelis, you're happy."

"I should have been there," Michaelis said.

"There be other wars," Stavros said. "Don't worry."

The others didn't let this opportunity to celebrate escape. The men fogged an ouzo milky white and another, then demanded that the slab of *bastourma* they'd been saving for Christmas be sliced and fried. Oh, how that garlicked bellymeat sizzled, filling the air with its sting. Eleni prepared her specialty, a halvah pudding of farina and roasted almonds, heavily dusted with cinnamon. Even the old lady brightened for the first time in weeks, when Eleftheria knelt before her and covered her face with kisses, saying, "Mommah, Mommah, we've won a great victory. There is peace at last."

There was a grunt and Eleftheria turned on her brother, saying, "And the peace is good for us, isn't it, Michaelis? Say!" so commanding him to help cheer the old woman, who hadn't been feeling well.

"Only the last peace is good," Michaelis said. "This one is for us to prepare for the final war, the one which will make Anatolia Greece once more and our land and villages ours again. *Embros!*" he barked, as he strode out of the apartment.

"At the Kaffenion Cappodocia tonight," Seraphim said, "there are mad dogs."

MARCH 1914

He watched her survive the winter. Through the cruel months she sat at her window over 136th Street, her hand on the radiator. Many a dead-cold night she endured half asleep, staring into the black and drawing what heat she could through her hand on the old gilded fixture.

In the morning her toes were icy. Stavros would rub her ankles and feet to pull the blood down and make it circulate again.

"Why you look at me that way, Mommah," he said the morning of a heavy snowfall. "What you thinking?"

"Why you put me here this country?" she said.

"Because on the other side Turks killing Christians."

"I never had trouble with the Turks. Even on the streets."

"Now they pull out their knives again."

"Why you brought us here?" she persisted. "Idea was Constantinople, where many Anatolian Greeks stay, not here, where only strangers. And cold! What is it you wanted, coming here? Give me answer, the truth this time—what you want here?"

He thought about it, really for the first time, and what he said surprised him as well as his mother. "I want to be an American," he said. "I want to be powerful. I want to be an American. I want to be rich. I want to be an American. I want to be boss in this world. I want to—"

"Ho! Peh, peh, peh! I knew you were crazy. Now you talk of being tyrant over the world? My God, my God!"

"The rug-business world, yes!"

"Poh, poh, poh, poh!"

"Don't laugh. In America, everything possible."

"All right. Enough, enough." Her eyes went blank as she turned her head away. Looking out the window now, she focused uncertainly on the orphan children in the great yard opposite and on the comings and goings through the street below. She seemed to be staring through space and into memory.

He saw that her face was gray and wasting, ordered Eleni to bring herb tea at intervals through the day and force the woman to eat. "Eat an egg, Mommah," he'd command before he left for work every morning and when he came home at night, the first thing he'd ask was: "You eat your egg today, Mommah, in the name of the Virgin?"

"Maybe make me piece dry toast, Eleni-Fofo," she'd say, linking the names to make sure one of them attended her.

"That's all she eats!" Stavros protested. "Vacilli, make her eat an egg, this stubborn old she-mule."

"Egg gives strength," Vacilli said, "so naturally she won't eat it. She wants to die here, in that chair, damn fool."

Her cheekbones shone like yellowing ivory under the parchment skin. She was starving herself.

The old woman slept in her chair, her hand on the radiator. Alone in the front room at night, she was taken over by dreams and delusions. She'd mutter, curse, argue, say harsh things, imitate a man's gruff voice calling from a distance, then say a word that sounded like *"Amessos!"* say it twice: "Immediately, immediately!"

Stavros would steal in and sit opposite, observing her where she sat by the black window. "What you saying there, what you dreaming, Mommah?" he'd ask. He never got an answer. Yes, once he did, but it explained nothing. "*He* was not afraid of the Turk," she said. "They were afraid of him."

"Who, Mommah?" he asked.

She looked angry, but it wasn't at him. "*He* would not have put me on a boat to a country of strangers and die to spite me the day the boat sailed. *He* would not have left me sitting here all night alone at this window of ice."

Stavros knew whom she was scorning—her husband. But the other man? It couldn't have been a lover lost. Vasso had been with only one man in her life, Stavros had no doubt of that.

The weeks passed. By the middle of March, Vasso was not even responding to Stavros. Not knowing what to do, he offered silent prayers—for spring. Perhaps the new year's "opening," as Greeks called the spring, perhaps the old miracle of the warming sun which woke all other creatures who'd slept through the cold would reach her and bring her back.

Late in the month, the soiled snow still fringed the side streets of the island of Manhattan. Finally, just as Stavros began to believe that the city would never be warm again, never again clean, there came a downpouring of rain, followed by two days of scorching sun. The gutters down the hill of 136th Street carried a cascade of water that flushed them clean. The patches of snow in the backyards shrank, then disappeared. Behind the building where the Topouzoglou family lived, the stiff body of a cat, locked out during a January snowfall and forgotten, was uncovered. Schimmel, the janitor, removed it with his coal shovel.

For the first time in five months, windows were thrown open. This had an effect: Vasso's body responded. On the blessed Sunday of Easter, a warm, gentle day, Vasso took her hand off the radiator and didn't put it on again.

Stavros saw it happen and decided, as the morning warmed, to take the old woman out of the house. He ordered Eleni and Fofo to dress her for the street.

"Her legs not so strong," Eleni warned him.

"What you expect, sitting all winter?" Stavros said. "Get her ready, we're going."

On Broadway, running between 136th and 135th Streets, there was an island of cobbles and paving between the lanes of traffic. It provided a place for some benches, painted green; there were also four small trees. These are now gone.

It was to one of these benches, under one of these trees, that Stavros led his mother. "Look up at this tree, Mommah," he said. "Look up and see! Spring is in the sky."

Vasso sat heavily, then slowly lifted her head and looked through the bare branches to the warm blue sky. "When I was dying," she said, "I thought of Vacilli. The others are . . . whatever they are. What can I do? But Vacilli . . ." She raised her hands uncertainly.

"When were you dying, Mommah, God's sake? What the hell kind of talk is that, dying?"

"This winter, many times. But I didn't care. You know what they say —cry when you come into the world, laugh when you go out." She laughed, showing the gaps where teeth were missing.

"Never, Mommah. I need your help. What can I do with these girls? I have to find husband for them before I marry. What I know from this kind business?"

"It's Vacilli needs help," Vasso said. "He is like your father, a weak man. Also something"—she touched her temple—"here, not . . . uh . . ." She waggled a hand. "When I'm gone, you must take care of him."

"I had same idea," Stavros said. "But for you, you must do something now. Look!"

He reached into his coat pocket and pulled out the kind of rag good wives make of old shirts and discarded underwear. "This is from Vacilli's body," Stavros said. "See here where you shorten the sleeve?" Then he ripped off a narrow strip about a foot long and offered it to her.

"Now do like you used to do, Mommah. To this tree here. Your son needs help, help from you and from God. Stand up! Come! Up!"

He helped her to her feet and steadied her. Then, standing on the bench, he pulled the lowest branch down until the end twig with its three plumping buds, as tender as a young woman's nipples, was within his mother's reach.

Vasso knew what to do. With fingers still stiff from the cold, she tied the strip of cloth to the twig. Then she crossed herself, saying, "Christ Risen, Lord of my soul, hear me. My son has need of your help. Hear me. Help me!" Whereupon Stavros released the branch and it sprung back to its position, holding high the strip of cloth.

The ritual completed, they sat on the bench, side by side, the man with the defiant face and his mother with the look of scorn, watching the flow of alien traffic.

"Look those Turks," Vasso said, shaking her head in disapproval.

Stavros laughed. "They're not Turks, Mommah. This is America here."

"Same thing." She spit.

"When you rested," Stavros said, "we walk to the bakery, buy two dozen French pastries assorted. I get you one napoleon, the kind you like —remember with the cream filling? Oppa! It's spring, Mommah. Easter! Christ has risen and it's time to eat French pastries."

But she wasn't listening. "I want explain you something before I die," she said.

"Oh, Mommah, again? The dying business?"

"This winter I saw the dark place waiting for me and I knew I wouldn't see my home again."

"You will, Mommah. I promise you. Did you forget?"

"You promise many things, Stavros."

"I promised I'd take you to Kayseri in Anatolia to our old home, where you can see the great white mountain, Aergius, again and—"

"I don't want to see that damn white mountain."

"That's what you asked me, isn't it? To go there again?"

"That's not where I want to go," she said. She was looking at him steadily, without wavering, as she spoke. "When I was dying, I thought: *There is one thing I must tell Stavros before I leave,* and it is this. Get ready." She closed her eyes and said, "Your father, he was a lazy man and he was a cowardly man. That's why the boys, your brothers, are the way they are."

"And me?" Stavros was shocked.

"You are different piece goods. You are not his son."

"Don't say bad things about Father, please, Mommah. He was a good man."

"Never mind good man business." She looked at him. "You don't remember how he was in the bazaar, sitting in front of that small hole he called his store, waiting for customers, maybe one every day, when he's lucky? Meantime, gossip, talk, one coffee, another coffee, couple games backgammon—you don't remember? He made lazy boys of your brothers. 'Turk works with his back, Greek with his brains.' How many times he said that? Only you, you went to hamal school, you became a man."

"Please, Mommah. Father was a saint. Don't talk—"

"Yes, a saint, and we're paying for it." She looked at him angrily. "I didn't say it before, but now, when I'm finished, I must tell you: He was a lazy man and he was a cowardly man."

Finally Stavros's anger revealed itself. "Then tell me why you holler 'Immediately, immediately' in your sleep to him?"

"Who heard me saying *'Amessos, amessos'* to him?"

"Everybody heard it. And the trembling in your voice like you're 'fraid."

" 'Fraid from Isaac? Never! When he was alive, I pay him proper respect, I'm sure, always. But fear—never; no fear of him." Then she said it again, *"Amessos, amessos!"* and again Stavros heard the tremble in her voice and saw the fear of respect in her eyes.

"I been seeing my father," she said, touching her head with a finger. "I never talk to you about my father?"

"Why? Why you never spoke of him?"

"Because I been angry at him all my life. Not a good thing." Again she looked at Stavros as if she was judging him. "Now, before I die, I better tell you. He was like you, that's what I mean—*he* was your father. It jumped over Isaac, your soul. So you can say you are his son that way."

She closed her eyes and began to talk, and he didn't know how much of what she said now was truth remembered and how much fantasy that time had spun. But a great stream was released. Stavros learned the cause of the tremble in her eyes and in her voice.

It was the memory of this man whom Stavros had never met because he lived far from Kayseri, offshore of Anatolia, on a high point of the island of Chios. By trade he was a boat builder and he never left the place by the water where he worked, or his home over the harbor of Chios.

Except once. When he'd brought his daughter, aged seventeen, across the narrow channel of Aegean water to Smyrna, to put her in service with a prospering merchant, his hope being that she might be found there by a man looking for a wife and prosperous enough to take Vasso without a dowry. There she'd worked, a children's nurse in a respectable home, until Isaac, a decent, reliable man in his middle years, come to Smyrna to buy cotton goods for his store in Kayseri, had seen her and decided she was what he wanted for a wife.

She never saw her father again.

"I wrote him I was getting married," she said, "but he didn't come. Three months later I got a letter from my mother saying my father sent me his best wishes. Last I heard. Best wishes!"

"And I'm like that?"

"Yes. That's the way he was, and that's the way you are—what can you do? A man who wouldn't come to his daughter's wedding. You're the same—that kind of man."

"What do you dream when you say, '*Amessos, amessos*'? That?"

Now, sitting on a traffic island within this stream of Manhattan traffic, she spoke at last to her eldest son of her childhood home.

It was on a ridge of a series of ridges, and it had a view of the circular harbor below and of the sea beyond.

Her head back, her eyes closed, she spoke of the sounds that inhabited that place and still inhabited her memory—sounds of the water running night and day, coming down a pipe from the cool spring above and emptying into a wooden tub in the family's yard. She spoke of the roosters boasting and the hens clucking and scratching, the dogs barking and quarreling and the donkeys braying, here and there on the neighboring ridges. She spoke of the wind off the water, always that wind, the *melteme*, whistling off the sea.

She spoke of the grapes, purple and red, hanging from the frame over the outdoor table where her father ate, the sun ripening and sweetening them, week after week, and of their "boiling" in the wine barrels, for her father made his own wine every fall, and of that other drink, stronger than the wine, the mouth-burner people called *tsiporo*—oh, how that smell stung her nostrils even now!

"Is this a place to live?" she asked, looking at the traffic and the Broadway buildings with their winter's coat of grime.

"And *'Amessos, amessos!'* " he said. "What was that?"

"He'd come up from the boatyard after work," she said, "bringing shellfish home, whatever the boats had brought in, sweet clams or those tender prickly ones like thistles—they were his favorites. As he mounted the last piece of road up the rocky hill, he'd shout to my mother—and to me—letting us know that he was coming and that he wanted his ouzo ready and the cold well water in a jar by his hand and his dinner, hot, and the bread she'd made that morning beside it.

"And we'd shout, *'Amessos, Baba, amessos!'* and run to have everything ready for him. I'd stand behind his chair as he opened the shellfish with his curved shuck knife. I remember those soft little sea thistles, how he'd make them naked with his knife, and when the juice from the lemon halves hit them, oh, how they'd clench and quiver! Then down his throat they'd go, with the ouzo just behind.

"After dinner, he'd tell stories as the wind came in from the sea, the clean wind, not like here, with smoke and dirt. How can you compare that life with this? Or to where your father, Isaac, took me, either, that house where you were born? Yes, you could see the great white mountain, but the place where we lived was flat, and the dust in the summer was to my ankles deep and there was no flow of water, only a well that dried up every June or earlier—once in April, yes, in April!

"In my father's place, we never closed the doors or the windows at night. There were Turkish people there, but they respected my father because they feared him. But your father, Isaac, was afraid and every window, you remember, in the house where you were born had bars. As soon as the sun fell, the shutters were closed and locked. It was like a jail."

She opened her eyes at last, laid her head back on the top of the bench, and looked up at the piece of Vacilli's shirt in the little tree. "Your father was not the man for me," she said. "After so many years, now I can say that. I say it to you because you are the head of the family and you must know who you are."

Then she looked directly at Stavros and her eyes had an accusing glint. "I want to tell you this too." And she spoke very slowly, stressing each word. "He treated me like a servant, Isaac, your father. A servant he found me; so he treated me. I had no admiration for your father, not ever."

"Why, then, did you marry him?"

"What was I to do? A girl without a dowry, abandoned by her own people who only wanted to be rid of her, to 'sell' her—that's how the Turks say it. So he sold me. Isaac sent him one rug, six by nine. That was my price."

Now she took Stavros's hand and she kissed it.

"I paid your father respect, don't think I didn't. He had nothing to complain of from me. I paid him respect even though sometimes it was hard. But . . . but I'll say it again. He was a cowardly man. I needed to say that to you before I died. Now I feel better."

"He was a gentle man, Mommah. Say it that way."

"Who paid for that 'gentle'? You did. With your money. I can't imagine that my father would have taken the abuse from Hassapoglou that Isaac did. How often I thought of that during those days in Smyrna. My father would have strung Hassapoglou Effendi's entrails on a stick and roasted them over a slow fire to take *mezeh* with his ouzo."

"I will take care this Hassapoglou one day," Stavros said.

"I believe that. Because you come from my side. You are an island person, you don't come from the flatlands and the bazaars." She looked fondly at her eldest.

"You're not going to die, Mommah, I won't let you. Come on, get up. We'll walk to the bakery. Come, come."

"I wanted to tell you who you were so you'd have pride in it. There are village people and there are island people and you are an island person. There are merchants who sit all day in the bazaar and tremble at the sight of a Turk, like your father, and there are men who live by the sea and are not afraid of anyone. That's what you are. I give you advice, last words. Don't wait for your brothers, do it yourself. They're afraid of everybody here, like they were there—what's the difference? When they're insulted, they say nothing. You're different man."

She closed her eyes, having said what she'd wanted to say. She was contented.

Stavros kissed her and said, "Come. Now napoleons."

"I'm tired," she said. "Talking too much."

"You not tired," he said. "You look good! First time. Get up! You're an island person. Get up."

They walked to the curb and waited for an opening in the traffic.

"So when you say you will take me back to that house under his damn white mountain, I don't want to go there again."

"I know where to take you now. I will take you to your island, to Chios. You will live your last years there, looking at the sea, and you will —when your time comes—you will lie there, high on a hill, at peace. That I promise."

Taking her hand, his arm under her elbow, he led her across the half street. She walked more confidently now than before she had spoken. Some of her strength had returned. Stavros saw her eyes shining.

They walked to the bakery and they walked home. The children saw that she had revived and greeted her with kisses. They had an Easter party and she ate half a napoleon.

AUGUST 1914

At the end of the fifth day of a record-breaking hot spell, a Saturday when every child in the city was out on the street and their elders—those who couldn't afford a trip to the mountains or the shore—were on their tenement roofs or sitting on the stoops, Seraphim, the most dutiful and the most reliable of the Topouzoglou "boys," the one who managed the household and whom everyone in the family trusted, this conscientious and decent man, just turned thirty-three, disappeared.

When they realized what had happened, no one of the family could guess where he might have gone or why. He'd simply vanished.

"Long live Greater Greece! Long live Greece in Asia!" The young priest threw these final words at the congregation as if the fate of their fatherland was in the hands of each man there, then, crossing himself quickly, he opened the gate of the tiny pulpit nest, perhaps ten feet off the floor, swept down the curve of narrow steps, paraded across the center aisle and past the men standing shoulder to shoulder there (heavy men, men of substance, their hands folded before them) and along the seats on the side where the women worshiped (proper women, women in black dresses, their faces partly covered). Gliding under his long black robe, he passed through the gilt door to the inner shrine where two great white candles stood sentinel, and so out of sight. The door closed, a silence remained and a delicate scent, the incense of the ritual.

Stavros was as astonished as anyone else by the young priest and by what he'd said, less a sermon, it had been, than an incitation. It was as if he'd usurped the high pulpit, not been granted its privilege. The man beneath the habit was spare, his body taut, eyes dark and threatening. A ringlet of heavy black hair fell over one temple and a taunting smile challenged those who were listening: You can't have expected what you heard from me!

Father Rondiris, when he'd introduced Father Achilleas Galoyeropoulos to his congregation that Sunday morning, had explained that he'd come with a letter from the archbishop of Smyrna, which designated the young priest as his representative in the United States, dispatched on a most important mission, and asking the priest of every Greek Orthodox church in the new land to offer Father Achilleas his pulpit for one Sunday. His Eminence's wishes were respected, of course, despite the youth of the newcomer and a racy vigor to which the good Greeks of the congregation were not accustomed.

Once out of sight, Father Achilleas's pace did not slacken; his purpose was not accomplished. In the vestibule at the side of the altar, he pulled off the ceremonial garments, attached Father Rondiris as escort (a brotherly embrace), and passed into the body of the church, crossing behind the men who'd chanted scripture and were now folding over the heavily encrusted covers of their hymnals. They rose from their crescent of high seats as the priests passed, inspecting Father Achilleas with wonder. Perhaps they were remembering, with a twist of envy, their own days of fire. They had never before heard such militancy from the pulpit of their church; it had been a demand for participation, not a plea for help. The young priest had wakened the congregation's guilt.

Stavros's family, at the rear and to the side, having come to consult Father Rondiris, waited. It was the custom each Sunday for the worshipers, exhausted by the end of the service, which lasted from nine until one, to rush from the church for their homes and the warm ovens, where the roasts of lamb and the great pots of rice with raisins and pine nuts waited. But Stavros saw that today this was not happening. As the young priest approached, the crowd moved forward, not back, gathering around him in thickening numbers until Father Achilleas was forced to stop.

"Your place of birth, Father, where is it?" asked a middle-aged Greek with the heavy-jeweled rings and the clothes of an affluent merchant.

"Aivalik," Father Achilleas said. "You know where that is?"

"It's on the coast," another man said. "Am I right, Father?"

"Yes. Across from the island of Lesbos and its city, Mytilene," the young priest said.

"The citizens of Aivalik are famous," the man went on, speaking to the group gathering around the young priest. "They have never shown the Turk their backs—am I right again, Father?"

Stavros could see that Father Rondiris was trying to get his attention, and he gestured back. The family had come to the church for help. There had been no sign of Seraphim through that entire week. Even Stavros was concerned and Vasso had taken to sitting at her window all night, watching the street below, falling off to sleep and waking again to curse the son who was costing her so much worry.

Stavros didn't like the priest Rondiris or his church, but there was no one else he could turn to for help. It didn't occur to him to go to the police.

Now Father Rondiris had taken his young companion's elbow and was trying to move him forward. "There they are," he said, "waiting for you. The Topouzoglou family, you were asking for. Fine people. You will see."

Again the progress of the pair was blocked.

"You've brought us hope, Father," a man said. "I've been waiting so many years to hear what you said from there." He pointed to the pulpit. "Thanks to God, all Greece will be Greece again."

"You spoke very well," another man said, "and I can understand that the people in Anatolia must feel as you feel. But in Greece proper, the people there, what do they say about the eastern lands? Are they ready to risk their lives for this?"

"They speak as he speaks," the old priest, Rondiris, hissed. He seemed impatient, angry. "*Aye-air-ah! Aye-air-ah!*" he whispered, raising his fist and stamping his feet in place as if he were marching.

"I for one am going," a heavily built man said. "I made up my mind while you were speaking. I will put my lunch counter in the hands of my wife's brother who has one leg, damn fool, and I will go there and fight for the fatherland. I am ready to die, even that!"

"They will be glad to see you there when you arrive." Father Achilleas noticed the man's protruding belly and smiled. "But first you must practice running. You have to catch the rooster before you can cut his throat."

"I know, I know." The man struck his belly with a fist. "Please don't imagine me the way I am now. It's because of where I spend my days, behind that lunch counter. I get nervous and I eat!"

"The truth is," Achilleas said, and again there was a kind of arrogance in his manner, "what we need from you first is not bravery—courage is for the young to show now. What we want from you is money. To buy the best new weapons for our boys. Automatics!"

"*Embros!*" Father Rondiris said, "Forward!" And taking Father Achilleas's elbow, he tried to push him toward the Topouzoglous.

But the young priest had more to say. "Money now is as important as blood." He was speaking to all the men around him. "The archbishop is waiting to hear your response to his message. There is only one way our future can be solved: by speaking the language the Turk understands." Father Achilleas made his hand into a fist and thrust it forward. "*Aye-air-ah! Embros!*"

Father Rondiris made a gesture of drawing a sword out of a scabbard. "*Embros! Embros!*" he shouted.

"After the war," a man asked, "tell us, Father, who will decide what is decided?"

"A war," Father Achilleas said, "is how history moves forward and justice is reestablished. When we win, it will be up to us to decide. For instance, Smyrna. There are more Greeks than Turks there! It is only just that it should be the heart of the Greater Greece that is coming. But we will be fair. Remember that democracy was born in Greece, in ancient Athens."

Again he felt Rondiris taking his elbow and this time he yielded. "Where are they?" he asked.

"There. Waiting for you." Father Rondiris pointed. "Hurry, before they leave. The man there, the oldest son, he's a rough skin!"

A woman stepped directly in their path. "What you were saying from up there before," she said to the young priest. "You don't mean our men should take three, four wives, as the Turk does? You said that as a joke, of course."

"Never mind, never mind that empty stuff now," Rondiris said, waving the woman off.

Achilleas held back. "It was a joke, yes. Also a warning. The Turk grows, we shrink. They take three or four women, we take one wife. They make a dozen children, we are civilized—we make three, perhaps four. Are we too civilized for this crisis? A great war is coming, a holy war. We will need many soldiers . . ."

The last of this he'd said over his shoulder as Rondiris pushed him forward, so the woman missed the end of the explanation.

"I think he does want our men to take three or four wives," the woman said sourly.

Men gathered around her. "He expects us to do our duty more often," one of them said.

At last the two priests broke through the congregation and found themselves before the Topouzoglou family.

"This fine family," Rondiris said with a wave of his arm, "they are the Topouzoglous from the Cappadocia province of Anatolia. You've heard of the city Kayseri? The people from there are too clever. For instance, today they come to my church all together for the first time in many months, so something bad must have happened. When things go well, these people don't come to church." He turned to Stavros. "You! Sir! You are being introduced to Father Achilleas Galoyeropoulos who comes from the archbishop of Smyrna himself. So kiss his hand. Quick!"

There was an awkward silence. Father Achilleas didn't offer his hand, nor did Stavros reach for it.

"Let's go in a corner where it's quiet," Father Achilleas said. "I have brought a message to you from the archbishop, and in my room I have some little things he gave me in memory of your dear father." He turned directly to Vasso. "Dear *Valideh* Topouzoglou. You remember me? From Smyrna? From the cathedral, Aghia Fotini? You saw me there many times."

"Yes, yes, of course," Vasso said.

Stavros could tell that she didn't remember the young priest. "She doesn't know you," he said.

"She will, give her little time," Father Rondiris said. "Now. I brought you together. Talk. I have to make a baptism."

"Wait!" Stavros said, holding on to his arm. "We came here to speak to you, not this one."

Demosthenes and Michaelis and the two younger girls had pressed around the young priest. "Stavros," Michaelis said, "we know Father Achilleas very well."

"May you be happy," Eleni said to the young priest and smiled.

"I remember you," the priest said. "You've grown up!"

Eleni blushed.

Stavros took Father Rondiris by the arm and led him aside to where Vasso waited. There he told him why they'd come.

"Yes, yes," Father Rondiris said. "And his name, dear mother?"

"Seraphim," Vasso said.

"Beautiful name! Seraphim! One of the singing angels, six wings over God's throne." He turned to Stavros. "I understand. I see what kind of family you are. A family exists when, if someone disappears, someone worries. You're all here? Good! I know, dear mother, sons don't always behave the way their fathers teach. America, America, eh?"

"Maybe he die somewhere," Vasso said.

This idea shocked Stavros; he hadn't considered such a possibility. "Should we go to the police?" he asked the priest.

"No, no, not necessary," Rondiris said. He took Vasso's hand and kissed it. "God will watch over us. I will write other priests, five beautiful letters this afternoon, with my own hand. Believe me, we have many churches, many places. My brothers in Christ will find your son, dear lady." He turned back to Stavros. "Don't bother the police. All Irish over there. You come to church, you do right. Greek to Greek! I have much experience"—he made a sly gesture, the twist of a crooked finger at his temple—"with these secret matters. Wait for word from me." And he hustled off.

The young ones were still around Father Achilleas.

"Father Achilleas has been telling us about Father's grave," Eleni said to her older brother.

SEPTEMBER 1914

The deposit he'd been dispatched to make in a downtown bank consisted of five checks to the order of Sarrafian Brothers, totaling $8,922. On the way back to the office on the trolley, Stavros divided this figure by the amount of his weekly salary, forty dollars. Now that Young Morgan was gone, Stavros wanted to be considered the number two salesman behind Big Morgan, with an appropriate salary. He determined to demand a raise once again, and if the answer was no, he'd deliver a warning, one he practiced as the trolley car rolled and rattled. "If you don't—give me—I open—our own store—and day will come—watch out—I ruin—your company!"

Anger warmed him. Perhaps the time to open his own store had come. His brothers knew the trade now and Stavros knew the market. What reason to delay further? Money. Yes, they'd do better starting with more cash and more stock, but—

He knew what Mr. Ara Sarrafian's answer would be: "Talk to Morgan Perry." Well, he'd go straight to Big Morgan, that side of beef, and give him his ultimatum.

As soon as he opened the door of the office, however, Stavros knew this wasn't the moment to ask Perry anything. The store manager had visitors. It was a Wednesday, and Mrs. Norma Perry had come in from Mount Ivy, New Jersey, to enjoy a matinee with her daughter, Althea, and the girl's fiancé, Freddie Farrow, a young stockbroker.

They seemed to be enjoying a family quarrel, so Stavros skirted the edge of their group, heading past them to give the bankbook and the stamped deposit slip to Emily Barton, the company treasurer.

"What they doing here?" Joe asked her.

"Spending money," she answered. Years ago Miss Emily had had a liaison with Morgan Perry and since the day he'd called it off, she'd hated his wife.

"I don't want to go, Mother," Stavros heard Althea say.

"Why not, dear?" Mrs. Perry was proud of her patience.

"Because I don't like the theater, it's silly."

"Ethel Barrymore silly!" She turned to Freddie Farrow, who had already been established as mediator in their family quarrels. "There you are, Freddie!" she said.

"Well, then, trivial," Althea said. "It's certainly that."

"The only people Althea takes seriously are the poor," Mrs. Perry said to Freddie. "That's what they taught her at Vassar." She turned back to her daughter, who had noticed Stavros and was waving to him. "Believe me, my dear, they are just like the rich, only more stupid."

Stavros nodded at Althea, whom he'd met there several times.

"Which—may I also say this, dear?—is the reason they're poor," Mrs. Perry said.

"Mother," Althea said, "I am not going to the theater, so don't waste your breath."

"Now, Althea, do stop raising your voice! It's vulgar. Let's be reasonable and do what I ask. There isn't a girl in your set who wouldn't give her birthright to see Miss Ethel Barrymore—"

Althea jumped out of her chair and walked to the back of the store, where Stavros was taking off his suit coat and hanging it up.

"Yes, there is, and her name is Althea Perry," she said.

"Darling," Mrs. Perry called after her, "Freddie has met us here in the belief that we are going to take him to a matinee. You don't want to disappoint Freddie, do you?"

"Freddie doesn't like the theater either."

"I don't mind not going, Mrs. Perry," Freddie said.

"Freddie says that," Mrs. Perry called back, "because you've already managed to terrorize him. Well, even if he says he doesn't mind, I mind. I mind for him. It's inconsiderate, it's bad manners, and—who's that back there with you in the dark?"

Stavros didn't offer to identify himself.

"I'd better go pick up the tickets," Freddie said, "or we'll have to rush our lunch. Althea!" His fiancée had found a magazine and didn't look up. "Althea, pay attention! We'll to to Lüchow's and have an apple pancake."

"I will most certainly not go to Lüchow's," Mrs. Perry said. "I hate that heavy German meat with all the fat left on. And you will certainly not go and pick up the tickets, Freddie. You are not an errand boy. Why are you so damned humble?" She turned to her husband. "Morgan, send somebody immediately to the Empire Theater to pick up our tickets before they sell them out from under us as they did the last time."

"Give me something to do quick," Stavros whispered to Miss Barton, "before he send me out again."

Then Stavros heard, "Joe!"

"Shit," Stavros said in Greek. "I'm busy, Mr. Perry," he said in English.

But when Perry insisted, Stavros walked slowly and defiantly over to the group.

Althea had climbed on a pile of five-by-three Sarouk mats, where, keeled over on an elbow, she was looking at a copy of *Collier's*. She smiled at Stavros as he went by.

"Darling, your knees," Norma Perry called to her daughter.

"What about my knees?"

"Cover them. That's what your skirt's for."

As Stavros walked up, Mrs. Perry said, "Joe, meet Mr. Farrow."

"Freddie, meet Mr. Arness," Althea muttered to herself so everyone in the place could hear.

"Miss Barrymore is such a lady," Mrs. Perry said to no one in particular and everyone in general. "Just to watch her walk, sit, and talk is an education and a delight. Miss Barrymore's manners are instruction you sadly need, Althea dear. Morgan, would you give this young man the money for the tickets? He's waiting. Let's not be inconsiderate of others. Yes, her manners are perfect. Not Althea's, Freddie, Miss Barrymore's. And Morgan, we'll need money for lunch. No, I will not go to Dinty Moore's, don't even suggest it. Let's go to Delmonico's. Morgan, why don't we have some of these lovely carpets in our home? Ours are all so ratty."

Just then the door to Fernand Sarrafian's private office was opened cautiously and Mr. Ara, who'd taken refuge there when he'd heard Mrs. Perry's voice in the corridor, peeked out.

"Ara Sarrafian!" Mrs. Perry cried. "You come out here this minute!" She turned to Freddie. "He's so shy with women," she whispered. "Poor man!"

"How are you, Norma," Mr. Sarrafian said, as he tried to think of a reason not to come out.

"Come come, Ara," Mrs. Perry said, "I'm not going to attack you." She laughed. When Mr. Sarrafian still hesitated in the doorway, she lowered her voice again. "He's so shy, Freddie, yet he's worth millions, untold millions! I do wish he liked me. Why don't you like me, Ara? I have great respect for you."

"You have respect for anybody who has money," Althea muttered, loud enough for all to hear.

"Dear madam," Mr. Ara said, "I like you very much."

"I'm so relieved," Mrs. Perry said.

"Oh, Mother," Althea said from her little hill of Sarouk mats. "Stop flirting."

"Flirting! Althea, how dare you? You're really a very vicious girl. Morgan, I'm going to have to have a serious talk with your daughter. You've let her run wild. And Vassar didn't help." She turned back to Mr. Sarrafian, who was retreating again toward his brother's office. "Oh, Ara, you do recommend Delmonico's, don't you? For lunch?"

"My brother Fernand favors it," Mr. Sarrafian said. "But for me, it's expensive. I've given it up."

"Althea darling, cover your knees. Please!" Mrs. Perry said. Then, turning back to Mr. Sarrafian, she said, "They're her best feature. She has my legs. But still—I mean, she is engaged. Freddie, what are you doing?"

Freddie was taking money from Morgan Perry.

"I don't mind going, Mrs. Perry. Joe says he's—"

"Morgan, are you really going to allow that? I've come to have luncheon with Freddie, not to send him traipsing all over town on unnecessary errands."

"Joe," Morgan Perry said, "here. It's the Empire Theater."

"On Fortieth Street and Broadway," Mrs. Perry added. "And bring the tickets to—Morgan, we can certainly afford Delmonico's just this once —to Delmonico's, Joe. We come into town so infrequently, Morgan."

Stavros pocketed the money and went back for his straw hat.

"I'm coming with you," Althea whispered to him as he went by. "I can't stand these people another minute."

Mrs. Perry went to Mr. Sarrafian, offering a smile. "Speaking of Vassar," she said, "did you hear about Althea's honor? This past June, she was elected to the Daisy Chain."

"Wonderful," Mr. Sarrafian said. "What is that?"

"The Daisy Chain at Vassar! You mean to tell me you don't know what that is?" Althea was imitating her mother's voice. "It means that she was recognized to be the prettiest girl in her senior class of more than three hundred assorted Christers, bookworms, and social reprobates."

Stavros, again making his circle of evasion around the group, hustled for the door.

"Wait, Joe," Althea called. "I'm going with you."

"Althea! Don't you dare," Mrs. Perry said. "We are going to lunch at Lüchow's—I mean at Delmonico's. Althea!"

"I don't want to go to lunch anywhere," Althea said as she slipped out the door. "And I'm not going to the theater!"

Mrs. Perry called, "Morgan! Will you please do something about your daughter!" But it was too late. She turned to Mr. Sarrafian. "You see, Ara," she said, "how he's spoiled her!"

They were passing the Waldorf, a hulking brown building at Thirty-fourth Street on Fifth Avenue, he marching at his own pace, she, a little behind, tagging along.

"Are you Armenian?" she asked.

Joe stabbed her over his shoulder with a furious look.

"I'm sorry," she said. "That question offend you? You don't like Armenians? None of my business? But then why do you work for them?"

Stavros didn't answer.

"Stupid question? Well, sorry—just think of me as ignorant," she said. "I was brought up by a mother who believes that all she needs to get by in this world is a set of good manners and a lawyer to protect the investments her father left her. Aren't they terrifying, my mother's manners? Weapons, they're weapons! You know what I'm trying to say?"

"No. Why you walking with me?"

"I like to meet people out of a different world," she said, "even when they don't answer. What are your parents like? Well, all right. I prefer silence to the sound of my mother's voice." She did an imitation: " 'Joe, this is Mr. Farrow.' Automatically he is mister and you are—what?"

"Goat. Your father calls me."

"I've heard him on the subject."

"Hey! What's the matter with you!" He pulled her back to the curb. "Look out before you cross the street. You get killed here."

"Thanks. You notice how my mother bullies him?"

"He should hit her."

"Wouldn't do any good. She's come to the conclusion that she married beneath her. But go back a generation and a half, and Mother's people were just micks who were lucky to escape the potato famine. How quickly people become snobs! What? You said something?"

"Yes. Horse coming. With wagon. Look where you walking."

"Oh, thanks. What are you, Joe? Now that I know you're not Armenian."

"Greek. From Anatolia."

"Where's that?"

"Asia. They call it Turkey on the map, but it's Greece. From the oldest days. You ever read Homer?"

"Yes, sure. Did you?"

"No. But he was from there."

"We had a course in ancient cultures, but I didn't learn that. Four years of college and I don't know something as important as that."

"You making fun of me?"

"No. Of myself."

"Look out! You get killed crossing the street this way. What's the matter with you?"

"Now you're doing it too."

"What?"

"Scolding me. Everybody's always scolded me. All my life people have been correcting my behavior. When I was a chubby little girl with a huge round belly—this is funny, listen. My mother was offended by the way I looked and she gave me this horrendous nickname—do you want to hear it?"

"Why not?"

"The little white gorilla! What she meant was that I was always clambering over the furniture and rolling on the floor and exhibiting my privates. Gorillas, of course, aren't burdened with modesty. What's the matter? You look cross."

"The way you talk," Stavros said, "not right for a woman."

"My mother's reaction precisely. So she engaged a nanny, an Englishwoman, Miss Lucy, whose job it was to make me behave properly—you know, keep my skirt down and close the bathroom door when I went. All I remember of Miss Lucy was that she used to say, 'Now, Althea! Now, Althea!' And that she was always plumping the pillows after I got off the sofa."

"Look out! The wagon!"

"Thanks. My mother still says it—'Now, Althea! Now, Althea!' Oh, how I hated that name. I asked my friends at college to call me Sally. Freddie still does, except when he's mad at me. But I seem to be part of the world now, so I'd better face the music. Althea it is! I'm going to be a social worker. Did I tell you that? Starting in two weeks. You know what they are?"

"No."

"People who work with poor families to help them."

"Tell me, you got lotsa money?"

"You mean I've been too protected all my life? That can be a curse, I know."

"Curse! Money? You don't like, give to me. I like money."

"Actually we're not wealthy. My grandmother, they say, has quite a bit. For which my mother is waiting. But my father—my mother is disappointed in him. You noticed that? Look, I'm going to ask you a favor. I don't know why you should do it, but—here. As soon as I start to work at the OCS, would you ask me to your home sometime?"

"What you want to come there for? We don't need charity help."

"I mean, just to meet your people. I want to get to know a lot of different people who aren't like my family and friends, to be out in the world and look around! I want to travel a lot too. Later. Oh, no—oh damn! Now they've sent Freddie after me."

Freddie Farrow was running toward them.

"Doesn't he run beautifully?" she said. "He used to be captain of the cross-country team at college. No, don't go away, stand over there against the building and wait. He's probably going to scold me too. If you're here waiting, he won't go on and on. You won't leave, will you? Promise!"

Before Stavros had a chance to say "Goodbye," Freddie had come up.

"What did they do—send you after me?" Althea asked.

"I came on my own," Freddie said. "I'm really sore at you." He looked at Stavros.

Stavros walked away a few paces and turned his back, but he didn't leave. At first he couldn't hear what they were saying; then they forgot he was there.

"And if you didn't want to go to the theater," Freddie was saying, "why did you have her come into town? That was pretty inconsiderate of you, don't you think?"

"Freddie, I didn't expect to carry on the way I did. I intended to be polite and obliging, go to the damned lunch and see Miss Barrymore, whom I rather like—do everything Mother might ask—and then she says something, and I'm off!"

Her voice had risen again. Freddie looked around at Stavros, whose back was turned.

And who was thinking: *My God, are these the only problems such people have?*

"But why make fun of her voice and her manner? She can't help how she is. Why keep after her all the time?"

"She embarrasses me. To be her daughter embarrasses me."

"But she's your mother, Althea, and you're not going to change that—"

"I know. Today I got angry because from the moment she pranced into the store, she was humiliating Father in front of all those men whom he has to boss—"

"Don't you think your father can take care of himself?"

"He used to be able to, but since my brother died, something's happened to him. And she pecks at the weak spot and pecks at it, and now, lately, he doesn't say anything; he just takes it."

"You know whom you hurt most? Him. After you left, he walked back to his desk and poured himself a drink. Secretly."

"I'm so sorry for him. Freddie please, you're right—please go tell her yes, I'll have lunch with her at Delmonico's and I'll go to the theater and I'll be just the girl she'd like me to have been."

Freddie nodded, looked at Stavros, nodded again, and smiled.

"And tell Daddy that I love him," Althea said. She turned to Stavros. "Come, Joe," she said. "We'll go for the tickets. Freddie, when I start work in the city, Joe's going to invite us to his home."

"I don't say that," Stavros said. He turned to Freddie. "What she wants to see my home for?"

"She wants to go slumming," Freddie said.

"That's not fair, Freddie! That's goddamn rude of you, Freddie."

"I meant *with* you. I meant other places, *with* you," Freddie said.

"You take that back, Freddie."

"It's all right, don't worry," Stavros said.

"Of course, Mr.—Joe. I didn't mean that the way it sounded," Freddie said.

"Apologize!" Althea commanded.

"I do. I do."

My God, Stavros said, speaking to himself. *Look how she talks to him. These women, like bosses with their men!*

"I'll meet you at Delmonico's," Althea said to her fiancé. "Let's go, Joe."

She started off and Stavros followed her. They walked side by side without a word, she an alien American with golden hair, a fine brow and cool green eyes; he shorter, square-built and slightly bowlegged, his face the face of a knife-puller, his dark eyes stricken with unsatisfied hungers.

The lobby of the Empire Theater was done in red plush and there were ceiling-high mirrors of rather cloudy glass which added a romantic luster to whoever was reflected. Althea waited before one of these glass panels while Stavros went for the tickets.

When he brought them to her, they stood together for a moment, not knowing what to say, and since they weren't able to look at each other, they looked at their reflections in the tall pier glass.

Look at us, she was thinking. *He's like a picture in the National Geographic, a true Oriental. All he needs is a fez. He's so mysterious. And I—so washed out, so pale . . .*

Stavros was thinking, *Don't be damn fool—girl like this . . . !*

"Don't forget your—I mean, what I asked you," she said.

"We have some troubles home now," he said. "Other time maybe."

"Whenever," she said. "And thanks."

Then he said it. "That's your husband-going-to-be, right? Why you talk to him that way? Not right!"

He turned and left her. She stayed where she was, looking at her image in the glass and the empty space beside it.

OCTOBER 1914

Stavros finished first. He raised a palm over his plate when Fofo offered to fill it again, then settled back to consider the others around the Topouzo-glou dining room table. It was Isaac's name day, an occasion the family celebrated as religiously as it did Christmas. Everybody, Stavros thought, liked the *tass kebab*. Freddie liked it, Althea liked it—or pretended to. Father Achilleas certainly liked it; he'd broken off a crust of bread and was mopping his plate clean.

Stavros had allowed his younger sisters to sit either side of the young priest, and now he regretted it. *He's not going to take one of my sisters,* Stavros thought, *if that's his idea.*

"Achilleas," Eleni said—too anxiously, Stavros felt. "How was it?"

"My mother doesn't make it better," Achilleas said.

"I made it," Eleftheria boasted.

"I'm sure you learned from your dear mother," Achilleas said in Greek.

"You didn't say anything, so I was worried," Eleni said.

"When children are silent at the table," Althea said to Stavros, "it means they like their dinner."

Stavros shrugged. Althea kept addressing her remarks to him. *If she wasn't high-class American girl,* he thought, *I'd get wrong idea.*

"Well, Mr. Farrow, how 'bout you?" Fofo said, getting up, a signal to the other girls to start clearing. "You like the food here?"

"Very, very good," Freddie said. "What was it, exactly?"

"Puree of eggplant," Althea said. "Right, Stavros?"

"Yes," he said. She was looking at him again, in that strange, fixed way. She seemed as anxious for his interest as his sisters were for that of the young priest.

"And the meat," Althea continued, "has to be lamb, never beef. Such a delicate flavor. There is a slight burnt taste to the eggplant. I like that. Next time I go into one of those restaurants, I want to order it. What's it called?"

"In one of those restaurants," Stavros said, "it don't taste the same."

"It's called *tass kebab,*" Achilleas said to Althea. "You see"—he turned to the rest of the company—"there again, both those words are Turkish.

As I was saying before, we are so close in so many ways, the Turks and us."

"Do you people put yogurt on everything?" Freddie asked.

"It's good for the digestion," Vacilli said. "Isn't it, Mommah?"

"What? Vacilli, my lamb, you're asking me what? Something?" Vasso said in Greek.

Vacilli repeated the question in Greek.

Vasso nodded, laughing, then shook her head. "No, no," she said. Then: "Maybe. Sometimes. Yes."

"Now, Achilleas," Eleni said, coming into the room with a stack of dishes, "tell the story." The dishes had been used earlier. Now, having washed and dried them, Eleni put them out for the dessert.

Fofo came out of the kitchen with a great flat tray of a sort of short-bread soaked in honey. Eleftheria followed with another dish containing soft rectangles of compacted sweet cream.

"Glory to God," the priest said. "*Ekmek kadayeef!* You women are certainly workers."

"Now, Achilleas," Eleni said, as she sliced the dessert and began to dish it out, "we're waiting to hear your story. But first tell me, how big a piece you can eat?"

"I don't eat sweets," the priest said. "A small piece."

"Give that piece to Freddie," Althea said. "He has a sweet tooth like a child."

"I told my dentist to pull it out, but he wouldn't," Freddie said.

Stavros laughed and the rest joined in. "You have to learn to like this kind of food, Freddie," Stavros said. "You'll be taking buyers for lunch and so on."

Four weeks ago an unexpected thing had happened. Freddie had quit his job on "the street" and accepted a position beside his father-in-law-to-be at Sarrafian Brothers. He was learning the Oriental rug trade from the bottom up and with great enthusiasm. Unexpectedly, Stavros had taken to the newcomer; they'd become friends, saw each other after hours. The Anatolian had told Freddie stories about his life as a hamal. Freddie had responded with envy. "My life's been so tame," he said again and again.

"Now everybody eat!" Fofo said.

"The story," Eleftheria said, "Achilleas, the story!"

"Miss Perry and Freddie," Eleni said, "Father Achilleas is going to tell us how it happened that there isn't a single Turk in Aivalik, the city where he was born. Even though it's in Turkey and there are Turks all around."

"Aivalik," Eleftheria said. "I know where it is."

"You never heard of Aivalik," Stavros said, "till just now from him." He pointed to the young priest. "You two girls! *Aman, aman!*"

"What's that 'You two girls ! *Aman, aman*'?" Eleni said. "What's the matter with us?"

"You flatter Achilleas too much. It's not good for a priest. He has to keep his humble face, you know."

"I'm human," Achilleas said. "I enjoy the flattery."

"We can see that," Stavros said.

"Stavros," Eleftheria said. "I did hear of Aivalik. We went to school in Smyrna when we were there. Aivalik isn't far from Smyrna. It's very close."

"It's not close," Eleni said.

"It's both close and far away," Achilleas said. "Depending on the wind. It's a two days' journey to the north by caïque if the wind is from the south. If the wind is the one they call the *melteme*, coming from the north out of a blue sky, then it takes a week, or more. Two, three. No one can tell." He turned to Althea and said, "Aivalik is the only city in all Turkey where every man is Greek. Not a Turk lives there, and this story is about how that came to be. We don't know if it's true; like all good stories, it may be a little exaggerated.

"In seventeen hundred and seventy-three, so they say," Achilleas began, "there was war between the Turk and the Slav to determine who would control the entrance to the Dardanelles, the place they call the Hellespont, made famous later by Lord Byron. A great sea battle in which many lives were lost decided that war. Many fine ships went down between the island of Mytilene and the island of Imbros which lies across the mouth of the Dardanelles."

"Who won the battle?" Michaelis said.

"It isn't important to the story," Achilleas said. "It happened that a young Turkish sailor who'd been badly wounded was thrown into the sea by the explosion of a *topp.*"

"A shell, in English," Demosthenes explained to Althea.

"All around this sailor, the sea was full of broken masts and the planks from destroyed decks. The sailor was lucky because he found a cabin door and for three days he clung to it, and three nights too. Finally, weak and in danger of dying, he saw the land. With the last of his strength, he made it to shore. It was on the edge of our city, where I was born."

"Aivalik!" Eleftheria said.

"Yes, the city of Aivalik. There the sailor crawled like a dying animal up from the water's edge to the nearest house and managed to strike the door before he fell flat to the ground. Glory to God, the door opened and the sailor saw it was a priest looking down on him. His heart fell. He thought because he wore the uniform of the sultan, he would be refused welcome, especially from a priest. But the priest took the sailor into his home and he said to his wife, 'Feed him.' She was a good woman and gave the young sailor the care she'd have given her own son. Slowly the Turk regained his health; it took a few weeks. When he had his strength again, the priest gave him money so he could make the journey back to his home in Constantinople. There he was greeted as a miracle, for they'd given him up for dead."

"Tst-tst-tst," Vasso said. Though she hadn't understood a word, the story had touched her, for Achilleas told it with gestures.

"Time passed," he went on, "and this sailor became wealthy and powerful, a great general. Hasan Bey Djerlieri Mandaloglou Pasha was his name. Oh, he was famous! And in the turn of events, he was appointed governor of the island of Mytilene, which is just across the sea from Aivalik —on fine mornings we can hear their roosters. The day came when this pasha decided to look up the priest who'd saved his life so long ago. He put on his finest uniform, covered with decorations and ornaments of heavy gold. At his side he fastened a great curved sword in its scabbard, which was encrusted with precious stones. He called for the most powerful warship at his command and sailed across the water to the city of Aivalik. There he recognized the little house of the priest, and followed by his warlike retinue, he marched up to it. When the priest, now weak and toward the end of his days, saw the great pasha and his company of warriors, he trembled in fright. 'I didn't do anything,' he pleaded. For he didn't recognize who this pasha was.

"Whereupon Hasan Bey Djerlieri Mandaloglou Pasha dropped his great sword to the ground and one by one, his decorations, and even his tunic, and stood before the priest as a naked man. Then the priest knew him and they embraced like brothers. 'What can I give you?' the pasha said. 'I don't want anything,' the old priest said. 'But I must give you something,' and now it was the pasha who pleaded. 'I owe you my life. Speak, I beg you. Jewels? Property? Money? Anything you want. A new church, even that?'

"Then the priest was quiet as he thought of what would be best for all his people. And he said, 'Grant me this: that no Turk will live in Aivalik. Let it be a Greek city.' When he said this he had no expectation that his wish would be granted since it was so bold. But the pasha did not hesitate. '*Oldu!*' he cried."

" 'It's done,' " Demosthenes translated for Althea, who had tears in her eyes. But she looked at Stavros.

"From that day to this," Achilleas said, "for almost one hundred and fifty years, no Turk has lived in Aivalik. Which is why the Greek school there is the best in the Eastern world and my own people are the proudest of all the Greeks. When the Turk comes into that city, he comes as a visitor and by day only, as if he is entering the city of a foreign country. That's the story."

The company around the dining room table was quiet.

"That Turk wasn't like any Turk I've known," Eleni said.

"The best man I ever knew was a Turk," Stavros said.

"Except Father," Fofo said. She crossed herself.

"Except Father," Stavros said.

"That is the city where I was born and raised," Achilleas said. "There I was educated and learned my English. From there I went to Smyrna and entered the priesthood. God blessed me to serve His Eminence the archbishop of Smyrna, the man I most revere in the world. It was he, the archbishop, who sent me here to do work for him, and when I was leaving he gave me something for this family, which I brought with me, a remembrance."

He reached into a small bag of black cloth which he'd hung by its strap over the back of his chair.

"My archbishop," he said to Stavros, "didn't forget your father." He held up a small photograph, and the boys, Michaelis and Vacilli and Demo, gathered around and the girls took the opportunity to press in behind Achilleas's chair, to lean on his shoulders as they looked at the snapshot.

But Stavros still sat in his chair at the head of the table, ignoring the priest and the token he'd brought.

The two men had been posed in front of the cathedral of Aghia Fotini. They looked into the lens as if to be judged.

"Father looks so small," Demosthenes said.

"By that time," Michaelis said, "they'd worn him down."

"This was taken by one of those little men who stand in the street before the cathedral to make photographs of visitors," Achilleas said, "about a week before you all left on the boat. Your father had come to say goodbye."

"It already started by then, the bleeding," Michaelis said.

"Here, Mommah," Vacilli said, taking the photograph from Achilleas's hands and holding it out to her.

"After," she said. "When everyone has looked, then." She got up and went into the kitchen.

"The archbishop is so handsome," Eleni said.

"Take it." Achilleas offered the photograph to Stavros.

"I don't want it," he said.

No one knew why and he didn't explain.

He's so mean, Althea said to herself.

"It was made the last time they saw each other," Achilleas said to Stavros, "and the archbishop wanted you to have it. He said it was one of the first things I should do when I came to this country."

"Now you done it," Stavros said.

"Does it offend you?" Achilleas said.

"No. But—" He was silent.

"I know you didn't want me here," Achilleas said. "I had to hint and finally even to ask." He turned to Eleni. "Have I done something to offend him?"

"That's the way he is," she said. "You have to get used to it."

Althea had been studying Stavros. "What's bothering you anyway?" she asked. When he looked at her, she wished she hadn't spoken.

Freddie thought it an indiscreet question, indiscreetly put. He looked at his watch. "I told Mother we'd be there at four-thirty, Althea," he said. "We ought to leave pretty soon. She'll burn her roast."

"You're not really going to eat again today, are you, Freddie?" Althea said.

"I can't hurt her feelings, Althea."

"We were there three weeks ago," Althea said.

"I've got to go, dear. She's an old lady. I'm all she's got and I promised. . . . She waits for me, you know?"

"I know," Althea said. "Can I see the photograph?" she asked Achilleas.

"Where's the coffee? Fofo, the coffee!" Stavros got up, taking the photograph, and walked into the other room. There he put it face down on the table.

"Now what did I do wrong?" Althea asked Eleni.

"Nothing," Eleni said. "Please understand—that's the way he is."

"He doesn't want it passed all over the place," Freddie said. "It's an intimate photograph with sad associations and he doesn't want it handed around to strangers." Then he whispered, "Come on, Althea, let's go. She's expecting us."

"I wasn't going to pass it all over the place," Althea said.

Everybody had drifted into the front room where there were carpets and small rugs rolled up and bound with lengths of rope or piled neatly into corners in honor of the family holiday.

Achilleas made a point of sitting next to Stavros. "I have another photograph, especially for you," he said, reaching into his habit. "It's only a snapshot, not very clear, I'm afraid. I took it myself." He handed Stavros a dim snapshot. "You'll want to see this one I'm sure."

Stavros looked at it. "I don't see anything. What is it?"

"It's where he's buried," Achilleas said, "The grave marker your brother Michaelis put up had fallen over. There—see it on the ground?"

Stavros didn't look at it again. He handed it to Vasso, who shook her head and put it on the low table at the side of her chair, face down.

"Thank you for bringing them," Eleni said. "It's so kind of you. We all thank you. Even those who say nothing."

Achilleas turned directly to Stavros. "I thought you'd particularly want to see it."

"Why?"

"Since you weren't there—"

"Look at it," Michaelis said, picking up the photograph and thrusting it at his brother. "Since you weren't there."

Althea saw Stavros's face tense and flush. But he took the photograph, looked at it briefly, and put it down again.

"In America they bury animals better than that," Michaelis said.

"There's nothing sacred in a dead body," Stavros said. "The only thing to do is forget."

"The Turks bury their people better," Michaelis said.

"That's enough, Michaelis," Stavros warned.

Althea saw Michaelis drop his eyes and turn away. *They're all afraid of him,* she said to herself.

"The archbishop sent me to the Wali after your family left," Achilleas went on, "to ask permission to move the body and—"

"We don't want the body moved," Stavros burst out. "I will move it myself one day. I don't want strangers touching it."

"I was worried," Achilleas went on, undeterred, "because the land is crumbling along the edge of the ravine." He picked up the photograph and pointed. "The body might then be exposed. There are dogs there, in packs, who don't get enough to eat, wild dogs who eat each other when they are hungry."

Althea could see how engorged with blood Stavros's face had become. *Like a bomb about to go off,* she thought.

"The Wali," Achilleas said, "refused permission."

Fofo spoke. "Don't talk about it anymore, Father Achilleas. My brother don't need reminders on this subject."

"Very well," the young priest said. "I'm sorry if I've offended."

Eleftheria brought in the coffee on a tray. She put it down in front of the handsome young priest and smiled at him shyly.

"Eleftheria," Eleni said, "Achilleas prefers his without sugar."

"I know," Eleftheria said, "I made his special and separate." She pointed a tiny pink finger. "This one, Achilleas, is for you."

Twenty minutes later, Althea, despite several urgent requests from Freddie to leave, was still there. A drama was developing and she was not going to be pulled away.

"Why do you dislike me?" Achilleas said, confronting Stavros directly.

"I don't like priests," Stavros said.

"Why?"

"They run only with the rich."

"That's absolutely false. Why do you say things you know aren't true?"

"I worked as a hamal on the piers of Constantinople for two years, suffering every hardship, and in all that time I didn't see one priest."

"They were there. You probably didn't want to notice. Our Orthodox priests kept the Greek language alive for hundreds of years when our people suffered under the Turk."

"Among the hamals," Stavros said, "when you get down that low, Turk or Greek, at the bottom it's the same."

Which is what Althea had been reading about the "disadvantaged" in a book her social work supervisor had loaned her.

"That is not true," Achilleas said. "There is a great difference. The Turks are a people of small intelligence and they always will be. They are close to the animals."

"I trust them as much as I do the Greeks," Stavros said.

"Yes, some of them are good, gentle people. But the Greek works while the Turk sits in the shade, smokes his nargileh, and makes children. More than he can feed."

"He prays five times a day, wherever he is. Haven't you observed?"

"Oh yes, of course, they're religious, they celebrate their holy holidays by teaching their seven-year-old sons how to cut the neck of a lamb. The first thing these children learn is how to pull a knife across a throat. The Turk comes from a race of nomadic shepherds who had—science has proven this—smaller brains than we have. For that reason they are inevitably less intelligent. They are not equipped for decision making. That is why they need us. We will conquer them very soon—but for their own good. We will not be cruel and vicious masters as they have been."

"All that is not what I've seen. In the end, the Turk is not my enemy. The people who build your churches, they are. All rich men are the same. They have the power, they take advantage, whatever race they are."

"Now I understand. You want to destroy the rich!"

Stavros thought for an instant, then smiled and said, "No. To take their place. I want to be one of them, because they own the earth."

"Can I tell you what I see in your face?" the priest said. "Above all else, strength. You have suffered a great deal. Your brothers have not. Perhaps Michaelis here, yes, but much less. It has made you strong, that experience. What else do I see there? Recklessness! Close to courage, but not the same. It's all on your face. Also some coarseness, even brutality. And much cunning, the kind the hunted have. You have the face of a wolf. Born of desperation. There is also a certain indifference to pain, which will be useful in the coming emergency."

"What emergency? There is no emergency here, not for us," Stavros said.

"You don't read the papers?"

"Michaelis reads; he tells me what I want to know."

"When I read him the papers, he falls asleep," Michaelis said to the priest.

"Perhaps Michaelis read you yesterday that the Turk has entered the war on the side of the Germans. Did he? So despite our king—who is a relative to the German Kaiser and favors him—we must enter on the Allied side. Why? Because the people of England and France and Italy are people like us. Christians. Civilized. And because they are going to win."

"A better reason," Stavros said.

"When they win, it will be the end of the Ottoman Empire. The Sick Man of Europe will die at last. At that instant, there will be a vacuum. With the blessing of the Americans, with the arms furnished by our great allies, the British, the French and the Italians, we will fill that vacuum. All Greece will be all Greece again."

"That is what is called the Great Idea," Michaelis said to his brother. "I read all this to you but you fall asleep."

"Are you a priest?" Stavros asked Achilleas. "Tell me the truth."

"Do you doubt it?"

"You speak like an officer recruiting for the Greek army."

"We Greek Orthodox priests, we don't pretend we're not interested in the politics of our people. We're concerned with everything our people are concerned with."

"You're too young to be a priest," Stavros said. "You have no beard and you have no judgment."

"He's not so young," Eleni said. "He's two years older than my age."

"For a woman, age is different," Stavros said. "Also he's too handsome for a priest. He looks like a singer of love songs."

"A girl your age," Demosthenes said to his sister, "is usually married by now."

"I would be—I would be—" Eleni said.

She began to cry and left the room.

"She has a suitor," Fofo explained to Achilleas. "In Smyrna. He wants to marry her."

"Does she want him?" the priest asked.

"Of course," Fofo said. "You can see that."

"What do you want here?" Stavros said. "This is a happy family. We don't need you. You can't get money from us."

"What he wants here," Michaelis said, "is to remind us that the Turks killed our father and that we are Greeks."

"So he's done that. We realize."

"Not you," Michaelis said.

"Because I don't care about his ideas," Stavros said.

Now again he ignored the priest and spoke to his brothers in Greek. "I will accomplish Father's will," he said. " 'You will bring your brothers out of danger and to your side,' he ordered me. 'As the eldest,' he said, 'it is your responsibility to set them up in business.' When I have done that, I will think of other things. Now we have some money in the bank; soon we will have enough to have our own store. Then—if what this priest says is true, if there is what he calls a vacuum—it will be an opportunity for us. Then we go back, not as soldiers but as merchants. At that time I will revenge my father. I will make the people who were his masters my slaves.

Those whom he feared will fear me. I will be rich and they will be poor. That is what Father cared about, not what happened to his body when he was dead. All that kind of thing is what priests feed on. They perform ceremonies and sign documents and collect money. His body is the same as what is left of an animal after its death. Garbage. Don't look that way at me—I'm telling you the truth. From experience. His spirit, his memory, that I will worship. Now"—he turned to Achilleas—"Achilleas Galoyeropoulos, I don't want to hear more from you. This is my house and I heard enough. I don't want you here now."

No one spoke. No one looked at anyone else.

And Althea felt the same fear the others felt.

Achilleas got to his feet.

"One thing before I go," he said. "About what I saw in your face. There was something else. Kindness. There is kindness hidden there. That will be useful later, after all the other things have been used. We don't conquer to persecute anyone. We conquer to love. To bring love to the conquered. That is what Christ is, love on earth."

He smiled and made the sign of the cross over them. "We Greeks within the next ten years will make the greatest civilization on this earth."

"One thing remember," Stavros said. "From this family, no one who will go to a war."

Achilleas didn't respond. He turned to Michaelis and said, "Why don't we walk together on Riverside Drive. The river is so beautiful."

"Oh, yes," Michaelis said. "Oh, of course."

"And you." The young priest turned to Eleni, who was standing in the doorway.

"I was waiting for you to ask me," she said.

"And you, Eleftheria, my little bird," Achilleas said.

"I was coming anyway," she said.

They all laughed.

Althea looked at Stavros, a face clenched to show no reaction.

"Come on, Althea," Freddie whispered.

"The men are going to play poker now," she said. "I want to watch." She went to Freddie and embraced him. "I'll write her a lovely note tomorrow and explain," she said. "I'll promise that next Sunday, no matter what, I'll go there! With flowers! But now let's stay. You play too. You love poker. Come on, you'll take all their money."

"Oh, my God." Freddie gave up. "Isn't she a terrible girl?" he said to everyone. "I just can't, dear. It would hurt Mother." He smiled. Was he embarrassed? "Stay and enjoy yourself," he said. "I'll explain everything to her."

She kissed him. "I'll wait here for you," she said. "Oh, Freddie, you're such a dear!"

The girls having put on hats for their stroll along the river, Father

Achilleas opened the apartment door for them and found Father Pericles Rondiris outside, peering at the faded numbers on the door. The old priest held a package in his hand, a gift of *keurabbieh*—white dough cookies, heavily sprinkled with confectioner's sugar and still warm.

He also brought news. A letter had arrived the previous afternoon from a fellow priest whose church was in "Noo Georgie, city of Bassac, Passakee, something, my eyes no good. You must take ferryboat, then train, then God knows what. But don't worry, plenty Greeks over there." As best he could, Father Rondiris read them the priest's letter, which contained the information that Seraphim was living in Passaic and had married a Miss Amalia Zymaris. "Poor fellow!" Rondiris added, shaking his head.

He gave Stavros a piece of paper on which his daughter, Diana, had written the address of the Zymaris family. This gave him the opportunity to call the younger priest's attention to the excellence of his daughter's penmanship. "Can be usee-full," he said. "She also make *keurabbieh* special for you."

Did he resent her coming along? She'd come as if he'd invited her to, as if that had been their understanding. It was much too bold, he thought. Is that the way they were, the children of the privileged classes? What was it she wanted? If she'd been a waitress or a seamstress he'd have understood, but—

They were on the back deck of the ferry, watching the city recede. Pretending to look downstream, his eyes crossed her face, returned across her body.

She caught him. "What do you think of me?" she asked.

"Too thin," he said.

"Not my looks. I mean I'm . . . so impatient and hateful to my mother. I know it's wrong, but I simply can't help it. And my father, I've lost respect for him. Since my brother died, he's been going down and . . . down."

"You should obey your parents."

"Would you? My parents? Of course not. If my mother could see me with you here, she'd suspect all kinds of things, all of them bad. Yet I'm very happy. To be with you."

"Don't complain so much. They put you to the college, didn't they? You're lucky."

"I suppose. On the other hand, I know nothing of the real world. Speaking of which, do you have a girl?"

"No."

"What do you do?"

"Once a week."

"Then you do have a girl?"

"Not one. Different ones."

"Oh."

"I pay."

"Oh."

"Quick. Finish. Goodbye."

"Well—maybe we'd better move up front. We're coming in."

They walked through the ferry gate and into the station building of the Lackawanna Railroad. Their train was waiting.

"I'm not too thin," she said. "I weigh one hundred and seventeen pounds."

It was a fifty-minute ride. At the Passaic railroad station he showed her the slip of paper Pericles Rondiris had brought him. "You have idea where this is?" he asked.

"Leave it to me," she said.

They set out on foot. She asked a few questions, and in time they came to an area of great dyeworks. There they found the home of Bodos Zymaris. She'd led Stavros right to it.

When no one answered his knock, Stavros walked around the house and there he found the owner seated before a rustic table in his backyard, waiting for his Sunday dinner.

Bodos Zymaris looked up. A dog growled, but from where? Stavros couldn't see the animal until it suddenly rushed out from beneath a kind of daybed in the shade of a ragged cherry tree.

Zymaris's brusque intervention—"Hodja!"—saved Stavros from being mauled by a large German shepherd. A plump woman in her late twenties ran out of the house and struck the dog with the side of a frying pan, backing him under the daybed, where he cowered. But he never took his eye off Stavros, and soon he was growling again.

Stavros took in the backyard. Behind the table where Zymaris sat, slicing a cucumber into a pitcher full of *aryan,* was his daybed, dressed with a brightly colored Oriental spread and provided with green and red pillows.

"What the hell you want here?" Zymaris said, stirring the water-thinned yogurt, the ice and the cucumber slices together. "You selling something? This is Sunday. I'm eating my dinner. Get out."

Zymaris refilled his glass from a bottle of ouzo. "Amalia!" he shouted. "Where's the food?"

"Where's my brother?" Stavros said.

"What? What you saying?"

"My brother. Where is he?"

"Talk to her," Zymaris said, pointing to the kitchen door. "Don't bother me on that."

The young woman came out of the house carrying a large plate of *mezedes*—sardines and anchovies, slices of *bastourma* and of Genoa salami, feta cheese, and *Kayseri payneer,* celery and scallions—and in her mouth she gripped the side of a small straw basket filled with dark, peasant-style bread sprinkled with sesame seeds. She put the food before her father, who started eating at once. He offered Stavros neither a seat nor a glass of ouzo.

"He came to see him," Zymaris said to the woman.

She nodded but avoided Stavros's eye and went back into the kitchen. Zymaris ate. The dog growled.

"Say, Mister Zymaris," Stavros said, "how 'bout it? I'm talking to you."

Zymaris didn't look up.

"Where is he?" Stavros said. And receiving no answer, he called out, "Seraphim! Seraphim!"

Silence. Only the quiver in the German shepherd's throat.

"What's that smell here?" Stavros said, speaking above the dog's growl. "Shit from the dog?"

"Maybe it's your brother," Zymaris said without interrupting his intake of food. "He smells."

The dog made a little move toward Stavros, baring his teeth.

"You come near me, you son of a bitch, I cut your throat." Stavros reached for his knife; he also backed off.

Zymaris laughed, shaking his head scornfully. "You frighten of damn dog too," he said, "same like your brother."

Challenged, Stavros started toward the animal and then there was a shout from above and the sound of a roller shade. Stavros looked up and saw his brother at a second-story window.

"Look out!" Seraphim called down. "He bite you. Stay away from him!"

"What you doing up there?" Stavros said to his brother. Then to Zymaris, "Shut up that dog."

"Hodja!" Zymaris shouted, and the dog whimpered and was quiet.

"What the hell you doing up there, Seraphim?" Stavros repeated.

"I'm in my grave here," Seraphim said. "Forget about me." He pulled down the shade and disappeared from sight. Stavros could hear him coughing.

Zymaris laughed, wiping his oily plate with a slice of brown bread.

"Hey, Mr. Zymaris, big eater! What's the matter—you got him locked up there or what?"

"He's not locked up," Zymaris said. "But I don't eat with him here." He struck the table. "Amalia," he called out. *"Chorba!"*

"What are you, some kind Turk?" Stavros said.

"Crete, I came from Crete." They both heard Seraphim coughing and looked up. "You know he's crazy, your brother. Look at him now."

An edge of the window shade had been pulled back and Stavros could see one of his brother's eyes.

"Come down here," Stavros called out. "Seraphim, I'm waiting."

"Forget about me, Stavros. Go home," Seraphim said, and then the edge of his face was again covered with the window shade, and Stavros knew that shame was overcoming him.

"What he said?" Zymaris asked. "I can't hear when he speaks."

"Baba is a little deaf," Amalia said from the kitchen doorway.

"What? What are you talking? My hearing is perfect. I just don't hear useless things."

"Oh, Baba!" his daughter said, laughing.

"How can foreman be deaf? If foreman is deaf, he lose job. It's him. Amalia, *chorba!* Ever since he got here, everybody whispering, everybody sneaky like Chinaman. Look, see how he hide behind shade? Is he saying something? Who knows? You can't see his mouth."

Stavros walked to the table, picked up a glass, wiped the rim with the end of his little finger, filled it with ouzo, and drank it. Then he sat down opposite Zymaris.

"I know he complaining to you," Zymaris said. "About what? Eh? I kill that son of a bitch." His voice rose to his rage. "He ruin my daughter! I went to priest last week. 'My daughter make mistake,' I say. 'She marry crazy man. Help! What I can do?' 'Beg God mercy and grace,' goddamn racketeer priest say. 'That's all you help?' I say. 'You talking divorce?' he say. 'Not allow!' So now look, there he sits. Hey, you, hiding up there, you are my daughter's ruination. Also you spoil my dinner!"

Zymaris was a very heavy man and he was breathing hard.

"My fault," he said. "I see this new man working dye plant, other division, Greek boy, they tell me; looks clean. I thought maybe I find husband for my daughter at last. So I make terrible mistake, I bring him here. Next thing I know, every night she going to meeting Daughters Penelope! You got idea? He there with her. Amalia, where the hell is my soup? Since he been here, she forgetting, she forgetting many things. Then one day, she smiling, he smiling, they come together. 'We want marry, Baba,' she say. So I say, 'Sit down here, boy!' And I talk to him, that son of a bitch, hiding up there. Why he hiding all the time?"

"From the police," Stavros said.

"So I study him good. And I make up my mind. I say, 'Amalia, don't marry that man; something wrong that man.' " He stopped. He looked at Stavros. "What you say before?"

"About what?"

"Police. You say that?"

"Yes. He has good heart, this boy, but— Tell me, police come yet?"

"No."

"Like you say, it's your fault, you let them get marry." Stavros poured himself another ouzo and put it away.

"What can I do?" Zymaris said. "Daughters Penelope. Young people, smiling together. So I say, 'All right, you want him, go 'head, marry. I take care of him, don't worry.' Right, Amalia? I say that?"

"Yes, Baba." His daughter had reappeared carrying a bowl of lentil soup dripping at the rim.

"Where's yogurt?" Zymaris said. Then to Stavros: "You see how she's forgetting since he's here?"

"I didn't forget, Baba," she said, running into the kitchen. "Coming, Baba!"

" 'But one thing,' I say to her, 'I have no wife now—' Mrs. Zymaris, fine woman, die, you understand. So I say, 'Go 'head, marry, but promise me one thing: You live here with me, take care Baba his last years, like always.' I say that, Amalia?"

"Yes, Baba," she called from the kitchen.

There was the sound of a car from in front of the house. It braked suddenly.

"What's that?" Stavros said.

"Maybe the police," Althea said from where she'd been watching at the edge of the yard.

Zymaris stopped eating.

Althea moved to look around the corner of the house and came back. "Just a neighbor," she said to Stavros.

"Who's this woman?" Zymaris said.

"A nurse," Stavros said. "She knows this situation."

"What's that police you mentioning here? What they want?" Zymaris said.

"Who knows?" Stavros said. "Different things all the time. That's why he change job, change job, change job."

"Please don't whisper about me down there," Seraphim said from behind the shade.

"You see?" Stavros whispered in Zymaris's ear. "Come down here, Seraphim," he shouted back at his brother.

"Don't wait for me, Stavros," his brother said. "I'm sorry I give you trouble. Forgive me that."

"So I made mistake," Zymaris went on. "But one thing, she gave me her word: 'I stay by your side, Baba, don't worry. I take care you like always.' Right, Amalia? You say that to me?"

"Yes, Baba," she said, coming out of the kitchen with a jelly glass of yogurt which she set before her father. "I didn't forget," she said.

"You worrying about police I see," Stavros said to Zymaris.

"No, no, no. In Crete we don't pay 'tention damn police." He looked up at the window, where Stavros could once again see one of his brother's eyes watching. "So I say to him, 'You marry my daughter, O.K., what the hell! I get you better job, dye plant, my division.' Amalia, I say that?"

"Yes, Baba," Amalia said as she gathered up the dishes he'd wiped clean.

"I am foreman there, you understand. So I get him better job. More money too. He work under me, learn dyes, so forth, so on."

"That's a wonderful thing you did for him. But I don't think he—"

"He don't appreciate."

"Tst-tst-tst," Althea said.

"Never did with me," Stavros said.

"Also he don't like her cooking. Can you imagine? One thing you must make sure." He was spooning yogurt into his lentil soup. "Before you marry woman, make damn sure you like her cooking. After, too late. No divorce possible, priest say."

Amalia turned and hurried into the kitchen; she was sniveling.

"Next thing I know I got crazy man here." Zymaris leaned forward to whisper in Stavros's ear. "He get marry with her, but he don't sleep with her in bed. She tell me he sleep on floor."

"What you think of that, nurse?" Stavros said to Althea.

"Just what I'd expect," Althea said.

"Where she sleep?" Stavros said to Zymaris.

"Stavros!" Seraphim called out from behind the shade. "You whispering again!"

"In her bed," Zymaris whispered. "What you think! She is clean young woman, not animal. She has fine bed from her mother."

Amalia reappeared in the kitchen doorway and looked up at the window. "Seraphim," she called, "you want me bring dinner there?"

"What you got?" Seraphim asked.

"Steak," she said. "Nice steak."

"I'll try some soup," Seraphim said. "Bring it here. Maybe fix my cough." She ran back into the kitchen.

"What the hell is this?" Stavros whispered. "He make servant from your daughter."

"Same thing with his sisters," Althea said.

"I'm getting disgusted here," Stavros said. "I'm going." He turned to Althea, "Come on, nurse!" he said. "I give up on this man!"

He started to stand up, but Zymaris grabbed his arm and held him.

"No, for God's sake, stay; help me this problem." Then he shouted at the window. "Come down here. Come talk to your brother. Sit by the kitchen over there, eat your dinner, and talk to your smart brother." He turned back to Stavros and whispered, "Yes, like you say, he make servant from a woman."

"I know," Stavros said, "but there's a reason."

"Seraphim, Seraphim, come down," Amalia said, and there was a softness in her voice.

Seraphim pulled the shade back and looked down, but he didn't answer. They could hear him coughing.

Zymaris turned to Stavros. "What's that reason you mention?"

Stavros looked at Althea. "He has big ideas of himself," he said to her.

"We call it megalomania," she said.

"See him up there now," Zymaris said. "See what I mean? Like Chinaman, spy all the time, say nothing, maneever, maneever—what big idea?"

"Shshsh!" Stavros said. "Listen."

"What?"

"He's saying something."

"Who to?"

"He speaks to God," Althea said. "Every day!"

Seraphim was in fact speaking to God, and through Him to his brother. "I am man of honor," he said. "I make mistakes, I will pay."

"What he saying?" Zymaris asked.

" 'I am man of honor,' he said," Althea explained. " 'I will remain here. I will pay.' "

"Son of a bitch."

Stavros could hear his brother now, a kind of lament. "I should have stayed other side. I was happy man there." Then Stavros heard: "Stavros, Stavros, Stavros!" And then, "Forget about me, forget about me." He was coughing again.

"What's he say? Is he saying something?" Zymaris asked.

Stavros touched his temple with his two fingers, looked at Althea and shook his head.

She said, "Shsh!" and put her forefinger to her lips. They all listened.

"All my life, Stavros, mistake. Turks don't bother me, but I listen our father, Stavros, I make journey across those roads, eating dust like it was halvah, and from the harbor, Smyrna—you weren't there, Stavros—such fish I ate from that sewer water and vegetables rotting, even the hamals don't touch those vegetables we ate there."

"What's he talking now?" Zymaris said.

"He wants to know if I brought him his knife." Stavros touched his temple again. "Like what you say, he's crazy."

"I had that idea, first time I see him. But she wanted him."

"You brought the knife," Althea said. "Give it to him."

"What he needs knife?" Zymaris asked.

Stavros pulled his square-end blade partly out of the inner pocket of his coat and showed it to Zymaris. "He forgot to take it with him," he said.

The man behind the window shade went on talking. "On the boat, Stavros—another mistake—every day I was sick. My stomach hold nothing. But through my suffering, I hold idea, damn fool, that here I will find —what? What was I looking here, damn fool?"

"Don't give him that damn knife," Zymaris whispered.

"So you see what happen here?" Seraphim said. "Why did I do it? Marry? Fine woman, good heart, but why? Hard on? What they call it, desire? Better like you, with the whores. One a week. Pay! Finish! But you know, summertime . . . warm nights . . . Passaic River. There's park over there. It's dark and . . . another mistake!"

"What's he saying now?" Zymaris said. He'd stopped eating.

"He says he thinks he's going crazy." Stavros looked at Althea. "He's worried about that."

"Yes," Althea said. "What he might do."

Zymaris dumped the entire contents of the yogurt jar into his soup and stirred it vigorously. "Will I be cursed all my life with this man here?"

"You see what it is, my fate here?" Seraphim said. "You see, Stavros? She's good woman, Amalia, all right. But who she gives dinner first? Not her husband. Him! In Daughters Penelope hall she say nothing to me about father. Only after, I find out she has father."

"What's he saying? Why don't he talk so I can hear him?"

"He say your daughter trick him into get married," Stavros said.

"But he begged her—hey you, you son of a bitch, you beg her marry!"

"Be careful what you say," Althea warned in a whisper, " 'Son of a bitch,'—he doesn't like that."

"Yes, I beg her," Seraphim said. "I make that mistake. And my life ruin. So O.K., now I pay. Don't worry, Mr. Zymaris. I am man of honor. Give me invoice, I pay price goods." And now he spoke out boldly. "Mr. Zymaris, remember this—I don't run away. I will stay here, in this window, the rest of my life, don't worry. Mr. Zymaris, you can be sure of that much."

"What? What?" Zymaris said. "He talking to me now?"

"He said he will stay in that window the rest of your life," Althea said.

"Oh my God, help me!"

"I will stay here," Seraphim went on, his voice rising and swelling, "breathing this terrible stink air, Mr. Zymaris, eating your daughter's food. Yes!" Suddenly Seraphim began to shout. "Everything stink here! Everything. I want to say this before I die."

He threw up the shade and it rattled around its roller.

The dog ran out and began to bark up at the window.

"Everything stink here!" Seraphim shouted. "From that goddamn dye plant. The air stink, the house stink, the food stink, my bed stink, that dog —oh my God! Even the water, everything! And you too, Amalia, little girl. I'm sorry, the truth is, you smell bad!"

Stavros turned away and shook his head.

"But, Mr. Zymaris," Seraphim shouted, "you stink worst of all! Stavros, why you telling these people I'm crazy, eh? You shouldn't do that, Stavros. Don't worry, Mr. Zymaris, I am not crazy. I am man of honor. I will not run away. Then one day, for your sake, I will climb roof and throw myself down so your dog—you, stinking Hodja-dog—can tear my flesh with your long teeth. That's what you're waiting down there for, right? You wolf should be in zoo. Go 'head, bark, bark!"

He pulled the window shade down and the backyard was silent.

"You heard that?" Stavros asked.

"I heard all right," Zymaris said.

In the kitchen doorway Amalia was sobbing.

"Don't cry, Amalia," Seraphim said, pulling the shade back an inch or two. "Don't cry, little girl. I won't take you from your father."

"Amalia," Stavros said, starting for her. "Tell me—"

The dog, coming in a rush, had the end of Stavros's shoe in his jaws.

"Look out!" Stavros slashed at the dog with his knife.

"Hodja!" Zymaris shouted, and the dog whimpered and crawled back on its belly under the platform, wagging its tail frantically.

"Amalia," Stavros said gently, "tell me truth, dear girl. Excuse me, but —you sleeping in bed. Where he sleep?"

"On the floor," she said.

"Tst-tst-tst," Stavros said.

"Animals sleep on floor," Zymaris said.

"The king of Japan," Althea said, "sleeps on the floor. It's an Oriental custom."

"But this man is not a king," Zymaris said.

"Those people, Japan, they also crazy," Stavros said.

"You didn't put enough onion this soup," Zymaris said, pushing his plate away and wiping his mouth. "That's why it taste like nothing. Come on," he said, "bring the steak!"

"I just put it on," she said. "Two minutes before."

"Then it's already cook too much."

She started back into the kitchen, but Stavros detained her.

"Amalia, wait," he said. "Tell the truth. Excuse me this question, but . . . this boy here, he knows nothing from women, no experience—not like you and me, Zymaris, you understand. So tell me, Amalia, he fix you up like husband?"

Amalia offered her full repertory of embarrassed sounds.

"I know what you mean," Stavros said. "How he can fix you up from floor—right?"

"Amalia, the meat, I can smell it burning."

The young woman dashed into the kitchen.

"So don't worry," Stavros said to her father.

"Don't worry?" Zymaris said. "Why not?"

"Because if he don't fix her up like husband, you lucky. Because then—"

Amalia reappeared in the kitchen doorway. "I turned it over," she said.

"Amalia," her father said, "so your father understand situation here, tell me, he fix you up like husband? Yes or no? The truth?"

"After we marry? Nothing," she said. "He do nothing."

"You understand why I'm saying to you you lucky?" Stavros whispered to Zymaris.

"Don't whisper down there," Seraphim shouted.

"I understand," Zymaris said to Stavros. "Sure, go 'head—another ouzaki, eh? But maybe something happen before—that's what I'm worry."

"That's different proposition, before," Stavros said. "That is monkey business before. After priest, that is marriage. How long they marry? Amalia, how long?"

"Two months," she said, "tomorrow."

"So you see," Stavros said.

"I don't need baby here," Zymaris said. "Crazy man baby."

"I don't think he fix me up that way," Amalia said.

Stavros turned to Zymaris. "You lucky man," he said.

"Amalia, the meat!" Zymaris said.

She ran into the house.

"Fine girl," Stavros said.

"Sure," her father said. "So one day he tell me he quitting job. I say, 'Seraphim, you better hold job, because where you get money to live?' 'You will give,' he say, 'dowry.' That's when I hit him. 'Dowry!' She stop me or I'm going to kill him."

"Maybe that's why he asked you to bring his knife here," Althea said.

Bodos Zymaris looked at her, then at his empty soup plate. "Everything taste bad today," he said. Then he whispered to Stavros, "I don't need baby here, you understand?"

Amalia appeared in the doorway. She was crying and holding a handkerchief under her eyes. "He didn't fix me up," she said. "He don't bother me after we get marry."

"But what about before?" Zymaris said. "Stupid, what about before?"

"I can't remember exactly what happen there. In the park by the Passaic River at night—who knows what happens?"

"Sure," Stavros said, "who knows? He has no experience from this, my brother. In dark, what he can find?"

"I can't remember what happen," Amalia said.

"You lucky," Stavros said. "You want crazy man husband, Amalia?"

She looked away. "I like him," she said. "I like him." She was weeping now without a sound.

"Don't cry, Amalia," Seraphim said from above. "Don't worry, I don't take you away from your father."

"What the hell he mean by that?" Zymaris said. "How can he . . . ?"

"You trying to understand crazy man," Stavros whispered.

"What the hell is the matter with him?" Zymaris said to Althea. But his voice was gentle now because his daughter was so sad.

"He say he miss his family, poor fellow," Amalia said. "That's what he say, poor fellow. And he's 'fraid from you, Baba."

"Good," Zymaris said.

"Shshsh," Amalia said. "Here he comes."

There was no sight of Seraphim. But the German shepherd, belly to the ground, was creeping toward the door, growling and baring its teeth and gums.

Then Seraphim appeared in the doorway, sidled along the wall, and sat in a chair against the side of the house, as far from Zymaris as possible.

Amalia quickly pulled an empty crate up to the chair. "I fix up your dinner here," she said.

Seraphim and Stavros stared at each other. Seraphim shrugged apologetically and looked away.

"I brought you the knife," Stavros said.

"What you want with that?" Zymaris said.

"How 'bout nice soup?" Amalia said. "Lentils soup."

"Amalia, never mind him. Where's my meat?" Zymaris said.

She darted back into the house, trembling.

"Here!" Stavros said, throwing his brother the knife. He turned to Zymaris. "Well, Mr. Zymaris," he said, "I'm going. I can't do anything more here. He will pay for his mistake, you heard him. He's man of honor. I have to catch train now, goodbye. If police come, don't worry, he knows how to hide." He got up. "Come on, we go," he said to Althea.

"Wait a minute," Zymaris cried. "I don't need crazy man here. Get him out! Out! I don't want him here!"

"But he's married here," Stavros said. "You hear what priest say? No divorce!"

"I make divorce!" Zymaris said. "Priest not necessary. Nothing happen—right?—so no marriage. Get him out."

"Too bad," Stavros said. "I thought we were rid from him. But suppose—listen, Zymaris—suppose Amalia she's . . . you know."

"If nothing happen with Amalia, finish. If something happen, also finish. We forget everything, both sides—right? I want nothing from you, your side, family, so forth. Get him out. Business finish."

"Divorce?" Stavros said.

"Divorce," Zymaris said.

They shook hands.

Amalia came out of the house with a large plate holding a huge porterhouse steak for her father. She stopped by the chair where Seraphim sat and showed it to him. "I have one for you too," she said. "Big! Just like this one."

"He's going," her father said.

She looked at Stavros.

Stavros nodded. "Get up," he said to his brother. "You have nothing to pay here. Get up, Seraphim!"

Seraphim slowly got to his feet.

"You going?" Amalia asked.

Seraphim looked down at the ground.

"Come on, Amalia," Zymaris said, "give me the meat here. It's getting cold!" His voice was gentle.

She looked at her husband. Then she whispered, "I can't leave my father, you know that."

Seraphim nodded. "I know," he said.

"I wish it was like at the beginning, before we got marry, before I brought you here. But . . . now . . ."

"Goodbye."

"Amalia!" her father said.

She gave him his steak.

Stavros took Seraphim by the arm and pushed him roughly toward the side entrance of the yard.

And Seraphim said no more.

The German shepherd growled. "Hodja!" was the last they heard from Bodos Zymaris.

The brothers didn't speak on the train home, but when Seraphim went to the toilet, Althea said to Stavros, "I think he loved her. It's too bad."

"Mind your business," Stavros said. "You people don't understand family."

A north wind had come up. The ferry ride over the Hudson stirred something in Seraphim. He praised Amalia. "Clean girl," he said. "Good heart. Good manners."

"Never mind good manners," Stavros said. "In that house she soon be cutting you up for steak and serving you to her father—with good manners, guarantee. I save you, you son of a bitch, don't you understand that yet?"

Seraphim didn't answer.

"Well, you don't say nothing? You don't say thank you, nothing?"

Stavros waited for Seraphim to speak, but his brother, looking intently over the choppy water toward Manhattan, was silent. He said only one thing, just before their ferry pulled into its Manhattan-side slip. "I learn plenty 'bout dyes. There are some beautiful colors, roses and blue like the sky in summertime. I have idea we can make Oriental rugs, more beautiful, with softer colors. What you say?"

"Tell Vacilli," Stavros said.

"You see," Seraphim said a little later on the subway, "I stop coughing now!"

On the dining room table the stud poker game was still going on.

Seraphim kissed his mother, then sat in. No one seemed surprised to see him back, no one asked where he'd been.

Althea watched Stavros walk to the window, kiss his mother's forehead, then stare off into the dark. When he turned around, he'd made up his mind. "Enough cards tonight," he said, walking up to the dining room table.

"We finish this hand, O.K.?" Demosthenes asked.

Stavros messed up the cards on the table. "Come in here with me," he said. The brothers grabbed for their bills and change. They were still counting their losses and winnings as they entered the front room where Stavros was waiting for them.

"Maybe you people learn something today, maybe not. But I tell you this—I don't go to Jersey again save you from troubles. That's finish! Anybody want to move out, all right with me. Go 'head. Now."

No one spoke.

"I'm waiting," he said.

They looked at each other. They all held secret grievances.

"Your father, his dream was we all stay together—but maybe impossible. What? Michaelis—you—speak!"

"I don't remember that was his dream," Michaelis said. "He didn't say anything 'bout that to me. When he say that?"

"He talks to me now," Stavros said. "At night, when I sleep half, he comes to me. So I am speaking for him. When time comes you boys marry, Father will give me word. Then I go to Greece or, God willing, Anatolia, find right one for you."

Demosthenes, the youngest, was bold enough to ask, "How will we know when he gives you word for that?"

"I will tell you," Stavros said. "But if you like your way better, go 'head. Now. Because now I am disgusted. You, Demosthenes—yes, you. What you say? You go? You stay? What?"

"What are you talking?" Demosthenes said. "Sure I stay. What you so mad about all the time, making that terrible face?"

"Vacilliki?" Stavros said. "What 'bout you?"

His mother answered for him. "He stay with me," Vasso said.

Stavros nodded, then turned to Michaelis. "I am reading your mind, boy. My advice to you, stick to what you know. Rugs, that is what you know. Politics? Nothing. War? You be killed. Guarantee! You are not fighter. You are not strong man. Your nature is to be smart. Read books, newspapers, fine! Good for the brain! Ideas, so on. That is how Anatolian people survive. We watch the heroes die. 'Tst-tst-tst,' we say. 'Too bad, too bad!' Meantime they dead, we safe. To run is our wisdom. Heroes die. Cowards live. You listening?"

"You have forgotten," Michaelis said. "You have all forgotten."

"I forgot nothing," Stavros said. "Hard days taught me many lessons. I know the life." He took out his square-end knife. "I kill one man with this. I have not forgotten how. With this and with my brain, I will protect you as long as you are in the family. But if you run outside again—anybody!—I don't go New Jersey look for you! Finish! Now, Michaelis, what you say?"

They all saw that Michaelis had a divided heart, but what he said was, "I stay."

Stavros accepted the half pledge. "When you change your mind, let me know," he said.

Then he got up and walked to where Seraphim was. He stood in front of him and said, "Get up." Seraphim stood. "You the one I trusted most before. So what you say?"

Seraphim was trying to find words, when Stavros struck him across the face.

Then he reached out his hand, palm down.

Seraphim bent his head and kissed the back of Stavros's hand. "Thank you for the trouble you spent for me," he said.

Then Fofo came up. "The money you made Jersey," she said. "Give it!"

Seraphim reached into his pocket and gave Fofo all he had, a sum in excess of two hundred and seventy dollars.

Crouched in a corner, Althea watched it all. She was very still; didn't want to chance being noticed and asked to leave. Even she could see that Seraphim was happy to be back.

"Now I tell you something," Stavros said. "We have 'nough money in bank now. Also carpets, stock, in this room, maybe seven, eight thousan'. Also U.S. Treasury bond, ten thousan' dollar. I'm going to find place for us, start our business."

Now the women put food on the table, leftovers, but to Seraphim they tasted better than anything he'd eaten in the home of Bodos Zymaris. What his sisters gave him tasted like home.

APRIL 1915

Stavros chose to open the family store on April 7; it was a day to celebrate.

The war in the trenches of Europe had created a boom in the rug business in the United States. Through this year and the next, the mood among the *khalidgides* in the American rug market was of self-congratulation—merchants and traders took credit for the accidents of history. America's peace policy was praised by all those patriots who, with a speed that exceeded their wildest hopes, were building fortunes. Their confidence in the future was absolute.

The opening of I. Topouzoglou Sons, Oriental Rugs and Carpets, was ceremonious. Stavros had taken Seraphim, the nominal president of the new firm, and Michaelis, the vice-president, to Rogers Peet and chosen identical suits for them, modeled on what Mr. Ara Sarrafian wore when he was expecting a valued customer. Vacilli, in charge of touch-up and repair, was dressed in the bib apron of his trade. There was one employee, a man of all work, Silo, a swarthy Peloponnesian, who, having had trouble finding employment because he was deaf, was prepared to accommodate himself to intermissions in pay.

The space Stavros had rented, some two thousand square feet, had three pillars in a row straight back from the entrance door. On the pillar nearest the door, on this opening day, Seraphim, standing on a chair, was nailing up a small "mat," two feet by two feet, whose design was a swirling eagle clutching an American flag in its talons. At Stavros's insistence, the eagle was being placed facing the entrance; in the Sarrafians' store, in a comparable position, the same bird assured American buyers that they were entering an establishment operated by men who, despite their names, were devoted patriots.

Near the center of the store in the largest open space in the establishment, Stavros, also on a chair with a hammer in his hand, was attaching another small mat to a pillar. This tiny rug had been woven, on Stavros's commission, from a photograph of Isaac Topouzoglou. The Teheran weaver who specialized in this kind of work had made of the family patriarch a romantic figure of large vision and boldness as well as considerable physical strength—none of which qualities, of course, Isaac had possessed.

No one walking in at that moment would have guessed that the man in his shirtsleeves standing on that chair was the important man there; that this establishment was Stavros's particular triumph, the culmination of fifteen years of effort; that the goods on sale were pieces he had selected and caused to be accumulated, and that he, Stavros, owned what he certainly deserved: sixty percent of the company.

Stavros had sold Joe's Shoeshine Parlor to buy more stock for the place, and this contribution had been recognized.

The other shareholders were his four brothers, ten percent each. Only the youngest, Demosthenes, had dared to ask for a letter contract. Granted with a smile. The "gene-ee-use lawyer," as Stavros had dubbed Demosthenes, didn't understand his big brother well enough to recognize the threat in that smile. "I could do this very well without you, but you're my youngest and most childish brother, so here you are. Thank your father's memory."

Stavros got down from the chair, looked at his father's image rendered in the wool of Bactiari, and was satisfied. He put on his suit coat and sat at the single desk, in the small open space at the back that was to serve them all. A bottle and glasses waited the ceremony's climax; he poured himself a sip, rolled it over his tongue, then another, as he watched the store. Satisfaction possessed him as he tasted again the flavor of his triumph.

He even considered history. That morning, again, the newspapers had reassured him about the future. The German submarine blockade of Europe was tightening, and although this horrified the moralists who spoke of "civilized warfare," it did not disturb this determined Anatolian who'd put every cent his family had into rugs and carpets. Yes, the arrival of goods from the Orient had been cut down to a trickle, but the goods he and his brothers had in stock were already worth three times what they'd cost. Stavros also knew where and how to get more; his years in the underbelly of Constantinople had made him familiar with alternate routes of trade: Alexandria, Haifa, Beirut and the growing ports on the Persian Gulf, Bushire and Bandar Abbas.

Meantime he had every intention of continuing as an employee of the Sarrafians. The salary from that job, while not large, was regular and reliable and made it possible to reinvest all income from sales of the family's goods. If he had any compunction at being simultaneously involved in two enterprises, it was reflected in the location he'd chosen for his family's store —10 West Thirty-third Street, seven blocks north of Sarrafian Brothers. Stavros felt better with that separation between them.

There was another advantage in continuing at Sarrafian Brothers. From that lookout in one of the busiest of New York's rug markets, Stavros would be up on the arrival of every out-of-town buyer with a fresh supply of money. If it happened that this person couldn't find precisely what he wanted at Sarrafian's Stavros would direct him to where he could.

But he was in no hurry to sell. He liked the heavy rolls of carpets, the great piles of throw rugs around him in the store, "hatching their eggs," as he'd say in Turkish. He knew that the worth of Topouzoglou Sons was going to go up, ten percent a month, double in a year. He'd rather swap a carpet that another merchant wanted badly for three pieces that would swell his stock. If his brothers believed that when the store was launched they'd very soon have pockets jingling with money—and they'd been talking that way—Stavros had other ideas. He smiled at the naive hopes of small men. In time, yes, of course, they'd all be rich, possibly very rich. But that would happen when he chose; for now, the "boys" had to be disappointed. Again Stavros was prepared to hear their complaints and ignore them.

The space the Topouzoglou brothers rented was tiny compared to the 21,000 square feet of floor the Sarrafians had, and their stock, worth perhaps thirty thousand dollars, was pitiful alongside the older firm's "well over one million." Stavros had watched how Seraphim—careful, methodical Seraphim, now recovered from romance—had arranged their goods so that the place would look as full as possible. But there was still a great deal of uncovered concrete floor.

It was not disturbing. Not to Stavros! Not that year! He looked forward confidently to the day when his store would be glutted with goods. The only thing he dreaded was the possibility that America might allow itself to be pulled into the European conflict; that might make problems.

At a quarter to ten his thoughts were interrupted. The front door was thrown open by Demosthenes, who immediately stepped aside and ushered in Vasso, the matriarch of the family, dressed as ever in black, and accompanied by her eldest daughter, Fofo. Following them came the priests, Pericles Rondiris and Achilleas Galoyeropoulos, and on the arms of the younger priest in a way that worried Stavros, the two young women of the family, Eleftheria and Eleni. The group was immediately greeted by Seraphim and Vacilli, each of whom kissed the right hand of the older priest, Rondiris, then that of their mother.

In the middle of their space the brothers had opened their most treasured carpet, a nine-by-twelve silk Keshan worth more than anything else in the place—"piece I wouldn't sell a king," Stavros had said. It was a lovely azure blue, with an intricately designed medallion at its heart and several rich borders, all woven in lustrous thread, eighty knots to the square inch. It had been worked over by Vacilli until it glowed like a fire of embers powdered with its own fine gray-blue ashes, a perfect blend of soft, harmonious colors.

Father Rondiris was led to the very center of this treasure's medallion. He raised both arms, a gesture to summon the flock, and there, amidst the devoted, he knelt, lifted his eyes to a brand-new electric light fixture, and said his prayers of dedication.

"May the God of the Orthodox," Rondiris intoned—it was close to song—"He who agonizes with the agony of the Greek people, now far from their rightful homes—"

He stopped. "Where's Stavros?" he said.

"In the back," Stavros said. "Better off here."

Father Rondiris chose to let this pass. "O God of the Orthodox," he chanted, "pay special attention, I beg you, to the business of these young men. They are good boys, I can tell you that much, devoted to their dear mother and with respect for the memory of their father, Isaac, now dead so long that less sincere men would have forgotten him. These are your most humble servants, who—"

"Humble? I hope not humble," Stavros muttered.

"Shshsh!" Father Achilleas said sharply.

"Humble, you don't make money," Stavros said.

"Tst-tst-tst, shsh!" Father Galoyeropoulos came back and Eleni joined in.

"Go 'head, go 'head," Stavros said to Rondiris. "And Eleni, never mind that 'tst-tst-tst' business with me. Finish, Rondiris, for God's sake. Tell Him bring good business here—main thing."

Rondiris, trying to keep his peace with Stavros, nodded but chose his own words. "O God of the faithful, bless this business and give it success and good profits which these boys, in my humble opinion, deserve. We all thank you for your support and for your help over the years, help without which—"

"Nobody help me," Stavros said. "Everything I did with these." He held up his hands. "Excuse me, Rondiris, maybe I say a few words here. Stay there," he said to Rondiris, who was on his knees.

Then he said: "My father, Isaac-Papou, who sits in heaven at the right hand of Jesus, I am speaking to you. You sent me here with nothing but these bare hands, nothing else. Because you believed in me, Father, I owe you everything." He advanced toward the small portrait of his father, woven in wool. "You've been waiting a long time for this day, Father, I understand that. You must have suffered from me many terrible hours. I did the best I could. I had some other problems, which it is better to forget now. Some of your sons lost faith. One of them even asked for letter contract his share this store, imagine that, Father. After all my years sacrificing here. But what the hell, I give it to him. After all, he is your son."

At this, Stavros looked at Demosthenes until he was sure Demosthenes understood. It was a warning. "And what other people say," Stavros said, "who were close to you one time"—a swift glance at his mother—"now I decided forget those things. Everything past, now, finished!"

Father Rondiris was still on his knees, waiting.

"Because now we're here. I brought them all here, as you wished, and it is your name on the door. We did not change it. We did not make it easy for Americans, as most foreign donkeys do. You asked for this and you have it."

Now he was singing, even more boldly than the priest. "Your sons at last . . . are together here . . . in your service. May they be worthy of you! Maybe they learned by now . . . at last . . . that each one by himself . . . is nothing. Nothing. Only together . . . under the leadership . . . which you gave to me . . . are they strong. Only I can be successful alone. Do they know that? I hope so. We will become here, out of many, one. In your name."

Rondiris was trying to struggle up from his knees.

"Wait, Rondiris, wait. I finish right away," Stavros said. "I am speaking to my father, who is unhappy—not with us, because this is a day of celebration for him. But I know what it is—without the help of your photographs, Achilleas. Your grave there, Father, the place where your body lies—not your soul, which is at the right hand of Jesus and rejoicing today—but the shell of your body, where you once lived: I don't need that damned photograph, Achilleas. I know without it that my father's grave is a disgrace and an insult to us all, but most to me, the eldest son of that sainted man.

"But, Father, listen to me from where you are in that seat of honor. I am going back to that place one day and I will bring some of the strength of this great country with me. I will have the greatest weapon of all. Dollars! I will also have a knife, a curved blade of fine steel which I will use just once, to slit open the belly of the man whom now I spit out of my mouth."

He spit and said, "Hassapoglou!

"I will split his belly open there, where the graves are crumbling, spill his entrails on the ground for the wolves to feast on. I will cut out his eyes and give them to the crows, that man Hassapoglou, and his tongue to the rats, Hassapoglou who stole the money I worked my years and lost my youth for, the money I sent to the East. He ate it there, Hassapoglou. I will cut his dearest part from off his belly and stuff it into his mouth to silence him forever. And leave him there to rot."

He rested for an instant. They were all silent.

"Then I will take your body back to its home, dear one, in a fine carriage with two strong but gentle horses, take it to the foot of the great white mountain of Kayseri, where you were born. I will buy you a hectare of land there and a Christian monument. It will show you seated in a glade, our Lord Jesus at your side. It is spring and you smile at each other in friendship. I live for that day, to see that. Then my service to you will be done."

Now Stavros, who was not religious, crossed himself three times and shouted, "Silo, bring the wine."

And Rondiris got up off his knees—with Stavros's help.

Silo came forward with the tray that Stavros had prepared. It was dry sherry, the drink Mr. Ara Sarrafian favored when the brothers returned from their summer vacations. Drinks were poured and enjoyed. Fond hopes and wishes were expressed, in voices barely audible because there was an air of fear in the place. Or was it awe—awe at the intensity of the emotions Stavros had revealed.

Only Eleftheria went to Stavros and kissed him, for she was the bold one of the women, she feared no one. Then Stavros went to his mother and knelt at her feet, took her kiss and kissed her in return. He saw she was troubled in a way the others were not, and he asked her what it was. But she shook her head and wouldn't say. He cradled her hand and kissed it many times, tears in his eyes, to reassure her that he hadn't forgotten the promise he'd made to her, which was a different promise.

Eleftheria and Eleni were singing a song they used to sing in primary school. As they sang, Vasso whispered to Stavros, "The Turks will be angry when they find this out."

"What will they find out, Mommah?" he asked.

"That we start new store here," she said, her face tense with apprehension.

"But Mommah, this is America. There are no Turks here."

"Don't fool yourself. They're running in the streets, just like before. I see them from the window."

Stavros didn't know how to reassure her; suddenly she'd retreated out of reach. "Listen to the girls singing," he said.

She nodded, then said, "We must marry the girls off before it's too late."

"Next thing I do, guarantee," Stavros said. "Don't worry, Mommah! I will marry them all, one by one, to good men. Fofo first."

Now the two younger girls—Eleftheria, the bold one, and Eleni, the modest one—arms raised, heads thrown back, faces pink with girlish ecstasy, were dancing as well as singing, circling the young priest, with handkerchiefs floating from their hands as they turned.

"From now on, *embros!*" Stavros shouted, "*Paradisos.* Everything perfect! *Aman, aman!* But not on the Keshan. No dancing on the—Silo! For God's sake, roll up that Keshan!"

MAY 1915

Stavros's problem, that May, was to marry off his oldest sister, Fofo. This done, he could see to it that the other two were married in turn, and then, relieved of the responsibility for their support, he himself could marry a proper Anatolian girl and begin his dynasty. He'd warned his brothers, particularly Seraphim, that they were not to think of marriage until all the girls were "sold." Seraphim understood. "That's the right way," he said. But Eleni and Eleftheria weren't able to conceal their impatience. "What's she waiting for, Fofo?" Eleftheria said to her brother. "A millionaire?"

Fofo was holding everything up and knew it; she felt guilty about it and at the same time resentful. When Stavros tried to talk to her about the problem, she wept and left the room.

He was determined to meet this problem as he did others, frontally and at once. There was a rug merchant in the building where Sarrafian Brothers had space, a man who had just lost his wife. He was at least a dozen years older than Fofo, but that was the preferred marital gap, so Stavros invited the man to tea. If everything went well, he'd ask him to supper, but tea was an important first step since it gave the woman in question an opportunity to show off her capability for baking sweet pastries.

When he told Fofo what he'd done, she nodded. By then her back was to the wall.

"So you thought everything over?" he said. "Good idea."

"I thought over you want me out from here," she said.

"You always have a home here, Fofo, you know that."

"A woman cannot have two homes."

"It's time for you to marry. You're thirty-five next month, am I mistaken?"

Her face puckered. "What it cost to keep me here?" she asked.

"That's not the reason, the reason is your life. It's time for you."

"I know more about rugs, how to find them, buy them, sell them, than any of the boys. I work harder than all of them together."

"I appreciate. The truth is you should have been a man. But you are not."

"So what's your hurry get rid of me?"

"No hurry, no hurry," he said, then pressed on into the heart of the matter. "Now I beg you, be a good girl when Mr. Yeremia comes tomorrow, make nice *beurek, keurabbieh,* and so forth. You know what I'm talking. I want to say that everything he sees on his plate, you made it."

Fofo was in love with her brother. "I don't want to leave you," she said.

"Where you going? Same city, no? Every afternoon, every Sunday, coming home, no?"

"I saw him in street with Seraphim, from the window I saw him. Too old for me maybe."

"That's a question."

"Also I don't like him," Fofo said.

"How you know you don't like him, you didn't talk to him yet close? Now I give you some advice, God's sake. Don't eat garlic tonight. Also this: Here is America, women not supposed sweat here. So shave under arms. Take my razor, wash good there after. Understand?"

"I smell bad to you too?"

"You smell all right to me. But I'm used to you. This man stranger. Also when you sit, keep your front up—"

"I have nothing there."

"He doesn't know those things yet. Smile—see, like this. Smiling, show your teeth. Come, show me! Good! Listen everything he says, nodding all the time like this. 'You're right,' 'Very good,' 'Of course, of course,' all the time nodding and smiling like this. When you give him pastry, *baklava, keurabbieh,* and so forth, say it's poor stuff. You know his dear mother made better. Wife too, now dead. Hope he likes it all the same, hope it brings him little satisfaction which will make all your trouble worthwhile. Ask him is he comfortable, then when he says yes, bring him anyway pillow for his back, make him more comfortable. You listening me, Fofo?"

"I don't want to leave you. Find me man like you first. Who is there?"

"Nobody, right! That's enough talk. Bring me my supper."

"What kind business he has?" she asked Stavros a few minutes later as she put a roasted knuckle of lamb before him.

"I told you. Oriental rugs like us, and carpets."

"I know you told me that. What I'm asking is what kind business— good business, bad business?"

"We find that out tomorrow first thing, don't worry," Stavros said.

She spent the entire next morning cooking delicacies, then carefully arranged them on two large plates, poured honey into the heart of each offering and powdered each dish with baker's sugar. Then she lifted her plates to a high shelf above the large wash tanks in the kitchen where, she believed, they'd be safe from cockroaches, and went off—she still had four hours but was anxious—to see what she could do about her appearance.

The sight of herself in the mirror did not encourage her. She envied Eleftheria her breasts, but there was nothing she could do about her own —she absolutely refused the suggestion her mother, Vasso, made. "We always put two stockings in there, roll 'em up, one each side."

She put on her one decently preserved dress. She hadn't worn it in two years and, having grown thick and heavy in the *abeeseenoh*, felt every time she moved that a seam would burst. But she had no other dresses to choose from, so she resolved to move as little and as carefully as possible.

The plan was for her not to greet Mr. Yeremia at the door, but to make an entrance after he was seated and her sisters and Vacilliki had put him at his ease. When she came in, carrying the two dishes of sweets, she brought a fragrant aroma into the room. She sat across from Mr. Yeremia, who was very heavy about the middle, she noticed, and smiled at him in the way Stavros had taught her she must. She began nodding at everything he said and saying, "Tst-tst-tst!" and "Peh, peh, peh."

Stavros hurried in a quarter of an hour late, having received the reluctant permission of Morgan Perry to leave before closing time; the occasion was that important. He embraced Mr. Yeremia as if they were old and true friends—which they were not.

Eleftheria served the tea, Eleni passed the sugar and the lemon slices, Fofo the sweets. It seemed that the two younger girls were taken with Mr. Yeremia—or were they just helping their sister, since they had an interest in getting Fofo married? Fofo thought they were behaving rather flirtatiously; she wished that Eleftheria, especially, would smile less seductively.

Stavros took over the meeting. "Our father was fine man," he said. "Very intelligent, had fine store, bazaar, Kayseri." He looked sternly at

Vasso, putting his forefinger to his lips to make sure she didn't contradict him. "He had a son, myself, so he wanted a daughter." He pointed to Fofo. "When she came, she was so pretty that he named her after the goddess of love, Aphrodite, understand? Fofo, short name for Aphrodite."

Everybody looked at Fofo. There was some uncomfortable laughter. Had Stavros made a joke?

It seemed, for an instant, that Fofo would leave the room.

Stavros saved her. "She is fine woman. She runs this whole house. Everybody depend on her. Any trouble, she takes care. Look at those pastries. She made everything herself. No bakery goods here. No grease, all pure butter—right, Fofo?"

"Sweet butter," she said.

"Now, that's our side of problem," Stavros said. "We touch on everything, right?"

"You didn't touch on problem of dowry," Mr. Yeremia said.

"This is America here, you understand that?"

"Same time, I am Anatolian. I have those customs in mind now."

"Now, yes, when it's convenient, sure, those customs. Tell me are you citizen here?"

"Yes, three years citizen."

"So this is America. Now my turn ask you. How much money you have? She's used to everything the best—right, Fofo?"

"Right, everything the best." She looked at Mr. Yeremia.

He pulled his vest down to cover his stomach.

"So, we have five brothers here, we watching out carefully what kind situation she go in. How much you got, plain language?"

"Enough."

"For whom enough? That's not plain language, please."

"Maybe twenty thousan' cash, maybe forty thousan' stock, present market prices. Who knows?"

"I have permission, maybe, come look at your store, the stock?"

"Welcome. I buy you lunch."

"Fine. Proper way. Next question: You marry before, I understand, wife die."

"Yes," Mr. Yeremia said. "Poor woman."

"Tst-tst-tst!" They all made that sound.

But Stavros stuck to business. "Children?" he asked.

"No children," Mr. Yeremia said.

"What's the matter you?"

"Nothing. Fall of dice, I suppose."

"Fofo expecting children—am I right, Fofo?"

Fofo shrugged. "If possible," she said.

"I give her children," Mr. Yeremia said.

"You think you can do that?"

"What you think? Look at me."

"I'm looking, but who can tell from looks?"

Mr. Yeremia pulled his vest down again. "I guarantee," he said.

"And if not?"

"If not? Fall of dice."

"Because I'm thinking, man married many years no children, natural thought, what's the matter over there?"

"You want I bring you letters from certain . . . certain parties—ladies, you understand? What you say? Forgive me, Miss Aphrodite, but your brother, he's asking difficult problem here. I am normal man, guarantee. But I go here, I go there, my business, many stores all over U.S.A."

"How old are you?" Stavros asked.

"Fifty," he said. "Plus," he added.

"Plus what?"

"Two, three. Why that so important here?"

"Why you answering in that strange way?"

"Because you ask too many private questions."

"But marriage, it's private business. We have right to ask everything here before—right? Because your answers are tricky. A little bit. No?"

He looked at Fofo. He wanted to know what she thought of the man.

Fofo looked very sour. She didn't want to leave home.

"Who's making decision here anyway?" Mr. Yeremia asked.

"We all are," Stavros said.

"No, I am," Mr. Yeremia said. "My decision. I have many chances, you know. Many women look on me hopefully."

"And what is your conclusion from that?"

"My conclusion, I don't need sit here and answer questions like police court. I am an American citizen.

Fofo stood. "I have little headache," she said. "You will excuse me, sir."

She did a little dance, half bow, half curtsy, and left the room. They heard the door to her own room close.

The conversation turned to more general topics of interest to rugmen. "Tell me, Yeremia," Stavros said, "we can talk better now other matter decided—forget it, right? You importing goods, and if so, how you get them here?"

"Present time, I'm scrounging market here. Where the hell can I buy goods with war everywhere and how the hell I get them here?"

"That is my secret and I tell that nobody. But we have our own company now, my brothers: Isaac Topouzoglou Sons. Remember that name! We will buy goods and we will bring them here. I have ideas that problem."

There was a heavy silence.

Stavros sighed and yawned. "Worn out today," he said.

"Me too," Mr. Yeremia said. "I go." And he went.

Later, when Stavros expressed some disappointment at the afternoon's result, Fofo said, "How could I know if I wanted him or not with Eleftheria throwing her skirts in his face and laughing at everything he said?"

They all enjoyed the sweets.

JUNE 1915

Stavros had learned many things observing the brothers Sarrafian; one of them was the uses of honesty. To anticipate suspicion in the matter of his business, he had cards made up which carried this message: "The brothers Topouzoglou, Seraphim, Vacilleas, and Michaelis, sons of Isaac Topouzoglou, deceased, are proud to announce the opening of their Oriental rug establishment at 10 West Thirty-third Street where they will offer buyers of the trade the finest selection of Oriental rugs and carpets at reasonable prices."

Along the bottom edge of this austerely designed card, there was printed in small type: "This enterprise has absolutely no connection with Mr. Stavros Topouzoglou, well known as Joe Arness, salesman of Sarrafian Brothers, Inc."

The first announcement went through the mails to Mr. Ara Sarrafian. The second, Stavros took himself to Miss Emily Barton and asked her to make sure it was placed in the private office on top of the personal mail waiting for the return of Mr. Fernand, the "big boss."

A few days later, on the twelfth of June, Mr. Fernand Sarrafian returned from Florida and entered the store to receive the congratulations of all. He'd had a close call—he'd booked passage to England on the *Lusitania,* a voyage that luxury liner never completed because, as of May 7, it rested on the bottom of the Atlantic Ocean.

Mr. Fernand was able to enjoy, in his own cynical way, the declaration of President Woodrow Wilson ("Professor. No brains!"): "The American government will, of course, follow its policy of holding Germany to strict accountability for the loss of life in this disaster." Mr. Fernand smiled. "Berlin, I'm sure, very worried by this," he said.

Mr. Fernand was not a patriot, not of any country; he was attracted by power, not by sentiment. The waving of a bright flag meant nothing to this perfumed nomad. He distrusted expressions of patriotism. Furthermore, he expected Germany to win the war. Soon.

On this particular morning, after reading the news of the war in the trenches, he threw down the newspaper and picked up Stavros's announcement. The old Armenian chuckled as he read it, coughed his nicotine cough, and called in his brother, Ara, and the store manager, Morgan Perry.

"You seen this?" he said, holding up the card.

Ara responded with a gesture of bewilderment tempered by indifference. But Mr. Fernand, a student of human character, was interested in probing further.

"He seems to be assuring us," Mr. Fernand explained, "that he has no intention of stealing our customers. I hadn't realized the fellow was so honest. Had you, Morgan?"

Morgan Perry read the card again. "No, sir," he said. "Not that honest!"

"Better keep an eye on him, Morgan," Mr. Fernand said.

"I've already got my eye on him, big boss," Perry said.

Neither Sarrafian ever commented on the announcement, or chose to ask Stavros in the months that followed how his brothers' enterprise was faring.

In its first year, I. Topouzoglou Sons did passably well—it paid all expenses. Its chief shareholder even let some money leak down to where the "boys" waited with cupped hands. But for the most part, Stavros had been quick to commandeer what take there was and reinvest it. He built the stock. Now the gray concrete floor was entirely covered—that was the immediately visible change—with *mahl*. The store began to look too small instead of too big for what it contained.

Of course his brothers were not content with what they were allowed to put in their pockets. The old lady heard their grumbling. "What's that noise every night?" she asked her eldest son. "Who's fighting around here all the time?"

"Your sons," he told her. "They got what they wanted, but they're like dogs: When you give nothing, they lie quiet; when you throw them few bones, they fight who gets the biggest."

His brothers may not have been content, but the change in Stavros was evident to everyone around him. Before going to work at the Sarrafians', he began each day in the store on Thirty-third Street, and it brought spring to his step and flash to his eyes—a new kind of dash and daring.

Unfortunately, this change in him edged over into arrogance. Stavros's temper had always been quick. Now he'd developed Mr. Fernand's faculty of looking straight through people who were of no use to him. Suddenly everyone at Sarrafian Brothers was finding him intolerable.

Mr. Fernand Sarrafian was in his private office with his brother one morning when he became aware of an unusual disturbance in the store. In one of the spacious bays where goods were displayed to buyers, Stavros and two portly men in summer suits and straw hats were standing around a large pile of nine-by-twelve carpets, talking animatedly. Standing idly by were the porters who open rugs for the inspection of buyers.

"What's happening out there?" Fernand asked his brother.

Ara looked through the small window cut in the wall. "What is that

—an argument?" he said, speaking to himself. "What the hell's Joe doing now?" He rapped on the pane to summon Morgan Perry, who was slumped over his desk, checking accounts due.

Perry was perfectly aware of what was happening; in fact, he had allowed it to go on in the hope that the Sarrafians would finally lose patience with Joe and fire him.

"Why don't you stop that?" Ara Sarrafian asked Perry.

"Just give me the word, boss," Perry said.

"What's he selling those fellows?"

"The Chinese nine-by-twelves we got in eight months ago and haven't been able to move. Selling, you hope."

"What might be the subject of their discussion?" Mr. Fernand asked.

"Don't ask me, sir," Perry said. "Why don't you let Freddie handle customers like those fellows? Look!"

One of the porters, an old trusted employee who kept Ara in touch with the office gossip for an extra five dollars a week, had noticed his master's face in the window and indicated Stavros with a lift of his chin.

"If they don't go for the price," Ara said, "cut it twenty-five cents."

"The price was O.K., last I heard, but maybe now they've changed their mind. We're lucky to get that stuff out of the place at any price."

"So what's he arguing?"

"Leave it to him, he'll find something. He's going to lose the sale in another minute, boss. Honest, let me send Freddie in there."

"All right," Mr. Ara said. "Time being, tell Freddie take over there. Send Joe in to me."

Ara turned to his brother. "Morgan thinks we should fire the little Greek," he said.

"Let me chat with him," Mr. Fernand said. "He's got a big family, I understand."

They watched through the window as Stavros hustled up to Morgan Perry and they could hear him say, "What do you want? Don't you see I'm making business there?"

Perry didn't answer him, but called to Freddie Farrow, who was rearranging stock at the other end of the floor. "Freddie, come take care of Mr. Singleton and Mr. Gordon. They're looking over those fine Chinese nine-by-twelves—you know the pieces."

Stavros boiled over. "Did you call me away so you could do that?" he demanded. "What the hell's going on?" Through the window to the private office he could see the two Sarrafians watching.

"The big boss wants to talk to you," Morgan Perry said, then turned his back.

Mr. Fernand liked his private office rather dark. What light there was came from two copper lamps, Egyptian globes which he had purchased in the great marketplace next to Cairo's ancient university. They were

inlaid with circles of colored glass, tiny moons which filled the room with
an eerie and—to Mr. Fernand—comforting glow.

"Sit down, Stavros," Mr. Fernand said when Stavros hesitated in the
doorway. "Sit, my miserable Anatolian!" He pointed to a place at the end
of the banquette.

Stavros knew that in being asked to sit, he was being favored, but
instead of putting him at his ease, this made him more nervous.

Mr. Fernand fell back on a mound of pillows and drew a small curtain
across the window which afforded a view of the store. Ara nodded to his
brother—a suggestion that he be the one to conduct the inquiry.

"We heard some commotion outside," Mr. Fernand observed with a
smile. "You were discussing something, so it seemed, with our buyers.
What was it? My brother and I have been wondering."

"They were looking for argument with me," Stavros said. "I didn't
bring up subject."

"What subject was it that you didn't bring up?"

"About the war. They're from Kansas and—"

"Atlanta, Georgia," Morgan Perry said from the half-closed door.
"Double A. Dun and Bradstreet."

"Whatsa difference—Georgia, Kansas? They saying America should
stay out. They don't realize, damn fools, that there's Atlantic Ocean and,
on other side, world where we have important commercial interest. I
didn't say 'damn fool' to them, of course."

"And you are of an opposite persuasion," asked Mr. Fernand. "You
believe that we should . . . ?"

"Of course. And no one had to explain me, sir. I follow events every
day. You read paper this morning?"

"I generally do," Mr. Fernand said.

"If you did read any paper this morning, you see that bomb was
thrown into Preparedness Day parade."

"Yes, yes," Mr. Fernand said. "But what, I must say, astonishes me is
that as recently as a year ago—no, considerably less than a year ago—your
convictions were opposite to the ones you're expressing today. It seems
that the only consistent thing about you is the level of your excitement—
and your voice. You don't have to shout in here, you know."

"I know," Stavros said, and he was quieter, though it took an effort.
"But, Mr. Fernand, when the situation changes, I change also. You think
that's wrong? Of course not. You're an intelligent man—"

"What the hell has the war got to do with the rug business?" Morgan
Perry said, stepping in from the doorway.

"Thank you very much, Morgan," Mr. Fernand said. "We don't need
your help for the moment."

Perry backed through the door.

"And do close the door please, Morgan," Mr. Fernand said, "as you go. Thank you."

"What price you quote Mr. Singleton and Mr. Gordon from Atlanta, Georgia?" Ara Sarrafian said.

"Two dollar fifty a square foot. We paid dollar, five freight on boat Shanghai." Stavros pulled back a side of the curtain to see through the window to where the buyers were talking with Freddie. "I better go back," he said. "They tried start a fight with me so I'd get nervous maybe and cut the price. But they'll buy at our price, don't worry."

"Freddie's there," Morgan Perry said as he closed the door. "We're not worrying."

"Were they objecting to the price?" Fernand Sarrafian asked.

"I told you, sir, it was all set. In fact, they—"

"So why the hell, my boy, were you arguing?" Fernand said.

"Last I heard," Ara Sarrafian said, "the price Chinese carpets in New York City has nothing to do with this war."

"Mr. Ara, you're wrong, you are wrong!"

There was a knock on the door.

"Mr. Sarrafian," Freddie Farrow said, "it's all set. We got our two, fifty."

"Damn fools," Mr. Fernand commented with a smile.

"They're taking all thirty-eight pieces too. O.K.?"

"Very O.K.," Mr. Ara said.

"I knew they'd come up to us," Stavros said. "It was only a matter few more minutes for me there."

"Come in, Freddie," Mr. Fernand said.

Freddie came in, pulling up his trousers and tightening his belt.

"I don't like the way you dress, Freddie," Mr. Fernand said.

"People have told me that before, sir, yes, sir," Freddie said with a laugh.

"We're raising your salary ten dollars. Also, go out tomorrow and buy yourself a suit with a vest, a nice gray. Give me the bill. You're a successful salesman now. Also some shirts. Pin stripes are nice. What you're wearing makes you look like a grammar teacher in a high school."

"Exactly," Stavros said, with a short laugh.

"They asked me to have lunch with them. What will I do?" Freddie said.

"I made reservation," Stavros said, "at the Bosporus."

"I told them I thought you had," Freddie said. " 'Too oily,' they said. They want to take me to Dinty Moore's for corned beef and cabbage."

"Dinty Moore's!" Stavros said. "My God! All right. So let's go."

"He'll go. You stay," Mr. Fernand said with a pleasant smile. "I want to have a chat with you, Stavros."

"Oh, thank you, sir," Stavros said. He smiled at Freddie. "Have a nice lunch," he said.

"I'm sorry, Joe," Freddie said. "It wasn't my suggestion, Dinty Moore's."

"Don't worry about it," Stavros said. "I got to talk to Mr. Fernand here."

"Ara," his brother said. "Why don't you go say goodbye to those fellows? They'd appreciate it. Stavros may be more comfortable with what I am going to say if we're alone."

"If you need me," Ara said to his brother as he left, "call me."

"I'm going to help you," Mr. Fernand said to Stavros, as he gentled a fresh Melachrino into his ivory holder, "by reminding you of certain facts of our life in the United States of America. Also some facts about your own nature, concerning which, it seems to me, you remain in ignorance."

"Yes, sir," Stavros said. "But first let me say this: I understand my mistake. Though Mr. Morgan Perry, he exaggerate it. He's my enemy—never forget that, sir."

"Now, now, Morgan is not only an employee but an old and trusted friend. He has served us well and now that he is so miserably unhappy because of his son's death, we must comfort him, not talk against him."

"I try to do that, sir, but it's not easy. So please—"

"So nothing! Preserve a silence. Try to listen. It's an accomplishment you should try to cultivate. You would be less often the victim of disappointment if you would accept the fact that you are not the same breed as many of our best customers, especially those from states with Indian names—for instance, Iowa, Missouri, or, if you prefer, Kansas."

"Just a minute, please, dear sir. You're wrong. They all like me."

"Our customers have good manners! You wouldn't know if they didn't. So, back to Freddie. You are intelligent, if self-deceiving. You must have noticed that he is of the same breed as—for instance—those men out there."

"Excuse me, sir. Again you're wrong."

"Again?"

"Yes. Those two customers are not the same piece goods as Freddie. They Jewish, sir—Mr. Singleton, I think; Mr. Gordon, guarantee! That's all I have to say."

"That can only mean one thing for us: that they prefer to be served by a Gentile."

"Right! That's me—sir," Stavros said.

"I suppose it's possible that you are," Mr. Fernand said, with a flourish of the fragrant Melachrino, "but not to look at. I have noticed that when you talk to them, they don't seem to be impressed."

"I have answer to that, but holding it back, as you ask me."

"Thank you. You see, Freddie, with no experience and a limited intelligence, is a far more effective salesman—in this situation at least. He makes the right impression."

"How long that impression last? Tell me that much."

"Long enough to sell thirty-eight nine-by-twelve Chinese of a very mediocre quality," Mr. Fernand said, as he parted the small curtains and looked through the sealed window into the store where Freddie was helping Mr. Gordon into his suit coat.

"But, sir, forgive me interrupting again, but I had sale all made when Mr. Morgan Perry, under advice from your brother, reasons I— Never mind. I'm sorry I spoke."

"I am not finding it easy to talk with you, Stavros."

"From my side, I am enjoy listening to you, sir."

"You are aware, of course, that since young Morgan died his father has not been the same man."

"Oh yes, sure, that's why I talking him gentle now. Otherwise—!"

"That was a terrible thing, of course, nothing worse is imaginable than the loss of a son. I lost two boys by my first wife—to the Turks in the 'ninety-six massacres—so I am ready to face the fact that my old friend Morgan has, for the moment, lost a good deal of his heart and most of his energy. He sits at his desk like an old sick dog—"

"Except when about me. Then his bite come back."

"He has lost his spirit. So I am obliged to think ahead. We need someone suited to the kind of customer we had today. Now! You must be far ahead of me—"

"Far ahead? No! *With* you. I'm listening very patient. As you ask me. Satisfied, sir?"

"Have you, for instance, noticed that when those sheiks from Kansas or wherever come in here, my brother stays off the floor? Even Ara! The owner! Personally, I show myself only to the very old ones who've known me long enough to have become accustomed to my nose—I'm no more handsome than you—and my manners, which are much better than yours. The greatest favor you can do yourself, my friend, is to accept the fact of who you are and who you are not. This is a white Protestant country and Freddie is one of the favored. What have you got to match his clear blue eyes? And he has no contrary opinions, certainly none that he holds strongly enough so he would wish to debate them."

There was a knock on the door.

"Who is it?" Mr. Fernand said. "I'm busy!"

"It's me again, sir."

"It's Freddie, sir," Stavros said. "Shall I let him in? What you think?"

"Oh, come in, come in, Freddie my boy," Mr. Fernand said.

Freddie stood uneasily in the doorway. Stavros eased back on the banquette, now apparently at complete ease.

"They want me to go to the ball game with them," Freddie said. "This afternoon. They have a box right behind third base. What'll I do?"

"You know something about the Yankees, my boy?"

"I was born knowing about the Yankees. Doc Ayres is pitching for the Senators; it turns out he's from Georgia too. They particularly want to see Peckinpaugh play—Roger Peckinpaugh, the Yankee shortstop. They've heard so much about him. I said I couldn't, of course, but they insisted I put it up to you. I'm sorry, sir."

"Sure, sure," Stavros said. "Go ahead."

"By all means," Mr. Fernand said. "Go. Go, my boy."

"We get along without you," Stavros said.

"You're sure it's all right?" Freddie asked Mr. Fernand. "Because I told them I really didn't think I could."

"You must go," Mr. Fernand said.

"You must!" Stavros agreed.

"Well, all right then," Freddie said. "Can I say something? I mean, to Joe, sir?" Mr. Fernand spread his hands, a generous acquiescence. "Joe, Althea wants you to come to her place and have dinner with us tonight. She said she misses seeing you, she says you're avoiding her."

"Why I should avoid her?" Stavros said.

"Of course he'll come to dinner," Mr. Fernand said. "What else has he got to do? Go on now. Play a good game."

"I'm not playing, sir, just watching." Freddie laughed as he went out.

For the first time since he'd come into the office, Stavros was silent.

"What's the matter?" Mr. Fernand said.

Stavros scowled. "I don't want to eat with them," he said.

"Why?"

"She's his woman."

"Oh! Can't blame her! What a nice boy! He's afraid he hurt your feelings so he invites—"

"My feelings not hurt."

"Of course they are. You're human, aren't you? Partly?"

"I'm not like these people here."

"Well, learn to be. Especially in the case of someone as nice as Freddie. What a fine young man! He's what we need on the floor. People will never believe he is overcharging them, it's impossible. With you and me, the contrary! People immediately suspect us. Which is why you and I need a mask named Freddie. Baseball! I hate baseball! I went once. In ten minutes I had a terrible headache, thank God, and left. But Freddie, he knows the names of the players. Peckinpaugh! I never heard of Mr. Peckinpaugh, have you?"

"All you have to do," Stavros said, "is buy a newspaper."

"My friend, you are still resisting the facts. Freddie has their mentality. He even looks like their sons—or what they wish their sons looked like.

Yes, and like their priests, their bankers, their teachers, their judges—everyone they were brought up to trust. That is Freddie's advantage over you! Even over me."

"But what the hell he knows about rugs?" Stavros said. "Everything on that he learn from me."

Mr. Fernand ignored this. "Of course, in time, Freddie will learn to take advantage of this advantage. He will begin to enjoy the fact that he can fool them. Then watch his face change. The buyers may even begin to wonder if he is overcharging them—which, of course, he will be. But they will still buy from him, and at our price. Simply because of what he is. The first thing a salesman has to sell—always remember this, my dear boy—is himself. After that, it's easy. What's the matter? What are you thinking?"

"If what you say is true, what the hell I'm doing in this country? Tell me that."

"Which, my miserable Anatolian, is the question we all have to ask ourselves at regular intervals, we recent arrivals. Do you want my opinion?"

"Why not?"

"A fellow like you, here, has to be an anarchist, a boxer, or a gangster."

"How 'bout you—sir?"

"I had a lucky strike. It happened I was in the right place at the right time, with the right information. I don't give myself credit for any extraordinary brains."

"I do. Myself, I'm talking. I'm smarter than Freddie or Mr. Morgan Perry or even your brother!"

"But you're not smarter than me."

"In one department, yes."

"Which is?"

"I tell you how to save this business. If you maybe listen."

"I wasn't aware the business needed saving."

"That's what I mean. I see further than you because I see up from the bottom. I know you have other interests, much bigger ones, and that you leave everything in your brother's hands. But something going wrong here and maybe even he's beginning to see that. I seen him lying on a pile of rugs when he thinks no one watching and he looks very sad. Also, he drinks. You know that. And I know what he's sad about. The business is going down. What he don't know is that it's his fault."

"How his fault?"

"He should be doing the opposite of what he's doing. He should be buying everything he can find. In Persian market, Turkish market, anywhere, here too, also Iraq, Greece, Egypt—what the hell, anywhere!"

"Why?"

"Because if Germany wins this war—which is possible if America stays out—goods from the Orient are suddenly going very short. Man who has rugs will survive, others go bankrupt. You—yes you—better listen to me, I am speaking about this place. You are sitting on your money. Is not your nature to do that. It's your brother's nature. Am I right?"

"This time you may be right. This time."

"Suppose the Germans win the war—is that possible?"

"Certainly."

"The first thing they do? Build railroad to Baghdad, from there Teheran. Road to the East! Then the products of the East will go to Berlin first. You listening to me? Sir? When you buy there you have to pay big profit to the Germans. This is idea which changed my mind on the war. You don't seem to have found this idea yet. Very simple. Why not? I'm surprised!"

"Don't be fresh, Stavros. So we'll trade with the Germans."

"At double the price. Even now Turks control the ports. Constantinople. Smyrna. Ask my father. Send urgent telegram to his grave and ask him. They killed him. How? By taxing him to death. That kind torture Turks harbor officials know very well. But think! If they are ever on the winning side this war, oh my God, Mr. Fernand! You will be paying not double—triple! That's why I telling those fools from Kansas, America must win! For business reasons! We must get into this war and make sure right side wins!"

"But how can we buy goods now? There's a war on."

"There are people who can tell you how. Find someone not like your brother. A desperado! A criminal!"

"Like you?"

"Who knows? Yes. You need man who knows terrain, knows the goods, and is ready take few chances. Even with his life. War is business. Big wars big business."

"How do you know that?"

"Mr. Fernand, Freddie was born knowing about the Yankees, I was born knowing this." Then Stavros looked at Mr. Fernand intently and said, "But I couldn't work with your brother."

"What did you say?"

"I said, sir, that I could not work with your brother."

"That's enough now," Mr. Fernand said. "Go to lunch."

"Have I spoken clearly?"

Mr. Fernand had to laugh. "You mean have you made it clear that you have something against my brother? Yes, you have."

"I see you're angry. So go ahead, fire me. Only do yourself favor—keep in mind the advice I gave. I was born in a house with three looms, Mr. Fernand. My three sisters wove every day. I can still hear the sound. I worked rugs myself for fifteen years and now your brother Ara sends in that big Welshman, who hollers at me so the whole store hears and pulls me off a customer as if I was hamal, sends in Freddie Farrow, a man who doesn't know one weave from another. You hear Mr. Morgan Perry yelling, 'Freddie, go in there!' Whose orders he's carrying out? Your brother's! Imagine what those buyers think about me now. How I can sell them anything again? What respect can they have for me when they hear how he shout on me? 'Hey, you hamal!' Greeks have pride, you know, Mr. Fernand. Not like Americans. Your brother insult me. I never forgive him. Go ahead fire me. Going to quit anyway. You want me to like your brother? I don't."

"I doubt if there's anyone you like," Mr. Fernand said. "You are a bitter, angry man—"

"Please don't say anything more, sir. One person I respect—you! I don't want to change my mind on that. I don't know you well enough to truthfully say I like you. But maybe we get to know each other better—first thing, you should listen my advice. I've been on the bottom. There you learn! I have suffer. I know the market. Not only here—over there. I know goods, I know prices. When right time come, I can go anywhere and I will. I can handle thieves and murderers and— You complain I don't listen. Complain about yourself not listening."

"Perhaps I will. Another time."

"No. Now. There's no other time. I won't be here much longer."

"Don't threaten me with leaving, Stavros. If you want to leave, go ahead. Tell Miss Emily to draw your check, an extra two weeks."

"I don't want extra two weeks, thank you."

"Now be quiet. Go to dinner. That's a fine girl who invited you. Bring her flowers when you go. I had a delightful conversation with her yesterday. Come, come—calm down. Yes, that's a very unusual girl— Say, look who's here!"

A tall, handsome young man, with light golden hair and piercing dark eyes, was standing in the doorway, looking a little bewildered.

"You haven't met, have you?" Mr. Fernand said. "This is my son, Paul."

They shook hands.

Mr. Fernand winked at Stavros. "Looks just like an American, doesn't he?"

Stavros noticed that Mr. Fernand Sarrafian, who held a mask in front of every other feeling, couldn't conceal the pride he felt in this beautiful young man. And he thought—he was to remember this—*That young man looks like anyone but the son of Fernand Sarrafian.*

"I'm not staying," he said when she opened the door.

"A fine way to walk into the home of a friend!" Althea Perry said.

"Freddie? Where's Freddie?"

"Just called. What are you mad about now? The game went fourteen innings. Of course he couldn't leave your customers. He told me you were coming and he told me you'd say you couldn't stay and he told me to knock you down, jump on you, and if necessary tie you up. Are you ready for that?"

"Today? No."

"He said Daddy was mean to you and that you'd be angry. You sure look it. I'm sorry. Daddy's not been himself since . . . you know."

"Why he punishing me? I liked your brother."

"I know. Sit down. You want something to drink? People are all drinking cocktails now, but all I have is the bottle of applejack Freddie brought back from his class reunion. I can run down and get you a pitcher of beer—"

"Not going to stay."

"Yes, you are. Freddie will be mad at me if you're not here when he comes. He told me what happened. He feels sick about it."

"Don't talk about it, talk about something else. How's your job?"

"It's an education. Oh, the trouble I've seen. I've got a new Greek family, by the way. From Turkey. Want to meet them?"

"No."

"Some of these people I see, they'll do anything. Like wild animals. I was visiting one family and I left my purse on the table while I talked to the mother—her husband had disappeared—and when I left, my money was gone and the only other people in the place were two little girls, twins, maybe ten years old."

"What you do?"

"Nothing. I figured they needed it more than I did."

"Damn fool!"

"That's what I thought later, when I didn't have the fare and had to walk."

She went to the stove, knelt, and looked into the oven.

"What you cooking? Smells good."

"You'll like it. It's called Indian pudding, a sort of hot dessert made with molasses. I told Freddie to bring some vanilla ice cream to go on top."

"Not going to stay."

"Yes, you are. I don't see you anymore. You stay away from us."

"In the store every day I see Freddie."

"Then it's me you stay away from. Are you angry at me? Or with everything in general?"

"Everything. Hate to go home at night. I walk in the door, tak! Somebody coming with their troubles."

"Are their troubles still your problem? They're grown up now."

"That news don't reach them yet."

"You're not their father."

"Everything they blaming on me. Everything that don't fit their idea how supposed to be here. So it's up to me to fix! Complain, complain, complain. Now fighting with each other, also."

"Why don't you tell them to go out on their own if they're not happy with you?"

"Because I had this idea, all of us together, what my father would want. That's what I tell myself. Who knows now?"

"Maybe you made a mistake. You know what I tell the families I'm sent to help? If you're not happy together, break up. Oh, if the social service people knew what I say! Is there a law saying you must stay together if you're miserable? My mother and father . . . Let's not even talk about them."

She came back from the stove and sat down next to him.

"Why don't you break loose?" she said. "Your brothers will get along."

"Who's going to look after my three sisters?"

"Women work too, you know."

"Have to wait they marry some damn fool support them rest of their lives."

"Any candidates?"

"Achilleas, the young priest, he wants Eleni, looks like. But now he says he's leaving and going to become a soldier, the kind who works behind the lines in secret. Priest-spy. Imagine! The archbishop of Smyrna sent him here to raise money for their big idea but now—"

"What big idea?"

"Greater Greece they call it. All Greeks, everywhere, one nation. He was in black clothes when he came and I thought he was priest. But soon I notice he don't speak like priest. War on earth, not peace on earth, that's all he's thinking. Our priests not like yours. They mix up in everything. You ever hear 'bout the unfinished liturgy?"

"No. Tell me."

"Four hundred years ago, more, when Turks captured Constantinople, their soldiers enter cathedral of Santa Sophia while liturgy going on. Priest there, when he see Turkish soldiers shaming his altar, walked into a small opening and closed the door. When the Turks try to open, they can't do it. No one, in all this time, been able to open that small black door. That's the story, anyway. So then this: They say when Greeks take Constantinople back and Santa Sophia become Christian cathedral again, that door will open and the same priest will come out and finish the liturgy from where he stopped."

"That's some story!"

"It don't matter it's not true, it's the hope Greeks live by."

"You too?"

"No. I only look to myself. I don't hope for nothing from anybody! I'll have some of that apple whatever it is now. What is it?"

She walked to a cabinet and produced an unlabeled bottle. "They freeze apple cider," she said. "This is what doesn't freeze." She poured. "Say when," she said, "and thank you for telling me that story."

"Maybe you understand me better now. Trying keep family together is my part trying keep Greek people together. So we don't mix in with everybody else and disappear."

"But it seems to me that you're angry with your family all the time, scornful and resentful and—forgive me for saying this—you actually seem to despise them. You're constantly all charged up with rage. It will end with them hating you."

"Let them. I'm still in the right."

"And because you hate the way you're living, you hate everybody else."

"I know. I do. I hate everybody. I hate your father, I hate my job, I hate the place where I live, and I—"

"Tell me this, please, because I worry about you, I really do, I worry. Can a life be of any value if it's lived entirely on one emotion, and that emotion is anger? You know why I worry? Because it seems to me that hatred kills the hater. Isn't there anyone you don't hate?"

"You. Which is why I don't come near you." He got up. "I better go now," he said.

She didn't protest this time. Or move.

"What you thinking?" he asked.

"I'm remembering your face when you told that story. You have such sweetness in you."

"Baloney!"

"Yes. I always knew it, but just now I saw it."

"That's what you were thinking?"

"And that you have beautiful eyes, soft, brown . . ."

"Salami! But only person on earth I talk to, you! You know that? You're only friend I have. Who I trust."

"I'm your friend. I always will be."

"You're only person on earth who sees any good in me. Even I don't. My father did, but he died. Now there's you."

He didn't look at her or she at him.

"Why don't you marry?" she said. "Any girl who wouldn't like you is crazy. There must be twenty. Aren't they all over you?"

"Nobody I want. And about marry—to have family my own, first I must get rid of my father's family." He turned to her and said, "Oh my God! I have dreams disappearing, leaving them all and going somewhere far away. Want to go with me?" He laughed, nervously.

"What are you talking about? What would Freddie say?"

"A joke, my idea of a joke! But that's the truth. I have dreams of going to some new land where I am alone and without a donkey's load on my back. I read about Australia in a magazine I found in a trash can. I used to read about America same way when I was boy in Constantinople. A lady I knew there, she had these magazines from here and she was kind to me."

"Did you love her?"

"She was married."

"Were you lovers?"

"You could call it that. I've thought of turning into a thief too. Don't tell anybody." He laughed. "Or do, I don't care. Something terrible is going to happen to me. I actually gone into hock shop on Canal Street other day and ask price on pistol. The man said he couldn't sell it to me without a license. And you want to know who I'd hold up first?"

"My father."

"No."

"Mr. Sarrafian?"

"No."

"Who?"

"You. I'd hold you up with my pistol and I'd grab your purse and run to Australia with it."

"You wouldn't have to hold me up for money, Stavros. I'd give it to you."

"No. I want to hold you up. You should see checks I deposit three times week for Sarrafian Brothers, and the payroll check I cash on Friday morning, size of that check for Mr. Ara Sarrafian's pocket money! He spends more on weekend for himself than I spend my whole family in month's time! And he won't give me raise. 'Talk to Mr. Perry,' he says. And Miss Barton—you know who she is?"

"That woman in the back of the store?"

"His secretary-treasurer. She likes me. She say I never get raise, forget it."

"You make love to her too?"

"She has man friend, maybe married, who knows."

"Like the lady in Constantinople who was married and kind? Isn't everybody kind to you? And married? It always seems to be a woman who belongs to someone else that attracts you."

"You have crazy ideas 'bout me. I don't think much about women. I got other troubles: my family, and job where I can't move ahead. How can I worry about women? Mr. Fernand Sarrafian told me today I scare the customers—because I'm not like Freddie."

"Is that why you looked so mad when you came in? 'Where's Freddie?' you said. Like that!"

"I like Freddie, but today he—never mind."

"What I was going to say is that if you had a nice lady friend—I mean, a wife—who looked after you and gave you pleasure and relieved you of all that . . . all that anger, well, then, wouldn't you be happier?"

"Another burden, another expense, another trap!"

"But you must do something. Don't you have anyone?"

"I told you before. Once a week."

She laughed nervously. Then she went to the stove again and, kneeling, opened it.

"I had a regular woman one time. Two months. Free. Wife of rabbi."

"Another wife?"

"You don't get into all that love trouble when they're married. They have to be careful too. But this one, she began to stay all night and I had to talk to her in the morning. I didn't like talking to her. She spoke bad about her husband. Then she began to discuss possibility leaving him, asking me those certain question—you know what. It's better to pay."

"Want to taste this pudding? Just a mouthful?"

"No, I'm going."

"A mouthful. Come here. Taste it. Come on."

She spooned out a little and blew on the steaming pudding as she walked slowly toward him, extending the spoon to his mouth. "Come on," she said. "Open up!"

He did. Her other hand touched his chin. He took the spoon into his mouth.

"Good?"

"Yes."

"More?"

"Yes."

"Please stay."

"Please don't ask me."

"Why won't you? The truth."

"The truth? It makes me sick to see people happy. I can't stand to see lovers in the park or boys and girls walking holding hands. It makes me ache places I can't talk about, you understand? Has Freddie told you about all that? I get worked up, you understand?"

"You're going to find someone. Soon."

"Think so? Ho-ho! What you know?"

"I know that. Because you need it so bad. Girls respond to that more than anything."

She returned to the stove and turned her back to him. "I can feel how bad you need it," she said, placing the pudding on top of the stove. "I can feel it from here."

Then some sort of determination came over her. She turned and looked directly at him and said sternly, "But first you must stop all that other."

"What other?"

"Paying for it. You mustn't do that anymore. You don't have to do that."

"Well, then what? What would I do? Tell me?"

He got up and walked slowly toward her.

"There's Freddie coming," she said. "I recognize how he runs up the stairs. He bounces like a little boy."

"Go on," he said, "tell me. What would I do?"

"He's so sweet. He loves to run the stairs. Up or down, either way. It doesn't make any difference."

"Well?" he said. "Althea? Well? What?"

Freddie burst into the room with the ice cream. "Hurry," he said. "It's melting."

Stavros turned his back to Freddie. He had to.

Althea quickly took the ice cream while Freddie opened the door to the upper compartment of the icebox. Althea thrust the ice cream in; Freddie slammed the door.

Then, standing there, they kissed until Althea noticed Stavros watching and broke away.

"Sorry I'm so late," Freddie said. "But—fourteen innings!" He looked from Althea to Stavros. "What have you two been talking about?" he asked.

"You stole my job today," Stavros said.

"What?" Freddie said.

"You stole my job today, Mr. Peckinpaugh. You made a donkey of me today, my friend not my friend."

"What could I do?" Freddie said, "The boss told me to—"

"Stavros, please stop it," Althea said.

"What you could do, you son of a bitch"—and Stavros was even angrier now because Althea seemed to be protecting Freddie—"what you could do is say, 'Joe taking care customer very good, don't need help, it seems, go 'head, Joe, take care of the gentleman from Kansas City.'"

"Atlanta, Georgia," Freddie said.

"Don't be smart blue-eye with me, Freddie; you know what I'm talking about. That was your chance to be true friend and walk away. But no, you grab my job, made damn fool of me, and—"

"Stavros," Althea said. "Stop! Right now. Stop!"

"Then you come in Mr. Fernand's office, you come in, you come in, showing Mr. Fernand how good you're doing out there, those damn Chinese nine-by-twelves which I sold already before, job finish, but you taking credit there, coming in with baseball game information, Peckinpaugh and so forth, corn beef restaurant and so forth. You're not my friend. I see that now. Friend like you, I spit in their face."

"Stavros," Althea said, "I want you to leave."

"Yes, friend like you, I spit in his face." Stavros walked up to Freddie as if he was actually going to do it. But he didn't. Instead he said, "Finished between us—understand the word? Finished!"

It had all come down on him so suddenly and with such force that Freddie still didn't understand why Stavros was so angry.

"Got to pee," Freddie said and left the room.

Stavros slowly put his coat on. Trembling with anger, he thought the coat was inside out when it wasn't, and he struggled with the sleeves as he moved toward the door.

Althea came to help him. "Stavros-Joe," she said, "but really! Really that wasn't very nice. You should be ashamed of yourself!"

"You be shame yourself," Stavros said. "How you know what happened? Why you don't shut up when you don't know nothing what happened? Why you don't keep your mouth shut, damn fool woman?"

At which Freddie came out of the toilet, and he was still buttoning his fly as he said, "Let me tell you something, since you seem to be begging for it. In the first place, if you want to sell a customer from anywhere in this country except New York City, you'd better learn, at last, how to speak the language—which is English, in case you've forgotten, not whatever it is you speak. Then Mr. Sarrafian might not have to take you off a customer."

Freddie, in his own anger, towered above Stavros, who was still struggling with his coat and its tangled sleeves.

"And why do you imagine," Freddie went on, "that any customer from anywhere would enjoy your condescending manner? What height, tell me, do you condescend from and how the hell did you get up there?" He turned to Althea. "You should see him, Althea. He walks up and down like some kind of crazy rooster with his toes pointed out, strutting splay-footed, like this, with his elbow swinging like this—look, Althea, look—and his head turned to one side, eyes to the ceiling. I don't know what's up on the ceiling that he's so interested in. I don't know!"

Freddie strutted up and down in front of her, swinging his elbow and looking at the ceiling, and Althea had to laugh.

"Then he squints at the customers," Freddie went on. "What is that, nearsighted, the way you look at people, as if the very sight of them offends you? I notice you keep sniffing at them too. What's that about? You don't like their smell? What's all that superiority based on? I've been there a year now and I've found that contrary to your opinion, you're not the only one who knows something about rugs. Every porter in the place knows as much as you do. And Garabet, the repairman, twice as much. I think you're a big bluff. Tell me, did you ever sit at a loom yourself or put a paintbrush to a border? Althea, are you listening? Look at him! Who the hell does he think he is, taking me down that way? Maybe he can make his family tremble, but at one hundred and forty pounds or whatever, all there is to him is that splay-foot strut and the swing of his elbow, back and forth, back and forth, bluff, bluff, bluff!"

When Stavros sprang, Freddie was waiting for him. He picked Stavros up as he'd learned to do on the wrestling team at Williams College and held him high in the air for an instant before flinging him down on Althea's sofa. Stavros bounced up like a rubber goat and butted Freddie in the stomach, driving him back against a chest of drawers. A cut-glass bowl, holding Althea's makeup trifles, buttons, pins, and an accumulation of pennies, fell and smashed on the floor.

"My grandmother's bowl!" Althea said. "You broke my grandmother's bowl!"

That was the limit of her patience. She ran to a corner, found her field hockey stick, and shouting, "Out! Get out!" drove Stavros through the door.

Freddie, backed to the wall, watched his rival's exit with satisfaction.

When Stavros heard the door being bolted, he walked down the stairs. Outside the building, he crossed the street and sat on the steps of the apartment house opposite, looking up at the window of Althea's place and waiting there until the lights went out.

"I want Fahma," Stavros said.

"Fahma is with someone," Thea Marie said in Turkish. With needle and thread she was reattaching the shoulder strap of a nightdress.

"I'll wait," Stavros said.

"Take one of my daughters," Thea Marie said.

Stavros looked at the girls. "I wait," he said. "Make me a coffee."

The woman went to the two-burner stove.

"Not too sweet," Stavros said.

"By now I know how you like coffee." Thea Marie was as big as a drill sergeant and nearly as tough, but her establishment was intimate, homey. It was, in fact, her own home and that of her two daughters. Fahma was her young niece. Immigrants, Lebanese, they had arrived in this country some years before, unprotected, and were protecting themselves the best way they could.

"Who's Fahma with?" Stavros said.

"Nice clean man. He's a Kurd, maybe. A little old, he shouldn't take long."

"What's all that noise from outside?"

"The police station next door, they're celebrating something."

"Crazy cops, what are they laughing?"

"They got a raise yesterday."

"Put some music. I need music tonight."

"You don't look well. What's the matter?"

"I could kill my best friend tonight, Thea Marie."

"Why don't you get married in a church like a good Greek? It'll save you all this trouble. And expense."

"Who will I marry?"

"Plenty girls looking."

"That much I know. Every Greek merchant who has a long-nose cow for sale invites me Sunday dinner so I can look her over. But I like them with golden hair, Thea Marie. That's my difficulty. I like American girls with golden hair, goddamn it!"

"So find an American."

"I found one, but she's with someone else. Right now. While we're talking here."

"American girls, they're not reliable. I advise you to marry Fahma. Well, what are you looking? You could do worse. She's a good girl—my niece, but a good girl. Here, take your coffee."

"Look, now she's with a Turk."

"What have you got against Turks? This is America here, forget all that old stuff. I know what you want, a virgin. You Greeks! Dreamers! There are no golden-hair American virgins who'd marry someone like you."

"Why not?"

"Why do you make me say things like this? Because you're five-and-ten-cents store. Look, three-dollar girl you're waiting for now. When you have your kind of money in America, you're shit. I like you but you're shit."

A short, heavy Turkish man in his middle years came in from the hall that led to the bedrooms. He went to the window and looked out.

"It's going to rain," the man said in Turkish. "That's why I hurried. Six minutes only I took, Auntie."

"Fast, slow, it's the same. Tomorrow we eat the same."

She held out her hand. The Turk gave her two dollar bills. She waited. He gave her another.

"I kiss your mother's eyes," she said.

"Inshallah!" He turned and left.

Fahma came in, pulling her robe off one shoulder to examine it. "He bites," she said in Lebanese. "He doesn't do much else, but he needs to bite my shoulder. Look what he did!"

"Stavros waiting for you, dearie," Thea Marie said in Greek.

Fahma sighed. "I see him," she said. Again she sighed.

"I don't like that sound you made, Fahma," Stavros said.

"Come on, dearie," Thea Marie said. "That bite, she'll be gone tomorrow."

"Joey," Fahma said, "my mother's sick. She needs medicine. I want to go home and I have to find a drugstore first. Where will I find one open this time of night? My mother keeps trembling as if she's cold. It's not cold, but she keeps trembling, poor thing. I'm worried."

"Ten minutes," Stavros said. "If you give the Turk six, you can give me ten."

"Please, Joey, I'm worrying."

"Something bad happened to me tonight," Stavros said. "I want to change the taste in my mouth."

"I'd be like a corpse tonight, Joey. You don't want that."

"You be my medicine tonight, Fahma. Then I'll find a drugstore open for you and take you home in taxi."

"Joey, see how pale she is," Thea Marie said. "Come tomorrow."

"I'll give you a good fuck tomorrow," Fahma said. "Like the first time."

"Go on, be a friend, Joey, take her home. I won't charge you tomorrow. She's a good girl. Take care of her, Joey."

"All right, all right! Nothing works for me tonight! Go dress. Go on. Somebody's coming."

Two policemen walked in, unbuttoning their coats. One was very young, the other stocky.

"Fahma!" the young cop cried as he unbuckled his pistol harness. "It's my birthday today, so I get first divvies. I get Fahma."

The older cop wasted no time; he pulled the younger of Thea Marie's daughters out of her armchair and led her down the hall to where the bedrooms were.

"Take this one," Thea Marie said to the young cop, pointing at her other daughter. "Fahma's going home."

"After me she's going home." He threw his pistol and its harness on a table. "It's my birthday, Auntie. I'm twenty-five today, and I want Fahma."

"Her mother's sick," Thea Marie said to the young cop. "This man, he's taking her home." She indicated Stavros.

"In twenty minutes he can take her," the young cop said good-naturedly. "How's that, mister? Quick enough, twenty minutes?"

"They have to find a drugstore first," Thea Marie said. "Her mother's waiting for medicine."

"I'll get one of the boys to drive them to Sheridan Square, there's an all-night drugstore." He turned to Fahma. "Come on, little brown mouse," he said.

Fahma looked at Stavros.

"She's going home now," Stavros said to the young cop.

"Who are you?" the cop said. "Who says she's going home?"

"I say," Stavros said. He walked up to the cop.

Thea Marie intervened. "Go in with him, Fahma," she said. "No arguments here tonight."

"It's up to you what she does, isn't it, Auntie?" the young cop said. "It's your say—that's how I understand the situation here—not his." The young policeman stared at Stavros. "Am I right, Auntie?"

"It's my say," Thea Marie said. "Not his."

"So tell the man," he said, pointing to Stavros. "Because I came in here feeling good and I don't want to go out feeling bad."

"Not necessary," Thea Marie said. "She go with you." Turning to Fahma, "Last for tonight, dearie," she said. "Go on."

Fahma walked down the hall.

"You live in this neighborhood?" the young cop asked Stavros.

"Uptown," Stavros said.

"So get uptown," the policeman said. "Don't be here when I come out."

The cop followed Fahma down the hall.

Thea Marie looked at Stavros. "What can I do?" she whispered. "We live under their shoulder. They protect us here."

Stavros went to the cop's holster and, unbuckling the strap, pulled out the officer's service pistol.

"Joey, what are you doing?" Thea Marie whispered. "Joey, put that back!"

Stavros turned on her. "Mind your business," he said, waving the pistol at her. "Sit there," he said, and walked down the hall.

It was surprisingly quiet.

"Shit on them both," Thea Marie said to her daughter in Lebanese. "Let them kill each other."

After a time, the young cop backed into the room. His shirt was off, his trousers were unbuttoned, and he was holding them up. Stavros had a pair of heavy-soled police shoes in his free hand.

"Don't make a sound," he said, "or this will be your last birthday."

"You'll hear from me later," the cop said.

Stavros lunged at him, pistol first, and the young policeman stiffened from fear.

"Don't say another word," Stavros warned. "Do what I say. Drop your pants on the floor. That's it. Now step out. Pick them up and give them to me. Those things too, your drawers, take them off. Go on. Now, here —throw them over my arm. That's it."

The cop followed instructions.

Fahma came into the doorway, tying her robe.

"Get back, Fahma!" Thea Marie said.

Stavros slowly lowered the pistol a little below the cop's heart. From fear and anger, the man's penis had drawn up into his body.

"Look at that pimple!" Stavros said. "How you going to fuck her with that? Tell me. Hey you, Peckinpaugh, I'm talking to you. Look at that, Auntie, what he's got there!"

The Lebanese woman didn't say a word.

"Now, in there," Stavros said, backing the young policeman into a closet. "Go on. Close the door, Auntie," he said. "Now you, police, in there: Any sound you make will be your last sound."

Stavros turned to Thea Marie. "When you hear me in the street," he whispered, "let him out."

Holding the policeman's clothes, he ran swiftly and silently out of the apartment. Soon they heard him shout from the street and Thea Marie opened the closet door.

"Why didn't you stop him?" the policeman yelled as he came out of the closet.

"Same reason you," Thea Marie said. "He's holding your pistol."

The older cop came in from the hallway, asking, "Did something happen?" When he saw his mate naked from the waist down, he began to laugh. "What happened to you?" he said.

The young cop told him and he stopped laughing. An older man, a veteran, he turned on Thea Marie, and his voice was hard and official.

"Who is he?" he demanded.

"He comes in here, I don't know him, some crazy man from uptown."

"Uptown where? You." He turned to Fahma. "Uptown where?"

"May my mother die," Fahma said, "if I know and I don't tell you."

It was pouring rain by the time the subway stopped at his station and in the two-block walk to the apartment house, Stavros got soaked through and through. Although he'd thrown the policeman's shoes and drawers away as he ran from Thea Marie's place, he'd kept the trousers, wrapping them around the pistol to conceal it.

He entered the apartment stealthily, turning the key in the lock as silently as possible. Just inside the door, he stood still and listened. He made a habit of coming in that way—several times he'd overheard one of his brothers criticizing the head of the house.

What he heard this evening was a woman crying bitterly.

Slowly he stripped off his coat and shirt, kicked off his shoes, and peeled off his stockings. Picking up a towel in the bathroom, he walked on down the hall. It was Eleni crying. She was sitting in the front room, and sitting next to her was Michaelis. Standing was a person Stavros did not immediately recognize: Achilleas, no longer in priestly black, an ordinary person again, in a suit coat too small for him. He moved uncertainly, swaying and smiling as he waited for Stavros's reaction to the change in him.

"What happened? You shaved too?" Stavros turned away from Achilleas and asked Michaelis, "His clothes? What is this?"

"I left the church this morning," Achilleas said.

"Is he drunk?" Stavros asked Eleni. She didn't answer. "He doesn't look any better this way," he said. "Still like a singer of love songs."

As he left the room, Stavros could hear Achilleas laughing. In his bedroom, Stavros rubbed his hair and face with the towel, then crouched at the side of his bed and pulled out his father's cowhide valise, which he hadn't opened for years. It was full of Isaac's clothes, and down beneath them Stavros hid the young cop's pistol. He decided it was better to burn the trousers, so he went into the kitchen, where he found there was still a fire in the coal stove.

Before he put the trousers in, he searched through the pockets and found fifty-nine dollars. Remembering the way the policeman had talked to him, he put the money in his pocket.

Achilleas came into the kitchen, looking for him.

"Why you got her crying?" Stavros said to him. "Be careful, she's my sister. What you do to her?"

"She's crying because I'm going back," Achilleas said.

"Good. When?"

"Now."

Stavros walked by him and into the front room. Achilleas followed.

"He's leaving," Michaelis said.

"Also he's drunk," Stavros said.

"There's more," Michaelis said. "Tell him, Eleni."

"I want to wash my face first," she said, and ran into the kitchen.

"I'm a former priest tonight!" Achilleas said. He did an awkward pirouette.

Stavros ignored him. He kissed his mother where she sat at the window and then he noticed Eleftheria in a dark corner. "What are you doing back there by yourself?" he asked. "You should be in bed, it's late. You crying too? What's the matter with everybody here tonight?"

Stavros sat next to his favorite and put his arm around her shoulders. "Stop crying, my little bird," he said, pulling her close. "I'm here now."

Eleni came back, her eyes red and swollen.

"He's going back," she said, beginning to cry again. "But he won't take me with him."

"Good!" Stavros said. "Now stop crying in the name of God."

Achilleas seemed unaffected by Eleni's tears or by anything except his own happiness. "You must come back with us, Stavros," he said.

"Back with us?" Stavros asked. "Us?"

"Michaelis. He's coming too."

"No, he's not," Stavros said.

"Greece has broken in two," Michaelis said. "It's to be decided now on which side she will enter the war."

"Who will decide that? People like this?" Stavros pointed scornfully at Achilleas.

"We will all decide," Michaelis said. "By what we do."

"And don't do," Achilleas said. "Our king, that squash head, is a cousin of the Kaiser. We will send him back to Berlin in a box. Greece will enter the war on the side of the British and the French. They are our friends.

We can trust them. Then—America! She will have to come in, and with her in the war, the Ottoman Empire will smash like a pane of glass thrown from that window onto the sidewalk." He slapped his palm on the table like a political orator. "It's time for all Greeks to—"

"I am not a Greek," Stavros said. "I am an American citizen. When this country goes to war, I will go too."

Michaelis looked at Stavros.

"Why do you look at me that way?" Stavros challenged his brother. Michaelis didn't answer. Stavros turned on Achilleas. "Now get out," he said. "Go on! We don't want you here. Get out!"

"You an American!" Achilleas shouted. "You? A citizen? Here, where people treat you like a servant? Where they laugh at you and give you their leavings and treat you like a hamal? For more than a year I've listened to you week after week, coming home angry and complaining, and now you still say, 'I am an American'? What?"

Stavros didn't answer.

"What happened to you?" Achilleas said. "Where's your pride? In heaven your father's ashamed of you." He spat in Stavros's face. "That's from your father," he said.

Stavros leaped on him, throwing him backward. His hands were around Achilleas's neck and he was banging the former priest's head down again and again.

Eleni tore at his hands. "Stavros, don't," she cried. "Stavros, he's my husband, we were married today. Listen, Stavros, listen: We were married today. Let him go."

Slowly Stavros released Achilleas; letting him fall back limply, he walked away. Then he came back and looked down at the inert man, realizing what his sister had told him.

Eleni had lifted her husband's head and was now cradling it in her lap. He was having trouble breathing.

"Look what you've done!" she said to her brother. "You've killed him."

Stavros went into his bedroom, closed the door and fell on the bed.

A few minutes later, Eleftheria opened the door quietly and looked in. He nodded and she came and sat next to him. "Don't trust him," she whispered. "So many times he told me to wait for him, said it was me he wanted."

"He's too handsome," Stavros said.

"He took me out walking night before last," she said, "and he said to me—"

Eleni broke into the room. "I thought so! What has she been saying?" she demanded. Then she turned on her sister. "Get out of here before I scratch your eyes out!"

When Eleftheria didn't move, Eleni darted at her and Stavros had to hold them apart. Then he pushed Eleftheria through the door.

"I hate my sister," Eleni said.

"I think Achilleas, he's at fault," Stavros said.

"I don't want to hear any more against him," Eleni said. "Whatever happened, it's over now, we're married. So I'm not going to let anybody talk against him. Not even you, Stavros. Please."

"How is he?" Stavros asked. "Has he recovered?"

"You twisted his neck," she said. "He looks strong but—he's not. I didn't tell you something about him. He's been married before. You know priests can marry only once. So he took off the black for me, may God forgive me. He loves me, of that I am sure. I know that he loves some other things, yes, perhaps more, one thing sure more—his politics. Greater Greece, he loves that more. But I will love that too and we will be together. He's the one I want, Stavros. You must love him with me. Please, Stavros. If you want me to be happy—do you?"

Stavros nodded slowly.

"Then go to him," Eleni said. "Speak to him like a brother, like he is what he is, my husband."

Stavros sighed, nodded, sighed again.

"Do it now," Eleni pleaded. "He's afraid of you. Everybody's afraid of you. If you attack him again, or if he thinks you will, he might leave, and if he leaves, I will leave with him. Forgive me, but that's the truth. So do it now, please. Get up. Come on, for my sake."

Slowly, heavily, Stavros got up. "You were married today?" he asked.

"Yes. By the priest Rondiris. He didn't want to marry us. He's afraid of you too, what you might do to him."

Achilleas was sitting in a chair, rubbing his neck. "You hurt me," he complained when he saw Stavros. Then he stood up and backed away and said, "Please, I have a headache. I'm sick. I drank too much. I can't take any more, not tonight."

Stavros went to his brother-in-law, put his arms around him and embraced him. "Since that's the way it is," he said, "what can we do? So come on."

He kissed Achilleas on both cheeks.

Then, still close, he whispered something no one else heard. "What you said before about me here, you were right. You said the truth."

When he knocked, she opened the door a crack.

She was wearing a light robe, sea green, he could see through to the flesh-colored cotton gown. The green showed off her golden hair, almost white in the sun from the east window. Her upper arms, which he'd never seen, were even whiter and they were plump—"as a *lokoum*," a Turk might have said. Stavros had a Turk's obsession for whiteness in a woman.

She was barefoot, and when he lowered his eyes, he noticed how slim her feet were.

"What are you doing here?" she said. "You look terrible."

"No sleep," he said.

"Go home this minute and get into bed," she said. "I'll have Freddie tell Father—"

"Is he here?"

"Father? Oh, Freddie. Of course not."

"I want to come in. Two minutes. I have to say something."

"I'm rushing off to work. I mean, I will be as soon as I shower and—"

"Two minutes."

She let him pass, pulled the front of her aquamarine robe over her breast, folded her plump white arms, further protection, curled her fine thin feet under where she sat in the old brown Morris chair, threw her hair back out of her eyes, and waited for him to speak.

"Bad time to come, I know that; excuse this, please." He looked at her and smiled. "You're different," he said. "Not like you were last night."

"Who ever is?"

"Last night I speak like damn fool to Freddie. Maybe he deserve it, my opinion yes. But main thing—I broke your grandmother's bowl." He looked around for it. "I want to pay for new one," he said.

"Freddie took it. He thinks he can get it put together. It's one of a kind, there's no way to replace it. Anyway, it doesn't matter."

"When he take it?"

"Last night." She laughed. "You think he slept here?"

"No, no!"

"Is there anything particular you wanted to say? Besides what you've said?"

"That's all," he said. But he continued to stare at her, turned away, turned back.

"You look so worried," she said. "What's the trouble?"

He made something up quickly. "My sisters. Time for them get married. I'm head of family, so this is my job. What am I gonna do?" He laughed. "Don't want to hear about that, hah?"

"I'd like to sometime, but now"—she looked quickly at the wooden clock on the mantel—"I really must go."

"Sorry I was damn fool last night. Wanted to tell you that much."

"Well, I'm glad you came by." She rose to her feet. "I'm glad you said what you said."

He was on his feet too, standing irresolutely, still looking at her.

"I have to shower now," she said. "I'm already late."

"Where you going?"

"To work."

"I take you with taxi, quick, catch up time that way."

"You don't want to do that, it's over on the east side, far out of your way."

"That's what? Nothing! I have nothing to do."

"Better not let them hear that, son, or they'll fire you."

"Who fire who? I'm only man in store understands anything on rugs."

"Not according to Freddie last night. My, you do have big ideas about yourself, don't you? Sorry! Look, I'm sure you don't want to take me where I'm going just because you broke—or caused Freddie to break—an old family bowl I was sick of looking at."

"Absolutely! Guarantee! Please do me favor. I owe you because I make damn fool myself here. Go 'head now. I sit here quiet and wait."

"Five minutes," she said, running out of the room. She closed the door to her bedroom, then opened it, inches. "Leaving the door ajar," she called, "in case you have an interesting thought while I'm dressing."

"No thought," he said. "Just waiting here quiet."

That was when he fell in love, felt the sensation he'd never felt before. He always remembered what happened in those next minutes, even though, as a matter of fact, nothing happened. He watched her shadow moving across a wall, heard every sound she made as if it were magnified many times—the scraping of the silk robe against the cotton nightgown as she took it off and threw it on a chair, and the sound the gown made as she pulled it over her head.

Then there was the sound of the bathroom door opening. "Won't be able to hear you now," she called. "Will be again in a moment."

She'd left that door ajar too and he heard the shower curtain being pulled across and the water falling on her body. He heard the washcloth rubbed against the bar of soap and slithering over her skin. Or was he imagining that? He wasn't sure, it was all a kind of dream. He heard her singing under the shower. He heard her turn the shower off and call out, "You still there?"

"Always," he said.

"Go on talking. I can hear you now."

He'd been talking on and off about his problem with his sisters, otherwise sitting totally still so he wouldn't miss the least sound she made. He thought he heard the towel rubbing against her skin and he began to speak again—so she wouldn't know how he was filling up with her. She must have touched herself with a perfume, because a sweet seductive odor reached him. He heard the snap of her underclothing's elastic, heard the rustle of her slip as it went over her head and was pulled down.

"Excuse me," she said. "Don't look."

Dressed only in a white slip with a camisole top, she dashed into the room, dipped under a table, came up with a package of laundry and ran back. He'd turned his head away but had seen every move, every posture, in the mirror opposite. He heard the sound of the brown paper parcel being ripped open and then, "Oh, damn! Button missing! Oh, well!" Then he heard the sound of a skirt going over her head.

When she came out, she was wedging her feet into shoes and still jostling her skirt into position.

"Let's dash," she said. "That was all very interesting what you said. Come on, I have to go!"

He'd been telling her about marriage customs in Anatolia, how all marriages were contracted by the two families, how on the day of the ceremony all the groom's people—generations—would march in procession to the bride's home, accompanied by a band of village musicians. The bride would be waiting and with her the presents the bride's family were contributing to the marriage, piled to the ceiling—the blankets and the sheets, the tablecloths and napkins and towels, the baby's clothes, they were already made and the things for the kitchen, and also the photographs of ancestors from both sides, the size of church icons—oh, how important they were, he said.

The band would play in the space in front of the bride's house and the family and their friends would dance—but men only, women didn't dance out of doors in Anatolia. They might be seen. The men, young and old, would take turns dancing alone to express joy and hope in front of the bride's home. "I can hear that music in my head," he said. "The flute and the drums, the old brass trumpet and the violin. But mostly the drums, how they beat!"

When the dancing had gone on for about an hour, the bride would come out of the house and the groom would take her hand; they'd walk slowly, side by side, leading everybody from both families to the church. The priest would be standing at the front door, stroking his beard and waiting to bring the couple to the altar . . .

Now, at the mirror, Althea was putting on her hat and a printed scarf, the long end thrown loosely over one shoulder.

"After the ceremony," Stavros said, "they walk to the young man's home, where feast is waiting and wine, family-made, plenty! Oh, those parties. Allah! They go on two, three days, believe me!"

"And the couple?" She was looking into the mirror, setting her hat at an angle, pleased with herself.

"First they stay downstairs with everybody, eating, drinking, so on. After, upstairs, alone, listening to the music, with each other, you know what I'm talking."

"And the music would go on all night?"

"For days. I've seen that myself. Days!"

"And the couple? Days!"

"Well—what else they have to do?" he said.

"With the girl, wouldn't it be—of course—the first time?"

"Naturally! Girl has to be from good family, father of boy look her over very careful."

"And the boy?"

"He's a man. Different. But both must be with both fathers' permission. Now, even from the grave, I have to listen my father when my time comes pick a wife."

She turned from the mirror. "Why are you telling me all this now?"

He was confused. "Didn't know I was—that I was saying—all that."

She bent over him, kissed him lightly on the lips, smiled, laughed, reached out her hand, took his, pulled him to his feet and they were out the door. Slam!

"Come, run! Run!" she called.

He ran after her, a boy again, in love for the first time.

When he got to the store, more than an hour late, he'd forgotten the racing form and didn't care.

"I know why you're late," Freddie said. "You had to be very upset by those awful things I said to you. Please regard them as the demented utterances of a fool, crazed by a woman and out of control."

"I was just there," Stavros said. "With her," and he walked away.

"This time of day!" Freddie said. "Hadn't she left for work?" Freddie was following him. "What were you doing there, this time of day?"

"She was late and I took her in taxi."

He saw the pain on Freddie's face and although he might once have felt some sympathy for him, now he felt only satisfaction.

"Why did you go there?"

"To pay for the bowl you broke," Stavros said.

"No, no, I'll do that—I'll be glad to do that, whatever it cost to fix. I deserve to be punished. I like you very much, do you know that? I've learned so many things from you—not only about rugs but about life, the kind of life I've never known. Look at me a moment, please. Please! Now forgive me if you can. Believe me, she truly drives me crazy. Because I know she doesn't love me, that she's capable of leaving me on a moment's impulse. Did she kiss you? I'm sorry! I still go on acting as if she does love me—I feel like a fool, but I don't seem able to get over it. She's got her hook in me, deep! So whenever I'm with her, I say and I do things I regret later. But never anything I've regretted as much as what I said to you last night. Because those things weren't true, many of them, do you understand? No, none of them were true!"

Stavros could see the havoc on his face.

"She's left a trail of victims like me," Freddie said. "But I live by this conviction, that I'm the one who'll beat the game, I will be there at the end to pick up the pieces. Perhaps that's all, but I'll be there. May I offer you a warning? Be careful, she's a man-eater even if she looks like an angel.

Tell me, did she kiss you? When you least expected her to? That's one of her tricks."

"To say goodbye. It was nothing."

"But you can still feel it. Am I right? The kiss? You see? She's a flirt. She needs to feel her power—over us, over men. It reassures her that she's not a nothing. I was brought up with girls like that. Something else you ought to know: She's expensive. Did she get you to loan her a ten?"

"What you think I am, damn fool?"

"You see, she's never spent money she's actually earned, only what she could wheedle out of her father's pocket. Or 'borrow.' It's always 'borrow.' 'Will you lend me?' she says to her catches. She owes me hundreds—no, maybe a thousand all told. That's a thousand I'll never see again."

Freddie could see this get to Stavros.

"I've got to go," Freddie said. "We're checking over the goods before we ship them to Atlanta. Have lunch with me? I'll tell you more."

"Some other time," Stavros said. "But sometime, sure."

The sudden surge of love within Stavros, the passion into which he'd plunged, had begun to subside—not from anything about Althea's being a flirt, Greek men have ways of controlling that, but from the reminder that she was expensive. That struck home.

The fact was that as the taxi stopped before the tenement which was her destination, she had asked him to lend her ten dollars and he had made the grand gesture gladly, and been paid with a kiss.

As the day went on and Stavros went over his memories of the girl and what Freddie had said about her, doubts and questions began to enter his mind. He was talking to himself all day. He remembered the light touch of her perfumed lips, but now he was wondering if he was being manipulated by that touch. Stavros was a man who knew when to be on guard.

When money was concerned.

"What can you get out of it?" Stavros asked himself. "How long can it last, anyway? If she flirts with me, she flirts with other men. What would father Isaac say? Because when she catches them, like Freddie, looks like she must find somebody else quick! Also if I take her to those restaurants she likes, Delmonico's, oh, *panaghia mou!* One dinner, place like that, week's salary! You have enough problems already, tough guy. Why hang your life on woman like that? This game those American girls play, love game, makes a man weak. You seen that few times, those wives from New Rochelle you fucked, how they talk about their husbands. Allah! Shame!"

And more advice from the core. "If you want to understand woman, the Greek brain says, look at her mother. This girl will be copy, guarantee. Go watch that old lady, study what she does to Mr. Morgan Perry. *Aman, aman!* Woman is boss in this country! You are Greek, never forget that. Also remember you getting along pretty damn good now without her kisses. Also remember, boy, you got enough problems at home. Put her out of your mind, damn fool!"

Before he left for home that day, he took Freddie aside and said, "My advice. Want it? Here! You will get her in the end. Guarantee. Don't give up. I give you my word, I won't bother her again. You're safe!"

It had not occurred to Freddie until that instant that Stavros had any intention of "bothering" Althea. And by the end of the afternoon, Stavros had no such intention. But there was this: In the days that followed, he continued to expect that she would communicate with him one way or another, would even suggest they see each other. He was waiting for that.

DECEMBER 1916

Sometimes when a single small piece of a large structure is removed, the whole structure collapses. The piece may have seemed of no importance to the whole, but when it's gone, every flaw in every other part is revealed and the structure falls apart. That was what happened after Vacilli's sudden death. It was hard to believe that his presence within the family had meant so much to so many people. The impression was the opposite.

A few weeks after the morning when Stavros visited Althea, he came upon Vacilliki sitting at the window in the same position he'd been in the night before. "For God's sake, good for nothing," Stavros shouted, "what am I crazy supporting you? Here, do something for your bread—take this goddamn rug to Benesch Household Furnishing, Broadway, One Forty-fourth Street."

"I have to touch up this border," Vacilli said.

"You have to touch up! Then why you're not touching up? Instead sitting there making 'Ach, ach, ach!' to the window."

"He has to put Aseptinol my legs," Vasso said.

"I thought I had clear contract with you people. Aseptinol business Eleni's job now."

"I don't like how Eleni puts it," Vasso said.

"Never mind you like, don't like. I want people making some money here. Am I only one who brings anything in? Didn't I say I expect everybody working? What you looking, Demo? You too. They tell me you take lunch hour two hours now. What the hell, two hours!"

When Demo didn't answer, Stavros's anger rose further. He took hold of Vacilli's arm and pulled. "Get up," he said. "Now say 'Ach, ach, ach!' because it hurts your arm—right. Now you have reason. So do me favor, do some work, please. Take this goddamn six-by-nine Hamadan to Benesch Household Furnishings, One Forty-fourth, Broadway."

"How I take it?" Vacilli said, and it sounded like a whine to Stavros, making him even angrier. "It's heavy."

"Take it on your bent-over back," Stavros said, "hamal style, like me, two years, Constantinople, working to bring you people here. Go, goddamn it. I don't want to see that rug here when I come home. I'm going crazy see you sitting good for nothing, idle here all day."

When Stavros got home from work that evening and was told that Vacilli was dead, he roared, "Why somebody don't tell me, make telephone to Sarrafian Brothers, tell me, for God's sake?"

"We didn't want to bother you," Demo said.

That remark, Stavros knew very well, was meant to be sarcastic, but he let it pass.

Demo left the room and Eleftheria followed him. Stavros heard her down the hall, and though he didn't hear her words, he knew she was protecting him. Eleftheria was loyal to him, he trusted her for that!

Eleni was weeping in the chair by the window where Vacilli used to sit. "He wants to leave here," she said, "Demo!"

"Let him go," Fofo said. She was, as always, in the wooden armchair by the kitchen door.

Michaelis and Seraphim were side by side on the banquette, their faces grave. They wouldn't look at Stavros. Did they blame him for Vacilli's death? Stavros wondered. He asked Seraphim what had happened.

"You seen him recent days when he dress up?" Seraphim asked. "No. He always wait when you leave for job. First he shave, taking long time, nobody hollering get the hell out of the bathroom by that time. After, he put on blue suit, one he got from Syrian millionaire in Smyrna, where he was waiter. He like that suit, put iron to pants every day, crease perfect. Every day he put on a fresh-wash white collar and beautiful blue tie, pearl stickpin—fake pearl, but looks good all the same. Shine shoes every day too. Then put on his black homburg, also from Syrian boss, you seen that homburg, what a hat!"

"Where the hell was he going," Stavros said, "all dress up?"

"To do the shopping," Eleni said. "Every day he bring in the oil, the rice, piece meat maybe, olives, butter, cheese—Fofo told him what we need. He had one thing figure out perfect: he come to bakery exact time when they take out oven fresh bread for that day. Then he come home, take off shoes, nothing else, put slippers, spread sweet butter on hot bread, three pieces always, sit by window, 'cross from old woman, and slowly eat. When he finish, he don't move, wipe mouth, stay looking out window, take ten-minute nap maybe, still neat, clean, good style. The baker give him name 'Count.' Vacilli liked that name."

"So when you tell him carry six-by-nine Hamadan to Benesch House-hold Furnishings this morning," Michaelis said, "he's not ready for that. He see himself like gentleman. 'Why Stavros want make me hamal?' he ask me."

"So then, at store, I get call from Mr. Benesch," Seraphim went on. " 'Better come look your brother,' he say. 'Something happen.' When I got there, Mr. Benesch, the old man, say look washroom, back of store. 'What happen?' I say. 'He come in here,' old man Benesch say, 'put my rug down and I could see something wrong. I keep store cold, save money but he's perspiring. Why you don't go wash your face, feel better? I say to him. He say, thank you, good idea, bowing his head, you understand, very fine man, that Vacilli, was gentleman. He goes in there, I hear door lock, last sound I hear from him. Half hour he don't come out. So we go in and he's on floor, his black homburg hat on white toilet cover, very neat. He die but he don't make sound, didn't want bother anybody, I believe. Even his face don't look like he was hurting, only that gentle smile, you know the one, make sure everybody knows he's not mad at them—what?' "

"With that smile, forgiving the world for treating him bad," Michaelis said.

"He didn't say anything bad about you, Stavros," Eleni said. "Don't worry about that, Stavros, don't worry."

"He say to me," Michaelis said, " 'Why Stavros want make me hamal?' "

Seraphim had a question. "Eleni, tell me, I see him and Mommah all the time whispering. When I come in, they stop. He sitting in chair, suit, collar, blue tie, pearl stickpin, handkerchief breast pocket, so forth, like they waiting for train to go somewhere."

"Like they waiting for chauffeur car," Eleni said. "The Count!"

"But where?" Stavros said. "Take them where? Where they had idea to go?"

"They had some scheme," Eleni said. "Between them. But I don't know what. But, Stavros, don't worry. When he die, he didn't have anger against you."

"That smile was there," Seraphim said, "even when he was dead."

"You all know where they were talking to go," Michaelis said. And he left the room.

There were sounds of a quarrel from the hall. Stavros stood near the door of Demo's room, eavesdropping. Demo was packing to leave, it seemed, and his sister Eleftheria was trying to hold him in the apartment.

"He killed him," Stavros heard his youngest brother say. " 'Good for nothing,' he called him. Made him carry that rug like hamal. All people aren't the same—he didn't learn that yet, your brother! He hated Vacilli like he hates us all, wishes we were all dead and gone out of here. One by one, he'll kill us all. Why should I eat his curses and damn ugly looks? He's not my father!"

Stavros turned and walked back to the living room. "Let him go," he said to himself, repeating Fofo's words. "Good for nothing," repeating his own words, words he would regret having said to Vacilli all his life. "Where's old lady?" he asked Seraphim.

At the beginning of winter, Stavros had given up his bedroom to her. The room was back to back with the kitchen and had an opening for a stovepipe, and Stavros had bought a small coal stove to keep the room warm. She'd spent the cold days hibernating there, staring out of an opening in the partly drawn curtains although there was nothing to look at except the brick wall of the next building.

"We told her nothing," Seraphim said. "You tell her."

Stavros shook his head. "Later," he said. "When I find good time. Now tell her Vacilli left on business matters, long trip."

Days were to pass and they still didn't tell Vasso that her son was gone. Vacilli's funeral was not only private, it was secret. His mother was not there.

A week later, at the store, Stavros found out why Fofo had said, "Let him go!" when she heard Demosthenes threatening to leave. Silo, their Peloponnesian porter, who spoke Turkish better than he did Greek, kept in touch with the underbelly of the rug market. Many of the porters took lunch standing at a counter of the cheapest Armenian restaurant on Lexington Avenue. There one of Silo's friends had come to him with the information that Demo was taking customers to other stores when they didn't find exactly what they wanted at the family store—or sometimes, it seemed, even when they might have. Silo told Fofo, who told Seraphim, who told Stavros.

"I do same thing you do with Sarrafian Brothers," Demo shouted, his anger flaring out of control. "You don't pay any of us enough to live a decent life. What you expect from me?"

"What I expect is—" Stavros started.

"And don't yell at me that way. You're not my father. I don't care what you think or what you say."

"Give me money you took from stealing our customers," Stavros said. "Took!"

"No, not took, stole—what you stole!"

"Prove it," Demo said, "that I stole."

"Give it to me, the money!"

"I give nothing. I'm not your little brother to run over anymore."

"Give me the money," said Stavros, advancing.

Everyone in the store watched, faces pale.

"No. Try and take it. It's here. Not hidden in my shoe this time. Here!

In this pocket." He smacked the pocket at the side of his trousers. "And don't make those faces at me! I'm not afraid of your looks, *agha* tyrant. Everybody here is afraid of that face, but not me. And watch out—don't hit me—"

Stavros did.

Demo turned, walked to the coatrack, and put his coat on.

"I'm leaving," he said to Fofo.

"Go 'head," she said.

"Leave the house too," Stavros said. "Get out from there."

"I moved out a week ago," Demo said. "You didn't notice?" He walked to the door. "I left before you found a way to kill me too. But you don't notice anything about the rest of us, *agha*, do you? Anything that we're feeling. So now I must tell you. Everybody here hates you because you killed their brother. You sent him to die on a washroom floor carrying a rug like a hamal, too heavy for his strength. You show him that ugly face you got, shouting at him with that *agha*'s voice, pulling him up by his arm, poor fellow. This isn't Anatolia, *agha* tyrant, don't you know that? This is America. Which you will never be, American man. Better go back where you came from, that's my advice. Because you don't belong in this country, boy—never, never!"

"You too, blaming me what happened Vacilli?" Stavros asked Seraphim later.

"Sooner or later, he had weak heart, had to happen," Seraphim said. "So it seems."

But Stavros didn't hear the words; he read his brother's face and he knew that Seraphim, a kind, understanding man, blamed him too.

Michaelis was sitting on the floor, working on the corner of a Sarouk. When he saw Stavros coming in, he got up and started out. Was he answering Stavros's question? Did he blame Stavros too?

"Where you going?" Stavros asked.

The Sarouk job should have been finished that night, but Stavros no longer had the confidence to object.

Eleni came in, sat next to him, and took his hand. "The old lady," she said, "she says she knows where Vacilli is and what he's doing."

"Where?"

"It's a secret, she says. Then she smiles. Did you notice her new smile?"

A few days later there was a warm spell and they found Vasso on the street, walking slowly toward Riverside Drive and the Hudson. She was carrying a bundle wrapped in a large print handkerchief. When she was apprehended, she stood rigidly, would not move. Then she sat on a stoop and looked toward the river. She seemed to be waiting for someone to meet her, would not talk, would not move.

The family stood at a distance, consulting in whispers. It was decided in the end to leave her to Eleni, the only one she'd said anything to about what was in her head.

Later Stavros and Seraphim waited idly at home. Michaelis was at the Kaffenion Cappodocia again. Fofo was making dinner, but no one had an appetite.

"Where the hell is Eleftheria?" Stavros asked Seraphim.

"Helping Demo fix up new apartment," Fofo said from the kitchen. "She says he has a beautiful place. She envies him that place. Must be plenty money he's making," she said.

"How the hell he make it in rug market?" Stavros asked. "Not taking customers here and there, few pieces, that way impossible!"

"I think he has rich woman friend. She comes in from New Rochelle three times week, maybe," Fofo said. "Eleftheria whisper this to me."

It was dark when Eleni brought her mother home. The old lady went right into her room and Eleni helped her into bed. "She was waiting for Vacilli," Eleni explained later. "She had it in her head that he's buying tickets for boat back to Anatolia."

"What you said to her?" Stavros said.

" 'Good idea,' I said. Otherwise she don't come back here with me."

"I talk to her later," Stavros said.

"Better no," Eleni said. "She won't talk to you. She told me special, Stavros nothing! If you tell her you know her idea, she blame me."

Soon it became clear to Stavros that everybody in the apartment blamed him for what had happened to Vacilli. They all avoided his eyes now, even Seraphim.

"Why they all blame me?" he asked Seraphim finally. "Why?"

"He's their brother, they kiss his eyes in the coffin. Maybe you shouldn't have sent him that job—he wasn't strong man. What you think now?"

It was the misery all this caused him that finally broke Stavros's resolve not to see Althea again and sent him on a Sunday morning to her apartment. He remembered her gaiety—it could be a release from his troubles now. Perhaps because he was constantly thinking of Althea, he had done what she'd urged him and stopped his traffic with prostitutes. He replayed scenes with her in his dreams—how she'd pulled him up from the chair and to the door, how they'd run down the stairs together. He had wanted nothing—or thought he wanted nothing—except to look at her and suffer her teasing a little. Now he wanted her to flirt with him, just a little. Or even listen to his troubles. *I'll ask her did Freddie get bowl fixed,* he thought. *My excuse for coming there all of a sudden.*

"She moved out," the janitor told him. "When? Two weeks ago. Who knows where?"

The next day, Monday, Stavros asked Freddie, "How's Althea these days?"

Freddie was flustered. "The truth is, I don't have any idea where she might be at this moment," he said. "I told you what she's like. But even so, she . . . surprises me."

"What kind woman is that?" Stavros said. "Impossible!"

Two weeks later, Freddie showed Stavros a postcard, a view of a Salzburg street, and on the message side, in a bold handwriting: "Don't worry about me. I'm fine. Never better. Even happy. Please, Freddie dear, try to reassure Father for me. I depend on you."

"How can I reassure her father?" Freddie asked Stavros. "I don't know where she is, what she's doing there, or—" He stopped.

"Or who she's with?" Stavros said.

"I don't know," Freddie said. "Do you?"

"How the hell would I know? Show the old man the card, maybe."

"It won't help," Freddie said.

But he did show Morgan Perry the postcard and it didn't help.

"Let's see card you got," Stavros said to Freddie at the end of the workday, and he pointed out to Freddie that though the picture was of a Salzburg street, the postage stamp was Argentine.

This bewildered Freddie. "She's in the Argentine! How could that be?"

Stavros knew damned well where she was—he'd had a letter from her a few days earlier and said nothing about it. Althea had asked him to look after Freddie. "He's in for an awful shock," she wrote. "I know how hurt he'll be—after all, we were engaged. I should have written to him and I will soon, but I don't know how to explain what I've done or even what I feel. I can speak the truth to you. You're used to girls who disappear when the sun comes up."

A couple of days later, Freddie had an envelope clearly stamped Buenos Aires. It contained the program of the National Symphony Orchestra of that country playing under the baton of a Hans Müller. There was a photograph of the maestro, a Bavarian bull with the head of a Beethoven and an explosion of jet black hair. The copy, in Spanish— Freddie stumbled his way through it—noted that Maestro Müller at sixty-two was acknowledged to be one of the great virtuoso conductors of the world, "a genius who bestrides his podium like Jupiter on a precipice of Mount Olympus, surveying the world he rules." ("Spanish is a fruity language," Freddie said.) His specialty, the copy went on, was the *oeuvre* of Richard Wagner. He'd conducted the *Ring* many times and anyone who'd heard his *Tristan und Isolde* had to acknowledge that here was a man who understood the passion of love more deeply than other men . . .

No letter, but a scribble on the program in Althea's handwriting instructed Freddie not to show the program to her parents. "They wouldn't understand." She did add a personal note: "I'm very happy. I promise to write a real letter soon." There was an afterthought slanted across a corner. "You can show this to Stavros. He'll understand."

The message was clear to both men.

Stavros's reaction was one he could not confess to Freddie and perhaps did not fully recognize himself. It was the uneasy feeling in the bottom of his belly that he could have had Althea—if he had made the move. The reason he hadn't, in the end, was because she was his friend's fiancée. So he had left her to this German genius!

"I'm glad she's happy," Freddie said. "I'm happy for her."

"What's the matter with you—you crazy?" Stavros said, and he made up his mind to go after her hard the next time she was within reach. *I could have had her*, he kept saying to himself as he walked up Fifth Avenue through the last of the day's light.

And then there she was, turning into Forty-first Street, saying, "Got here yesterday." She didn't look like someone glorying in happiness. She seemed harassed and sickly under a suntan. She said she was going to a chemist's shop nearby and would permit him to go with her if he'd promise not to tell anyone she was in New York. "Please don't try to carry on an inquisition, one of those 'Tell me all about it' conversations. Walk with me if you want to, but don't ask questions."

He stood in a corner of a small, dark shop while she consulted the chemist. Stavros edged close to overhear the end of their conversation.

"How do you put it on?" the chemist asked Althea.

"Rub it into his scalp, at the roots. See my fingers?"

"Completely wrong technique."

"That's how his wife told me to do it."

"His wife! You believe her or you believe me? She thinks she knows everything better than anyone. If you don't want the tips of your fingers black, wear surgical gloves—here, take these. How often do you put it on?"

"Once a week."

"Wrong. Twice a week. Stroke it along his hair, like petting a dog. Like this." He touched her. She pulled back. "Why doesn't he let his hair go white? It's common with artists now."

"Vanity, I suppose." She shrugged. "How much?"

He gave her a slip with a figure. She looked into her purse, then went to Stavros. "Lend me fifteen dollars," she said. She didn't thank him.

They walked up Fifth Avenue—it had become dark and she was more at ease—without talking. At Fifty-seventh Street, she turned and said, "Thank you, goodbye. I've written Freddie a long letter, did my best. But —it's impossible."

"If I can help you on anything," he said. "You don't look good."

"Why do you say that?" She seemed angry. "I'm fine. Been traveling all over South America. What do you expect? Now don't follow me further. You're not to know where we're living."

"Whatever you say. Sure. Goodbye."

Hunching over, she hurried west on Fifty-seventh Street. He followed, of course, at a distance, saw her go into the Osborn Apartments at Seventh Avenue.

"Guess where she is now," Freddie said the next day. He was holding a letter. "Rio de Janeiro!"

"Rio what? She's where?"

"In Brazil. The letter was mailed two weeks ago. It's a real letter. So —forgive me, I can't let you read it."

"Why should you?" Stavros said. "Just tell me, is she all right, her health, so forth?"

"Oh, yes. She's been swimming at the Copacabana beach—it's famous, you know. As for the other side of her life, she says she's learned more in her three months with Maestro Müller than she did in four years at Vassar. It's a good letter. 'I just couldn't turn away,' she says, 'from this chance to know, intimately, one of the giants in the world of art, a true genius.' "

Then Freddie put the letter into his pocket. At the end of the day, he was carrying a recording he'd bought during the lunch hour—"The love duet from *Tristan und Isolde,*" he said to Stavros as they rode down the elevator and walked to the street. "Maestro Müller conducting. Certainly it's the greatest piece of love music ever written."

A few days later, on a Saturday afternoon, she called him at the store. "I want you to do something," she said. Her voice, asking a favor, had an imperious quality he hadn't noticed before.

"Tell me, I do it," Stavros said.

"He's sick, Hans; a sore throat. In fact, he's just about lost his voice."

"What's he need a voice? All those violins!"

"That's not funny. Actually, he's always scolding those violins. Hans is a perfectionist and these fellows have no discipline whatsoever. Americans are too independent, Hans says—they have their own ideas how everything should go. The point is that he wants a certain honey-brandy-lemon drink his wife makes, and I don't want to ask her to fix it. For obvious reasons. I hate her, of course, a slut with an air of culture. And she hates me. So could you bring me some honey? I don't know whom else to ask. I still owe you some money; I haven't forgotten."

She'd asked him to leave the jar at the backstage entrance to Carnegie Hall, but his curiosity brought him to the lobby of the Osborn, where he declared that he had a delivery to make and that it had to be put into the hands of Mr. Hans Müller's secretary and no one else.

When she opened the door, he saw blue discoloration around one eye.

"What are you doing here?" she whispered. "I told you the—"

"I knew where you were, why go Carnegie Hall?"

There was a heavy voice from inside, made heavier by a throat cold. It was a voice accustomed to command. "Close the door, Althea. You're making a draft on me! You want me sick again? Close the door at once!"

"It's the deliveryman, Hans," she said. "With the honey."

It was her little-girl voice; Stavros recognized it.

"Pay him and conclude—what's the delay? Listen to my throat. How am I going to conduct, tell me that?"

"I'm going to fix it for you, Hans. Immediately," Althea said.

"I don't want you to fix it. Bring the honey here; my wife will fix it."

"What happened your eye?" Stavros said.

"None of your business," she whispered, pulling the honey out of his hands. "Now please go."

He was set in the doorway, not moving. "He do that your eye?" he said.

"What kind of honey did you buy, Althea? Althea, I'm talking to you." This in a woman's throaty contralto.

"Greek, I believe, Mrs. Müller," Althea said. "Oh, yes, Hymettus. Greek."

"German honey is better, from Black Forest," Mrs. Müller said.

"German honey," Stavros said, "is shit!"

"Shshsh!"

"Why doesn't she ask me, Hans, when she buys something? I have experience in these matters."

"Step back," Althea whispered to Stavros. "You're blocking the door."

"I'm going to kill that pimp do your eye like that," Stavros said.

"You're getting the wrong idea," Althea whispered. "This eye was an accident. I'm happy here, understand that? Happy."

"What are you whispering here?" Maestro Müller had bulled his way into the entrance hall. "Who is this fellow?"

Hans Müller, a huge man, wore a heavy robe of loden cloth, a muffler, and a skullcap with a purple tassel.

"The delivery, Hans, from the store," Althea said.

"So what's the whispering? Must you flirt with everybody?"

"Oh, Hans, please."

"Did you pay him?"

"Just now."

"Then why are you continuing the contact?" He looked scornfully at Stavros. "Whispering and so on. Get him out!"

Before Stavros could respond, Althea said, "Now, Hans, stop it, don't be silly, please!" She looked at Stavros and said, "That will be all, thank you." Then she headed into the apartment, pulling the maestro by the hand after her, and when she turned to close the door, it was with a look of pleading that made Stavros walk away without another word.

From this incident, Stavros concluded that American women were like

Anatolian women in one respect: They liked to be hit by the men they loved.

"Look," Freddie said a few days later, holding up another letter. "She's in Caracas, that's Venezuela." He seemed by now to be completely in the spirit of Althea's tour with the maestro.

"What the hell's the matter with you, damn fool?" Stavros said.

"I've accepted the situation," Freddie said. "I must learn not to be jealous. That's an uncivilized emotion."

"Honestly God, I think you're crazy."

"Because I want only what's good for her?"

This brief conversation removed whatever guilt Stavros may have felt about going after his friend's fiancée. He bought another jar of honey.

"They left the city. Another tour, I suppose." The man at the desk was surly and indifferent. With Stavros's quarter in his grip, he brightened a little.

"What will I do? I was told put this in her hands," Stavros said, "only. I'll get fired if I—"

"Go upstairs and deliver it to his wife, Mrs. Müller. I'll ring her."

Mrs. Müller, an amazon in her early forties, had obviously been drinking, and Stavros was bold with her. When she allowed him to enter, he started with: "Remember, Mrs. Müller, I brought honey last week . . . ?" Then he looked around. "Oh, look what's here!" he said.

The room was a museum of photographs of her famous husband. Every inch of wall space was covered with him.

Mrs. Müller was digging into her handbag. "I can't find change," she said. "How much was this? Two dollars? The smallest I have is a twenty."

"I see you're a good and faithful sister, so please accept it as a gift."

"I'm not his sister, I'm his wife!"

"That young woman told me you were his sister. I apologize. Now I see these pictures, this great man here, and I feel sorry for you."

"Well, you're certainly a most unusual and generous delivery service."

She smiled at him, poured herself another glass of sweet sherry. "Sit down," she said. "You look like a gentleman. Sit there. Some sherry?"

A half hour later, Stavros was being very direct. "I've seen this situation hundred times in my work," he said. "A good wife sacrifice her best years to a man, then some little girl with noodles in her head comes along and takes him away."

"She will never take him away from me," Mrs. Müller shouted. "I know floozies! None of them mean anything to Hans. He takes them, one after another, then throws them away like the wrappers of chewing gum. Only I remain, forever."

"How can you be so sure?" Stavros said.

"Because he told me. He's bored with this one already. He already has a new interest. This Althea is a fool! 'Look out,' I tell her. 'Your days are coming to an end.' "

She laughed and poured herself another sherry. Then she lay back on the sofa and invited him to come near. "I can't hear you from there," she said. "And you speak so well. Turn that light down. My eyes are sensitive!"

Stavros had nothing better to do. And it occurred to him that this woman might be useful in the course of time.

"Mexico City," Freddie announced two weeks later. But he didn't sound so happy. "I keep having this feeling, call it an instinct, that she's somewhere here in the city. Instincts aren't reliable, of course, but—what do you think?"

"You have a letter in your hands says Mexico City, no?"

"To be truthful, Althea's best friend, Maud Erhenbrecher, hinted at something. Have you any idea where Althea stays when she's here?"

"How would I know that? And suppose you found out—what would you do?"

"Nothing. That's the hell of it. What could I do? Can I read you this letter? It's very painful. She wrote it when she was drunk."

"I don't want to hear it if it's so bad," Stavros said.

"Please! Listen. Then tell me again to give up on her." He read: " 'Don't you see, dear Freddie, I would never be faithful to you—or to anybody. The truth is, I will never stay with one person. I want to suck all the juice out of life, like one of these mangoes they have down here. Every experience a human being can have, I will have. I'm drunk, so I write the truth. I want it all. I want to live the life a man lives, I don't want to live like a woman. So forget me. I would kill you.' "

Freddie looked up, avoiding Stavros's eyes, folding the letter away. "What do you think of that?" he asked. "I want to be understanding and patient, but—"

"Only one thing to do."

"What is that? You're my friend, tell me what to do."

"Go where she is, find her, beat her. Anatolian style. You think she's different? Wrong. All women are like that. How many women you been with your life?"

"One. Althea."

"So you know nothing. I been with thousan'. And I tell you don't trust, not one of them. Anatolian men, they learn one thing from the Turk: women, what to do."

"What is that? I want to learn."

"Turk say, when you come home at night from work, first thing beat your wife. Even if you don't know what for, she will know. You understand that philosophy?"

"That's awfully cynical."

"What's that, cynical? It's the truth. Only way. This man, the German genius—guarantee he beats her. But I give you one more guarantee. She won't stay with that heinie pig."

As soon as work was over, Stavros rushed to the Osborn Apartments, but the doorman, after he'd taken the quarter, told him that Müller hadn't returned. "You want to see his wife?" he said. "She'll be glad to see you."

Two weeks later, Freddie was ecstatically happy. Everybody at Sarrafian Brothers noticed it and everybody guessed why.

"You were right," he said to Stavros, embracing him. "She didn't."

"Didn't what?" Stavros asked. But he knew.

"Didn't stay with that German."

"Where is she now?"

"With me! Didn't tell anybody. She asked me to protect her. She's very tired and rather discouraged. I told her not to answer the doorbell. When I get home, I take her to dinner and we do the shopping. The heinie's hired detectives—they even went to Mount Ivy and asked Mother Perry where they could find Althea. Mrs. Perry says she felt rather flattered." Freddie laughed. "Anyway, one thing is certain—she is forever and ever through with Müller."

"Did you hit her?" Stavros asked.

"Why should I hit her?"

"So she won't do it again. You mean you took her back without—without a . . . ?"

"I'm so happy, I don't want to spoil it."

"What's to stop her doing same thing next week with another genius? If she was mine— Look, let me explain few things to her, all right? I go make her realize what's right and what's"—he held up his open palm and wagged it—"what's wrong. I tell her what should happen to her for what she did to you. Let me do this job for you. A pleasure for me—guarantee I teach her how woman suppose behave with a man."

Freddie laughed. "What are you so angry about?" he said. "I'm the one she did all this to, not you."

"I'm giving my best advice. Go home now, beat her first, then have nice dinner."

Freddie embraced Stavros. "You're still such a foreigner, my friend," he said. "This is America, not Asia."

Two weeks later, he showed Stavros another card. "She's in Veradero," he said.

"What is that?"

"A beach. In Cuba. He rents a house there at the end of the winter each year, to rest up."

"I told you it would happen again."

"The last thing she said to me before she disappeared was: 'I'd do it again, take whatever he gave me and be grateful.' "

"What did you do?"

"What could I do?"

"I told you, but you don't listen."

"Stavros, I refuse to believe that the kind of thing you're talking about is necessary. Anyway, as of this moment, I've given up on her." He looked at her postcard with its view of the blue Caribbean. The man was breaking down. "Want to read her card?" he said to Stavros.

"I don't want to read nothing from her," he said. "I give up too."

Of course he hadn't, quite the opposite. He'd had a hidden feeling all through this episode, one he couldn't admit to, even to himself. Althea's behavior with Maestro Müller attracted him deeply. When he thought of what she'd done—the speed of it, the boldness, the total recklessness, the absolute surrender of herself to this old man—he was filled with desire.

He devoted hours to a consideration of the nature of sexual relations in Western society, came to the conclusion he'd started with, that the only way to keep a woman in line was to do what the Anatolians do: Run off a string of pregnancies, then dress the woman in black and beat her every time her eyes lifted from the ground.

APRIL 1917

On the sixth of April, 1917, the United States of America declared war on Germany. The next move was up to Stavros. Up until a year earlier, he'd told everyone that when these great belligerents closed in conflict, he would offer himself to the American army. "They take me, I go. Any job," he used to say.

Now he spoke somewhat differently. "My brother, Demo, he's young man, all right," he said to Freddie. "But me, forty-one, maybe forty-two for army? What's the use?"

"Besides, you have no obligation," Freddie said.

"I have big obligation," Stavros said. "When I come here, fifteen years ago, I fall on my knees and kiss the ground. I owe this country everything. Someday I pay back in full. But now—"

"Come to the enlistment office with me," Freddie said. "I'm thirty-three and they probably won't take me, either, but I'm going to give them their chance. If they don't, I'll try for the ambulance corps. Althea finished my life here."

"You pay too much attention one woman," Stavros said. "Althea! Althea! How 'bout I get you other woman, right away? And that ambulance business—what you want, get killed? Enjoy life! Make money!"

Against Stavros's advice, Freddie applied for admission to the ambulance corps.

Then Althea was back, again with startling speed and suddenness, and again with Freddie. But this time she hadn't run away from Müller. He had dismissed her. "He's with someone else now," Freddie said.

"At last," Stavros said, "she find out what kind donkey-fucker he is."

"She doesn't hate him, if that's what you're trying to say. With him, every love affair ends in a friendship. She told me how kind and considerate he'd been when he was informing her that it was over."

"And now she's back with you?" Stavros said.

"Yes. And we're so happy," Freddie said. "If they want me in the ambulance corps now, they'll have to come drag me."

JULY 1917

On July 29, the government of Greece, having resolved certain internal problems and made certain choices, declared war on Germany, Bulgaria, and Turkey.

Greeks everywhere in the world were summoned to the flag.

Silo the Peloponnesian inadvertently told him where Michaelis was. He misheard something Stavros said at the end of the day and said, "Michaelis? He's with the others at the Kaffenion Cappodocia."

Stavros's brother Michaelis had not slept at home the night before. Nor had he come to the store that morning.

"With what others?" Stavros asked Silo.

"Those going back."

Stavros turned to Fofo, who by the last light at the window was touching up little wool flowers in the border of a Hamadan "antique." She'd taken Vacilli's chair.

"Did you know this, Fofo?" Stavros asked. "Michaelis is . . . ?"

Fofo didn't look up, shrugged, shook her head.

"Seraphim," Stavros roared. It was near the end of the working day and Seraphim was in the back, primping his new mustache at the small mirror attached to the first-aid cabinet.

Seraphim didn't lie. "Michaelis told me," he said.

"Why you don't tell me, man of honor?"

"He made me promise don't tell no one."

"I'm no one?"

"Especially you," he said. "Well, what can you do, Stavros? He made up his mind; they're probably gone by now."

The Kaffenion Cappodocia was located in an old brick building which had been a shirt factory twenty years before. The enterprise had failed and the second floor, cleared of all machinery and equipment, had been converted into a social club for Anatolians from the province of Cappodocia. Its walls had been papered with views of the valleys at the foot of Mount Aergius, but these had faded now, and the planks of the wooden floor, imperfectly fitted and worn smooth as silk, had buckled. Bunched around each of a dozen tables were identical rickety chairs of the kind found in small streetside cafes in the mother country. The place was lit by five naked bulbs hung in a pentacle.

The air was full of cigarette smoke and the sour smell that comes from burned-out tobacco. On the tables were leavings: fruit peels, curled and brown, broken crusts of bread, parings of cheese, sardine tails in their oil. Also bottles, empty or near empty. On some of the tables were backgammon boards, left as they'd been when the game broke up, the counters and dice scattered; on other tables, dirty playing cards. At the back was a small partition behind which the owner made "Turkish" coffee, the invariable refreshment, but at the moment he was staring into space, exhausted.

Normally the Kaffenion Cappodocia would be buzzing with life at this hour, but on this sweltering night it was quiet. But not empty—far from it. There may have been one hundred and fifty men there, past the point of weariness, numb, talking in low voices. Some were sitting at tables, others were asleep on the floor. Near each man was a pack of his belongings—a suitcase or merely a bundle wrapped in a cloth. Those who were sleeping on the floor used these as pillows.

At one side, two tables were joined together and on them was a plump priest, asleep on his back; under the tables, another priest, even heavier, his legs splayed.

Stavros was looking everywhere for Michaelis, but he couldn't find him. The men there were, for the most part, strangers to each other, and when Stavros said the name "Michaelis Topouzoglou," it aroused no recognition. Pushing his way out of the place, he stopped to take one last look around and felt a pull at his trouser leg. His brother was lying on the floor.

Michaelis seemed embarrassed. "We've been here since yesterday noon," he said, standing up and brushing the dirt off his trousers.

"What you waiting for?" Stavros said.

"The boat. They're loading cargo in Boston. It's taking longer than they expected."

"It's like a stove here. Let's go to the air."

"Our captain told us don't move."

He led his brother to a corner where there was a table with two men asleep under it. The men sitting around, all fifteen or twenty years younger than Stavros, were chewing over the issues of the day. Despite their state of exhaustion, they seemed excited, even elated.

Michaelis pulled a pair of chairs into a corner. Nearby, two men were teasing a cockroach. The insect would scuttle toward the wall, where it had a hiding place, and just as it reached there, the men would turn it back with the edge of a straw fan. They were marveling at the persistence of the creature.

"When they heard about the declaration of war this morning," Michaelis said, "those men at the table in the other corner, they did something to the Konya, the Turkish kaffenion on Allen Street, and it's made them happy. Hey, you, Kucho," Michaelis called, "what you do to the Konya this morning? Here is my brother, tell him."

Kucho had trouble explaining, partly because he'd been drinking continuously since noon of the day before and partly because he laughed so hard every time he thought of what they'd done. "Pukh! Pukh!" He made the sound by exploding his lips. *"Bomba!"* he said, standing up and throwing out his arm, then slapping one hand against the other to indicate the contact of something thrown against a wall. *"Haemma!"* he shouted.

These empty volcanoes, Stavros thought, *shouting and laughing as if they're going on a holiday. Children's games! They don't know what life is. Wait! Damn fools!* But then he saw Michaelis's face, glowing with eagerness, and all he said was, "Did he say *haemma?* Blood?"

"His uncle is a butcher," Michaelis said. "They threw pails of blood over the door and the windows of the Konya."

"But since America declared war on Germany," Stavros said, "that place has been closed, no?"

Michaelis laughed. "These men consider it the first victory of the war," he said.

"I notice one of his legs is shorter than the other, your friend Kucho. Is he going to the war?"

"Oh, yes! He's very quarrelsome. The Greeks don't care about age and so on. The American army would refuse you, but our people, they'll take anyone with a strong spirit."

Stavros didn't respond to the suggestion, if that's what it was. "Are all these men going to Greece?" he asked.

"God willing."

"But not you."

"I too."

"No, you're not." Stavros waited, and then said, "I told you you're not going."

Michaelis stood up, his face drawn white.

"Sit down," Stavros said, "and tell me: You signed papers?"

"I did," Michaelis said. "So it's goodbye."

"Nobody's moving yet, so sit down."

"The train leaves at six." Michaelis looked at a clock on the wall.

"It's already seven-thirty," Stavros said. "Did you say train?"

"We're sailing from Boston in the morning." He sat, seeming more confident. "It's a Greek ship," he said, "the owner's contribution to the war."

"And this boat, it goes to where? Piraeus? Athens?"

"Patras. Where we'll be taken into the army. I too. All this was planned weeks ago, long before the declaration of war."

"I knew nothing about it," Stavros said. He looked at Michaelis, who didn't speak. "The Greeks are crazy," Stavros said. "Three million people, total, so they declare war on Turkey; then that wasn't enough for their pride, so it's Germany too, and then Bulgaria. They forgot Austria."

"They're not so crazy," Michaelis said. "They waited until America was in."

"Tell me," Stavros said. "That sweater you holding—isn't that the one Eleni been knitting last two months?"

"It's the one."

"Then she knew you were going? For two months?"

"Yes."

"The others?"

"They've all known."

"Why didn't they tell me—someone?"

"Nobody tells you anything, don't you know that? They're afraid of you."

"Well, they should be. I'm head of the house. They'd run crazy if there wasn't someone they were afraid of."

"But when you're afraid of somebody, you hate them."

Stavros didn't respond for a moment, looked around, and then said, "What did you say? Just then? Now?"

"I said they all hate you at home. Your brothers and—"

"And . . . ?"

"Your sisters too."

"After all I've done for them?" Stavros said.

"I'll tell you what you did for us. Start with Fofo. You made her your servant. She's almost forty now. She'll never find a man; her life is finished. Vacilli? You made him a nursemaid, buried him with his house slippers on. Demo? What? A liar. A thief. He was so afraid of you, he didn't have the courage to ask for more money so he steals. Now he steals from the United States Army. He'll end in jail. Seraphim? You took his wife away. You think he's happier for that? Without her? What you think he should feel for you—love? Consider you his benefactor? Now, like you, he has no-body. You owe him a wife. Eleni? You prove to her she was marrying a man who couldn't protect her. Was that brotherly act? Eleftheria, the little kitten who sits on your lap? You watch her like cop. Every time a man comes near, you chase him off. In the end, after her youth is spent, you will sell her to a merchant with a cigar breath, someone with whom you do business, no doubt, twenty years older at least, all of which she knows very well, which is why she hates you."

"Not Eleftheria!" Stavros said. "Not the others, either. But not Eleftheria."

"She more than the others," Michaelis said. "You'll find out. One by one, they will all leave you, like me, without a word of thanks. Then you will be alone, which I think is what you want."

"Why don't they tell me themselves if this is their feeling?"

"No one has talked truth to you in years. What is there to say? You are what you are."

Stavros turned away. On the wall behind him he saw a lithograph, *Byron Taking the Oath of Allegiance to Greece,* and across from it, a pair of old prints, *The Death of Patroclus* and *The Vengeance of Achilles.* Then he faced his brother again.

Michaelis could see that Stavros was very angry, but he didn't care. "I think you enjoy that people are afraid of you," he said. "But the day may come when you need some help from us, some kindness, perhaps only that, and we won't be able to give it to you because of how we feel. You brought us here a family, you made us servants. We worked like niggers for eight years and all I got to show for it is anger."

"So I did everything wrong?"

"I don't know what you wanted from us. None of us know. You used to say, 'This is America, here is freedom.' But you ordered us around like it was the old country, telling us what we must do, what we must think, what is right, what is wrong—"

"It was the responsibility my father put on me."

"At first, perhaps that was it. But soon it was what you wanted. Power over us! To use us. For your good business. All you think about is putting money together, like the Americans here, same philosophy! You made us work for eight years, accumulating money, and what we have now, I suppose, is one very small part of a very small store."

"What is that 'I suppose' business?"

"Only Demo was smart enough to ask for a paper to prove it. Now he's out, I suppose."

"You suppose again?"

"Yes. Suppose, like now, we go a different road from you? Suppose we disagree, suppose we quarrel? Must we beg you for our share? I believe that's what you want, that we beg you."

"But I'm your brother. After all the quarrels and the disagreements, we are still brothers. Aren't we?"

"No. We learned the truth—that you don't understand us and we don't understand you, that you don't care about us—so we don't care about you."

"What don't you understand about me?"

"What you want? Tell me. What eats you? Nothing Father said; I
knew him better than you. It's some idea you got here. You see, now that
I'm leaving I can ask things I was afraid to ask before. Why do you want
us to be like you? To live like you? You have nothing. You work all day,
every day, and once a week you have a whore. Is that a life? You're
surprised now that everyone keeps secrets against you. Why? You know
they're all afraid of you. But I believe that's what you want. More than
love, you want us all to fear you. Well, now you have your wish!"

There was an outbreak of singing in one corner of the kaffenion. Men
were rising to their feet. Here and there other men joined in. It was the
political song of the moment, a triumphant chant against a king who'd
tried his best to bring his country into the war on the side of his cousin
the German Kaiser.

> We chased him out.
> King Constantine—
> That dirty thief.
> That big mouth—

"I think our captain is coming," Michaelis said.

Men were lining up at the entrance door; there were shouts and com-
mands.

"Goodbye," Michaelis said.

"You're not going, Michaelis." Stavros held him by the arm. "I listened
to you," he said, "you're going to listen to me."

"It's too late, Stavros. I signed papers. Finished!"

"Tell them you changed your idea. Tell them your brother said no.
Tell them you're afraid. Tell them to call you coward. We Anatolians
survive by watching the brave die. I have not heard sounds of joy coming
from a grave. Michaelis, listen to me. You let some pimp-hearted politicians
in Athens steal your life? Think! Behind them are the priests—like those
two in the corner—and under their black robes, pockets jingling with the
rich man's money! You're going to let them send you where there's a Turk
waiting with a bullet to shoot into your heart—a Turk, a boy like you,
whose father was a hamal and who has nothing against you but is saying
only what you said: 'I signed a paper.' I'm speaking to you as a hamal now.
I carried the rich merchants' loads until I envied the donkeys. But I didn't
make the money; they did. Patriotism is something the rich invented.
There are no patriotic hamals; they have no reason to go to war, to fight
each other. Tell me, Michaelis, you see any rich men here tonight? Anybody drive up to volunteer in a Pierce Arrow with a chauffeur? Where is
Mr. Paul Sarrafian tonight you imagine? You imagine right; in a warm bed
with a warm *dolma,* a young woman, soft like a squash, and he's the meat
in the middle. Michaelis, this patriotism business, don't let it make a victim

of you. Singing songs together, marching together—see, they're starting
—going to die together—"

"Michaelis! Michaelis!" It was Kucho calling. "Come!"

"I'm coming," Michaelis called back.

"No, you're not," Stavros said. "I've got to say this, too. You're not
a strong man. You're like your father, not put together for hardship. Your
body is like his. You won't come back, Michaelis—"

"I worked as a fisherman for two winters, Stavros, and I never missed
a night on the water."

"I'm trying to save your life, Michaelis."

"I don't want you to save it."

With a sudden twist and a pull, Michaelis was loose and running across
the room to where Kucho was waiting for him. There he entered the
crowd of volunteers where their numbers were thickest.

Seeing Stavros run after his brother, the volunteers gathered around
Michaelis to protect him.

"Michaelis, you're not going," Stavros said. He was pushing men out
of his way so he could reach his brother, but they blocked him, and
when he tried to make his way through, they held him off and cursed
him. Others, hearing the sounds of commotion, rushed up to block Stavros off.

At the door to the stairs, the captain appeared and shouted a command.
From below there were whistles and more shouts.

The volunteers lined up. Michaelis, guarded, protected, was in the line
near the wall. Some men at the head of the column began to march; then
they all filed out along the wall and down the stairs. They were singing
now, in a low, threatening tone.

And Stavros understood there was no way he could save his brother.
When the place was empty, he sat in a corner and watched the owner
begin to clean up. Outside—now from a distance—he heard the low,
threatening song in time with the shuffling of feet. Then all was quiet.

AUGUST 1917

One reason they rented a house in Atlantic City was the worsening
condition of Vasso's legs. Below her knees, dark brown circles—ulcers—
had reappeared under the skin, and they didn't heal.

On a Saturday morning in August, when the sun had already warmed
the sand, Stavros brought her to the beach in a taxi. Seraphim had gone
ahead, carrying a wicker armchair which he put down at the edge of the
tide. They seated the old woman in the chair and her heavily veined hands
gripped the armrests.

Seraphim knelt to take off her black woolen stockings which he pushed into his coat pocket. Then he rolled up the bottoms of the long "winter" underwear which Vasso wore on even the hottest days.

This done, Seraphim and Stavros pulled off their shoes, hiked up the trousers of their "business" suits, and carried Vasso in her chair into about four inches of water. Eagerly she dropped her feet from the front rung into the cool salt surf. The gentle, evenly spaced waves lapped halfway up her calves.

It was a perfect day, the sea receding to the sky; where sea and sky met, there was a blur, not a line—a soft blue mist.

"Hot!" the old lady said.

"Hot is good for you," Stavros said.

"Where's my fan?" she said.

"Demo took it," Seraphim told his brother. "For his lady friend." He pointed to where Demosthenes was lying on the beach. There was a girl with him, fanning herself as she looked over the crowd of bathers.

"See that woman he pick up!" Seraphim said. "New one again! Where he find that kind business? So quick!"

"Go take the fan," Stavros said.

Seraphim hopped to his feet and left.

"You hear from Michaelis?" the old lady asked.

"No word yet."

"Where's Eleftheria?" she asked.

"With those people there," Stavros said to her.

Eleftheria was sitting with an Italian family: a short, stout man, the head of the house, his plump wife, and their four sons. She seemed at home among the husky boys, all of them of medium height or even shorter, but powerfully built.

"What kind people there?" Vasso asked.

"You see what they are," Stavros said. "Italian dagos. He's a contractor, she told me, he build up some kind school here."

"You hear from Michaelis?"

"Nothing yet."

The old lady pulled up her skirt and her underwear further. "Feels good," she said.

"Doctor said best thing."

"But I can't sleep. I dream and that wakes me up. Which way Kayseri from here?"

Stavros pointed across the water. "Straight there," he said. "I have bad sleep too."

"What's the matter your dreams?"

"Not dreams exactly; everything. Rondiris told me Achilleas is back home, in Athens, with his wife again. I don't know what to say to Eleni, she didn't listen my advice before."

"Say nothing. Good news makes you happy, bad news forget. You hear from Michaelis?"

"Not a word, Mommah. But soon, I'm sure. I tell you when."

"How's business?"

"We pay expenses. Salaries? Some weeks we take, other weeks, starvation. Good thing we live together."

"Vacilli good boy."

"Yes, Mommah."

"Seraphim good boy."

"Good boy, honest, but no ambition. Demo plenty ambition but on wrong things."

"Where he gets money girl like that?"

"From United States Army with his tricks."

"You talking to him now?"

"I'm talking but I don't change my mind."

"Don't tell Eleni anything. Maybe Achilleas change back."

"I don't like that man, Achilleas."

"He's priest, you have to like him. Where's Eleftheria?"

"Over there with those Italian wops."

"Which one likes her?"

"The small one with the big nose. He's got black hair at least; all the others red-head and getting bald. You ever hear red-head Italians and getting bald? Look, she's waving to you. Wave back, Mommah. Here."

He lifted her arm and swung it from side to side. "Good!" he said.

Fofo came up to the edge of the water. "That Greek-lost-his-wife you want me talk to, Stavros, he's old man!"

"Never mind old man," Vasso said, "you better get marry soon, you getting old yourself."

"You smell him, Stavros?" Fofo said. "He smells."

"It's hot today, everybody smell," Stavros said. "He has good business, Camden, New Jersey. We sell him from Sarrafian Brothers. Also from our store, we pull him in, sell few thousand."

"I don't care if I get married or not, pig like that pig."

"Go put bathing suit on, talk to him," Stavros said.

"Leave her," Vasso said. "She has your father's legs."

"Like me," Stavros said.

"On a man, who looks?" Vasso said.

"I'm going cook supper," Fofo said.

"You get married!" Vasso said.

"Not today," Fofo said, and left.

"She's getting old, Stavros."

"What can I do? She doesn't like anybody. Not only she's smarter than they are, she's stronger. I don't mean her body. She wants to make up everybody's mind, they should obey her on everything. Men don't like that in woman. Eleftheria, she's too strong too. Only Eleni here is like woman. Normal."

The old lady yawned. "Well, what can you do?" she said. "Men are donkeys mostly. Stupid!"

"I got nothing but trouble, Mommah. Sometime I wish I left us on other side, what you think of that?"

"You forgot already what it was there. That's what you told me. Now you having same idea, change your mind?"

"I don't forget there, I realize here. Seraphim O.K. but no pep. Vacilli? His whole life gone, putting Aseptinol your sores, so forth, so forth, he should have been woman! He was not for this country! Poor fellow! Michaelis, the smart one, damn fool fighting war! Don't wait for help from him—right? Demosthenes? I hate to tell you what happened to him here. I'm getting crazy with these people, Mommah, I'm getting mad. Fofo! You see situation: What am I going to do with her? Eleni? That damn pretend-priest, he lie to her, she don't take my advice 'gainst him. So what happen? Cross, double cross. Now look Eleftheria. Who she's with? Italian, that little short one with big nose, he's shorter than she is and I don't like his hair, it's curly like nigger. I don't want to fight all the time, Mommah. Twenty years I work. My whole life. But this country belong to the people it belong to. Why should they give me part of what they have? Meantime, I have no life here, no happiness! I didn't tell you, I like certain girl, one I brought to dinner that night long ago—remember? But she's with some-one else—you saw—and I can't go after her because why should she be with me? What have I got to give her? I'm nothing here. A foreigner with a small business! Push, struggle, sweat! But—I tell you this much. Some-day, yes, someday believe me, I have certain big ideas. I know I can pull plenty money out from here. Someday, yes, I will—Mommah?"

The old lady was asleep.

He went on speaking to her. "I know what you thinking, Mommah. We go back now, right? Sure. The war be over soon, Turkey finish, Ottoman Empire *kaput!* Who knows, maybe things better for us there. That your idea? You die there better? Hey, sweet old lady? We go, huh? What you say? So many things better there. I remember. Sure. They don't want us here. Look what happen your family in this country! Disaster! I work twenty years, where is my happiness? Twenty years! How much longer it should take? Now I give up. What you say, dear old lady? We go? What? I should decide? O.K., I decide. We go!"

Stavros looked out over the water in the direction he'd pointed when Vasso asked where Kayseri was. A fish broke the surface, a flash and a ripple.

"Shshsh," he said to Eleftheria. She was coming up with her young man, who was indeed shorter than she was. "Mommah's sleeping," he whispered.

"This is my big brother," Eleftheria whispered to her companion. "This is my friend Johnny Coniglio," she said to Stavros.

Stavros didn't offer his hand.

"Shake!" Johnny said.

They shook hands.

"Go help Fofo with the dinner," Stavros said to his sister. "You leave her alone in the kitchen."

"Oh, sure," Eleftheria said. "Johnny is coming to dinner tonight," she said.

Not only was Johnny at the dinner table but Demosthenes had done something difficult for Stavros to forgive: He'd brought his whore—which is what Stavros from his experience judged her to be. In the harsh light of the dining room fixture, the color of her hair looked like what it was.

"You use peroxide?" Eleftheria asked.

"Yes," the girl said. "You like it?"

"Beautiful," Eleftheria said. "On you."

"Her name is Diana," Demosthenes said. "Everybody, Diana!"

"Johnny," Eleftheria said, leaning against Coniglio flirtatiously, "you like her hair? Shall I make mine too?"

"I put big stick to your behind," Stavros said.

"Don't listen to him, Johnny; Stavros, he's an old-fashioned man. What do you say?"

"I like your hair the way it is," Johnny said. "Very much."

The old lady began to chuckle. They all looked at her.

"Fofo," Stavros said, "she has to go."

Fofo and Seraphim got up and helped the old lady from the table, led her to the stairs and up.

She left a trail of her water.

"You're so sad tonight, Stavros," Eleftheria said. She ran around the table and jumped on his lap. "Cheer up," she said, throwing her arms around his neck. "This is summer and summer is supposed to be a happy time." She kissed him on the cheek. Then she smiled at Johnny Coniglio.

"He must be in love," Eleni said. "In love, a person is either very happy or very sad. Sometimes both at the same time."

"Are you in love, brother of mine?" Eleftheria asked. She was hugging Stavros, but it was clear to everyone that it was a way of flirting with Johnny.

"Don't do that," Stavros said.

"Oh, she's so sweet," Diana said.

Stavros glared at her. Then he got up, pushing Eleftheria off his lap.

"Did I say something wrong?" Diana asked Demo.

"Everybody!" Johnny Coniglio said. "Come on, we go for ice cream cones."

The old-fashioned drugstore was full; Saturday night.

"The owner here, he's a Greek too," Johnny said to Stavros.

"Too many Greeks this country," Stavros said.

"I also want a quart and a half of chocolate and tutti-frutti mixed," Johnny said to the counterman when he brought their cones. "Let's take it home and surprise the old man," he said to Eleftheria, reaching in his back pocket for his wallet.

"No, no, I pay," Demosthenes said. "Everything family dinner tonight."

"Where you get so much money all of sudden?" Stavros said.

"From your taxes," Demo said. "I got enough."

"I know you got enough. Question is where you get it?" Stavros said.

"Please, everybody be nice," Eleftheria said. "I'm so happy tonight."

"Don't be mad," Diana said, and she took Stavros's arm.

He threw it off and walked out of the place.

Diana burst into tears.

Eleftheria began to cry as well, and she embraced Diana.

"Why did he do that?" Diana said. "Why did he do that to me that way? What did I do wrong? Somebody tell me."

"You did nothing wrong," Eleftheria said.

"I know how he feels," Eleni said. She went to the counter where the man was holding the cones. "I'll take his to him," she said.

She took a strawberry cone, ran out and down the street looking for her brother, calling, "Stavros, Stavros!"

He was on the boardwalk, sitting on a bench and looking over the water. "I don't want ice cream tonight," he said, but took the cone she offered him. "Where did Eleftheria go?"

"She's still in the store."

"You see who's got her?"

"I don't think he—what did you say? Got her?"

"If the women in this family would listen to me, if they would pay attention old-fashion way, they be better off."

"But this is America, Stavros, my heart."

"I wish on these things it was the old country. Lotsa ways better there."

"But Eleftheria has a right to pick out her own."

"You had a right too; now where is he?"

"I don't know. But wherever he is, he's thinking of me. He's the one I want if he's here, and if he's not here, he's the one I want."

"You think he says the same thing?"

"I'm sure."

"You were made to suffer, Eleni."

"Why? You know something different?"

"No, of course not."

"There is such a thing as faith. If you have it for the one you love, their touch in your imagination is better than someone else's touch in life. Do you know that?"

"I know that."

"You're in love too, I can tell."

"I'm not in love—"

"Deceive yourself but not your sister. Althea! She's so beautiful. Not like that Diana. Clean. Also beautiful. When she came to dinner, I watch everything. What's the matter?"

"I have headache. Here, finish this." He gave her the cone.

"When you're in love like me, you can feel who else is."

"So then tell me—Eleftheria, is she?"

"I think so."

"Couldn't she do better than that little . . . ?"

"Who can explain a mystery? Everything else in the world is clear what to do, but not love. You need money? Work. Religion? Pray. Education? Read. Cooking? Learn from mother. You can teach everybody anything but—"

Suddenly he got up. Then he sat down.

"I know," Eleni said. "I talk too much."

"Don't tell me Demosthenes," Stavros said. "You call that love?"

"Men are different," she said. "They're not pure. Except you. I believe you can love." She laughed. "I believe that," she said. "Now I'm going home. I write Achilleas a letter every night. I'll tell him our talk."

She kissed her brother on the cheek and went.

He sat on his bench for a long time after she was gone. Then he stretched out, closed his eyes and listened to the sound the water makes as it moves in and out.

Then he was asleep, or half asleep, the way he always slept now—uneasily, dreaming.

When he woke after a couple of hours, he decided to walk along the boardwalk. He walked slowly, gravely, his hands clasped beneath his coat and behind his back, a businessman in love.

He was thinking of Eleftheria. Where was she? What was she doing? How close had she let Johnny Coniglio come? Eleftheria was a properly brought up girl, a family girl. She wouldn't permit any quick intimacies. But in America, as he'd learned, people change. She'd been on the beach all summer with Fofo and the old lady—and with him, with Johnny. She certainly behaved as if she'd known him a long time. And well. Even his family—she seemed at home with them.

The setting of the sun hadn't cooled the air. The heat seemed to have soaked into the wide wooden planks and been stored up there.

He heard sounds from the sand beneath the boardwalk, and recognized what they were, but curiosity brought him to the boardwalk's edge. Lying on the sand were lovers in an embrace. Stavros stopped, walked on, looked back; he could only see the lower half of the bodies as they coupled.

Must be something different when you love the one you're with, he thought. *I never had that.*

He turned away, his thoughts heavy as he walked along the boardwalk.

Althea and Freddie, was it possible? Like what he'd just seen? Perhaps. But that other man, the old man . . . ?

He couldn't believe it.

Did Eleftheria love that little Italian?

He didn't want to imagine them together.

A little later, however, he did imagine it; he saw them so vividly that when he came to Johnny Coniglio's street, he turned off the boardwalk and down into the crowded settlement of homes.

In the police station later that night, no one told the same story. The one thing they all agreed on was that Stavros had come on his daughter in an intimate embrace. (The police kept calling Eleftheria his daughter. No one bothered to correct them.) The Coniglio boys said that the young couple had been sitting quietly in chairs on the side porch. But the next-door neighbor, who'd watched the whole scene from his dark bedroom window, said the lovers had been lying on the grass under a tree and that the young lady, contrary to custom, had been on top of the young man. The sound of their love play had broken this man's sleep and, outraged, he'd telephoned for the police even before Stavros appeared.

Eleftheria and Johnny were not in the police station to set the record straight; they were at the Southside Hospital in the emergency room.

No one disagreed, however, about Stavros's first action: He'd pulled Eleftheria to her feet and slapped her unmercifully while she covered her head with her arms and screamed. Then he took her by the ear and tried to pull her out of the yard and to the street, as she struggled and screamed for help.

The father of the family, Anthony Coniglio, an esteemed builder in that community, who'd been brought to the police station for his testimony, was treated with the greatest respect by the desk sergeant. He said that Eleftheria's cries for help had wakened him, he'd looked out the window and seen his son, Johnny, doing what was only right, going to Ellie's rescue. Mr. Coniglio had no idea then who the girl's "assailant" was, so he'd immediately called for the police and was told they were already on their way.

Yes, Johnny's brothers said, they'd gone to help his fiancée—that's how

Eleftheria was known in the Coniglio family. All they'd hoped to do was help her get free. But the man had not listened to reason, he'd struck and kicked at them viciously, below the belt, they said, then taken the girl by her long hair (not cut from birth) and was dragging her away. Still, at that time, there was something just a little comic about the incident, this "nut" trying to drag a violent and noisy young woman down the street by the hair, it was like a "funny paper."

But when Johnny didn't manage to free his girl—the man simply wouldn't listen to reason—his three brothers rushed in (one in the pajamas he was still wearing at the police station) and surrounded the "crazy Greek." Even then the incident was more like a kind of rough game—so they said.

The neighbor in the darkened window above, however, thought it less funny; the boys were powerfully built and he knew them to be cruel at times, "bullies," he called them. They circled around the struggling couple, darting in and out, a kind of bear baiting as they began to block Stavros from moving off with his sister. They were taunting and insulting the man, laughing uncontrollably, pulling at his clothing and his hair while his sister struggled to get free.

It was then that he'd produced a knife from somewhere in his clothing and threatened them with it. Now the game they played was: Who can take the knife away from the madman. The brothers feinted and snatched at the man's arms, then his hand, then at the blade itself. They jostled the man, knocking him off balance, turning him and turning him to make him dizzy. The Greek responded by making passes with his knife, but the boys moved closer and still closer, laughing all the time, still shouting taunts and insults.

Then it happened. One of the boys leaped on his back and the others closed in, Johnny pulling at the man's hand to set Eleftheria free. The neighbor above had not seen how it happened—it was dark under the tree and there were so many bodies crowded together—but he distinctly remembered that Johnny suddenly stepped back and clapped his hand to his face. There was blood coming from between his fingers.

Everyone realized that something serious had taken place. Stavros dropped the knife. The fight stopped. His brothers gathered around Johnny Coniglio, who had a long, deep knife slash across his cheek.

It was at this moment that Stavros made a mistake. Instead of going to Johnny with some show of concern, he went to his sister and, once again, tried to pull her away. At this, Johnny's brothers went after him, and now their attack was deadly. They were out of control.

The neighbor in the window, who didn't like the Coniglio family, said that the father had come out and, seeing what had happened to his youngest son, spurred the others on instead of trying to restrain them. They took turns beating Stavros, finally knocking him off his feet and onto the ground, falling on him there, kicking him and giving him a terrible beating with feet and fists.

Stavros had fought back as best he could, but he was overwhelmed; soon he couldn't defend himself. The beating went on.

Only the young woman understood what was happening, the neighbor said, and she tried to pull the Coniglio boys off, but there was no way for her to intervene through the hailstorm of fists and kicks. Stavros was a fox on his back, covered by a pack of hounds going for the kill.

The arrival of the police saved him; they'd come just in time.

When he got to his feet, he staggered and fell. He was in a state of collapse. But dazed as he was, the first thing he did when the police had restored some kind of quiet was to call for Eleftheria to come home with him immediately. He lost his footing, fell, got to his feet again, and repeated his command.

She was examining Johnny's cut, and when she saw how deep it was and that he'd probably be scarred for life, she became hysterical and, facing her brother, cursed him in Greek in the most violent tone of voice. There was no sound except her shrill, furious voice shouting words in a tongue no one understood.

Except Stavros.

The police knew that the first thing to do was to get Johnny to a hospital; he was holding his cheek together. They rushed him into one of their cars. Eleftheria, having had her say, ran to go along.

Everyone else went to the police station, not because they'd been ordered to or even invited to, but because, under the leadership of Mr. Anthony Coniglio, they wanted to make sure that Stavros "got his."

There the various stories were heard. The fact that there wasn't a mark on any of the boys, while Stavros had to be supported at the sergeant's desk while he was booked, made no difference. He had cuts too, his brows had been split and the blood was running into his eyes. His nose seemed to be broken. His body, a quick examination revealed, was black and blue.

Booked on a charge of attack with a deadly weapon, Stavros was glad to be taken to a cell, where he was safe and could lie still on a cot. He didn't complain or protest; he passed out.

At the police station, the neighbor won the everlasting hatred of the Coniglio family (he moved to another part of the city six months later) by saying that Stavros had been completely justified in using his knife to hold the boys off. They would have killed him, he said; the Greek was lucky to have gotten off so easily.

When Seraphim, the brother he trusted most, came to see Stavros in jail the next morning, he brought the news that Eleftheria had declared she was not returning home, ever. She'd arrived very early, guarded, so it seemed, by several stocky, redheaded Italian men, and taken all her clothing away. Johnny, she told them, was in the hospital, where they'd had to sew up his cheek with twelve stitches.

The bail figure the judge set later that day was ten thousand dollars. The father wanted Stavros punished to the full extent the law allowed. The charge was changed from "attack with a deadly weapon," to "intent to kill."

A peculiar knife—none of the police had ever seen another like it: "must be foreign-made with that square-end blade!"—had been found, bloodstained, on the lawn at the side of the Coniglio home and retained as evidence.

To everyone's surprise, Stavros asked Seraphim to notify Althea Perry where he was and what had happened. Then he told his brother to go back to New York and take every member of the family with him; he didn't want help from them—in fact, didn't want to see them.

The family obeyed.

Stavros didn't speak to the guards or to the prisoner across the aisle. He didn't eat and "was altogether odd," the sheriff in charge remarked, "very strange. He keeps talking about Peckinpaugh. Who is he? The shortstop?"

Late the next afternoon, a Monday, Althea appeared. She'd found a bondsman and arranged for Stavros's release. She also brought him a piece of good news—or was it good? She couldn't tell from Stavros's reaction.

A deal had been made. In light of the fact that Eleftheria had vowed never to go home again but to stay with her lover in the hospital until his long cut began to heal, then accompany him to his home, where they would be immediately married, he in turn, Johnny Coniglio, had notified everyone concerned that in the interest of harmony and their future happiness, he would not press charges—this over the violent opposition of his father. But the runt was a strong-minded runt and his bride-to-be was equally determined. They wanted no revenge; they had each other and needed nothing more. The matter was closed, they said, and they were perfectly ready to go off and live by themselves if their decision didn't please Johnny's father.

Mr. Coniglio had to accept their decision or lose a son. However, in smaller things he was not so generous. He expected payment, he said, for the three large windows Stavros had broken—though no one else could remember Stavros going near the windows or into the house, where, so the man claimed, an antique light fixture had been cracked. "That crazy Greek really had to go out of his way to break that one," the elder Coniglio said.

Althea advised Stavros to accept these obligations. He nodded, but she wasn't sure he'd heard. She realized he was having a kind of breakdown. He couldn't talk clearly, his body ached everywhere, and he had a fever. Some terrible and painful change was happening inside him, she could see that.

He kept looking at her and she could feel his need for sympathy. She also saw that he had no way of asking for it—she knew that Stavros was incapable of ever asking for anything.

She took him to the house the family had rented. There was no one there. Everything was in disorder, even the kitchen, as though the inhabitants had panicked and fled.

She made him dinner. He did ask for Indian pudding, and she explained that she didn't have the "makings." "Tomorrow, if you still want it," she said. "If we're still here tomorrow."

"We be here tomorrow," he said. He kept looking at her from the sofa where he was lying, but he didn't speak. When she asked him why he was looking at her that way, he shook his head.

At last he said, "I don't care anymore. About any of them. I try my best here, I lose. O.K., I lose. Finish!"

She tried to comfort him, but he wouldn't listen.

Later he said, "We came to this country too late, I think. The ones who got here first, they own it. The ones with blue eyes. Like Freddie."

His mind seemed to wander. He slept, woke, spoke, slept, woke.

She told him he should go upstairs and to bed.

"Then you'll leave," he said.

"I won't go," she said. "I promise. Tomorrow, not tonight."

Upstairs he undressed before her, turning his back. He would have done that with his mother or his sister Fofo. She saw that his body had great black-and-blue areas.

He was asleep almost immediately. She sat very still for a moment to make sure. Then she started out, small slow steps on tiptoe. That woke him. "You know who Peckinpaugh is?" he asked.

"What?" she asked. He seemed delirious. "No," she said.

"What have I got to beat Freddie's clear blue eyes?" he said.

"I don't understand," she said. "What do you mean?"

"That's what Mr. Fernand Sarrafian ask me." He laughed, but it hurt. "Don't leave me now," he said.

"I'm sitting right here."

"I made a mistake bringing them here," he said. "Yes, we are safe, but this country belongs to your people. You know that."

"This country belongs to anyone who takes it," she said.

"Also we come with wrong philosophy. Family life not for here."

"You should not work with anybody," she agreed, "or for anybody. You're a man meant to be alone."

"No, no, no. Don't go! You're not going to go?"

"I told you I won't go. Don't you believe me?"

"I need you," he said. He'd closed his eyes in order to say that.

She knew how hard it was for him to speak those words. She couldn't believe, an instant later, that he'd said them.

"I'm not going," she said.

He seemed passive, unable to assert himself. The man who'd been so urgent in his demands, so absolute and beyond denying with so many other women, was incapable with her. Now he looked at her as if she was all he'd ever wanted in the world, as if the whole struggle of his life had led to this instant. But he couldn't move toward her. He couldn't ask for what he wanted most.

She turned off the light—to escape the look in his eyes. "Try and sleep," she said.

In the dark, he was remembering how the old man he hated—the conductor, her lover—had treated her. Brutally. And that he, Stavros, had determined to do the same the next time he had her alone. He'd planned it in detail so many times, rehearsed what he'd say: "What the hell you think, you play with me like you play with Freddie? I'm different type man, not like your people. You are the woman I want so don't play your flirty games with me, bitch! Come here, bad girl! Come to me!" And so on.

Then he'd imagined how he would attack her, beat her until she crawled to his feet, helpless and completely submissive, begging for mercy.

But all he could say now was: "My body hurts." Again he seemed delirious.

She sat next to him and stroked his thick, coarse hair down to his neck. His head was very hot. She left her hand on his neck, gently rubbing it.

He smiled at her touch. "Your fingers are cool," he said. "So cool. Oh!"

He tried to turn a little, toward her, but he couldn't. He groaned, then smiled and shook his head. "Goodbye," he said. "I'm going now."

She took off her clothing and got into bed with him.

He clasped her. Now he felt no ache in his muscles. He was freed of pain.

His body was hotter than usual.

She liked it burning. She chose to become part of his delirium.

He had the strength that only the desperate have.

"Don't hurry," she said. "We've got all night."

Later she said, "Please don't hurry."

Then, "Wait," then, "Please wait. A little more."

Afterward she was tender with him, a child in his mother's arms.

She sang to him. She sang, " 'I don't worry, I don't care.' "

"What's that?" he said.

"A silly song. 'I don't worry, I don't care, I don't marry a million-aire!' "

They stayed there the next day. They sent no messages, they didn't touch the telephone. They talked, they ate together, they lay together.

They stayed another day.

She understood him at last, understood he was not for her.

He thought the opposite. He remembered her words: "This country belongs to anyone who takes it." Those words gave him a reason now—

the only reason, it seemed—to stay here. "She's all that I want here" is what he told himself.

They didn't communicate any of this to each other. She didn't want to hurt him. He feared rejection.

She found that his life's struggle was really not comprehensible to her. They had nothing to talk about. But he did truly need her and that stirred her. She was dealing with a convalescent. The name of his illness was bitter disappointment, and she was the cure.

"I'm finished here," he said. "I'm leaving America."

"No, you're not," she said.

In his delirium of fever he said many other things, but she didn't believe any of them. She was giving him comfort when he needed comfort. A gift, two days of her life.

They stayed another night. And a day. "He's sick," she said to herself. "He needs to be nursed."

The next morning, he still had the fever, and except for that fever it wouldn't have happened as it happened. He didn't altogether know what he was doing, and she was ready to enter an irrational world.

She placed the room's white wicker bed lamp on the floor in a corner and covered it with a worn pink towel. She pulled the shades down. The room became a land where a fairy tale was taking place.

She suggested they stay another day; it was her idea. By now she'd realized that what was happening was a two-way comforting. If she was giving him a gift, he was giving her one too.

Sometimes when they made love she'd pull the sheet up and over their heads; they coupled in a twilight tent, hardly speaking.

His hunger for her never gave out. His body did, but not his desire. She'd never known anything like it. It's because of the fever, she thought.

She loved his burning body. That special heat suited her mood.

She kept remembering Müller, how he'd mounted her, spent, and walked away. Soon he'd be at his table, reading a score out loud, humming and chanting, pounding out the beat with his knuckles, articulating each instrument, scolding imaginary musicians. She hadn't realized until then the depredations Müller had made in her confidence. And when it suited him, he'd dropped her.

Freddie hadn't helped her get over Müller.

When she was sure Stavros was asleep, she spoke to him. "You gave me my confidence back," she said. "Thank you," she said. She was certain he hadn't heard. If he had, she was certain he wouldn't know what she was talking about.

Exhausted, she'd fall asleep. He'd wake her by entering her. Perhaps, she thought, he knows that we won't ever again be together, that these few days are the last days, so he's getting all he can.

She kept terminating the affair that way—in her mind.

Sometimes his behavior amused her. He'd "put" her places; put her head to the foot of the bed, put her on the floor so his feet were against the wall, put her on her hands and knees along the edge of the white wicker chaise. She especially liked it when he put her on top of him.

Yes, true, she also liked being on top for the reason he said: She was boss up there. Instead of what she'd been with Müller—a slave. She realized how much of what she was yielding to in that twilit world was an attack on Müller. These nights were dedicated to purging the humiliations she'd suffered from the maestro.

But there was something more than that, and finally she had to recognize it. Stavros would set up a continuous rhythm of ecstasy in her, one that kept coming in waves, one wave following another in an unrelenting rhythm. "You're the only one who's ever done that to me," she said.

Again she wasn't sure he knew what she was talking about. But she knew this: that he couldn't get enough of her and that he'd given her her confidence back.

"All white meat," he called her. Yes, she was that special thing for him, white without another tint, his dream of Eros come true.

In the middle of the night, when she believed he was asleep, she'd walk through the whitewashed rooms of this empty summer cottage. When he came after her and caught her, she said, "Yes, here. Do anything you want to me anywhere you want."

Need met need. "I've never felt that before, what you do to me," she said, "waves that don't stop."

She noticed that this man who spoke so scornfully of priests, who never went inside a church, who wouldn't tolerate the family icons in his bedroom, called on God and the Lord Jesus when he finished. "Oh, God!" he'd say. "Oh, God! Oh, God! Oh, Jesus!"

Afterward, in the calm, she asked him what that meant, that he called on God during his ecstasy.

"Maybe because I'm sick," he said.

He kept reminding her that he had a fever. Perhaps, she thought once more, he knows that when he's better we'll separate and he'll lose me.

Sick or not, he was at her again. And again. In the middle of the third night, the tension in her head exploded and her nose started bleeding.

"Look," she said. "I have a nosebleed!" She was proud of it.

In the morning, she'd try to recover her aloof superiority.

"We ought to be getting back to the city," she said.

He didn't answer. She didn't press her suggestion.

During the fourth day, she found the small lump, a mound of fat and flesh, in the middle of his back. It was a bullet, he told her. "Why don't you have it taken out?" she asked. "It doesn't bother me," he said. "Also it reminds me." "Of what?" "That I owe a bullet." "To whom?" He shook his head, would not say.

When he slept, he dreamed. "She is America," he said to Isaac, his father. "I lost her. Now I have her again."

He realized Althea had been listening. He wouldn't explain whom he'd been talking to or what he'd meant.

"I'm all in your hands," she blurted in the darkest hour of their last night. "I belong to you." Later, cool again, she regretted saying that. She didn't want to be in anyone's hands again.

She determined to put distance between them.

On the way to the railroad station, when he spoke to the taxi driver, she realized that the manner of his speech embarrassed her. She didn't take his arm when they walked into the station. When he reached for her hand, she slipped it free as soon as she could.

Did he notice?

They sat side by side in the train. She looked out the window, trying to understand what had happened. One feeling she was able to identify: anger at Müller. She kept thinking of her time with him, going over and over her humiliation. "You got rid of him for me," she said to Stavros. Not out loud.

But as for the rest of it, she found she was being devoured by this illiterate man, even when he wasn't touching her or looking at her. It was too much. She was relieved that whatever had been happening with him was about to finish. Penn Station would be the end, that would be that!

"You belong to me now," he said as they left the train.

She gave him a quick smile but didn't answer.

Stavros knew that the decisive moment was coming—either there, in the station, or later, when he'd taken her home so she could resume her daily routine and he his.

"Thank you," she said when they stood at arm's length under the vault of Penn Station. People hurried past on their way to their regular lives. "I want to see you every night from now on," he said to her, putting it as plainly as he could. He waited for her answer.

She dropped her eyes and laughed nervously.

Finally she managed to get back to her apartment alone and to the security of her job. She'd been ill, she explained. "You certainly lost weight!" her boss told her. "You're so pale," her closest colleague observed. "Soak a cloth in tea and put it under your eyes," another friend suggested. They were glad to have her back, and Althea, now at ease, felt freed of an embrace that had been much too tight, one where more was being sought of her than she wanted to give. She'd been losing herself, she thought.

Myself! she thought. *Whatever that is.*

Yet as she went about her day's work she recalled that rhythm of ecstasy she'd known, the waves like those of the sea. Those memories persisted all through her day, like the waves themselves, ever returning.

Stavros went back to Sarrafian Brothers. "I had small troubles, few days," he said to Mr. Morgan Perry. "Business matters."

"What kind of bowlegged business matters could you have had more important than holding your job here?" Perry asked.

Stavros grinned, daring Morgan Perry to fire him. He almost said, "Fucking your dear daughter is what bowlegged business," but he realized, at that moment, that he was not supposed to talk about Althea, that their relationship was a secret.

I wonder if she'll tell him, he thought. *Well, she'll have to soon, she'll have to.* But the very thought that Althea might find it difficult, might even hesitate, made him angry.

He recalled that coming back on the train, she'd sat as close to the window, away from him, as she could slide, and that she'd looked out the window all the way home.

What had she been thinking? Was she embarrassed to be with him? That thought came like a flash.

"Family business; means none of your business," he said to Morgan Perry. He was ready, even eager, for a fight at last.

But Freddie came up and they shook hands. Freddie had been standing close enough to hear "family business," and he knew it had to be more than a routine family matter. Stavros had been absent five days.

Didn't Freddie suspect that Stavros's absence might have something to do with Althea? Apparently not, no sign of that.

When Stavros went home, Eleftheria was not there. They'd not heard from her and they were worried. He told them all—Seraphim, Eleni, Fofo, and the old lady, though Vasso did not listen and may not have heard— not to concern themselves further about Eleftheria. She'd done what she wanted; it was her fate and it was all right with him. Then he told them that all of them could do what they wanted now, whatever that happened to be. "I'm not your father," he said. "No more. Finish, that!"

He was pleasant, even kind. He smiled at them all, kissed his mother, and left the apartment.

Althea had stayed at the social services office to finish reports that her five-day absence had left undone. It was past eleven when she got home.

He was waiting outside her building.

She was surprised to find that there was no question in her mind what she would do. She took him in.

Early the next morning, she saw that his face had tightened; he said, "Tell him new situation here."

"It's too early," she said.

"Call him," he commanded.

She didn't move.

"All right," he said. "I tell him. In the office. In front of everybody."

She didn't speak, went to make coffee.

He came up behind her and spoke softly. "Althea," he said, "please do me favor. Tell Freddie, finish the business. Sooner or later—why not?"

She still hesitated, but finally she called Freddie at home and told him what had happened. "Yes," Stavros heard her say, "I'm probably seeing him again tonight."

"Probably!" Stavros said to himself. "Probably!"

When she hung up, he asked her, "What Freddie say?"

"Nothing," she answered. "He'd stepped out of the shower and hadn't turned it off."

"He must have said something. No? Something?"

" 'Oh!' he said. 'I see,' he said. Things like that."

"That's all?"

"What's the problem? You don't believe me?"

He went into the bathroom. "Don't be damn fool, lose your temper now," he scolded himself. "She's good girl."

When he came out a moment later, he kissed her. "I believe everything you tell me," he said. It was part hope, part truth.

She responded with a smile and a shrug.

He rushed home to change his clothes. The old lady was in her chair, bending over to watch the life in the street, more stooped now. Was she aware that there'd been defections in her family? Or was she resigned? Had she given up?

Still he wondered, had Althea been telling him the truth? He didn't want to be suspicious of her, but he was. He remembered again how she'd sat in the train, shunning him. And just now, when he'd left her place and she'd come into the doorway to say goodbye, a neighbor from across the hall had come out of his apartment to go to work. "Hello, Althea," he'd said. She'd closed the door quickly without answering, leaving him in the hall with the stranger.

Why had she jumped back and closed the door that way?

One thing at home heartened Stavros. Since the Zymaris incident, Seraphim had changed for the better. He had put on weight with grace, was dressing more carefully, his hair trim, his shoes shined. He looked what he was, a merchant beginning to prosper.

"I want to talk to you," Seraphim said. "Sometime, maybe. Soon?"

"Sure, why not?" Stavros said. "Everything all right with the store?"

"Oh, yes, O.K. now," Seraphim said. "No hurry. Soon. Personal problem." For the first time it occurred to Stavros that Seraphim could make good on his own.

On the way downtown in the bus, Stavros thought: *Suppose the situation was reversed, suppose I was where Freddie is now, out in the cold. What would I do?*

"*Aman, aman!*" he said out loud, shaking his head.

No one had ever stolen a girl from Stavros because he'd never taken the chance of having a steady girl. But if he had, and another man had stolen her, even a close friend, and this close friend had just left the bed of this woman and they'd met the next morning . . . !

But Freddie was another piece of goods. Stavros couldn't imagine what Freddie would do, but what he didn't expect was that he'd do absolutely nothing beyond what he did every other day. Freddie smiled, said, "Good morning," and when he sent one of the porters out for coffee as he always did, he sent out for Stavros too as he always did. Stavros waited for Freddie to acknowledge in some way that there'd been a shift in their relationship, but to judge from his behavior, there hadn't been. Freddie was still . . . Freddie.

"This is America here, damn fool," Stavros said to himself. "Civilization!"

At the same time he noticed that Freddie was very strong around the shoulders and thick through the chest; Freddie kept himself in shape. Stavros also observed that Freddie was very handsome—not less handsome than he'd thought; more. There was, above all else, an enduring confidence about him, the confidence of a race and a class in command; their world was the only world—it couldn't be shaken by the erratic behavior of one female person.

So Stavros waited. Toward the end of the morning, Freddie said, "Why don't we eat lunch together," a question put as a statement, and Stavros nodded and Freddie passed on. But that, of itself, had no significance; they often ate lunch together.

This time Freddie took Stavros—surprise!—to the Williams Club. On the walls of the dining room was history—group photographs of the football teams down the years, all boys with the same look Freddie had, perfectly fit, perfectly trustworthy, perfectly confident. Along the bottom of each picture was the year of the team and its record against Amherst and Wesleyan.

That room made Stavros an outsider.

Through the meal—Swiss steak—Freddie talked about Williamstown, how beautiful the mountains were in the fall of the year ("We'll drive up sometime") and how dramatic the breakup of winter was in the valleys below. He hadn't appreciated the place, Freddie said, when he was there, but now he realized what it had meant to him. He spoke about his fraternity, Zeta Psi, and when Stavros asked, explained what a fraternity was. Yes, they were most certainly snobbish, he said, but he also had to acknowledge that some of the happiest times he could remember had taken place at the Zeta Psi house.

Stavros wondered, *Why's he telling me all this?*

Freddie ordered dessert and coffee. "Try the blueberry pie," he said to Stavros. "It's very good this time of year."

Stavros said, "I was there when Althea talked with you this morning."
Freddie said, "I know."

"Well," Stavros said. "You mad?"

"No," Freddie said. "I mean, she's Althea after all, isn't she? Still experimenting. With life, with everything. You're part of that. Don't you really think? No comparison intended, of course, please don't misunderstand this, but it's the same as her interest in social work among the poor. How long will that last? She's said it so many times herself: She wants to try everything she hasn't been able to in her sheltered life. Her people are very strict, you know. Well, you've seen Mrs. Perry."

"Old man Perry used to fuck Miss Barton, every Saturday afternoon, you know that?"

"No. Really? Well, well! Still, with their daughter they were very strict."

"And this Mrs. Perry, tell you the truth, I close my ears, look the way she moves her *golo*"—Stavros slapped his behind—"she's a belly dancer I knew in Constantinople."

Freddie laughed. "Yes, she's a card, all right," he said. "By the way, has Althea told them about you?"

"Not yet," Stavros said.

"But she intends to?"

"Sure, what you think?"

"What do I think? I think her behavior is still a bit of a shock to her parents, considering how she was raised. When I first began seeing Althea, it was home by ten, weekends eleven-thirty."

The waiter brought the pie and poured the coffee.

"Thank you, Russ," Freddie said.

The waiter presented the check, face down on a small silver tray. Freddie reached for his Waterman pen and signed.

"Much oblige, Mr. Farrow," the waiter said, and left.

"She'll come to her senses one of these days," Freddie went on, as if he hadn't been interrupted. "I mean, I understand perfectly well what this is—it's like that other incident, with Maestro Müller. She's a curious child finding out what goes on in the grown-up world. A little late, but oh, you kid! You saw how long Müller lasted!"

Stavros noted that the blueberry pie was staining Freddie's tongue a rich blue.

"The attraction of opposites again—you know how long those last. I don't have to tell you, do I, because you're a very mature and experienced man."

"No; tell me."

"She'll return to me one day, she's said so herself, in fact, she's asked me to wait for her." Freddie smiled. "I'm sorry," he said, "that we both have to go through all this."

The hamal had an impulse to overturn the table. Instead he said to himself, "This is civilization, you better get used to same."

"You see what I mean?" Freddie said. "I do hope so, because I don't want to lose your friendship. It's been one of the most interesting friendships I've ever had—your stories about life in Constantinople, for instance. But since we're talking about it now, I feel obliged to tell you the truth."

"Yeah, the truth, that's what I want to hear," Stavros said.

"The truth is that in the end she will do the same thing to you that she's done to me. Twice now. But I will be there to pick up the pieces, because I have more of a certain kind of character. It's just a matter of self-control until that day comes."

"But now—last few days—what you think?"

"I don't think her connection with anyone now, including—yes—me, could be faithful. She's looking over life's possibilities. Let her look, say I. She has a right. Personally, I admire her for it. It's reckless, of course, but it's a passing thing, a phase. You will be a very interesting episode in her life when she looks back."

"That's all?"

"You asked for the truth. It's what they call an infatuation. A fling. Enjoy it while it lasts, my friend. And we'll see."

"What do you feel, Freddie? Tell me."

"I just did. I'm going to wait her out," Freddie said. He looked at Stavros steadily and calmly. Then he looked at his wristwatch. "We'd better go," he said. "Lunch always takes longer here."

Back at the store, Freddie was all smiles. But he left early, well before closing time.

When Stavros called Althea at the end of the day, she told him to come late. "Freddie rang up," she said, "and asked to see me to talk things over. What could I say?"

"You could say no," Stavros replied.

"He's so nice, Freddie," Althea said. "And I was so abrupt with him this morning. He told me he had a very good talk with you, though he did all the talking, he said; you hardly opened your mouth. He doesn't seem upset at all. Did you think he was?"

"I don't understand these people."

"Well, let's see what happens."

"You want me come over tonight or what?"

"Stavros, are you jealous?" She laughed. "It sounds as if you're jealous."

"If you don't want me to come, I don't come."

"Shut up, silly. Come about eleven. O.K.?"

Actually, it turned out well; Stavros had a chance to talk to Seraphim. His brother had a couple of proposals to make.

"The name of the company," he said, "Topouzoglou Sons. For these Americans here, impossible to say. Things are difficult enough without that."

"You want to call it what?"

"The Anatolian Oriental Rug and Carpet Company Incorporated," Seraphim said. "Sound big!"

"I think it over," Stavros said. "Let you know."

"Also something else," Seraphim said. "My name. Impossible. I want to change it. Seraphim! What the hell is that? Here?"

"It's the name your father gave you."

"On the other side, he give it. Over there people don't laugh when they say it. This is problem for me, Stavros, not you. No 'I think it over' business on this. I am changing my name. Finish!"

"To what?"

"Sam. Sam Arness. That's my name."

"Hey, you—come on, you!"

"That's my name now on. I want success here. Sam Arness!"

There was nothing Stavros could say. The truth was that Seraphim's —Sam's—assertiveness took a load off his shoulders. As he walked to Althea's place, he felt freed of responsibility.

"Well?" he said when she opened the door. "What happened?"

"What do you think?"

Stavros flopped on the bed, pushed off his shoes and stretched out. "He try to jump on you?" he said, as a joke.

"How did you know?"

"Did he?"

"He took it for granted."

"And? So? What happened?"

"Look!" She showed him a dark blue mark on the soft place just above the elbow of her left arm. "I tried to be as easy on his feelings as I could, but he's damned strong and pretty angry too, no matter what he told you. Did he really take you for lunch at the Williams Club?"

"What an icebox, that place! So? What happened?" He touched the bruise on her arm. Then he said with more surprise than anger, "Son of a bitch, huh?"

She sat on the edge of the bed, leaned over, and kissed him. "They don't allow women there at lunch," she said. "So I never got to be taken there."

"So what happened? Huh? He really tried for it?"

"Why are you so surprised? Come to think of it, what else could he do?"

She reached behind him, lifting him up enough so that she could help him off with his jacket. "He'd been drinking all afternoon." She laughed as she loosened his tie, then undid the buttons of his shirt.

"What you laughing?"

"He's reversed the situation, hasn't he?"

"What situation?"

"Ours. It's your move now, sir!" She laughed again, a sort of excitement.

"My move? O.K."

She pushed the shirt off his chest, then off his shoulders. "We've got to give him time to digest this," she said, unbuckling his belt. "Meantime just act the way he acted. Nothing to get excited about and so on."

She pulled his pants down and off, taking the socks with them.

"Wait a minute," he said. "What's your hurry?"

"I've been waiting all day," she said. "Don't be mad at him. He's a decent guy and this is tough on him. Very!"

Stavros said nothing.

"Get into bed," she said. "I've been cold all day. Warm it up for me. Go on, get in."

He pulled off his underpants, slid between the sheets, then reached for the bed light.

"Leave it on," she said. "I like to look at you. Your skin, it's so smooth everywhere except—I'm sorry about this." She touched the little mound of fat and flesh under his shoulder blade. "That bullet hurt?" she asked.

"After so many years? No. Leave it alone. You didn't tell me what happened with Freddie."

"I did."

"Not exactly."

She kissed the place where the bullet was. She was the first woman he'd ever allowed to touch him there.

"Did he say bad things about me?" she asked, as she pulled off her dress.

"He said you're experimenting with me. Don't."

At the window, she drew the shade down, then hesitated, pulled one edge away from the frame and looked down at the street.

"What you looking?"

"He's out there."

"Where?"

"On the steps of that publisher's across the street. Come here."

"I don't want to see him."

"Poor guy," she said.

She released the shade, then sat on the edge of the old Morris chair and undid the garters of her garter belt.

"You didn't tell me what happened with Freddie," he said.

"It takes a lot of energy to hold that man off," she said. "He's very strong."

He watched her. "He better not come up here," he said.

"Oh, he wouldn't do that, not Freddie. He wouldn't think it right."

Standing, she pulled the garter belt around so the clasp was in front, and undid it.

"He's hurt and can't really believe he is," she said, pulling off her pink bloomers. "Imagine yourself in his shoes."

"I'd come up here quick," he said. "Quick!"

"I know." She ran, holding her breasts, and jumped into bed, covering Stavros and herself with the sheet. "He's always been the most admired and the most—actually he was voted that: Most Likely to Succeed. It's in the class yearbook—he showed it to me. But it didn't make him proud, it worried him. You see, the only way he can take this is to pretend he's above the whole thing. At the same time, he's out there—poor guy!"

"Teach him good lesson," Stavros said.

She hugged Stavros hard, kissing him, but he didn't respond.

"Don't be mad at me," she said. "I haven't done anything disloyal."

"You don't tell me—how far he get?"

"How far? With what?"

"With it. With you. How far? You said he tried and—"

"He got nowhere. Shut up about that. I belong to you now. Come on, don't turn your head away. I've been waiting all day for you. Stavros!"

"Tell me first, how far? Exactly."

"He threw me down on the bed and held me there. That's where I got the mark on my arm, I suppose. Then I laughed him out of it. It was the only way. He's strong."

"That kind strong means nothing. At night in a bad place, where anything goes, I'm stronger."

"I'm sure. You're so cute when you get mad."

"I'm not mad and I'm not cute."

"Then if you're not mad, what's the matter now? Does it make you nervous, him out there?"

"No. I hope he's there every night, all night."

"Then what is it? That 'experimenting' remark of his—that upset you? Suddenly you're cold to me. Nothing happened. He got nowhere. And listen—pay attention, Stavros. Look at me! I like you better."

"For tonight anyway."

"Tonight anyway, yes. What do you want me to say—forever?"

"I don't know. With you I don't know."

"If I say it, will you say it?"

"No."

"What would it cost you? Let's hear how it sounds. I'll say it first. Forever. There! Now you say it."

"No. Not tonight. Not yet tonight."

"Oh! It's moved. At last." She took it in her hand. "You mean thing. Where've you been?"

She got on top of him, straddling him.

If he suspected she was trying to reassure him, he didn't care.

Later, when she saw he was about to fall asleep, she slipped out of bed, tiptoed to the window, raised the shade high, then the window itself. She stood there looking out, perfectly framed against the night.

"He still there?" Stavros said.

"Yes."

"Where?"

"Where he was, sitting on the steps. There's somebody with him now, talking. You think they're talking about us?"

"With you standing there naked, sure that's what. What the hell you doing there?"

"He can't see. It's dark in here."

He got out of bed and went to the window and looked out at Freddie. Then he touched her on both hipbones, pulling her gently back to him.

"What?" she said.

"Bend over," he said. "Come on. It's my move now. Bend over."

She did.

"Now look at him."

"No."

"Yes. Now. Look at Freddie! Look at Freddie! There! Now I'm experimenting too. Hm? Huh? You belong to me now, hah? Tell me. Say it."

"Yes, I belong to you. Yes. Don't stop. I do. I do."

Later, in bed, she put her arms around his middle—he was asleep long before she was—and pulled his hard round buttocks into her dark place. "Oh, God, how I take to you!" she said. "What am I going to do? How can I escape?"

The next morning she made him breakfast; she'd bought rolls on the way home the night before, and bitter English marmalade.

"When'll you tell your mother?" he asked. "And Mr. Morgan Perry?"

"Give me time on that one," she said.

"What you need time for? What's the problem?"

"Don't push me on that, Joe," she said. When she was mad, she'd call him that, Joe. But then she regretted her tone, and said, "I bought a toothbrush for you here."

"All right, I brush my teeth," he said. "Then I figure out what I say to your dear father. I'll do it myself. Mustn't hurt his feelings—everybody sensitive except me, right? So how about this? Dear Mr. Morgan Perry, come in, sit down, something to drink, please? My father unfortunately not here but I will explain our side this problem, so listen carefully, dear sir, I beg you. I have announcement. I been you know with your daughter, lucky girl, very nice, and now, next step naturally, I must make up my mind, if agreed by my father and permitted by her father, you, Mr. Perry, then I should marry her. But before my family takes this important step, we must ask two things: First, how much dowry comes with your daughter, dear Mr. Perry, how much you giving me take your crazy damn daughter off your hands, hah? What? Nothing! Deal's off! My friends, we are Anatolian people, we don't take woman without dowry. This is America, you say? Not for me, I have many other chances. Now second problem. Is she clean girl? High-class, clean? I understand from gossip, recent history, that famous man, he try her out, then show her the door. Don't forget that story, dear Mr. Perry. Remind your wife on that. We're not talking about absolute virgin here. Are we? If I take her off your hands, honored sir, who knows what he left inside, that heinie pimp. Oh, dear sir, dear lady, don't get mad. Only trying tell the truth."

"Oh, shut up," Althea said. Then she burst out laughing.

As he was leaving, Stavros said, "I don't want him up here again."

"You don't want what? Did I hear you right?"

"I don't want you to let him up here again. That's what I said."

"Was that an order?" she asked. "This is my place."

"You heard what I said?"

"I heard."

"O.K." He turned and left, closing the door. Then, before she could lock it, he came back in. "I know," he said, "I don't talk right. I don't understand how to talk to woman. Only bad ways. I'm brought up certain style, you know, boss of my family, so forth, nobody must get fresh with me. In that situation, I had to give orders, like a boss. I'm sorry I talk rough to you. I trust you. I want you to know that. O.K. Now I say it. Forever."

She laughed, threw her arms around him, and kissed him.

OCTOBER 1917

Fofo was waiting for him at the store. She looked rather happy, which was unusual for her. "Come I show you," she said. Seraphim, now Sam, watched from a distance, smiling. A secret was about to be offered to Stavros, one that Sam already knew.

Fofo led Stavros to the window where Silo, their Peloponnesian porter, was working on a rug. Stavros went reluctantly; he didn't like to observe Silo's work, first because it reminded him of Vacilli and his share of responsibility for Vacilli's death, second because Silo's work was so inferior to Vacilli's that he was reminded what a craftsman they'd lost when they'd lost Vacilli. He also didn't enjoy talking to Silo because the man was deaf.

"We want to get married," Fofo said. "Silo!" She raised her voice. "I'm talking to him about it now, so listen."

"Who wants to get married to who?" Stavros said. Then he understood and called out, "Sam!" then: "Seraphim! Come!"

"Silo and me," Fofo said. "We want to marry."

"What for?" Stavros said.

"What people get married for?" Fofo said.

"Nobody yet explain me that," Stavros said. "You talking real business here with me?"

"I'm asking you permission. I want to get married. To him."

Silo nodded, but kept working on the corner he was touching up.

"I resigned job head of family from you people," Stavros said. "Do what you want."

"I still want your permission. Sit down, we talk. Silo." She raised her voice. "Give my brother your chair. I bring you stool from the back."

"Seraphim!" Stavros called again, calling for help. Then he looked at Silo, who seemed in his usual frame of mind, neither happy nor unhappy. Having Stavros's attention, he tipped his work up to display it. Stavros shrugged. "Can't match original colors," Silo said, "these pieces."

Stavros dropped his voice, speaking to Fofo. "Vacilli could," he said.

"Vacilli is dead, may Jesus watch over his soul," Fofo said.

She was serious, Stavros realized, so he inspected Silo seriously for the first time. Here was a peasant of honest weave. But coarse, coarse!

Seraphim—Sam—came up. "What you want?" he said to Stavros.

"Situation here," Stavros said.

"I have customer," Sam said. "I know this situation. What can you do?" And he walked away.

Stavros looked from Silo to Fofo. "You know this man is common porter?" he whispered.

Silo, not hearing, but pleased by the attention, nodded.

"There's a disgrace on that?" Fofo asked. "You say many times, marry, marry—so here! What you expect I catch? Look at me, look at him."

Silo nodded.

Stavros, not knowing what to say, finally said the conventional thing. "He wants dowry?"

"A raise, maybe," Fofo said. "Like dowry. Instead of."

"Can he hear us?"

"Now? No," Fofo said. "But don't look at him that way. He's not stupid, he can read your face. Also think carefully. I warn you he has many chances with women." She raised her voice. "Silo!" she said. "Am I right? Many women like you. Am I right?"

Silo smiled and nodded. "Too many," he said, turning to Stavros. "But I only want Fofo—that's who I want."

So Stavros went ahead. "How much money you have?" he asked.

"In the bank?"

"Where else?"

Stavros had dropped his voice and Silo hadn't heard the question. So Fofo answered, "Three hundred twenty dollars. Talk loud."

Stavros shrugged. "Three hundred twenty is—"

"Three hundred twenty," Fofo said.

"You have piece land, something, family house, other side, something?" he shouted.

Silo smiled and said, "Nothing."

Stavros shook his head. "Nothing," he said. "He has nothing."

"I don't care," Fofo said on the edge of rage. "I want him. Don't try to stop me!"

"Fofo! Quiet!" Silo said, a sharp admonition, reinforced with a raised forefinger. "Don't talk to your brother that voice!"

Fofo's palm flew to her lips. Silo's command and this response impressed Stavros, but still he had to ask once more. Dropping his voice, he said, "Are you sure? He's a common porter."

"I'm sure. Don't lose him! Please! I beg you. One thing my life, I beg you."

"You like him like a woman?" Stavros whispered to his sister.

"Oh, yes. He hit me couple times, but what the hell, I like him."

"O.K." Stavros said.

"Good," Fofo said. "Now about the raise. Instead of dowry you have to give him raise."

Stavros gave his consent to this too, but did it in the manner of his model, Mr. Fernand Sarrafian.

"Tell him talk to Seraphim," he said.

"Why can't you just give Seraphim order to—" Fofo was terribly impatient now, but so was Stavros.

"Tell him talk to manager here, Sam Arness. Finish!"

Then Stavros went to Silo and embraced him, like a brother. "Man smells bad," he said to himself.

Later he told Seraphim to throw Silo another ten. "Could be worse," he said.

"Could be much worse," Seraphim said.

NOVEMBER 1917

Then there came "that dreadful Sunday," as Mrs. Morgan Perry tagged the day in her memory.

"Explain me," Stavros had said one morning, sitting at the alcove table waiting for Althea to bring him coffee. "I noticing your parents don't invite me."

"You know why not?"

"That's my question. Why not?"

"You're hard for them to swallow."

"Swallow? That much not necessary. Ever ask them their opinion on this?"

"I did, actually. Once."

"Once? Maybe. Maybe never."

"Are you calling me a liar?"

"Yes. I see your face." She turned toward the stove and the coffee. "Now you're hiding your face," he said. "Tell me why you don't ask them."

"Stavros, you're making a big something out of nothing."

"Not nothing for me. I'm being insulted. I'm going to find out what goes on here. Now. I buy them Sunday dinner. How 'bout that? Greek restaurant. Clean one. Pantheon. Forty-fourth Street, Eighth Avenue. What? Why not? We talk private, corner table, straighten everything out. Where's my coffee? What you saying?"

"I'll figure something out. The coffee is coming."

"You figure out nothing. This is third time I ask you this simple problem. So finish! Sunday. I buy dinner."

"He won't come into town on Sunday."

"Saturday then. Don't make problems here, Althea."

"She hates Greek food."

"When she taste Greek food, Mrs. Morgan Perry? Tell me that much."

"She doesn't have to taste it. She has her opinion: It's greasy. She's very wrongheaded. I promise you you'll like her less after you meet her."

"I already meet her and already I like her less. That's what I want fix up."

"Look, why don't we start by taking him to lunch, right here in town?"

"No. I made up my mind. We're going there. That's proper way, Greek style. Go to home girl's parents, you and me together. What the hell, they should have invited me already. What am I, nigger here? Their daughter take me to her bed, they don't ask me to their house, proper way? 'Come in, come in, welcome, glad to see you,' so forth."

His voice was pitched high, in imitation of a Greek woman welcoming a visitor through her front door.

"Stop acting, Stavros. Calm down."

"Why you don't want me meet your mother, hah?"

"Where did you ever get that idea?"

"I see your face. I understand what you're thinking. You don't want me—"

"All right. I give up. We'll go out there Sunday. I'll arrange it."

"Good! Mount what? Where they live. Mount something."

"Ivy. And you'll regret it."

"Don't worry. When I make up my mind act polite, everybody like me. I get new clothes too."

Whereupon Stavros Topouzoglou, known in the rug trade as Arness the Anatolian, also known as Joe the Hamal, went into a shopping frenzy. Every night he appeared at Althea's with packages containing clothing, items he'd hustled to buy in his lunch hour. They generally brought questions of taste to her mind. Whenever she challenged his choices, Stavros would answer, "Mr. Fernand Sarrafian wear exact same thing."

On Sunday morning he shaved twice. Into the tub, which he'd run hotter than usual, he dropped half a cup of her best salts, a first indulgence for him, and slowly lowered himself into the steaming water to plan the day ahead.

How would he present himself to Althea's mother? She was the one to win over. So, what to wear? The weather was still mild, so he chose his checked gray suit, a model as close as he could find on any rack to what Mr. Fernand had worn (his custom-tailored, of course) on his way to the track when he'd passed through town two months before. Stavros had taken the vest of the suit to a tailor and had him sew on the same cloth-covered buttons he'd admired on Mr. Fernand's vest.

Next question: shoes. Which? Black shoes, with which he could wear the spats he'd bought, or those others, gray suede uppers over black leather bottoms? He put on one pair, then the other, then a different shoe on each foot, and got up on a chair to look into Althea's bureau mirror.

"Wear your plain black ones without those damned spats," she yipped from the bed.

He decided on the suede uppers. "Latest thing," he said.

His most difficult problem was the collar. He'd bought wing collars of various heights to provide a base for the blue polka-dot bow tie such as Mr. Fernand favored. He tried these collars on, one after the other, finally asking Althea to get the hell out of bed and hold a hand mirror so he could judge from the side.

"Doesn't it cut into you?" she asked. "That wing collar?"

"Which one?" He was putting on a straight collar.

"All of them. Daddy gave them up."

"Mr. Fernand not."

"That's better. Leave that straight one on. It looks better on you too."

He pulled off the straight collar and ripped it in two, then picked up a wing collar and his polka-dot bow tie. "Tie this for me," he said, handing it to her.

"I've never known how. Why don't you wear an ordinary up-and-down tie?"

He pulled the bow tie out of her hand. "Never mind. I do it," he said. "You criticizing me on everything today."

"Sweetheart, precious, sugar, we don't need to leave until eleven o'clock. We have to have breakfast first, for instance, then—"

"I'm going out, get shine."

"You've got a shine. Your shoes are blinding."

"I know what you want," he said. "I should look like hamal."

He came back from the shoeshine parlor an hour later, a yellow rose in his buttonhole.

He carried his father's cane when they left, and inside his pocket, the snapshot of Isaac taken with Chrysostomos, the archbishop of Smyrna, which he planned to show Mrs. Perry. He was sure it would impress her.

On his head, he tipped a derby lined with red satin.

"You're going to wear that?" she demanded. "To Mount Ivy?"

"Why not? People there out of date? What's the matter with my derby hat, hah?"

"I don't dare say."

"Why you don't put your blue dress? Go 'head, put your blue dress. Proper style this situation."

"You always want me to wear that dress. It's not the only good dress I have, you know."

"I seen the others. They make you look like some kind fast filly."

"Your derby makes you look like a racetrack tout."

But she put on the blue dress. And so, on this beautiful fall day, they caught the ferry at the foot of Forty-second Street, bound for the Jersey shore and the Lackawanna Railroad. It was a kind November so they leaned over the rail and studied the great river pouring south between the city and the cliff.

"This is the first Sunday since Atlantic City," Althea said, "that you haven't made love to me"—she kissed his cheek—"morning, noon, and night."

He frowned, took off his derby, patted his hair down. "You brought my comb?" he asked.

"I miss you," she said. "I miss you even when I'm with you."

Stavros, recovered from the beating in Atlantic City, had returned to full vigor. He delighted in Althea, wanted her every time they were in the same room, and soon she was ready for him whenever and wherever they were. Which is how he wanted her to be—always his, always open.

He loved to watch her undress, to lie back on the bed in the posture of what she sometimes called him, "Pasha," his arms folded under his head and a greedy look on his face, lips pouting, as he watched her take off garment after garment, revealing his treasures. He was enraptured by her white skin and her long straight legs—he'd never seen legs so white, so slim, and so perfectly turned.

She reveled in his admiration, played up to it, undressing more slowly than she did when she was alone, prolonging it every way she could.

Once when she'd stayed in the shower for what he thought was much too long, he went in after her, fondled her under the fall of water, then pulled her out and threw her on the bed. They did it soaking wet. She still remembered those moments, and sometimes stayed in the shower longer, hoping to arouse him again to that pitch of violence.

He encouraged her to be aggressive. She'd never before been that demanding with a man. She knew very well that sex was the one sure bridge between them.

They'd done it once, as the impulse overtook her, in the stacks of the neighborhood library. The head librarian at her desk on the ground floor, hearing sounds strange to her, sent for the janitor. "I think there's someone hurt in the stacks," she said to the old Serb, who'd been mopping the floor with ammonia water. He went off, grumbling, to where he'd been told. By the time he arrived, the lovers were leaning against a wall of books, breathing hard and resting.

Incidents like that recurred. Often they had to do with danger, running the rim of risk, along the border of what Althea called "hamal land." Increasingly they were efforts to shock members of the society around them. Sometimes it seemed they were asking to be caught.

She participated in these vengeful impulses as eagerly as he did. More and more often, she initiated them. In their imaginations there were two particular targets: Althea's parents. The lovers were partners in revenge, she on her mother, he on her father.

Often she felt a strange thing during these errant and bizarre incidents: She imagined that her mother was there, witnessing them.

Once when she'd been invited to a bridal shower for a college chum and knew that her mother was to be present, Althea brought Stavros along. On that occasion, Mrs. Perry gave Stavros an elite freeze. Althea paid her back. She'd had three tulip glasses of champagne, or she would not have taken Stavros up the stairs on the pretext of showing him the details of the fine old house where the celebration was taking place, then, quickly, slipped into the bathroom and pulled him in after her.

Everybody with any experience of life—this included Mrs. Perry— could see what had been going on when Stavros and Althea came down together, holding hands, to rejoin the celebrants.

When the train arrived at Mount Ivy, they found the day so agreeable that they walked to the First Presbyterian Church where they were to pick up Morgan Perry and ride home with him.

"Glad to see your father, at least, go to church on Sunday," Stavros said.

"Suddenly you've become too, too respectable," Althea said.

"My father, every Sunday, in the church. Used to be."

"Not this one's idea," Althea said. "My mother's a member of the parishioners committee and she insisted—oh, did she ever insist—that her husband do what the other committee women's husbands do: take a Sunday school class. Also, and not so incidentally, it was my mother's device to keep her man on the straight and narrow. You can't teach the Bible with a load of booze in your belly."

"I don't like the way you talk about your parents. You don't show respect."

"I don't mind my father," Althea said.

He looked at her from a high moral plateau and quickened his pace.

They entered the Georgian parish house. It had a basketball court, mostly below ground level, which was used for dances. Above were executive offices for Dr. Kenworthy, his assistant, and his secretary, as well as a large reception room. On top, dormers provided light and air for a row of classrooms where the Sunday school classes were convened.

Althea went straight to the room where her father was holding his class. They could hear him through the door, explaining the differences between—he ticked off the names—Presbyterians, Methodists, Episcopalians, and Baptists.

Althea opened the door. Morgan Perry sighted her over his shoulder and nodded. When he looked down, Althea noticed the open book in his lap.

Perry lifted his head. "The Presbyterian Church," he declared, "is traditionally Calvinistic."

Althea reached back, pulled Stavros into the room, and pushed him toward the rear of the classroom.

Perry's eyes, red-rimmed, confronted Stavros.

"Continue, continue, Mr. Perry," Stavros said. "Don't worry, I sit here quiet and listen everything. Hello, boys and girls."

Morgan Perry had lost his place in the book. Now he found it. "The theological system of Calvin and his followers . . ." He turned a page, lifting his head quickly to see what Stavros was up to, and Stavros favored him with a fat smile. ". . . emphasizes the doctrine of predestination, limited atonement, total depravity, and the irresistibility of sin."

Then he slammed his heavy palm down on the desk. The class, which had been laughing, was silent.

"Shshsh!" Stavros said.

Althea knew the signs. Her father's straining face was fish-belly gray, his eyes blood-soaked. "Father, what you mean is—" she started to say.

"Please don't march into our room like that, Althea," Morgan Perry said. "There's a Bible class going on here."

"We be quiet like two mice, don't worry, Mr. Perry," Stavros said. "Go on, boys and girls, pay attention to Mr. Perry. Sit down here quiet, Althea."

"Why don't you take your gentleman, Althea—it will be at least another half hour—and show him the church. If he's interested."

Stavros got up, awarded the class a sort of bow, and strode out of the room. If his feelings were hurt, he controlled them.

"Absolutely soused last night," Althea whispered as she shut the door.

"I notice every chance you get you insult that man," Stavros said. "Now remember, we control ourselves today."

In the church, Dr. Kenworthy and Mrs. Bryant, his director of music, were following their custom: After each Sunday's service, they'd perch side by side on the edge of the organ's bench and play four-handed Bach. Here and there in the hall, a few people sat listening. In the front row, Mrs. Bryant's husband, Chief Dan Bryant of the Mount Ivy police, waited, arms folded, head and neck stiffly erect.

Althea and Stavros walked slowly back along the rows of pews. The floor sloped gracefully up. The pews, made of several kinds of wood, had recently been polished; they glistened. The windows of colored glass looked as if they'd found inspiration in the illustrations of children's books.

"Cost plenty money, church like this," Stavros said. "Very high-class!"

"Here. These stairs lead to the balcony, where we can sit and listen to the organ." As they climbed the stairs, she continued: "Sorry Father was rude to you. Imagine that man teaching Bible!" From the balcony they could see the devout musical couple at the organ, but not the people scattered about the floor, listening. "And our dear Dr. Kenworthy," she went on, "look at him! Playing a Bach devotional with his knee smack up against Mrs. Bryant's, and her husband, that gross cop, in the front row looking like a public statue representing righteousness. I always want to release a horse fart in this holy atmosphere."

"Althea, I don't want to hear these dirty ideas here. This is church."

They'd come to a heavily carpeted open space behind the balcony's four rows of pews.

"What a fake you are," she said. "No more religion than a rabbit." She knelt quickly. "You know," she said, "down here, no one could possibly see us." She pulled at his arm.

"Get up, Althea. Last time I'm telling you behave yourself! Get up!"

She did. "You don't want to mess your suit, is that it?"

She pulled his body against hers and kissed his mouth. "No response," she said. "A piece of refrigerated liver has more warmth. Where's my hamal boy hiding today?"

"I see you gone crazy suddenly," Stavros said. He turned and hustled to the stairs.

Althea smiled.

Mrs. Morgan Perry's specialty was Manhattans on Sunday at one. She made them by the quart in a cut-glass pitcher and they were eighty-twenty strong.

Stavros was surprised at their strength. "This is for *levendis,* this drink you make here, Mrs. Perry," he said, plucking up his trousers crease before he crossed his legs.

"Why, thank you very much," she replied, laughing. Stavros could see that she'd made up her mind to be cordial. "A very graceful compliment indeed. Hear that, Morgan?"

Morgan Perry grunted, sipped on his drink, blinked his eyes.

"What does it mean, sir?" she asked. "Leh . . . what?"

"*Levendis.*" Stavros made a gesture with his fist. "Like a cannon inside."

"She's trying to get you drunk, Stavros," Althea said, "so your vicious side will reveal itself."

"Don't pay any attention to her, Mr.— But then it's hardly likely that you any longer do, having been together for . . . for how long?"

"Seven weeks," Althea said. "Actually," she went on, turning to Stavros, "this is the one day of the week Mother doesn't mind if Father gets tanked. After all, he has all afternoon and all night to sleep it off."

Mrs. Perry sighed and turned to Stavros. "So you haven't been able to control her manners, either," she said.

"I control her very good later," Stavros said. Then he turned to Althea, raised a forefinger, and said, "That's enough now, Althea. Finish!"

"That's the way to treat 'em," Morgan Perry said. "Rough!"

"She's getting a little crazy when she come here," Stavros said to Mrs. Perry. "But I control her, don't worry." He gave his hostess his best smile. He was sure they were getting along. "I see you drinking same thing," he said.

"My mother was Welsh," she said. "Welsh women drink, Mr.— Particularly our family. And will you, in the name of all that's decent, help me with your name?"

"Call me Arness," Stavros said. "Not correct name, but easy to say. Other name, Topouzoglou, impossible for American people. So Arness. Say it.

"Arness."

"Wonderful! Now, I'm glad you mention your family here. I came to talk to you about my family. Because when you look at me, you see only what you see. Not much, maybe, but—" He reached into his inside pocket and carefully brought out the snapshot Achilleas had brought for the family. It was the kind made by quick-job, sidewalk photographers along the Kordon of Smyrna. "I want you realize I come from good family. Here is my father, photograph, you see. Here, take it."

"Which one is he?" Mrs. Perry said, looking at the snapshot.

Stavros laughed, completely at ease now. "The priest is my father's friend, Chrysostomos, archbishop of Smyrna. Fine man, will be saint someday, guarantee. Father small one there, Isaac Topouzoglou."

"Well, well, very interesting. Here, Morgan." She handed the photograph to her husband. "Isaac, you say? So you're of the Jewish faith? Althea didn't tell me." She sipped at her drink.

"No, no, what you talking, Jewish? Greek. Anatolian Greek. Only true Greeks. We keep our women by ourselves when Turks come. In Greece, mainland, they mix up—who knows who's what over there?"

"I see, yes. The women of Wales are said to have rebuffed the English soldiers too."

"That's one thing you can never be sure of, the behavior of women when we men are not on guard. Right, Joe?" Morgan Perry put the snapshot down on the table next to his chair and picked up his glass, drank it dry, and reached for the cut-glass pitcher.

"Remember what you promised, Morgan," Mrs. Perry said, and turned to Stavros. "So then, you're Turkish?"

"No. I just explain everything to you. You don't listen?"

"But your father's hat. I've seen that in the *National Geographic*. It's Turkish. They call it a—a what?"

"Fez. Correct. Our Greek Anatolians wear that because—"

"So they can slip in and out of Turkish society without being identified," Althea volunteered.

"Wait a minute," Stavros said. "That don't sound good."

"Well, you are a slippery race," Althea said, "based on firsthand evidence."

"Persecuted there five hundred years, what you expect? Also, Althea, I told you shut up, no? Hey, Mr. Perry! What you doing there?"

Morgan Perry had put his glass on top of the snapshot. Stavros leaped to his feet and pulled the photograph from under the glass. There was a wet circle on the face of the print. "Why the hell you don't look where you're— Excuse me, Mrs. Perry. Give me towel here, napkin, something."

The Perrys had an Irish pair in service, mother and daughter. The mother-maid had appeared with a small silver dish on which English soda crackers topped with a cheddar cheese spread had been arranged, and she was offering these around together with small embroidered napkins. Stavros snatched one of these to wipe off the picture of his father and the archbishop.

"You'll stain those napkins, Mr. Arness," Mrs. Perry said. "They're linen."

"Then get me towel," Stavros said. "Somebody—you, Althea, maid, somebody. Hey, maid, towel!"

The daughter-maid came in as her mother retreated to the kitchen; she was carrying another silver dish, this one containing assorted nuts, shelled and salted.

"Goddamn it," Stavros said. "Excuse me, here, Mrs. Perry. I can't get it off." He turned to Morgan Perry. "What's the matter with you? Why don't you look where you put your glass?"

"Say you're sorry, Morgan."

"I'm sorry," Morgan Perry mumbled, then shrugged and drained his glass. "All right, I'm sorry," he repeated. Then, as Mrs. Perry nodded approval, Stavros heard Perry grumble, "Just a damn snapshot, isn't it? After all."

"Althea," Mrs. Perry interceded quickly, "Mr. Arness should certainly be interested in seeing your childhood room. There you'll find the most exquisite dolls' house, Mr. Arness, a genuine Tailleur, hand-crafted in France. Microscopic details. Go on, Althea, take Mr. Arness away."

Stavros, waving the snapshot to dry the wet ring, glared at Morgan Perry, who said directly to him, "What's all the fuss about? It's not a Rembrandt, just a damned snapshot."

"Morgan!" Mrs. Perry said, and then quickly turned to Stavros. "This dolls' house, Mr. Arness, is absolutely unique. You won't find another like it anywhere, so there's no use looking. And the dolls it contains are completely out of the ordinary."

"What are you talking about?" Stavros looked at her and then at Althea.

"The dolls' house, dear," Althea said. "In my room."

"She wants us to go up there?"

"Yes. So why don't we?"

"Do Turkish people give dolls' houses to their girls?" Mrs. Perry asked. "Well, Althea, what are you waiting for. Take him to your room, dear. Remember, just to *your* room."

"Just to my room. Don't worry, Mother," Althea said. "I'll restrict the mad Greek carefully."

"Althea, you're a horrid girl. How could you?" She drained her glass. "How could I what?"

"Suspect me of such a thought. It's simply that I'm not sure Rhoda had the time to tend to everything upstairs this morning. I'm sorry about your snapshot, Mr. Arness, and so is Morgan, despite what you may have thought he said a minute ago. Morgan is sometimes a naughty boy on Sundays, he gets so pent up all week in that dusty store. Althea, what are you waiting for?"

As Althea pulled Stavros toward the stairs, they heard Mrs. Perry say to her husband, "Now, Mr. Morgan Perry, I'll have a word with you. If you don't mind!"

"Naturally they sleep in separate bedrooms," Althea said as they reached the second floor. "His is at the end, and she occupies what they call, with good reason in this case, the master bedroom. There."

Althea opened the door to her old bedroom, which was halfway between the rooms of her parents. "Lie on the bed and calm yourself," she said. "You're shaking."

He was trembling with rage. "They hate me," he said.

"God, you're so intense. Of course they hate you."

She flung him a towel and he proceeded to mop at the snapshot, but it was too late. The water ring was there for good.

"In the animal kingdom, which is where we are, strangers hate strangers. Like dogs when they meet. Humans the same. We're all full of hatred, it's got to come out. Take your feet off the bed."

Stavros didn't like the way she was giving him orders so his feet stayed where they were. On Althea's bed was a spread with a matching comforter, both printed with the same design—fairyland. Mrs. Perry's favorite country.

"Well, you know all about hatred," Althea said. "You even hate me when you make love to me. You should see your face then. It scares me —which, I suppose, is why it thrills me so much."

"She called me Jew."

Althea laughed. "You thought you'd walk in here and they'd fall all over you. Why did you believe they'd even like you? Only I like you. Don't you know that?"

"I get her yet, your mother."

"Oh, baby, dear little baby, give up." She got on the bed with him, stretching alongside. "Let's eat quietly, listen to their chatter and go back to our city. You're never going to—"

"I get that woman yet. I got idea how."

"You talk too much. I mean now. Close your eyes." She raised herself so that her face was over his and she kissed him. "What does it merit you, as the Bible says, if they do like you? It would be pretend, nothing more. Let's eat and go home." She ran her hand up and down his body. "I'm still mad at you, don't forget."

"Shut up, I'm thinking."

"Because this is the first Sunday you didn't make love to me and I'm awful mad and awful needy—Big Pasha, are you listening to me?"

"No. I didn't give up on these people yet."

"I spent my whole life with her and nothing I ever did made her like me and nothing she ever did made me like her. Can't you see that they can't take you? Oh! There! See! Good morning. Look, there's life there after all, even on blue Sunday."

"Leave it alone."

"I thought you said it belonged to me."

"Sometimes. Not now."

"No, now. We have time. While she's scolding the old man. Please, Stavros. I'll lock the door."

"There's no lock on that door."

"Oh, so you had the same idea."

"Stay away from me."

"I can't stay away from you."

"I'm thinking."

"That won't last long. Be like me. Be content to be disliked by every-one. Don't you know that we're both impossible? That's why you're stuck with me. Please, Stavros, I want you now," she whispered. "See there, what's happening? You want me too."

"Automatic with me. Means nothing. Leave me alone."

"No." She covered his face with kisses. "Please," she said.

"You're messing my tie."

She pulled it loose.

"Goddamn it, stop! What you doing there? Mother of God! What a woman!"

There was a knock on the door.

"What?" Althea barked. "What is it?"

"It's me, Althea. Mother."

Althea leaped off the bed and Stavros, coming off the other side, adjusted his clothing as he went to the mirror.

"Come in," Althea said, opening the door. "You don't have to knock. What did you think we were doing in here?"

"Fixing my tie better, Mrs. Perry," Stavros said. "Come in, come in, please. I been thinking about you. I made up my mind something and I will tell you now."

He flipped his hand away from his hip as if it were hinged there, did it twice, an Anatolian gesture of command. "Althea, go down talk to your father!"

Althea backed to the doorway, then decided to remain there, watching.

Mrs. Perry was briskly straightening out the bed. "This brass bed," she said, "is part of the family, the oldest thing in the house." She snapped the bedcover, then looked closely at the place where Stavros's feet had been.

"Mattress pretty hard; maybe brass too." Stavros made an unsuccessful joke.

"We Welsh don't like soft beds," she said, slapping at the place on the cover.

"I'm glad to see you take good care those things," Stavros said. "You seen Althea's apartment? Everything there, wrong places, clothes lying around—"

"Underwear on the floor and behind the bed," Althea interjected.

"So forth, so forth," Stavros went on. "But don't worry. I put my sister Eleni, she keeps everything very nice, teach Althea how take care house proper way."

"Stavros," Althea said from the doorway, "Mother has two maids working full time; that's why everything is so damned orderly here."

"Go downstairs, Althea. I told you that already. I want to talk to your mother here."

Mrs. Perry whirled the bedspread into a ball and threw it on the floor in a corner. "I might as well send the bedcover out for a good cleaning," she said. "Now we'll all go down, please. Poor Morgan is alone there. Oh, Althea, he's so ashamed and contrite. Like a little boy, so sweet. Bring Mr. Arness. Come!"

"Stavros, please," Stavros said. "Say Stavros."

"We're going to have a wonderful dinner. Your favorite, Althea, roast beef and Yorkshire pudding. Can you smell it, Althea?"

"Make my meat well done," Stavros said. "Greek men, they like—"

"An outside cut should do him, don't you think, Althea?"

"Forgive me. Sometimes maybe I talk too fresh, Mrs. Norma."

"My Irish father was a highly charged individual, Mr. Arness. I'm quite accustomed to a bit of arrogance in a man. Unless a man has some spark of temperament, even a threat of discord—within reason of course—he's not to my taste."

"Agree. American men too weak. You say, 'Morgan, shut up!' he shut up. You understand? No insult intended."

"Morgan on Sundays, that's another matter."

"But Greek men different. Every day."

"Yes, yes, I can certainly see that."

"Mrs. Perry, I don't know what happen, but your daughter, she's crazy about me."

"I know what happened," Althea said from the doorway.

"Althea, will you get the hell away from here? Go downstairs. Now!"

Althea backed out of their sight.

"Yes, yes, Althea," Mrs. Perry said. "Do what he says." She looked at the bed, now without its cover. "You two will stay off this after dinner, won't you?" she said.

"Mrs. Perry," Stavros said, "I like your daughter. Greek custom is talk to father of girl first, but I talk to you because I have idea you boss here. Right? Especially on Sunday. What you say, hah?" He laughed. "I want your daughter, Mrs. Perry. I have chosen her from many women. I want she make me baby, you understand?"

"What? What did you say?"

"No, no." He laughed. "That's what I wanted to explain. Everything legitimate, marriage, everything proper way, don't worry. I will make you family, Greek style, children who respect parents and grandparents, *yaya, papoo!* You will bless me one day."

"Is she pregnant now?"

"No, no, not yet." He laughed again. "That's why I wanted to explain everything. Legitimate. You're worried that I will one day find other girl, leave your daughter with big belly. Don't worry on that. My proposition to your family is high-class, best for her."

"Have you discussed this with Althea?"

"First you, then Althea."

"But, Mr. Arness, I'm sure that—"

"Stavros, please, call me." His voice dropped to a whisper and he held Mrs. Perry by the elbow so close that she could feel the heat of his breath on her cheek. "You understand because you're not damn fool, that Althea has some bad things in her past. But don't worry. I'm not old-fashion Greek *vlax* man. I understand modern customs. Past is past. I will take her as she is—if you give kind permission. Now, what's your answer my proposition?"

"Well, I really don't know what to say. Here you are expected to talk to the girl first. Have you?"

"That will not make problem. She will do what I say. She likes me!"

"So it seems."

"What do you mean, dear Mrs. Norma, 'it seems'?"

"Only that it does seem," she said, and stopped. "Come. I must bring you to the table. Beef is not improved by waiting, you know."

"Never mind beef. I'm not finished here." He held her by the elbow. "I know what else you're worried. Naturally. Because you're not damn fool, you're worried that I have no—"

"My elbow. You're squeezing my elbow, Mr. Arness."

He released her. "Thank you," she said, and left the room, brushing off the top of the extra chair with a sweep of her palm as she passed it.

Stavros hurried after her and caught her on the stairs. "Mrs. Norma," he started.

She didn't slow up, so he had to make another dash, circling around her to block her progress. "One more minute, please. Other natural thing you worried, I know very well too. You see I understand worries of mothers."

"Perhaps you should talk to Mr. Perry."

"No, you. I respect you. You're worried I have no money, right?" Astonished, she stopped. "You're smart to worry on that. I have very little, but that's temporary condition. In ten years, guarantee I will be richest man in rug market here, millionaire! I am only man Sarrafian Brothers who understands rugs." They were moving again, approaching the room where Mr. Perry and Althea were waiting, so he dropped his voice. "Mr. Perry good salesman," he whispered. "But he understands rugs, nothing! Nobody that store who speaks English understands rugs. I am only one with that combination. I grew up with a loom next to my bed where my sisters worked every day. I know how rugs are made and where, who makes them and how to tell value. I also speak English. Good."

This declaration amazed Mrs. Perry.

As they entered the living room, Althea and Morgan, who had been whispering, stopped.

"Morgan!" Mrs. Perry said, brightly. "Here is Mr. Arness. Now. Please."

"Yes, yes, I see. Well, Joe, I'm sorry about your father's picture. I may have sounded a bit sarcastic before—that's the Welsh in me. So let's forget the whole damned thing, shall we?"

"Next time be careful where you put your glass down," Stavros said.

"So," Mrs. Perry said with some relief. "Dinner! At last! Come, Althea dear." She hooked her arm in her daughter's. Her face was flushed. Stavros could see that he'd had a powerful effect on her, even though he wasn't certain what that effect was.

"What were you two talking about?" Althea asked.

"Mr. Arness has assured me a number of times that I'm not a damn fool."

"Be careful; he's pretty cagey and quite seductive. Believe only half of what he says. That's his charm."

"He also told me about his plans for you. That he wants to—well, a number of things, the first of which seems to be marriage."

"He's joking," Althea said.

"Half," Stavros said.

"Tell the other half," Althea said, "never, never, never!"

"Everybody has their plan," Stavros said. "Free country here, remember?" Then he turned to Mrs. Perry. "I didn't explain my plan to her yet; plenty time."

"Can we please put aside the jokes and eat dinner?" Mr. Perry said.

Mrs. Perry put her arm around her daughter's waist, and as they turned the corner into the dining room, Stavros heard her whisper, "You're not pregnant, in the name of God, are you, Althea?"

"By every sign, Mother, no. Of course not."

Then Mrs. Perry lost a little of her control and said loudly, "You're not going to marry him, are you? Him!"

"I have no such plan," Althea said.

Stavros looked at Althea and smiled. "I told you, Mrs. Norma, we don't discuss this problem yet."

"Well, don't you really think you should before you make announcements like the one you made upstairs? Don't you really think you should? Now sit down. No, there!"

"You worry too much, Mrs. Norma. Everything will happen like I want and like you want too. I explained all this to you. I understand your worries."

"Stavros feels," Althea explained, "that he owes that to me now. It's an old Anatolian custom. The man, if he is fairly young, adequately vigorous, and has some promise of advancement—all of which merits Stavros possesses—believes he is conferring a great favor on a woman when he offers to marry her."

"Correct!" Stavros said. "Very good, Althea."

Morgan Perry, already seated at the head of the table, said, "Let's eat."

"Then would you say grace, Morgan, the best you can. Now don't be angry, Morgan. That was a joke to lighten the atmosphere. So proceed."

"For what we're about to receive, O Lord, make us truly grateful. And it better be good. Amen."

"Oh, Morgan!" Mrs. Perry laughed, then turned to Rhoda, the mother-maid, who stood waiting in the kitchen doorway with her daughter, Rhonda, beside her, and said, "All right, Rhoda."

The dinner was served by a unique ritual of service in the most protracted fashion possible. Rhoda, the mother-maid, came out first, picked up the cold plate from in front of Mrs. Perry, carried it through the swinging white door into the kitchen, and came back with a warm dish, which she put in front of Mrs. Perry to replace the one she'd taken. The daughter-maid, Rhonda, then performed the same ritual before Althea. Then came the men's turn, plate by plate. There was a pause livened only by faint sounds of ladylike scuffling from the kitchen.

If Stavros was impatient, he was also impressed. He made up his mind that when he came into his wealth, he would have two maids and teach them this routine.

Mrs. Perry filled the silence. "Althea," she said, "you remember poor little Rose Barnaby? The treasurer of our garden club for so long? Surely you remember dear little Rose. Well, she—"

"Died," Althea said.

"Yes, poor dear, quite unexpectedly, no warning. We were very close, poor Rose and I."

"Mother is president of the Mount Ivy Garden Club," Althea explained to Stavros.

"Congratulations, Mrs. Norma," Stavros said.

"Rose did one final arrangement that—I was going to say deserved, and perhaps it did—the first prize for our fall meet. Actually it was quite a simple arrangement—some winter grass, sorrel, ground pine and one really exquisite sprig of what is to be pussy willow. That victory made Rose's life complete and happy at the end."

"Very nice, very nice," Stavros said.

Mrs. Perry went on speaking to her daughter. "We wanted to give her the first prize so I took second prize. I have a photograph of my arrangement if you'd care to have a look at it, Althea?"

"I like to look," Stavros said.

"Ah, here we come," Mrs. Perry said.

Rhoda came through the white swinging door from the kitchen carrying a six-pound roast of beef on a large silver platter. Rhonda followed with a pewter gravy boat awash with beef gravy thickened with flour.

Stavros, noting that Morgan Perry seemed to be in something of a fog, volunteered, "I carve, Mrs. Norma, if you want. What?"

"No, thank you, Mr. Arness. Morgan! Morgan!"

"Rhoda," Mr. Perry said, "I've told you time and time again this knife does not cut."

"Morgan!" Mrs. Perry exclaimed, as Rhoda ran out of the room. "Gently, gently."

"Well-done for Stavros," Althea said.

"There's no well-done on this roast," Morgan Perry said, "I hope."

"The end piece, then," Althea said. "Perhaps that will do."

"Do you mind waiting, my girl, until I've had a look at what's there? I haven't put a blade to it yet."

Rhoda ran in with another knife, and in good time, Morgan Perry cut off the end piece and held it up to Stavros. "Joe," he said, "is this satisfactory to you?"

Stavros wanted to be agreeable, but what he said was: "Greek men don't eat meat when there's blood showing. When you cook beef our way, Mrs. Norma, it takes all the grease out. I understand from your daughter you don't like greasy food. Or is it only Greek greasy food you don't like?"

"He may have you there, Norma," Mr. Perry said with a gruff laugh.

"Rare for me, please," Mrs. Perry said. "A few slices in, Morgan, if you will."

"And Althea? Your wish?"

"In even further."

"Do me favor," Stavros said. "Tell your women take end piece and give it some more fire."

"Of course," Mrs. Perry said. "In just a minute."

Rhoda had come in with a silver dish full of peas livened with tiny white onions and sprigs of parsley. Rhonda followed with another silver dish, containing a great mound of mashed potatoes. Both maids went slowly from one person to the next, starting with Mrs. Perry.

Stavros waited, a model of patience.

"Rhoda," Mrs. Perry said, "as soon as we've helped ourselves to the vegetables, take that end piece and put it back in the oven."

"No, no, no," Stavros said. "Put under fire, under gas fire—you have that here? You want me come in kitchen, show you?"

"Really, that won't be necessary, Mr. Arness."

"Burn it a little, Rhoda. I like taste of burnt meat, Mrs. Norma." Stavros still seemed convinced of his power to charm Mrs. Perry.

"Norma, we're not going to wait for him, are we?" Morgan Perry answered his own question by beginning to eat.

"Start, go on, enjoy yourselves," Stavros said. "I have some subjects to discuss here. You eat, I talk."

They all helped themselves to potatoes and peas and thick beef gravy and began to eat. Each of the women was dreading what Stavros would say next but not Morgan Perry. "Beef should be pink!" he said, challenging Stavros.

"I'm from other side," Stavros said. "Pink we don't eat."

"Probably a way of insuring that the meat has not spoiled, eh?" Mr. Perry said. "That it, Joe?"

"Do you have refrigeration in Turkey?" Mrs. Perry said.

"We bring ice down from Aergius, mountain with white top near our home. When I was boy, I did that. I went up with wagon and cut the ice. That's where I learned to work hard. Nineteen years old, I already bring more money home than my father. Work my muscles every day. American boys, from what I see, they don't know how to work. Like Freddie, your formerly sweetheart, Althea—when there's work with hands, Freddie, he has brain other places."

"Be careful what you say about Freddie," Mrs. Perry said. "I am particularly fond of Freddie."

"So am I," Morgan Perry said.

They both looked at Stavros for an instant and it was clear, even to Stavros, that they wished Freddie were there in his place. But he didn't back off. "I teach my brothers and sisters to work," he said. "We work twelve, fourteen hours a day. Right in our house."

"Althea told us about her visit there," Mrs. Perry said. "Forgive me if I say that it sounded a bit like a sweatshop—you know those awful places one reads about in the evening papers."

"Not awful. Very good. That's why we rich someday. All we need is capital. The rest I do. Go on, eat. I teach them something else, my family. To love this country. I notice people here don't 'preciate what they got. Only people come from other side 'preciate this country proper way. People who know some trouble one time, they know they're lucky to be alive here. People coming out of danger, they appreciate America—right, Althea?"

"I suppose that's true," she said.

"Take my word," Stavros said. "I'm glad I'm not eating yet. Now I have chance to tell you, Mr. Morgan Perry, that I worry about Sarrafian Brothers store. It is going down. Mr. Ara Sarrafian, sick all the time and don't bring in customers, proper way. Same time, we're not importing new goods—"

"There's a war on, for Jesus' sake," Mr. Morgan Perry said.

"Right! So after this war, there will be big demand. Our stock too small. We will lose our chance."

"There are no rugs to be bought now," Mr. Perry said.

"I know where to find. Listen to me, I tell you how I will save Sarrafian Brothers—"

"Excuse me a minute," Mr. Perry said to his wife. He threw his chair back and, staggering a little, left the dining room. Mrs. Perry wasn't surprised when he came back carrying a tumbler full of straight bourbon whiskey.

"Morgan," she said, "I'm warning you—"

"Warning me what?" he said. He stood behind his chair, legs apart, defying his wife. "What is your warning to me, dear?"

"You know what," she said.

It looked for an instant as if he might throw his drink at her. Instead he drank it, all of it, and sat down, breathing hard from rage.

Rhoda came in with a plate and, on it, Stavros's piece of meat. When she showed it to him, he shook his head. "Don't be 'fraid, Rhoda," he said. "Burn it a little, go 'head."

Rhoda looked at Mrs. Perry, who responded with a delicate shrug of her shoulders, and Rhoda went back to the kitchen.

"What's the use getting mad with me, Mr. Perry?" Stavros said. "Maybe this time I'm right, not impossible. Last year profits not same as year before. Am I right that much?"

"Father," Althea said, "just for the hell of it, why don't you listen to—"

"What the hell have I been doing?" Mr. Perry said. "Haven't I been? Listening? What I can't do is be grateful that this man, like Jesus the lamb of God, is favoring us by walking among us!"

"O.K.," Stavros said. "Then finish! I say nothing! I am not responsible for the future. I tell you this—you, you too, are not working hard enough to bring new business to Sarrafian Brothers store. You're satisfied bring back cost plus expenses. I am not satisfied with that. I could make our store the biggest in the market and the richest. Freddie, he is hopeless case. Why not say it? He's a good heart, so on, sure, but in business they eat your good heart with one swallow, our competitors. It's up to you, you're manager there, but you do nothing. Mrs. Norma, I see she thinks I'm getting too fresh. Hey, Mrs. Norma, don't worry, almost finished. You see, I'm hamal still, crazy man from those hamal days." He laughed uproariously. "And still crazy," he said.

Mrs. Perry looked at Althea and shook her head in a kind of commiseration.

"Forgive me for what I'm thinking," Morgan Perry said as he gulped down the rest of his meal.

"I know what you're thinking. Don't worry, I'm used to it."

"How 'bout some dessert, Norma?" Morgan Perry said.

"Father," Althea said, "Stavros hasn't started his dinner yet."

"Well, I've finished mine," Morgan Perry said. He lifted his glass to drain it, but it was empty and he slammed it on the table. Then he said, "Excuse me," got up, and started out of the room. "Stretch my legs, get some air," he said.

"Morgan, you come back here this minute," Mrs. Perry said. "Now sit down like a good boy and be a decent host. Mr. Arness, like it or not, is our guest here today. Morgan! Sit!"

He smiled at his wife, promising revenge later.

"I don't talk business no more," Stavros said. "Don't worry, Mrs. Norma."

There was a silence. Then Rhoda peeked around the edge of the white swinging door to the kitchen. "It's still on the fire," she said to Mrs. Perry, "getting smaller and sort of dark. Can you smell it?" She gave in to the giggles.

"Fine, fine!" Stavros said. "Bring her in."

"May I have some dessert now, wife?" Morgan Perry asked.

"No," his wife said. "You will wait for the rest of us."

"Rhoda," Morgan Perry called out in the voice he used to coach the parish football team, "come back here. Now! Take my dish and carry it out. Then bring me a clean, deep saucer. And the ice cream in a large bowl with a great deal of chocolate sauce. Do it now, because I'm telling you to. Don't look at *her*. *I* pay your salary. So be quick about it. Hop to."

"Allah!" Stavros said, under his breath.

Picking up Mr. Perry's plate, Rhoda rushed for the kitchen. But her mistress's voice stopped her in the doorway.

"Morgan," Mrs. Perry said in a voice that was not unpleasant, "you had two rather large Manhattans before dinner. Just now you consumed a supply of bourbon whiskey equal to twice what must have been in each of the Manhattans. You know perfectly well from your experience that when you take alcohol in quantity, then indulge your addiction to sweets, you invariably come down with a crippling headache. When you do, don't expect the least sympathy from me. Now, Rhoda, go do what Mr. Perry asked."

"Too much ice cream no good," Stavros observed. "But as you say, Mr. Perry, what the hell, we live once. Am I right?"

"Now, while I wait for my dessert, may I say what's been on my mind?" Morgan Perry said. "Norma and Althea, why do we have to continue to pretend that everything is cordial here, that we're old good friends? Joe, the truth is that I can't stand the sight of you and my daughter in the same room, let alone sitting side by side on the sofa with your heavy hand in her lap. So why don't we stop being hypocrites? I'll start a new era of truth. Joe, I find you crude. I always have and I still do. You are crude! And vulgar. There—I've said it and I feel better!" He looked at Stavros, smiled and waited.

Stavros smiled back. "And you, Mr. Perry," he said, "are drunk."

Whereupon Rhoda and her daughter, Rhonda, hurried in, the mother with an enormous white island in a sea of chocolate and Rhonda with a large bowl which, skirting her mother, she deposited in front of Mr. Perry.

"Father," Althea said, "I'll never forgive you for today."

Slowly Morgan Perry helped himself to the ice cream, then looked at the company, taking their measure. "Well, Norma," he said as he filled his mouth with the first spoonful of sweet ice cream and bitter chocolate. "What do you say?"

"Say to what, Morgan?"

"The hypocrisy in my home on this day. Do you understand what I've been saying?"

"Yes."

"Do you agree?"

"Yes."

"Peh, peh, peh, peh, peh," Stavros said.

"Which is Greek for what?" Mr. Morgan Perry demanded.

"That's the sound an Anatolian rooster makes when he's mad," Althea said.

"After I finish this," Mr. Perry said, "I will go to my room and have a long, quiet nap and think about the perversion of truth in our world and what a relief it is not to pretend. I may even talk to my class about it next Sunday." He finished his ice cream, stood up, bowed to the company, then fixed on Stavros. "The truth is, my man," he said, "that I want you to stay away from my daughter. I warn you that if you continue to—"

"Father!" Althea said. "Stop that! This minute!"

"I said it and I mean it," Mr. Perry said, and left the room.

"The aspirin is on the shelf in my bathroom, dear," Mrs. Perry called after him in her bright voice.

Rhoda came in with Stavros's meat. "It sure shrunk," she said.

"I don't want it," Stavros said, and no one urged him to eat.

Mrs. Perry, ignoring Stavros, turned to Althea. "After dinner," she said, "I simply must go out and finish work on my mulch heap. Why don't you take your feller"—she didn't look at Stavros, merely nodded her head in his direction—"and show him my garden. Be careful where I've put in bulbs, they're marked with tiny white stakes. I'm afraid men don't notice those things unless they're pointed out. Then show him the sundial in the rose garden. It tells the time, Mr. Arness, so accurately you can set your watch by it. Or catch your train."

"We're taking the four-eighteen back to the city, Mother," Althea said. "Don't concern yourself further about us."

"Mr. Arness may enjoy seeing my garden." She still didn't look at Stavros. "Do you think you'll enjoy seeing my garden, Mr. Arness?"

"No," Stavros said.

"Oh?" Mrs. Perry said, quite pleasantly. "Oh?" Then she called, "Rhoda," and when the mother-maid hurried in, she said, "You can take my plate and Miss Althea's." She looked at Stavros's plate, containing the meat he hadn't touched.

"Perhaps he'd like some scrambled eggs," Rhoda said.

"I don't think so," Althea said. She saw what was happening. Stavros was sinking back into the hamal world. That look was there.

"I don't know what he wants," Rhoda said as she left the room.

Then Stavros said, "Why you people treat me this way? Nobody answer my questions, no one look at me when I talk. You talk to Mr. Perry and you talk to Althea, your face turns from one to the other like this." He swung his arm in a broad arc. "You treat me like I know nothing. Mr. Perry, his insults—those I'm used to. But I want to be friends with you. Your daughter hates you, Mrs. Perry, but I tell her, 'Your mother not so bad,' so why you don't act polite with me, at least that much?"

Rhoda came in to pass the ice cream and Mrs. Perry helped herself. When Rhoda offered a dish to Althea, she shook her head, and the maid went out.

"Why you treat me like this, Mrs. Perry?" Stavros said. It was his final effort. "We cannot be friends, I understand that now, but polite, why not? Tell me?"

"Well, you've asked for it," Mrs. Perry said. "That I refused to talk directly to you or even look directly at you, I'm afraid that's true. Althea is my only child. I did have a son; he died, as you know. After that, all my hopes were pinned on Althea. I have devoted my life to her, to see that she had the best care, the best education, the best friends. When she graduated from college, there was never a mother more proud. I don't think my hopes for her were unreasonable. I truly believe she could have been many things—the wife of a great industrialist, or of the publisher of a great newspaper or of a prominent educator. After all, her great-grandfather was a college president. Why, she could have been—and I don't believe I deceive myself about her worth—the wife of the President of the United States and done him honor."

She'd begun to cry.

"Mother, really," Althea said. "That's enough."

"Well, he asked me," Mrs. Perry said, "so I'm obliging him. I'll feel better, actually, once you've both heard me say these rather hateful things than if I—well, what your father said—deny them or swallow them."

Again she turned and looked squarely at Stavros. "Yes, she could have been all those things. What does she do instead?" She indicated Stavros with her flattened palm. "You! Do you expect me to be happy about that? I am not. I am bitterly disappointed. In fact, revolted, stirred to hatred and fury."

"Peh, peh, peh, peh, peh," Stavros said.

"I tried my best today," Mrs. Perry said. "Give me credit, Althea, I did try, today, to be— But Morgan was right. I couldn't, I could not."

She wasn't able to go on. Then she seemed to recover, looked at Althea, and said, "Poor little soul. Look at her, Mr. Arness! How beautiful she is! When she was born, she had an aureole around her head, golden hair and a heavenly light in her eyes. I said to myself, 'This girl can win anyone.'

Yes, she was an angel, and now she's in the gutter with you." Looking at Althea, she said, "Poor little soul." Then: "I'll change my shoes." And crying bitterly, she left the room.

Stavros, head up, undid his bow tie, ripped his collar off, unbuttoned his collar band and his coat, then looked at his plate with the piece of burnt meat on it.

Althea said, "That's all, Rhoda," to the woman, who'd come back to see if anything more was required of her. Then Althea got up and went out through the door, calling back to Stavros. "We can still take a walk if you like. There's time, and it's a beautiful afternoon."

He didn't answer. Instead, after a moment, he strolled out of the dining room and went up the stairs to the door of Mrs. Perry's room and knocked at it discreetly, even respectfully. There was no answer. "Mrs. Perry," he said, "it's Topouzoglou, Stavros Topouzoglou." He listened for an answer, but there was none. He heard the sound of a shoe falling to the floor. "I want to say a few words to you, Mrs. Perry. Please listen." Then he raised his voice so that the person inside the room had to hear, as well as Althea, who was coming up the stairs, and even the maids who were cleaning up the dining room.

"I want you to know, Mrs. Perry, I come from an ancient race of men who have suffered for centuries without losing their pride. We are noble people, poor, yes, but men of honor. Better than you! I found that out today. We have manners, not you. We would not, no matter what we feeling, insult a guest in our house. We have generosity, not your husband. I can't even compare you with the hamals, those penniless animals who sleep where they work on the docks of Constantinople—my brothers in misery they were for two years. I was one of them—no clean food to eat, no roof against the storms, no hope. But they have more friendship and generous feelings to each other than you and your husband. Your daughter, I must tell you, is fortunate to be with me, not the other way. Don't forget that. I am not honored by her. She is honored by me."

Mrs. Perry swung the door open looking rather cheery. She had on her garden shoes, heavy brogues with thick rubber soles and welts along the seams. She'd changed to a tartan wool skirt and a heavy Donegal sweater. "Off to my mulch pile," she said gaily.

She tried to swing around Stavros but he blocked her path.

Challenged, she looked up at him and her smile was defiant. "Well, I certainly cleared the air, didn't I?" She tossed her head in what must have been, when she was a girl, an enchanting gesture. "Excuse me," she said.

"One minute," Stavros answered. "Your daughter, you know," he persisted—and now she sensed the danger in the man—"she has been in many beds, with many men. Not one, not several, but many. She is not clean girl. But I will take her."

Mrs. Perry slapped Stavros across the face. Hard. When he smiled at her, she slapped him again. "Go 'head," he said. "Again, go 'head! Once more!"

Exhausted, Mrs. Perry stood where she was, head down, trembling.

"To slap my face, Mrs. Perry, means nothing. It does not hurt me. Only hurt you—and Althea; see where she's watching there. What I said about Althea, it's truth, but it means nothing to me, because I love your daughter like a wife. That's why I asked you for her."

Mrs. Perry pulled the door to her bedroom closed and now Stavros stepped aside to let her pass. She went down the stairs past her daughter, out of the house and into the garden.

Stavros didn't look after her. He threw open the door to her bedroom and went in. He walked here and there, reconnoitering, inspecting the evidence of this other culture. Then he stepped to the woman's bed and stretched out on it, which is where Althea found him.

"See why I hate her," Althea said to him. "I keep thinking of awful things to do to her."

He reached out for her.

"No," she said.

"Better than the church floor," he answered. "Also same thing. Come here. Althea!"

When she didn't yield, he forced her. The old-fashioned way, the Greek way—he on top, her neck bent back.

His shoes were on the spread, and when he lifted his head, he could see through a window to where Mrs. Perry, in her garden, was working on her mulch pile. This sight gave him satisfaction.

DECEMBER 1917

Fofo and Seraphim had undertaken a crusade to preserve Stavros as their family's head, to keep him theirs. He didn't grow aware of the effect his declaration of freedom and indifference had had on his brother and sister until he noticed that every time he entered a room, their conversation stopped. He smelled a conspiracy, and that it had to do with him.

. One night after he and Seraphim had stayed on late at the family store shooting craps with some of the other small merchants in their building, Althea said to him, "I had a nice visit with your sister this evening."

"Which sister?"

"The one who just got married, the old one, she came to see me."

"Fofo? What she want?"

"To get to know me better, she said."

"Fish story," Stavros said. "What the hell she got on her mind?"

"She told me how important you were to them, how deeply your father—yes, him again—had trusted you, how hard you'd worked to bring them all here—"

"Bee's wax! What else? Must be some reason. What?"

"Then she asked me about Delmonico's, how the food was there, and so on. What could have put that into her head?"

"I told her we'd gone there."

"And the Brevoort too?" Stavros nodded. "She wanted to know what they charged for everything on the menu. I couldn't figure out what she—"

"Since she got married, that woman, who knows what she got on her mind?"

But Stavros knew very well. Fofo was very tight-fisted with the family's funds, and Stavros had had to draw double his weekly allowance from their treasury when he'd taken Althea to Delmonico's and to the Brevoort.

"I think she's worried that you're spending too much money on me," Althea said.

"That's my business what I spend," Stavros growled. Then he quickly slid around the subject. "I had complaints about Fofo too. Her husband says she goes to bed with corset on. I had to explain to her this is America, also she should wash more. American women don't sweat, I told her."

A few days later, Althea said, "I had lunch with your brother."

"Who? Seraphim? What's going on my damn family?"

"I think they're all afraid they'll lose you because of me."

"What the hell Seraphim want?"

"It wasn't him; it was the young one—the cute one."

"Demo? Cute?"

"Very. All dressed up in his uniform."

"What the hell he want?"

"He said he wanted to comfort me, you might say. 'Pay no attention to the family's feelings,' he said. I said, 'What family feelings?' He said, 'They're old-fashioned people, don't let them bother you, those—' What's a *vlax?*"

"Damn stupid peasant from backcountry, lives with animals."

"That's what you are, so says your brother Demo. Incidentally, he let me pay for the lunch."

"I'm going to step on that cockroach."

"Be careful. That cockroach is wearing the uniform of the United States Army, he's protected."

"What he wants from you?"

"I believe—now don't get mad—I believe your little brother Demo has designs on me, that he may be waiting for me to get tired of you and—"

"You mean other way, no?"

"That would do it too. He wanted to make sure I knew, without ever saying so plainly, that if either thing happened, he was very ready and very able."

"I'm going to kill that criminal. First thing in the morning."

"He also informed me that you've never stayed with one lover in your entire life."

"And you have?"

"He didn't say that. In fact, he was sure of the contrary—that in this case, with you, I definitely wouldn't. It seems I'm a constant subject of conversation in your house, and your brother Demo, your sister Fofo, and, so she informed me as we parted, your brother Seraphim believe you owe it to your family to honor some Greek maiden lady from a good family under a crown of June flowers—as you described it to me once—and so resume your proper position as head of the family."

"I know. They been crossing my path with young Greek cows again; thick hairy legs, behinds like casaba melons, noses as long as a baby's foot, thick black hair, even a small mustache one of them had—everything I don't like in a woman."

"It's your father's wish, it seems, and when your father wishes, even from the grave, you obey. So, Demo said, I should keep alert to other possibilities."

"I don't like the smell from Greek women."

"As a wedding present, I will give you a full gallon of a powerful French perfume—gardenia, that's it! It comes from a very white flower and will replace all other odors."

On Christmas Eve, Althea went to Mount Ivy for a "quick supper," and Seraphim and Stavros went home on the subway together. As they came up into the street, Seraphim took his brother's elbow and pulled him west on 136th Street instead of east. "Come, I show you what I been talking," he said.

They walked into the wind from the cold river.

Seraphim, so everyone believed, had the most regular life of any of the boys, which is to say that no one knew anything about him. He hadn't been coming home to supper the last few weeks, but always slept in his own bed at night. He'd leave home before anyone was up—to open the store, he said, and check the mail. What he did during certain hours between closing time and opening time, no one could say. He himself revealed nothing. Stavros, for instance, had no idea where they were going now, and, respecting Seraphim's character, decided not to ask questions.

"I told her I might bring you," Seraphim said. "I think she making nice dinner."

Stavros hadn't even guessed there might be a "she" in Seraphim's life.

"I met her at the French bakery on Broadway," Seraphim chose to explain. "Where we buy pastries. She likes her bread as it comes out of the oven, warm. So now, every morning, I go pick up couple loaves and we have breakfast together, nice warm *baguette* with butter and honey."

"Who?" Stavros said. "Who the hell you talking?"

"Why you getting mad all of sudden?" Seraphim said. "I have sweetheart, that's who!"

"Since when? Who is she? I mean, congratulations first, but who is . . . ?"

"Don't worry," Seraphim said quickly. "No marriage business here."

He turned into the vestibule of an apartment house, just one building back from the river and a little cleaner, a little showier, and a little more expensive than the one where the Topouzoglou family lived. There was an elevator, for instance. "Hello, Mr. Sam," the operator said. "Sorry, you're going to have to walk again, the motor's being fixed."

"Merry Christmas, Benjamin," Seraphim said, slipping him a dollar bill, and the brothers slowly mounted the stairs.

They were waiting to greet them, a mother and two daughters, twins. Behind them Stavros could see a Christmas tree, richly decorated, and underneath it a mass of presents in gaily colored paper tied with bright ribbons. "Here is Louise," Seraphim said. "And here's my brother, the eldest! Stavros his name."

Louise reached out a pink palm. She was a small woman with soft graying hair, parted in the middle and pulled back into a knot. She looked to Stavros to be a schoolteacher or a librarian. It turned out that she was a music teacher. Her two daughters also offered their hands and murmured, *"Enchantée."* They were—who can tell with a woman, Stavros thought—maybe twenty-four or -two or -six. But not pretty—Stavros noted that immediately.

One of the twins rushed into a back room, then reappeared with a robe of a light silk cloth printed with an Oriental design—Persian, Stavros thought. The other twin had come up behind, holding dark red woolen slippers.

"Thank you, Simone, thank you," Seraphim said. The girl with the robe held it up and he slipped it on. Then he sat and the other twin, Janine, knelt at his feet, took off his shoes and put the woolen slippers on his feet. "There's another exact pair of their father's slippers inside," Seraphim said to Stavros. "He always had two of everything. Would you like them? Why not?"

"Oh, don't worry, don't worry," Stavros said. "Too much trouble." He turned to Louise. "Beautiful tree," he said. "We don't have one. What can we do? Mother sick."

All three women made a sound of sympathy, "Oh, ooh, oooh."

"But yours is so beautiful, it makes me happy," Stavros said.

Louise blushed as if it had been a personal compliment on her appearance. "Thank you, thank you," she said. "You're so kind."

Seraphim pulled the silk robe tight around his belly and sat down at the head of the table as if he owned the place and everything in it.

The table had been set very neatly, even handsomely. Everything was in place. *Althea keeps her place a mess,* Stavros thought, *doesn't wash the damn dishes at night, she's used to too many servants all her life, doing everything for her.*

"Everything very nice, orderly, on the table," Stavros said to Louise.

"It's how Sam likes it," she said. "He's very *propre,* and insists that we be too. Doesn't he, girls? Sam is quite strict along certain lines." The twins murmured, assenting. "As was my dear husband," Louise said.

"She likes me because I'm like her husband," Seraphim said. Then he turned to Louise. "I'm hungry," he said. "Let's eat!" The head of the house was speaking.

"Right away, dear. Come, girls. Sam is ready."

Everything there, Stavros could see, was done to please Seraphim, a habit that the mother and her daughters had developed from serving the dead man. Seraphim had fallen into great luck.

Stavros sat next to Louise, and she and the girls bowed their heads, and she whispered something to Seraphim, whereupon he murmured what must have been a prayer—was it in French? Stavros knew that his brother was not in the least religious, but he was also a very practical man who wouldn't take the least chance with something so good.

As soon as the prayer was over, the twins ran into the kitchen and came out to present a hot sardine dish with a spicy sauce. It didn't look good to Stavros but when he tasted it he wanted more. "Very tasty," he said to Louise.

"Thank you, thank you," she said. "You're so kind, just as dear Sam promised you'd be."

The sardines consumed, Louise turned to Stavros and said, "I hope you like *gigot*—do you like *gigot?*" Her voice was soft and her smile enticing, and Stavros could see why his brother liked her.

"That's leg of lamb," Seraphim said.

All the women got up, cleared the table quickly and retreated to the kitchen. Stavros looked at his brother and said, "You got it pretty damn good here!"

Seraphim smiled and nodded. Stavros noticed he was getting fat under his chin.

The women came back, nimbly as elves. The meat, vegetables, French bread, sweet butter, warm plates were on the table, one, two, three. Now Louise was at Stavros's side, leaning over to show him a bottle of wine. "From the Jura section," she said as if she wanted his approval. *"Vin jaune. I hope you'll approve. Sam likes it."* She was very serious now and very close. Stavros saw that she was considerably older than Seraphim, but her hands, her ears, her nostrils, were pink and delicate, perfect. "My husband

and I came from that province of France," she said, indicating the bottle of wine, "from Besançon, which we thought was a city until we saw New York. New York is a city!"

"Here, Mr. Arness," one of the twins said to Seraphim. "We had the knife sharpened for you."

Seraphim, looking very grave, cut a slice. "The knife will do," he said. He continued to slice, evenly, carefully, as the women watched with admiration. "Doesn't Sam carve beautifully," Louise said. Then she leaned forward anxiously. "No, Sam," she said. "Keep the outside piece for yourself." She turned to Stavros. "Sam likes the outside cut," she said.

"My brother likes it too," Seraphim said.

"Then, of course, we must give it to him." Louise smiled at Stavros. "Janine!" she said abruptly, and her voice was stern. "Don't put gravy on Mr. Stavros's meat, he may not want it. Ask him first." She turned to Stavros and again she smiled. It comforted Stavros, that soft smile.

For dessert they had a chocolate pudding out of the oven. Stavros had smelled it steaming all through the meal, the smell itself a treat. Meantime, before that delicacy, there was a salad of lettuce, each leaf left whole with a coating of oil and lemon and whatever else, Stavros didn't know—spices, he supposed. And there were two kinds of cheese, one soft, one hard, with which they finished the wine.

"We have another bottle," Louise said.

"Don't open another bottle," Stavros said.

"Open it," Sam said.

Both girls ran for the kitchen.

After dinner, they sat in the parlor, where the furniture was gathered around a piano. The girls sat and looked at Sam, waiting, apparently, for some expression of his wishes.

"The girls have been practicing their Mendelssohn allegro, four hands," Louise whispered, leaning to Stavros; "Sam loves it. It would make him so happy if you asked for it."

Stavros did. "What you been practicing?" he asked. "Let's hear!" Twin armchairs faced the piano. Stavros and Seraphim sat side by side. Stavros had never felt so close to his brother.

Midway through the movement, Stavros's head nodded. *Damn music, too long,* he thought. Then he wondered if Louise had noticed, looked at her quickly. Her eyes were closed—not in sleep; in rapture.

Seraphim, declaring that he needed a breath of air after the heavy meal, said he'd walk his brother home. Louise said, "Of course, *cheri.* It will give us a chance to clean the table so everything will be nice when you return."

"You're smart man, Seraphim," Stavros said to him on the street. "What is she, Louise? Your age?"

"Older," Seraphim said. "Don't worry, no marriage business. Maybe ten years older."

"When you get married," Stavros said, "you must bring children."

"Too late for Louise, that," Seraphim said.

"Otherwise very good," Stavros said. "Every night like tonight, good dinner?"

"Every night," Seraphim said.

"You giving them money?"

"You think I'm crazy? Those women don't ask money. They all teach piano-playing lessons, have more money than me and you. I put all my money into our business, I buy stock. Prices going up, going up."

"You fucking that old woman?"

"Sometimes, yes. She likes me; what can I do?"

"You fight sometimes?"

"What's there to fight about? Louise, she's always like you saw her. American women fight, not Louise."

"You talking about Althea now, American women?"

"You decide. Maybe you like one of those girls tonight. They're taught how to be for a man exactly, guarantee. They looking for husband now too."

"Very nice, very nice, but—" He made a face, meaning "not pretty." "Besides, idea for me is Greek girl, isn't that it, Anatolian girl? No?"

"Honestly God, Stavros—Greek, French, whatever, you must find wife like those women there. Better Anatolian girl, all right, sure. But her character, she must keep you calm, like me here; clean, quiet woman who's not jumping up and down all the time, here, there, all night, wear you out, worry, fight, going crazy. You see why I'm calm? Louise! Women can be devil, you realize that? Eating you. That woman you have, ideas on everything. Excuse me. Before she's through she will eat your liver. I warn you, look out."

Stavros stopped walking. He seemed to be thinking. Then he said, "Seraphim, mind your business. I look out for mine."

He walked away, went into a bar, had a drink, then went downtown to Althea's. There was no light from under the door. Was she back? Asleep? Stavros slid his key into the heavy steel lock, shouldered the door back. The only light in the room came from the lamp in the street below.

Althea wasn't where she should have been, waiting for him. "Althea!" he called. It was past ten. "Althea!" The tone of Stavros's voice was that of the traditional domestic despot. "Althea!" Stavros shouted again, as if he expected her to respond by scuttering out of hiding, begging forgiveness.

He switched on the light. There was evidence she'd left in a hurry; the room was everywhere disordered. He kicked the door shut and looked into the bedroom. "Didn't even make the bed," he grumbled out loud. "Breakfast plates still on the table, egg yellow getting hard, bread knife in the butter, bread left out for who—the cockroaches, maybe?

They be here, guarantee, any minute. They heard the news, I'm sure."

He walked to the bathroom door. "Look," he said to himself, "where she leave her rag!" The hamal word for women's underdrawers was "rag," and there, in a basin in the washbowl, Althea's rag had been left to soak. "Where the hell your idea, Miss Society, that I shave in the morning, with this here? Tell me that much?" he asked Althea who wasn't there to answer. "Where? Hah?" He turned to the room. "Look!" he said. "Disaster!"

The cumbersome Morris chair, Althea's heirloom of oak, was covered with a tangle of clothing—dresses, skirts, blouses, belts that she'd apparently tried on and decided not to wear. "Thea Marie's whores keep their cribs better!" he said out loud.

He recalled the perfect order Louise had imposed everywhere in her place. How the hell was he going to straighten this woman out? Maybe bring Fofo or Eleni over, teach her the proper way to keep a place for him? Would she ever become what he wanted? "Trouble with you, Althea," he scolded her in his gruffest voice, "you have too many servants all your life. Now hopeless case, I'm afraid. Too late!"

Suddenly his mind swerved in another direction. Suppose he made the bed, washed the dishes, put everything in order? Maybe then when she got here and looked around she'd be ashamed and understand at last what he expected of her.

And why had three cups been used for coffee? He dumped the breakfast dishes in the kitchen sink. "What the hell! Cover everything with water, let dirt get soft!" The bed? He'd never liked the way Althea made her bed. He'd show her, tuck the bottom in tight as it should be. As for the clothes she'd chosen not to wear, he gathered the mess in his arms, flung it all on the floor of her closet, and slammed the door.

He took off his jacket and hung it carefully across the back of the Morris chair, pulled off his necktie, stretching it to flatten the wrinkles, lifted the mattress and tucked his trousers under its weight so whatever crease remained might be sharpened by morning. Pulling off his underclothing, he hung the shirt on one arm of the chair, the drawers on the other, and across the front edge, he laid out one of his stockings. He liked to air his clothing since he didn't have Eleni to provide him with fresh garments in the morning.

Into the other stocking he stuffed his paper money, then pushed the little bundle deep into the pillowcase on his side of the bed, a precaution he'd continued taking, over Althea's ridicule. She hadn't succeeded in laughing him out of that one!

He stacked her pillow on top of his, propped his body up, and faced the door, waiting, an ambush in the dark. And as the minutes went by, he became angrier.

Then he heard laughter from the street below, the laugh that always unsettled him, the same coarse sound one hears through a wall behind which clandestine lovers are sporting.

In an instant, he was at the window over the street. Below, a Ford, a runabout two-seater, top up. Althea had just stepped out of it; an arm from under the canvas top was pulling her back, the cause of her laughter. She slammed the door shut. Then she leaned over the barrier and he could see that the conversation with the person inside was continuing.

Stavros went for his trousers, preparing to go down to the street. Then he thought to test her, to see if she'd lie. He'd get back into bed, wait, say nothing about what he'd seen.

Apparently she expected him to be there, because she entered without switching the light on. The room was still lit only by the lights in the street below. She stopped and looked at the bed, where he confronted her, eyes open.

Her eyes, it seemed, had not yet adjusted to the dark. "Are you asleep there," she whispered, "or sulking?" He didn't answer. "Sorry to be late. Long way out there, as you know. And back! In the dark! Are you asleep?"

"No," he said.

"Good," she said. His surly tone hadn't affected her; she was accustomed to it. "I'll be right there," she said. "I'm thirsty."

As she pulled her sailor blouse over her head, she walked into the kitchen. "What's all this in the sink?" she said. "What a mess you've made!"

He watched her undress, watched her drop the skirt of blue serge on the floor, then, after a quick glance in his direction—was she doing something wrong again, by his standards?—she folded the skirt on the Morris chair. "I'm a little drunk," she said, as she loosed the cords of her camisole top and pulled it off.

Althea didn't need a brassiere, not yet, and he never had enough of looking at her breasts. She knew this, turned her back to him, smiling, taunting him, he thought.

Naked now, she walked to the closet for her nightgown. "What's all this on the floor?" she asked. "Did you throw my clothes on the floor? Why did you do that? What's the matter with you? Are you mad at me again? Or are you sick?" The gown went on, over her head; its hem hit the floor.

"I'm not sick," he said.

Now she understood. "Oh, Lord!" Then, angry, she said, "Again? Really, Pasha! Don't scold me tonight. It's Christmas and I've got a present for you which I'll give you in the morning. Be nice to me tonight. I'm so tired. You know I need nine hours' sleep every night and I haven't been getting it. . . ."

She was on her side of the bed. She reached toward him and pulled her pillow out from under his head, dropping him, unceremoniously, to her level. Which made him angrier. Which made him want her. She needed to be put in her proper place.

Perhaps she knew what he had in mind—and why—because she moved as far as she could away from him. And he went for her. After a moment, she opened her legs, submitting to him.

"It hurts," she said. He didn't relent. "It hurts when you just push it in like that. Wait a little. Stavros, stop it. Stop!"

No longer tumescent, he rolled off.

Her eyes became accustomed to the dark; she could see how angry he was.

"You're supposed to wait a little," she said. "I wasn't ready. What's your hurry, anyway? Do you have another engagement tonight?" He didn't respond. "Why don't you let me tell you when? It's better that way."

He got out of bed. "I'm too big for you," he said.

"Not at the moment," she said, laughing.

He picked up a handful of pistachio nuts from a bowl, his favorites.

"Tell me," she said. "Why does it affect you so drastically when we have the least little difference?"

"Little?"

"Well, yes. What did I say? I asked you to wait until I was—"

"Where you been so late?"

"Oh, that's it! At my parents', where else?"

"Where else, yes—where?"

"That what you're mad about? That I was late?"

"It reminds me, when you tell me, 'You're supposed to wait a little,' and 'Let me tell you when' and so on, how many different men you've been with."

"There weren't that many."

"And the way you laugh—"

"I can't help how I laugh. I always laugh that way."

He stepped in front of the mirror. Between his thumb and the forefinger of his right hand, he squeezed the plumpness in his middle. "For me, one is many," he said.

"Yes, you're very handsome," she said. "What are you doing there—reminding yourself?" She began to laugh again. "Your sisters have really spoiled you," she said. "Too many compliments about what a great man you are. Come back here."

He turned away from the mirror, and from her, and cracked open a pistachio.

"May I ask you this without upsetting you? When you get out of bed next time, darling, could you remember not to throw the covers off that way? It's a grand gesture, to be sure, but it leaves me completely uncovered. Could you remember that? Maybe?"

"Sure. Why not?"

"Yes. Why not? And when you do come back to bed, please don't bring those pistachios with you. That's not a criticism. Just a request, modestly put."

"I understand. Not necessary explain everything to me."

"Come on back, darling, please, sweetheart, wonderful man, greatest lover in the world, please come back. If you come back I'll give you your present now. I'll give you anything you want. Come on, Stavros."

He couldn't tell if she was mocking him, but slowly he swaggered back to the bed. Standing over her, he said, "Why you so late tonight? Tell me the truth."

"Oh, you know, it was a party, Christmas and all, and they opened the presents tonight, because I was there. I brought mine home—I'll show them to you in the morning. Stavros, come on, get in the bed. Also I wanted to make it up with my father."

"Did you? Make it up with him?"

"He won't talk to me. Mother did. He talked to Freddie. Pasha, please!"

She lifted a triangle of sheet and blanket on his side. He condescended to get in. She slid over next to him, put a leg over his.

He didn't respond. "You drink a lot, again," he said.

"It was Christmas, for God's sake! They had a great bowl of punch! You remember how my mother is with alcoholic beverages: She knows how to pour! Remember?"

"You're smelling," he said.

"I know, I know. So what now, Stavros? What?" She took hold of his penis, caressing it, then lifted his testicle sac on top of his legs. Then she pulled gently, stroked gently, looking into his face with the light of desire in her eyes and a mischievous twist to her mouth. "You know," she said, "when you want to enter somebody's home, darling, you really should knock first, then wait, until the door opens and the host, whoever she is, invites you in."

"Not in Greek village," he said. "There you're sure you're welcome, so you go right in."

"Well, I'm not a Greek village. Am I?" She continued to fondle him, but after some time, when he didn't respond, she gave up. "What's the matter?" she asked, like a little girl disappointed by the behavior of an adult she'd trusted.

"I can't fuck you when I'm mad at you," he said.

"I don't believe that," she said, moving away. "Maybe you don't like me anymore. Is that it?"

"Not when you're like this," he said, getting out of bed. "You're too damn fresh."

"You uncovered me again," she said.

"You're there, cover yourself."

To Stavros she sounded just like her father, Morgan Perry, giving orders at the store. He picked up another handful of pistachios, cracked one after another. Then he walked to the window, his back to the bed and looked down into the street.

"I know why you like to come into me before I'm ready," she said.

"Why?"

"Because it hurts me and you like to hear the sound I make when I'm hurt."

"I can't help it. I'm bigger."

"Bigger than whom?"

"Freddie. Anybody. Many women told me that."

She didn't speak.

"Well, what you say?"

"I didn't say anything. You want me to say something?" He didn't respond and she said, "You want the truth?"

"Always!"

"Like hell you do. No man does—about that. You're thicker, Freddie's longer. There."

"Other women tell me thousan' times—"

"How wonderful for you. But tell me, does it matter, all that? The size and so on? I'm hardly aware of it. Oops. Sorry!" She laughed again. "Sorry, I didn't mean that quite the way it sounded. Look, Pasha, you're a wonderful lover, please come back, my prince. Let's not go to sleep mad at each other again. I've got something good for you, so will you—will you please stop cracking those damn pistachio nuts? You're dropping the shells on the floor. And do not bring them back to bed with you."

At the window, he cracked another nut open. "Why you lie to me before?" he said.

Her laughter this time sounded nervous. "About what do you think I lied?"

"About why you're late, where you been, so forth."

Once again she laughed.

"What you laughing all the time now lately? You nervous?"

"No. And I'm not laughing at you. I'm just laughing. It's the way I am."

"Also scolding me all the time."

"I'm not scolding you all the time."

"On everything. Don't eat nuts, don't throw the blankets up, come away from that window, wait a little, I'm not ready, the kitchen is a mess, the closet too, look at this sink! Who the hell made the kitchen mess, tell me that much? Also, tonight, suddenly it hurts, it hurts. Also 'Let me tell you when to put it in.' Where you get that damn idea?"

"It's just so you won't hurt me."

"All of a sudden, last few weeks, you complaining about that; never before."

"Well, it's about time I told you the truth, isn't it?"

"Plenty girls don't tell me that 'it hurts' business."

"I'm very impressed. And contrite too. Come back. It won't hurt now, I promise you."

"Now I don't want you."

"You don't want me most of the time now."

"Because you don't do it like once you did. For instance, you not wet down there today like always before. Why?"

"I'm not a machine. Sometimes I like you more, sometimes less. You know, I think all this is camouflage for something else. Tell me the truth —why are you mad at me tonight?"

"You know why I'm mad at you. I don't have to tell you that."

"No, I don't know. Tell the truth."

"Why did you lie to me?"

"About what?"

"About where you were."

"I didn't lie to you. I was at my parents', Mount Ivy."

"You didn't come home by train."

"I didn't say I did."

"But you didn't say how you came."

"Do I have to tell you everything?"

"Only important things. The car you came in, it's still down in the street here."

She didn't answer immediately.

"At the curb," he said. "Whose is it?"

"He said he was going into the bar around the corner on Seventh Avenue."

"Who said?"

"Freddie. How did you know I came in that car?"

"I saw you."

"Why didn't you tell me when I came in? What's all this secrecy and detective work and questioning? All right! So Freddie brought me home."

"He took you out too."

"You're some detective! How do you know that?"

"Three cups for coffee here when I came. You spent whole day with him."

"My parents like him. They invited him. He suggested I ride out with him."

"Why you don't tell me that before?"

"Because I knew you'd behave as you're behaving."

"I got good reason. Now tell me this: Freddie, he—"

"Save me your police inquisition, please. I'm sick of it."

"Don't get fresh with me, bitch!"

"Don't talk to me that way! And if you're waiting for me to apologize, don't. Because I have no intention of—"

"Freddie, he touch you? Tell me that—he grab hold of you?"

"He didn't grab hold of me, because I didn't let him."

"But he tried to get you?"

"He always does."

"Since he always does, why you went out with him? Since you expect he would again."

"Because it was a hell of a lot more convenient than going out there on the ferry and in the train, wouldn't you say?"

"What I say is you still playing your old game with this Freddie."

"I do like him, but not in the way your twisted mind works."

"My twisted mind. All right. My twisted mind wants to know, since you expected that he would—"

"I didn't say I expected that he would. I said—"

"You said he always does. So you expected."

"This time he got more drunk than usual. You know my mother and alcohol."

"I know you too. You smelling like a bum today, lady, and your chin, she's all red tonight, lady, all rough and red."

"That's from you. Last night! Trying to make love to me when you couldn't. Freddie has no beard to speak of. This is from you! Oh, God, I'm sick of this. I'm sick of it! Every day something. I'm sick of you. All this fussing about love when the fact is you rarely touch me now—"

"I touch you when I like you which is when I like you."

"All right. You don't like me, I don't like you. That straightens everything out in a hurry. I'm sick of you too, you got it?"

"You smell of booze tonight—what you expect?"

"What about *your* smells? That Near Eastern smell from rugs or goats or olive oil or garlic or something! It may fetch Anatolian women, but it doesn't fetch me, not anymore. I don't have to explain anything to you, and I won't. I'm sick of your constant suspicion and your questions, your spying and your distrust and your everlasting hatred."

She closed her eyes, she was silent. When she spoke again, it was in her small-girl's voice. "Why are you doing this?" she said. "Why do you want to lose me?"

"I do nothing," he said. "You did everything."

She went on as if he hadn't spoken. "Why do you want, bit by bit, to drive me off? Because I can't take it anymore. I'm not threatening—I simply can't. You're making me lie to you. I'm afraid to tell you things I would and should, ordinarily, tell you easily, because I'm afraid of provoking another of these storms of suspicion and resentment. Which I can't take anymore. I can't! And I won't!"

She stopped, breathing hard. When she spoke again, it was in an even softer tone. "Please, please, please, see what you have here—because otherwise, it will soon be too late. One day you'll come in and I won't be here. I've thought about that, leaving you. Not for another person and—oh— not for Freddie. You're jealous of Freddie! Why do you think I left him? Because I wanted him? What's the matter with you? You're the one, don't you know that? Look at me, look at me. Can't you see that?"

Rising from the bed, she went to him and put her arms around him. The doorbell rang.

"Who the hell is that?" Stavros said.

He'd been walking around the room in agitation. Once he'd had the impulse to dress and had started toward the chair where his clothes were, but then he stopped. Now she held him tight in her arms.

The doorbell rang again. Ignoring it, Althea said, "The reason you can't make love to me the way you used to, darling, is because you're so full of anger against me. But why, suddenly over these last weeks, I don't know. Tell me. Because all I know is that you hate me so violently that you can't make love to me."

"I have," Stavros said, "many times."

"I know. But then it got more and more—until now— Why do you hate me so terribly that it's paralyzing you? It can't be something personal, because I haven't done anything. Is it because—you keep grumbling about this—you feel foreign here and I'm part of what makes you feel that way?"

"Well, sure, everybody in this country against me. You too!"

"I can't understand that. I've done everything to let you know that I like you better than anyone who was born here and grew up here, and why do you—"

The doorbell rang again—two short bursts, one long, another short.

Now Althea paid attention. She ran for her bathrobe.

"Who's that?" Stavros asked.

"Morse code for F."

"F? Freddie? Don't let him in here," Stavros said.

Again the doorbell rang, two shorts, a long, and a short.

"I said don't let him in," Stavros said.

"Stavros!" Althea said. "He's a friend of mine. I can't ignore him, I can't just turn him away."

"If you let him in here, I'm going."

"Stavros, this is my place. Damn it! My place!"

She pressed the button that released the street door. Then she turned and looked at Stavros defiantly. If she had cowered or raised an arm to defend herself, he might have struck her.

"Don't you dare do what you're thinking of doing," she said. "If you ever hit me again, it will be the last time!

He looked away.

Then she softened. "He must be terribly drunk," she said. "He was drunk driving home, we were all over the road. Finally I had to steer the car from my side. When we got here, he decided to go to a bar. He's in awful pain. Please try to understand. He's the way you were in Atlantic City when your sister turned against you. Try to remember that. How you were when I came to you. That's the way Freddie is now. I was engaged to him. He can't understand what's happened, why I prefer you. You don't have to talk to him. All right, I won't let him in. I'll open the door just a crack, keep the chain latched. I promise. Then I'll send him away. I'm so sorry for him."

Freddie was at the door. His knock was urgent.

"All right, Stavros?" Althea said. "Please! Try to understand. Will you? Please?"

"I understand," Stavros said. "But you understand too. You lied to me what happened all day today. I tell you again, you let him in, I leave. Now you been also saying bad things to me. I don't forget those things you said to me tonight—when you should be shamed instead." Stavros, naked, got into bed.

Althea did as she promised, opened the door a couple of inches, keeping the latch chain in place. Then what she saw made her quickly unhook the chain and open the door wide.

"Come in here, Freddie," she said. "Oh, Freddie, you awful, awful fool!"

Stavros watched Freddie walk slowly into the room, his eyes fixed on Althea, as a man hypnotized might do. Then he extended his left hand toward her. The back of it was ripped in deep scratches and was bleeding heavily. In his right hand he held a broken barroom glass with which he scored the top of his left hand again. He made no sound, no exclamation of pain, only offering Althea the symbol of the torture she was causing him. It was an accusation.

"Oh, Freddie," Althea said, pulling him by the elbow into the bathroom. "Give me that broken glass. Freddie, what have you done!"

Stavros heard the broken glass drop into the wastebasket. They were out of sight now, but he could still hear Althea's murmured reproaches— her voice loving, soft, maternal—her whispers of concern. He didn't move. He heard the bottles in the medicine cabinet clink. Then Freddie must have said something macabre that amused Althea, because she said, "Oh, Freddie!" again, and laughed the laugh that had been upsetting Stavros all night.

Perhaps she knew the effect that laugh might have on him, for she— or Freddie—closed the door, shutting Stavros off.

He went to the Morris chair and swiftly began to dress.

Althea must have been dousing the lacerated hand with iodine, because as Stavros was pulling on his trousers, he heard Freddie complain in his

drunken voice and Althea say, "Now, Freddie, please! Just hold still!" And
as Stavros was thrusting his arms through the sleeves of his shirt, he heard
Freddie again, murmuring something that made Althea laugh again and
say, "Freddie, don't do that. Be a good boy. Hold still!"

There was a silence as Stavros pulled on his stockings and laced his
shoes. They were taking a hell of a long time, Stavros thought, and then,
as he was putting on his suit coat and starting for the door, there was a
thud, as of a body being thrown against a wall, and he could hear Althea
saying, "Freddie, you stop that—stop it this minute!"

What followed happened so quickly that Stavros himself couldn't have
described it five minutes later when he was out in the street. Again Freddie
said something that made Althea laugh, and at that, Stavros burst into the
bathroom. Freddie, who had a large white pad over his bleeding hand, was
bending over Althea, whom he'd pinned against the wall. He was so drunk
he was unaware of Stavros's entrance.

Stavros ignored him. Taking Althea by the arm, he pulled her, struggling through the bathroom door and flung her into the bedroom. While
she writhed with her considerable strength, not afraid of him now, defying
him, he held her with both hands and shook her hard.

Then she bent over and bit his hand, and Stavros struck her across the
face with an open palm. Freddie roared in from the bathroom to rescue
her.

Stavros picked up the serrated bread knife from the breakfast table.

"You stay out of this, Freddie," Althea shouted. "Stay out of this!"

Neighbors began to be heard, coming into the hall from the other three
apartments on the floor.

Althea was right up against Stavros, face to face, defying him. "If you
ever, ever hit me again," she said, "I will hurt you where it will hurt you
most." She poked at his chest with her finger. "In there! I will talk about
you, tell what I know!"

"Only one way you can hurt me," Stavros said. "Like you're starting
now, doing business with another man. But that you won't do long,
because the legs you walk to his bed, those legs I will break! You understand me?"

"All right. Now we'll see. From this minute on, I am not with you.
We're through. So don't you dare ever, ever, ever, hit me—"

Stavros hit her again, harder.

Badly shaken, Althea held her cheek and called, "Freddie! Help!"

"You hollering for him?" Stavros said. "Against me!" Holding the
bread knife, he turned to Freddie, but he seemed more dazed now than
dangerous.

"Look out, Freddie," Althea screamed. "He's got a knife."

"Let him come, let him come," Freddie said. "Welcome, boy, come to me!" Freddie had picked up the kitchen chair and was holding it, legs pointed toward Stavros.

Someone was knocking on the door from outside, calling, "Are you all right in there? Hey! In there!"

"Yes, yes," Freddie called back. "We're fine here, thank you. Just a parlor game we're playing." Then he turned to Stavros. "Come on, old friend. I'm waiting for you."

Stavros turned slowly and faced Althea. "I see everything now," he said quietly. "I understand everything." He nodded his head several times at her, then turned to Freddie and nodded at him. "O.K.," he said. "Sure!"

"Come on, boy, I'm waiting," Freddie said. "You have a knife. Let's see what you can do with it."

Stavros dropped the knife at Freddie's feet and left the apartment.

The following Sunday morning, Stavros went to call on her.

"You might have telephoned first," she said. "I haven't even brushed my hair."

"You look all right," he said.

She thought him surprisingly calm, and they talked together quietly.

"What I can't understand," he said, "is the following: How, when you're with me, you can be friends with a man you've been with before? Take a ride in his car, take him to your parents, so forth?"

"They invited him." She wondered why her tone was so apologetic.

"But you belong to me," he said, using the present tense of the verb, which signaled to her that in his opinion, their quarrel was over.

Surprised, she smiled, and that made him uncomfortable.

"What you smiling?" he asked.

She shrugged, and pulled the front of her bathrobe together.

"I have to tell you something," he said. "I believe a certain way on these things, I can't help it."

"That I know." She smiled again.

"So from now on, you must treat him like stranger"—he hesitated, then said it—"if you want to stay with me. When he says something to you he thinks is funny, you must not laugh. When he comes into a room, look the other way, or maybe better, leave the room. Then he knows you finished with him. Not like now. Imagine what he's thinking now. You understand what I'm talking? I can't help it, that's the way I am. Why you laughing again?"

"I was thinking: How about the way I am?"

That made him pause. They stared at each other. Then she got up and moved to the kitchen. When she came out, she had a glass of ouzo, which she'd fogged with water. "Too early for this?" she asked. "I understand what you've been saying to me."

"Then all right, what the hell, I take it." He looked at her, took the glass, shrugged, and smiled. "What the hell," he said.

He drank the ouzo. She went back into the kitchen and he heard a familiar sound. When she came out she had a full bowl of pistachio nuts. "I thought you might come back to the scene of the battle," she said.

A half hour later they were in bed. And so they went along, as people do, having nothing better at hand. But although what they'd said to each other that Christmas night may have been forgiven, it wasn't forgotten.

MARCH 1918

The crack in the structure of Sarrafian Brothers that Stavros had been waiting for finally came. Mr. Ara disappeared. One Monday morning he didn't come into the store. Morgan Perry told Freddie that Ara had gone to Arizona for the sun, suggesting that Freddie pass along "this minimal information" to the other employees so that they wouldn't think anything more serious had happened.

Stavros, born to doubt, knew damn well there was more to the story. He'd noticed, with a bitter heart, that before his departure Mr. Ara had held a series of private talks with Freddie and Morgan Perry, as well as several with Freddie alone, keeping him late after work and using the privacy of Mr. Fernand's dark back office. "The seat of power is being fitted to Freddie's ass," Miss Emily Barton said.

So the change, about which Stavros had been so anxious, had not been in his favor and seemed to be a final blow to his ambitions at Sarrafian Brothers. But he needed to know exactly what was happening before he decided if there was still a chance for him, and he turned to Emily Barton, letting her see his disappointment at the turn events were taking. Several years earlier, he had spent a few well-spaced evenings with Miss Emily, and always for practical reasons. It was she who first revealed to him the politics of the store, and he'd devoted himself to her until he'd learned all that he could. Then he pulled away. "Talks too much," he told his brother Seraphim. But now this was precisely what brought him to her again; he wanted her to talk.

His show of renewed interest led to a dinner which Miss Emily prepared in her own apartment. Her hospitality extended to her bed. There, she advised Stavros to return immediately to Althea—she'd sensed a certain cooling—and do everything he could to make that liaison firm. "Your future in the firm will finally depend on Mr. Fernand, and he likes Althea, he always has. I've noticed how his eyes light up when she comes into the store. A word from her at a critical time might mean a great deal for you. A word from her boosting Freddie would cook your Greek goose."

The situation as she presented it sobered Stavros. "You telling me," he asked, "that Mr. Ara not coming back? That he is what he looks like with that big gas belly, very sick man?"

"That big gas belly," Emily Barton said, "is his liver. And liver trouble is booze." Mr. Ara, she said, for as long as she had known him, had had a date at five o'clock every afternoon—with himself for a drink, or two, or three, the reinforcement he apparently needed to face his family in New Rochelle.

People acquainted with the Ara Sarrafian family would agree that it was one of the happiest they knew. There had been an ugly rumor once connected with Mr. Ara, but Mrs. Ara, while her husband was in Carlsbad with his brother Fernand, fired the "nigger maid in question." That was that, and the drama of their lives subsided.

Until the war interfered, Mr. Ara took his break from this happy marriage in the summers. He met his brothers in Constantinople, there checked the stock that Oscar, the youngest, had bought in Persia, which took all of a morning, as well as what other buyers had bought in Turkey and Afghanistan, which took the rest of that day. The rugs of Chinese manufacture were sent directly to New York without inspection. Chinese rugs, in the opinion of the brothers, were like the Chinese themselves: You couldn't tell one from the other. So one long session did it all. After which, the "boys" would enjoy a few days together at the Pera Palace Hotel and its tiled *hamam.* Then Mr. Fernand sent Oscar back to Teheran and took Ara to Carlsbad.

Mr. Fernand had great sympathy for his brother Ara; he knew how serious liver trouble could be. The great specialist he procured for Ara warned him in the most absolute language that he must never "touch" alcohol again, that it would endanger his life if he did, and Mr. Fernand's severe expression reinforced this professional advice. His program for his brother took hold in Carlsbad. The brothers, at Mr. Fernand's expense, stayed at the most luxurious and expensive hotel and took the waters. They patronized the casino, where Ara would lose his hundred dollars regularly while his brother, who seemed bored and indifferent, won and won and won. But Mr. Ara was not depressed by his losses; his loving brother had arranged for him to enjoy the services of a comfortable and undemanding female companion, recently arrived from Vienna. There was this startling development: Mr. Ara still had the five o'clock habit, but what he did at five was to consort with the lady from Vienna. After which he'd sleep, a boy in her arms.

All this was gossip and hearsay, but Emily had some evidence: Three summers running, she'd sent checks to a certain address in Vienna. These checks were signed by Mr. Fernand. "After all," he'd said to her, "I have the strongest possible reason for keeping him well; not only is he my brother, but he runs this store for Oscar and for me. Whom else would I get?"

Once Ara returned to America, the five o'clock drink habit resumed and the symptoms of his disease became more obvious. His face was redder than ever and he made unnaturally frequent use of the toilet; he was always disappearing in that direction. People also observed that he was holding his side, where it had swelled. Then one morning, so Miss Emily heard from a terrified Mrs. Ara on the telephone, Mr. Ara had fainted, in fact had experienced a small seizure, his face twisting up into a tension of the greatest pain. Later he vomited "some black stuff, coffee grounds it looked like." Whereupon he fell back on his pillow, staring at the ceiling without blinking.

Emily Barton had tracked down Mr. Fernand at the Ambassador Hotel in Los Angeles and he'd taken charge from there, arranging the trip to a sanitarium in the sunland, a place famous for treating what seemed to be Ara's malady. Mr. Fernand said he'd meet his brother in Phoenix and to tell Mrs. Ara not to worry.

Emily Barton didn't like Mr. Ara, but she told Stavros the story with sympathy. "Thank goodness Mr. Fernand is with him now," she said. "He'll take care of him. He'll also come here and deal with our problems."

"When? When's he coming?" Stavros wanted to know.

"Soon. Morgan Perry talks to him every day. He's going to do something about the store. I'm sure Mr. Ara will never come back. Yes, there's a big change coming. But don't worry," she said. "Mr. Fernand will know what to do; he has a brilliant mind. I should think his success in his own business proves that."

"What is his own business?" Stavros asked.

"That proves how smart he is," Emily Barton said. "No one knows what he does."

Then she advised Stavros that he had two choices. First, to leave Sarrafian Brothers as soon as Freddie's appointment was openly announced, thus making Mr. Fernand aware that choosing Freddie would cost the firm Stavros's knowledge of rugs, markets, and prices. The second choice, an extension of the first, was to win Mr. Fernand over to his side. "If you have any chance to get Morgan Perry's job," she said, "which I doubt, it would be through and because of Mr. Fernand. I once thought he liked you, but with that man you never can tell. He's smart!"

She walked Stavros to the door, demanding yet another embrace, then trying to pull him back. Fat women, Stavros noted, in contrast to fat men, were often insatiable in sex. He put her off, but she was still kind and supportive, urging him once again to hold on to Althea if he could. "I don't like the way you talk about her now," she said. "She could be very useful to you."

Stavros shrugged. He preferred to appear unimpressed by Emily Barton's advice.

Stavros was let into a handsomely appointed parlor by a woman even a friend might have had difficulty recognizing: Thea Marie. It was her new place, far larger and far richer than where she'd operated before. So was Thea Marie, far larger and far richer, and she'd had her thinning hair dyed red.

"Yes," he said, "I like this place much better. How the hell you make money, place like this?"

"I got rich customers now, politicians. High-class girls too. College graduates—they make most trouble—society women, wives, everything. I got a new one for you special, just came in. A Greek."

"I don't like Greek girls," Stavros said, looking around. "Who? That one?"

"Yes. You interested?"

"I want to talk to you first. Private business."

"Oh," she said. "Come see my room."

Stavros looked around. "Nice place, plenty money here," he said to himself as he followed Thea Marie from the parlor. "I'm in the wrong business maybe. Oh, look at this!"

Thea Marie displayed her bedroom with pride. It was her dream come true: a canopied bed, lace curtains, and photographs of Beirut, her birthplace. "And look," she said, "what I had done: my grandfather and grandmother, painting by oil. Very expensive, but I can afford it now. What's the matter with you? You sick? Sit down there. You look bad."

"I had few disappointments business. But that is business—right? Goes up, goes down. My problem personal. What? I can't do it anymore."

"Can't do what?"

He pointed to the canopied bed. "That," he said.

"You mean sleep?"

"What? No."

"I ask because that would be serious. The other thing, for a man like you, your age, it comes and passes."

"I hope so," Stavros said. He was keeping his head down, his eyes turned away.

"You can believe me," she said. "Who has more experience these problems, you or me?"

"You. That's why I came here. I don't know what's the matter with me, all of a sudden—no, not all of a sudden—six weeks now."

"Maybe it's her," Thea Marie said. "Whoever."

"Maybe. I don't know, is it here or there?" He pointed up and down.

"Your head first. What's trouble there?"

"Nothing. But then, something. I keep thinking she has bad opinion of me. She said something once when she was angry. Then I think of all the other men she's had. That stays on my mind. They are rich, some of them, and famous, one of them. Maybe I appear like nothing to her. I'm suspicious. Even when she tells me she likes me the way I am, I'm suspicious."

"Maybe she means it—maybe she likes you the way you are."

"Maybe. But there's this expression on her face all the time now, sort of funny smile. I mean, like I'm funny and don't know it. Understand? Then another worry: I never know where she is during the day. It's her job; she's not in the same place all the time. I never know how to get her during the day. She gives no information. Where she goes, what she does. I think she wants her business should be mystery from me. You think she's doing that on purpose?"

"Women do that. I like whores better; if I don't know where they are or what they're doing, I put them out, get other ones their place."

"Then I noticing things about her I didn't before."

"For instance?"

"Suddenly she has new way kissing me. Not like anything she did before. Where the hell she learn that? I ask myself. She touches me new place too. Something new all the time, you understand?"

"She trying to get you excited?"

"Maybe. But I wonder where the hell she pick them up all of sudden, these new ways get me excited? Also, something very bad. You paying attention? Used to be even when I got mad at her I could fuck her. But now, when I'm mad—nothing!"

"Didn't this ever happen to you before for a few days?"

"I didn't come here, few days. Six weeks, nearly, I can't do it. It lays there, you understand, like dead *barbooni* fish! She must be going crazy. Beautiful young girl like that, used to it regular!"

"What she say?"

"Says she can wait."

"Well, that's nice. If—"

"If true, right? That worries me. You see, I thought at the beginning it was only for few days, can happen to anyone. But now six weeks, different situation."

"What she think the reason is?"

"She said it's because I hate her and I'm pretending I like her. She says prick never lies. Where she get those ideas?"

"Sounds like college girl!"

"Yes, goddamn it. Why I get mixed up with college girl, tell me that, so many ideas on everything?"

"But what she said about the prick—she's got a point there. Maybe you don't love her anymore. So she's looking around?"

"No, I watch her for that. She's my woman! If she go with other man, I kill him, but her first!"

He got up and walked around the room in a fury.

"Sit down," Thea Marie said. "You walking like a bear."

"Goddamn it, goddamn it, help me! It die all of a sudden and I'm worried. I'm going to kill somebody if it don't get better."

"You try with other girl?"

"That's why I come here, to find out my trouble, how bad it is."

"How old are you?"

"Forty-two. I got to find out. Am I finish?"

"You see that new girl? Before?"

"I told you, I don't like Greek girls. Thick black hair everywhere."

"She's from the Argentine, this one. Half-Greek. Clean, I guarantee. Try her. I'll tell her what to do."

"Don't you have some kind girl with yellow hair?"

"Will you let me do my business my way? Please! Men over forty, sometimes they like child girls. This one looks like saint, clean, innocent. Try her, see what happens. Stay here, use my room. You get in bed first, turn off the light, relax ten minutes, maybe sleep a little, better if you can. She will come in the dark. You won't see her face clear. Then she will get into bed. If you're asleep, she will wake you."

Early the next morning, Stavros left Thea Marie's bed, paid off the half-Greek from the Argentine—she didn't look like a child in the morning light—and went uptown to the family store. Letting himself in, not turning on the lights, he sat quietly in the gentle dark. Waiting for his trusted brother Seraphim, Stavros had a very short but very restful sleep.

The sight of his brother sitting alone in the empty store startled Seraphim. "What happened?" he said. "Something? What? Bad?"

"Did she call last night?"

"Althea? No."

"Good. Well, my brother, you were right. It's her, Althea! Is my trouble. Last night, I was with Greek girl, very young, and I was"—he laughed—"perfect. Better. I did it to her three times. That little girl. Oh, she knows! How she knows! Everything. First Greek girl I like. I began to wonder why the hell I stick with Althea, only her, so long. This girl, she woke me up."

"How many times I told you?" Seraphim said. "You got the wrong girl there!"

An hour later Stavros burst into Althea's apartment reinvigorated, cleansed of his uncertainty, his confidence restored.

"I told you," he said to her in that Anatolian voice of unchallengeable authority. "It's not me, it's you. You made me like that six weeks. You did it!"

Althea looked away and didn't answer.

"Hey, you!" Stavros said. "What you say to that? Because last night I was like *petra* there, a rock. What you have to say to that?"

"What have I to say to that?" She thought for a moment, then answered, "I say, What's the difference? I say, O.K., it's my fault. Tell me what the girl was like."

"A Greek, half, from the Argentine. I don't know, seventeen, sixteen. She brought me to life. I still got it. You were killing me, but I saved myself. I fucked her three times."

"Good," Althea said, quietly.

"Why good! Why you say good?"

"Because I fucked Freddie three times, so we're even."

"You making fun here?" Stavros said.

"I warned you—what you do, I do. Three times, three times. And since you always ask me, he's better than you. Remember you asked me that? Stronger, bigger, and better!"

Stavros hit her hard across the side of the face.

Althea staggered, straightened up. She gave no sign of pain, and when she spoke she seemed absolutely calm. "I can't fuck you anymore either," she said.

Stavros hit her again. She fell sideways, caught the corner of the table, straightened up. She looked at him and smiled her smile, the one he hated. "Go ahead," she said, "hit me all you want, it doesn't change anything. I can't fuck you anymore either. There it is!"

Blood seeped between her very white teeth.

"Aren't you going to hit me again?" she said. She touched her lips with her finger, looked at the blood on it. "Oh, look," she said. "I'm glad," she said. She smiled at him, the smile he wanted to wipe from her face. "Now you'll be able to, I'll bet," she said, "because now I'm a stranger again."

She was right. He pushed her on to the bed, and when he fucked her —he fully dressed, she with her bathrobe parted—she neither resisted nor participated. It was as if it didn't matter to her, one way or another—a sure sign that it was over. But he didn't know that.

When he was through, he fell asleep. As she got ready for work, he was still asleep. She took her clothes into the bathroom and, looking into the mirror, she was shocked. The bleeding had stopped, but her face was beginning to swell and it was red in blotches. She considered not going to work, but she thought, *It's the fact of my life, this face, the way it is now.* She dressed and left without waking him.

That night, Stavros came back to Althea's apartment, even more angry than he'd been in the morning. It had just become known that Freddie had received the boost in pay which signified that he was next in the line of succession. The news spread quickly through Sarrafian Brothers, then to the other Oriental rug enterprises in their building. Within the hour, Freddie's friends were congratulating him and Stavros's friends were expressing their sympathy.

When he let himself into the apartment, Stavros found a stranger there. "Who the hell are you?" he demanded.

"My name is Maud," the young woman said. "I was Althea's roommate in college. She asked me to come in and pack some of her clothes for her."

Maud was an extremely energetic, utterly capable little person, just over five feet tall and appearing years older than she was. As Stavros was to find out, she was amused at the drama and tensions that resulted from her friend's erratic sexual behavior. Maud herself was a virgin; it was a way of life she preferred.

"Pack up her clothes! For what? Where she going?"

"That I can't tell you," Maud said. She was arranging skirts carefully along the bottom of a large suitcase on the bed.

"You have to tell me. Where?"

"Don't be absurd," Maud said.

He marched on her. "Listen, Miss, I want to know where she is now and where she thinks she's going."

Maud laughed, then faced Stavros directly, six inches shorter. Adjusting her glasses on the bridge of her nose, she said, "You mean you're threatening me with some sort of violence? That really would be a compliment!"

"What?"

"Now would you please step to one side. I need to get into that closet."

She proceeded to fill the large suitcase and a small valise, wrapping shoes in shoe bags and folding lightweight dresses neatly to make sure they weren't creased where they shouldn't be.

"Somewhere hot?" Stavros said. "I see that."

"Well, that's a sign of some intelligence. I'd be impressed if it weren't so absolutely obvious from the clothes I'm packing that a child would quickly have come to the same conclusion. Now just stand over there, please. This chest of drawers is next. There! Thank you!"

She went on packing as if he weren't there.

Stavros didn't know what to do.

"May I tell you something?" Maud said. "If you really care for Althea's welfare in the years ahead—and I'd rather believe you do—you must recognize, even though it's probably too late now, that Freddie could have been and perhaps may still be the only solution to her life. Freddie, if I may invite your displeasure, is a much better man than you or most of your sex will ever be—honorable and clean-hearted. I cannot understand—excuse the candor, please—why Althea chose to give herself to a series of—I do hope you'll forgive me for this—extremely eccentric choices. Does that make you mad? Surely you must know what everybody else does—that you're an extremely eccentric choice for a girl like Althea. Excuse me— passing through to the bureau again. Thank you."

She carried a load of underclothing past him to the small valise. "I mean," she went on, "if Althea had been sensible about her life and taken my advice, she'd be living now in a comfortable home with a couple of beautiful children—physically, she and Freddie are a perfectly matched pair; if they were horses, who'd hesitate to mate them? She'd also have, by now, all the protection from uncertainty that Freddie could give her and you cannot. Let's leave it that way. And instead of—you'll agree with this, I'm sure—that puffed-up windbag, the musician, and that other one— Did you know about the Negro? He was a friend of Freddie's, went to Williams with him; a brief liaison, that one. Did you know about that?"

"No," Stavros said, "I didn't know . . . about that."

He was shocked, Maud could see, but perhaps less so than she'd hoped.

"There were others too," she said, "whom I'll not name. Now she's really got herself into a mess and I certainly don't intend to go into that with you. But perhaps something can still be done—"

"What the hell you're talking about, I don't know."

"Just as well. I have to get by again. Thank you."

Vigorously, she stuffed stockings into the suitcase.

"At least she's made one good resolve. To turn her back on you. When you hit her the second time, she said, that was the end. 'I came to my senses,' she said. A little late, but certainly a step in the right direction, don't you agree? I mean, for her. I haven't the foggiest idea what it might mean to you, and candidly, I don't care. Oops! My glasses keep falling off. Must get them fixed before we leave. There! I guess that will do her."

She turned to Stavros. "Don't look so downhearted," she said. "I suspect that on a day not too distant, you'll see that it's the best thing for you too. You should marry one of your own kind, don't you think? I mean, you surely don't believe you could manage a girl like Althea. Can't do it by beating her, you know. I despise what you did to her. Despise it! The side of her face where you hit her is terribly swollen, it will be for weeks. Where did you get the idea that was the way to treat a woman?"

"Sure I beat her! How she knows what's right, what's wrong, if I don't beat her?"

"My God, where did you get those ideas? What kind of people do you come from? Is it common practice among your people to— Oh, what's the point?"

She closed the larger bag, locked it, and slid it off the side of the bed. "I wonder if you'd carry this bag downstairs?" she said. "It's a bit heavy for me. And get me a cab. Won't take you but five minutes. Will you? Thanks. I'll take the small one. Returning to the subject of Althea, you can do one decent thing for her at last."

"What?"

"Disappear. Here, let's go, let's go. I'll lock the door. Go on down."

Stavros leaned close to her. "She did it to Freddie," he said. "Behind my back! The monkey business."

"Nonsense," Maud said. "Althea stays with the one she's with until she's no longer with him. In that sense, she's a one-man woman. At the same time—well, she's a complete romantic. You simply can't believe everything she chooses to say. But romanticism is for sophomore year. By the time you're a senior, you have to face up to final choices. Althea, I believe, has learned that now. She won't need to have all kinds of sordid drama swirling around her to make life—what? Interesting? Are you really? Interesting? Here, I'll lock the door!"

She dug a key out of her purse.

"Well, anyway," she said as she turned the key in the lock, "it's over now, thank God!"

APRIL 1918

Mr. Fernand Sarrafian was enjoying his spring in the flowering desert. This man had long ago learned to make the best of whatever circumstance he found himself in, and since he had to look after his brother Ara, and since it was impossible, because of this and the war, for him to spend that April under the chestnut trees of the Champs-Élysées, Fernand found what pleasure he could in Phoenix and its more leisurely ways. The joys of indolence, however, did not dull the edge of his wariness or gentle his cynicism; he never forgot the lessons his experience had taught him: Trust no man, no government, no god. "Don't worry," he was fond of saying. "Things will turn out bad." A cheery remark.

He particularly didn't trust the federal government of the United States of America and its postal service. When the time came for his brother Ara to affix his now shaky signature to certain tax forms and a revised will, Fernand decided to protect all concerned against accident and have an emissary from the East get on a train, carrying to Arizona the packet of legal and financial papers which required Mr. Ara's signature.

Mr. Fernand considered Stavros to possess all the more formidable yet useful qualities of a gangster, so he chose him in preference to anyone else to bring the papers safely West, wait while signatures were inscribed before witnesses, then carry them back to the New York headquarters of Sarrafian Brothers where a lawyer and an accountant were waiting.

Mr. Fernand considered his choice of Stavros an honor; Stavros thought it an insult. His pride was stung; he'd been reduced to an errand boy again. But he felt a little better when, Ara having affixed *Ara Sarrafian* wherever the little penciled *x*'s were waiting, Mr. Fernand informed Stavros that he was taking him to dinner.

The train to back East would not arrive at Phoenix until about one o'clock in the morning, which gave the two men time for a leisurely dinner at a private club. Mr. Fernand, wherever he traveled, soon found himself invited to partake of the privileges and advantages of a "club," and always one which served alcoholic beverages at all hours; this was the critical consideration.

"The wines available here, my cantankerous Greek friend," Mr. Fernand informed Stavros that evening as they sat at table, "are not within my capability to ingest. I believe we will do better with their native whiskey, diluted and sparked up with White Rock water."

So they drank a whiskey from Kentucky, Blue Grass bourbon. "You fancy it, I hope?" Mr. Fernand asked.

"No," Stavros said. "I don't like the taste."

"I'll get you a couple of bottles to take back East," Mr. Fernand said. "It does take some getting used to." He signaled the waiter for refills and asked for the menu. Then he turned to Stavros and studied him. "What's the matter?" he asked. "If the question does not intrude on your peace of mind."

"With me? Why?"

"You seem even more surly than usual tonight."

"What you expect? You make errand boy out of me again, bringing me here."

"I thought you might enjoy the change of scene."

"Too late to do me those kind of favors, Mr. Fernand. I'm leaving."

"Your train doesn't pass through until one o'clock. We have time for a nice dinner and—"

"I mean the company, I'm leaving your company."

"Oh! Really. Well, then—I'm fortunate for this opportunity to have a farewell chat with you."

The waiter brought menus. Mr. Fernand studied his.

"Tell me," he said, eyes on the print. "Am I supposed to take your last declaration seriously—that is, literally—or is it the opening salvo of another of your offensives to obtain a raise in pay?"

Stavros looked at his menu. "What's this here? New York steak? I come here for New York steak!" Then he looked at the big boss, no longer as a man in whose employ he labored. "When you make up your mind pay me what I'm worth and give me right position . . ." He folded the menu. "O.K., New York steak."

"I'll have the same, waiter—mine blue, his dark brown." He turned to Stavros. "You were saying, when I make up my mind . . ."

"Then send Freddie for me."

"Don't you ever give up?"

"I give up hundred times already."

"You've never given up and you haven't now."

"This time, yes. Last chance for you."

"So then—just to keep the flow of conversation going—tell me your idea of what you're worth and the position you believe you should be accorded."

"Second question first. Put me in charge Sarrafian Brothers store."

"But I have my brother and Morgan Perry and—"

"Those men dying."

"How dare you talk that way! Are you totally lacking in human compassion?"

"All right, little human compassion. Send those two men to Florida, away from their wives, who are killing them."

Mr. Fernand had to laugh. "And Freddie?"

"He don't like Florida?"

The old man laughed again. "And to continue this idle speculation, tell me what you'd require as compensation if I was fool enough to put you in the executive position you're demanding. Head of the company, is that what you ask?"

"Yes. And forty percent of the profits."

The old man laughed uproariously. "You are a good one," he said. Then he began coughing uncontrollably.

Stavros ignored his condition. He was devouring the bread and butter pickles and making sandwiches of the hot chilis. "You're an intelligent man," he continued. "You see Sarrafian Brothers gone to hell now. Stock less than half what it was when the war started. You know what that means. You're not stupid."

"Thank you. Much obliged," Mr. Fernand said.

"I'm giving you friendly advice only. I have no interest now. We have our own company, my brothers and me. As soon as war is over, I will go into Turkey and Persia, take our capital there, and begin buying."

"Your capital? How much is that?"

"Maybe fifty thousan'."

"Maybe less."

"I will make it multiply. In two years I will take Sarrafian's place as the big outlet store, New York market."

"Oh, please, give us at least three years of continued supremacy."

"Because I will have the goods to sell and you will have nothing, still be scrounging market, what you can pick up there. That's what I was going to do for you, go there as soon as those countries open again and buy. But your damn fool brother, he has a short nose and can't see past its end. As for Freddie, send him back to Wall Street. Market going up soon, any damn fool can make money there, but in our business it's time for courage and action. These people you have there are not men.

They're finished. Tell me which of those men even fuck their wives!"

"Don't wait for kindness from the young!"

"I'm not young. I'm forty-two. You see, now that I've quit your company, I talk straight to you. I'll tell you something else. Inside your heart, you know I'm right."

"Didn't you notice," Mr. Fernand said, "that my brother is perfectly healthy again?"

"Too bad. I mean for the business. You understand what I mean?"

"Don't wait for kindness! But you'll have to admit, even though it's your ingrained disposition to hate everyone in the world above you, that—"

"Why should I like your brother? Anytime it came to a choice, he preferred Freddie over me. He put Morgan Perry to humiliate me on the floor, Sarrafian Brothers store, again and again. I say nothing but I don't forget."

Mr. Fernand chuckled. "You're a mean little bastard," he said.

"Oh, yeah, sure, what the hell. Anyway, I agree one thing—he's looking maybe little better, your brother."

"That's generous of you."

"Main thing, you took him away from his wife."

"Did you notice his belly is down, on the right side? Far down?"

"That's good?"

"My God, you're ignorant. That's where his liver is, the seat of his trouble. Not only has it returned to normal, but his headaches have let up and his constant thirst. What all that means is— Am I boring you? You're looking at that blonde? Forget her. She's far past the reach of your financial resources."

"One day they'll crawl to me, those golden hair girls!"

"As Shakespeare said—you read Othello?—first put dollars in your purse. By the way, I understand Althea has left you, am I right?"

"Nervous girl. She make mistake. She come back."

"My God, are you arrogant! Anyway, back to my brother. He hasn't touched a drop of this miserable stuff"—he lifted his glass and sipped whiskey—"not for six weeks. And—can you keep anything private? You nod but I doubt it. Oh, what the hell. My brother feels so good now that he even consulted me about divorcing his wife and daughters. That's how good he feels!"

"First sign of intelligence I heard from him. I've got to ask you question. How did you do it? When he left New York, I thought Mr. Ara was taking his last trip. How did you fix him up so quick?"

Mr. Fernand settled back, signaled for the waiter, and said, "I did what I always do—get the best people to help me. I brought a specialist from London here."

The waiter was bending over him. "Yes, sir?"

"A package of Melachrino cigarettes please."

"We don't have that brand, sir. Camels? Lucky Strikes?"

"I can't smoke those."

"I brought you some," Stavros said. "Forgot to give them to you before." He pulled his valise out from under the table—and from under the feet he'd kept on it to keep it safe.

"Ah," Mr. Fernand said. "How can I thank you?"

"Don't bother yourself. I don't need your help anymore. Here, smoke."

The old Armenian laughed, nodded. "I'm surprised how much I enjoy your company," he said. "I thought this would be a chore tonight, but—"

"Well, what the hell—you done the talking, you enjoy that."

The old man laughed again as he split open the box of Melachrinos. "What was I talking about this time?"

"Who knows?" Stavros said. "Always something. Oh, specialist from London."

"He examined my brother," Mr. Fernand said, "and he gave me his absolutely candid opinion. 'We don't entirely know how to deal with this condition yet,' he said. 'Someday soon we will, but your brother may be gone by then. Meantime we have to do our best with what we have. For your brother, no alcohol is fundamental. Also no sugar. And here's a prescription. The strictest surveillance to insure that he doesn't break through my restrictions. This program, if you're rigorous about it, will produce a temporary benefit, nothing more.' 'Isn't all of life temporary?' I said. We shook hands and he was gone, leaving behind a very large bill."

"You can afford it," Stavros said. "Mr. Ara, he agree no booze?"

"Did you notice that large man in white standing behind my brother?" Mr. Fernand said. "I was able to temporarily separate an officer from the police force here and install him on twenty-four-hour duty. There have been several contests of will and strength between them. Ara is clever about getting what he wants, and what he wanted—until recently—was the hard stuff. My policeman needed all his cunning and strength to keep Ara from running a scoundrel with a bottle past his nose. Now Ara has become a teetotaler and wants to divorce his wife and daughters."

Mr. Fernand even took Stavros to the railroad station. "Since I don't ride a horse," he said as they waited for the train in the chill desert air, "since there is no casino here, and since I don't enjoy reading anything except a favorable balance sheet, I get lonely. Even you looked good to me tonight. I cannot believe that I am clinging to your most disagreeable company. . . . Well, here comes your train."

"I want to tell you," Stavros said, feeling friendly now. "As soon as this war over, I'm going back to other side, where I came from."

"So am I," Mr. Fernand said. "This country is uncivilized. By the way, I want to say in parting that I had the impression all through dinner that everything you said to me was part of a carefully planned manipulation."

"Same to you and many of them," Stavros said.

The train roared up. Mr. Fernand screwed a Melachrino into a snub-length amber holder, lit it, and looked at Stavros affectionately. As the conductor lifted the gate for the passengers and Stavros picked up his bag, Mr. Fernand said, "Don't make any foolish moves now. Remember, I have big capital, not your fifty, forty, whatever."

"All aboard!" the conductor called.

Stavros made no response to what the old man had said.

"And I may even have some plans for you. For instance, you're right about one thing, that it's time for bold moves. I may have a plan. I said that because—well, companies are like people: They live, they die, they are born again. So perhaps I'll be having a chat with you soon."

"Send for me to the Polo Grounds," Stavros said. "Send Freddie." Stavros mounted the steps. At the top, he turned and winked at Mr. Fernand.

"Goodbye, son," Mr. Fernand said.

That word, "son," to his surprise, thrilled Stavros. He decided not to quit his job at Sarrafian Brothers.

They saw each other again much sooner than either expected.

"Life is a balance bar," Mr. Fernand said to Stavros as he entered the office of Sarrafian Brothers ten days later. "One side goes up, the other goes down."

Mr. Morgan Perry had been discovered to have cancer of the colon.

"I'll have to rely on you, Freddie," Mr. Fernand said, "perhaps with some assistance from our cantankerous Anatolian, to keep this place operating until my brother returns next week. You'll be surprised, Freddie, how well Ara looks. What do you say to that, Topouzoglou?"

"He look O.K.," Stavros said.

"Greeks know enough to avoid superlatives," Mr. Fernand said.

"I'm awfully glad—I mean about Mr. Ara. That's wonderful," Freddie gushed.

If Stavros had believed that any special warmth had been kindled between him and Mr. Fernand in Phoenix, he saw no sign of it now. Still, he could not forget what the old man had said at the railroad station.

Even after Mr. Ara returned, Mr. Fernand faced a crisis. Yes, Ara looked well, but there was a strange, shifty light in the corner of his eye that did not suggest stability. As for Morgan Perry, Mr. Fernand consulted the Perry family doctor, fired this doctor, brought in a specialist for another opinion, went to another specialist, whom the first specialist recommended, who verified the opinion of the first two: "It's simply a matter of time."

The next step was up to Mr. Fernand.

For a time it seemed as if the brothers Sarrafian might turn to the third brother, Mr. Oscar; he'd been sent for months before, and had finally arrived from Persia. Stavros assumed that Oscar Sarrafian was going to take Mr. Ara's place, but the instant he saw the man, he was relieved of this concern. Mr. Oscar, at three hundred pounds, was what the Greeks call a *phagas*, an eater. His breathing was labored, and he dropped into a heavy sleep the instant he entered a taxi, falling back in the seat and more or less fainting. He often held a brown bag in his lap, which he would open as soon as he woke, to devour the entire roasted chicken it contained.

It was evident to all that Mr. Oscar embarrassed his brother Fernand. Without ceremony, Oscar was sent back to the pilaff in Teheran.

There was a further crisis. Emily Barton had the bad news first and revealed to Stavros that Morgan Perry had to have an operation whose purpose was to create a passage nature was denying him, to void his wastes. Now Mr. Fernand moved swiftly, handling the situation in his most characteristic manner. He threw a party, declaring a holiday—Morgan Perry Day, as it were—to celebrate the manager's thirty years of service to Sarrafian Brothers. Everyone knew it was a retirement party, the end of the road.

The moment of change was at hand.

The baseball season had started just in time; this game was one of Morgan Perry's few genuine passions and attendance at a game became the central event of Mr. Fernand's Morgan Perry holiday. Everyone at the store had the Saturday off, with pay, and everyone was provided with a ticket to the game and invited to the celebration which was to follow.

Morgan Perry came to work that day all dressed up, wearing a gaily striped bow tie and the straw hat he favored in the summer, indoors and out. He already looked thinner, wasted, and needed the support of the person whose arm he held.

Althea. She had returned from wherever she'd been. Stavros had heard rumors two days before that she was back, but when he'd called her apartment, no one had answered. From the street outside, he saw that the window shades were down and the windows shut. When he called Mount Ivy, Mrs. Perry answered the phone. "She's not here," she said. "Don't ever call again."

Althea looked "perfectly beautiful," everybody told her, and "so young!" But to the Anatolian, his ex-lover seemed thin, even desiccated. "How she look to you?" he asked the big boss, Mr. Fernand.

"Depends which side of the East-West cultural line you're on," the old man said. "American people fancy their girls as you see her, bony. Coltish, let's say. So do I."

"She look sick to me," Stavros said. "Where's the suntan and so forth?"

Needing to talk to Althea privately, he edged closer and finally came alongside, but he didn't get to speak more than a few clumsy words. Althea was always talking to somebody else, and Stavros knew this couldn't be accidental.

"I wanted to write you letter," he finally blurted out—Mrs. Morgan Perry was rushing up—"but no one knew where you gone to." He looked straight at Althea's mother and raised his voice. "Maybe they wouldn't say it to me, where you were—what you think?"

Althea didn't respond.

"I wanted to tell you what damn fool I was that morning, you remember? That morning?"

"We remember," Mrs. Perry said. "When you hit her." She took her daughter's arm.

"Forget it," Althea said. "I have."

Mrs. Perry led her daughter to Mr. Perry, who was sitting at his desk, drinking from a small silver flask. He put it away when he saw his wife and daughter approaching. He began to fuss through the drawers of his desk, pulling out all sorts of forgotten things. Stavros remembered Emily Barton's telling him once that Morgan Perry even kept a pocket-sized pistol there.

Mr. Fernand had planned the celebration in his biggest style. There was a sign over the entrance to the store: SARRAFIAN BROTHERS CLOSED ALL DAY SATURDAY FOR MORGAN PERRY DAY. Then, along the bottom, in small type, the reminder: REOPEN MONDAY. Mr. Fernand's new Rolls-Royce plus three taxis were to take everybody—the humblest porter was not excluded —to Dinty Moore's, Morgan Perry's favorite restaurant, for a lunch of corned beef and cabbage. From there the cavalcade was to go to the Polo Grounds, where the Yankees, who'd got off to a poor start that season, were to play the Philadelphia Athletics.

While the assembly was gathering, Miss Emily Barton went around with a tray of sherry glasses filled with Bristol Cream. Stavros kept looking for another chance to speak to Althea alone, but she stayed at her father's side as if they were long-separated lovers. Althea, Emily Barton told Stavros, had returned that very morning from Florida on the sleeper.

Mr. and Mrs. Morgan Perry, Althea, and the Reverend Kenworthy, the tall, handsome, athletic pastor of the Perrys' church in Mount Ivy, rode uptown in the Rolls; the rest of the party, including Mr. Fernand himself, followed in the cabs. "Oh, when the rich decide it's an advantage to be democratic!" Stavros said to himself.

At Dinty Moore's, Mr. Fernand had taken a long table next to the glass partition in front of the kitchen, and was seating the group as if the Morgan Perrys were throwing the party. He enthroned Mrs. Perry at one end of the table, then went to the other end, pulled back the chair, and called for Morgan.

He wasn't at hand. Freddie pointed. Morgan Perry was at the bar near the entrance door, head down, drinking alone.

"Morgan!" Mrs. Perry called. "Morgan, please, we're waiting for you."
Morgan Perry didn't move.

Everybody was looking at him.

The Reverend Kenworthy, sitting next to Mrs. Perry, was whispering
to her. He stood up and hustled to the bar, placed himself next to Morgan
and ordered a shot of whatever Morgan was drinking. They were shoulder
to shoulder, the man of God talking to the doomed man.

Mr. Fernand, unperturbed, seated the rest of the company while wait-
ers began putting out dishes of green olives and celery and cole slaw.
Others came on, holding high frosty pitchers of foaming pilsner. But Mr.
Morgan Perry and the clergyman were still at the bar, talking earnestly
over another double.

Then something astonishing happened. Big Morgan—and he looked
his nickname at that instant, so upright and fierce was he—turned to the
long table where the entire company was waiting for him. Everybody
could see he was searching for someone. It was Stavros; he wanted Stavros!
Big Morgan stretched out his arms and came toward the Anatolian, his
hands outstretched, offering himself in friendship. He was in a glorious
mood now, and after shaking hands with Stavros, he shook hands with
Garabet, the repair man, and Vartan, the touch-up man, then he dashed
to where Althea was seated and kissed her passionately, again and again.
He was saying farewell to them all. Althea knew that—Stavros could read
the pain on her face.

At last Morgan Perry was in his seat at the head of the table, ordering
drinks for everyone, kidding the Irish waiter about having no ouzo, ignoring his wife's "Now, Morgan!," turning on Stavros to demand if he could
take Irish whiskey, and when Stavros, to keep things going, nodded,
ordering him a double old-fashioned made of Jameson's; then he ordered
the same for the other men and grenadine cocktails for the ladies. And Mrs.
Perry kept saying, "Now, Morgan! This is really Mr. Fernand's party, you
know, Morgan," and so on.

But Big Morgan said it was his party, the last he'd ever have, and he
was going to enjoy it. Stavros watched him with admiration, as he drank;
no old-fashioneds for Big Morgan, but doubles, straight, to make sure he
stayed happy.

After the home-style strawberry shortcake, the procession of automo-
biles was to carry everyone to the Polo Grounds, but Morgan Perry
insisted on riding in the same cab with Stavros and Mr. Fernand while his
wife—her parting words were: "Now, Morgan, you behave yourself!"—
got into the Rolls with the Reverend Kenworthy and Althea. Which gave
Morgan an excuse, if he needed one, to dash back into Dinty Moore's,
waving everybody to go on ahead, he'd catch up. Stavros, sent in by Mr.
Fernand to bring out the guest of honor, found him despondent at the bar,
gulping another double while his silver flask was being refilled. But he

seemed happy enough when he rolled out of the restaurant, tucking the flask away in an inside pocket. Stavros thought there was something so boyish and so desperate about the man that for the first time he liked him, admiring how he was fighting off death that way!

Morgan sat between Stavros and Mr. Fernand and was almost immediately asleep. "I can hear you when I sleep," he'd said, chuckling, "so be careful what you say." Then, speaking to himself, his eyes shut, he murmured, "Now, Morgan! Now, Morgan!" Stavros could feel the weight and the warmth of the sleeping man and he knew that if they had come together under other circumstances, without prejudices, they could have been friends. He even liked the man's anger at him; it was something Stavros could have felt if a daughter of his had become involved, outside marriage, with a foreigner.

At the ball park, Mr. Fernand had reserved four boxes, one behind another. On every seat was a souvenir program with a page inserted, across the top of which had been printed, in Old English type: *Mr. Morgan Perry's Thirty Years Of Loyal Service* And then: *Thank You, Thank You, Thank You* over the signatures of each of the three Sarrafian brothers.

"I like Mr. Morgan Perry," Stavros said in astonishment to Mr. Fernand, who was sitting with him in the last box of the four, the one farthest from the playing field.

Mr. Fernand, it soon appeared, had a reason for sitting in the topmost box. As soon as the first Philadelphia player had grounded out, he turned his back to the playing field and produced copies of the *Wall Street Journal* and the *New York Herald* and prepared to enjoy the outing in his own way. "Good idea, these," he said to Stavros, handing him a bag of peanuts. It had been Freddie's suggestion to put a bag on every seat. Then: "Oh, look, he's waving to you!"

Indeed he was. Mr. Morgan Perry had been placed, of course, in the box directly above the roof of the Yankee dugout, along with Mrs. Perry, Freddie, and the Reverend Kenworthy. Behind them, in the next box, were Althea, and her friend, Maud, and Mr. and Mrs. Ara Sarrafian, close enough so they could lean forward and be impressed by the Reverend Kenworthy's knowledge of baseball. But Morgan, restless, had wheeled around in his chair, looking for Stavros, and when he found him, he waved wildly for him to come down to their box, closer to the action. Stavros could read Mrs. Perry's lips: "Now, Morgan. Stop it, Morgan."

Stavros waved back. "I think he gone crazy little bit," he whispered to Mr. Fernand.

"Thank God it's a happy drunk," Mr. Fernand said, unfolding the *Wall Street Journal.* "Look, he's sending the preacher to change places with you. No, she's holding the dear reverend; Freddie's coming up."

"What you want me to do?" Stavros asked.

"Go on. He's got that flask in his inside pocket. See if you can take it away from him. I don't want him falling down at the party."

Freddie came up and Stavros went down. Mrs. Perry gave him a resentful look and pulled her chair as far forward as she could. When Stavros started to slide into Freddie's chair, Big Morgan stood, pushed Stavros into the seat next to his wife, and sat behind him, his hands on his shoulders. He smiled at everybody. "We must educate these foreigners to our customs," he said.

The Yankees had a big inning and Morgan thought it was due to his cheering them on; every time they scored, he celebrated by raising his silver flask. He did this less and less surreptitiously. During one rally his frantic wife snatched the flask out of his hand. When Morgan made a grab for it, she passed it to the Reverend Kenworthy for safekeeping. But Morgan Perry, not a respecter of the cloth, not on this day, pushed his hand into the reverend's pocket and pulled his flask free. Mrs. Morgan's patience was about to give out, but Big Morgan was grinning like a boy who'd stolen a plate of cookies.

I could be this son of bitch's friend, Stavros thought. *I could be an American.*

Then it was between innings and Morgan got to his feet and said he had to go to the Men's and Mrs. Perry was unbelieving. "Now, Morgan," she said, "who do you think you're kidding?" "You don't want me to do it here, do you?" he said, laughing at his great joke. Then he thrust his face up to Stavros's—was he hostile again? Stavros wondered—and said, "Come with me!" Stavros went along just to nettle Mrs. Perry.

Except for one drunk vomiting discreetly in a corner, the Men's room was empty. Morgan Perry pulled out his flask and offered it to Stavros first. "In sweet friendship's name," he cried. So, in sweet friendship's name, Stavros had a pull of the stuff. Then Big Morgan had a final drink, bottoms up, and as he swallowed he looked at Stavros in a peculiar way that made the naturally suspicious Anatolian suspicious again.

Morgan tucked the empty flask away and put his arm around Stavros's shoulders as they went to their section, then down the aisle to their seats. He had begun to sing a song—a Welsh backcountry song, Morgan said, one his father used to sing. His father, he said loudly, had been a coachman, a common driver. Then he confessed that he was not good enough for his wife, goddamn it, he'd always been a disappointment to his wife. "But what the hell, none of us are good enough for our women, are we? You too," he said. "I had such hopes for Althea once, and look what I get. You!"

He smiled as he said that, and Stavros wondered: Didn't he know that Althea had quit him? Was he too far gone to remember, or hadn't she told him? Back in his seat, Morgan fell asleep again; and when the game was over, Mrs. Perry woke him. Although Morgan Perry was known for holding his liquor—he'd practiced every weekend of his adult life—he was not in perfect condition as they left the ball park; he was obstreperous and clearly dangerous.

Waiting for the cars, Stavros supported Morgan, who punched at Stavros's biceps, smiling a taunting smile. Was he looking for a fight? Meanwhile Mrs. Perry was having an urgent conversation with Mr. Fernand and must have convinced him that if she and her husband were alone for the ride downtown, she might be able to deliver Morgan to the party in some kind of shape. Clearly, she was the only one who could prevent him from adding alcohol to the alcohol already in him.

Stavros saw Mr. Fernand kiss Mrs. Perry's hand, then hold the door of the Rolls open for Morgan. Stavros led him to the door, the drunken man hugging Stavros's neck with his heavy arm. "The last of the rebels!" he shouted. "You and me!" Mrs. Perry followed him into the car, not looking at Stavros, not a flick of a glance. Althea had got in with the chauffeur where she would be separated from her parents by a glass partition. Mr. Fernand whispered some urgent directions to his chauffeur— they could only have been: Don't bring him to the store until she's got him a little sober.

The others had to wait almost an hour for the guest of honor—all but the Reverend Kenworthy, who made excuses and left the others to deal with his Sunday school teacher.

They arrived soon after, and the instant Stavros saw Morgan Perry's face he knew that something terrible had happened on the ride down from the Polo Grounds. In that one hour the man's face had grown drawn and desperate; it had begun to waste. Stavros could see the yellowing bones shining through the skin. It was evident that Morgan had had a shock of some kind; it was also evident that he was indeed dying. Here now was a different man—or more accurately, the man Stavros had always known.

A tremor of fear possessed Stavros. In Constantinople, during his hamal years, he had learned to respect his irrational inner voice. "It tells you when danger is coming," a dockside mate of his had said. "Only animals and hamals have this. One day it will save your life."

When Morgan Perry, wife at his side, walked through the door, instead of going to where all the guests were rising from the piles of Sarouk and Hamadan three-by-fives to greet him, he stopped in front of Stavros and looked at him with a question born of hatred in his gray-green eyes, a question he didn't ask. His wife had to pull him away and point him to where people were waiting to offer their gifts and good wishes.

What had happened during that ride downtown? Had the drunken man grown sober? Unlikely. What else could have happened?

The Reverend Kenworthy followed the Perrys into the store. How had he got back in their company? Why did Stavros think that a bad sign?

The crowd of guests swarmed around Morgan Perry, speaking the best words they could. He seemed dazed and unresponsive, like a man walking out of an auto wreck. Looking past the others, he studied Stavros.

Stavros stood, not moving, by the door. The instinct was overwhelming him, warning him—of what? That in this place, at this moment, danger was near? Nonsense. It was absurd to be paying attention to an animal instinct awakened by a glance from the cold eyes of a drunken man!

But the voice from his hamal days persisted: "You're surrounded by enemies. Look to your life." His brain throbbed with the pressure of a deep, irrational fear. If he were an animal, he would be scrambling for his den deep in the earth.

He could see Emily Barton at her desk, waving a small, handsomely wrapped package. He remembered that she'd bought a tie for him to give Morgan Perry—her idea, not his. She was reminding him that the time had come.

As Stavros turned to close the door, the Reverend Kenworthy was making excuses to Mrs. Morgan Perry. "I just hated sneaking out that way, but you know our trains, how they run—or rather, don't run." He laughed guiltily. Stavros heard Mrs. Perry getting her way: "What a lucky chance, catching you at the door, you bad boy, just as you were escaping into the street. Now come, he wants you next to him. Yes, I insist." She dragged the reverend into the thick of the crowd where Morgan was receiving his presents.

"Here! Give it to him," Emily Barton said, coming up to Stavros. "Hurry! It's from Sulka's."

So Stavros, remembering Morgan's friendly behavior to him throughout the day, hurried to where the big man was accepting his presents— a watch inscribed with an extravagant sentiment, a framed photograph of the office staff with everyone's signature, a leather desk set, sumptuously embossed with initials in gold script—all of which he accepted with a nod and a mumble, while intently watching Stavros as he moved forward to offer his gift.

"Best wishes," Stavros said.

Morgan said nothing, his gray-green eyes cold with an unasked question.

"Why you looking at me all of a sudden that way?" Stavros asked.

Morgan shook his head slowly from side to side.

Mr. Fernand, standing behind the table where the drinks were, was tapping the thin rim of a champagne glass with a silver spoon. Everyone turned to pay attention except Morgan Perry.

"Please?" Stavros said. "Say. Hah?"

"I saw from the beginning what you were, boy," Morgan whispered.

"Morgan," Mr. Fernand called in his thin, rheumy voice. "Dear friend Morgan, I am speaking for my brothers and, with their kind permission —may they find my poor words acceptable, *evalah!*—for everyone who's come here to honor you. Now! Please join me, dear friend. Here, at my side! Look, you have a thousand friends! Come. Next to me! You must say a few words."

Morgan Perry didn't move. Mr. Fernand called for help. "Norma!"

Stavros had edged his way behind Althea. "You angry at me too?" he whispered.

"No," she replied as she turned away.

"You're angry," he said. "Why?"

"At myself." She gave Stavros a thin smile.

"That smile," he said, "I remember. When you were fighting the janitor in your building, you gave him that smile."

She hurried to help her mother. Norma Perry pulled the presents out of her husband's hands, handed them to Althea, hooked his arm with hers, and gripping the elbow of the Reverend Kenworthy, pushed the two men to where Mr. Fernand was waiting.

Stavros noticed she whispered something to Mr. Fernand; a warning, he guessed. He came up behind Althea again. "Anyway, be polite," he said. "Why not?"

She gave him another thin smile. "Why not?" She walked away. And this time Stavros didn't follow her. Could this be the same girl? He remembered her from their nights, how the waves of feeling rode over her!

Everyone had had strong drink. There were over a hundred men from the rug trade there—Armenians, Turks, Anatolian Greeks, Jews, Syrians, Persians, Egyptians, even some Americans; associates and competitors, buyers and sellers. These men had known Morgan Perry over a quarter of a century and they were shocked at his appearance. It frightened them; it made them anxious.

Mr. Fernand reached out to bring Morgan Perry to his side. Morgan, pulled off balance, seemed to falter. Everyone saw him reach for the Reverend Kenworthy's support, then reply to Mr. Fernand's solicitude: "Don't worry. Best shape of my life! First time I'm clear on everything. Let's go. What's the program? Here, Althea, fill my glass. It's been empty so long, it's dry."

Althea, who had been arranging the cologne, the cufflinks, and a cable-knit cardigan sweater on the gift table, took his glass, defied her mother's look, and gave her father the drink he'd asked for.

"I've never been able to speak publicly," Mr. Fernand said when they were all in place and quiet. "Thanks be to God, Reverend, it's not been essential so far in my long life. But today, for the first time, maybe I'll try a few words. This modest celebration gives me a chance, and you, my dear friends, the opportunity to make known—if it's not already evident to our dear Morgan—how much we love him."

Mr. Fernand, having said this, began to applaud—not at what he'd said, but because he wished to arouse the general company to applaud Mr.

Morgan Perry. Which they did, except for Mrs. Perry, who was now sitting alone at one side of the gathering. Stavros caught her looking at him—a glance, quickly turned away, which could only be called vengeful.

Did their feeling have to do with Althea? Stavros wondered. If so, they should have been delighted; Althea wasn't talking to him. It must be something more. For Morgan to change so utterly, what did he know now that he hadn't known at the baseball game?

Mr. Fernand was finishing. "The Turkish people—certainly not a great people since they lack both culture and grace—do have their human side. It is their custom when they take leave of a companion to say what I will say to you now, Morgan, my esteemed friend." Whereupon Mr. Fernand raised his arms in a gesture surprisingly theatrical and said, *"Guleh! Guleh!,"* adding, "Laughing! Laughing!" Then he explained. "Do you all know the story of the camel driver who asked his beast if he preferred to go uphill or down, and the camel replied, 'What happened to the level road?' Morgan, as you travel the rest of your journey, may it be what we Easterners call 'a camel's road,' level and pleasantly winding, and may there be, at regular intervals, splendid oases where cool, clear water can be found. So my dear friend, as you start down your camel's road, I say to you, *Guleh! Guleh!* And may the springs of love be waiting for you wherever you go—and speaking of love, it's what everyone here feels for you."

At this the Reverend Kenworthy applauded vigorously, as a signal to everyone, but Morgan suddenly threw his arm tightly around the reverend's neck, and God's minister was still. That was when Stavros saw that Morgan Perry had not sobered, but had arrived at the second stage of drunkenness. Again he was holding out his empty glass to his daughter.

Everyone was waiting for him to speak now; it would be the high point of the celebration. Most of the guests had found seats again and were giving Morgan their most respectful attention.

"Yes, yes," Morgan Perry finally managed to say, and then couldn't go on. Instead he looked at Stavros, and Stavros realized that whatever was keeping Morgan from proceeding did have to do with him.

"Yes, yes," Morgan Perry started again. "Speaking of love, yes, speaking of love . . ." Then he dropped his head, raised it, looked at Stavros, and murmured, "Somebody'd better tie me down. Really." No one spoke. His head sank and he said, "Althea, did you forget me?"

She brought him his drink.

"Althea!" Mrs. Morgan Perry protested too late. "I give up," she said, and when she saw Morgan raise his head to speak: "Now, Morgan, all you have to say is 'Thank you all very much!' and we'll be on our way."

"That is not all I have to say," Morgan Perry said. Stavros noticed how red his face had become. Anger had pumped through his heart and he was breathing hard. "And I won't be on my way anywhere, Norma, until I'm through saying . . . what I have to say here."

Again Morgan looked at Stavros, as if the words he was about to say held a unique meaning for the Anatolian. "This may be my last chance to say anything, boy, or do anything that has to be done before I go . . . not home, Norma, but . . ."

He left it there, smiled at his wife, taunting her, then spoke to the crowd. "How flattered I am that more than a hundred of you big-bellies, the richest merchants in our trade, have come to say goodbye to me. I know the reason you're here, old friends: to witness not the end of a business career, but the termination . . . of a life. I'm honored that you care this much. Thank you."

Despite himself, Stavros found he was liking Morgan Perry again.

"I have cancer," the man said. "All through here." He swept his hand in a wide path across his abdomen.

"Oh, Morgan!" his wife said.

"I didn't know it until a few months ago," he continued, "although without a doubt it's been there for years. I lived a pretty good life until that time, so there's no need to feel sorry for me. Fact is, many of you may have the same affliction and don't know it yet. Just as I didn't. What I wish is that someone had told me what I'm about to tell you. You want to hear? Is anybody in a hurry?"

There were confused murmurs in several languages: No one knew what to say. Many were embarrassed by the personal nature of what Perry was saying.

"Three doctors examined me," he went on. "They came to the same conclusion—that there was nothing they could do. Which is to say that they didn't know the cause or the cure. So they gave up on me. Now they want to operate. Imagine that! A scalpel in the hands of a surgeon who hasn't the faintest idea of the cause or the cure! Why should I agree to that? Meantime I keep getting large bills from these same doctors, posted on the very day they've said to me, 'We don't know what to do!' "

Morgan laughed, quite at ease now, raised his glass to the guests and offered a toast. "Astounding fortune!" he said, and drank, three long swallows.

Mr. Fernand who had slipped behind Stavros, now spoke in his most discreet tone. "Perhaps, dear boy, you'd better excuse yourself from the rest of this celebration."

"Why you say that?" Stavros asked.

"His wife was talking to me rather anxiously—about Morgan's attitude to you. So perhaps—"

"Mr. Fernand—run from trouble! Me? You know me better."

"Well, then, fine, fine. But we'll do our best, won't we?"

"Our best? For what?"

"Not to aggravate the man." He turned toward Morgan, who was downing the last of his drink. "That's his third, damn fool!"

There'd been some restlessness and laughter. Now, as Morgan Perry finished drinking, the laughter stopped.

"It's all right, laugh," Morgan said, putting down his empty glass. "Best way to take it. Life's a laughing matter. You may soon be laughing at yourselves."

"Morgan!" his wife said. "These people don't want to hear all this."

"I found the cure for cancer," he said to the guests. "You want to hear what it is?"

"Oh, Morgan," Norma said, "even the doctors don't—"

"Well, do you?" he demanded of the guests. "Or don't you?"

There was a rumble of embarrassed assent in several tongues.

"Hear that, Norma?" He smiled affectionately at all the guests. "After all," he said to them, "you're my friends, have been for thirty years, so any vital discovery I've made I feel obligated to pass on to you." He tapped his abdomen. "I've learned what caused this—at the price of my own life. And since I know the cause, I know the cure. Be patient. Yes, do sit down. I see this is making some of you nervous."

Again Stavros couldn't help liking the man.

"You remember I had a son?" the man said. "Young Morgan—remember? He was everything to me." Then a sharply spoken command. "Remember him!" There were murmured responses, some in Turkish, "*Eee chojuk! Eee chojuk!*"

"Thank you, thank you. Those remarks, even though spoken in a foreign language, are appreciated by me. Some people think I'm prejudiced against foreigners. They're right." He laughed. "But not when they behave!" He raised his empty glass. "Astounding fortune!" he said. "Time for the truth. The truth is that most of you will remember me with hatred. Fine! So tie me down! I was saying, about my son—God betrayed me. God took Young Morgan away. For no reason. I was a good churchgoer all my life; I even taught Sunday school and made my children go. This act of God, this betrayal, upset me. I even resorted to asking for advice from this one." He threw his arm again around the neck of the Reverend Kenworthy, who was standing ready to support him if he faltered. "That's how desperate I was. Although I don't believe anybody can help a man with a loss as terrible as the death of a son. No help for that, is there?"

There was no way Stavros could help caring for this doomed and tortured man who obviously hated him. Morgan must have read Stavros's face, because he said, "I see you're remembering Young Morgan, Joe. Is that what I see?"

"We were friends," Stavros said.

"He understood you," Morgan said. "I don't. Every time I thought I did, I paid for my mistake."

"Now, Morgan, that's enough," his wife said, rising from her chair. "I'm going home."

"Goodbye," he answered. "Astounding fortune!" And he lifted his glass, which Althea had quietly refilled. "I'm going to stay here, Norma, as long as I have listeners and there's booze to be had. I think all these men here, to look at them, may be under the same gun I've been under for years and didn't know it. I see a lot of swelling bellies here; that's the first sign. So be patient, all. I'm coming to it. The cure! The cause and the cure! Patience!"

He sipped his drink and said, "About my son. After his death, let me tell you, I wanted to curse God. I wanted to revile Him. The anger got stronger and stronger. But I silenced it. And let me tell you, it took the kind of effort they call superhuman for me to forgive God. 'We must accept God's will,' Ken here used to say to me." Morgan tightened his hold on the Reverend Kenworthy's neck. "And I did. I didn't curse God for taking my son; I praised him. I accepted that he was right. 'Bow your head in humility,' Ken told me, and I did. I forgave God."

Morgan sipped at his drink and there was a silence. "Damn Him!" he said, and he had to make an effort to continue. "Because the day I decided to forgive Him, that day, I felt the cancer for the first time." He passed his hand over his abdomen as he had before, the same long, slow path across the swelling there. But this time his face was all hatred. "I felt my belly tightening around the great lump of anger," he said, pounding his abdomen with his fist.

"Daddy, don't do that," Althea said. "Please."

He didn't hear her. "This hard lump is my willpower holding in the anger. I made this!" He pounded his abdomen again. "The more I praised God—Ken, listen to this!—instead of damning Him, the bigger and the harder this damned cancer became!"

"I will have to talk to you about all this," the Reverend Kenworthy broke in.

At the front door there was a stir. The door swung open, and two men in ragged clothes, unwashed, unshaved, looking like tramps, entered.

"Man's hope is a deceit," Morgan was saying. "Perhaps God meant us not to trust our hopes."

Stavros felt he should know these men. Did he? From long ago?

Morgan turned to the reverend. "What do you say to that, Reverend Ken?"

"God means us to hope, of course," Ken said. "We must trust God's love."

Stavros remembered. There had been a letter from Michaelis some weeks before, from the island of Chios, to inform him that two men who had been working behind the Turkish lines were coming to America for reasons Michaelis would explain later.

"Well, I have a contrary opinion," Morgan said. "God's love failed me. My boy died."

"God's love hasn't failed you," the reverend said. "Has it, Norma?" Mrs. Perry looked back at him scornfully.

Stavros remembered what Michaelis had written. "For the love of our country, protect these men, feed them and give them shelter." Were these the men? They were standing just inside the door now, looking around the store for . . . for him? They were clearly of his own race. He nodded to them and smiled.

"God failed me!" Morgan said. "He failed her too." He pointed at his wife. "She said to me what you did, Ken, that Young Morgan's death was God's will. But the difference is, she believed it. I didn't and I pretended I did. I held my anger in and—it's here still!" He gestured toward his swollen abdomen. "Yes, I forgave Him," Morgan Perry said, "when what I needed was to curse Him, even kill Him, if such a thing is possible. I sang his damned hymns in church and squeezed in my anger so this"—he drew his hand across his abdomen—"got harder and bigger, until now it's an iron bar. The more dutiful and God-fearing I was, the more I—" He jerked his hold tight on the reverend's neck.

"Don't!" Kenworthy said sharply. Then he whispered, "Stop it, Morgan! Let me go now, please. Now!"

"No!" Morgan said. "You have to face this with me. You have a responsibility in this matter. You misled me, Ken."

Garabet, the repairman, was at the door talking to the strangers in a low voice. Stavros hurried up to them, and said, "How are you?" to the taller of the two.

"Thanks to God," the man said. "I'm Simeon Hadjopoulos."

"And you?" The other man was much shorter and very thin.

"Glory to God," he said, but didn't give his name.

"I ask you for an explanation, Ken," Morgan was saying. "Is life anything more than a series of accidents? Can God's cruelties be explained? You know they can't, don't you? But I don't blame Him anymore. I betrayed myself, and because of that, I got what I deserved. This! A bill comes—always. Well, I got it. The bill for betraying myself! It's come!" He finished his drink, put the glass on the table, looked at Stavros. "Somebody'd better tie me down," he said. "This is your last chance. Come on. I mean it!"

There was silence. Nobody laughed. Nobody moved.

"Your brother Michaelis sent us to you," the taller of the two men whispered to Stavros. He was a sailor, and to judge from his cap, a captain.

"Last chance," Morgan Perry said. "Well? Nobody? Then I'll go on. Now—since I know the cause—I come to the cure."

It was Norma's last chance. Perhaps she knew what her husband had in mind. "Morgan, stop it!" she said. "There's no need to be so personal and so blasphemous!"

"I thought you went home," Morgan Perry said.

"Your feelings, your theories, don't interest anyone here. You've simply had too much to drink—with the help of your daughter. Everybody can see that you're very, very drunk. So please, this is a party. I mean, shut up!"

"You shut up," he said. "About drink: I tell the truth only when I'm drunk. Drink releases all that's best and honest in me. Since today may be my last day on earth, everybody will have to bear with me, or— Well, the door's not locked, and I don't see anyone leaving. Do you, Norma?"

He raised the glass that Althea had refilled again, smiled at the guests, said, "Astounding fortune!" and emptied it. Then his eyes swung around until he found Stavros at the door. "Joe!" he called.

"I'm listening," Stavros said.

"Good! Because now this concerns you, Joe," Morgan said. Then he turned to the merchants. "Yes, drink and my desperate circumstance have, at last, released the truth in me, and you'll do well to listen carefully, because now I'm about to tell you my secret—what I learned from my experience: not from a doctor, not out of a book, not out of the Bible, but from living. Here it is! Joe, pay attention."

"I'm listening," Stavros repeated. He was leading the two strangers to a pile of Bokharas. The thin one—the "ferret," Michaelis had called him, his real name Efstathis, Stavros remembered—wouldn't sit; he was too interested in his new surroundings. The tall, handsome captain, Simeon, was exhausted and glad to rest.

"With my son dead," Morgan said, "I put all my feelings onto Althea. She's the only person in the world I love, so when I see her hurt, I have murder in my heart, Ken, not love. She was my hope to continue our family after my death. It's not the same, of course—the name of my family won't continue—but I decided to make the best of it." He was looking at Stavros as he spoke.

"What's he saying, all the time looking at you?" Simeon whispered to Stavros.

"Foolishness. He's cursing God," Stavros said. "Years ago, he had a son who died." Simeon crossed himself. "Tell me," Stavros said, "how's Michaelis?"

"He didn't write you?" Simeon asked. "He lost an arm."

"Even when she made an attachment I completely disapprove of," Morgan Perry continued, "I did my best to be understanding, didn't I, Ken? I obeyed God's will, didn't I?"

"How did it happen?" Stavros asked. "The arm?"

"Just below the shoulder," Efstathis said, "the left arm."

"He landed with some men in Aivalik, where there are still many Greeks. At night they moved down to Pergamum, where they blew up large ammunition supplies in the old Roman temple there. They didn't all come back. Your brother was lucky."

"Even as late as this afternoon, I was—what, Ken? love your neighbor? yes—I was trying my best to obey God's will."

"Where's he now?" Stavros asked.

"Still in Chios. The monastery, Nea Moni, on the mountain above the city where the bones of the martyrs are."

"What are you women whispering?" Morgan said suddenly. "Stop it!"

Everybody turned to where Althea and her mother were standing, and in the sudden silence, they heard Althea's hoarse whisper. "What did you tell him that for? Why did you do that, damn you, Mother."

Mrs. Perry became aware that people were listening. "Now, Morgan," she said, "don't you think that—well, there's so much delicious food. Everybody! Why don't we eat?" She spread out her arms, a model hostess, and moved toward the table where the food was.

"Yes," Mr. Fernand said. "Delicious cold meats from Reuben's! And caviar!" But no one stirred. The absolute sincerity of the doomed man and his pain had pervaded the room.

"That's when the question came up in my mind," Morgan said. "What will my reward be for obeying God's will? For being Christian when I should have been a murderer? What's my reward for letting my cancer grow bigger and bigger this way? What will be the final bill for that?"

"I'm hungry," Efstathis whispered to Stavros. He was looking at the buffet table.

"They delayed treating the wound," Simeon said. "It got infected. In Chios, the doctors didn't know what to do. It was turning green. They took his arm to save his life, the doctors said."

"I tried to accept her lover," Morgan said. "Against my true feelings. What will the bill be for that?"

"Why's he looking at you that way all the time?" Simeon asked again. "Does he hate you?"

"He's sick, poor man," Stavros said. "He's going to die."

"I'm hungry," Efstathis said.

"I couldn't stand the sight of him," Morgan Perry said. "But I choked down my anger. I was a God-fearing man, wasn't I, Ken? Wasn't I, Norma?"

Mrs. Perry had poured herself a drink. "Too late, too late," she was muttering.

"Go to the table," Stavros said to Efstathis. "Take food, but quietly."

"Yes, there's a price for everything," Morgan said. "You always get a bill, don't you? Your advice, Ken—it's been killing me! The price is my life."

Efstathis moved swiftly to the table where the food was.

"I'm going to go to Chios," Stavros said. "Bring a good doctor."

"He's coming here," Simeon said.

"When?"

"Soon."

"No, no," the Reverend Kenworthy said, "you mustn't believe that. God will reward you."

"Well, Ken, this afternoon, coming down from the ball park, I got His bill in full! I learned what God's reward was. And you know who's going to pay that bill? Not me, no; not my wife, no. The innocent one, my daughter."

"I must bring him here, to a good hospital," Stavros said.

"He's on his way now; he's on a boat," Simeon answered.

"An hour ago," Morgan Perry said, "in Mr. Fernand's Rolls-Royce, I was told what God's bill was—not to be paid by me but by my daughter, Althea."

"Daddy, stop it!" Althea was speaking for everyone to hear. "Please don't, for my sake! I've forgotten about it. It's finished now, Daddy! So forget it. It doesn't matter now."

"I'm almost through, my darling," Morgan said.

He was staring at Stavros, at last distracting him from his conversation with Simeon.

"Well, now, my friends, I will get on to what you've all been waiting for. What is the cure?" Again he looked at Stavros. "I've decided not to allow the cancer to grow further," he said. "Today I made up my mind that the cancer will die and I will live. I will not contribute to its growth. Perhaps it's too late, but—I will—give it a try."

He was breathing very hard now and it was clear to everyone that he was preparing himself for an act he hoped would clear his life of shame, and that he was approaching this crisis with fear and uncertainty.

"This"—he indicated the presence in his belly—"is nothing but a lump of anger and hatred that I didn't release when I should have. It's in there eating me alive because when I should have liberated it, I held it in. It's in there now and it's devouring me."

"Too late," Mrs. Perry said, glass in hand. "Too damned late!"

Morgan Perry turned to the Reverend Kenworthy one more time. "The truth is, Ken, that I went against my nature. I have no forgiveness in me, Ken. I'm not a charitable man, I'm not a compassionate man, I'm not a forgiving man. I have no mercy. I am not kind. I am like your God. I hate my enemies."

He turned to Stavros and said, "Joe, from the moment I first saw you, I wanted to kill you. That's the truth. I can't say why. But I pretended. I pretended as late as this afternoon. I hated you more than I ever let anyone see. When you took up with my daughter, I wanted to kill you then but I didn't—because—because—it seemed she liked you. Now she's found you out. So I'm free of that! Joe—I warned you many times. Go back where you came from, I said to you. You don't belong here, I said. You thought I was speaking in jest, eh?" He couldn't go on, he was breathing so hard.

"What's he saying now, with that face to you?" Simeon said.

"He's saying I should go back to Anatolia, some such nonsense! Come, get up. I'm leaving. We'll find a restaurant." He put his arm around Simeon and started for the door, swaggering, his head thrown back, his free arm swinging, in a posture of total defiance. To Morgan, it was a challenge.

"That's what Michaelis told me to tell you," Simeon said, as they walked toward the door. " 'Come back to Anatolia,' he said I should say to you. 'Your country needs you. You're missing its days of glory. History is being made and you're selling rugs.' I say it too, Come back, we need you, all your brothers need you!"

"Joe!" Morgan called.

Stavros turned and stood in place.

Morgan appeared calm now. "I believe," he said, "I believe that I will be cured, that the lump will disappear and I will be my true self again." He closed his eyes for an instant. "I refuse to die. I became sick by obeying God's will. I will cure myself by breaking it."

There was a fumbling movement, his hands were somewhere in his clothes, and at that instant, Althea shouted, "Daddy, don't!" Then she shouted, "Stavros! Look out!"

Efstathis, the small, wiry man, had leaped on Morgan Perry's back and was reaching over Morgan's back for his hand. Morgan wrenched his body around and threw Efstathis clear. Everyone could see the pistol as he aimed it.

Simeon threw Stavros to the gray concrete floor and covered his body with his own.

"Get away, get away!" Morgan shouted at Simeon. He held the pistol ready, waiting for an opening.

At the moment the hammer hit the back of the shell, Efstathis was on Morgan's back again, clutching at his hand as the pistol fired.

Garabet and Vartan, the touch-up man, were on Morgan Perry too, bearing him to the ground.

No one knew where the bullet had gone, as the guests ran for the door.

Gripping the hand that held the pistol with both of his, Efstathis dug his teeth into the flesh of it, then slammed it on the ground until the gun came free. He grabbed it and sent it skittering across the floor like a stone scaled over water. Then he was choking Morgan, banging his head on the concrete floor. Garabet and Vartan had to pull him off.

Mrs. Perry, in her chair at the side, hadn't moved.

Stavros, relieved of Simeon's weight, got to his feet. He could see Althea kneeling at her father's head, cradling it, saying, "Daddy, Daddy, I love you, I'll never leave you, Daddy," despite the fact that it was obvious her father couldn't hear anything at all.

Mr. Fernand kept his head. He hustled up with his chauffeur, instructed Garabet and Vartan to lift Morgan to his feet and drag and carry him across the floor, out of the store and down to the car. Within a minute they were gone, Althea with them. And Mrs. Perry.

Then it was quiet. No one knew what to do. Some people did the natural thing and began eating the rich party food.

Simeon came up to Stavros and handed him the pistol, saying, "You hold this." Stavros put it into his pocket. Then he helped the two men from the island of Chios to food, putting sausage and cheese and caviar on their plates. The little fellow particularly liked the sturgeon, which he'd been picking at while Morgan was speaking; Stavros loaded his plate with more of it.

As they talked, Stavros found out about his brother, how important he'd become in the behind-the-lines operations of the Greek forces, and how respected. A leader! And again he was told that Michaelis expected him to join in the fight that was just beginning. Every Greek had to!

But the men were in no condition to talk. "Can you show us a place where we can fall down to sleep?" Simeon asked. Stavros told them they could lie down in the back of the store, on folded carpets, stay there until morning when he'd come back.

He sat for a while watching them sleep, making certain no one disturbed them. Finally the store was empty, but Stavros still watched over the sleeping men.

"Who are my friends?" he asked himself. "With whom do I feel the deepest bond? Who saved my life? Who covered my body with his?" He looked at the exhausted men, sleeping in his care. *I am an Anatolian,* he thought. *And will always be.*

He still couldn't believe that someone had tried to kill him. Morgan Perry, a murderer! Yet why not? Two different species. How could they live together?

He walked around the empty store, looking for the bullet that had been meant to kill him, and found it lying on the floor under the window, a small, blunted blob of metal. It was like an orphan, so innocent now that its strength was spent. He put it into his pocket to remind him who he was and who his friends were. And who his enemies.

The next morning Stavros hurried to the store. He'd cleared out Demo's room and was going to accommodate Simeon and Efstathis there. Since it was Sunday, he expected the store to be dark and empty, but he found Mr. Fernand on his knees before the safe in his office. The old man, to spare them the trip to New Jersey, had taken the Perrys to his town house on West Sixty-eighth Street. They'd been up all night, tending to the drunk and hysterical man.

"Despite that performance he put on here," Mr. Fernand exclaimed, "they were able to talk him into it!"

"Who talked who into what?"

"He's going to have the operation. Straight off. I remember distinctly his assertion that he would not expose himself to the sacrificial knife in a surgeon's hand. But those women got to him. Turn your back."

Having adjusted his spectacles, Mr. Fernand began to spin the dial that would release the door of the safe. Stavros turned his back.

"Personally I distrust all doctors, especially the expensive ones. They'll kill him for sure," Mr. Fernand went on. "But he asked for it and I was able to arrange for him to get into a hospital today. That was some trick, on a Saturday night! Those hospital administrators—all Jews—they didn't know me. They obliged Fernand Sarrafian to show the color of his money. So I had to come down here, to get into this safe. Poor Morgan . . ." Stavros heard the sound of the safe door opening. "Despite all his bluster, the man is terrified of his wife. And the daughter—a fine girl, I'm sure, but straight out of college—she still believes medicine is a science. Between them they had the man groveling. I've never seen anyone more contrite. He kept calling for your forgiveness. You must go to him sometime—it would have to be at the hospital—and tell him you forgive him."

"I don't," Stavros said. "He tried to kill me."

"What would it cost you to say the words?" Mr. Fernand said. "Compassion, my boy! One day you may need it for yourself." Stavros heard the safe's door close. "You can turn now," the old man said. "By the way, who might those two derelicts be, sleeping on the floor in Vartan's corner? Some of yours, to judge by their appearance."

"They saved my life," Stavros said.

"I saw. Nevertheless, they're unacceptably dirty. Get them out immediately. I can't stand anyone that filthy in my place of business. It lowers the tone."

Stavros repeated what Michaelis had written about the men, and Mr. Fernand was impressed. He surprised Stavros with his knowledge of the war and his passionate desire to see Turkey beaten to the ground.

"Don't mistake me," he said. "Strictly for business reasons. The Turks are only a little worse than any other race of man. I might except the British; they steal with more style. But I do want to see the Ottoman Empire dismembered. Then we can deal with its components to our advantage. What exactly did your two relatives do?"

"They're not my relatives, and what they did is blow up a bridge at the moment an ammunition train on the way to Smyrna was crossing. They can't stay in the Smyrna vilayet now; sooner or later they'd be suspected and shot. So Michaelis put them on a boat to America. Michaelis himself lost an arm in the fighting there."

"Fortunes of war," Mr. Fernand said with a shrug. Then he did something that impressed Stavros. He asked him to wake the men and greeted them as if it were a state occasion. "We're all in debt to your bravery," he said with a slight bow. Then he told Stavros to take the men home in the Rolls, and with his own hands, he wrapped some of the left-over food, saying, "They must be terribly hungry; besides, there's so much here. Perhaps your dear mother and your charming sisters will enjoy it. Women, I've found, are partial to rich food."

"Without your car," Stavros said, "how will you manage?"

"I propose to take a nap on the sofa in my office. For some mysterious reason, I've always slept better in my offices than in any of my homes. Besides, I have those women bedded down in my place. I find dear Norma excessively distasteful. Wynn, my chauffeur, is waiting downstairs. Ask him to return and wake me at precisely a quarter past twelve. Our appointment at the hospital is at two."

So Stavros and the two dynamiters rode to 136th Street in style, the men sleeping all the way. Here are two penniless heroes, Stavros thought, who risked their lives for a cause they believe in, riding in a chauffeur-driven limousine that only a man who believes in nothing could afford.

The next day they were still sleepy and hungry; they'd eat, fall asleep, eat, sleep. Michaelis had arranged passage for them on a Lebanese freighter that made stops all along the north shore of Africa, with long waits for cargo at every port of call. The food, once they were past Gibraltar, had been mealy and rotten. It was a choice of being sick or being hungry; they'd been both. The only thing their stomachs had been able to hold was tea and a kind of hard bread. "Like wood," Efstathis said.

Simeon told the news. "Everyone is expecting a landing by the Allies in Smyrna," he said. "The Turks expect it, of course, and they're getting ready. The train we blew up was bringing supplies and a new military commander to Smyrna. Also six hundred fresh troops from Sivas." The two men had made their way north along the shore in their fishing caïque until they were opposite the bridge. There a friend provided them with a donkey and helped disguise them as fig farmers. The cache of dynamite was exactly where it was supposed to be, and after waiting for the sun to set, they moved inland to the bridge, working all night to set the explosive in place; the train was to pass at dawn. Both men were fishermen and knew dynamite—they used it to bring up fish.

Simeon then described how the great bridge, with the train on it, had swung slowly and gracefully through the air—it was a thing of beauty, he said. The train had fallen off sideways, falling faster than the bridge down into the ravine where the stream flowed. They were moving away as fast as they could, to cover the distance back to their boat before the light was strong and the countryside awake. Behind them they heard a great explosion and imagined that everyone on that train had been killed. Then came a fire, followed by an even greater explosion. This certified that the train carried ammunition.

Once at sea, they went on fishing until their fish well was filled with *barboonyah*, the red mullet that was a favorite fish of the middle-class Turk. They sailed then back to the fish market along the Smyrna waterfront and heard the news of the bridge and the train and what the Turk was going to do about it.

The authorities had moved quickly. Five hostages were taken and a date fixed: They were to be shot at noon in the square near the cathedral of Aghia Fotini unless whoever had done the job at the bridge surrendered. The five hostages were the five most respected and honored men in the Greek community; one was a close friend of Simeon's, and godfather to the one girl among his five children.

Simeon considered surrendering—it shamed him to think of innocent men being shot in his behalf. But he received a directive from Michaelis that not only was he not to make any romantic gestures, he was actually to attend the execution, in this way allaying any suspicion that he might have been involved. Simeon debated with himself. He had no one to consult with—he was under strict orders not even to talk to his wife. In the end, he obeyed Michaelis's order. "Everyone is afraid of your brother," he said to Stavros. "Since he lost his arm, he has become the kind of man everyone fears."

Simeon described the ritual of execution, how he stood among the curious and the committed and the families of the men, and what a dreadful cry went up when the hostages were brought to the square in a large wagon. The sounds of protest persisted until the Turkish soldiers turned their weapons on the crowd and fired over their heads.

The five men were brought down from the wagon and turned to face the crowd. The Turkish commander again asked that whoever had committed the terrible crime, or anyone who knew anything about it, should step forward; they preferred not to shoot innocent men, he said. The blood of these five would be on the heads of whoever had destroyed the train.

It was then that the godfather of Simeon's daughter looked at Simeon for an instant. Quickly Simeon looked away, turning his eyes to the one hostage he did not know; four of the five were men he'd greeted on the street all the days of his life.

It was half an hour before noon, and the hostages stood there, with the Turkish commander seated upon a little square platform at their side. The commander smoked nine cigarettes, and every few minutes he again begged the guilty ones to step forward. No one did. At noon the five men were shot, their eyes uncovered.

If anyone had believed that the Turk would be satisfied with this revenge, he was mistaken. The search for the saboteurs continued. Michaelis slipped into the city one night from his headquarters on the island of Chios, and then slipped out before morning. Told of the intensity of the search, he decided to remove Simeon and Efstathis from the danger zone. The two men put out in their caïque as if they were going for fish, but they made their way to Chios, where Michaelis told them the surprising news: They were going to America. There was a storm coming, Michaelis said, and the story would be spread that they'd been lost at sea.

Simeon's feelings about this were mixed; he didn't want to leave his wife, his daughter, and his four young sons behind. Michaelis ignored him. He had important work for them in New York City, he said, although he couldn't tell them yet what it was.

Now they were here and they still didn't know what this important work was. They were waiting for Michaelis to arrive. "He was all right. He gets along with one arm," Efstathis assured Stavros. "He can still use his pistol."

J U L Y   1 9 1 8

"What she wants?" Stavros asked Maud.

"To talk to you."

"For what?"

"I can't imagine. All she said was: 'Go to the store. Tell him I want to talk to him.' "

"To play games again, maybe. Hah? On, off, in, out? So forth?"

"Come tomorrow afternoon, she said."

"Ah! Tomorrow afternoon! But how about I'm busy tomorrow afternoon? We're shorthanded in the store now."

Maud turned and looked at the three great bays of the Sarrafian Brothers store. They were empty except for a pair of porters, sitting on a large blue Persian, clipping out the white ends of the webbing knots which had come through when the carpet was washed. It was what they did when there was nothing to do.

"I can see you're busy," Maud said.

"These Sarrafians, they don't know how to make rug business in new conditions now," Stavros said. "Old men, too rich, they don't give damn."

"I heard," Maud said, "you're the only one who knows anything."

"Don't be so smart, Maud," Stavros said.

"She says she'll phone Mr. Ara and ask him as a favor if you can—"

"Never mind favor business; no favors, please."

"She's already done it. It's arranged. So if you can convince yourself to come, come."

"I'll think about it."

"I'll tell her you're not coming." Maud turned toward the door.

"Where is it? She? The hospital?"

"In Mount Ivy. Grace Memorial. They moved Mr. Perry after the operation so it would be more convenient for Mrs. Perry."

"That woman will be there? Guarantee I don't go."

"Do whatever you want. I happen to agree with you; it's pointless. I told Althea so, but she insisted." And Maud walked out of the store.

All that day and during the night, awake and asleep, Stavros lived out the scenes he imagined would take place at Grace Memorial—how aloof he'd be, how distant, unbending, unapproachable, and how she would beg for his forgiveness. He rehearsed the ironclad conditions he would set for their reconciliation. The premise was always the same: Althea wanted to make up with him.

"What makes you think," he'd say, "that you can call 'Come,' like you're calling a dog, and I run? Hah? Only reason I go is maybe your father dying. Tell you truth, 'bout time. That son of a bitch, he try to kill me, and next thing I know you're on the floor, holding his head and telling him how you love him. You expect me to say, after that, all right, we make up? Nothing doing. Hamal philosophy: When man wants to kill you, kill him first. Only thing save Mr. Morgan Perry, he's your father."

This continued into a dream. He was on the Constantinople waterfront confronting a certain stevedore boss he remembered, warning him, "I'm cautious man, I don't let my feelings show, like Mohammedan woman, I'm wearing my face covered. When you insult me, I swallow it like a dog—gulp, down! Then, I'm silent. I wait. You dump that big load on my back, I carry it. But when I get to the wagon and drop that heavy load at last, better pay me in heavy *droosh*, because I took your load, twice so much as you put on other hamals, I carried it with your curses behind me. But when night comes, my *agha*, sleep with your eyes open, because I still carry the knife, see!"

The next morning he went on speaking to Althea as he dressed. "I don't like the way you tell me come to the hospital. You don't say please, you don't say if you maybe have time and so on. You give command. This afternoon! Quick, I want to talk to you! About what, you don't say. But I got idea. You think it's so easy make it up with me? If I come see you now, woman, I do you big favor. Understand that? No! You send that insect, Maud, to give me your orders. Me! Who the hell you think you are, you women?"

Meantime he was putting on his new black suit, the one he'd bought to be ready for big buyers when Freddie would let him take them.

"Where you going today?" Eleni asked at the apartment door as she handed him his new black hat, a homburg. "To a funeral?"

"Not mine," he said. "Go bring Father's black *bastooni* here."

He had to stoop low to kiss his mother goodbye. She was permanently bent over the Turkish language Bible in her lap now. "You look like plenty money, plenty money," she said.

"Yes," he said to himself as he rode the ferry across the Hudson, inspecting his image in the heavy plate-glass windows. "Anyone can see that I'm a man who needs no favors from nobody. You want to pretend you're too good for me, Miss Althea Perry, go 'head; you'll find out few things today!"

To maintain his mood and his attitude, he took a taxi from the Mount Ivy railroad station to Grace Memorial Hospital, overtipping the driver as if he was already what he hoped he appeared to be—a plutocrat come to accept the apologetic explanations of a suppliant.

He swaggered into the hospital, an important man demanding immediate attention. It was a small hospital, run by nuns in gray habits. Everyone seemed busy and cheerful, murmuring like bees working over a field of flowers. Obviously they were trained to bring cheer and hope to a sinful world gone awry. At the desk, no one questioned Stavros's right to see Mr. Morgan Perry. Stavros might have been His Excellency the ambassador from Cappodocia; in this alien place he felt more Anatolian than ever.

Up the stairs and down the hall, there were no sounds above a whisper. Inquiry drew kindness. The halls seemed cleaner than necessary. There was an old man with a red face pushing a mop on a stick. He finished at one end, turned, sighed, and started back the way he'd come. Stavros tiptoed around him.

The door to Morgan Perry's room was open. Stavros saw Althea by the window, the afternoon sun across her back, an unopened book on her lap. She wore a dress of yellow cotton, her favorite color, but on this day it made her look sallow. Morgan Perry lay on his back, looking at the ceiling. At his side was a man Stavros had seen before.

"So Sister Theresa said," the Reverend Kenworthy was speaking, "—and you'll have to take my word for this, Morgan; remember these are Catholics here. You know?" He chuckled. "Here is what she said." He glanced mischievously over his shoulder at Althea, then leaned forward, one hand over his chest—like an old woman, Stavros thought, keeping her tits out of the soup—and placing his mouth next to Morgan Perry's ear, he whispered whatever it was he'd overheard Sister Theresa, whoever she was, say. Then he pulled back and started to laugh and laugh, while poor Morgan—he looked so weak and drawn—tried to laugh, couldn't, choked and coughed and turned to his daughter.

"It hurts when he laughs, Ken," Althea said, turning her head. She saw Stavros. "Excuse me," she said to the men, and started out of the room.

"Althea!" the Reverend Kenworthy said. "I only have a few more minutes here."

"I know," she said, looking at Stavros, then dropping her eyes.

"I really should be out of here now, Althea dear," the reverend said. "I have appointments. You'll have to take over bedside."

Stavros could hear it in his voice: The man was trying to prevent her from coming out to meet him.

"Won't be more than two minutes, Ken," Althea said.

"Make it three," Stavros said to her when they were in the corridor.

"There's a sitting room at the other end of the hall," Althea said.

"How is he?" Stavros asked.

"As well as can be expected. That's what the doctors say. I can't make them out, whether they're telling the truth or trying to make me feel better. I told them, 'Give me the plain facts, please,' but that seems difficult for them to do."

"They operated and . . . ?"

"Took out some of his intestines. They say the operation was successful. But they always are. Until. They keep saying, 'He's going to be all right,' but he's lost I don't know how many pounds and doesn't gain them back. You saw how he looks. He's all sewed up across the stomach. Inside too. I'm sorry I helped talk him into this operation. You saw—it hurts when he laughs. Also when he breathes."

"So what the hell that priest—" Stavros turned his head toward Morgan Perry's room. "Why he makes him laugh?"

"Father's supposed to stay cheery, not to worry. That's why Ken—"

"Look," Stavros said. "He's watching us from the door."

When Kenworthy realized that Stavros had seen him, he withdrew into the room.

"I know," Althea said. She hadn't turned her head. "They're worried about me. What I might do next. Everybody's been making me feel that it's my fault what happened to Father. All that worry about you and me —they keep hinting that's what did it. You should hear my mother on the subject."

"Well, maybe it is. The worry. Who knows?"

"That's what I think. Who knows?"

"The doctor, what he says?"

"The same. Doctors say the same. Are you listening to me?"

"Sure. Why not?"

"I can't tell from your face, ever."

"I was thinking that's how my father died too. From worry. Maybe we're supposed to go through life without worry; what you think?"

"I don't know. I don't know anything anymore. Ken Kenworthy isn't quite as gentle as he seems. He's after me all the time, with steel in that soft voice. 'Take care of your father, dear Althea,' he says. 'Love your father. You're all he has,' he keeps reminding me. 'He needs your love more than medicine,' he says. 'I love him,' I say. 'If you really loved him,' he says, 'you wouldn't have hurt him for all those months!' Did you see his face when he saw you just now?"

"I saw it."

"He believes that every time Father sees you, the cancer spreads."

"Your father didn't see me. He was looking up at the ceiling."

"I wouldn't put it past Ken to tell him."

"Tell him I'm going back to Anatolia. I'll do him a big favor, disappear."

They'd come to the sunroom at the end of the hall.

"People in there," Althea said. "Let's go outside."

"You don't look good," Stavros said when he saw her in daylight. "Pale. You lost plenty weight too, looks like."

"I've been sick," she said.

"With what?"

"I'll tell you some other time."

At the emergency entrance, an ambulance was emptying, an old lady on a stretcher.

"The summer," Althea said, "goes so fast."

"So I came here, like you asked," Stavros said. "What is it you want to say to me? I tell you one thing first. You did many bad things to me —disappearing, no explanations, talking bad against me, insults. God knows what. Not easy for me to be with you again. I don't think I can again."

"Oh, that's a relief!" she said. "Oh, what a relief!"

"What? What is?"

"That you didn't expect to go on with it, either. I couldn't do anything else, you know."

"What do you mean, you couldn't do anything else? What did you do?"

"I told him I wouldn't ever see you again. Before his operation."

When Stavros didn't react, she repeated. "My father. I told him that."

"I understand," Stavros said. "You had to say it—right? The situation and so forth."

"No," she said. "I meant it."

Stavros looked at her, trying to see from her face if she did really mean it.

"You mean . . . you're saying . . . finish?"

"Yes."

"Then why . . . why you ask me to come here?"

"Come around here. Under this tree. There's a bench."

He kept staring at her, incredulous.

"You know my situation," she said when they were seated. "My father is not only sick; his mind is going. He can't talk in a straight line anymore, or think. Can't concentrate. He's also unemployed. That's what that big party was about. He's been fired. We live and will have to live—unless I do something—by whatever charity Mr. Fernand chooses to hand us. My mother has no money. She's waiting for Granny to die, for whatever money she'll inherit there. But what am I good for? College taught me nothing useful. My social work? Pays nothing, of course; it's for girls from the Social Register who want a taste of 'real' life. So I finally had to take a hard look at myself." She laughed a little. "The fact is I've been spoiled. I like good clothes and a car and someone to make my bed and do my laundry and charge accounts wherever I want and to eat every so often in a very expensive restaurant. What's more, I found that I didn't really expect to ever change my style of living. You listening?"

"Sure. I want to say something to you."

"Let me finish, please. I have something to tell you. So, facing the facts about myself, I decided I'd have to do what other girls like me do—depend on a man to support me. Find someone, marry him, treat him well, be a good wife, provide him with children, tie him down in every conceivable way and so make my future secure."

"I want to say something."

Althea could see that Stavros's eyes were moist. Was he hurt? she wondered.

"Please," she said, "let me tell you this and then you. The reason I asked to see you is—I want a favor from you."

"Anything you want, Althea."

"Please don't talk about us."

"I don't."

"I mean, in the future. Ever. What was between us. Because I . . . because . . ."

"Because why? What happened?"

"I think I've found somebody. That is, somebody found me. Either way. He just showed up when I began thinking this way; that's what happens, isn't it? I think he likes me and he's a fine man, I know, and he's . . ."

"Rich?"

"Very. If you think I'd marry anyone who's not rich, you haven't understood me. He's very rich. I'll have a nice apartment, high off the street, with beautiful furniture and fine curtains cutting off noises from the street below. That's what I want most—heavy, pearly gray curtains, curtains and quiet. We can travel and I'll have a servant or maybe two, and charge accounts at Lord and Taylor and Altman's, and—here's the most important thing—he will look after my parents. He's said so."

"You talking about Freddie?"

"Freddie! No, I mean rich! Not like Freddie. Freddie may someday be rich. I mean now. Rich! So my parents will be secure for the rest of their lives and my father will never worry again. You understand now? That's what I had to say to you. That's all."

Stavros said nothing.

"You had something to say to me?" Althea said. "I'm sorry. But I did have to get all this out. It was hard. But now—you had something to say? To me?"

"I wanted to say—"

He couldn't say it.

"Yes," she said. "Yes?"

"That you're the only girl—"

"Yes?"

"That I ever love. The only one."

"Oh, I'm so glad to hear that!"

"I didn't know what the word meant before you. What it meant, that word."

"I loved you too," she said. "But it's finished. Might as well say it. Finished."

"I'll tell you one thing. You'll never find another man like me. Never."

"Oh, Stavros, don't say that."

"Never!"

"Stavros, dear Stavros, wish me well, wish me well."

"Who is it?"

"I can't tell you—yet."

"You'll never find another—"

"Can't you wish me well? Is that how you want to leave it?"

"How the hell can I do that? I'll have a hole in me the rest of my life from you."

"I'm sorry."

"And you—you from me."

"All right. If you want. So be it."

Neither of them moved. They stayed sitting silently side by side under the tree.

Now her tone grew firmer. "When it got down to it," she said, "and he was about to go into the operating room, and I knew he might never come out alive . . . do you understand?"

"What a damn fool I was!" Stavros said. "I thought he was beginning to get over it—about me. At the baseball game, remember how he was? Joe! Joe, come sit next to me—here, Joe! Then one hour later, at the party . . ."

He'd taken something out of his pocket, and now he showed it to her, in the palm of his hand.

"What is that?" she said. "Oh, that's . . . ?"

"What he tried to kill me with. I found it on the floor."

"You carry it around?"

"Reminds me not to trust people. I still don't know what happened. On the ride downtown in that damn Rolls, he became a different man. What happened? You know?"

"I made a mistake," she said.

"You? You said something to him?"

"I'd said something to my mother. Before. I told her I'd gone to Puerto Rico."

"What's the harm on that?"

"Why I went."

"Why? What?"

"You don't know?"

"No."

"I thought you'd figure it out. Why I suddenly—When I disappeared that way, with a girl friend, I thought you'd know why."

"I don't know now."

"We were going to have a child."

"Oh!"

"I thought for sure you'd figure it out. Anyway, I told Mother, which was a mistake. I made her swear she'd never tell anyone, especially Father. But my mother's word—when she's angry, she goes crazy. She'll do anything! She saw how friendly he was being with you at the ball game and —well, I don't know if she made a decision or it just came blurting out. In the Rolls. Maybe she decided to set him straight about you once and for all."

"Oh!"

"You really didn't guess that—you really didn't?"

"We don't have that in Anatolia. In my family. Never."

They were silent for a time, then he lifted his head and looked at her with the most absolute hatred.

"So you kill it! My"—he hesitated—"my son. You killed him out, hah?"

"Why do you say it that way? That's so ugly!"

He hit her across the face as hard as he could.

She stood, hand to her cheek, dizzy. She was holding back tears through sheer will.

He lowered his head, looking at the ground beneath the bench.

"You shouldn't have done that," she said. "Now we're not going to be friends." She started toward the hospital, then stopped, turned directly to him, and said, "That's why I'm pale." A determination born of desperation came over her. She moved back toward him a step. "I had an infection. It's not certain that I can ever have children. The man I'm going to marry —I don't want him to know anything. That's why I asked you never to mention what existed between us and what's happened—since. Now, Stavros, listen. Listen!"

He didn't move or speak.

"I want you to give me your word on that. I want your word. Now. I want you to say it." Her face was drawn and pale and hard as slate.

Bent over, eyes to the ground, not moving, he said, "I'll never speak a word. Go ahead. Finished!"

"Thank you," she said.

She walked back into the hospital, leaving him on the bench under the tree.

SEPTEMBER 1918

The summer of 1918 was an in-and-out time for Mr. Fernand Sarrafian. He'd show up at the office, no one knew from where, then disappear again —out of the country, Miss Emily Barton told Stavros.

"How he cross the water?" Stavros argued. "Submarines still there."

"That old Armenian has friends; it would surprise you who," Emily Barton said. "They carry him anywhere he needs to go."

Stavros dropped his voice. "For instance where?"

"Don't be so clever," she said. "You know I can't tell you where. But wherever it happens to be, he keeps in touch with Morgan Perry's health. First thing he asks when he comes in is: 'How's Morgan? What's his weight now?' You know he lost thirty pounds feeding that cancer."

One mid-September morning, Mr. Fernand reappeared and called Stavros into his office. "Learn a lesson," he said. "Love is the great medicine."

"So they say, boss," was Stavros's routine concession. "What brings you to speak wisdom this morning?"

"That young Miss Althea," Mr. Fernand said. "She performed a miracle. Through her spiritual devotion, she completely restored her father's health."

"Glad to hear it," Stavros said.

"I hope so," Mr. Fernand said, "because I intend to bring him back here."

"All right with me," Stavros said. "But remember, the sight of me may make him sick again."

"No longer," Mr. Fernand said. "Wait till you see the man. Also I'm relying on you that what happened before won't happen again."

"*I* didn't do anything. He tried kill me."

"Let's not mention what you were doing for months that bedeviled my friend Morgan's soul. Let us not look back, shall we not?"

"Whatever you say, boss."

"I spoke to Morgan about you. His contrition was—you know what that is, contrition?"

"No."

"When are you going to learn English? You're so ambitious but you don't know what contrition means. It means shame. His was overwhelming. He said he would beg your pardon and prove to you by his behavior that he knows the meaning of charity."

"Charity! What charity? *He* wanted shoot *me*, not vice versa."

"Put that day out of your mind, as he has, my boy. Morgan has been with the nuns for three full weeks. I got him a place near their retreat in Connecticut, and Althea—oh, what a wonderful girl; if only I had had a daughter like that girl!—she stayed at his side and believe it or not, wait until you see, performed a miracle. His operation appears to have been a perfect success, and they tell me there isn't the least threat of recurrence —which there generally is."

"I don't want to make problem for the man."

"O.K., quit if you want to. You're right. His life is the main thing."

There was a pause in this conversation while Stavros allowed Mr. Fernand's suggestion to hang. Then he said, "All right, boss. You want me to go, I go."

"What's the matter—you don't want this job anymore?"

"You just now suggest I quit. O.K., I go. I finally gave up on you, anyway. You're hopeless case—excuse me, boss."

"That's pretty high and mighty of you."

"High and mighty is you, not me. But since you read history, you know that high and mighty people, countries also, all coming down now."

"So you consider yourself the wave of the future, do you?"

"Yes, sir, boss. One by one, we will take away your customers."

"We?"

"New, future merchants."

"That is to say, you."

"Right. I advised you what to do so many times. Now I give up."

"You forgot to mention that you're making a pretty good income from another source."

"Just making living there."

"You're lying. Ara tells me your brother's enterprise is doing, not *pretty* well, *very* well."

"Ara knows everything, I'm sure."

"So when it comes right down to it, you don't need this job here."

"It has some uses for me."

"You know, you're an arrogant little son of a bitch!"

"Anything you say, boss. You call me what?"

"Arrogant! Too fresh!"

"That's because you are so used to people falling on their knees to kiss your *abeeseenoh* that you can't take the truth—so you call the truth that word you said."

"The uses we still have for you—what are they?"

"I learn what's best to do by watching you do the opposite."

"You scoundrel! Why do I tolerate you?"

"Because you know I like you, boss. And because one day soon you will get smart again and give me the position I should have here. If you don't, I'll destroy your company."

"Did I hear you correctly?"

"I'm sure. Or else you wouldn't be looking at me with that face."

"Sarrafian Brothers is one of the three largest—"

"I know what you were. I also know history, how quick it moves!"

"How the hell could you destroy us?"

"The American way. Get financing elsewhere. Outbuy you at the source, undersell you here. Look out, boss!"

Stavros laughed and after a moment Mr. Fernand joined in.

"I should fire you," Mr. Fernand said. "But I haven't the time today; I'm meeting a friend at the track. Maybe I'll fire you so you can come with me. Ever go to the horses?"

"Can't today. We've got a big buyer coming from Chicago. He's a squash head, but I better stay here. That Freddie is liable to sell him too cheap."

"You didn't really answer my question before. Why do you continue here?"

"Because someday soon you will realize that I, only I, can save your business. I have plan, now that the war is almost over and Ottoman Empire is breaking up—"

"In other words, you hope to get capital from me."

"I'm glad you said it."

"I appreciate you, you know. You have many of the qualities I had as a young man. Also some of the same thoughts I do now. My problem is that I don't like your character. Personally, you disgust me."

"What's the difference, if I can bring in the money? Your stock is down to—"

"All right, all right, I heard that. We'll talk."

"You always say that. But this is time to act, not talk. You should listen to me, not try get rid of me. Your brother is half asleep, getting worse all the time. You must be seeing what I see."

"As I was saying, Mr. Perry will be coming back, and despite the fact that Freddie and Althea have broken off, I've asked him to do everything he can to make Morgan's return here as easy as possible. I ask you the same."

The old man had changed the subject and Stavros knew it wasn't the moment to crowd him further. "I will shake his hand when he comes in, and so forth. Don't worry."

"He needs more than your 'and so forth.' Think of this man with compassion. Make him feel your sympathy."

"I will try."

A week later, Morgan Perry came in for a visit. Gone was his beefy swagger. He was at least thirty pounds lighter. His eyes had a peculiar reflective shine, as if he knew some secret about life and death that most people were denied. Even his voice had gentled. He offered his hand to Stavros immediately. "Put it there," he said, then assured him that he regretted what he'd done, but was sure Stavros would understand since he'd be especially aware of the stresses Morgan had been under. "I want us to turn our backs on what's past," he said.

Stavros said, "O.K., ancient history!" and added that he had other girls now, so Mr. Perry shouldn't worry about anything more between him and his daughter.

Of course he hoped that Perry would repeat this to Althea. There were nights when he hurt, he wanted her back so badly. He was doing his weekly whore again, as well as some amateurs, no charge, but he felt, every time, that they were acting. With Althea . . . He could hear her still, the sounds she made and her face when it happened. Althea exploded when she finished. It satisfied him as much as it did her. He had to make a terrible effort to put all that out of his mind, especially how she used to look at him when it happened and how she kept on trembling.

Then, in a week, there was Morgan Perry back at his desk, the office manager, looking out over the floor. He left the buyers and the sales to Freddie and sometimes even to Stavros—if he had to. Big Morgan—that "big" didn't suit him anymore—seemed a little absentminded. His body had been drained thin, but it was sounder than his mind. He seemed to be dreaming. He was making plans and schemes none of the others in the store knew about, miscorrecting old Condit the bookkeeper's books, going over the mail again and again, and dictating to Emily Barton letters she showed to Mr. Ara, then didn't mail. He slowed things up and everybody knew it and everybody was patient.

Mr. Ara finally found him a job that would take him out of the office. He sent him here and there around the market to see what he could pick up in the way of stock. There had been no importation of goods since the sea lanes had closed down three years before and Sarrafian Brothers' stock had to be replenished by whatever could be picked up in the dusty corners of the trade. It was made the doomed man's special task to keep the piles of rugs high and the great rolls of carpet filling the corners. He even bought goods from retailers at exorbitant prices to maintain the old prosperous look of the store. Morgan Perry had many free lunches and received quite a few valuable gifts.

The forced cordiality between Stavros and Morgan Perry didn't last. It lapsed, not into antagonism, but into silence. Their eyes didn't meet. And Stavros made no effort to improve things between them; it didn't matter to him. His brother Seraphim, known as Sam, and his sister Fofo, with Stavros behind the scenes, were doing well enough at their small store (which they'd renamed the Anatolian Carpet Company). Stavros's cause for impatience was that the family operation was such a small one—perhaps their stock was worth eighty thousand dollars now, no more. He knew it was the time to strike big.

One October morning, after playing poker all night, Stavros arrived at the family store to find Simeon and Efstathis waiting for him. They said they'd been up all night, arguing, and since Stavros hadn't come home, decided to try for him downtown. But Stavros was very sleepy and had drunk too much, and the last thing he wanted was to listen to a quarrel between these two. Over the last weeks, they'd become increasingly antagonistic toward each other.

Simeon had found out why Michaelis had sent them to the United States and why Michaelis himself was coming. With the collapse of the Ottoman Empire imminent, there were going to be a series of meetings to raise money in America for the cause of Greater Greece. Michaelis was to speak, he and certain other leaders who would come to New York from the field of action. They would present to the affluent audience of big-bellied Greeks from whom they wanted funds the two saboteurs who had carried out a heroic act in the name of the cause now known as the Great Idea—the redemption of all lands where Greek people lived to join under the flag of Hellas.

"As soon as I stand up as a hero in front of all those people," Simeon said now, "what do you think? The Turks won't hear of it? They won't have their people there? Your brother Michaelis, he doesn't care; he's a machine, you might say. But you, Stavros, you're a human being. Please listen. I know you're sleepy, but—"

"I'm a little drunk."

"I can see that, but please try to listen. As soon as the Turks hear about it, or see me, worse, they will say, Ah ha! There he is, the one who blew up the bridge. Let's find his wife! Let's bring his children in and see what they look like." He turned to Efstathis. "Then what do you think they'll do, Efstathis? Eh? You know very well what they'll do. I don't care what you say; I am going back. I am going to find a little caïque and take Sarroula"—he turned back to Stavros—"that's my wife; and my children —I have four boys—and I am going to take them out of Smyrna. I only hope I won't be too late. Give me money. Your brother brought me here, risking the life of my family. He doesn't care. Efstathis doesn't care. But you—be a brother to me! Send me back. There's a boat, southern route, I can get on it if I buy the ticket today. I can't sleep. I am going crazy from worry. Pity me, Stavros." He began to weep, unashamed. "Be a Christian," he said.

"I heard enough; here!" Stavros said, reaching into his pocket, full of the money he'd won at poker. "How much do you want? Here, a hundred dollars. Go buy your ticket!"

Simeon fell on his knees before Stavros and kissed his hands.

"One hero here is enough," Stavros said, looking at Efstathis.

"Don't worry about him. He has no wife." Simeon turned to Efstathis. "That piece of dried fish you have—you don't call that a wife, do you?"

Efstathis, that small, tense man, didn't speak.

Simeon was exuberant. "I know what you're worried about," he said to Efstathis. "But how can they capture me? I will sleep in my boat, I will go out only at night. If they find me and bring me in, I will take out my knife and cut off my tongue, in front of them."

Efstathis was silent. He turned and looked at Stavros who saw that he was so angry he couldn't talk. Why? Stavros wondered. Did he want money too?

"I'm going to sleep now," Stavros said. "Go get your ticket, Simeon. I don't want to hear any more about it."

"They will make you talk," Efstathis said to Simeon.

"If the worst comes to the worst," Simeon said, "and you lose your wife, you should bless me. How many times you told me when we were tending the nets that you hated her? You will find a beautiful young girl here, an admired hero like you! All the girls like *andartes!*" He laughed.

"Don't tell me about your knife and how you'll cut off your tongue," Efstathis said. "They will take your knife first thing."

"What would they want with your wife?" Simeon said. "That piece of dried fish. I'm the one who needs to worry, being such a hero and leaving my wife behind. I have to get her. If they catch me, we will go down together, not me here safe and she—whatever they will do to her." He was advancing on Efstathis in a fury. "Get out of my sight! I don't care what you think."

The phone rang and Stavros ran to pick it up. Simeon was still shouting so angrily and loudly that Stavros had to ask Freddie to repeat the message that Mr. Fernand wanted to see him right away.

"They're waiting for you in there," Freddie said, pointing to Mr. Fernand's private office.

"That's better than me waiting for them," Stavros said.

Freddie didn't laugh. As Stavros walked through the bead curtain, he followed close behind. "You're following me like a cop, Freddie," Stavros said, smiling. "What's going on here?"

Freddie looked at Mr. Ara, who was sitting on the banquette. Behind him stood Morgan Perry. He'd gotten even thinner. *Poor fellow!* Stavros thought. Then he looked around for Mr. Fernand, but he wasn't there. No one said anything. Stavros sat on the other end of the banquette. "Might as well be comfortable," he said.

"Get up," Morgan Perry said. "This is Mr. Fernand's private office." Stavros got up, slowly.

"What's so funny?" Morgan Perry said. "Why are you smiling?"

"I have some thoughts," Stavros said.

"What do you do during your lunch hour, may I ask?"

"Who wants to know?" Stavros looked at Mr. Ara, who stayed silent.

"He does." Morgan Perry pointed to Mr. Ara.

"I eat lunch," Stavros said.

"You eat lunch?"

"When I'm hungry. I sit in the park if it's sunny."

"And you sit in the park?"

"And I talk to Miss Barton sometime." Stavros smiled again. "Get latest inside information, Sarrafian Brothers."

"Don't get fresh with me, boy. I'll break you in two," Morgan Perry said.

Stavros had to laugh at this. "You sick man, Mr. Perry," he said. "Better don't have those ideas. Also it's not good you get excited. I don't want to do that to you. Right, Mr. Ara?"

Nobody said anything.

"Well, what are we doing—playing games here?" Stavros asked. "You got something to ask me, ask it. Come on, nice and quick, let's go, kid!"

"What did you do last Tuesday at lunch hour?" Morgan Perry asked.

Stavros tried to stay calm. He looked at Freddie and winked. "What is this, lawyer game here?" he said. "Prosecution trial? Who remembers last Tuesday? Freddie, what you do last Tuesday—you remember? Maybe I talk to Miss Barton last Tuesday, Mr. Perry," he said.

"Don't do that, Joe, please," Freddie cut in. He'd moved behind Morgan Perry and touched his own stomach with a fingertip.

"O.K.," Stavros said, "but meantime maybe somebody tell me what's going on here, please?"

"What's happening," Morgan Perry said, "is that Mr. Ara Sarrafian and his brother, Mr. Fernand, want people here they can trust."

Stavros knew that Morgan Perry in his time had pulled down some nifty commissions on the side, but he took his friend Freddie's advice and let it pass. All he said was, "Allah!"

"What do you mean by that?" Morgan Perry wanted to know.

"You know. Turkish word for God," Stavros said. "Turks say it when they need help quick—'Allah!' Meantime goodbye, I think I go now. Excuse me, gentlemen—"

"Before you go," Morgan Perry said. "About Tuesday last. I see I'm going to have to tell the truth for you. Last Tuesday, during your lunch hour, you took our old and good customer Mr. Charlie T. Hogue to the store of Nassibian and Sons, and there you—"

"How do you know that?" Stavros was surprised.

"And there Charlie Hogue bought twenty pieces of fine Kerman carpet, gross maybe fourteen thousand dollars, maybe more. Your commission on same, maybe seven hundred, right?"

"Wrong."

"Where's that letter?" Morgan Perry turned to Freddie.

Freddie looked toward the round copper table in front of Mr. Ara at the other end of the long banquette.

Morgan Perry picked up the letter, put on his glasses, and read aloud: " 'The Hogue Emporium and Dry Goods, Kansas City, Missouri. Dear Mr. Farrow: With reference to your inquiry, I must answer yes, your Mr. Joe Arness did—' "

Stavros had been looking at Freddie. "Dear Mr. Farrow!" he said.

"Mr. Ara wanted me to find out," Freddie said.

"Dear Mr. Farrow!"

"Well," Freddie said, "you've been doing it for a long time now. I think for your own sake, Joe, you ought to stop. I mean, it's dishonest, and sooner or later somebody was bound to catch you at it."

"Later or sooner, even dumb people like us," Morgan Perry said.

"Anyway, it's a lesson to you," Freddie said. "Don't look at me that way."

Stavros couldn't take his eyes from Freddie.

"I don't like my part in this," Freddie said. "I was only doing what the boss asked me to do."

"That's all right, Freddie," Stavros said, "I understand." Then he turned to Mr. Ara, who still hadn't spoken. "We didn't have the rugs he wanted in stock," Stavros said.

"We have plenty Kerman," Morgan Perry said.

"Not the colors he wanted," Stavros said to Mr. Ara.

"Then it was your job," Mr. Ara said, breaking his silence, "or so it seems to me—Freddie is your friend; what do you think, Freddie?—then it was your job to persuade Mr. Charlie T. Hogue that the colors we have are the colors he wants. Freddie? What do you think?"

"That's what I'd try to do," Freddie said.

"I tried that," Stavros said, speaking to Mr. Ara.

"You're a liar," Morgan Perry said. "He's lying, boss."

"Don't, Joe—Joe, don't. Stavros, be quiet! Sit! Quiet!" Mr. Fernand was in the office now. Stavros had no idea how long he'd been there.

"You're looking better, Morgan," Mr. Fernand said. "Don't aggravate yourself. So the boy lied, Morgan. Not an unusual thing in business."

"You see, sir," Morgan Perry said, "it's just as I told you."

"You were right, Morgan, it looks like. Thank you. I'll talk to the boy now. You, too, Freddie—thank you."

"That's why I fired him," Morgan Perry said.

"When did you fire him?" Mr. Fernand said. He turned to his brother. "Is that your decision, Ara?"

"I don't want dishonest men here," Ara said.

"We respect that philosophy," Mr. Fernand said.

"When did you fire me?" Stavros asked. "Mr. Ara—I mean you."

"He's doing it now," Morgan Perry said.

Mr. Ara looked at his brother anxiously.

"Is that right? Mr. Ara?" Stavros asked. "You putting me out?"

"What do you need—a brick wall to fall on you?" Morgan Perry said.

"Shshsh, gentlemen, gentlemen," Mr. Fernand said.

Nobody spoke.

"Well, then, since Mr. Perry talks like cop," Stavros said, "and my old friend Freddie writes letters, so on, so forth, my turn to speak. The truth, plain language. Sure I been taking your customers. Many times, many years. Since we started, my brothers, our place—whenever a customer don't find what he wants here, I send him there. Or somewhere. Sometimes, yes, lunch hour, I take him myself, make sure he goes to right place. Also I will say this, Mr. Sarrafian." He was speaking directly to Ara. "You stole ten years my life without paying me what I was worth, so now we're even. Tie score, Freddie, right? And now I had enough of you, all of you, so shut up! All of you. Shut up!"

"You're fired!" Mr. Ara screamed.

"You been drinking again," Stavros said. "You drink too much, Mr. Ara; you don't know what you're doing sometimes these days!"

"I don't want to see your face in here ever again," Mr. Ara said. He stood up and started toward Stavros.

"What you coming to me for?" Stavros said. "You're an old man, sick, drinking like fish, Morgan Perry too. You're finished, both of you. Goodbye forever—right!"

Mr. Fernand had his arm around his brother. "Well, fine, Ara, fine, he's fired. Fine, Ara," he said, as if he were singing a lullaby. "Now I wonder if I could have my office, gentlemen? Fine, Morgan; go ahead now. Thank you, my old friend. I'll talk to the boy about some other matters. Words spoken in haste don't last."

"I meant everything!" Stavros said.

Mr. Fernand ignored him. "Thank you, Freddie. You go too, please. We'll talk later, Ara. By the way, Morgan, give my regards to dear Mrs. Perry. Tell her I admire the way she raised her daughter; she must be an excellent mother. She's feeling better, I hope. Is she? Better?"

"A little, maybe. Just nerves. My condition, you know. Well, boss, sorry to bring this up in front of you this way, but you see we can't trust this one. Maybe, God willing, this will be a lesson to him."

"Maybe, Morgan. Who knows? Maybe. Goodbye."

Then they were gone.

Mr. Fernand looked at Stavros and laughed, shaking his head. "Have some pistachios, damn fool," he said. "Come on, eat something." He poured himself a raki and began to strip the wax off a slice of roe. "I heard what you said about Miss Barton as I came in. It wasn't nice to tease a man who's dying about such a thing."

"If he's not sick, I cut his throat."

"Shshsh! Damn fool. This is America! Where do you think you are?" He fogged his raki with water. "Tell me, have you had an intimacy or two, maybe, with Miss Barton?"

"With that old woman?"

"Thirty-five doesn't look old to me. Did you?"

"Maybe once last year. She told me plenty about him, Morgan Perry."

"I don't want to hear it." He saw Stavros looking toward the roe and the raki. "Help yourself," he said.

"My father," Stavros said. "This was big favorite with him."

"Then take more. What are you doing this afternoon?"

"Work."

"It's Saturday."

"My family, we work Saturday. All day. Now especially."

"Now especially? Oh, yes, you've just been fired. So come on, we'll go to track." He hummed a tune. "I heard from my spies that the sun will soon be shining." He pranced out a fox-trot step.

"I don't bet," Stavros said.

"All Greeks bet. About the other business, it's simple. You told a lie and he caught you. My dear little friend, it's like fencing: Never leave yourself open. Always tell the truth. It's the practical thing to do. For a few hundred dollars, you gave that man a gun loaded to kill you. By the way, I want that seven hundred dollars. We pay your salary here; you work for us, including your lunch hour. Not for Nassibian on commission basis. You hear?"

"It was only five hundred and seventy dollars and I haven't got it anymore."

"What did you do with it?" He poured still another raki.

"I spent it. Yeah, give me one too. I don't want the job here anymore. Don't worry about it."

"Don't change the subject. What did you do with five hundred and seventy dollars? Tell me that. The truth, for a change."

"I bought two Sarouk, slightly damaged, seawater. My sisters working on them now, Fofo and Eleni, making them better than new."

"When you sell them, you owe me the money."

"Then I owe you."

"Come on, we go to the track. I provide capital. I like you, damn fool. Anything you lose, I pay. Anything you win, yours. O.K.?"

"Can't waste the time. I go home help my sisters."

"I make you more in one afternoon than you make here in a week." Stavros interrupted. "You guarantee?"

"I guarantee. You son of a bitch!" Then he made a very affectionate gesture toward Stavros. He walloped him with his open hand across the side of his face. It was what Stavros's father used to do when he was angry with his eldest, used to do in a way that made Stavros love him more.

"Come on, for God's sake," the old Armenian said. "Remember this: Misfortune is good for the character. There is no more effective goad to action. Now that you're a man of leisure, now that you have regained your precious freedom, enjoy it. Come on, we go. The sun is shining and I have very few friends."

Mr. Fernand had to pick up a certain Mr. Alan Aylesworth, and he told his chauffeur to go a roundabout way, along Riverside Drive. "I love to look at the river on a fine morning. It's a majestic river; reminds me of the Rhine, where I spent some weeks of my youth with a fräulein of uncertain virtue. . . ." He rambled on, enjoying his own chatter, while Stavros sank into the heavily cushioned seats and wondered what the hell he was going to do now. Then Mr. Fernand looked at Stavros. "What's the matter with you?" he said. "You haven't learned how to enjoy life yet?"

"I didn't like what that Morgan Perry—"

"Oh, come, come. That man is finished—can't you see that? People get desperate when they're dying. And he has more than one reason to hate you. You ever hear about a father's jealousy? It's worse than a lover's. And his wife, whom I asked about? She's not sick. She stays in her bedroom all day, drinks sherry. He sleeps in another room. When you're that miserable, you have to let it out somewhere. You didn't learn that yet? Come on, cheer up. Maybe this is good—maybe big things will open up for you now. You didn't get tired of that lousy job at our store yet? Tell the truth?"

Mr. Aylesworth was a tall, angular Englishman in his late sixties, who was wearing a Harris tweed jacket, medium-gray trousers of flannel cloth, and a sweater, even on this very hot autumn day. He greeted Wynn, the chauffeur, as an old friend.

At first Stavros didn't listen to their conversation—he had his own troubles—but then Mr. Fernand brought Stavros into it.

"Our young friend here, Alan, has an understanding of what we've been talking about, political vacuums. He says that as soon as the Ottomans collapse there will be a vast commercial vacuum and that is the precise moment for the incursion of predators, that means you and me, Aylesworth. Jackals like me, lions like you—yes, that is the time for power to move in. Eh, you, liar, you listening?"

"Half," Stavros said.

"He's just been fired," Mr. Fernand said. "I've had trouble convincing him that it's the best thing that could have happened to him."

"He's trying make me feel good," Stavros said to Mr. Aylesworth. "Not necessary, Mr. Fernand."

"He understands the nature of war too," Mr. Fernand said to Aylesworth. "For instance, that it's continuous, never stops, and is alternately commercial and military, then military and commercial, so it goes, on and on."

"Let me out here," Stavros said suddenly, putting his hand on the door. "I don't want to go to the goddamn track. I have to figure out what the hell I'm going to do next."

"Sit back," Mr. Fernand said. *"Eeeraht ol!* You need thought, not action. Reconsider your life. Consider alternatives. This is an opportunity, what happened today, to look at your whole life again."

"I do that every morning," Stavros said.

"Besides, Mr. Aylesworth is a financier. You can learn from him. You may even be able, if you get over your sulk, to interest him in your ideas, if not your personality. He has, Mr. Aylesworth does, an appreciation of the alternating currents of history. He swims in those currents—something you have not yet been able to do. Perhaps this is your chance. And perhaps yours, Aylesworth. I might be a marriage broker here. You always need desperate young men, don't you, Aylesworth? He looks like nothing, I agree—short, crooked, mean-looking. But listen to him, to his passion, his anger. We have a monster with us here, Aylesworth."

Aylesworth laughed. "Our friend Fernand," he said to Stavros, "likes nothing quite as much as the sound of his own improvisations."

"By the way, Stavros," Mr. Fernand said, "Aylesworth here is a great friend of your mother country, Greece, and of your premier, Mr. Venizelos."

Soon they were sitting at a table on the upper boundary of the clubhouse enclosure, out of the sun, watching the parade of the crowd.

"There are days," Mr. Fernand confided to them, "when I'd give the rest of my life for one real stiff one like I used to get. Other days, I prefer lunch. I am going to have, may God help me, spaghetti Caruso. What do you gentlemen want? Have the same. It's very good here. What are you looking at, Stavros? Oh, the girls, the girls! The girls are getting prettier, I'm getting older. Swish, swish, this way, that way, the head, the tail. You shouldn't tease Perry about poor Miss Barton. A long time ago, that. Also he's too sick."

"Every Saturday afternoon, he used to."

"I know every Saturday afternoon."

"If he weren't sick man, if he talk to me that way I cut his throat."

"Don't expect pity from the young, Aylesworth. Oh, look where he's looking now. You fancy that one, Stavros, eh? Ohh! Look at that one—oh my God!"

"I like them all."

"Then why blame Morgan Perry? Why shouldn't he have had a Saturday sweetheart? Life, it's impossible. We do the best we can. He's a good —well, he used to be a good salesman, the best maybe for American customers."

"What you don't know is he steals too."

"No pity, the young, Aylesworth, no pity."

"Why he expose me like criminal court judge? Where you think he got furniture for his house?"

"He got it from Caldwell and Abramowitz, Newark, New Jersey. He got it because he did them some favors—first chance special goods and so forth, so on."

"He tell you that?"

"He didn't have to tell me. I know. He did favors for some other stores too. Cost me nothing. The stores pay. Everybody steals. Watch the monkey in the zoo. Only thing I ask is, don't do too much. I'm not going to live long enough to see the human race change. My advice to you, foreign born especially, in the beginning be honest. At least for a while."

"I can't afford that," Stavros said. "Honesty is for the rich. Seven hundred dollars, that's nothing for you. But my whole family works three months, they don't save up seven hundred dollars. So I make it one lunch hour, when I see chance."

"What did you do with seven hundred dollars? By the way, you lie before—right? Now it's seven hundred dollars?"

"Right."

"So what did you do?"

"That's my business. Look there!"

"With the red hair? That's her hair, it's like that all over."

"How do you know?"

"When you have money, you have information. You want her, you can have her."

"I don't have money buy that kind goods."

"It's my present to you, going-away present. Courtship, so forth, not necessary. All right? You accept?"

"Then you will want something from me."

"What do you think you have that I could want?" He swiftly changed the subject. "I think you still like that filly—young Miss Perry. Right?"

"Wrong."

"My advice: Forget her. Waiter! Two spaghetti Caruso. Aylesworth, what do you want? He's asleep. He does that; before you know it, he's asleep. Like a cat. Make it three, waiter. He'll eat it. And three Scotches, White Rock. Yes, young friend, forget Mr. Morgan Perry's daughter. Such as that is not for you."

"I found that out."

"She is feature-race stuff. Big purse. Belmont Stakes. Not for you."

Stavros was looking at the girl with the red hair all over. "They'll crawl," he said.

"Who? What?"

"Never mind. I don't want Miss Perry, believe me."

"You don't want her because you can't have her. Advice: Don't want something you can't have. You can buy any woman, if you have the money. But let's look at your bankbook. Can you show the proper figures?"

They'll crawl, thought Stavros as he watched the girl with the red hair all over flip her eyes here and there. He watched her as she walked away.

Mr. Fernand took this in. "Poor things," he said. "They have no way to earn a living, so they have to live this style."

There was the sound of a distant bell. Alan Aylesworth woke and began to look at his program. "Who do you like in the first race, Fernand?" he said.

Stavros was looking at another young woman.

"Now, that one—excuse me, Aylesworth, we'll go to the paddock, I have a friend there, he may say a few words to me. Look what this man is hungry for. That's a Murray, damn fool. Her father owns one-third of Southampton, Long Island, shore line. Also owns number-five horse, second race. And he owns her. No, sorry; he sold her. She's getting married next June to one-half of Newport, Rhode Island, shore line. Wait a few years, make plenty money, then maybe she get tired of her husband, her husband tired of her. Even then, what would she want with small bow-legged hamal goat? Ha-ha-ha. Girls like that you can't have; resign yourself."

"They'll crawl," Stavros said out loud.

"Crawl? To you? Get money first, my boy. You don't understand this country yet."

"I don't spend money for girls."

The waiter brought the drinks and Mr. Aylesworth got up, holding his glass. "Let's go to the paddock," he said.

"Hey, hey! Don't drink Scotch like that, boy. Sip. Look, Aylesworth, it's all gone already. Waiter, bring one more here. Come on, get up, we go to the paddock. Waiter, in ten minutes we'll be back for spaghetti. Put plenty cheese, right? Here's dollar, for your dear daughter."

At the paddock, Stavros looked at the horses carefully and made his judgment. Then Mr. Sarrafian advanced him ten dollars and he made his bets. Mr. Sarrafian did not look at the horses. He talked quietly to a man in the corner of the stalls, a little old man with the face of a used lemon. Then he communicated the information he'd received to his friend Aylesworth and they made their bets.

While they ate, Mr. Sarrafian and Mr. Aylesworth's horse came in second and Stavros's out of the money.

"We both lost," Stavros said, as he finished his spaghetti.

"We played place," Mr. Fernand said. "Advice!"

For the rest of the afternoon, Stavros played only the horses Mr. Fernand played and at the end of the day, after he'd paid back his new patron, he had one hundred and eighteen newfound dollars in his pocket. "I will come here again," he announced.

They found Mr. Fernand's Rolls. "Wynn," Mr. Fernand said to the chauffeur, "there's a young lady, friend of Mr. Aylesworth . . ."

"She's in the car," Wynn said.

Mr. Fernand turned to Stavros. "That young lady with the red hair, the one you liked," he said. "She'll be coming directly to my home. My farewell present to you."

Stavros was amazed. He'd had three Scotches during the afternoon and his eyes shone. "When did you . . . ?"

"Her husband will arrange it," Mr. Fernand said.

Then he got in. Aylesworth was beside a young lady who was either very short or slumped low in the seat. "By the way," Mr. Fernand said, as he held the door open for Stavros, who settled in a jump seat. "I'm glad you are finished with Miss Perry, as you said, feeling nothing and so on, because I talked to my son, Paul, and he told me the good news. They are engaged. I am—you know how I admire that girl's character—I am very happy."

So he bought her, Stavros said to himself. He'd learned the lesson Mr. Fernand had been teaching him all afternoon.

The front door of the West Sixty-eighth Street town house was trimmed on either side with long, narrow lights, and through one of these Stavros could see a small Japanese sitting on a three-legged stool. Had he been waiting for them to arrive? Stavros had guessed it! Mr. Fernand's butler and houseboy. Yes, when you have money, they wait for you at the front door—oh, how they jump and hustle when they hear your feet on the stoop!

Mr. Aylesworth had taken the outside steps in a bound, his energy on display for the young lady he'd brought from the track. She was a plump pullet and as short on her feet as she'd seemed to be sitting. They were ill matched physically but Stavros guessed they'd find a way to get together. Lillian was her name and she skipped through the door the old Japanese was holding open. She'd been there before, it was obvious; perfectly at home, she sang "I love you, Kyushiro," as she kissed him on the cheek and danced by. Was she a musical comedy star?

Stavros waited outside for Mr. Fernand, who was giving parting instructions to Wynn. "When the young ladies are tired of us," he said, "you will take them home. Now go have your dinner and give my best wishes to your excellent wife."

The redhead Stavros had noticed at the track was in the foyer, sitting on a long colonial bench, waiting patiently as if this were an employment agency. Mr. Fernand had started for her, but Kyushiro had immediately slipped a womanly hand under the old man's coat. "You're perspiring again," he scolded, as if sweating were a voluntary act. He produced a fresh linen handkerchief and when the old man waved it off, mopped Mr. Fernand's brow and neck himself. It was apparent from Kyushiro's concern that Mr. Fernand was susceptible to colds. Then Kyushiro scooted back to the door, locked it, and was flying past, up the stairs, like a ghost up a chimney.

Mr. Fernand greeted the redhead graciously, murmuring, "Lucy, how nice of you to trouble yourself with us this evening," then inclined his body toward the stairs to indicate that she should proceed to the rooms above. Eager Aylesworth and his catch were already out of sight; Stavros could hear them joshing far above. Mr. Fernand began to mount slowly, the stairs evidently a strain. Lucy followed. Then Stavros. They moved as if in royal procession. The lady's livelihood was at the level of Stavros's eyes as he followed her; she was carrying Mr. Fernand's gift to him up the stairs. A whore—what else?—but who would know it to look at her! "Imagine!" Stavros said to himself, "her husband brings her to Mr. Fernand's house! America America!"

It was generous of the old man, Stavros thought, to pimp for him. But then what was it out of his pocket—a few dollars? Still, he'd noticed Stavros's interest at the track and arranged for her. Perhaps it was to take the sting out of what he'd told Stavros about Althea and his son, Paul.

"Thanks very much, I accept your kindness, old man," Stavros said to himself. "I will gladly spread those legs and remember you gratefully as I do. There, between, I will try to forget Althea. Was that your idea, old man?"

Halfway up, there was a landing, and Kyushiro rematerialized, holding a floor-length brocaded robe. Mr. Fernand turned to be fitted and Kyushiro whisked off the old man's Palm Beach jacket and let it drop to the floor. Then he slipped on the robe, rounded by Sulka (Stavros could read the label) to fit the stooped shoulders. A couple of tugs, up and across, covered the old bony chest. Kyushiro, chattering like a monkey, whispered and scolded as he pulled a small embroidered cap over the old man's small bare skull. Finally he thrust into Mr. Fernand's hands a China silk handkerchief which gave off a sweet scent. "Use it!" he ordered. And the old man did, drying his forehead again, then his wattled neck where it met his chin.

There was a delighted scream from above, then another, then laughter. Kyushiro vanished, fuming. Mr. Fernand laughed. "In love, the English hurry," he said. And he patted Lucy's hand. The redhead looked at him and smiled faintly—as yet, she hadn't looked at Stavros. Perhaps, thought Stavros, Mr. Fernand hadn't told her whose gift she was. She was certainly a fine piece—good goods! Mr. Fernand had bought her for Stavros just as he'd bought Althea for his son.

"When they became interested?" Stavros asked, and when Mr. Fernand seemed not to understand his question, added, "Althea and your son?"

"The first time he saw her he was interested," Mr. Fernand said. "My son is not blind. Althea, as you well know, is a beautiful girl. I knew Paul wanted her even before he told me so." Having caught his breath and rested his heart, the old man continued up the stairs, his retinue following as before. "I've told you how much I admire her," Mr. Fernand said. Turning, he noticed Stavros's expression and smiled. "Time brings many surprises," he said. "Eh? We agree?"

"What's that smell?" Lucy said.

"I have a new cook. He's showing off. Are you hungry?"

"She's been here?" Stavros asked. "Althea?"

"Not yet," Mr. Fernand said. "But the engagement party will be here, and I suppose there will be a June wedding at her grandmother's in Southampton."

"Sounds good," Stavros said.

"I'm glad you think so," Mr. Fernand said.

Stavros couldn't imagine Althea here, nor could he imagine her with Paul, whom he'd seen only once. Paul had been quiet and vague that day, and to tell the truth, he'd seemed stupid, almost defective. They hadn't spoken.

The dining room was à la Turka, divans covered with red velvet around a long low table, and scores of pillows of multicolored silk. Stavros couldn't imagine Althea here either. Then suddenly, yes, he could, now he could, rolling and laughing among all those pillows.

Mr. Fernand had sought the ease of his divan immediately, but after that he wasn't hurrying, not even wishing for anything, taking things as they came. *Money waits,* Stavros thought.

There was a sound from above, a commotion of cloth and plump limbs; then two young women came charging down the stairs, Kyushiro driving them from behind as if they were sheep and he a toothy little terrier nipping at their rears.

Mr. Fernand had picked up one of the three newspapers that Kyushiro had arranged neatly on the coffee table, glanced at the headlines, then lowered it and smiled in a kindly way at the girls being propelled from his house. "Don't be impatient with them, Kyushiro," he said. "Life is not easy for them." Then he turned to Stavros. "There go Emily and Agnes, whose accommodations have an uncertain flow of hot water. They asked to use my bathroom—"

"They don't ask nothing," Kyushiro shouted from below. "They say you give O.K. They lie."

"Kyushiro is not kind to women," Mr. Fernand said.

The door below was slammed, then bolted, and Kyushiro came up the stairs as if he had wings, saying, "Yes, yes, all the time patience, kindness, but I have to clean up after those bitches—you should see how they leave the bathroom. They were in there together for almost two hours. Doing what? Ask God." And he was out of sight above.

The girls had gone by so swiftly that Stavros had no impression of them; only that they'd waved to Lucy as they passed and she had waved back.

The old man had raised the paper and was reading again.

"I want my bath, Kyushiro," he complained loudly.

"Well, you have to wait," the Japanese called from above. "They use all the hot water. Bad girls!"

It was difficult for Stavros to imagine Mr. Fernand engaged in sexual activity, but the whole place suggested . . .

"She'll like it here," he said to Mr. Fernand. "Althea, I mean."

"You really think so?" the old man said. "I often can't tell if you're sincere. My own impression is that she is basically very straitlaced and—"

"She give that impression but—"

"Certainly her upbringing was strict. This place"—he waved his hand, indicating the upper regions—"befits an old man with more money than he will be able to spend the rest of his life. It's arranged for pleasure."

"She likes pleasure," Stavros said. "Take it from me."

Mr. Fernand frowned at Stavros. "I think we should all forget the past," he said. "Not pull it back to memory again and again. Regret is a wasted emotion, my boy. Nothing is permanent in this world, and in the end nothing can be relied on. Change is the order of the world."

"Money buys everything," Stavros said. "That is the order of the world."

"An unkind remark," Mr. Fernand said. "At the same time, true. Women have no way of acquiring the wherewithal, and their term of beauty is so short, they must do what they can. When they can. That is why they gravitate to the magnet and that magnet is not sex, but money. We mustn't look down on Althea for that. On the other hand, when you are in the opposite chair, as I am, you must take advantage of the circumstances—women's nature and their needs—since it is a law of nature."

"I have to be somewhere else in an hour," Lucy said.

"Ah, but you shan't be there, my dear. You shall be here," Mr. Fernand said. He turned to Stavros. "We mustn't begrudge Althea her ease of mind," he said. "Nor be unkind about her natural concern for her future. Don't you agree?" He was looking intently at Stavros now, his eyes hard as marbles.

"I agree," Stavros said. "I congratulate her. Through you. She made wise move."

"I hope you mean that. I really don't know when you're sincere. The only important concern I have in life after all these years is my son's happiness, present and future. Everything else is a kind of game for me. The boy came to me late in life, he's the only one I have, and I'm afraid I spoiled him. And . . . he has some other problems."

He stopped as if he'd said too much, smiled at Stavros, nodded, picked up a newspaper and began to read.

The little redheaded hen sat on her eggs, patiently. She still hadn't looked at Stavros, but he'd inspected her thoroughly. Now he made a tiny sound and she looked at him, then back to the old man reading, then back to Stavros. She shrugged. What did that mean?

The old man must have noticed this exchange, because he said, "Don't be impatient, dear friends. You will have much time together. And alone. Kyushiro is making certain the bathroom is in perfect order, as well as airing and reordering the bedroom, so that when we go up, it will be immaculate."

"We?" Stavros said.

Mr. Fernand smiled at him over the top of the *Evening Globe.* "There is space above for us all," he said. "More than enough."

Stavros stretched himself out on the divan à la Turka, legs folded ankle to crotch. Time passed. The redhead yawned.

Mr. Fernand had said "we." Did the old man—who was seventy-two, at least—did he still indulge? Stavros had asked Freddie this once, and Freddie had told him what Morgan Perry had said in answer to the same question: that yes, it did come to Mr. Fernand, the moment of arousal, but as an unanticipated guest, gratefully welcomed. When it was delinquent or long absent, the old man had a recourse: two girls, sisters—of course, the ones who'd just left—were trained to provide the old man with a service Mr. Fernand had learned of from an old Arab merchant-sheik in east Persia. Mr. Fernand, according to Morgan Perry, had schooled the sisters to work as a team, he perfectly passive, they doing the "work" on glans and prostate simultaneously, until the old man had what satisfied him —an emission, don't call it an orgasm. Which is why the old man's butler kept the young women Stavros had seen in attendance. It was Kyushiro's responsibility to have what the old man needed ready when he needed it.

Mr. Fernand suddenly put down his newspaper and said, "It seems that the statesmen of the world are planning a political rearrangement, or as I'd prefer to put it, a redistribution of economic resources and markets. Your Mr. Venizelos, my little patriot, his voice is being heard everywhere. It's natural for you Greeks to want to change the world in your favor, you've been skimped for so long you're famished for power. But I will confess to you that I have often wondered—privately, of course—whether it makes any real difference. I can get along as well with one government as with another. I've seen so many governments come to liberate some of the people by murdering some of the people and—"

He'd noticed that Stavros's eyes had wandered to the wall behind him.

"The photograph you're looking at is a representation—rather flattering, I'm afraid—of my esteemed parents. And those smaller ones, the row either side of the fireplace, are of myself when I was young and adventurous. They were taken in Persia when oil was first found there, and it was that discovery and perhaps a bit of my ingenuity in negotiation, if I may say so, that changed the history of the world. I don't like those pictures. I'm going to take them down. They remind me!"

Kyushiro rushed down the stairs. "Come, come," he said. "Bath ready."

Mr. Fernand got up slowly, folding the newspaper and replacing it neatly on the table. "All my life, I've seen the same words thrown up like fireworks by both sides—liberty, brotherhood, justice for all, freedom for all. Every army marches under the flag of God, and both sets of soldiers, before they go into battle to be killed, are equally blessed by equally holy men in equally eloquent language in every known tongue. Each side is sincere and— What, Kyushiro, what?"

Kyushiro had pointed him toward the steps and given him a little push.

"Yes, I know, Kyushiro." But he went on with his quiet ruminations. "I've watched and waited while power changed hands, this way and that. In the aftermath, everything stayed the same." He stopped on the steps. "Ortak," he called. Kyushiro tried to push him on up the stairs, hissing and whispering, but Mr. Fernand waved his hands impatiently like an old woman and refused to budge.

A man with a white apron bound tightly above a melon belly was standing in a service doorway, bowing his head in salaam.

"Yes, Ortak, fine," Mr. Fernand said. "I will have my bath and then my massage and then I want what you probably don't have—lamb chops."

"I have them," Ortak said, "of course. Baby lamb."

"But these young people, their stomachs are hardier as well as more impatient. Invite them into your kitchen and see if you have anything there that pleases them." He turned to Stavros. "I will leave you two to make each other's acquaintance. Lucy, you will enjoy the company of this young man. But don't allow him to go too fast. Let's not hurry tonight, Lucy. You understand me?"

"Yes, Mr. Fernand," Lucy said.

"First eat something. I will have my bath."

Then he was upstairs and out of sight, and from above Stavros could hear the sound of a stringed instrument being tuned, and he remembered being told by someone that Mr. Fernand kept a musician living in his home, a man whose only duty it was to be there in the evening when the old man entertained and provide him with the melodies he loved, those of the Ionian isles, the Italian modes wedded to the Turkish.

Lucy and Stavros were alone except for Ortak, the cook, who was waiting to show them his kitchen, parting his hands, smiling, inclining his body toward the area behind him.

"Before we eat," Stavros growled at Lucy, growling to let her know that he understood what she was, a whore, "go find room with a door. You know his house, you been here before. Come on, come on—food will wait."

"Didn't you hear what Mr. Sarrafian said? Not to hurry," Lucy said. "He's taking his bath; he'll be mad if we do what you say." She looked at her wristwatch.

"What's the difference he's mad?" Stavros said.

"The difference is he pays my rent. Look, the cook's waiting for you. Don't you want to eat something?"

Ortak was still in the doorway, looking anxious. When Stavros turned to him, he bowed once more, then inclined his body from the waist toward the kitchen, his large, soft hands following.

"You come too," Stavros said to the redheaded whore. "We mustn't hurt his feelings."

When they started for the kitchen, Ortak darted back out of sight. As Stavros walked through the door, the cook was lifting a lid off a large shallow pot, to invite inspection. The *kazani* contained a serration of small shrimps arranged like sleeping lovers, side by side, spoon style, in a fragrant sauce, both sheet and blanket, of fresh tomatoes and bay leaves. The redhead bent over to sample the aroma, hanging her muskmelons over the steaming dish. She was bigger than Althea there, Stavros could see that. *Althea, that bitch,* he thought, *that betrayer, allowing herself to be sold like a common whore. What's the difference? She jumps where the money points just as this one does, shaming me, shaming what we've been to each other.*

There were two other large pots, enough for a feast. In one, young artichokes sat on their bottoms surrounded by pearls, baby onions pulled out of the earth early to allow their neighbors to grow to full size. And there was a pot full of little zucchini, piled in soft stacks, orphans plucked off their parent vines before their time of seeding and stuffed with a preparation of minced lamb and spices. Stavros could smell the cloves and cinnamon in the steam.

"What will you eat?" he said to Lucy.

"I can't eat this food," she said. "It gives me heartburn." Then she looked at her watch again and made a little sound.

Stavros took her wrist and twisted it, then undid the strap. "You're spoiling my temper looking at this damn thing," he said, putting the watch in his pocket. "What do you work, by the hour?"

"I sell my time," she said. "Give me my watch."

"You sell your *golo*," Stavros said, "not your time. You think people buy you for your conversation?"

"There's no need to be ugly," she said, turning away from him. "What's *golo?*"

"What you sit on." Stavros turned to the cook. "Give me everything," he said. "I want to taste everything you have."

Stavros knew this kind of man well. To be ordered brusquely was the pleasure of his life, a sign he was needed and respected.

"I make all this food. From early morning, I market, I cook," he said. "Wasted! His honor wishes lamb chops, I will place lamb chops before him."

"Come, come," Stavros said. "Stop complaining. He pays you well, doesn't he? We're all whores here, we jump where money points. Come, I'm hungry."

"Go sit down, sir; please, dear sir. I'll bring everything."

From above, where the musician had tuned the strings of his instrument, came the sound of an *amanee*. It had a sour and bitter taste, that music; it rankled in the Anatolian's heart. "Oh, Althea!" he said to himself.

"What kind of music is that?" the redhead asked. "It's so . . . so uncivilized."

"Turkish," Stavros said. "They're the most civilized people in the world, the class Turk who make that music. Because they don't hide their anger. That musician, whoever he is, is telling Mr. Fernand he's shit, and the old man don't know it."

Stavros had heard that "uncivilized" sound in many a Constantinople hashish cellar in his time as a hamal. Now it brought back memories and awoke his anger. "Althea is a whore too," Stavros said.

"Do I know her?" Lucy asked.

"No," Stavros said, "I know her. She's class of whore who gets more than you."

The redhead was offended. "How do you know what I get?" she demanded. "I get fifty dollars here tonight, plus a hundred a week regular. He already paid my husband that. Who makes more? I ask you." She minced to the sofa and sat staring straight ahead, then looked at her wrist. "If you don't give me my watch back toot sweet, dearie, I will have to tell my husband when he comes for me and he will take it from you." Then, as an afterthought: "He works out with Jim Londos."

Ignoring the threat, Stavros ambled to the large photograph of Mr. Sarrafian's parents. It was tinted pink and rose, like the cover of an Italian bonbon box, but in every other respect it was ordinary. What astonished Stavros was that it was so familiar: the father in his black suit of worsted wool staring straight at the camera, the mother standing behind her master, ring hand on his shoulder, looking at him as if she was waiting for an order. Her hair was pulled back, peasant style, and in every way she was as plain as possible, still insuring, as she had from the beginning, that no other man would be attracted to her. They were Armenians, of course, but they could have been Greek, Turkish, Bulgarian, Lebanese, Rumanian, Syrian, Serb, Montenegrin, even Italian. Their social level was little above the one on which Stavros had grown up: They weren't *rich,* any more than Stavros's parents had been rich. Both were wearing their single set of "good" clothes, at other times wrapped up in paper and packed in a chest of rosewood. These clothes were brought forth only for an occasion like this one or, say, the wedding of a child or the funeral of another, and finally for their own funeral.

Stavros realized that his host, who now had at his command every pleasure he could imagine or the world afford, had started from circumstances little more favored than Stavros's own. He also suddenly understood that the event of that morning, his dismissal from Sarrafian Brothers, was indeed what the old man had said it was: a blessing, a chance to reconsider the course of his life and see that anything was possible for the man who used his energy with daring. The only curse was a "regular" job.

Ortak hustled in with silver and dishes and the basic condiments, arranging a place for Stavros at the head of the table, before the divan where Mr. Fernand had sat. "Ready, honored sir!" he cried, and hustled back into the kitchen.

Stavros was about to walk past three other snapshots, framed together and hung at the side of the ornate green tile fireplace, but he thought he recognized someone and stopped to examine them. The top picture showed a barren and rocky hillside, a vast and forbidding arena, empty except that in the foreground three men sat around a rug on which a small white tablecloth had been spread. They were having a picnic, it seemed; there was wine and the remains of the kind of repast one welcomes on a camping trip—bread, cheese, sausages, milk chocolate. One of the men could have been an Indian or a Persian, he was that dark, and he wore a long black robe and a fez. In his lap was a tiny white dog. The second man was clearly an Englishman, for he wore a pith helmet and sported a barracks mustache. His coat was neatly buttoned and on one hand, a glove. His other hand hung at ease over the back of a large hound, alert at its master's side. The third man, more at his ease than the others, it seemed, was Mr. Fernand. He might have been forty-five at the time and was dressed in a suit that would have been appropriate on Regent Street—the foulard tie held a stickpin—except for one thing; he wore puttees to bind the bottoms of his trousers.

The second photograph had been taken in the same place some time later. The hills behind were the same, vast and barren, but now the foreground was fully occupied. Mr. Fernand and the Englishman were mounted on horses and both wore business suits and homburg hats. Surrounding them was a company of swarthy men, perhaps two score, again Persians, Afghans, Kurds, or perhaps Turks, some of whom carried the tools of the surveyor's trade. At the side of Mr. Fernand's white horse stood a servant, also in white, carrying a flagon for water and a glass. Mr. Fernand, even then, made sure of his comfort.

The third photograph showed the identical barren hills, but now the hollow where the picnic had taken place was filled with a great shed of black metal. Behind it was a derrick, perhaps one hundred and fifty feet high, out of which black smoke—no, oil!—was erupting. Apparently the photo had been snapped at the instant of triumph, the fulfillment of the effort suggested in the other two snapshots. Mr. Fernand was alone now, in the foreground, looking quizzically into the camera, a slight smile on his lips, as if he was thinking: Didn't you know I would finally? Perhaps that was his thought, for the Englishman had disappeared.

"You gave me too much," Stavros said to Ortak.

"What am I going to do with it?" the cook complained. "What you don't eat, leave."

He watched Stavros eat. After a moment, the girl stole in behind Stavros and she must have been hungry, because she leaned over and picked a curl of shrimp off his plate and sucked it into her mouth. When she tried it again, Stavros hit her hand with the flat of his knife.

"You have no manners," she said.

Kyushiro reappeared. "He like you upstairs now. Come."

"I'm eating," Stavros replied.

"You can eat later."

"I eat now. I like my food warm."

Kyushiro turned to the girl. "Quick, you—upstairs," he said in the highest pitch of voice he could manage. "You explain to him why this one doesn't obey orders." Lucy bustled past Kyushiro and ran up the stairs. Again she looked at her wrist where her watch had been.

Despite himself Stavros did hurry, even told Ortak that he didn't like sweets although sweets were what he lived on. And when he went up the stairs, he trotted.

Mr. Fernand was in bed, covered with a white sheet that was pulled up to his very white face. Between his lips there was a white cigarette holder clasping the only spot of color, the glowing end of a Melachrino. It bobbed up and down as he whispered to Lucy, who was sitting on the edge of his bed, head down, as if she'd been reprimanded. Mr. Fernand brightened when he saw Stavros. "She tells me you found our kitchen satisfactory," he said. Then he waved his hand to a large and exceptionally wide sofa opposite his bed. "Lie down there," he said. "Be comfortable. We'll have a chat while I have my massage." Then he said to the girl, "Lie next to him."

The girl did what she was told; it was her training. She loosened something in her clothing and curled on the sofa like one of Ortak's potted shrimps.

Mr. Fernand gestured Stavros to the sofa again, but instead Stavros walked around the room. He noticed that Kyushiro had laid a sheet on the floor between the bathroom and the bed, a clean white sheet. He peeked into the bathroom: towels all over the floor, a bouquet of flowers on a table.

"I know you're feeling bitterness and pain now," Mr. Fernand said. "Such a moment is not bad necessarily. It can, in fact, be a very creative time, depending how a man takes it. As you correctly noted with reference to my brother, secure comfort can be stifling, the enemy of ambition. But there"—he curled his arm toward the sofa again—"there is certainly the best way to recover from your deprivation. Your former lady and your employment both gone within a short span of time! But you will be amazed how quickly the human animal forgets. And moves on. Go comfort yourself."

"I just ate," Stavros said.

"So satisfy your other appetite. Don't you like the young lady? You did at the track."

"Of course, I like her. But I just ate."

"Do I seem to be hurrying you?" Mr. Fernand asked.

"Yes," Stavros said.

The musician changed to a new melody in a new mode.

"Oh!" Mr. Fernand said. "Perhaps that's it, the presence of a stranger. Of course!" He made a gesture to the musician, who quickly left the room. "Strangers present! I forgot. Now, there. You no longer consider Kyushiro a stranger, do you? You must have realized that he is a completely impersonal being who has seen a great deal and forgotten it all. Haven't you, Kyushiro?"

Kyushiro ignored the question. He took the cigarette holder out of the old man's mouth, then placed two small moistened pads of cotton on Mr. Fernand's eyes and pulled the white sheet off the old man's body, exposing it completely.

"Go lie down with the lady; she's waiting for you," Mr. Fernand said. "Come. As you see, Kyushiro has rendered me blind."

"Few minutes," Stavros said. "What's your rush?"

"She tells me you were studying my photographs." Kyushiro had doused him with alcohol and now was sliding his moist palm over the wrinkled body, spreading the cool liquid. "Ah! Good," Mr. Fernand said. "What a blessing! So cool! You must try this sometime."

"Your photographs," Stavros said. "Where was that?"

"Western Persia, many years ago, an area completely without charm. Nevertheless the source of many fortunes, including my own. Those snapshots, I hope, didn't leave you with the impression that I was once an intrepid adventurer. The fact is that I don't like the wilderness. I prefer Maxim's in the Rue Royale."

"Seems you operated O.K. in that wilderness."

"Again the fact is not what it appears to be. I discovered nothing. My contribution, if you can call it that, was to facilitate conversations. I knew who needed to talk to whom and I was able, thanks to the art of hospitality which I learned at my mother's table, to bring them together. My mother had a large family and kept us all harmoniously happy. I learned there that if you bring apparently discordant elements into the same room, serve them beverages which contain alcohol in moderation, and follow with savory foods, you are already more than halfway—" He lifted the moist pad off one eye. "What are you looking at?" he said.

Stavros said it. "At you."

"Are you shocked?" The old man chuckled.

"Yes, sir. I am."

Mr. Fernand Sarrafian, who looked so exquisite in his clothing and carried himself like royalty, was, without his clothing, a physical disaster. He seemed completely dried out, his skin a web of wrinkles covering the entire surface of his body. Except in two places, he was thinner than it could possibly be healthy to be. His knees were bony and unpadded. His teats sagged to wrinkles. His arms were racks from which hung folds of loose flesh, like miniature household curtains on rods. The Japanese, who was working on him, had now reached his penis, which he lifted by a corner of the foreskin. It was small, like a boy's, and singularly lifeless. But there was the first surprise: the bag which held the testicles seemed swollen and strangely reddened, which made the penis look even more withered and white.

But the biggest surprise was the man's belly. It was large and round and firm; not bloated, firm! Possibly it was the only healthy part of his body because it had continued to be a seat of pleasure for him.

He was still looking at Stavros and chuckling. Then he put the pad back over his eye.

"You've never seen an old man's body before, apparently. What did you expect?"

"I don't know," Stavros said.

Mr. Fernand raised his hands. "I want you to take particular notice of my hands," he said. "You'll find a lesson there for you, hamal. Do they look like they have ever done a day's work? I've relied on my cunning. I'm talking about cunning! A jackal, lacking the strength of the great predators, needs cunning. I was born with it."

"Those three photographs," Stavros said. "You must have had idea there was something under that land of rocks which people would pay fortunes for. No?"

"No. Other people had the knowledge you speak of. I anticipated nothing. I discovered nothing. I had no fresh thoughts. I merely recognized the ingenuity of others and provided the capital for the necessary operations."

"Come on, do same thing for me," Stavros said. "Come on!"

Kyushiro turned Mr. Fernand over, spread-eagled, exposing his wrinkled, flabby buttocks. The Japanese began scuffing the skin, bringing blood back to parts that seemed lifeless.

"Perhaps, perhaps," Mr. Fernand said. "There's a good deal of unemployed capital now, due to the war. Yes, we must talk about your ideas sometime."

"I been talking my ideas to you so many years. Now when I get fired you pay a little attention."

"Yes, that's the way it happens. I am famous for that. I'm 'slippery,' they say. Slippery! It's nothing more than a way of protecting myself. When you have capital, you are the object of constant exhortations, pleas, requests; your arm is forever being tugged at, eyes seek yours, pleading, desperate eyes; and in less rigid civilizations people rush at me, fall on their knees, and press their lips—which can't be clean, can they?—to my hand. I have to hurry to the hotel to wash."

Stavros got on the sofa and stretched out alongside Lucy.

The old man lifted a pad again. "Good," he said. "Perhaps now we can have a civilized chat and not talk about money and finance and affairs of business. Lucy, you like your cruel ugly man there?"

"Yes, Mr. Sarrafian."

"You have my blessing." And he replaced the pad.

Lucy came close, throwing a leg over Stavros's leg.

"Here's a question I have meant to ask you," Mr. Fernand said. "You Greeks now, it seems, have ideas of empire. A big word. That is natural, I suppose, considering your glorious past. But tell me how you can have it better than you've had it under the Turk? Every good position in Sultan Abdul-Hamid's government—I know this from the most personal experience—was held by an Anatolian Greek. Excepting the army, of course. But politics, commerce, industry, finance—wherever there was money moving, I would find one of your race moving it. You say the Turk was a cruel master? Nonsense! They were your dray horses. All you Anatolians had to do was call, 'Cluck, cluck, *embros!*' then sit back and let the animals pull the load. The Turks did all the work. You were administrators, with hands like mine. These!"

"I was hamal for two years—"

"I'm talking about your nationals. They enjoyed the middle-class life. How will you be able to improve on that? Tell me?"

"We will have our country back," Stavros quoted his brother Michaelis, "and we will have liberty."

"Oh, those words again. Patriotism. Liberty. I'll tell you the truth: It doesn't seem to me that you speak from a sincere feeling. In my opinion, you have no interest in politics. Or the fate of anyone else on earth. You want what I used to want—power. Specifically, the power money brings. I recognize myself in you. That's why I have always been interested in you. But please—leave those big beautiful words to the politicians. Mr. Venizelos and the rest. Tell me your true feelings if you can. Do you truly know anything you feel yet, and if so, do you dare say it?"

"I hate my goddamn position in life. I want change."

"That's better. But change? I am cynical about change. I am for the dismemberment of the Ottoman Empire, but it's not for the reasons your Greek leaders say—liberty, equality, Greater Greece, and so on. If they said empire . . . Empire! I would agree to that."

"Then why you're on our side?"

"Simply because the emerging victors will be more hospitable to my interests. I already have assurances of that. But I am cynical enough to wonder if, in your case, you will be any happier? The Turks were a slave class who lived in the illusion they were masters. Now the Greeks seek to make them a slave class who know what they are. Can you expect them to continue so docilely? Everyone understands the nature of war now, that it has nothing to do with flags, fatherland, patriotism and so forth. It's about one thing only: Who's going to live better? Who's going to enjoy the wealth of the world, the raw materials, the markets? Who?"

"You know I'm not damn Greek," Stavros said. "An Anatolian—who knows what he is? As much a Turk maybe. I am also citizen here. But for practical reasons. I am not an American."

"Then what would you call yourself?"

"A nothing. A man like you, with no country. A hamal, that's me. My only interest is—my own interests."

"That is the only intelligent and honest thing I've ever heard you say."

"But this I know. Big change is coming. Explosion. After that nothing will be the same.

"It has already happened. You are late."

"But not too late. This explosion will leave a place—empty Anatolia —where no one has the power. Who will move in, that's the question?"

The old Armenian started to speak. "I will answer that—"

"No, Mr. Fernand, listen for change. You never stop talking. Pay attention to me. I and my family have maybe eighty thousand dollars and we can get that much more, sure. Credits. I will go into my old country soon as the sea is quiet and roads of trade open—even before. I will buy goods when people are starving and will work for the ends of bread. For nothing, even; for shelter. Maybe it will be three years like that, maybe five. In that time I will buy goods to my last penny. I will give peasants in Turkey—and Persia too—money they need for looms, wool, dyes. They will work for me. Hard. They will bless me and they will be 'fraid of me. I carry a hamal's knife so they won't try cheat me. The goods they make I will put on boats and send here." Stavros noticed that Mr. Aylesworth had come into the room. "You gentlemen should finance me," Stavros said. "New business empires are going to be made by animals like I am. I could invest a million dollars there quick and a year later what I brought here will be worth ten. It could save your sleeping company, Mr. Fernand. But looks to me you like better to sit on your money—your brother, I mean. What's the matter with the man, suddenly drinking like fish, every day five o'clock again?"

"Perhaps the strain of respectability has finally become too much for him."

"The truth? He's finished. You know it. What you need now is man who carries a knife. You and your brothers and friends are too soft for this time, too happy with your fifty-dollar whores and your massages. You sit on sofas, cross your ankles, eat baby lamb, have cars with chauffeurs and girls to suck you off. You go to track every day and what's the difference, you win? you lose? But for me, every dollar, when it grows means I'm stronger. Red ink in ledger, like drops of my blood. I saw your old photographs, where you said you were not adventurer at that time. Imagine now! I saw your body, what you are. Want inside information on that? Ask this whore, Lucy. She tell you only power you have left is power of money. You people are buyers and sellers. Only. In time like after war, a time of big change—maybe more revolutions coming, who knows—you need me. Someone like me. Other people must do dirty work for you. You have to find those people or you be wiped out. Oh, I see you not listening, Mr. Fernand, slippery Mr. Fernand. So then I talk to you, Mr. Aylesworth. About going to Anatolia after coming Ottoman disaster and making there hundred, two hundred, three hundred small factories to weave Oriental carpets because—oh, the hell with you both."

"I heard what you were saying," Mr. Aylesworth said.

His girl, Lillian, behind him in the doorway, spoke to Lucy. "We have to be you know where half an hour ago," she said.

"Shut up," Aylesworth said. His attitude toward the young lady had certainly changed. "Can I borrow Wynn?" he asked Mr. Fernand.

"He should be downstairs waiting," Mr. Fernand said. Kyushiro came to him, holding up a soft, light robe of camel's hair.

"If you ever draw up a prospectus," Mr. Aylesworth said, "I'd like to have a look at it."

"I don't need your favor, Mr. Aylesworth," Stavros said.

"I thought you were asking for it. The fact is, I'm a great friend of Greece. I know Mr. Venizelos very well, he's been on my boat many times and has stayed, during his days of discouragement, in my villa above Nice. He spoke of Greece as the Albion of the Eastern Mediterranean and he has spoken about the vacuum of power when the Ottoman Empire collapses. Your ideas are not new ideas, my friend. Who will control that part of the world? The Italians? The French? Who can rely on either of them? Yes, we British are interested in anything that will develop on the ruins of the Ottoman Empire, and if you ever—"

"Where are you going now?" Mr. Fernand interrupted. He was in his camel's hair robe and Ortak had sidled into the room, bringing him ouzo in an onyx glass. "I'm still not hungry, Ortak," he said, "but I will be, don't despair."

"We're playing cards tonight," Aylesworth said, "as soon as I can get rid of her. The Metropolitan Club. Why don't you join us?"

"I'll take my ease here tonight," Mr. Fernand said. He looked at Lucy.

"I'm going to stay a while, Lil," Lucy said.

Mr. Fernand's look was a kind of blessing upon her.

"They'll be awful mad," Lillian said.

"Tell them I've got a headache."

"Only wives get away with that," Lillian said.

"Come, come, stop the chatter," Aylesworth said. Then he turned to Stavros. "What's your name again?"

"Joe Arness," Stavros said, "here. Stavros Topouzoglou there."

"I wouldn't mind at all having another chat with you. Meantime, why don't you get your ideas down on paper: capital requirements, operating costs, so on."

"By then will be too late."

"Let me be the judge of that," the Englishman said.

"What are you talking about?" Mr. Fernand said. "He's my employee."

"Well, then, perhaps we can do something together," Aylesworth said. "Rascals and desperadoes like this fellow—he's right, their time is coming. Hey? Come, my sturdy little pack animal. *Embros!*" He gave Lillian a push and she went out the door before him.

Stavros lay back on the sofa. Lucy seemed to have discovered a fondness for him. She moved as close as she could.

"Not your employee now, Mr. Fernand," Stavros said.

"I know," he said. "My brother fired you, but I have the last word there. He'll take you back."

"Nothing doing!" Stavros said. "You had right idea before. My time coming now. I thank your brother for firing me out!"

Mr. Fernand made a sign, a wave of his hand across his eyes, and Kyushiro turned off the lamp he'd needed for the massage. Only a soft, shaded glow was left in the room. Kyushiro shuffled to a corner and lit two small stands of incense, watching them until he saw threads of scented smoke rising; then he left the room.

It was quiet in the bedroom now, a twilight. The warmth and the aroma of the scented alcohol, the incense and the perfume from Lucy, the weight of her soft full breasts, her plump leg over Stavros's groin, all were making him relaxed and contented. He wanted nothing for the moment except to stay where he was through the night. He began to wonder if he might ask—or suggest—that Mr. Fernand go downstairs to eat his dinner. And leave him alone with the woman; his needs were becoming urgent.

"Yes," Mr. Fernand said. "I'm impressed. I've studied history, the course of nations, all my life. You seem to know it by instinct. For instance, that it's a time now for enterprise and daring . . ." and Stavros wondered why he'd suddenly changed toward him. "You have the instincts of a jackal," Mr. Fernand said, "no insult intended. It happens to be my own gift. People like you and me recognize when the great predators, England and France and America, have brought down their prey. Our instinct tells us that there will be enough meat there for us too. So then we move in."

Lucy put her mouth against the side of Stavros's neck and held it there, sucking at him.

"My son, Paul," Mr. Fernand was rambling on, as if to himself. "I wish he had some of your energy and restlessness. You don't bear my son any ill will, do you?"

"Not him; her."

"You mustn't hold it against her. Be realistic. I'm trying to teach you to be realistic; I have no hope you'll be fair. She was only looking out for her future security. It's natural, particularly with her father dying." He waited. Stavros said nothing. "Don't look for pity from the young," Mr. Fernand said, as if to himself. "You see, my son, Paul, he's had everything he needed from me, so it was impossible for him to want anything. He only had to ask and he had whatever it was he wanted, so badly did I feel about separating him from his mother. I wish I hadn't won that damned custody suit; my lawyer was too good, so ruthless. So was I then. At any rate, the easiest thing for me to do was write a check. Anything was better than listening to his pleading voice—even when he was grown, that little whine out of such a big body. I'm used to it now. I've forgotten what I once wished for him—"

Lucy was getting bolder, loosening Stavros's trousers.

"I worry about him, though—yes, I still do," Mr. Fernand said. "But why should he have ambition? He's never needed to make an effort, so he never learned how."

Lucy bent over and put it into her mouth.

Mr. Fernand was looking at the ceiling. "Maybe Althea can do something for him," he said. "That's my hope. What do you think?"

He looked toward them now. And smiled, softly.

"What's your hope?" Stavros said.

"That she may give him a little of what you have," he said. His voice was as casual as ever, but his eyes were on them. "What do you think?"

"Don't know," Stavros said.

"I'll tell you something," Mr. Fernand said, watching Lucy's movement. "Your problem is the lack of a talent I call adaptability. You seem to be fond, as most young people are, of rigid positions. Let me tell you something, my boy: When people begin to refer to you as slippery, you will know you've arrived."

"Maybe," Stavros said. But that was all he could say. Lucy was working him up and down and his breath was coming shorter and harder.

"What Paul needs, perhaps— Are you listening to me?"

"Trying to."

". . . is a connection with someone who has what he lacks, even a partnership with someone—like you."

"What he could bring"—Stavros took a breath—"to this—partnership?"

"Money. Intelligence. Taste. The odd thing is that he is extremely quick and bright. Yes! He knows a little about absolutely everything."

"Don't know him," Stavros said quickly. It was all he could get out.

"Yes," Mr. Fernand went on. He was watching the sofa keenly now, sympathetically, as it were, responding to the rhythm there. "If the circumstances were different—" Stavros was aware of how openly Mr. Fernand was observing what was taking place, but he didn't care anymore. "If the circumstances were different— Are you listening?— I'd really try to make you partners. I would."

"Oh!" Stavros said. "So?"

"What would you think of that?"

"We could—I guess. What—circumstances—different?"

"But still, we might . . ."

"Might?"

"Talk about it. At another time, of course. Are you listening?"

"No."

Lucy had begun working faster. Stavros touched her head to slow her. It was too good to lose.

"Kyushiro! Kyushiro!" Mr. Fernand was calling.

The little Japanese slid through the door. Lucy's eyes shifted and she lifted her head.

Stavros pushed her head down.

"Kyushiro," Mr. Fernand said again, his voice uncharacteristically soft, surprisingly young.

Lucy tried to move. Stavros held her where she was.

The old man was whispering to his servant. Stavros could hear it, a murmur in the distance. Then a shuffle of slippers.

Stavros was getting near. The tremble was not far off.

Kyushiro was leaning over the head of the sofa. "He wants you now," he whispered to Lucy. "Come. Come!"

"Go away," Stavros said.

The servant tapped Lucy on the shoulder. Stavros pushed him away, but when he did, he released his hold on Lucy, who got up and hurried to the old man. At his bedside, she took off her clothes, dropping them on the floor.

Then Stavros lost control of himself. There was a rush of pressure to his head, as if it might burst. It had happened to him before, so he knew what was coming—a moment when he could do anything and cared about nothing.

He got up. He couldn't see clearly—couldn't see what was happening at the bed.

Kyushiro came up to him, bowed, smiled. "Go now—please, sir," he said. "This is all for you tonight, sir. Time to leave here."

As Stavros went to the bed, he pushed the ancient Japanese out of his way. Lucy had uncovered the old man again—Stavros could smell the tang of rubbing alcohol—and was settling in beside him, her plump breasts pillowed on his chicken's chest. His eyes, looking up at her, were those of a young man. In that instant, Stavros understood Mr. Fernand and the reason for everything that had happened that night. From that look in the old man's eyes, Stavros understood his hidden soul and his secret needs. Mr. Fernand didn't want to die. That is what kept the life in him.

Kyushiro was tapping Stavros on the shoulder. But Stavros felt nothing. He seized Lucy by the wrist and she cried out. When he pulled her off the old man, she cried out again. Stavros dragged her over the soft, heavy carpet toward the door. Except for her cry, she didn't resist. She knew danger when she saw it.

There was a sharp shout from the bed. Stavros didn't hear the words; they were coming from too far away.

Lucy heard and began to struggle for the first time. Stavros took her by the hair as well as the wrist. He dragged her and she was helpless. Again the shout from the bed, and her resistance strengthened. Stavros lifted her in his arms and carried her toward the door. "Be still," he warned.

"Kyushiro!" the old man barked. "Kyushiro!"

Stavros had the naked girl over his shoulder. Holding her there with one arm, he pulled the door open and went for the stairs. Up or down? Up.

"Mister! Mister!" Kyushiro was following.

Up five or six steps and the Japanese was closing in. Stavros turned and put a foot to his chest and pushed. When Stavros looked down, Kyushiro was sitting on the floor at the bottom of the steps, holding his head. He looked up at Stavros reproachfully. Stavros laughed. He'd begun to feel fine again. He heard Kyushiro say, "Why you do that to me?"

Now she wasn't struggling. Her arms were around Stavros's neck.

At the head of the stairs there was a door. The room it opened onto looked as if it had been decorated to please a woman. There were lace curtains and a dressing table with three mirrors. The bed and an armchair were covered in a pastel material of spring flowers.

Stavros kicked the door closed and carried Lucy to the bed. She jumped up and ran to the door. Stavros didn't try to stop her—everything about her now told him she wouldn't try to escape. She locked the door. When she came back, Stavros tried to pull her head down to where it had been, but she shook him off. "Don't you want to fuck me?" she said.

"Yes."

"Well, then . . ."

"But they'll be in . . ."

"Don't worry. There's no hurry now," she said. "They're afraid of you. He wouldn't send that little yellow head after us." She began removing Stavros's clothes, slowly and carefully. "And if he did, that smart Kyushiro, he likes his safety. He won't come up. Here, help me."

Stavros lifted himself and she pulled off his trousers.

"That old son of a bitch was playing games with me," Stavros said.

"Of course. He's an old man. What did you expect?"

She folded Stavros's trousers and hung them over the arm of the chair. Below, all was silent. Not a sound anywhere except the traffic in the distance.

She was very open to Stavros, even eager, not like a whore.

Later, when they were quiet, Stavros listened. "Still not a sound!" he said.

"I told you, they're afraid of you." She laughed.

"Well, good."

"Keep 'em that way."

"Maybe I got you in trouble?"

"No, he'll scold me, that's all, just scold. He enjoyed what happened. I know him well. When I go into his room now, he'll act like a child whose mother left him. 'How could you treat me that way,' he'll say, 'after all I've done for you.'" She laughed again. "He's kinda sweet."

"What will you say?"

" 'I'm sorry, Mr. Sarrafian,' I'll say," and her voice was sugary. " 'I'm so sorry. But you know how those young men are.' 'I know,' he'll say. 'I know very well.' "

"And then?"

"Then I'll put my arms around him and put his head here, against my chest, you know. Have you any idea how he loves that? When I become that old wreck's mamma."

"And then?"

"The usual."

"He'll fuck you?"

"Don't you know anything? He can't. He'll do what he can do. His thrill is here." She touched her head. "You've got a lot to learn. The truth is, he's already had enough for tonight. He may even be asleep when I go down."

She kissed him.

"How old are you?" she said.

"Forty-two."

"You should know more. You're a boy, you know that?"

"And you're a beautiful girl."

Stavros turned over on her.

"Don't do that," she said. "I really have to go down and pretend I'm sorry."

"Let him go to hell. Come, I take you home."

"No, thanks very much. My husband's downstairs, said he would be. He's very dependable. I'm not a whore—you understand that, don't you? I mean not everybody can have me. I want you to know that. If I like someone—you—I don't ask for money."

"Well then, what are you if you're not . . . ?"

"I have regulars. And he's the best. He doesn't tire me out and he doesn't leave marks—look what you did, look here! And here! Bad boy!"

"They go 'way."

"Say you're sorry."

"Why? I'm not sorry."

"Bastard! You know he likes you! You trying to get something from him? Money?"

"How you know?"

"Everybody is trying to get money from him. I'll speak a word for you."

"Don't bother. I don't need it."

"You know you're a terrible little bastard. Terrible!"

"I give up on him. He's just an old cock teaser."

"If you're worried that he might be angry at you because of what you did, don't be. He likes that. The excitement." She laughed like a child. "Oh, he had plenty tonight. I better hurry down there."

She jumped out of bed, her tits bouncing so she had to hold them. She looked at her face in the mirror, touched her hair here and there.

Stavros went after her, putting one arm around her waist, one hand on the place between her legs.

"Don't," she said. "Please don't do that again. Please!"

Stavros pulled her back to the bed. This time it was quick.

"You son of a bitch," she said.

She ran into the bathroom. Stavros followed her. She had a washcloth and was wiping herself.

"What's he get out of all this?" Stavros asked. "Like tonight. He didn't have to bring me here and go through all this game."

"The thing he likes, what pleases him deep in his soul, you might say, is to take a young woman away from a young man. And that is not possible for him unless he arranges it."

"You've done it before?"

"Three or four times. But you're the first one who did what you did. The others wanted his money more than they wanted me. That's why I could tell he respected you. He wants you to move in here with him. Did you know that? He's lonely here and— Did he ask you yet?"

"No. We fight all the time."

"A man like that only respects you if you fight him. They step all over the meek. You watch, next time you see him, how he'll play up to you. Tell him to go to hell, and whatever you want from him you'll get. Take my word. Well—goodbye." She kissed Stavros the way you kiss a friend. "Anytime you want me," she said, "I won't charge you."

"You didn't get all my stuff off—look."

"The old man likes that. Then he can scold me and I'll beg his pardon and kiss him and hold him in my arms and say, 'I'm sorry, Dad, don't ever let me do that again, Dad, because I like you best.' Then I'll say sweet things to him till he's asleep—if he isn't already."

At the door, she stopped and kissed Stavros again. "Did I please you?" she asked.

Stavros nodded.

"Well, why the hell didn't you say so?"

They walked down the stairs, she first, naked, Stavros behind her.

Kyushiro came out of Mr. Fernand's room. He stood to one side as they passed and gave Lucy an angry look, but bowed low to Stavros Topouzoglou. "Effendi!" he said.

When Stavros stayed out late, even then, in his forty-second year, he'd unlock the apartment door as quietly as a thief and steal in on his toes, a habit from his youth in Anatolia when he hadn't wanted his parents and sisters to think him a "bad boy."

He expected silence; it was close to four in the morning. What he heard was a low rumble like the sound of a heavy sea heard from far away. It came from Demo's old room where Stavros had lodged Michaelis's saboteurs. *They don't have the Turk to fight here,* Stavros thought, *so every night they fight each other.*

Stavros's first mission at whatever hour he came home was to check on Vasso. Generally he'd find her asleep in her chair at the window. Everyone in the family was convinced that her time was near and that, when it came, they'd find her hunched over in that chair, stiff.

This night her chair was empty. Her heavy old Bible was on the seat, and on the side table, a bowl of sunflower seeds, the husks in an ashtray.

He turned back down the hall. The bedroom Vasso had chosen to occupy had no opening to the outer world. Even though the apartment was on the fifth floor, she kept the small window to the back yard closed and locked, fearing that a Turk might climb through at night. Her room drew its air from an even smaller window onto the long hall. Stavros found it open a finger's width, and on the four cloudy panes the flickering light from the oil lamps which burned before the old-country icons on the plate shelf.

Noiselessly, he pushed the door open. The old lady was sitting in an old oak armchair. He tiptoed to her. The family joke was that her funeral would be expensive because a special coffin in the shape of a question mark would have to be ordered. No one could remember when Vasso had last straightened out. He bent over her; she was alive, breathing, her lips in a stubborn pout.

At that moment, Stavros heard Michaelis's voice. He was back! He was with Simeon and Efstathis! Stavros rushed out, then into the room where his brother was, to embrace him at last.

There were four men there. Simeon stood with his back against the wall farthest from the door. In a chair facing him sat Michaelis. He'd aged, and looked thin and tired; there were white streaks in his hair. On the edge of one bed Efstathis crouched, intent, a sharp-toothed weasel facing prey it had cornered. Sitting on the bed near the door was Seraphim; he seemed to be an observer, interested but not involved.

When Stavros came rushing in, Michaelis looked up quickly, and realizing that his brother was coming to embrace him, held up a hand and shook his head.

Stavros stopped; he'd walked in on a trial.

The hand Michaelis held up to stop him was his only one. Where the other arm would have been, there was a stump with a sleeve pinned up to cover it. "Damn fool, didn't listen to me," Stavros said to himself. But his next thought was relief that Michaelis's loss meant he would not be going back to the war and risking his life again.

"So when they take you," Michaelis was saying in the quiet voice of a prosecutor who believes he has a perfect case, "what then? What will you tell—"

"*If* they take me," said Simeon. "*If!*"

"Very well. If they take you," Michaelis said quietly, "what will you say then, my old friend?"

"Nothing!" Simeon said. "Nothing."

"Shshsh!" Seraphim said, pointing to the wall of Vasso's room. "Not so loud, Simeon, please. The old lady, she needs to sleep, you know, Michaelis."

"Come tell us," Efstathis whispered. "How will you answer their questions?" He moved quickly, slipping behind Stavros to close the door to the hall.

"What questions?" Simeon said. He seemed impatient and angry, even threatening.

Michaelis and Efstathis looked at each other.

"Never mind this now, Michaelis," Stavros said. "Come, tell me, eh, man, when you arrived here? Hah?"

Michaelis put his forefinger to his lips. "About midnight," he said to Stavros. "Later, all that." Then he turned to Simeon. "You know the questions they'll ask," he said.

"I was one blood with those people, risking our lives together," Simeon said. "You think I would name them now to the Turk?"

"The first question they will ask," Efstathis said quietly, "who was with you at the bridge? 'You didn't do that alone,' the Turk will say. 'Who was with you?' "

"I will cut my tongue out before I answer that question," Simeon said. "But they will not see me. I will slip into Smyrna at night and next night I will put out to sea again with Sarroula and the four boys, under canvas, looking as other fishermen do."

Stavros noticed that Simeon kept turning to him, as if for help.

"You had a daughter, I remember," Stavros said. "A *lokoum* of a girl!"

"Thank God I sent her to Aivalik before," Simeon said. "To Aivalik where there are only Greeks still, glory to God!"

"Shshsh!" Seraphim said. "Simeon, please, you forget again." He pointed to the wall.

"Your next-door neighbor," Efstathis whispered. "He's *Ottomanli*. Tell me, he won't notice? That you're home again? He won't talk about your sudden return?"

"They've made everyone talk," Michaelis said. "They know how to do that."

"But not me; trust me," Simeon said, looking at Stavros again.

"Do you trust yourself?" Efstathis asked. "When they take you to that room below the surface of the ground, you trust yourself to be silent in that room? Tell me the truth?"

For an instant, Simeon hesitated.

"I don't trust myself," Michaelis said. "That's why I stay in Chios, on the island, go into Smyrna only when the moon is dark and leave before the sun."

"I wouldn't trust myself," Efstathis said. "Why should I trust you?"

"I will speak with sincerity," Simeon said. "I will tell them that a storm with an edge like a knife ripped my sail and carried me off, all the way to Poros, lucky to be alive, and so to Andros. I made it there with the oars alone."

"That's the story we spread through the fish bazaar," Michaelis said. "But if they once see you and take you to question, then—"

"When I talk they will believe me." Simeon pounded the wall with his fist. Then he looked at Stavros for help.

"That's enough now, boys," Stavros said. "Michaelis! Enough! Finished!"

"Of course, Stavros is right," Seraphim said. "Leave Simeon quiet now, boys." He turned to Stavros, speaking deferentially to his oldest brother. "What is your opinion on this, Stavros?" he said.

"He has nothing to do with this!" For the first time Michaelis raised his voice. "He knows nothing about this!" he shouted. "Also"—he turned to Stavros—"you're drunk. How can you talk about this, about a man's life? Aren't you drunk? So don't talk here. Get out." In a surge of feeling, he raised his arm, his one arm, high, a gesture of threat, and said, "This is not your affair. So be silent here! Go sleep! Go!"

"Michaelis! You raised your hand to me!" Stavros said. "To me! You raised your hand!"

Michaelis didn't answer. After a moment he turned to Seraphim and once again, with a great effort, was able to speak quietly, to say, "Go to your room, Seraphim."

Stavros felt his brother's outburst as a challenge he did not want to let pass. His cheeks had chilled and his anger sobered him. He wanted to respond as he knew he should, but remembering his brother's lost arm, said to himself, "He's your brother. He gave an arm to his country!"

"Listen, Michaelis," Simeon was saying. "If I stay here as you want and weeks pass and I'm not there, they will go to my wife and say, 'Where is he? Where has he disappeared, your husband? What happened? Is he dead? Then why are you not in mourning?' You know how they talk."

"Yes, they treat women badly, the Turks," Seraphim said. "You know that, Michaelis."

"So?" Michaelis said to Simeon.

"They will begin to ask her other questions," Simeon said. "For instance, 'Where was your husband the night the bridge went down?'" He imitated a Turkish officer: "'Eh, you woman! What you say to that, hah?' Then they will take her to their headquarters for questioning, and you know what's next."

"What's the use of all this talk?" Efstathis spoke only to Michaelis. "He must not leave here."

"You raised your hand to me, Michaelis," Stavros said quietly. Michaelis did not ask to be forgiven.

"I told you," Simeon said, "and I'm telling you again, they won't take me."

"Michaelis, I'm talking to you," Stavros said. "You raised your hand to me."

"We're talking 'if,' " Efstathis said to Simeon.

"If they do, I will say what I told you and nothing more."

"Even when they put the hot iron to you?" Efstathis said.

"Even then."

"Or in you?"

"Nothing!"

"When they cut off your *nikolaki* and put it in your mouth?"

"Don't say those ugly things, Efstathis," Seraphim said.

"And as you begin to bleed from where you piss. Then?" Efstathis said.

"Especially then. I will say nothing." Simeon gripped the end of the bed.

"When they take your wife to the barracks," Efstathis said, "the one where you are, and give her to the soldiers. And tie you to a chair so you will miss nothing of what happens there. Then? Then? When you see her dying after they've all used her, dying. Then?"

"I will protect my brothers."

"When they throw your eldest son," Efstathis said, "the boy Manolis, the handsome one, with the eyes like olives, when they throw him into the barracks to take the place of your wife. Then?"

"Why don't you trust me?" Simeon screamed.

"Because we see your face when you answer," Michaelis said. "I had a dream last night," he went on, and he was quieter now, the weariness of many months showing. "Remember, Simeon, when they caught little black Yanni, the fig farmer who brought you the donkeys? They took him for questioning to that room under the ground—"

"He wouldn't talk," Efstathis said. "Yanni? Never!"

"Why do you say that, Efstathis?" Simeon seemed on the point of attacking his partner. "You mean I will? Eh? Is that it? So now I see what you think. No more talk with you. I'm finished with you!"

"Shshsh, Simeon!" Seraphim said. "You will wake them all here."

"Seraphim, go! Get out. Now!" Michaelis said. He turned to Stavros. "You tell him. Tell him to go," he commanded. "And you too. Go!"

"You raised your hand to me, Michaelis. I have not forgotten that," Stavros said. He could see that Michaelis was another person now, that he'd killed men and could again, even close friends if it was important.

"Seraphim," Stavros spoke gently, "do as Michaelis asks, be a good boy, go. I want to speak to him alone."

Looking reproachfully at Stavros, Seraphim started out of the room. "These men are barbarians," he said to Stavros. "Our brother too—yes, I mean him. They are torturing Simeon. Before they kill him." He turned to Michaelis. "You became a barbarian, Michaelis," he said as he left the room.

Stavros noticed that Michaelis felt no need to defend himself. Nor did his expression change. His brother's very character challenged Stavros, made him need to assert himself, to put Michaelis back in his place. But he remembered the arm and what Michaelis had given up for his country and he determined to wait and speak to him later, quietly, brother to brother.

"No one has ever frightened me," Simeon said, trembling. "No one can make me talk," he said. "Michaelis, we're friends so many years—have you ever seen me frightened? We did two trains before the last one. Him! Efstathis, that little animal, he was frightened. I, not! Come, you animal, admit the truth."

"I have a wife too," the small man said. "If they take you, they will ask you first who was with you at the bridge, and when you finally say my name, they will find her in the kitchen of the French Club and—"

"What's all this suddenly about your wife?" Simeon said. "I never heard a sweet sound from your mouth about her before. Now suddenly, 'my dear wife'! She's like a dried mullet, your wife. Did she bring you children? Not one! You'll be happy when she's gone; don't pretend with me because I know you."

" 'When she's gone'?" Efstathis said. "You hear that, Michaelis. 'When she's gone.' "

"I heard it," Michaelis said quietly. "So then, Simeon, you must think it's possible, you have it in your mind that it's possible they will make you talk, is it not so?"

"No! I will be like Yanni. I will be brave as he was!"

"I didn't finish that dream," Michaelis said. "There, Yanni, in the end, told all he knew."

"Michaelis, the only thing I care about in this rotten world now is my wife, Sarroula, and my children. They are the last of my family, all that's lasted. I am going there and I'm going to take them out."

"Forget it, that idea," Efstathis said. "You're not going back."

Stavros saw that the tall, handsome man was losing control. "I will risk my life once more," he shouted. "For them, not for you! If I stand on that platform next week at your side there, Michaelis, a hero, the Turk will be sure to see me. Even now, the streets here are full of Turks, dark people with big noses and heavy hair—"

"Those are Jews," Michaelis said. "There are many Jews in America."

"No, no." Simeon held frantically to his point. "They are Turks." He was trembling now. "They will send word back. 'Find this hero's wife,' they will say, 'and his sons.' What they would do to them, I prefer they do it to me."

Now Stavros felt enough in control to speak. "Michaelis," he said, "I'll forget now what you did, raising your hand to me, your father's appointed. So pay attention to what I say. This Simeon, he is a good man. He blew up three trains for you, putting his life in danger. Is this the way you pay him back? Are we going to kill our friends now? Is that what it's coming to? Also he saved my life. I'd be dead except, at a certain moment, he threw his body over mine to protect it. I owe him my life, which means you owe him— Are you listening to me?" Michaelis's face had not changed. "Michaelis!" Stavros said. "I was talking!"

Michaelis's face was set and did not respond.

Simeon jumped to his feet. "No more!" he shouted. "I'm not asking your permission now. I'm going." He tapped his coat, the inside pocket over his chest. "I have what I need. I'm going."

Again Michaelis was speaking quietly. "Where would you find money to buy such a ticket?"

"He gave it to me," Simeon said. "Your brother is a human being; he gave it to me."

Michaelis looked at Stavros, studying him, then turned his back to him and spoke to Simeon, matter-of-factly. "You see, Simeon, how these things happen? Just now, my old friend, just now, when you talked, you betrayed my brother to me. It will happen there too."

"Let whatever happens happen," Simeon said. He reached under the bed, pushing Efstathis out of the way roughly, and pulled out a small bundle wrapped in a large blue handkerchief. It contained what he had of value—his fishing knife with the wooden handle so it would float if it fell in the water, a wrinkled snapshot of his parents, another of his wife and children taken years ago, a small compass, his beads of amber, and a gold crucifix on a leather lace. He checked all these items through. Then he had something else in his hand, polishing it on his trousers.

"Here," he said, offering Stavros a small, time-darkened icon of Saint Nicholas, the seaman's saint. It was on wood and perhaps four inches by three. "A token!" he said. "Thanks."

"Then you did give him the money." Michaelis spoke calmly to his eldest brother. "The passage money, he got it from you?"

"Yes," Simeon said. "He's a human being; you are not."

He started toward the hall, but Michaelis was there before him, his back flat against the door, blocking it. "I don't believe it," he said, "that Stavros gave you the money. But if he did, you—brother—Stavros—you listen. Tell him—if it's your doing—tell him you want your money back."

"The money is spent," Simeon said. "I bought the ticket. Here!" He pulled a ticket out of his inside pocket. "I don't have the money; I have the ticket." He waved it for all to see. "Passage on the *Eastern Khan*. Even now it's loading cargo, and when it sails I will be on board. No one will stop me—not you, Michaelis, with your one arm; not you, Efstathis, weasel; no one."

Efstathis turned to Stavros, crouching, facing him. "Are you going to stop him?" he said.

"Be careful what your brother asks you to do," Simeon said to Stavros, as he stuffed the ticket back into the pocket over his heart. "You can't stop me, either."

"Simeon," Michaelis said. "They have already shot five men for your sake, men you knew all your life, shot them because of you, and now you're going to—"

"I don't care about those men," Simeon cried. "They're dead. My family lives! My sons, my wife, my—"

Michaelis made a quick reach into his back pocket. By the time the pistol came out, Stavros had his wrist, twisted his arm, shook it, snapped it like a whip. When the pistol dropped, Michaelis reached to pick it up.

And at that instant, as Eleni entered the room, Stavros clasped Michaelis behind the neck with one hand and behind the knee with the other and flung him across the room against the wall, where he collapsed on the bed, stunned and in pain.

As Simeon passed through the doorway, Eleni, with a cry, rushed to Michaelis. "Oh!" she said. "Oh. Michaelis? Stavros, what have you done to him? Stavros! What did you . . . ?"

She flew at Stavros, striking him in the face again and again with her fists.

Stavros left the room. And the apartment.

As he stood on the curb at Broadway, looking for a taxi, Stavros felt his face where Eleni had pummeled him. Eleni! The gentlest bird in the family coop! To hell with her too. At that moment Stavros made up his mind never to live in the family apartment again. Several times in the past he had rented apartments, hotel rooms, and furnished rooms when he needed privacy, but he'd always returned to his mother's side.

Now he needed not privacy, but the opposite. Part of his larger, most desperate design was to pursue Mr. Fernand and Mr. Aylesworth, on both of whom he believed he'd made an impression; to pursue them relentlessly until he got from them what he needed—money, gold, silver, letters of credit, banknotes, bullion, backing—or failed to get it. It was time for a final drive, now if ever; time was sliding out from under him fast.

The first thing he'd do was look into the invitation Lucy had passed on to him; if Mr. Fernand really wanted Stavros's company in the house on Sixty-eighth Street, he could certainly have it. *Amessos!* Immediately! To be close to that old man every day might prove very useful. For some reason he couldn't understand—was it disappointment in his own son, Paul?—Stavros knew that the old Armenian had a fondness for him. Why not adopt him as a father—some such thing—if he could get that close? As for Mr. Aylesworth, he'd find a way of getting that one's favor, he'd surely find a way.

But it was four-thirty in the morning and he needed a bed for what was left of the night. There was only one place where he could certainly find shelter, where he was ever welcome, where there was always a bed that could be emptied for him and where he'd be treated with admiration and affection, with warmth and true friendship: Thea Marie's.

The establishment was closing. Thea Marie had retired, but she came out of her bedroom when she was told who was there. Her hair was up in a net and her face scrubbed; she looked like the mayor's wife. Quickly she arranged a place for Stavros to sleep and a girl for him to sleep with.

Gladys, the girl, was English, eighteen, she said, with baby fat still on her bones and a tiny face topped with an enormous mop of caramel-colored hair in heavy natural curls. She was sleepy and didn't want to be bothered, but finally she obliged him and, when he woke and found her in bed with him, obliged him again. She looked so fresh and so innocent, her breath was so clean—baby's breath for a fact—that Stavros decided to offer her as a present to Mr. Aylesworth.

The arrangement with Thea Marie, made over breakfast, was simple to conclude.

"She could use a day off," Thea Marie said.

"Day off! What you think I'm talking about?"

"You said he was an old man."

"You should see him. Near seventy, yes, but thin, like damn horse jumper! Cavalryman! Won't be day off, guarantee. Give me more coffee. Good coffee here!"

Then Thea Marie brought up a subject that surprised Stavros. "That policeman," she said, as she poured, "the one whose pants you took in my old place; he's looking for you still. It wouldn't be to your advantage to meet him."

"I forgot about him," Stavros said.

"He hasn't forgotten you. It hurt his pride, what happened. They still tease him about it. Other cops keep stealing his pants every chance they get; their idea of fun. He believes the only way he can get back his honor —it's become a matter of honor, you know how those Irishers think—is to track you down, and he swears he'll do it."

"Tell him forget it. *I* have."

"But he hasn't. He wants to beat you up. In the station house."

"I buy him another pants."

"That's not what he needs, another pair of pants."

"All right, I give him back his pistol. No, I won't. Maybe I need that soon. What's he want from me?"

"Maybe two hundred dollars, if I could give him that."

Stavros gave Thea Marie an appraising look. "How much of that for you?" he said.

"Half," she said. "I'd have to do a great deal of talking. And give him some of my new girls. It may take a while, several meetings."

"So you're a whore too."

"What did you think I was?"

"A friend. You were only person left I trusted."

"That I am not honest, this disappoints you?"

"The opposite. It excuses who I am. Oh, well, God probably intended it this way." Laughing and in great spirits, Stavros returned to his breakfast.

"So, all right—agreed then? Two hundred dollars—one for me, one for him?" Thea Marie said.

"No. Nothing for him, nothing for you."

"I warn you that—"

"I want to see what you'll do. I'm curious."

"I will tend to business."

"As ever?"

"Yes. Finished between us, then? Eh? No? Still friends?"

"Sure thing! I want to see how far a friend will go in the end."

"Have some more coffee."

"For instance, will you tell him where he can find me?"

"I may, one of these days. When I need money. I can get an equal amount, I believe, from him."

"You're fine business woman! Will be very rich!" He got up. "About Gladys. You will send her?"

"Of course. Forty dollars."

"Lot of money!"

"She's just off the boat. Ten for her, thirty for me."

"But you not just off the boat."

"I have overhead. You liked my coffee and the bed last night? I have other, older, cheaper girls if you like. Do you want to see—"

"No, no; Gladys. She's what I want." Stavros reached into his pocket. He had only forty-eight dollars there, but he was determined to pursue the favor of these men at any and all costs. The collapse of the Ottoman Empire and the arrival in Anatolia of the Greek army and the Allies were imminent. He had to get financing quickly or go there with just what he and Seraphim and Fofo, the family, could spare for investment overseas. Stavros's reach was much bigger. He gave Thea Marie the forty.

"Mr. Aylesworth's address," he said. "Plaza Hotel, room 508. Tell

Gladys to go there, right away, say she's present from me, then stay as long as he wants her."

"So it will be," Thea Marie said, putting the money in her apron pocket after counting it carefully. "Sorry for our little difference." Stavros was laughing. "Why do you laugh so?"

"I was imagining them together, this old bony Englishman with that cavalry mustache, he's at least sixty-five, probably more, riding this child, eighteen."

"Fifteen," Thea Marie said.

"What a picture of how the world is now. Goodbye."

He hesitated, kissed her, and headed for the house of Mr. Fernand Sarrafian.

OCTOBER 1918

Lucy hadn't been mistaken. Mr. Fernand welcomed Stavros to his home on Sixty-eigth Street. At first the new guest was wary—the hospitality was so warm that it seemed excessive. Stavros knew that there was a reason, unstated, well-disguised, for everything the old man did. What could it be this time? Why this sudden flood of cordiality? Stavros, a suspicious person, kept looking for causes.

His host noticed that it took Stavros a few days to surrender to the luxury. "You'll become accustomed," Mr. Fernand promised; he'd spoiled younger men of limited means before. He instructed the entire staff of his house to provide Stavros with anything he wanted, whether he asked for it or not. And after a few days, Stavros came to accept it all; in fact, to count on it as normal. He'd sleep mornings until he heard Kyushiro entering the room with his soft-slippered swish. He began to enjoy the sound of his bath filling, learned to pick up the scent of the tiny shower of aquamarine bath crystals as Kyushiro stirred them into the steaming water. In time—there was no hurry—the Japanese would appear at the side of his bed, bow and say, "Your bath, sir, waiting. May you be pleased." Stavros did not stir until this signal was given.

He soon learned that bathing the body is properly an indulgence, not a chore, so he lay there while the water relaxed his muscles and reached his bones. He'd play with his penis, make it stand, the red knob protruding from the surface, then let it return to the tinted warmth below. After which he'd clear his throat and Kyushiro would scamper in with a large Rock Island sponge and a bar of English Lavender soap. It had taken Stavros only a very few days to accept the suggestion that Kyushiro should lather his back, then pour pitchers of clear, fresh, warm water over Stavros's body to remove the froth of soap. After which Kyushiro disappeared, a dash out, a dash back with the thick towels he'd warmed for the houseguest. Then came a body cologne, which the dear old fellow spread lovingly. "You have softer hands than any woman I've known—except one," Stavros said. "And she is elsewhere." Kyushiro bowed. Powdering followed, and finally Kyushiro guided the onetime hamal's arms into the armholes of a white cotton robe, as if the newborn sybarite couldn't have found these openings on his own. And who knows, within a few days perhaps he'd have forgotten how.

In the bedroom, breakfast was waiting. The suit Stavros had worn the day before had been replaced by its mate, brushed and pressed. On a rack, a selection of neckties borrowed from Mr. Fernand's oversupply hung, as if vying to be chosen. Shoes? Gleaming! Shoehorn? In place.

So Stavros would be off—Mr. Fernand still asleep, of course—to the family store. He'd taken a far more commanding position there since leaving Sarrafian Brothers. His brother Sam, and his sister Fofo found him restless and testy, short-tempered. Plainly he was dissatisfied with the scope of the Anatolian Carpet Company and he made no effort to hide his feelings.

Without asking for it, he'd pick up news of Michaelis. It seemed that his brother was rarely home now. A copy of the *Atlantis* Stavros found on Seraphim's desk was informing the Greek-American world that Michaelis Topouzoglou, the army hero, had been a speaker at a rally in Boston's Faneuil Hall. The purpose? To raise money for the cause of Greater Greece. A resolution unanimously passed on that occasion demanded that no Turkish government ever again be allowed to rule the Greek race in the Ottoman Empire. And that those districts of Anatolia normally Greek in population be reunited with Greece.

"See! We have famous man!" Fofo had come up behind Stavros. "Eleni is the only one he talks to when he's home, so I can't tell you how he is." Stavros folded the newspaper and put it away, looked through the bills being sent out. "I'm worried about him," Fofo went on. "His color is the color of a dead fish belly. His eyes have a ring of red and, underneath, purple. He lost half his weight."

"Talk to him about that, not me."

"I do. 'What's the matter you don't eat?' I say. 'I eat enough,' he says, 'since I have only one arm to feed now.' He thinks that's funny. He laughs."

Stavros nodded. "And how's Eleni?" he asked.

"She don't talk, either," Fofo said. "Michaelis told me her husband went back to his wife and I said, 'Tst-tst-tst!' and you know what his answer to that was?"

"How should I know? Was I there?"

" 'Better his old wife, with whom he's finished,' Michaelis said to me, 'than a new woman, no?' "

"I can see what he means," Stavros said.

"You too! How my father's boys grew up this way? It's America does it! Glory to God, I got a clean man. Where you get that suit? Never mind, I know where. You used to dress like honest man. Now you smell à la Franca. I got idea you became Mr. Fernand Sarrafian's pimp, excuse the expression."

Stavros went out for lunch.

But everything that was happening within his family was incidental to Stavros's concern. He was waiting for a decision: Was he or was he not going to get the financial support he needed? Every sign of interest, of respect, even of affection, from the old man seemed to point to an hour —when was it coming?—when he'd say, "Yes! I will provide you with the money you need."

Finally Stavros allowed his impatience to be seen.

"When you going decide, God's sake, put up dollars I need for my plan?" Stavros asked him abruptly one day. He hoped to catch the old one off guard and perhaps get a true indication of his feelings.

"I'm deciding every day, but haven't decided yet," Mr. Fernand said.

"Because if not, I look elsewhere," Stavros said.

"If not, you should," Mr. Fernand said.

But why, if he was not preparing to finance Stavros, did he go on discussing with him the problems connected with setting up a web of small ateliers in Anatolia when it was liberated, and when the best moment would be to return there and create this small empire. Was it to advise his brother Ara? Mr. Fernand wouldn't rise to a mention of Ara, except to say, "He's still angry at you, Stavros!"

Always, in the end, Mr. Fernand was what he had called himself: slippery.

Stavros was to find out later that Mr. Fernand had a most specific reason for his concern over Stavros's plans, and not surprisingly, it was a business reason. He was reading reports from private investigators and scientists concerning the oil fields in eastern Turkey and Iraq, Syria, Cilicia, and Persia, but at the same time, Stavros noticed, he was reading reports and papers from certain sources on Oriental rug manufacture. Was there some relation between what he was planning on his gigantic stage and the move Stavros was hoping to make on a small one?

Mr. Aylesworth, who operated in the same arena, was often a visitor in Mr. Fernand's house, and when he was there, other guests came, powerfully built Englishmen of years and substance, empire builders. Stavros was never to forget how these men discussed the coming invasion of Anatolia by the Greek armies—the move already agreed upon between England, France, and the Greek premier, and approved by Woodrow Wilson. (Italy's attitude was equivocal; no one trusted Italy.) The only question unresolved was what cover would the great powers provide the

troop transports and how long would the maritime flank be protected by
the warships of the Allied navies. Mr. Aylesworth dubbed the Greeks
"Our heroic little brothers in skirts," and the other Englishmen would
respond with grunts of laughter and coughs of assent. "Brave men, brave
men," they'd mutter under their breath, as if already in requiem.

And after the more substantial, more correct, older men had left and
the business talks were over, there were always girls waiting upstairs,
who'd charge down with whoops of joy. They were purchased, of course;
ordered to appear at such and such an hour and dismissed abruptly when
done with. The girls favored this businesslike procedure. Stavros was the
only man under fifty there. Most were considerably older, and though they
showed off with the girls—an entrance through a door, the closing of the
door behind—when it came down to the business, the ladies themselves
told Stavros, very little happened and that quickly.

Stavros would direct one or another of the girls into Mr. Fernand's bed.
"He didn't bother me," they'd usually report. Mr. Fernand, it seemed, was
content to lie in bed with their warmth and softness pressed against him
until he slept. Sometimes he'd kiss them below the waist, lie with his head
at the mouth of the warm scented cavern until he felt drowsy and was still.
His demands were minimal, but it was important that these small demands
be respected. Mr. Fernand provided a small squad of girls with a reliable
living.

Stavros got what could be called the leavings.

In time he acquired a coterie of girls who, when they felt the need,
sought him out. In a circle where they made their living by satisfying the
uncertain appetites of old and tired men, Stavros was a prize. The young
women began to compete for him. He was flattered, of course, but here
was the odd thing: The more he got from them, the easier it was to come
by, the more he longed for Althea Perry.

He'd been unable to forget her. He remembered her contrary nature
with longing. Her unpredictability, her mocking humor, everything about
her that used to annoy him, now seemed attractive. The quick compliance
of the other girls bored him. He discovered that they were actually indifferent to sex. It was not Althea's body he missed, it was her passion—how
ardent, how completely giving by comparison. Stavros thought about her
all the time. He even asked her father-in-law-to-be how her engagement
was progressing.

Mr. Fernand smiled. "Why do you ask?" he said.

"Why? I don't know." Stavros realized that asking had been a mistake.

"Out of envy?"

"Yes, that's it. Envy."

"I told you, forget about her."

"I have."

"You haven't, it seems."

"Because I ask once?"

"The girls tell me you talk about her."

"They lie."

"Whores don't lie.

"So what's the difference?"

"The difference is"—Mr. Fernand had become very intent—"that I am trying to make a realist of you. You couldn't keep Althea in stockings. What would you do, ask her to eat dry beans every night? She did the best thing for herself, especially with her father going down so fast. So leave her alone."

"I am. Leaving her alone."

"Not in your thoughts. Do you dream about her?"

"No, nothing like that."

"You're lying. You dream about her."

"I can't talk to you today. I'm going home."

"You have no home to go to. Bessie and Erna are coming over. I want you here."

"You can't count on me like that; you don't pay me a salary."

"You want a salary from me?"

"No. We're making enough at the store now for my family to live."

"I'll give it to you.

"I don't want a salary from you."

"I can't tell if you're sincere. You lie constantly. You know you want money from me."

"Yes, I do. Big money. Not damn weekly salary. Big money! When you going to give it to me? When you going to stop teasing me? Give it to me, Mr. Fernand, now, so I can make plans. Time getting short. I want to go into Anatolia same day Greek army does. I'm tired waiting on you. I'm giving you up."

"Nonsense. There! You just lied again. Where would you go? Why don't you come into the oil business with me? I'll give you a job. Or Aylesworth will. He likes you."

"I don't know anything about oil business. I know rugs."

The front doorbell rang and Mr. Fernand started for the stairs. "Erna and Bessie!" he said. "Well, don't say later I didn't ask you. Oil is the coming thing." Halfway up he stopped. "I'm not through with you yet," he said. "You've raised certain suspicions in my mind. Remember that— about Althea. You're playing with my son's life there, you're on dangerous ground. Be careful!"

The next day he took Stavros to his personal tailor. He was throwing a lavish engagement party at the Claremont Inn and he insisted that Stavros dress properly—that is, as he, Mr. Fernand, dressed: black box coat, striped trousers and the rest. "This is going to be a rather dressy affair," he said. "After all, my one and only son and my dearest friend

Morgan Perry's daughter! When will anything like it happen to me again?
So you will dress as I tell you."

There was no time for a made-to-order suit so Stavros's clothes came
off the rack. Stavros thought he looked like a waiter and said so to Mr.
Fernand on the way home.

"Wrong again," Mr. Fernand said. "You're simply not accustomed to
seeing yourself decently clad. This clothing will properly distance you
from your past, which we shall never mention again—am I right?"

"You're always right, Mr. Fernand."

"Never mind that flippancy! Another lie! Will you agree with this
proposition: You shall never remind my son, that is to say, acquaint him
in any way—by a touch, a word, a glance, a tune whistled, a photograph,
a posture—that you once had what I must suppose you did have, though
it's distasteful as poison for me to imagine: a few happy moments together."

"I've forgotten them," Stavros said.

"You're probably lying again. But remember that your future with me
depends on how you observe this oath I'm asking of you."

"I agree with what you said."

"Swear now by your father's grave."

"I do."

"Say it. Swear."

"I swear."

" 'By my father's . . .' "

"By my father's grave."

Mr. Fernand had taken the most desirable dining space at the Claremont Inn, where a circle of windows commanded the majestic Hudson
River. He'd had the place completely redecorated in blue and white—
white for virginity, blue for a baby boy, the grandson he wanted. He'd
ordered all the furniture in the place removed and had created an arrangement of his own, two long tables placed in a broad V that opened towards
the view of the river so that everyone, as they dined on Indian curry of
spring lamb (the most expensive offering of the kitchen, at seven dollars
the plate), would be able to enjoy the view. The space encompassed by the
V was for dancing. A small orchestra, placed to one side, played throughout the meal.

At the apex of the V, there was a small center table, at which were
seated three people: Morgan Perry was at the absolute center. On one side
of him sat Althea, in white, flounces at the chest (her breasts were small).
She'd chosen the dress under Mr. Fernand's supervision. "After all, I'm
paying for it," he said. "I don't want any unpleasant surprises for my son."
On the other side of Morgan Perry was Mr. Fernand. He seemed to be in

constant conference over his shoulder with the major domo, and was directing the timing of every move from this position.

At the center of one of the side tables was Mrs. Morgan Perry. She was ecstatically happy—everything had turned out better than she could have possibly hoped. And at her side was the cause of her happiness, the groom-to-be, Mr. Paul Sarrafian. *If he'd been a man of the most modest means,* Norma Perry thought, *I'd still be happy. He's so damned handsome.* He was. That night, already quite drunk, Norma Perry was in a mood of unre-strained celebration. After all, the family's financial problems, which had worried her for so long, were now solved. Forever, she believed! Mr. Fernand had even paid for her new dress.

The other side of the V was a table made up entirely of Althea's schoolmates and their boyfriends. In its center were Maud, dressed in an astonishing garment, a suggestion of the sari there, and at her side, Althea's fiancé of another day, a man who knew how to accept the turns of fate, Freddie Farrow. There was no doubt of it, now that Paul was taken, Freddie was the catch of the evening.

Behind the small center table was another, covered in red plush. Here were the presents, the most prominent of which were the gifts of the groom's father to the bride-to-be. These were wrapped in silver paper which showed very well against the red. The light from a lamp had been focused on the treasure the couple was coming into.

It was clear to everyone that Mr. Fernand's most fervent attention was being devoted to Morgan Perry—it could have been supposed by a visiting stranger that the dinner was in his honor. Mr. Fernand had used the occasion as an excuse to give Morgan a set of matched baggage in buffed pony hide; he had promised the doomed man a holiday in Europe as soon as the travel lanes to the capitals of civilization were open.

Everyone was merry except Stavros. Seated at the far end of one of the V's, flanked by a couple of Althea's sorority sisters who'd arrived unes-corted, he was clamped shut and silent. The young women, since he was no longer pretending to listen to their conversation, were talking across him.

Actually the man was on the brink, and shame was pushing him over. Waiting for an excuse to slip away from the party, he kept his head lowered and gulped his food, washing it down with wine which he drank like water. Once he did glance up toward the focus of the celebration—he'd heard Althea's laugh, that laugh!—and his eyes met hers. Quickly recalling Mr. Fernand's stern warning, he looked to see if the old man had noticed. Apparently he had not; Stavros tipped his head down over the curry.

"Where is Mr. Ara tonight?" Norma Perry asked Freddie, speaking across the V. It was obvious that her consumption of liquor had been immoderate. Freddie tried, sympathetically, to pitch his voice for Mrs. Perry alone. "His wife, you know, she's a little . . ." He made a subtle gesture with a hand held low, a flutter to suggest that Mrs. Ara Sarrafian had had a breakdown.

Stavros noticed that Freddie immediately did what he had done, looked at Mr. Fernand to see if what he'd said met with the old man's approval. It was a habit Stavros had been acquiring and it was one cause for his shame.

"They're fine!" Mr. Fernand announced for all his guests to hear. "He sends you all, all best wishes."

But Mrs. Perry had her own explanation. "He's shy," she said. "Dear old Ara, like a blushing boy." She swayed, leaned against Mr. Paul Sarrafian. "Sorry," she said, smiling flirtatiously. "Oh, Paul," she said, "I'm so happy."

It was immediately after the main course that Althea rose from her place and—ignoring Mr. Fernand's "Where you going, dear girl?"— marched around to Paul, pulled him up by the hand and—still giving no explanation—led him into the open place between the flanks of the V. Everyone was watching and everyone heard Mr. Fernand say, "Of course, of course, they want to dance. Dancing will commence now, dear friends!" He raised his arm and snapped his fingers, an imperious gesture directed at the maestro of the orchestra whose eyes never strayed far from the fount of money.

But Althea had not left her seat to dance. She was leading Paul directly to Stavros. When Stavros looked up, Althea was standing over him, her fiancé at her side.

Stavros had the grace to stand. He lifted his glass and drank some of the wine—to suggest ease—while holding on to his chair with the other hand. Immediately—again—he looked to Mr. Fernand.

"I see absolutely no reason," Althea said, "why we shouldn't communicate like rational human beings. Stavros, I want you to meet my fiancé, Paul Sarrafian."

What Stavros thought was: *My God, how beautiful she is. Did I have that once?*

Paul found Stavros tricky; that was his first impression. He thought the man's smile strained, his eyes shifty. This last, about Stavros's eyes, was true. They kept flickering—uncontrollably it seemed—to Mr. Fernand, who was watching the encounter intently.

"No doubt," Stavros said, apropos of what he didn't know. "Glad to meet you, Mr. Paul. We met before, you remember?"

"Yes, I do," Paul said, offering his hand.

The maestro, having quickly instructed his artists to change the sheet music on their stands, now launched them into a lively fox trot.

Stavros had to put down his wine glass to shake hands. But since he was glancing toward Mr. Fernand as he did, the edge of his glass, descending, touched the rim of his dinner plate and tipped over, spilling the wine on the table cloth.

There was laughter, quickly hushed.

Stavros shook Paul's hand while, with his left hand, he mopped the soiled place in front of him with his napkin.

Suddenly Mr. Fernand began to applaud. Maud, sitting by Freddie, got the idea and joined in. Althea's sorority sisters were more explicit. "The first dance! The first dance!" they called.

Paul pulled Althea away from the man she'd been talking to so strangely, and, alone on the floor, they began to dance, a fine pair, perfectly matched. Everyone was proud of them.

Stavros's head drooped; he suspected that everyone was whispering about him. His shame became intolerable. He had an impulse to overturn the table—that would relieve him, break up the damned party and end his bondage to Mr. Fernand. But he didn't. What he did was get up and, not looking toward Mr. Fernand this time, disappear—leaving not through the proper entrance but through the service door. In the kitchen, passing as service, he felt at home. Outside, the cool air eased him.

He'd had a date to bring Lucy to the Claremont, but Mr. Fernand had forbidden it. "A whore at an engagement party!" he'd shouted in his high, squealing voice. "What's the matter with you? Where are your manners? Are you going to be a hamal all your life?"

"She doesn't look like a—" Stavros started to protest. He was recalling scenes in which this same old man and the redheaded girl were partners in intimacy. Fernand had had no compunctions about those parties. But then Stavros quickly warned himself, "Damn fool! Shut up! You want to throw away those years of trying to squeeze dollars out of that old man in order to win an argument over a whore?"

Hours later, Lucy and Stavros were sitting alone in the parlor of the house on Sixty-eighth Street and Lucy was scolding him. "You didn't say 'perhaps,' or 'maybe'—you're such a little liar! What you said was—"

"Be careful," Stavros cut in. "I had enough tonight. Be careful with me tonight."

"You be careful with me tonight," Lucy said. "You told me we were definitely going. 'Get yourself a new dress,' you said. 'Try to look respectable,' you said. Although some of these society women I've seen—I've been to a few high-class affairs, you know, where less frightened men took me—yes, those women stick their tits out, when they got them, further than me, some of those young society women I seen. So I went to Lord and Taylor, where you told me to go, and bought this dress. You want to know what it cost?"

"I'll pay for it," Stavros said. "Now shut up. I don't want to hear

another goddamn word out of you. Kyushiro, give me a Scotch." He
turned back to Lucy. "And when they get here, we're going."

Lucy didn't scare. "You mean you crave that old man's money so bad
you couldn't say, 'I promised Lucy I'd take her. I won't go without Lucy?'
Does he decide who you go with and who you don't?"

"He decide everything," Kyushiro said. "Your Scotch, Mr. Joe. No
more for you, bad girl! Now, behave yourself. I hear them coming in
downstairs."

"You promised me," Lucy said to Stavros. "You're not a man of your
word. Why did I have to fall in love with a terrible person like you? You're
such a hypocrite."

"And you're a whore."

"Same to you," she said, finishing what was left in her glass. "I love
you, but I lost respect for you. You're worse than me."

Stavros looked at her, making up his mind to dump her at the first
opportunity. At the same time, he was thinking, *The bitch is right!*

Then he heard people coming up, and got off the sofa to go to the head
of the stairs.

"You don't even want to be seen sitting with me," he heard Lucy
growl.

Which was when the others, invited in by Mr. Fernand for a nightcap,
entered the room: Mr. and Mrs. Morgan Perry, the future Mr. and Mrs.
Paul Sarrafian, the Reverend Kenworthy, Mr. Freddie Farrow and Miss
Maud Erhenbrecher, Mr. Fernand Sarrafian himself and his closest friend,
Alan Aylesworth, accompanied by an unidentified female.

Mr. Fernand ignored Stavros's greeting. He conducted Morgan Perry
to the large sofa, lowered him carefully to its center and was about to
plump down beside him when he decided to oblige Morgan and bring him
the Scotch he'd been pleading for.

Mrs. Perry headed directly for the bathroom; she'd taken on a heavy
load of liquor. Lucy, her face disarranged by her fit of emotion, headed for
the same place, bypassing Stavros and ignoring his whispered, "We're
leaving right away."

Stavros went to the table where the big boss and the liquor were. On
the way he passed and greeted Aylesworth and said hello to his female
companion, whose name he'd forgotten, although he'd fucked her some
months before. Now he was standing next to Mr. Fernand—who continued to ignore him.

He could hear the Reverend Kenworthy and Freddie discussing
whether or not it was acceptable for a man of God to indulge in social
dancing in a public place—a difficult issue which was not to be settled that
night.

"Don't expect a kind word from me," Mr. Fernand said, "if that's what
you're waiting for. After your disgraceful conduct at the Claremont. At

least behave yourself here. There's a minister of God present. Start by taking that woman you brought upstairs and out of my sight, if not out of the house."

"What about Aylesworth and his?" Stavros dared that much.

"Dont get fresh!" Mr. Fernand cut in. "I've told him the same thing. I advise you to be very careful tonight." And he turned his back.

Trembling with unreleased anger, drifting, directionless, Stavros found himself next to Maud, who was examining some paintings Mr. Fernand had hung on his walls. Without looking around, she commented, "Poor examples of very expensive artists." Then she turned, saw whom she'd been talking to and said, "Hello there! Who's that lovely lady you're with tonight? I must get the name of her hairdresser."

There was no way Stavros could respond to that without breaking up the party, so he swallowed his anger and edged away.

He saw that Althea was about to sit next to her father and pull Paul down beside her, but another erratic impulse overtook her and she marched up to Stavros, still determined, it seemed, to clear the air. "I noticed you left my party," she said. "Believe me, there is no need to be constrained with me any longer. I simply told Paul straight out that you and I had once been close. Now I feel so much better."

"Althea," Mr. Fernand called. "Come, dear girl, come sit between your father and me. We're waiting for you." He'd fixed a Scotch and soda for Morgan Perry but considered it too heavy and was preparing a lighter drink.

"You know how I am," Althea persisted to Stavros. "I detest intrigue."

"I know you very well," Stavros said, his eyes shifting to Mr. Fernand, who was making an urgent sign to his son, dispatching him after Althea. When Paul understood the message, he got up off the sofa and Stavros saw that his legs were very long and that they were unsteady.

"Good! Here comes Paul," Althea said. "I hope that, in time, you and Paul can be friends." She smiled at Stavros, very much as she once used to, then said, in a quick whisper, "Remember, I'll always be your friend. Don't ever change. And don't let that foul old man corrupt you. I don't like the way he talks to you. And about you."

"Good evening again." Paul came up carrying his load, Piper-Heidsieck.

"*Allah's maluk,*" Stavros said, as he thought over what Althea had whispered.

"What's that mean?" Paul asked.

"May Allah take care of you, something like," Stavros said.

"Do we really need Allah to look after us?" Paul said. He looked bewildered.

"Of course we do," Althea said. "Everybody does. Thank you for your good wishes, Stavros."

Then, perhaps to reassure Paul, she made this declaration: "I have never felt so happy and so excited, so protected and so safe in my life. Thank you, dear Paul, for all that!" She leaned forward, Paul leaned forward, and they kissed. Then, proudly, she led him away.

Mr. Fernand had watched the encounter and heard Althea's declaration. Now he hurried to deliver the Scotch to Morgan Perry. But his guest was asleep.

Which was when Lucy and Mrs. Perry reentered the room. They seemed to have struck up a friendship because Lucy was telling tales about her early years in a voice that commanded general attention. More and more people dropped their own conversations and listened to Lucy.

"First my father left my mother. When I was only four and a half years old. Then my mother decided to get rid of me because she wanted her men friends to come in and out—you understand? So she put me with my grandfather, who was a miserable hypocrite, a secret drinker, who used to beat me every Saturday night when he'd had his damned corn whiskey. And every Saturday night he dragged poor old Granny out to the barn. She'd come back with straw all over her back. He wouldn't do it to her in the house, that damned old hypocrite."

"You've certainly had an irregular youth," Mrs. Perry said.

"Stavros!" Mr. Fernand said. It was a whisper. Also a command.

Stavros knew what was expected of him, but some perverse allegiance prevented him from taking Lucy in tow and leading her up the stairs where Alan Aylesworth had escorted his female companion, to the second-floor sitting room for banished people.

"But now I see," Lucy was going on, "my grandfather was like everyone; people are all hypocrites. I mean everybody."

Everybody was listening to Lucy.

"Stavros!" Mr. Fernand said, a little louder.

"I wanted to come to that engagement party so bad!" Lucy said to Mrs. Perry. "And you said you liked my dress, didn't you? You said you did."

"Yes," said Mrs. Perry, looking around for help. "It's lovely."

"Joe!" Mr. Fernand said. This was plainly an order.

Stavros didn't move. He was watching Lucy whom he liked and Mrs. Perry whom he despised and wondering why he should lead Lucy away in disgrace. Maybe, he thought, he should take Mrs. Perry upstairs instead and there let her witness the stunts Mr. Aylesworth and his female companion would be performing.

"Of course you did," Lucy said. "So you wouldn't have minded if I'd come. But that old man, he couldn't dirty his—" She'd noticed Stavros approaching to silence her. "All right, all right," Lucy said. Then she drew close to Mrs. Perry and people heard her say, "I could tell you things about that old wreck—" but did not hear the whisper which followed. They did hear Mrs. Perry say, "Oh, my! Really? You don't say!"

"Yes," Lucy said. "And I wasn't good enough to come to his party."

Stavros, at last, took Lucy's arm and pulled her to the stairs.

"Where are you taking me?" she said.

"Come on, child," Stavros said. "They don't want you here either."

Lucy didn't resist. In a bright voice, she called over her shoulder to Mrs. Perry, "I think you're the only good person here. Can we have lunch together some day?"

"Of course, of course," Mrs. Perry said, quickly.

"Oh, good. I'll be so happy. I'll get your number and call. Soon! Soon!"

Then she and Stavros had disappeared past a turn in the stairs. Whereupon the whole room joined Norma Perry in a well-muffled laugh. "Dear Fernand," Mrs. Perry said. "Who, but who, is that creature?"

"They're pretty respectable down there tonight, aren't they?" Alan Aylesworth said when Lucy and Stavros entered the upstairs sitting room.

"Damned hypocrites," Lucy said. Then, turning to Stavros, "And that includes you."

"I know," Stavros said. He'd fallen into a chair and leaned forward so that he was staring at the carpet.

"And that thing you called me before," Lucy said. "You're one too. And worse than me."

"I know," Stavros said. "It takes one to know one," he said to himself.

"Are you sick?" Alan Aylesworth asked.

"I'm very O.K.," Stavros said. Yes, that is what he'd become. Well, now, enough! He'd take Lucy back to her place, then go to the family apartment and stay there. He'd not live in this house any longer.

"How does he stand that woman?" Aylesworth was saying. "I mean Mrs. Perry. No wonder the man is dying."

"Don't you dare talk about her that way," Lucy said. "She's the only warm-hearted person in this place." She began to cry, the tears filling her eyes. "I love her," she said. "We're going to have lunch."

Aylesworth looked at his watch. "I have an important engagement in the morning," he said.

Aylesworth's companion, who had an excellent figure, wasted no time showing it. She'd pulled off her dress and was now in her bloomers, but otherwise unbound. She sat on the tall Englishman's knee and put her arms around his neck.

"I have an important engagement tomorrow too," Stavros said. "And, Mr. Aylesworth, I hope it's with you."

Stavros, at a distance from himself, scornfully heard himself continuing the charade. "Can we please have a talk tomorrow?" he said.

"Of course, of course," Aylesworth said, "I'll find time for you soon."

Did he really expect help from that man? Stavros thought, as he heard himself say, "May I call you Alan, sir?"

"In these circumstances? Why not?"

"I must know soon, Alan, if I can look to you for—"

"This is hardly the time or the place for that conversation, wouldn't you say?" Aylesworth seemed to be studying Lucy, who was crying. "By the way, I neglected to thank you," he continued, "for that lovely girl you sent to my suite in the Plaza. What was her name?"

"I've forgotten," Stavros said.

"A delightful child. I'm in debt to your generosity."

"Always glad to please big man like you," Stavros said. But he thought, *How did I get into all this? How do I get out of it?*

"You're both hypocrites," Lucy said. And she was crying hard now. "I don't want anything more to do with either of you."

"And you're extremely pretty," Aylesworth said. Then he turned to Stavros. "I must tell you," he said, squeezing the waist of the near-naked girl sitting on his knee. "Tonight, I prefer your companion to my own. I've always had a *penchant* for a woman in tears."

Well, this one you can't have, Stavros thought. *She's too good for you.*

"Darling girl," Aylesworth said to Lucy, "don't cry anymore. Come to me and let me comfort you. Come."

Kyushiro had slipped into the room, as if he'd passed through a wall not a door.

"Get up," Aylesworth said, lifting his knee and dislodging the girl who was on it. "That's a good girl. Musical chairs. No? Stavros, all right? What? What?"

Kyushiro wanted advice. He'd just been told over the telephone that Mr. Fernand's brother, Ara, had died an hour before. Should he tell Mr. Fernand now? Or wait?

Stavros thought for a moment, then he said, "Don't do anything. Leave it to me."

"Thank you, Mr. Joe," Kyushiro said.

As Stavros left the room, he heard Lucy say, "None of you are better than me." She was crossing to where Alan Aylesworth was waiting for her. "I want you all to understand that. No one in this house! That's what my husband says and he's right."

Downstairs, Stavros took Mr. Fernand aside and in his most casual manner, as if he was giving him information about the weather, informed him that his brother had died.

In the emergency, Mr. Fernand's manners were perfect. "We shan't say anything about it for the moment," he said to Stavros. "But I would like to terminate this party."

"Leave everything to me, boss," Stavros said.

So Stavros took charge and came into his own. Mr. Perry's condition —he kept falling asleep—was reason enough for Stavros to send everyone home. Wynn and the Rolls were ready. The Perrys would drop Althea and Paul off on their way to Mount Ivy. Freddie would take Maud home; everyone liked Maud, except Freddie. A hint of what had happened brought Alan Aylesworth down the stairs escorting the two girls. Stavros arranged it all.

Lucy had something to say to Stavros. "I can't see you anymore," she said. "I've lost respect for you."

Stavros nodded. "I have to stay here," he said. "Alan, could you—?"

"Leave her to me," Aylesworth said.

When the house was empty, Stavros took Mr. Fernand upstairs. The old man needed the support. Stavros stood by while Kyushiro put his master to bed. "There is nothing we have to do tonight, absolutely nothing," Stavros assured him. This remark comforted Mr. Fernand. "Tomorrow, we go together," Stavros went on, "and I make all arrangements, don't worry. I take care everything, yours truly."

"Stay close," Mr. Fernand said. Stavros was surprised how upset the old man was.

"I'll be here when you wake up, boss," Stavros said.

Kyushiro, at a nod from Stavros, put out the overhead lights. The room remained in the soft glow with which Stavros had become familiar.

Stavros lay back on the sofa à la Turka. He saw the new situation very clearly and very simply. Ara had been one obstacle, Morgan Perry the other. Now they were both out of the way. Stavros had needed a miracle. Seven-eleven! The dice had turned up seven-eleven!

When Mr. Fernand was fast asleep, Stavros looked at the old gray face. He didn't have long to live either. Stavros had to get what he had to get from this man quickly.

He tiptoed downstairs to the sitting room. There he had a drink alone and contemplated the future. Yes, the skies had opened for him at last.

Stavros jumped out of bed at dawn. It was a brisk October day and leaning out the window he could see leaves flying in Central Park at the head of the street. Having purchased the *Times* to read the official final words about his ex-boss, Stavros tucked the newspaper under his arm and decided to walk from Sixty-eighth Street to the family store on Thirty-third. To celebrate this day of opportunity-arrived, he stopped in at Childs and ordered their specialty, the plump, white hot cakes, with extra butter and clover honey. Three cups of coffee intensified his impatience. Stavros planned to examine the morning mail at the family store for checks received, then rush back to the bereaved and stay at his side, nursing his spirits, helping him with the funeral arrangements, not leaving him until the organizational step, now inevitable, had been taken. That's why he had wakened so early, walked so briskly, consumed his breakfast so eagerly: to get back to Sixty-eighth Street and be at the old man's bedside, concerned and anxious, when he opened his old frog eyes.

The office of the Anatolian Carpet Company seemed smaller that morning, darker and dingier; it seemed bankrupt. On Stavros's desk lay a ticket. With a hole in it. And around the hole, a tattered fringe and a stain of blood. The ticket was for passage on the *Eastern Khan*. Stavros recalled Simeon's putting it into the pocket over his heart.

He wasn't content to take the subway to 136th Street; only a taxi could contain his rage. Not only had a member of his family challenged his orders, this effrontery had been flaunted by— It must have been that sharp-toothed weasel! He had thrown the dead man's ticket on Stavros's desk.

"Who did this?" he demanded of Eleni, holding up the ticket. She was in the kitchen, at the gas range. "I did," she said, lifting two fried eggs onto a plate. She walked out with the dish and a small basket of dark, seeded bread. "Now eat!" she said to Michaelis, who was at the dining room table. "All of it!"

"*Eleni*!" Stavros said. "Who did it?"

"You know my husband is there," she said, turning to Stavros. "You want him dead?"

"He's no longer your husband. When will you stop deceiving yourself? He's with his wife again—don't you know that?"

"That's not true!" she cried. "People say it, but it's not true! He's a priest, a fine man. He's not like you. He's clean in his heart."

"Shshsh, Eleni!" Michaelis said. "That's enough!"

"Then tell him not to say those things. My husband is pure. I would kill myself if I thought anything bad about him." Tears filled her swollen eyes.

"Sit down," Michaelis said to his older brother. "Have coffee."

"Who did this?" Stavros said, throwing the ticket on the table.

"What would you do if I told you?" Michaelis said. "Turn him over to the police? Simeon was one of my oldest friends, but I wouldn't turn whoever did it over to the police. Would you?"

"What does that mean?" Stavros said. "What do you mean by saying that?" Michaelis dipped the bread into the yolk of an egg and lifted it to his mouth. "Where's the little animal?" Stavros said. "Efstathis! He did it!"

"I can't tell you where he is," Michaelis said. "I'd be careful about him if I were you. At one time you could have managed him, no danger, but he's a desperate man now—as you were in Anatolia long ago. I'm careful with Efstathis myself now—what I say, even what I think."

"So he did it?"

"The truth? I did it." He put the yellow-soaked crust into his mouth, found it savorless, showered his plate with salt. "Before you decide to say or do anything further, please listen to me," he said. "For your own sake. I don't want to be your enemy."

Stavros walked into the front room where old Vasso was looking out the window. He kissed her forehead; she didn't look up. He decided to hear Michaelis out.

"Simeon knew our men, every one, who they were," Michaelis said. "Along the sea as far south as Kyrenia, north to the three harbors of Aivalik, east to Aidin and farther, along the road to the interior and the hills. He knew who carried the dynamite and who drove the donkeys to the places we marked on the map. If they had taken him . . . Can you doubt they would have? For years he'd been seen every morning in the fish market and along the docks. They all liked him in that city, even the Turks liked him. But they can do it to their fathers, the Turks, and would have to him, forcing out the names just as we would force the names out of one of theirs. The experience of centuries they have; they know where the body is weak. And now is the time we need our men most. If the Turks took our people, one by one, and put them to torture—*ish bitti!* Try to find new people then. How many people would risk their lives after that? Who's so crazy?"

"Finish your eggs," Eleni said.

Michaelis ignored her. "Simeon was right about himself—he said he was a brave man. But you saw here how he was trembling! He'd have given names when he was tortured, just as you would or I would when they hit the right spots."

Stavros was surprised how matter-of-fact his brother was. He watched him dip a crust of bread into the yellow of the other egg, lift it partway to his mouth, then drop it on his plate.

"That's why I brought him here," he said. "I saw him trembling. They'd see it too, wouldn't they? No? Could we accept that chance? That they might take him in and pull the names of our brave ones out of his mouth before they pulled out his tongue?" For the first time he looked at Stavros directly. "I'll tell you the number—one hundred and thirty-eight men would have been in danger of their lives because of you. Also their wives and their children. Because you had to play the big merchant with a kind heart and a pocketful of dollars. Here's a hundred, *palikari,* go jump in bed with your wife! Stavros the American! Big sympathy for those you see, but what about the ones you don't see, their wives and children? Eleni! Take this damned plate away."

"I want a doctor to see your arm," Stavros said.

"Never mind the arm," Michaelis said. "I don't need it anymore. And I don't have time to pass with doctors." He got up. "The toilet," he said, leaving the room.

"He says he did it," Stavros said to his sister. "You believe that?"

"If he did," Eleni said, "he killed one of his best friends."

"He looks sick," Stavros said.

"He doesn't eat," Eleni said. "Half an egg, a little milk in his coffee, sometimes a few dry figs, he likes figs. And he doesn't sleep."

When Michaelis came back, he was putting on a jacket. Eleni helped him.

"Michaelis," Stavros said, "you're getting sick. You don't eat. Why don't you sleep?"

"Because I'm thinking of you at night," Michaelis said. "What you were once, what you are now."

"I'm the same man."

"Oh," Michaelis said. "Good!"

"Of course. What are you talking?"

"When we first came here," Michaelis said, "I was so proud of you! My brother, the man who always carries a knife, the man everybody has to be careful when they speak. Patience he has none, so watch out how you look at him—he may not like the expression on your face. He protects his family and its name. And his father's sacred memory—that above all! I remember how hard your hands were in those days! Now look—the hands of a merchant. Where's their strength gone? Your face is soft and round. A man for a woman. Wearing pimp's clothes from the Armenian. What do you care about what's happening in the world outside? What do you care about your *patridah?* You're comfortable, you're safe, you're happy. You don't even take offense when I talk this way. All you care about is how to make money. Or which whore to pull into your bed. Did I make you angry at last? Here! Do anything you want to me. The fact is still that you placed in danger the lives of one hundred and thirty-eight good men and you didn't care."

He waited for an answer, then, getting none, walked into the front room and bent over to kiss the old lady goodbye.

She didn't look up at him either, she couldn't. "Where's your arm?" she said.

"It's on the garbage heap of a small hospital on your island, Chios. I don't need it anymore and I don't want to hear about it anymore."

She pointed out the window to the tree in the traffic island. "Long ago, I tie piece from one of your shirts," she said, confusing Michaelis with Vacilli. "That rag bring you back safe. So believe in God and his goodness. Also the devil and his cunning!" She chuckled.

Michaelis kissed her and decided to finish his talk with his brother, who hadn't said a word in his own defense. "Come back," Michaelis said. "Stavros, come back."

"To what?" Stavros said.

"To yourself."

When Stavros didn't respond, Michaelis gave up and left the room. Stavros could hear the door of the apartment close quietly behind him. He sat for a time across from the old lady at the window before deciding to ignore his brother's harsh remarks. They were insulting, even wounding, but what could you say to a man who had lost an arm and was determined, so it seemed, to lose his life.

Mr. Ara's funeral—a homey affair, surprisingly modest—took place in a chapel on upper Broadway owned and operated by an Armenian. The service was given an old-world flavor by the presence of a number of women in their sixties and seventies, whom few of the mourners, even members of the family, had ever seen before. They were dressed in black, of course, but this was in no way out of the ordinary; such women always wore black, shoes to hats, and showed up at every funeral of their set, no matter how remote the kinship. None of them had seen Ara in years, but they shed tears amply and remarked again and again that he was a good man—although if they'd been challenged they could not have recounted an instance of his generosity or precisely when they'd observed benevolence in his actions. As a group, they created a backcountry atmosphere, an air of sincere and lasting sorrow, as well as a spiritual continuity with another time and place.

There was another homogeneous group attending: Ara's competitors, the men of the Oriental rug market, some rich, all well off, but in all cases dressed as if they were just getting by: Anatolian Greeks and Armenians who spoke Turkish to each other. These men were of a similar physical cast—of medium height, with potbellies which were, in this culture, a mark of affluence, not an embarrassment. Unlike the women in black, these men did not shed tears. They seemed to be doing their duty, nothing more, and if they were thinking anything in particular, it might have been what Stavros remarked to Freddie: "I wonder who's next?"

Ara Sarrafian's bereaved family, a widow and three swarthy daughters with large noses and flashing eyes, made their appearance from the back under the protection of the Armenian priest who was to perform the mass, a tall man with an enormous head of iron-gray hair, who proved to have a fine singing voice. He supported the widow to the seats in the front row reserved for the family of the dead and then took his place on the dais behind a lectern.

Mrs. Sarrafian looked dangerously exhausted; she'd just come through eight terrible months. The death of her husband had been especially destructive of her self-respect, because she had experienced, at his last breath, a profound feeling of relief, which she felt was sinful. Still, a burden had been lifted. Mr. Ara, it was now possible to reveal, had begun to drink heavily again about six months before his death. No one knew why, because Mr. Ara took great pains to conceal his feelings—even from himself.

Mrs. Sarrafian, of course, was aware that Ara had resumed his drinking, and she concluded that her husband was trying to end his life. There was no one she could tell this to, no one from whom she could elicit help. Certainly she couldn't talk to the three girls about it; they had a difficult time as it was. Nor could she turn to Mr. Fernand for help or a kind word; Mr. Fernand had always despised her, she felt, and she was right.

One morning Mr. Ara began to groan in a quickening rhythm, louder than he ever had before, all the while holding one side of his large belly —the locus of his liver. Mrs. Sarrafian, hearing the distress in these sounds, bundled her husband into his bed and watched his eyes become glassy. She sat in the straight chair between the twin beds and waited. At five in the afternoon, his groans became more violent and much louder. Suddenly he opened his mouth and a foul odor filled the room. A small flow of a brownish liquid flooded out of a corner of his mouth. A moment later, he was dead. Mrs. Sarrafian got up, opened the window, then returned to the corpse. *I should kiss him,* she thought, but then didn't. She covered his face with a sheet and left the room. In ten minutes—there was a lively breeze that afternoon—the foul odor was gone.

Now, in his casket, her husband's face had been smoothed by the undertaker's cosmetics and his art; it was not an unpleasant shock for those attending to see the corpse on display, surrounded as it was by a great show of flowers, proof of how many friends the man had had among his competitors. But the ceremony was longer than it needed to be. The Armenian priest had made a mistake with this family; he believed that if he went on for enough minutes—Freddie clocked twenty-two—he'd be paid more generously. What he received was the envelope into which that morning Mr. Fernand had slipped a twenty-dollar bill. The enclosed card read "With all family appreciation": a warning to the priest not to expect anything more from any member of the Sarrafian clan.

When the ceremony was over, Mr. Fernand surprised Stavros by inviting him to drive downtown. After a few blocks ("They fixed up dear Ara very nicely, but personally I will prefer a cremation") he cranked up the window separating the chauffeur's compartment from the one where he sat with Stavros. Then he put his soft hand gently on Stavros's thigh and said, "I am considering inviting you and Freddie to become the managing directors of—"

"Not interested," Stavros said.

"For God's sake, I didn't finish my sentence."

"You said Freddie! Enough!"

"'I didn't make my proposition clear. I was going to say managing directors of Sarrafian Brothers, your names on the door, at the bottom, in gold letters. Why do you answer so abruptly and rudely, before you heard the terms which—"

"What's the money?"

"A decent raise, of course. I am a generous man."

"I haven't noticed that about you."

"Maybe sixty dollars a week. All right—what the hell, why not?—make it seventy."

"Percentage profits what?"

"Profits! What are you talking about? You said profits? That I can't even consider, profits! What kind of proposition are you making here?"

"I'm not making any proposition. You are. Mr. Fernand, if you offered me hundred dollars week and ten percent profits, maybe we could begin to talk."

"Forget it. Let's open another subject here. You will never get that from me. Profits are for people who have invested money, in this case my brothers and myself. Don't ask me for profits."

"So forget the whole thing," Stavros said.

"Suppose I strain myself and say eighty dollars? Finish! You can't get me there again, this one time, never again. Take it quickly, my boy, don't argue, let's finish the discussion."

"Without share of profits, ten percent, I wouldn't take that, or twice that, or three times that."

"I see you're still jealous of Freddie. Eh?"

"I like Freddie personally, why not? But business partner? What I need him for?"

"I have, over the years, explained this to you."

"I have found, in my own store, over the years, that was shit what you explained to me over the years, Mr. Fernand."

"You'll find out. You with the dirty mouth!"

"*You'll* find out."

"Look, my boy, you been talking like damn fool. You need me, not the other way around. Capital. You need capital, *don't you?* Your big idea?"

"I have other sources now." Stavros lied. "In a year I will have all your customers. You're too old and too bored and too lazy to do the job yourself. You want to go to Europe, lay in hot bath in the day, maybe get your cock sucked at night. And Freddie, he's not tough enough be good boss, you know that. The way business is going to change, not you, not him, have any idea what is necessary to do."

"My God, you're so conceited it's impossible. Listen to me. I'm your friend. I like you. It's obvious to me you're upset about something; the funeral perhaps, the sight of dear brother Ara's face in death—is that it? Or did something happen with one of your women last night? I won't let you decide now. Take two weeks. Think my proposition over and—"

"Don't need two weeks, Mr. Fernand. Answer is no. Here. Let me off here."

"Where are we, here?"

"Where I want to get off, here. Doesn't matter where. Let me off."

Mr. Fernand gave Wynn the instruction and the car stopped. Stavros stepped out, then turned and stood blocking the door's frame. He studied the small man, sunk in his plush upholstery, who'd been his employer, his model, and his hope for so many years. Having seen Mr. Fernand naked, he now saw him dressed in his Rolls-Royce. He understood the car as a piece of clothing, designed to conceal the infirmities and reinforce the standing of its owner.

But when Stavros held the door open, these advantages disappeared. Mr. Fernand seemed to feel a threat. "What is it? Stavros?" he heard him say. And when he continued standing in the door, studying the old man, he heard him call, "Wynn! Let's move on now, Wynn, shall we now, Wynn."

"I wasted so many good years on . . ." Stavros said, then stopped because it sounded like a whine or a plea and that wasn't how he wanted to express the disappointment he felt. Or the anger. He did that by blocking the door's frame.

It must have appeared to Mr. Fernand that Stavros was about to reenter the car because Stavros heard him call, "Wynn! Wynn!" and there was a hint of panic there.

"Don't worry, Mr. Fernand," Stavros said. "Just tell me one thing: what this car cost."

"Twelve thousand, I seem to recall. Built to my specifications," Mr. Fernand replied. "Why do you ask?"

Stavros nodded. "Because," he said. "Goodbye," he said. "You forget about me now, Mr. Fernand, big boss. We had enough together. Finish."

Then Stavros closed the door—it made a substantial click—and he walked away.

The next morning when Fofo and Seraphim arrived, Stavros was in the family store, striding the floor, slamming back and forth from wall to wall, like a man incarcerated. There was evidence that he'd spent the night there. He didn't speak to them, so they kept a distance and went about their morning routines. At about nine-thirty, Stavros opened the safe and took out the firm's books—the ledger, the stock book, the daybook, accounts receivable, the two bankbooks—as well as certain bonds which Seraphim had purchased to salt down their earnings.

"What you mixing up my books?" Fofo said.

"I'm thinking here," he said. "Don't bother me." Eyes fixed, eyebrows tensed, lips moving, he frightened Fofo. An hour later he announced he wanted to speak to them.

"We have customer," Fofo said.

"He's looking at three-by-fives, in the name of God, Fofo, cheap stuff. Let Silo sell him." Then he led Seraphim and Fofo into the farthest corner at the back of the store. "Where Demosthenes these days?" Stavros asked.

The question surprised them. "War finishing, for him it's disaster,"

Fofo said. "That damn rooster made fortune selling army goods outside. What he do now? God knows. Something crooked sure. Police catch him someday, guarantee!"

"I want to talk to him too," Stavros said. "Where's he living?"

"He has new woman, I understand," Seraphim said. "With beautiful house on water—Babylon, Long Island—boat, sport car, everything he wants. She buys his clothes, even, our dear brother."

"Seraphim, enough high-class shit from you," Stavros said. "I remember you getting certain benefits from woman yourself."

"You're bringing Demo back this business?" Fofo demanded to know. "He comes, I go!"

"Shshsh, Fofo!" Seraphim turned to Stavros. "What you want from us?"

Stavros told them, his eyes daring contradiction, challenging resistance. "My plan," he said, "I have it clear now. War finished, Anatolia opening again for business, I go there, first one in, give money peasants, they weave goods for us. Cheap! I know territory, I know goods, I know market here, what to order, designs, colors—"

"Same idea you talk Mr. Fernand many times, no?" Seraphim said. "We taking capital from him, good idea."

"No. Putting our money," Stavros said. "That's my idea now."

"But you told me Mr. Fernand, he's interested," Seraphim said.

"Yesterday he offer me money, I say 'Much oblige, never mind, we don't need your damn capital.' Why give him piece our profits? Better keep it all for us; we will make fortune, guarantee!"

"So where we going for money?" Seraphim said.

"I told you. From us! I will take what we have, borrow more, everything in the pot, double or nothing, triple or nothing." He made a familiar gesture, as if he were shooting craps. "Now the time to shoot!"

"What's your idea?" Fofo said. "Make gamblers of us? That's why you looking my books?" She threw up her hands in a violent gesture of frustration and disgust. "What we work so hard make here, you shoot crap with that?"

"Did I see you raise your hands to me, Fofo, with that 'Shoot crap?' " Stavros said. "You speaking to me without respect, Fofo, you know that? I talking nice so far, but no more! I tell you plain goddamn talk now. I own sixty percent stock this company. I ask about Demosthenes because, same as you, he holds thirteen, one third share of rest. But I am boss here, I have sixty, and I will do what I know is right for this business. Like I always done for this family. You people, goddamn, can't see ahead, only back! So I will do what this family needs. I will make us rich, American style. Then, after that, you can crawl back to me and say, 'Sorry, dear brother, we were wrong, dear Stavros, you were right; thank you for not listening to us.' I'm the only one who sees ahead here. O.K.? Got that?

"I see you getting nervous too, Seraphim. So now I talk quiet again, see, like this, quiet. Soft voice. Fofo, you don't respect me, never mind, I respect you as sister. I understand, this is big step for you. You're not man, like me. No courage! You're worried. For whatever reason, you're not thinking proper way this morning. So I give you chance to think her over. I will do what I want anyway, but—two weeks, think! Sixty percent, don't forget that! If you like my idea, good; if you don't like, all the same—I go ahead without. My beloved Fofo, you have to take chances in business. That's how fortunes are made. Not by sitting quiet on your eggs, like those lousy little hundred-dollar bonds you bought here, Seraphim. So think, talk between you. In two weeks I ask again, quiet, polite, with respect. Meantime I make our plans."

He marched out of the office, leaving the firm's books flung over Fofo's desk, along with scraps of paper he'd scribbled on and crumpled.

"Something happen to him maybe," Seraphim said, "talking that way."

Fofo put it more plainly. "We better find lawyer," she said.

NOVEMBER 1918

Stavros finally received what he'd given up waiting for, a message from Mr. Aylesworth. It was delivered by a factotum, a Scotsman so discreet that although Stavros had run into him several times, he'd never heard the man speak. The invitation for a social evening was Mr. Aylesworth's way, the Scotsman said, of "expressing his appreciation for the accommodations you've provided him. Oh, no, not a business meeting, nothing like that; just a nice chat over beef and a beer."

What other men of affairs called a business conference, Mr. Aylesworth as well as Mr. Fernand termed a "chat." To put whomever it was being held with off guard, Stavros believed. He'd finally concluded that anything either of these men said, especially if it was blandly put and seemed innocent of intent, was spoken for a purpose, a purpose that was never the one professed but another, more central to the man's ends. Despite his Anatolian cunning, it had taken Stavros longer than it should have to perceive that the more generous and openhearted the proposal of either man sounded, the more softly it dropped from the mouth, the more reason there was to be suspicious. Mr. Aylesworth and Mr. Fernand were equally clever in this respect, evenly matched. Stavros had enjoyed watching them tilt.

Still, in certain ventures, for certain purposes, they'd been business partners. "He's never so dangerous as when he's your partner," Mr. Fernand said of the Englishman. "He's a man unburdened by conscience: the reason the British are sitting on the wealth of the world, drinking their damned gin! Don't believe anything he says, my boy; he's a complete flirt."

"The time you have to watch him most carefully," Mr. Aylesworth said of Mr. Fernand. "is when he's your partner. For one thing, he's the most seductive cunt since Cleopatra, and like that antique lady, he is, in the end, a whore. Now, as you must have noticed, he's senile—and so he's even more disarming, more treacherous."

Nevertheless, the two men were fast friends and forever in each other's company.

The life stories of the friends had one surprising similarity: They'd both started as comparatively modest retailers in a humbler line. Mr. Fernand's father, a member of the Armenian colony in Constantinople, had, when the time came, followed tradition and turned over to his eldest son the conduct of the small family business, Oriental rugs and carpets. Mr. Aylesworth, as his tradition suggested, had married into his fortune, taking a bride for reasons more substantial than romantic love. His father-in-law, now in his eighties, was Manchester's most respected figure in household furnishings. On his sixty-fifth birthday, he'd thrown his business into the lap of his son-in-law—who was waiting to catch it.

In the case of both men, their energy and appetites were too great to be confined to a commercial enterprise where profits were modest. Mr. Fernand, in his youth, had traveled widely in Persia to purchase floor coverings. The road to the southwestern city of Bushire passed through a field covered with a black muck which in several places, Mr. Fernand noticed, was burning unattended. Inquiry revealed that the natives of the region used this viscous fluid as household fuel. Mr. Fernand was sufficiently curious to bring in a scientist, who made a guess: The infertile soil of the area capped a sea of oil so abundant that it seeped up through the surface sand. Mr. Fernand made discreet land purchases, discreetly found risk capital, used substantial sums to insure the friendship of certain government dignitaries, and in time, passing off the family rug business to his younger brothers, Ara and Oscar, rushed on to wealth and glory.

Mr. Aylesworth made his start retailing oil for household lamps, part of his father-in-law's business. Gradually Aylesworth moved into wholesale, a natural expansion. His great impetus was patriotic. A brother, who was in the Royal Navy, informed Aylesworth—discreetly, of course—that the day was hard upon them when every capital ship in His Majesty's fleet would be powered by oil. There'd be great need, great demand. Aylesworth had the confidence and the capital to plunge.

Hostage to his past, Mr. Fernand kept an eye on Sarrafian Brothers. Mr. Aylesworth still helped operate a chain of outlets for household furnishings; in fact, he'd brought the business up to date: "Allow us to make your house a home!" But both men's real interest was elsewhere: Behind their humbler masks, they'd become rich by arranging and organizing business alliances to pump the Near East of its wealth.

This reach of enterprise was beyond Stavros's capabilities, and he knew it. After he'd been rejected by Mr. Fernand, he had, for a few hours, doubted his optimism. But no one could doubt his resilience. He went at seven, the hour the Scotsman had given him, to the address he'd been given; early, Stavros thought—Mr. Aylesworth usually dined at nine-thirty or ten. *Maybe he got something in his mind—about time*, Stavros thought. *Maybe son of a bitch going to cough up dollars I need, maybe now he realize I'm better than that old Armenian thinks.*

"Thought we might have a chat over a bit of decent British beef," Mr. Aylesworth said. "Then go on to attend the Hellenic Rally. I have four places booked; the French consul and his lovely wife will join us. The evening's purpose, as you must know, is to raise funds for Greater Greece, a cause that has my full support. . . ." And so on and on about Greater Greece and Byron, Venizelos's Great Idea, the Elgin marbles, which Britain had saved from vandalism, and the traditional friendship between the people of Britain and "our little brothers at the other end of the Mediterranean."

The place where they met had no sign above the door, being less a restaurant than an eating club which members of the British colony in New York had set up so they could be at home over a supper table in an uncivilized city. "We have some very nice Scottish salmon tonight, sir," the waiter said. "And what's to follow, Ronnie?" "Beef and pudding, steak and kidney pie, sole of a sort. Have the beef." "Mine bloody!" "Very good, sir." "And if I know Greeks, our guest will have the outside cut." Ronnie hustled away.

"You can see," Mr. Aylesworth said, "this place is quiet. The boys who attend us here are Cunard Line stewards whose ships—troop carriers, for the moment—happen to be in port. They know how to serve you, you'll find, without being either servile or impertinent. By the way, it was awfully decent of you to turn the young lady with the lovely red hair over to me, dear Lucy; yes, there's a favor I shan't forget. As well as darling little Gladys. It was Gladys, wasn't it, at the Plaza? A bonbon, she was, that child. I do hope she's not neglecting her schooling."

"Happy you enjoyed those girls," Stavros said. "I'm at your service. Anytime. I have many connections here."

"I know. Your reputation precedes you, my friend. I may well call on you again, and very soon."

"Now I'm calling on you. I have plans, rough idea I already told you—"

"Ah, the salmon! And the beer, Ronnie? Ah, yes, good!"

"You can make fortune"—Stavros laughed—"I mean, another fortune."

"I remember very well what you have in mind. Penetrating the heartland of Anatolia now, at a time when— The bread, Ronnie, is it buttered? Ah, good! I was saying, before the peasants there have recovered from the depredations brought on by the war. Get them while they're desperate, what?" He mopped some beer from his mustache. "Very sound! Very sound! An industry of cottages, and so on. Why not? You see, I understood! Come, come, Ronnie—a vigorous hand on that pepper mill. We'll be reopening our retail house in Berlin very soon, before the damned heinie's able to reorganize himself. So we'll need all the goods we can get. Now, Ronnie, take care of Mr.— Would you allow me to address you as Stavros? Always had trouble with Turkish family names."

"Sure, call me Stavros, why not. Or Joe. Lotsa people call me Joe."

"I prefer Stavros. The other sounds, I must say, a bit as if you're anxiously trying to be an American—or to be liked. No need to be anxious, you know. Not with me. Of course we want you with us."

"You said—what?"

"Of course, of course!" Mr. Aylesworth filled his mouth with soft, pink salmon.

"Thank you, sir," Stavros said. "For me that will be a dream not a dream anymore."

"Excellent salmon, isn't it? You're not eating. Why do you keep looking at me? Eat! Yes, you have, it seems to me, just the combination of qualities the job requires: the home-grown paterfamilias and the buccaneer. Soft hands, sharp teeth."

"Can I tell you now why it's important we move fast?"

"May I, on the other hand, suggest we have our meal in peace? Mind you, I am eager to hear every detail, but—after all—we don't have to move tomorrow, do we?" He watched Stavros roll salmon on his fork, as he had done, and put it into his mouth. "That's the style! Enjoy your salmon. Certainly we can give an hour to the pleasure of eating." He raised his beer. "Will you drink to Britain?"

"I drink to anyplace where the money sitting."

"Well, then, to the Bank of England. Where the money is sitting." He laughed.

They drank together in an atmosphere of brothers-in-business. Stavros regretted having mistrusted the man. He did make one more try over the beef, but it was rather casual. "My idea, central office should be in Smyrna, best place for shipping. What you think?"

"Teheran, actually," Mr. Aylesworth said. "Center of the market. But at the moment, my idea is to enjoy an English cheese, a Stilton, perhaps. The only cheese I can eat, British! I detest those insipid French cheeses, near butter—so soft, so sweet, no fabric. Precisely what was wrong with their damned army!"

As Mr. Aylesworth signed his name on the check, he said, "Actually, I should tell you we have an office in Teheran now and a couple of chaps there buying for us."

"Then why you need me? For what?"

"They happen to be Persians. Persians dealing with Persians in Persia. That bears watching. I don't trust them. Awful nice chaps, actually, but—"

"Oh, a cop!" Stavros chortled, half-mockingly. "You want me for a cop!"

"I want you to watch them for me. Come, let's walk."

"A cop!" Stavros said on the sidewalk. "That's what I always wanted."

"So glad," Aylesworth said. "Why?"

"So people will be 'fraid of me, instead of other way."

But Stavros was troubled and wanted reassurance. "You know something, Mr. Aylesworth? When I told Mr. Fernand Sarrafian I wanted percentage, he act very funny."

"Percentage of what?" Aylesworth said, his breath coming evenly. "How funny?"

"What I mean—I'm asking you—a cop, he will get percentage profits?"

"I should think it's possible. Don't worry about it."

"I worry. That's why I didn't take job from Mr. Fernand."

"I gather you'd like a plain answer? Yes?"

"Yes."

"If you earn it, you will get it."

Stavros still didn't know where he stood.

On the stage of Carnegie Hall there'd been constructed a model of the *New Generation,* the warship being bought for the Greek navy by contributions from unredeemed Greeks everywhere. As Aylesworth was finding their seats, Stavros stood watching a group of men and girls, dressed in the costumes of Cappodocia, perform a folk dance to music played by a group of strings from Smyrna.

The two men took their seats and Mr. Aylesworth turned his attention to the stage. "You know, Stavros," he said, "the way your people cling to their past—the costumes of their grandfathers, the dances of their great-grandfathers—it makes one wonder if Greece will ever come into the modern world. . . . By the way, have you been to Teheran?"

"No," Stavros said. "That song they're playing—that's from where I was born."

"Oh, yes, yes. Very rhythmic! About Teheran—their cultural traditions are rather puritanical, you'll find, even by our British standards. There is an international set there, however, and the women seem to be rather neglected by their husbands. You should do very well." He chuckled. "I must say I have."

The dancers were running off into the wings.

"I remember my mother, from long ago, with other women, doing that dance," Stavros said.

The sides of the ship model opened onto a *tableau vivant*. A soldier, wearing a *fustanella* and a fez, was mortally wounded, it seemed, his sword broken, the blade on the ground, and bloody.

Stavros made up his mind to pin Mr. Aylesworth down: a percentage, yes or no, and what figure, and when?

The dying hero onstage was supported by another soldier, similarly clad. He was holding a flag, a white ground on which there was a single square blue cross, and he was shouting his defiance at the enemy.

"Mr. Aylesworth," Stavros said, "I must talk to you."

"You know that's rather touching, that tableau." Aylesworth chuckled. "So naive."

Behind the scene, a large group of men were singing a patriotic song, and most of the audience joined in. The stage lights were being switched on and off, creating an eerie effect on the tableau. Then suddenly the two figures from the War of Freedom rose, breaking out of their postures and striding directly to the edge of the stage. The light now grew strong and steady as the two soldiers, in unison, recited a poem.

"My Greek is not that good," Mr. Aylesworth said. "Are they speaking some sort of dialect? What are they saying?"

Stavros translated: " 'How long, brave men, shall we suffer as slaves, how long—' "

"Here are my friends!" Mr. Aylesworth had turned toward the aisle.

Stavros went on to himself. " 'How long shall we live alone, like lions on the mountaintops, how long—' "

"I want you to meet these people, Stavros," Mr. Aylesworth said. "His wife is a great favorite of mine, a charming—get up, Stavros; on your feet, boy." He pulled Stavros up.

The woman, a beauty slightly overripe, embraced Mr. Aylesworth ardently.

"Juliet," Mr. Aylesworth said, "may I present Mr. Stavros—er—Topouzoglou. Stavros, here is Madame Juliet Domarchi and Monsieur Henri Domarchi, the French consul in New York. Henri, *ça va?*"

"Too much wine, too much food, too much talk," Domarchi said. He sat, heavily.

"Juliet, here's a Greek, a present for you. May he be to your taste."

Juliet Domarchi smiled, shrugged, looked at Stavros carefully.

Stavros turned his back to her—she was directly behind him—and sat looking at the stage. M. Domarchi sat where Aylesworth had been; Ayles-

worth sat with Juliet. "Why are you late, Juliet?" Stavros heard him say.
"I've been waiting for you."

"I simply hated to leave where we were," she said. "What's been
happening here? What's he saying? That's Greek, I suppose. Mr.—"

"Stavros," Mr. Aylesworth said. "Madame Domarchi is asking what
the speaker is saying."

" 'Better an hour of freedom than forty years of slavery,' " Stavros said.

"Ah!" the French consul said. "Noble words. Could have been spoken
by a Frenchman." He yawned.

"What era are those costumes?" his wife asked. "They're so quaint. Sir!
You!" She tapped Stavros on the shoulder. "I'm speaking to you."

Stavros turned to inspect her, a hamal looking over an arrogant tourist.
"In 1821, Greeks won freedom from the Turk," he said. "That's what
they're showing there, 1821."

Another man, waving a sword, came forward on the stage and proceeded to sing.

"He's most heroic," Juliet Domarchi said, "and *tres mignon*. What's he
saying? Tell me the words. You!" Stavros ignored her. She poked him in
the back with a long, stiff forefinger.

"Juliet," her husband said, "you're interfering with Mr.— with his
pleasure."

"I'd really like to know what's being said," Juliet Domarchi protested.
"I didn't want to come here, but now don't you think it's simple courtesy?
Aylesworth? I want to know what's being said."

"Just watch and keep quiet," her husband said. "Wherever you go you
make a scene!"

"Juliet is quite right," Mr. Aylesworth intervened. "Stavros, I want
you to—"

Stavros swung around and shot the words at the woman as he heard
them, phrase by phrase. " 'Cover the ground with Turkish dead. "Allah,
help us," cry the dogs.' " He looked at the Frenchwoman steadily. " 'No
sweeter music was ever heard.' "

"Go on, go on," she said. "Go on, please."

" 'The bam, bam, boom, the glin, glin, gloun,' " Stavros said. Then it
was repeated. " 'The bam, bam, boom, the glin, glin—' " He stopped.

Juliet Domarchi was whispering something in Aylesworth's ear. They
looked at each other and laughed. Then she looked at Stavros.

"What she say to you?" Stavros said. His tone was threatening. "What
she say to you just now?"

"Nothing, nothing."

"She making fun here?"

"No, no, just a pleasantry. What's the matter with you?"

"I said, 'The bam, bam, boom.' " Juliet Domarchi swung her shoulders
from side to side like a marching soldier, her bosom following. " 'The glin,

glin, gloom.' " She laughed, leaning against Mr. Aylesworth. "But the man, he's so handsome!" She smiled at Mr. Aylesworth. " 'The bam, bam, boom,' " she said.

"That's enough, Juliet, *tais toi!*" M. Domarchi's eyes were heavy and closing.

The side of the warship's model had opened again and a man was revealed supporting an old woman dressed in black.

"Oh, my God, that too—*sa mère, sa mère!* They stop at nothing! I must know every word of this priceless conversation. 'The bam, bam—' "

"Juliet," her husband said, wearily. "*Assez!* Stop."

She whispered something to Aylesworth and he laughed. "Of course," he said.

"Tell me what he's saying." Juliet Domarchi prodded Stavros in the back.

"Don't do that," Stavros said.

"Oh, Stavros, come, come," Mr. Aylesworth said. "You're being extremely rude."

"I don't like women pushing me with their fingers."

"She's being playful with you, boy. She's flirting with you."

"You don't like this?" Juliet said, poking him again. "Even when it's so gentle? Like that? So soft?" She was being flirtatious. "You don't like that? 'The bam, bam—' "

Stavros, his body tense, looked straight ahead.

"Tell her what they're saying, boy," Mr. Aylesworth commanded. "Come, come!"

When Stavros did, his tone had changed; he was on the side of the people being represented on the stage. Their emotion was his now, and he spoke the translation with respect, defying the attitude of the people he was with. He turned to the woman. "He's saying, 'Kneel with me, Mother, and pray that I shall slay many—' " He broke off. "Why she's laughing?" he said to Aylesworth. "Is that funny? What is it makes you laugh, lady?"

It almost looked as if Stavros was about to strike Juliet Domarchi. Mr. Aylesworth put his hand on Stavros's arm and said, "Stavros, I insist you tell Juliet, who is my dear friend, what that man is saying."

Stavros bowed his head and then decided to make a final effort. He stood in the aisle and bowed low. Juliet applauded. People, diverted from what was happening on stage, laughed.

Stavros straightened up and spoke to Mr. Aylesworth. "Get up," he said. "I want to sit next to lady." There was an anxious pause. Juliet appeared to be thrilled. Mr. Aylesworth gave Stavros his place.

"He said this," Stavros spoke gravely; it was his last chance and hers. " 'Mother, pray that I shall kill many Turks. Mother, plant roses and black clover, sprinkle them with sugar and water and with musk. As long as they bloom, Mother, your son is not dead, he is fighting the Turk. But if that wretched day comes when the rose withers and the blossoms fall, then I shall be smitten too. Then do you wear black.' "

The unexpected happened: Juliet was silent. Then she said, "That's very charming. Don't be angry with me. I'm a foolish woman who's bored with her husband and had too much wine at dinner."

"Now I want to listen," Stavros said. "I don't want to talk." He smiled at her, a threat, and turned his head away.

An Englishman had come on stage, dressed in a costume of the same period.

"Who is that?" Juliet said.

"Lord Byron," Aylesworth said, turning around.

Byron was misrepresented as a burly man. He spoke with the greatest sincerity and force, proclaiming the eternal brotherhood of England and Greece. "We have always been brothers and always will be," he said.

Juliet tapped Stavros on the shoulder. "I told you don't do that," he said, jerking his body away.

"I wanted your attention." Juliet spoke sincerely now. "For an instant."

"He's speaking English; you understand English, no?"

"I want to ask you a serious question," she said. Lord Byron was reciting a poem about the glory that was Greece. "Do you trust the English?" she asked.

Stavros was aware that Aylesworth was turned in his seat, watching him. There was the twist of a smile on his face.

"I do," Stavros said, still looking at the stage. There was applause.

"You believe they're honorable?" Juliet asked. "You believe they will be steadfast in a crisis? There is sure to be a crisis; will they be honest?"

Stavros was so angry he spoke the truth. "No—not honorable, not steadfast, not honest," he said. "No more than you French. But English, French, you both have commercial interest in Anatolia now, further east too, so for that reason we Greeks can count on you. For the moment. Our interests—temporary, sure—are the same."

"Alan, you must admire this man," Juliet said. "He spoke the truth."

"Let me ask you," Aylesworth said to Juliet, "do you trust the Greeks, our allies?"

"As much as I do the English," she said.

Her husband, Henri, was snoring.

While they'd been talking, a man introduced as Tsolsimos, of the New York Committee of Unredeemed Greeks, had begun to demand of the audience that Constantinople be one of the cities reunited with Greece.

Juliet touched Stavros on the shoulder. "Do you mind me touching you gently?" she said. She seemed frightened of him.

"I don't want to talk anymore. I want to listen what he's saying. It's my—"

"Are you from there? That's what I was going to ask. Constantinople?"

"Yes. I am one of the unredeemed. I am an Anatolian."

"What does that mean, unredeemed?"

"It means we are separated from our home country."

"Oh, how terrible! It must be terrible!"

"It is!" Stavros said. He was surprised to hear his own voice, how ardently he'd spoken. "It is!"

Tsolsimos was speaking of Constantinople: "our eternal city," he called it, and said that its return to Greece would fulfill a dream of five hundred years. Juliet could see how moved Stavros was. "What's he saying, please, what's he saying?" she whispered insistently. "Please forgive me, but I must know what—"

"Don't talk anymore. I don't want to listen to you. Shut up!"

There was a silence. Aylesworth, furious, bowed his head. Juliet looked away. Henri slept. Stavros listened to the speaker.

". . . which is now a mosque but was once our cathedral, our church, Santa Sophia. When it is ours again, the king who lies there in marble, Constantine himself, will come back to life. And the priest who was singing the service in 1453, who disappeared when he heard the boot of the first Turk invading holy ground, shall come out of the small black door which no one has been able to open in all the years since, go to the altar, and resume the service where he had left off."

Stavros was crying. Not because of the story itself but at the memory of how his father had told it to him the first time.

"You have no right to speak to me that way," Juliet said. "Henri, you shouldn't allow him to talk to me that way." She saw that Henri was sleeping and turned to Aylesworth. " 'Shut up!' he said to me when I was only asking a natural question. I was very respectful. You brought me here, Alan, and I wanted to know what was happening. Was that wrong of me?"

"Certainly not wrong," Aylesworth said. "You had every right. He was rude. Stavros, what you said was unforgivable."

Stavros knew at that instant that he could no longer hope for anything from Aylesworth, and he no longer wanted anything from him.

A resolution demanding the return of "our eternal city" was proposed in English, and when a vote was asked for, it was accepted by unanimous acclamation. A roar! The entire hall of people seemed to rise to its feet, shouting approval.

Not Juliet. She shook her sleeping husband's shoulder. "Henri," she said. "I want to go. I'm going. Get up."

"Juliet dear, don't be upset," Aylesworth said. "He did speak to you crudely, but, Juliet—"

She was crying with anger. "I'm not accustomed to being treated that way, Alan. Why didn't my husband protect me? Why didn't you protect me, Henri? Wake up!"

The audience sat down. There was a roll of drums from offstage. Henri woke and looked at Stavros anxiously. "Did you insult my wife?" he asked.

"Yes. I insulted her!" Stavros said. "She talk too much. Tell her to shut up now."

The side of the *New Generation* opened again and there was a swelling roll of drums and a blast from four horns. Onto the stage rushed ten pretty girls, maidens all—you could tell because they were dressed in white.

"Oh, Juliet, look," Aylesworth said. "How pretty they are! Aren't they pretty? See how their eyes sparkle!"

"I want to go home," Juliet Domarchi said.

"Stavros, I want you to apologize to Madame Domarchi immediately," Aylesworth said.

Stavros's eyes didn't leave the stage.

As the drums rolled, the maidens scattered rose petals in the path of a brigade of wounded soldiers, perhaps forty men, who were marching forward to make a semicircle. Into which a priest advanced, a representative, a booming voice announced, of Chrysostomos, the archbishop of Smyrna. The priest held a silver vessel on three fine-link chains. It contained smoking charcoal over which an incense prepared by the monks in a mountaintop monastery had been sprinkled. The priest flung the vessel back and forth on its chain and everyone for rows back could smell the blessed presence. Then he chanted a prayer. The audience bowed their heads.

"I detest that smell." Juliet's head was erect and she looked at Stavros challengingly. She made no effort to control her voice and some people nearby shushed her. "And I detest you," she said to Stavros. "You have no manners. You are uncivilized, completely."

"*Skasseh!*" Stavros said. "Which means, choke." Then he ignored her. He was surprised at the strength of his feelings for what was happening on stage—and for his own past; these were feelings he hadn't had in years. He bowed his head during the prayer, not listening to the words, but remembering who he was.

"I'm going," Juliet said. "But before I do, I want one of you men who asked me here to speak to this savage in my behalf. I expect you to protect me, Henri, since you're my husband."

Stavros raised his head and saw a man in an evzoni costume march up and occupy the place where the priest had been. He held a small wooden box in the air. It was painted blue. Then he turned the box upside down on the forestage, emptying it of the soil it contained.

"Now what's he doing?" Juliet said. "Does anyone know what this is all about? Alan?" She looked at her husband. "Henri, did you hear what I said just now—to you!"

"What's he saying, what was in that box?" Aylesworth asked Stavros. Stavros didn't answer. A man sitting in front of Aylesworth turned and said, "He is going to speak to us from the soil of our *patridah*. He brought that box of earth from Anatolia to here!"

"You mean he brought that dirt all the way from . . . ?" Henri asked the man.

"Yes. That soil was blessed by Archbishop Chrysostomos."

Now came a parade of soldiers, casualties of the war, the maidens scattering rose petals in their path. From offstage, trumpets played the national anthem over the beat of the drums. The audience was on its feet, cheering.

So was Stavros, on his feet, cheering.

For there, leading the brigade, was his brother Michaelis, marching to the center of the stage and as near to the edge as he could get.

Stavros filled with pride.

Some of the men had lost an arm, some both arms, some a leg. Some were blind. One man had lost both feet and was marching on pegs where his feet had been, marching well and with confidence.

Stavros was an Anatolian again. And those with him were his enemies.

The man without feet not only walked, he strutted. Michaelis threw him a rifle and he performed an exercise with it, all the positions of the manual. He carried his head proudly, strutting, saluting, presenting arms.

"Oh, I can't look at this," Juliet said. "Why do they allow this man to — Henri! I'm waiting, Henri."

The girls in white were running down the aisles now. They carried baskets to collect money in.

Henri laughed nervously. "This is really grotesque, you know," he said to Aylesworth. He looked at the man parading on pegs and laughed again. "Juliet, you're right—let's leave. That's the simplest thing to do."

Michaelis was speaking to the audience as the baskets began to fill. "Can you compare anything you could give here to what these men have given? Can you?"

"*Aye-air-ah! Aye-air-ah!*" the man on pegs shouted between each phrase. There was a bayonet on his gun and he was thrusting at imaginary foes.

"Our country needs blood to become great," Michaelis shouted. "Our country needs your money!"

"Are people actually swayed by all this patriotic . . . ?" Henri Domarchi said, turning his head away.

Stavros seized him and turned him back toward the stage. "Here! Look! Look at him," he said.

Mr. Aylesworth had been very patient, but now he struck Stavros's arm hard so that his grip came loose.

"That's all I will take from him!" Henri announced, jumping to his feet.

"Curses and anathemas for those who ignore their duties," Michaelis shouted from the stage. He was thrusting his single arm at the audience in a gesture both exhortatory and threatening.

"*Aye-air-ah! Aye-air-ah!*" shouted the man with the pegs for feet.

"He's your employee, Alan," Henri said. "Why do you allow this?"

But Aylesworth remained cool. "Oh," he said, "sit down and be still, all of you. All this bluster properly belongs in a theater on Shaftesbury Avenue, of course. I've noticed, Juliet, that once one gets east of Torino —is it the climate? is it a racial thing?—people behave as if they were in grand opera. But that doesn't mean *we* have to behave that way, does it? What I can't take, Stavros, is your damned Greek self-pity. If you're wounded, I say, simply go about your business the best you can. That fellow with the amputated arm who's shouting at us—spare me, please! He can't bring the arm back, can he, waving that stump and yelling at us?"

"*Ella! Ella! Ella!*" Michaelis was calling out, striding from side to side. "*Thoseh! Thoseh! Thoseh!*" And in English: "Give! Give! Give!"

"Must he really push that damned stump in my face?" Aylesworth continued. "I'd admire him a good deal more if he said absolutely nothing, accepted what happened as part of the game—he turned the card over and it was a loser. I mean, war is war, isn't it? He knew the chance he was taking!"

A maiden in white was reaching out a basket to them.

"Give!" Stavros commanded. "You came here—now give!"

The Frenchman threw in a coin. Alan Aylesworth drew a wallet out of his jacket pocket and carefully examined its contents. Stavros snatched the wallet from the Englishman's hand, pulled out the money it held, and threw the wallet into the air. "*Zito*, Michaelis!" he shouted.

Michaelis, standing on the raised platform, could see his brother charging down the aisle throwing dollars into the baskets the virgins in white were holding, and could hear him shouting, "*Yassou*, Michaelis! *Zito*, Michaelis!" Michaelis hadn't known his brother was there. Later, when the rally was over and he was sitting, exhausted, among his fellow veterans and friends, he saw Stavros sliding through the crowd toward him. Quickly and without a word, Stavros kissed him, and Michaelis kissed his brother in return.

He'd been playing poker all night and into the morning so he got to the store long after it had opened. But he found only Fofo's husband, Silo. "They think it's happening, the old woman," Silo said. "They been looking for you—where the hell you sleeping these days? They say better come quick. They're all there waiting."

They were. Even his youngest sister, Eleftheria, the one he'd once loved the most, she was there, nursing an infant. Eleftheria looked twenty pounds heavier, a matron.

He'd opened the door of the apartment as he always did, these days, like a thief. He was standing in the doorway to the dining room for some seconds before anyone noticed. The whole family was seated around the table. In the center, two large cardboard boxes had been torn open— French pastries.

At the head of the table, where Stavros used to sit, was Demo, glowing with health. "We don't look ahead, this damn family," he was saying. "Leave everything to Stavros, that's the way we go. And him—same old way."

There were murmurs of guarded assent.

Demo, very well dressed, seemed in a class above the others. "The day of the Oriental rug is finished," he said with absolute certainty. "Everything will be machine made from now on here," he said. "We are up-to-date in this country, modern. Remember, if you're not ahead, you're behind."

"He learned a lot in the army," Eleftheria observed to the others as she switched the infant to her other breast, then picked up an éclair. When she bit into it, it gushed custard.

They saw Stavros in the doorway then, and looked at him without speaking. Finally some murmurs of greeting.

Stavros nodded. "The old lady?" he asked.

"Eleni's with her," Fofo said.

Stavros walked around the table to kiss Eleftheria and smile at the baby. "Nice-looking boy," he said. "Red hair!"

"A girl," Eleftheria said. "Elaine, like Eleni, but American."

Stavros nodded again and walked away. They were all irrelevant to him now, strangers.

He entered his mother's room noiselessly. She was in her chair, bent over the heavy, leather-bound Bible. The room smelled of Aseptinol and garlic. The old lady credited her long life to eating three cloves of garlic every day.

Stavros knelt at her feet. "Mommah!" he said. "Mommah!" She was completely unresponsive. He noticed that one side of her mouth hung lower than the other. He tried to jolly her, a rougher tone. "Come on, old woman," he said, "what the hell game you playing here? Come on, get ready, we're going back. I made up my mind. I'm taking you back."

There was no sign that Vasso had heard. In the darkest corner of the room, there was a movement. Eleni. "Too late for those lies now," she said scornfully. "She hears nothing!"

"Why the hell don't you put her teeth in?" Stavros said.

"They don't fit anymore," Eleni said. "She needed new teeth for three years, but nobody—nobody moved. Now she can't talk, so—"

"Get out," he said to her. "Hell out of here! I'm going to talk to her."

"Tell her about your life at the Armenian's. That she'll believe." And Eleni left the room.

After he closed the door, he spoke to his mother for a long time. The only light was the flickering from the oil lamps on the plate shelf. He told her he took the blame for not fulfilling his father's dream. He had brought the family over, as Isaac had wanted, but then the family had gone bad and he'd lost control. He'd given up on them, he said. And on the country too. He was going back now, he told her, to where he'd come from, where he was born. It was opening up there now, he said, big chance for business. So he was going and would take her: a promise.

That last he knew was a lie. Take her? Like this? But he thought that the lie, the one she'd wanted to believe for so many years, might resuscitate her.

"Mommah, remember how we used to cry, 'America! We're going to America!' Now it's the opposite way, with a different voice. You were right, Mommah, it ruined your family, this country. Everything Father wanted and I tried, it's gone. You were right, Mommah, on that."

She didn't respond. He'd been talking to himself. He stroked her face and her long gray hair, so lank and lifeless.

The very reason for his discipline and devotion would be gone when she went. What would those other people, his brothers and sisters, mean to him then? Or he to them? They were already strangers. He was sick of countering their resentment. If they hadn't been his father's and mother's children, he wouldn't be giving them a thought. The only one for whom he had respect was Michaelis; he at least possessed courage. Seraphim? A good heart. The rest? When his mother was gone, he'd wipe them off his mind. Let them seek for themselves, let them see what they could do alone.

He went into his old room. In a corner he found the *bastooni,* symbol of the charge Isaac Topouzoglou had laid on him. Once, also, it had been the symbol of his power. He looked in the mirror, proudly. He had the power still, inside him somewhere; he didn't need the damned stick or his father's word, his brothers' help or his sisters' support.

Because he knew how little they thought of him now, he strutted even more foolishly, more grotesquely, in front of the mirror, then turned down the hall to where he heard them murmuring and squabbling. Oh, the years, the effort he'd wasted on them!

He knew what they thought of him: Mr. Fernand's pimp, corrupted beyond redemption. But he made up his mind to give them one last chance. It would be his final duty, absolve him of his ultimate responsibility. For one last time, he would overlook what they thought of him and what they were.

They grew silent when he entered the room. It was obvious that they'd been talking against him. They looked at him quickly, then away. "All right, all right," he said. "I know you been talking bad things against me here; makes no difference. Hello, Michaelis."

Michaelis had come in; he was pale, exhausted. Stavros couldn't read the look on his face except that in some way he was making a judgment. Goddamn! Everybody was judging him. Enough of that, enough!

"The old lady, I saw her," Stavros said. "Yes, she's finished, looks like. Matter of time, you can see that. She hears nothing, sees—"

"You know why she got deaf?" Eleni said. "Listening to those lies you said to her about taking her back to other side. Now she refuse to listen to those lies from you anymore, so she got deaf."

Stavros nodded. "O.K.," he said.

"You want a napoleon?" Eleftheria said.

"No. I want to—I better say few words here." He started to sit, didn't. "I talk to Seraphim, Fofo also, two weeks ago. I told them my idea. Now is the time to strike, I said, go the limit, all or nothing, our chance to get in the big money. I said to Seraphim, I own sixty percent Anatolian Carpet Company. So I make up our mind take every cent we have, go back to other side and buy goods while they're cheap. Not a gamble, this. More like gold rush. I say to Seraphim and Fofo, I give them—and you now— last chance to get rich with me. Two weeks, tell me, yes or no. You want me buy out your share or you want to come in with me? I can do it without asking you. I put in capital, our company; remember where capital come from? Joe's Shoeshine, my place I sold for us. So I don't have to ask you nothing. Sixty percent over forty. I can do anything I want, so I'm doing you favor. Now tell me what you want."

He leaned on the *bastooni,* legs apart, and waited.

They said nothing.

"Say it yes, or say it no," he said. "Easy. Tell me—not so hard. Yes? No?" He looked at them and smiled. "I notice you're afraid," he said. "No reason. I'm your brother still. Say!"

Seraphim spoke up, softly, as was his way. "Beloved brother," he said. "We are happy the way it is now. I have good life, everything in good order. I don't want to be richer. Why take big chance?"

"You have these ideas from listening Mr. Fernand too much," Fofo said. "You understand what I'm saying, Michaelis, I'm sure. We talked about this."

Michaelis's face was of stone.

"No," Stavros said. "Mr. Fernand Sarrafian been listening to me. So come on, speak. Seraphim, I get idea you say no."

Seraphim nodded.

"Fofo?"

"No."

"Demo? I don't see you long time. You own ten percent this company. What—?"

"Don't talk so fast, what you owe me. Vacilli died; it's thirteen, one-third percent, not ten. Right?"

"Right. I forgot."

"Very convenient, you forgot. Now, you want to talk, I have many ideas what to do."

"I don't want to talk," Stavros said. "I pay you off, thirteen, one-third. So, Michaelis?"

"I don't care."

"Plain language, no," Stavros said. "Finish! So I go my way, you go yours. I'm not your boss anymore, and when Mother die, I'm not your brother. Finish!"

He brought up the *bastooni,* held it at the level of his eyes. "Father give me this to show his faith in me." He broke the stick across his knees and threw the halves on the table where the pastry was.

They looked at him as if he was insane.

"That's the end," he said. "Don't go by my face; I'm satisfied. What's the matter? You all look so worried. Frightened like chickens when they hear the fox outside. Tst-tst-tst! Oh my God, look at you here! Tell you what I'm going to do. I'm not going to pay you off. I'm going to give you the whole thing. Everything. My share, it's yours. The Anatolian Carpet Company belongs to you! Your forty percent is now one hundred percent."

Now they were sure he'd gone insane.

"Don't play games with us," Demo said.

"The business is yours," Stavros said. "I mean what I say. All I want, maybe, is that nine-by-twelve silk Keshan; I have idea 'bout that piece. So goodbye. You're free. I'm free. I don't want to be with you people anymore."

He strutted around the table, looking down at them scornfully. Only Michaelis held his head up.

"You people pick who's boss—it's up to you. Think of me dead. Leaving the country. Going back Anatolia. 'Set your brothers up in business,' our father said to me, so now I set you up in business. Finish. Here is his ring." He pulled it off his finger. "It means head of the family. Let someone else wear it."

He threw the ring on the table, then slowly, like a toreador circling the arena to the applause of thousands, he strutted into the kitchen. Finally and forever he had lifted their weight off his heart. In the kitchen, drinking an ouzo, he heard them quarreling in whispers. Demo's voice was the clear one. "He's insane," he said.

The question became who should wear the ring. They couldn't decide. Most of them wanted Michaelis, it seemed; Stavros couldn't hear what Michaelis's response was.

"First we must get a lawyer to make him sign papers," Demo said.

"I trust him," Seraphim said. "What he said, he'll do."

"Wait when he thinks about it!" Demo whispered. "You realize what he's given away? Wait till he realizes! Then see! You're not smart man, Seraphim."

Stavros began to laugh. He was free of them, free of everybody! He'd taken himself by surprise. Laughing, he asked himself, *What the hell did I do that for?* On an impulse he didn't understand—irrationally, without planning—he'd given away his whole life's earnings. But he wasn't unhappy about it, he was proud.

"He's always an honest man," he heard Seraphim say.

That's been my trouble, Stavros thought, *too damned honest.* For years he'd tried to convince old man Sarrafian of the business merit of a plan. With what result? A humiliating offer: half manager of the store at $80 per week and zero profits. Now he'd accept Mr. Fernand's offer—with a secret purpose: to wait on the ground for an opening when he could put some kind of pistol to that old man's head—the kind that made people move—not reason and good business sense but force, terror, panic, fear, whatever. He'd be ready now to exercise, when the chance came, a ruthlessness that would match the ruthlessness of the man whom he'd been trying so long and so unsuccessfully to impress.

"Didn't you see his eyes?" Fofo was saying. "Demo's right, he's gone crazy."

Stavros agreed, pouring himself another drink.

"Michaelis, you take the ring," Seraphim said. "Michaelis!"

Then they'd have a hard boss there, Stavros thought. *Michaelis will teach them right and wrong. Yes, take Michaelis, wear the ring, Michaelis.*

"I still love him," Eleftheria said. "He's my brother."

Not anymore brother, Stavros thought. *Too late for that stuff. You marry that dago husband, you watch while he beats me near death and now suddenly I'm your brother again. To hell with you.*

There was a burst of angry babble in response to what Eleftheria had said.

Also, Stavros thought, *thirty, forty thousand investment in Anatolia goods is not what I want.* He had to get a big sum fast, some way, how he didn't know. But he'd find it. Just the fact that he was no longer tied to them . . .

The angry babble stopped.

Now that he knew good intentions, sincere reasons, didn't work, it was time for the pistol. He had to point it at Mr. Fernand some way. And soon.

There was a complete silence, an eerie stillness. Stavros went to the door. The old lady, Vasso, had come down the hall on her hands and knees.

The girls rushed to her. She waved them off, but they lifted her into a chair at the table.

"A yogurt," she said. "Bring a yogurt here." Her voice was a croak, barely audible.

Stavros went to sit next to her. She gripped his hands, kissed them, then looked around at the others. They had no favor in her eyes.

Eleni put yogurt in a jelly glass before her mother, dipped a spoon into it, lifted the full spoon to the old woman's twisted mouth. Vasso waved her away. The movement of her hand was not vigorous but it was definite. She made a sign that she wanted to speak to her youngest son, to Demo. When he sat next to her, she whispered in his ear, a few words at a time.

Demo told them what she said. " 'Except for Stavros,' she says, 'we'd be selling charcoal . . . in burlap sacks,' she says, 'like Father did,' she says, 'in the Kayseri bazaar.' That's what she said."

Demo looked at the family. "She's an old woman," he whispered. "Doesn't know what's going on!" He exhaled violently through his pursed lips, a sound of impatience and of disgust.

"Take my share too," Michaelis said from where he stood in the doorway. "Thirteen and whatever! I don't want it. I'm going back with Stavros."

The old lady, who'd had her say, was eating yogurt.

"I still don't believe you did it," Stavros said. "It was him, wasn't it—that small ugly one like an animal? You're pretending for him."

"I did it," Michaelis said.

"Simeon was your friend!" Stavros said.

"That's why I didn't want Efstathis to do it. He was hunting for Simeon everywhere, but he didn't find him, thanks to God. Simeon was an excellent person; his pride would have been hurt if a weasel like Efstathis took his life."

"How did you find where he was?"

"I knew Simeon well, an impatient man. They kept holding that boat here, adding cargo, more and more, and knowing how he was, I guessed he'd be near the boat, perhaps even on it."

"And he was?"

"On the prow, looking downriver. I saw him even though it was very dark that night. Behind him they were still loading, the men pulling ropes and calling, *'Travah! Travah! Travah!'* The wind was from the north and Simeon must have been thinking that now, with the tide going out, would have been the time for the damn ship to cast off. He was always the sailor, a very impatient man on shore. So—well then—it happened. I did it."

He stopped, having told all of the story he intended to tell. They were sitting on the traffic island under the tree where the scrap of grimy cloth had once fluttered. The broad street was empty and dark and there was a cold wind.

"Well, then?" Stavros urged. "What?"

"Well, then . . ." Michaelis sighed; it wasn't easy for him to go on. "There was nobody blocking the plank from the dock and I walked up and forward to within a few feet. Nobody saw me. I was hoping he'd changed his mind, when, without turning his head, he said, 'I've been waiting for you.' You know, people who work in danger have instincts just as animals do. So Simeon spoke without turning his head, and I said to him, 'Simeon, I can't let you go, you know that.' Still he didn't turn his head, and I felt my love for him coming on and I realized I couldn't do it. Even holding the thought of the one hundred and thirty-eight men at the mercy of the Turk, I couldn't do it. To kill a friend! That way! It was too much to ask of myself. First let the whole world come down! I was about to leave the place when he turned and leaped on me, putting his arms around me, and my pistol was tight against his chest. That's when it happened. I mean, when I did it. He hadn't tried for the gun, you see, just clasped his arms around me, embracing me, not fighting me off. Perhaps it had become too difficult for him and he was leaving it to me what should happen. Then he had the bullet in him and he sat on the dock, nodding his head, looking at me as if he pitied me. After a time there was blood coming from his mouth and he fell over on one side, the way a ship does just before it sinks. The last time he looked at me, it seemed—maybe—he was thanking me for solving his problem for him. Maybe. Or do I think that because it makes it easier for me? That's why I can't sleep at night, remembering how he looked at me then."

They were under a street lamp and the beam from overhead sank Michaelis's eyes as deep as a cave and under his eyes the skin was dark and blue. It was then—when Michaelis reached for the edge of his collar to pull it up and protect himself from the cold wind—it was then that Stavros became aware that his brother's hand was trembling. Michaelis had taken on his victim's affliction.

Quickly Michaelis thrust his hand into his pocket. "Efstathis is still searching," he said. "I didn't tell him anything. I wouldn't shame Simeon that way." Then he was silent, head bowed, an exhausted man.

"I was so proud of you when you spoke at the hall," Stavros said. "Before all those people! No one admired you as much as I did. My brother! I felt some kind of new happiness at that moment because of how you spoke and what you were saying."

"You tried to be an American here," Michaelis said. "You forgot you were an Anatolian." He was about to say more, but he stopped and got up. "I'll go now," he said.

"Where?"

"I have a place in the home of a Greek family in Brooklyn. But I can't sleep there. I'm sleepy until I lie down." He looked at his brother, studying him. "First I get angry at you," he said. "Then I see you and . . ." He shrugged.

"I've taken a room in a hotel," Stavros said. "Come live with me. You'll sleep, I promise. There are two beds, side by side, and it will be like when we were boys—remember?—sleeping in the same room. We'll talk across the space between the beds, tell the old stories about the Turkish hodja, how he put his hat on the floor and how the guest mistook it in the dark for something else and what happened then; remember how we used to laugh at those old hodja stories when we were boys together? Come, Michaelis, come with me."

Michaelis surprised him. "Why not?" he said. "Maybe there I'll sleep."

They crossed the other half of the wide divided street, past the bakery, where, in the back, they were baking tomorrow's bread, and so to the subway. "Thank God you don't have to go into the army again," Stavros said.

"I'll go again," Michaelis said. "Until the war is over."

"With one arm! What army takes soldiers with one arm?"

"Our army. I speak Turkish; they'll use me to question prisoners. Besides, consider: Can I take Simeon's life and refuse to risk mine?"

DECEMBER 1918

Demo had found a lawyer; papers had quickly been drawn up. Both Stavros and Michaelis had to sign—Demo was still convinced that Stavros would, in the end, realize what he was giving away and think better of it. But Stavros, dressed in his new flashy style, showed up, accepted the pen, listened when the lawyer told him where to write his name, and leaned over, ready to sign.

It was Seraphim who broke. "Please, please, Stavros, think again what you're doing."

"Don't worry," Stavros said.

"He's a grown man," Demo said. "He knows what he wants to do."

"Say, brother Demo," Stavros said. "Where it says here about the silk Keshan? I don't see that one."

"Damn, we forgot about that. Sorry," Demo said. "Well, on that much you can trust us, sure."

"Sure I trust you!" Stavros said. "But write it anyway, what the hell? Come here, quick, smart lawyer, write it in here I get nine-by-twelve silk Keshan, color deep blue, number—what's number there, Fofo?"

"What you going to do with that fine silk Keshan?" Demo asked.

"Who knows, maybe I give it to the orphanage across from the apartment, we see," Stavros said.

Demo made his sound of disgust.

Fofo called out the number and the lawyer inserted in longhand that Stavros was to keep the carpet. "You all have to initial here," he said.

While they were signing, the front door of the store opened and in came a bizarre procession. Mr. Fernand Sarrafian led the way, wearing an Oxford-gray cloth coat and a black homburg. "Can we come in?" he said.

"Sure, sure, why not," Stavros said. He'd been meaning to go talk to his old boss and tell him he'd accept his humiliating offer.

Mr. Fernand stepped back to hold the door open for Morgan Perry and, with him, not the Reverend Kenworthy, but an old Armenian priest, a small, thin man with coal-black eyes and a full white beard.

Morgan Perry, who used to be built like a barrel, had shrunk by at least seventy pounds. His face was gray and his eyes shone like lamps. His appearance shocked Stavros. It wasn't only that he was frail, but there was a surprising spiritual quality about him. His eyes seemed to be looking past whomever he was talking to and his attention was never totally on anything.

Stavros went to the man who used to torment him and welcomed him. Morgan Perry nodded, smiled, looked around the store as if he didn't know where he was.

Stavros turned to Mr. Fernand, wondering why they'd come.

"Morgan doesn't want anger on his soul," Mr. Fernand said. "Other people's. He wants your forgiveness."

"For what?"

"He tried to kill you. He wants you to forgive him for that."

"I do."

"Are you sure?"

"I just said it."

"But you frequently lie. Say it to him so he'll believe it."

"I forgive you, Mr. Perry," Stavros said.

This time he extended his hand and Morgan shook it with his own, which was frighteningly frail.

"He doesn't want the burden of guilt on his soul," the old priest said. His English was accented, yet cultivated. "He has made a full confession to me," he added. "I am satisfied."

"But Morgan wanted to look you in the face and hear you say what you said," Mr. Fernand said.

"I'm glad he came," Stavros said. "And I meant what I said."

"I hope so," Mr. Fernand said.

"This time, you can be sure, I am sincere," Stavros said. "I can only hope in my turn that he bears no further anger to me."

"About what?" Mr. Fernand said. "Did you do something again?"

"About his daughter, before. And so forth."

"That problem has healed over," Mr. Fernand said. He turned to Morgan Perry. "Tell him what you are going to do," he said.

"About what?" Perry said hazily.

"The invitation. You know—the one you were going to—"

"I want you to come to their wedding," Morgan Perry said quickly.

"Althea's?"

"Yes."

"Not necessary for you to do that, Mr. Perry," Stavros said. "I have forgiven you for what you did. I have put all my past behind. Everything. I don't need anything more from you or you from me, so please—"

"He insists!" Mr. Fernand said in his most forceful, businesslike voice.

"But I won't be able to come," Stavros said. "In June I'll be in Anatolia, as I always planned."

"You got the money somewhere?" Mr. Fernand said.

"I told you I'd get it," Stavros said.

Seraphim turned away to conceal his amazement—or disbelief.

"I will leave present for Althea and your son, here in the store. Nine-by-twelve silk Keshan—fine piece."

"Very generous of you, very cultured," Mr. Fernand said. Then he came close to Stavros and whispered, "I miss you. What's the trouble, you didn't care for the accommodations in my home? There are other rooms. Choose the one you want. Kyushiro misses you too. Come back, damn fool!"

"No, no—but many thanks. No."

"Tell me where the hell you get the money? Or are you lying again?"

"We'll talk about that sometime, Mr. Fernand, if you like. I'll come to you and we talk. Why not? Now, about the wedding, I want to say—"

"We postponed it," Mr. Fernand said. "No, the other way, forward. It's not May now, it's in two weeks. January twelfth. There are reasons for that. We have spoken together about the problem, Morgan's health— am I right, Morgan?" Morgan Perry nodded. "Seems he be better able to stand the strain January twelfth."

Clearly, Morgan Perry was dying. Anyone could see that. He looked as if he wouldn't even survive the two weeks until the ceremony. He'd been coached in what he'd been saying, in nodding at every proposal Mr. Fernand or the priest made, but even while he was nodding, his mind was elsewhere.

"What about Mrs. Perry?" Stavros asked. "She and I . . . you know?"

"I discussed the situation with her," Mr. Fernand said. "I bring you her formal invitation." He handed Stavros a small white envelope with his name written in green ink across the front.

"Open it," Mr. Fernand commanded. "And read!"

The note was formal and it was cool, but there was no doubt about it. Mrs. Perry had been well coached too. "Will you do us the honor of attending the marriage of our daughter, Althea, to Mr. Paul Sarrafian on Sunday the twelfth of January, 1919," it said. And so on.

"I'll be glad to come," Stavros said.

With that, the little Armenian priest hustled up, took Morgan Perry by the upper arm, turned him around, and led him out of the store.

"You behaved very well," Mr. Fernand said. "You have acquired some culture in the time we've spent together." Then he led Stavros to one side. "Where the hell you get the money suddenly?" he whispered. "You lying? Sure. Well, don't worry; at that same occasion, on January twelfth, I will discuss with you the business proposition you made—"

"I have the money, Mr. Fernand," Stavros lied. He knew his man well.

"Never mind, never mind; we'll talk." Mr. Fernand smiled conspiratorially. "I was proud that you insulted my old friend Alan Aylesworth," he said. "He was furious with you!" He laughed as he started for the door.

Stavros hurried after him, opened the door, and as the old man passed through, bowed. Like Kyushiro.

JANUARY 1919

When Freddie Farrow happened upon the brothers on the train to Southampton that clear, cold Saturday morning the day before the wedding, Stavros was gratified to see him marvel. The Anatolian was dressed to outshine Mr. Fernand: the same striped ambassadorial trousers under a black box coat, a stiff white collar attached to a shirt of blue pin-striped broadcloth, a bow tie of blue polka dots. The difference was that Mr. Fernand's clothes, despite the most conscientious attention of the best fitter on London's Cork Street, hung from his chicken breast with all the verve of old rags, while Stavros, on this occasion, looked like a model advertising a gentlemen's tailor.

It wasn't simply that Stavros had arrived at those solid proportions some men develop in their middle years. Confidence did it, the confidence with which Stavros carried himself that day. And there was a reason for this aplomb. In Stavros's right trousers pocket there was a bulge, not quite hidden, made by a bankroll of tens, twenties, fifties, as well as, in its crisp green heart, four five-hundred-dollar federal notes.

Poker! In the days since Stavros had given his sixty percent interest in the Anatolian Carpet Company to his brothers, he had enjoyed a great run of fool's luck. No longer working by day, he'd improved his nights by becoming a regular at certain midtown high-stake poker tables. There he'd made himself a legend.

Not an accident, this. For many months, Stavros had cultivated a character: the joker of the poker deck, the fifty-third card, a fool so foolish that everyone forgave him for taking their money. "Flat Tire Joe" he was dubbed; it was a nickname he gladly tolerated. This dandy who was fate's patsy became known for his stories about himself in which he always appeared as the loser, the victim, and most frequently of all, the cuckold. It was a most successful psychological tactic, one he reinforced for the first

half hour of each night's sport by so overplaying mediocre hands, continuing to bet when he should have thrown down his cards, that he lost and
lost and lost. But as the night progressed, as the tobacco smoke thickened
and the attention of the other players lost its edge, the pots got larger, and
while Stavros continued to make a fool of himself with his clowning, he
raked in bigger and bigger winnings. The losers would take home stories
of this miserable fool, rejected by his family, ridiculed by his friends,
deceived by every woman he courted, a legendary loser at poker—except,
so it had happened, at that table late that night. Yes, everybody had a good
time playing poker with "Flat Tire Joe" and everybody lost.

Stavros was making much more money than he ever had by respectable
employment. And money was his tonic. He enjoyed the illusion most
gamblers do at one time or another: that their run of good fortune would
go on and on. He credited not luck but his new independence: no burden
of relatives, no sweetheart to bedevil him, no boss to serve; instead an
attitude toward the rest of the race that was free of responsibility, servitude,
or sympathy. About him now there was a continuous, desperate gaiety.
His dream of a commercial empire in Anatolia was no nearer to fulfillment,
but to judge by his behavior, his optimism had grown—not diminished.
People, apart from his poker crowd, began to find him arrogant. This
pleased Stavros. After all, his period of obliging Mr. Fernand and Mr.
Aylesworth had yielded him nothing but shame and humiliation. "Keep
the flag of your hopes flying," he'd say to himself. "And never fall on your
knees before anybody again." When you crawled you got nothing. Kismet
doesn't come to the humble man. Now let them complain you're too much
a rooster. Remember what offends people is what's keeping your soul alive.

Michaelis was his life's companion, and precisely because of his air of
needing no favors from anyone (he commanded his audiences to contribute to the cause; he did not beg). They'd moved into a modest suite in a
lower west side hotel where, since it was frequented by vaudevillians, the
rates were reasonable. The administration of this hotel, accustomed to
oddities, couldn't make these brothers out—if they were indeed brothers.
One was affluent; he was loose with his money. The other appeared to be
a common seaman, unemployed because he'd lost his left arm. This man
was silent and threatening. His appearance at the hotel was irregular
(Michaelis traveled here and there, speaking for the cause). Neither man
seemed to have an interest in a member of the other sex that lasted longer
than an hour.

Now, having agreed to attend the wedding of the young woman who
had once been his sweetheart, Stavros carried with him, by the inspiration
of that tonic money, not only confidence but a zany boldness. He'd
brought Michaelis along, an uninvited guest, to help unroll and display the
silk Keshan, Stavros's wedding present.

To sustain his high spirits, the pleasure he now found in everything, to insure that the *kef* didn't let up, Stavros had a bottle of ouzo uncorked on the woven straw seat opposite.

Suddenly Stavros jumped to his feet. "Michaelis, up, quick! We have young lady present here."

He made a game of inspecting the young woman with Freddie. He'd seen Maud before, of course, twice, but was looking at her now as if for the first time. Her features were so traditionally Anglo-Saxon that they were commonplace—the straight nose, neither short nor long, jutting over lips too tight for ecstasy; eyes as blue as the heart of an iceberg and clean of complications. Those eyes would be cool in any circumstance, Stavros judged. The only human thing he found about the creature was her irregular skin.

Stavros flashed the smile of a man enchanted. "Who is this goddess, Freddie?" he said.

"Meet my fiancée," Freddie said.

"We've met," Maud said.

"Where's fiancée?" Stavros made a pretense of looking around.

"There. Her! Meet Maud Erhenbrecher."

"Freddie, we've met," Maud said.

"This one? Impossible. She's too good for you, Freddie. Come, Michaelis, God's sake, we have Freddie's fiancée here. Stand up! Give your place. Quick! Really, this is your fiancée, Freddie? What a surprise! Congratulations! Both sides. Wishing you many children, all boys."

"This, dear," Freddie said, "is the man I've mentioned so often, Stavros Topouzoglou."

"Freddie, don't you remember? We've met," Maud repeated. "He has, as I recall, two names. What's the easier one?"

"Joe Arness," Stavros said. He inspected Maud again, shaking his head in wonder. "What can I do?" he said. "Other men get beautiful woman, I get nothing."

"He's making fun of me," Maud said to Freddie.

"Had two drinks," Michaelis said. "Maybe three. So, foolish talk."

"Absolutely not," Stavros said. "Sincerely yours." He yawned.

"Maud was Althea's roommate at Vassar," Freddie said.

"Well, then! Well, then!" Stavros grabbed a handful of newspaper and vigorously scrubbed the place next to the window where Michaelis had been sitting. "My apologies," he said, "for Long Island Rail Road. Damn train dirty. Here, young lady, Miss Maud, take this seat. You like ouzo, few drops? Give some color your cheeks; best medicine for that. Here. Sit. Don't worry, now clean. Sit."

Maud sat and thanked him.

"It's so nice running into you like this," Freddie said. "It's an occasion for friendship, isn't it? A wedding, I mean." He turned to his fiancée. "Stavros has been sort of mad at me—off and on—for five years," he said.

"Yes, true," Stavros said. "But angry after five years, foolishness. I am closing old books today, Freddie. New times coming!"

"Then you have talked to Mr. Fernand?" Freddie said. "About us?"

"Many times. Not recently," Stavros said. "Now, Miss Maud, dear young lady, I want introduce you my brother Michaelis. He gave his arm for you in the war."

"How terrible," Maud said. "I'm sorry."

"Me too," Michaelis said.

"Go 'head," Stavros said, "shake his other hand. It's O.K. That's it, that's it."

Maud gave her hand. "Very pleased to meet you indeed, Michaelis," she said. "Is that right? Michaelis? Michael in Greek?"

Michaelis bobbed his head, turned away.

Now a silence as Stavros had another drink, then still another, smiling like a demon in between. They were all reluctant, it seemed, to watch him as he drank. Maud looked out the window. "We're still in the suburbs," she said.

Suddenly Stavros was snoring, the uncorked bottle in his lap, clutched by the throat.

"That was quick," Maud said.

"Don't be mad at him," Freddie whispered.

"I'm not mad," Maud said. "He looks so unhappy I want to put my arms around him."

Stavros popped his eyes open. It appeared he had not been asleep. He winked at Freddie's fiancée. "You think I'm unhappy man? Eh? You like that, unhappy man, maybe? Some women like that. Put their arms around and so forth." He leaned close to her.

Freddie rescued Maud. "Stavros," he said, "Mr. Fernand has had this idea for us ever since Mr. Ara died. He must have told you something about it. Of course! That's why you're coming out today."

"I'm coming to celebrate *gamo,* Greek word for wedding. Also word for the business—excuse me, young lady."

"I'm sure Mr. Fernand spoke to you, Stavros." Freddie turned to Maud. "These Orientals are so full of guile," he said. "You can't tell what's true from what's false."

"That's right, young lady. Don't trust man from Orient! You got right fellow there."

"Come on, Joe, cut out all that Greek crap for a moment and tell me what you thought of Mr. Fernand's proposal."

Stavros might have been offended; if he was, there was no way Freddie could have known. Stavros began to hum and sing a lively dance tune, snapping his fingers, and soon he was on his feet in the aisle, where he did some steps, looking seductively at Maud as he turned. Suddenly, staggering slightly with the train's movement, he leaped into the air, slapping his heel with his palm.

"Sit down, Stavros," Michaelis said, in Turkish.

"O.K., boss," Stavros said, in English. "Much oblige for advice."

"I see you don't like this pimp." Michaelis gestured toward Freddie with his head. He spoke again in Turkish.

Stavros replied in the same tongue. "Where we're going, I like nobody."

"Then why we going?"

"Closing all books today. *Pezeven!*"

"What language is that?" Maud asked. "Greek?"

"Turkish," Stavros said. "Language of intrigue and mystery."

"Well, we don't understand it, Freddie and I, so it does seem rather rude that you choose to—"

"Maud is very outspoken," Freddie interrupted. "Just like Althea. Remember, Maud was Althea's roommate at Vassar."

"How could I forget?" Stavros said. "You told me."

He turned his face to the aisle, his back to them, and this time he did sleep; he slept through the rest of the journey. When they arrived at Southampton, he was, miraculously, dead sober.

"What the hell is Topouzoglou bringing out here?" Mr. Fernand said to Paul, who, wrapped in a beach blanket, was sunning himself in a deck chair on the glass-enclosed terrace of Mrs. Morgan Perry's mother's summer place. "Looks like a sailor from a ferryboat. What's he carrying?" The old man reached through the overcoat he was wearing for his distance glasses.

Paul opened his eyes, said, "Who knows?" closed his eyes, and said, "When do they serve lunch here? All I had, all morning, was a cup of inferior coffee."

The house, a classic white structure, stood at the far end of a long potato field. It had six fluted columns in front, a frozen flower garden behind, and was embraced everywhere by fine old evergreens. It was, as everyone was to say all afternoon, the perfect setting for the wedding of the daughter of a fine old family to a very handsome, very wealthy young merchant prince (who had never worked a day in his life).

Althea was waiting for Stavros at the front door. He'd forgotten how beautiful she was.

Freddie and Maud had arrived earlier in another taxi. Stavros could hear Freddie somewhere in the house, telling Maud its history. (Freddie had been there often and heard the old tales many times.) What had delayed Stavros and Michaelis was finding a taxi willing to carry the rolled-up nine-by-twelve Keshan.

Althea and Stavros shook hands. She was wearing a heavy Irish shawl. "This house was built for July and August only," she said. "Now get ready for a surprise. Are you ready for a surprise?"

Michaelis, carrying the Keshan over his shoulder, pushed the front door open.

"My present," Stavros said. "Happy birthday, I mean, wedding. Is that how you say it? Open her up, Michaelis."

Michaelis dropped the roll of carpet and took out his knife to cut the cords that bound it.

"What big surprise?" Stavros said.

"You're going to like him, that's the big surprise."

"Who?"

"My fiancé. You'll like him."

Mrs. Morgan Perry rushed in and saw Michaelis. "What are you doing?" she demanded. "Deliveries are in the back. Don't open that here."

Althea burst out laughing. "Mother, this is Stavros's brother Michaelis," she said. "Really Mother, you're such a goop! And that is a wedding present Stavros brought me. Now come on, give the boys a pretty smile and say hello."

"Hello," Norma Perry said. "And don't you ever look natty, Mr.— Stavros! What did you do—clean up in a crap game?"

"Stavros, where's your bag?" Althea said.

A servant, dressed in a summer-weight dress under a bulky home-knit sweater, had come up and was whispering to Mrs. Perry.

"We go back tonight," Stavros said. "I come to bring the carpet. Only."

"Like fun you're going back tonight. We have a room for you that was once occupied by Black Jack Pershing and a woman he claimed was his wife."

"Lunch is almost ready," Mrs. Perry announced. "At last."

Michaelis, holding the edge of the rolled-up carpet with one foot, kicked it open with the other.

"Damn it, don't do that! Look at that dust," Mrs. Perry said. "We just cleaned up here. You men! I give up. Let the dust settle, don't swish it around. I must say it's beautiful, the rug. Now, I want you boys to move the electric heaters for me from the parlor to the dining room. Come, come!" She slapped her hands together and stalked out of the room, her satin underskirt swishing.

In the parlor were four round electric heaters, and in the radiance of one of them Morgan Perry slumped, fast asleep, in his favorite armchair.

"Get up, Morgan," Mrs. Perry said. "Come, come, dear."

"What's for lunch?" the sick man said. He struggled to his feet, then flopped back into the chair.

"I have lobster," Mrs. Perry said. "Newburg."

"I can't eat lobster. I'll stay where I am."

"I'll order milk toast for you. Come, darling. Everyone will miss you if you're not at the table."

"They better get used to it," he said.

Mrs. Perry pulled him to his feet. "Drinks first," she said. "In the farmhouse."

The original dwelling—a farmhouse, dusty white—was dwarfed by the mansion which the late Mr. Murray, Mrs. Perry's father, had caused to be built in front of it, for the most part concealing it. The farmhouse, attached to the rear of Mr. Murray's showplace by a short passageway that opened on to the bottom floor of the old place had had every partition removed. At the far end of this enlarged space there was a fireplace from a more utilitarian day—it had pot hooks and a compartment for baking bread.

To satisfy his eye as well as an early dream, Mr. Murray had had another structure built, a facsimile of the old farmhouse, placed symmetrically behind the other side of the main building. In this twin he'd set up —a seventieth-birthday present to himself—a complete shop for working wood. His collection of tools was encyclopedic; he'd exhausted every catalogue. Here he'd planned to pass his last years, but an arrest of the heart left this dream unfulfilled. No one entered Mr. Murray's workshop now.

The single low-ceilinged chamber of the old farmhouse, dominated by a fire devouring four huge logs, was the only really warm room available to the wedding party on this winter's day. The heating system of the "mansion," even up where it was, full blast, was an expensive failure. The old lady, that January afternoon, sat in front of, almost inside, the old fireplace. At her feet, dozing, was her husband's poodle bitch, a favorite who'd outlived her master.

From ingredients on a cart wheeled before her by a matronly servant, Mrs. Murray had mixed a pitcher of Manhattan cocktails of a strength legendary in her circle. Although she filled the air with chatter, Mrs. Murray knew that she bored the members of her family, so she was grateful for the Topouzoglou brothers. A woman who'd crossed the Atlantic with her late husband every summer for three decades, she had a fondness for sailors, and so for Michaelis in his dark blue crew sweater. "Oh, yes, yes," she said to him, sipping from her Manhattan, "Mr. Murray and I were on the passenger list of the *Berengaria*'s maiden vogage." Sip. "You knew the *Berengaria*, of course."

"No," Michaelis said.

"Of course you did. Because of Mr. Murray's prominence, we were begged, literally begged, by the captain to sit at his table." She put away more of her drink. "But he was a retiring sort and preferred—"

"What is this drink?" Michaelis said.

"Would you prefer some other refreshment?" Mrs. Murray asked. "Perhaps you don't like Manhattans. I could make you a—"

"That's good drink, *vlax,* " Stavros said, laughing fondly at his brother. "Drink it."

This conversation was the only one going. As he drank his cocktail, Stavros noticed that Althea, sitting next to her fiancé and leaning against him, was not talking to her future father-in-law. Several times she hadn't responded to his reach for conversation, even with a turn of her head.

"What kind party this?" Stavros said at last. "Nobody talking?"

"Don't you find it a relief," Mr. Fernand said, "to be so comfortable with a set of people that you don't feel required to make conversation?"

"That's situation here?" Stavros wanted to know.

"Mr. Murray used to say, 'Never waste a sentence when a word will do it.' " The widow finished her drink. "Damn him!" she said.

The matronly servant had reentered the room, and after a nervous clearing of her throat and a pit-pat-pat of her feet, bent to whisper something in Mrs. Murray's ear.

"You don't have to put your tongue in my ear, Agnes," Mrs. Murray said. "I can hear you perfectly. Now, what were you saying?"

"Lunch is ready, Mother," Mrs. Perry said. "I believe."

"Well, I believe I will have a bit more of this holy spirit," Mrs. Murray said.

"Mother, lobster Newburg is not good cold," Mrs. Perry said.

"But I haven't finished expressing my thought, dear." The old lady allowed some irritation to show. "Shouldn't I, at seventy-seven, be allowed that deference? Cultivate patience, child; that was always your shortcoming. Rushing from one place to another, not enjoying the passing view. Ah!" She'd poured the last drops from the Manhattan pitcher into her glass. "All good things come to an end. Now, what was I saying? You see, you've got me all confused."

"Your husband," Stavros said, "he don't talk."

"Thank you, dear friend," Mrs. Murray said. "Well, that was all very well for him, that damned threatening silence, but I—for instance—I never found out in the almost fifty years of our marriage whether he was satisfied with his life. Or not. Or with me. Or not. At this very moment, I—"

"If he didn't complain," Mr. Fernand said, "he had no complaints."

"That's not true," the old lady said. "You know better than that, Fernand. Why do you say that?"

"It's my experience."

"But you're in error. Many miserable people don't complain. I knew I bored my husband from time to time." Mrs. Murray turned to Stavros and Michaelis again. "To tell the truth, most of the time. Perhaps it was I who talked him into his silence. That possibility must be considered. But I was unhappy and for that reason I—"

"What's the difference now?" Michaelis said.

"The difference is that some people in my own family blame me for his early departure from this life," the widow said.

"Mother!" Mrs. Perry said.

"Yes, let's leave well enough alone," Mrs. Murray agreed. "This is a day for happiness."

"How he made all this money?" Stavros waved his hand.

"Now, there is an example!" Mrs. Murray said. "He never told me. Even that! Not even that! He was secretive and silent, more so every year—"

"Mother," Mrs. Perry said, "do I have to remind you that Althea is getting married tomorrow?"

"Silver," Mr. Fernand said. "Silver mines and shares."

"Who we talking about now?" Michaelis said.

"Her husband, *vlax*," Stavros said, laughing at his brother.

"Where is he?"

"Dead. He died."

"So what's the difference?" Michaelis said. "Man's gone. Forget him."

"Did you intend that to be a rude remark?" Mrs. Perry appraised Michaelis. "I think that was a very rude remark."

"I think he intended it that way too," Stavros said. "What you say, Michaelis?"

"Old lady talk too much," Michaelis said.

Mrs. Murray rose to her own defense. "I was brought up to believe, young man, that it's the duty of the hostess, when no one else speaks, to keep some sort of social intercourse going."

She had to do it during luncheon too.

A table for eight had been set in the dining room of the big house. Freddie and Maud had decided to skip lunch.

At the corners of the chilly room, four round electrical heaters had been placed, their coils glowing like the stamen of tropical flowers.

Althea, seated next to Mr. Fernand, had managed to turn her chair so that her back was almost to him. Stavros noticed again that not a word passed between them.

"Why you not speaking to anybody today, Mr. Fernand?" Stavros asked. "Most of all, to Althea."

"She and I understand each other very well without a lot of chatter," Mr. Fernand answered.

"Speak for yourself," Althea said.

The silence grew heavier and, except for Mrs. Murray, complete. "I was very tense before my wedding too," she said. "It's a time for doubts. I suddenly doubted that my husband's people approved of me. These doubts proved to be justified. But by then it was too late."

"Mother," Mrs. Morgan Perry said, "shut up."

"What are you two whispering about?" Mrs. Murray turned on Paul. "Since I've got old, everyone seems to be whispering."

"I was telling Michaelis about the party some friends are throwing tonight. Who Gets What's Left they call it. Dividing the leftovers."

"Leftovers?" Mrs. Murray said.

"The young ladies of my past," Paul said, "now without solace."

"Where is this event going to take place?" Mrs. Perry asked.

"Oyster Bay. Three different houses—guests will move from one to another. The plan is for three nights and two days."

"Too bad you'll miss it," Stavros said.

"All my old girl friends will be there," Paul said. "Poor darlings."

"A goodly crowd, I'm sure," Mrs. Perry said.

"You can be sure," Althea said.

Paul chuckled. "They're coming from as far as Atlanta, Georgia!"

"Carpetbaggers," Althea said.

Paul chuckled. "Hate to miss it," he said.

"Why don't you go to Oyster Bay?" Althea said. "Last breakout."

"Certain sacrifices have to be made," Paul said.

"No one give party like that, my leftovers," Stavros said.

"The houses of prostitution would have to suspend activities," Althea said.

"Althea!" Mrs. Perry said. "Shame on you."

The maid, now serving as a waitress, had come in with a message for Mr. Fernand, and she leaned over to whisper something in his ear.

"Don't get too close when you whisper, Agnes," Mrs. Murray said. "What is it this time?"

"There's a Mr. William Wildberg at the door. He claims he has an appointment with Mr. Sarrafian—yes, you, sir."

"He's exactly on time," Mr. Fernand said, taking a gold watch out of his vest pocket and reading it.

"Well, damn it, finish your lobster first," the old lady said. "What in the world can be as important as enjoying a lobster? You know"— she'd turned to Michaelis—"these creatures are nothing but scavengers of the sea bottom, yet they have a taste as fresh and as clean as— Well, there's a lesson there somewhere, don't you think? Sit down, Fernand!"

"I'll be right back," Mr. Fernand said, leaving the room.

"Another damned fool," Mrs. Murray said.

Stavros noticed that Althea was trying to get her fiancé's attention, but he was telling Michaelis about a cruise he'd made years ago among the Greek Islands. She pushed her plate away.

"Finish your dinner, girl," Mrs. Murray said. "My God, no one is eating my lobster Newburg. Never again!"

Morgan Perry had fallen asleep at the table. Suddenly everyone noticed it. When Althea went to him and kissed his forehead, he woke with a guilty smile.

Mr. Fernand reappeared in the doorway, ushering in a large, bulky man. "This is Mr. William Wildberg," he said. "Dear Mrs. Murray, may I take him into your parlor and chat with him for a few minutes?" He waved a large envelope in the direction of Norma Perry, nodded and smiled.

"No," Mrs. Murray said.

"Some matters won't wait even for lobster Newburg," Mr. Fernand said. "You'll simply have to excuse me."

"I'll have to do nothing of the sort," she said. "You come right back here and finish this lunch. I had to chase all over the South Fork of Long Island for these damned lobsters."

"I really must read this over now," Mr. Fernand said.

"Well, this is the last time you'll ever be invited to my table," Mrs. Murray said. "And Freddie and his fiancée, not even troubling to come down! I'm disgusted with you all."

"Freddie said he's dieting," Mrs. Perry said.

"I think something else," Mr. Fernand said, attempting a joke to ease his departure. "Haven't you noticed, Mrs. Murray," his voice dropped to a whisper, "that the plainer a woman is, the more eager she is to engage in the games of Eros?"

"Fernand, I consider that a most disagreeable remark," Mrs. Murray said.

"Billy, come to my rescue," the old Armenian said to Wildberg. "Beg her indulgence."

Mr. Wildberg hunched his shoulders like a boxer, stroked his hair to cover a balding place, and murmured, "Excuse me, Mrs. Murray. Please." Then he added, "Hello, Mrs. Perry."

The men disappeared. A plate of cheeses was brought in, and coffee, with a tart of almond paste. Only the Topouzoglous enjoyed these special treats. It was twenty minutes before Mr. Fernand returned—an interval filled by a long harangue from Mrs. Murray excoriating the legal profession. "They're all scoundrels," she said in summation. "For the most simple reason that by the payment of a fee, you can buy their allegiance. That was the one subject on which Mr. Murray and I agreed. He despised lawyers as much as I do. I've seen this man Wildberg before. In a zoo. Did you see the lupine smile he bestowed on us as he left? He has the teeth of a wolf. Did you see his eyes gleaming? They're adapted to seeing in the twilight of a courtroom—oh here they come. Let's see if we can extract an explanation!"

Mr. Fernand led Mr. Wildberg back through the door.

"Well, gentlemen," Mrs. Murray said, "what heinous legal crimes have you been plotting? What are you about to do, Fernand, to mar the day before the day when your only son is lucky enough to be marrying my granddaughter? Well, Wildberg, speak. Stop trying to cover your bald spot with that splotch of hair you have left; it won't work. Come, let's hear your excuses."

"Isn't she a dear old lady, Billy?" Mr. Fernand said, laughing. "Especially when she tries not to be."

"Do you want me to wait?" Wildberg asked Mr. Fernand.

"If you would," Mr. Fernand said. "I suppose there may be some small changes. Sit where we were, in the parlor, and turn an electric heater directly on you. You'll find a book on the table which contains a catalogue of the sharks to be found off the south shore of Long Island. It will interest you."

When the lawyer had left the room, Mr. Fernand approached Mrs. Perry. "Here," he said, handing her the legal envelope. "This is really the best we can do." And as he sat down next to Althea, he said, "You might glance at it too, Althea dear."

Althea threw down her napkin and pushed her chair away.

"Oh my God," Mrs. Murray said. "Mutiny! Jailbreak! Panic in the teeth of a hurricane! I can't endure it further." Coughing, she prepared to get up from the table.

"Oh, Mother," Mrs. Perry said, "you're really making a mountain out of an anthill."

"I've had enough of you all. I'm going back by my fire. Agnes, you can take your orders from Mrs. Perry now." She tapped Michaelis with her cane. "You! Young man! You come with me."

Paul and Michaelis had been discussing the harbors of various islands in the Dodecanese chain, but the old lady was not to be denied. She led Michaelis off.

"Come, Stavros, I'll show you your room," Althea said, getting up.

"I'm leaving," Stavros said. "I came here to bring your present. Only!"

"You're not leaving. Not by any trick in your bag will you get away from me today."

Stavros saw anxiety in her eyes. Then he heard Mr. Fernand saying to Mrs. Perry, "I'll sit at your side while you read it. Just in case you have questions. Here!" He opened the envelope, unfolded a bound sheaf of pages, and put them into her hands. "You'd better say a word to Althea," he said.

Stavros got up and walked to Althea's side.

"Oh, yes," Mrs. Perry said. "Althea dear, I'll want to have a talk with you. So don't go running off somewhere." Althea hadn't moved. She stood squarely in the doorway, looking defiantly at her mother. "Althea," Mrs. Perry said. "Did you hear what I said? Paul! Paul, talk to her."

Paul turned and looked at his bride.

"Paul, when are you going to tell your father," Althea said, "that I won't, and that you don't want me to?"

"I'm going to talk to him," Paul said.

"When?"

"I want to speak to Freddie and Stavros first," Mr. Fernand said. "In the billiard room, in about twenty minutes?" He smiled at Stavros, then turned back to Mrs. Perry.

The bedroom to which Althea led Stavros was colder than any of the rooms he'd been in already. "Cold as William Wildberg's heart," Althea said. "But there are plenty of blankets. With Daddy's health what it is, we gave him the room directly above the furnace, the only warm room in this house."

"It's all right, I'm not going to stay."

"Yes, you are. Steal a heater tonight on your way upstairs, before Mr. Fernand gets them all. I'll steal one for you. Do you mind if I sit here for a moment? I don't require conversation; I just want to rest out of range."

"Sure, sit down." She did, next to him on the bed. "You're looking good," he said.

"Oh, I'm fine. Went to my doctor yesterday. He says everything's working again, as it should."

Still it seemed to Stavros that she was on the verge of a fit of tears. He could see her straining to control herself. "What's the matter with you?" he said.

"Let's not talk about it," she said. "Please."

"All right. No more questions."

"It simply turned out to be a very complicated business."

"Anything I can do? Like break someone's arm?"

"You can do this. Tell me you like Paul. If you do."

"He's all right."

"Well, moderate your enthusiasm, friend."

"I'm not going to marry him, so I don't have to—"

"Well, I am. But they are making it difficult."

"Who are?"

"You said you wouldn't ask any questions."

"Knock my teeth out if I talk again."

"I just want to sit here. Can you, for old time's sake and in a brotherly way, put your arm around me?"

"Why not?"

He moved toward her, but just then Mrs. Perry entered the room, without knocking. In her hand were the Fernand Sarrafian papers.

"Althea," she said. "Now I must talk to you. I want you to go with me to where your father is. He has most of the electric heaters in a circle around him and it's the one warm place except for the other house, where my uncontrollable old mother is. So come."

Then she turned to Stavros, as if she hadn't seen him until this moment. "Fernand asked whether you would please come to the billiard room; he wants to talk to you. I don't know whether you realize it, but he is extremely fond of you. In other words, you're a lucky man. Now come, pay respect to the aged. Freddie is already there with him." Stavros didn't move. "Are you going?" Mrs. Perry asked.

"Maybe, maybe not. I feel sleepy. Ouzo on the train, old lady Manhattans, wine for the lobsters . . . What's he want talk about?"

"That's for you to find out. By the way, your brother says he wants to go back to the city. If he does and you do, there's a train in about an hour—"

Althea exploded. "Mother, goddamn you. You yourself invited this man to the wedding tomorrow. He is a close friend, whether or not you like it. I loved him once and I still like him. *He* never asked me to do anything disgraceful, and—"

"I have my own ideas about that," Mrs. Perry said.

"And I want you to ask him to stay overnight. I want you to beg him if necessary, I want you to overcome whatever resistance he may put up; I want you to make him believe that he will be doing you a favor if he stays. Because I warn you, I am close to walking out on this whole thing. I can't take any more of it—believe me, I can't, and I won't. So now, damn it, you'd better ask Stavros in your best Miss Finch manner, say please, say you'll be honored, because if you don't I will get Paul and I'll push him into his car and we'll run off together and you won't get a cent. I asked him to do that, and we were just about to, because he is just as disgusted with this mess as I am. But we were what you and Mr. Fernand are not—we were considerate of other people's feelings—so we—"

"Oh, that's enough," Mrs. Perry said. She turned to Stavros. "You're welcome to stay here if you choose, Mr.— I've never been able to pronounce your name."

"Jesus! Is that the best you can do?" Althea said.

"Don't worry," Stavros said, "I stay tonight."

Mr. Fernand, it turned out, was a brilliant billiards player. When he saw Stavros enter the room, he said, "I'm taking money from this all-American boy." He smiled fondly at Freddie.

"He's already got twenty of my dollars," Freddie said.

"You want to play?" Mr. Fernand said. "I take your money too."

"I don't play," Stavros said. "The mother here, she said you want talk to me, so let's talk."

"There's nothing to billiards. You poke this white ball with the point of this stick in such a way that it will hit the other two, first one, then the other. See? You keep that up—click click, click click—a game of skill for gentlemen. Come try it."

"What's the subject of this conversation you want?"

"You won't mind, I hope, if I continue to play with Freddie as we talk?"

Stavros shrugged. "It's cold here," he said.

"I've become used to it. Now, everything important in life is simple. Ten for you, ten for Freddie—percent, that is. Eighty for the original owners, my dear brother's family, Oscar, me. You and Freddie will be partners in administration. I will retire to Europe now the war is finished. The name of the firm remains Sarrafian Brothers, in honor of my reverend brother and me. Also, it's good for business—a name recognized everywhere. That is my proposal."

"Like you say, everything important in life simple," Stavros said. "No."

"It's what you asked for."

"I change my mind."

"You mean no?" Mr. Fernand asked.

"That's what I told you he'd say," Freddie said to Mr. Fernand.

Mr. Fernand made a run of three. Then he missed.

"So tell me," he said, "Stavros-Joe, how much more you want."

"I don't want anything from you," Stavros said.

"It's me, it's because of me," Freddie said. "He doesn't want to be partners with me."

From above they could hear Mrs. Perry's voice raised in anger, and even louder, Althea's, responding.

"Is it because of Freddie?" Mr. Fernand said.

"I'm satisfied with my own company," Stavros said.

"But that is nothing, your company; it grosses maybe hundred fifty thousand a year. It's all right for your brothers—they are ordinary men—but you . . . So it is Freddie?"

"I don't want to make partners with anybody," Stavros said.

They could hear the voices of mother and daughter screaming at each other.

"But if you did go into partnership . . ." Freddie said.

"That's right," Stavros said. "Not with you."

"Why?" Mr. Fernand asked. "Think carefully."

"Because I once informed your brother Mr. Ara," Freddie said, "that Joe was stealing customers. Isn't that it?"

"I don't want partners," Stavros said. "But that too, what you did. Yes. Why you bothering me? I'm satisfied. I'm leaving for Anatolia next week. My plans are made. Ticket bought."

"How much you taking with you to buy over there?"

"That's my business."

"How much?"

"Fifty, sixty thousand."

"Sarrafian Brothers would provide half a million. In steps. You could become rich. Why do you prefer small-scale cheap stuff?"

Stavros smiled at him. "Because I am small-scale cheap-stuff guy."

"I don't believe it," Mr. Fernand said.

Directly above them, the sounds of the altercation between mother and daughter had reached a shrill climax.

"What the hell is going on up there?" Mr. Fernand said.

"Women!" Freddie said.

It was then that Stavros discovered Maud had been in the room all the time, sitting on the windowsill behind him. He hadn't noticed her until she said, "You know perfectly well what's going on up there, Mr. Sarrafian, and it isn't 'women,' Freddie. You know that Althea is right, she's right to be upset, so why do you say 'Women!' that way, Freddie, except to cater to him?"

"What are you so mad about?" Freddie said. "You know what I meant."

"Let's try the other room." Mr. Fernand put up his cue. "Come, Freddie," he said.

Stavros followed. He could read the disapproval on Mr. Fernand's face. "You're marrying a strong one there, Freddie my boy. Better stop her dead first chance, or else you'll have trouble." Then Mr. Fernand turned to Stavros and said, "I'll give you an hour to think it over, till supper. Go ahead, reflect carefully, and tell me how much more you want. Maybe I can do something for you. Use your brain on this one or you will regret it the rest of your life."

Which was the moment when Althea entered the room with the legal papers in her hand. She walked over to the corner, where William Wildberg was pretending to read, and threw the envelope into the crease of his open book.

"So you read it?" Mr. Fernand said. "See, it's not so bad, is it?"

"I didn't read it," she said.

Stavros could see the effort it cost Mr. Fernand to control his anger, "Would you like me to read it to you?" he said.

Althea, on her way out of the room, stopped, turned, and smiled at him. "You'd like that, wouldn't you?"

"Only in extremis," Mr. Fernand said. "Why don't you read it?"

At which Paul walked into the room, relaxed, still yawning from a nap.

"Because I talked to Paul about it and he said he is in agreement that I don't have to do such a degrading thing." She went to Paul and kissed him. "Didn't you, darling?" she said.

"Paul, I just want her to read it," Mr. Fernand said. "She has a notion of what it is and that notion is highly inaccurate." Then, remembering that Stavros was there, he said, "Would you excuse us, please?"

"Stay where you are," Althea said. "He's my friend—one of two I seem to have in the whole world. Anyway, I am not going to talk about it anymore."

"And I don't want to hear about it anymore," Paul said. His tone was imperious, and Stavros realized that what Althea had hinted at was true: the one person in the world Mr. Fernand feared was his son.

"I made this clear to you, Althea dear, a long time ago," Mr. Fernand said.

"You mentioned it, yes, perhaps twice. I didn't think you'd go on and on about it. Particularly because Paul doesn't insist, and if he doesn't, I don't see why I should."

"All I ask is that you read it. It's not what you think—"

Paul interrupted in the same imperious tone. "Read it, Althea! Take the damned thing, go into the other room, and read it! Then do what you want, I don't care."

"Really, dear Althea," the old man said, "it's getting very late in the day, and tomorrow—"

"*You* put it off and *you* delayed it!" Althea was wildly angry. "You acted as if it was a matter of no consequence, in your usual chatty way, dropping hints and smiling and shrugging it off, and now you've got me into a situation where soon it will be too late. It's your tactic, it's the way you work, I've watched you."

"Is that a way to talk to your father-in-law?" Mr. Fernand said, going to Althea and putting his arm around her. "I'm very hurt by your accusation, my dear. But I forgive you. Please remember that when I don't press, I'm trying to be gentle with you—"

"You were like hell being gentle—you were trying to get me in so deep that I couldn't back out."

Mr. Fernand turned and walked toward the door. There he encountered Mrs. Perry.

"Althea, I just called Mrs. Vaghi. She says she's made the changes you asked for in the dress—Althea! Wait till you see her in it, Paul; she's a vision! Heaven! Mrs. Vaghi wants to close up and go home, Althea, it's Saturday, and— Althea! are you listening?"

Althea turned on her mother like a cornered animal. "No," she said, "no."

Then Paul walked to where William Wildberg was sitting, picked up the marriage contract, strode back across the room, and thrust the envelope into Althea's hands.

"All he's asking is that you read it. He doesn't realize that it will make you madder at him, but that's his risk, one he's ready to take. Anyway, I don't want to hear any more about it. Read it, then say 'I've read it and I hate it,' and throw it away, tear it up, burn it, do whatever you want. This is the only thing I will ask of you—"

"And that's the only reason I'll do it," Althea said. "I will read it and then I'll tear it up and— Have you read it?"

"No! Then go get your dress. We're getting married tomorrow," Paul said, "whether or not, if yes, if no, if anything."

She kissed Paul, shook her head as if to say, "About time," kissed him again, and turned to her mother. "Now!" she said. "Where's Maud? I want her to come with me."

Mother and daughter left the room together.

"Come," Paul said to Stavros. "You promised me backgammon."

While they were playing their second game, which Stavros was winning as decisively as he'd won the first, Mr. Fernand came by and watched. He brought with him an electric heater which he put at his feet. "I want to go into town and see if I can find a few good Havanas," he said. "Paul, come."

"I'm playing backgammon, and you just want to get me off by myself. Well, it won't do you any good—and if you want to talk to me, do it here without interrupting my game. This whole thing is becoming more than I can take—"

"Shshsh," Mr. Fernand said.

"And I don't care who hears me."

Paul could see that his situation on the backgammon board was hopeless, and he said to Stavros, "That's twenty I owe you. Don't pay any attention to him." He pointed to his father. "One more, can we?"

"Why not?" Stavros said.

"Double or nothing?" Paul said.

"Why not?"

"Paul, do you remember," Mr. Fernand said, "a young woman with a sweet face that turned out to be exceptionally deceptive? I believe her name was Vivien, with an *e,* and she was all saintliness. She took me for a hundred thousand quid because you'd made some foolish promises which you didn't necessarily intend to keep."

"She was everywhere luscious," Paul said, "as well as having a very sweet face."

"I remember her face in a more venal mood," his father said. "Are you sure you want this man here to be a witness to all that I'm about to say?"

"No, I'm not sure. I wish you'd shut up about it. I've heard and heard about my drain on your finances and still I keep watching you get richer and richer. What's all your money for except to—? Damn, a one and two!"

"In time all that money will go to you. I'm only trying to protect what will very soon be all yours."

"Well, try less. I believe in today, Father dear; I don't even know if I'll still be here next week."

"Speaking of that," Mr. Fernand said, "do you perhaps recall Katherine—yet another saint? She was able to find some very hungry lawyers too —do you remember? I warned you about her, I saw the light in her eyes —they flashed the pound symbol and you said the same thing about her that you say now about dear Althea—that you are ready to kill yourself if you can't have her."

"Well," Paul said, pulling up his jacket sleeve and shirt cuff to display the scar tissue across his wrists. "Look."

Mr. Fernand didn't. "Four months later you told me you couldn't stand the sound of Katherine's voice, and that her body, when in heat, had an overpowering and not altogether pleasant odor."

"Listen, Father, Althea is the girl I want and I will marry her tomorrow whether she accedes to your pressures or not."

"Please don't threaten me, Paul. I don't threaten you, do I? Oh, I could. Billy Wildberg is over there pretending to read, and with his aid I can make some drastic alterations in my will and very quickly."

"I don't intend to live that long. I want Althea now. You never taught me any reasons for hoping to live— God, look; I've lost again. Oh, I'm sick of it!"

He stood up. "Give him forty dollars, Father," Paul said with a jerk of his head in Stavros's direction, and he left the room just as Althea, Maud, and Freddie came down the stairs.

Paul kissed Althea and took her aside.

"Perhaps we can have a game or two," Mr. Fernand said to Stavros. "I haven't played backgammon in years. Probably forgotten how. Let me see, where do these go? Here? Or there?"

Stavros showed him how to arrange the counters and let him throw the dice first. He threw a double six. Maud came and stood over Mr. Fernand to watch the game.

"Where's Paul?" Mr. Fernand asked her.

"He's talking to Althea. I'm sorry I burst out at you, Mr. Fernand, but I do think—"

"Mind your business next time, miss," Mr. Fernand said, his manner a lesson to Freddie who was standing in the doorway. "Don't mix in mine."

"Oh, Maud, will you please stop?" Freddie walked away.

"No." She turned to Stavros. "I told Freddie," she said, "that he simply ought to ask you directly and plainly for the truth. Mr. Sarrafian's offer means an awful lot to him. Why are you refusing it? What is it you want? More money? More percentage? I don't see why you keep Freddie in ignorance."

"It's easy. I don't want to be in Mr. Fernand's pocket, so I don't make partnership with someone who's already in Mr. Fernand's pocket."

"He told me what he did that you're so angry about," Maud went on. "I must tell you that he was absolutely right about that. You were being professionally dishonest, betraying the people who were paying your salary, and—well, damn it, you have no right to be angry at Freddie; he should be angry at you. But he isn't, he forgives you."

Mr. Fernand turned over the double-or-nothing die. Stavros didn't pick up his challenge; the old Armenian was too far ahead.

"You still here?" Stavros said to Maud. "Go away, will you? I can't concentrate with you here."

"I'm worried for Freddie."

"Let him talk for himself. What the hell, he lets damn woman talk for him?"

"That's not very gracious of you, that remark," Mr. Fernand said. He had Stavros boxed in.

"You are a boor; illiterate and vulgar and simply horrible," Maud said, and left the room.

It was too late for Stavros to do anything about this game. He wanted another. But just then Althea came in with her fiancé and said, "Paul and I will do the following: I will read Mr. Wildberg's masterpiece, although I warn you, if you think I'm unreasonable now, it's sure to make me really fume. Meantime I will get the dress, because Paul and I are going to get married no matter what. We're getting married tomorrow, and—"

"And I will ride into town with you"— Paul said—"and pretend that we're going for cigars."

"You owe me twenty dollars, I believe," Mr. Fernand said to Stavros as he rose to his feet.

A few minutes later, Stavros heard two cars drive off. He seemed to be alone in the house and it was quiet. Then Michaelis came in. "She's asleep," he said. "Mrs. — What's her name? Freddie tells me the old man made you big proposition and you refuse."

"To get me to work for him again," Stavros said, "he has to pay me much more. Also I think I will get more."

"I look these people over," Michaelis said, "and they are nothing. Where I was last few years, they don't last one week. I also think they know that. They know we are tough like iron and they need our strength. I think you can get anything you want from the old man."

"I don't want from him what he offers," Stavros said.

"Figure out what you want—how much money, what share profits, who's the boss, so on—then tell him, stick to it, and wait. That's my advice. He has to have you. That Freddie! He's like water, flows this way or that —how the land slopes. His woman runs him around like a poodle."

"The old man fools you. He looks soft, but—"

"He's afraid of his son; I saw that."

"Only one in the world. I don't know why."

"Another thing. He's afraid his son's sweetheart likes you. You were with her once, the old lady tells me."

"One year."

"Beautiful girl."

"That business finished."

"Old man's not so sure. That's why he keeps talking about money to her. That's his hold, he thinks."

"He doesn't understand her. Money is not important to her."

"Well, maybe. I'm not sure. Money, in this country, it's the pistol and the knife. They buy and sell people here. And Mr. Sarrafian senior, he knows the money-power business, how to talk money without saying the word. Right?"

"Right."

The matronly maid came in. "Mrs. Murray asked me to find you, Mr. Michael," she said. "She wants you to come back."

"That old lady loves me," Michaelis said. "Says she is going to leave money for me in her will." He laughed. "Same time, I went into the kitchen and all the servants complaining, no pay. Fish store man came in with bill for the lobsters. They don't have cash to pay. That's the kind of situation you have here. This family needs money and they hope to get it from you know where."

"What's your idea?"

"Since we are still in this country, play their game. Money's everything! Who gets the money? So . . ." He looked around.

The maid was waiting. "If you would," she said.

"Yes, I'm coming," Michaelis said, and went off with her, a new little strut to his walk.

Stavros was groggy from all the alcohol in his belly, so removing a heater from Morgan Perry, who was sleeping in the parlor, covered with a comforter, he went up to the chilly bedroom. The next thing he knew, he was being wakened out of a deep sleep by Althea, coming into his room with a swish of cloth. She was in her wedding dress.

"You look beautiful," Stavros said.

"How do you know?" she said. "You haven't opened your eyes yet. Come on, sit up and take a good look."

Stavros smiled at her.

"Like it?" she said.

"What it cost?" he asked.

"Now you're awake," she said, laughing.

"Who pays?" Stavros said.

"The father of the bride, traditionally," she said. "But every bit of the milk and honey that's flowing here today comes from the same source." Suddenly she deflated, flopping into a chair, seeming not to care whether she might be crushing her frills and her lace trim. "I can't make him out," she said, "that old man. I think I despise him, then suddenly I find myself laughing at his stories and admiring his experience and how intelligent he is on any subject. My God, he's so suave too, fascinating, and then, damn it, I like him. So when he puts his arm around me and kisses me, I kiss him back. Later I'm ashamed of myself. Now, this thing he wants me to sign—the very idea is insulting."

"Easy problem. Don't sign. Paul told me that—"

"But then the old man gets after him—"

"Mr. Fernand is afraid of Paul."

"In one way. Paul has tried to kill himself twice, and that must be a terrible thing over a father's head. Or a wife's. So the old man has to work subtly, gently. But in time he washes away Paul's strength. You see, the record is against Paul. He's been taken by women, they've made a fool of him. He's fucked and Daddy's paid. I mean, if it was some other girl and I was looking at it from the outside, I'd understand why Mr. Fernand's so anxious. Paul suddenly gets fed up, disappears, as it were, and the girls are left with—I've talked to one of them—nothing. Not even an explanation. So they get angry and take what they can get—a fat check. Which is why Mr. Fernand thinks of women as pirates in skirts. And there's my mother! I'm not surprised when I see how she fawns over him, because I know why she's so desperate. We're clean out of funds, our wonderful family. The hospital and doctor bills—and all the rest. I don't know whether you know this—how could you?—but mother is getting two hundred thousand dollars clear by that contract Mr. William Wildberg wrote. Clear!"

"What do you get?"

"I get Paul."

With a sudden show of gaiety, she jumped to her feet, swirled around, and looked flirtatiously at Stavros over one shoulder. "I love you," she said. "But not like I used to."

Norma Perry came in, again without knocking. "Oh, there you are. Now come. We've waked Father and he's as alert as he can be and is ready for you." She turned to Stavros. "You may come watch," she said. "That's going to be some expression on the old man's face when he sees this dress."

"He's not that much older than you, Mother," Althea said as they left the room, Stavros following them down the stairs.

Norma Perry had already reached the parlor when Paul, coming through the front door, with his father buzzing in his ear, saw Althea in her wedding dress.

"You're not supposed to have seen me in this," she said. Then there she was swaying, and twirling in place, as if for some reason she thought that her supreme attractiveness in the dress could settle all their differences. As she spun, she raised her arms to heaven, like a whirling dervish.

"Go ahead," Paul said to Mr. Fernand. "I don't want you here."

Althea told Stavros later that she'd believed for that one instant the same thing he did—that they'd had a quarrel, and that Paul was breaking with his father.

"I'll go see if I can induce dear Mrs. Murray to make up with me," Mr. Fernand said, chuckling. Both father and son had this habit of laughing to themselves as if at a joke no one else could understand or appreciate.

When he'd gone, Paul said to Althea, "Did you read those papers?" He said this in his most authoritarian voice.

Althea didn't answer.

"Did you?" he said.

"No," Althea said. Her face was flushed.

"You said you would," Paul said.

Althea didn't reply. She turned her face away and then looked up at Stavros, still on the stairs.

"Well, I did," Paul said. "Twice. Carefully. Did you know that your mother is making a quarter of a million dollars for herself out of that agreement?"

Althea nodded. "A little less," she said.

"Don't you think that's sufficient? How do you think that makes me feel?"

Althea shrugged.

"Try to see it from our side—from any side except your family's. Don't you think Father is right to make an effort to protect himself? What he's giving your mother is enough, don't you really think?"

"More than enough," Althea said.

"Well, then, sign it. I'm sick of it, I'm sick of the whole mess. Sign it, will you! I don't want to hear about it anymore."

"I won't sign it," she said.

"Yes, you will. Just sign it and get it over with."

Again Althea looked up at Stavros, who'd stopped halfway down the stairs.

"What do you want here?" Paul asked.

"I was coming to see expression on a certain old man's face when he saw his daughter in her wedding dress," Stavros said.

"Are you that eager to overhear our conversation," Paul asked, "that you sneak down like this?"

"I know your conversation," Stavros said. "I heard it all before."

"What's he mean by that?" Paul turned on Althea furiously. "Have you been talking to him about our situation?"

"No, you've been talking to him about—"

"Althea, will you please come into this room so we can talk together without an eavesdropper?"

If that was a hint, Stavros didn't take it. Althea needed a protector; he knew she wanted him there.

"He didn't intrude himself," she said. "I asked him to stand by me. I told him what I thought was happening. But I also told him that I thought you'd hold fast, that you were my friend."

Paul was more forceful than Stavros had suspected he could be. He took Althea by the arm and led her into the billiard room. Stavros sat on the steps, listening to the sound of voices and picking up a few words here and there.

"I want you to sign that thing . . ." Paul began, then nothing from her except, "No," then some further urging, near the peak of his anger, from him.

Mrs. Perry came into the hallway and sat on a chair near the entrance to the billiard room. She was doing the same thing Stavros was doing— listening in on a conversation that concerned her deeply. She hadn't seen him, but he watched her face; it showed the most murderous anger every time she heard her daughter say "No" or "I won't."

"He's an old man," Paul shouted, "and I've made life difficult for him in the past. I won't do it again. Anyway, what's it all about? Tell me, are you really marrying me for the money you might get out of it?"

Stavros thought he saw see Mrs. Perry nod.

"I'm not marrying you to be ashamed," Althea said.

Then Paul was screaming. "I'm sick of this, I'm sick of it." He was over the brink of hysteria. "I don't want to hear another word about it—"

"I will not sign any such agreement," Althea said.

"Then there won't be any marriage," Paul said.

"Don't threaten me, Paul!"

"I am. I am threatening you with the truth."

Mrs. Perry jumped to her feet and rushed into the room where the quarrel was taking place.

"Don't come in here," Paul said. "You're the cause of this!"

"Oh, Paul, I'm not, I'm not."

"Go on, get out," he said. "Yes or no, Althea?"

"I will not sign," Althea said. "I've told you so from the beginning."

"Then there won't be any marriage," he said.

"If that's the reason, it's O.K. with me."

"Are you sure? Think, now think!"

"Don't threaten me, Paul."

"Then it's finished!" he said.

He rushed out of the room and grabbed his overcoat from a chair near the door. Mrs. Perry ran after him. "Paul," she called, "Paul!" Her voice was like that of a child about to cry. He didn't even look at her. "Where are you going, Paul?"

"Oyster Bay," he said and was out the door.

Stavros walked down the stairs and Mrs. Perry turned and released her fury on him. "It's your fault—yours. You encouraged her!"

Stavros walked into the billiard room. At the far end, Althea had thrown herself into a deep armchair. She looked like a broken and abandoned doll.

"Aren't you cold?" Stavros said.

She didn't answer, and when Stavros started toward her, she said, "Don't!"

But Mrs. Perry didn't respect her pain. She ran to the chair at the end of the room and cried, "I knew it—I knew that sooner or later you'd find a way to wreck all my plans and hopes. It's the way you've been your whole life!"

Althea leaped from the chair and ran past Stavros and past Mr. Fernand, who was just coming into the room from the passageway to the old house. She spoke to none of them, but was out through the front door, and in a moment Stavros heard the family's old Marmon heating up, then rolling over the frozen gravel and out the gate of the Murray home.

Then there was Mr. Fernand, smiling at Stavros. "Oh, you!" he said. "I'm glad to see you. The old lady's asleep by the fire. A painting by Vermeer. Do you know his *Girl Asleep?* Of course not, you're a savage. Now perhaps we can complete our talk—over a game of billiards. Do you suppose?"

"No," Stavros said. "No suppose!"

As he went up the stairs, he could hear Mr. Fernand comforting Mrs. Perry. "She'll come to her senses," he said. "Don't worry, dear Mrs. Perry."

"She never has, thus far in her life," Mrs. Perry said.

"I'll talk to her. Let some time pass. Time works wonders."

Stavros fell on his bed. The ouzo and the wine and the Manhattans had got to him again. He barely had time to cover himself with an old gray beach blanket before he was asleep.

She lifted the blanket; that woke him. Her wedding dress made a sound like small dead leaves when she embraced him from behind. They used to sleep in this position, in the old days when she was his woman. There was a heavy chill in the room, but Althea's forehead was hot as with a fever. She was shuddering and trembling as she said, "You want it like that? I don't give a damn. Let it go. Forget it!" She wasn't speaking to him.

After a while she was quiet, so Stavros turned to her. "Don't look at me," she said, throwing up an arm to cover her face. "I'm a mess."

Why, Stavros wondered, do American women think they have to look perfect all the time? He liked her better as she was then, tired and sick and a little drunk. He liked her eyes, dark underneath. But she had her face down between his shoulder and his neck. Then she told him what had happened.

"When I got to Southampton center," she said, "there was his car parked about three feet off the curb in front of that bar all the boys go to —that long, dark bar. He was alone in the first booth with a couple of empties in front of him and a drink in his hand. I sat down across from him, but he wouldn't talk to me or even look at me. Suddenly he was a stranger. When he finally did speak, he actually sounded rather jolly, kidding the whole situation, relieved that it was over; it had been damn nonsense, he said, and a strain on his health. Now he felt better. As soon as I arrived he waved at the waiter, wanting to pay his bill and leave. I asked him where he was going and could I go with him. He looked straight at me for the first time and said, 'Go with me? Are you crazy?'

"He was looking at me stubbornly, the way a drunk does. 'We're lucky it happened,' he said. 'It was all a stupid mistake, wasn't it, the whole damned thing?' When I tried to tell him my side of it, I could see he wasn't listening. 'Sure, sure,' he said. 'I understand why you won't sign it. Your mother is getting two hundred thousand dollars and you're getting nothing. Simple!'

"Then he stood up and called for the waiter in a loud voice, but when he reached into his pocket to pay the bill, he said, 'I haven't any money with me. Can you lend me ten?' Then he had to laugh, it was so ridiculous. 'I don't imagine there are any pockets in that wedding dress, are there?' he said. 'Did you bring a bag?' 'No,' I said. 'I ran out of the house like this.'

"The waiter sent for the owner and we were left standing there. I had time to tell him again that it had nothing to do with my mother's two hundred thousand dollars, that it was a humiliating thing for me, that premarital agreement, and having that lawyer, Wildberg, in the house to get my signature the day before the ceremony. It was a crummy way to start life together; didn't he agree?

"'Humiliation works two ways,' he said. 'If you trusted me, you wouldn't care.' Then he said, 'I've noticed all my life that people behave differently when there's money involved.'

"By now I was ready to scream, because he wasn't believing anything I said. 'Listen to me, Paul, try and listen to me,' I said. But he stayed on his one track. 'Money changes everyone and it's behind everything,' he said. 'The first memory I have of my father, he was rattling coins in his pants pocket; it was a kind of music. All his life he's done that and people have danced to the music he made down there.'

"He turned to the owner, who'd come up to us—he was built like a toadstool—and said, 'I left my money in my father's pants pockets; will you trust me?' When the owner hesitated, Paul said, 'Of course not. You're right not to. You'd never see me again. Here!' He pulled out his cuff links and gave them to the man. 'They're gold,' he said, loud enough for every-one in the place to hear. 'Fourteen karat. You know what a karat is? Not the vegetable. Karat with a *k*. Here! Look!'

"As the owner was studying the links, Paul said to me, 'I've been here before, my darling, the same story with the same ending. That's why nothing you and your mother did surprised me. Don't get me wrong. I have great respect for money. When you don't have it, you have to wait while a little mutt like this little mutt here'—the owner didn't even look up—'who doesn't know what fourteen K means, frowns and squints, and you wait and hope he'll do you the big favor of accepting cuff links which are worth twenty times his bill.'

"The owner was taking his own good time, turning one link over, then the other, which gave me time to try to get through to Paul. 'Paul, I'm not like that,' I said. 'Don't you remember me? Althea? I'm not like that at all.' But he said, 'When it comes to fourteen K's, everyone's the same.' And when I said, 'Please, believe me, believe me,' he said, 'The only way I'll believe you is if you'll admit it.'

" 'Admit what?' I said.

"The reason you set out to get me is on account of money. When you'll admit that, I'll believe anything else you want.'

" 'But it's not,' I said.

" 'You'll never get anywhere in life until you learn to lie better,' he said. 'You're an inexpert liar, dear Althea. Just admit this much: I could have been any one of twenty men you know. I'll give you the list, if you want, and you can go after the next one down the line, because there's no reason why you should like me more than any of the others, is there really?'

"The owner said O.K., finally, as if he was doing us a big favor, so Paul turned to leave. 'I'll write you a very good reference, if you like,' he said to me, smiling that nasty Social Register smile of his. 'Be glad to.' 'Go fuck yourself,' I said. 'Won't have to,' he said, and started away.

"I was really angry by then, but I said, 'Where are you going?' 'To my farewell party,' he said. 'I'm going to get laid without feeling I'm the object of some mother's scheming. I really don't know how I let myself get into all this with you. I ask myself, was it sex?' He looked me up and down in this damned wedding dress—I hate it now. 'Is this what I was waiting for and dreaming about? Was it simple lust? I can't believe that; it's never meant that much to me. All that groping and clambering around in bed —it's nothing really, over in a minute. A few pushes, a grunt or two. A few whimpers from you—or whoever—then you're both asleep. When you wake up, it's as if nothing happened. It's certainly not worth ruining your whole life for, is it? Girls are interchangeable, you know. Aren't they? Tell me the truth—aren't men too? Interchangeable? They all have the same equipment and there isn't that much difference in how they do it. Is there?'

" 'They're not all the same,' I said. I was out to hurt him now. 'Some are better than others. A lot!'

" 'Well, I'll speak for myself,' he said. 'There are three or four completely interchangeable young ladies in Oyster Bay this evening who have overcome any illusions they may have had about me. Tomorrow morning, before I open my eyes, I won't even remember who it is in bed with me, and when I take a look I'll rest easy because I know she won't expect anything from me. I may stretch the member once again if she's lucky. I won't feel obligated or trapped or taken advantage of. I won't resent her. We'll even remain friends. You see, my romantic lady? I won't have to pretend and she won't, either. It was all something performed as we drifted down the stream of life, and come the dawn, it's over. No strain!' "

Althea stopped and sighed, then turned to Stavros, expecting sympathy.

"What got you so mad?" he asked. "Those few remarks, they made you so crazy?"

"Yes—well, no. More. I don't want to remember it all. 'All romantics are fools,' he said, 'but people like you'—that's me—'who pretend to be romantic for a reason, they're scoundrels. What you are is an adventurer, what they call a gold digger—and your mother is worse.' "

She looked at Stavros, outraged. "That's what he said—adventurer," she said. " 'Look at yourself in that mirror by the light of day if you don't believe me. You're smart enough and you used to be honest enough to know what you really are behind those frills and that expensive Belgian lace. Oh, that virgin white! Who do you expect to fool with that? For a time, yes, possibly. But in the end, my dear, all masqueraders get unmasked.' That's what he said, the bastard!"

She jumped up to her feet, undid some buttons at the back of the dress, jerked it roughly over her head, a white button and some clasps flying. She stood there in a white slip and to Stavros looked a hell of a lot better. All the time, she was telling the last of the story. " 'Goodbye,' he said, and he bent over to kiss me on the cheek before I could turn my face away—I didn't want him to touch me by then." She threw the dress on the floor, into a corner. "Then he was gone, just like that."

She was tired now, tired and still angry. She got on the bed with Stavros, no longer hiding her face or trembling, but her old hard-headed self. "I stayed and had a couple," she said. "Courtesy of a man who wanted to pick me up—some stunt, he must have thought, picking up a girl in her wedding dress. I was so mad at Paul I almost went with him. I'm still mad! After all the time I spent working on that man, all the plans I made, the houses we were going to build together—Nantucket in the summer, Hobe Sound in the winter, the upper east side of New York in between. I drew ground plans with him and furniture arrangements and we talked about the parties we'd throw and the fun we'd have traveling around the world together. I got catalogues and ship schedules and an illustrated atlas of the world. Damn, damn, damn—all those months I spent on him, all that effort."

"You ask me," Stavros said, "he was right."

"Who asked you? What was he so right about?"

"Everything! Everything you got so mad about. You were after him for what he said—his money, what else? You know that—his father's money."

"Who asked you!"

"The houses you were going to build! Where the hell is Hobe Sound, anyway? And the parties! The trips. You know what all that cost? Only with very rich man is that possible. Adventuress? That it? Right! Your ideas, his money—I know that dream very well. Nothing you imagined was possible without the money of that old Armenian who is, maybe, his father."

"I know you never liked Paul, you never saw in him what I saw in him."

"I saw it all right: same thing. What his father rattle in his pants pocket. Paul's not so dumb, it turns out. The man was right about your mother too, scheming all the time like a Chinaman. It was all high-class holdup, like in a Western movie! Come on, admit it, what he said. You feel better if you do."

"It's a lie, a damned insulting lie!"

"Sure, sure. And that was why you left me too. You could see your father going fast and there were those big hospital bills. I don't blame you, it's reasonable, no sin, to sell your *golo* in that situation. Only thing to do! When you looked ahead, all you saw was bills, so your brain began to work. 'That little Anatolian never going to be rich,' you said to yourself. 'I better find some big money, quick! Hey, Mamma! Mamma, what you say?' 'Same thing. Go 'head, my daughter dear, I find you good customer! Shoot the shoots! Go 'head, peddle what you got.' " Stavros had to laugh.

"Stop laughing," she said. "Stop laughing!"

"So first thing you forgot me. You were beginning to see your future. What it would be. You're not used to life without money, that possibility, it frightens you. Or maybe you had it figured out all the time. Yes, I think so."

"You think what?"

"You act very strong, big, independent and so on, but the truth is you always lived by other people. Somebody always support you. A man, I mean! That's the way you were raised. Go along for a while, have good time, take me, good time, that old man, the conductor, good time. God knows who else! Good time. But suddenly, it's getting late. So better be smart. Time now for Hobe Sound—where the hell is that?—and upper east side New York City. Get practical, kid, look around, make your big catch. You got one thing. You know where it is. Sell it!"

She struck Stavros across the face. "How many times did you tell me," she said, "that you wouldn't marry an American girl—hell, I would have married you in a minute. But no, we were all no good, all unreliable. We couldn't cook for one thing, and when it came to our morality, we were all beneath you."

"Now you prove what I said."

"Well, let me tell you—you're a hamal and always will be. You've got the mind of a gutter dog."

And being what he was—it was she who brought the hamal back, not he—Stavros hit her even harder than she'd hit him.

She was more surprised than hurt, Stavros noticed. In this country, he thought, the women slap the men when they get fresh, but the men don't hit the women. She sat there looking at him with the most amazed expression, and then she turned her face away and was crying, sitting on the edge of the bed, her back to him.

"I tell you something," Stavros said. "We're both the same—what he said you were. Adventurers, both of us. We know when the time has come to look around for new business. The old days are over for both of us. We're the same, partner! Hamals! Right! You too! Hey, you, hamal, here! Look here! That's enough, those tears and so on. Waste of time. I seen them before. Forget it, partner. World's not over yet. Come on."

Stavros pulled her down and she was warm and moist. He'd never been able to resist a woman who was crying or feverish, and she was both, her tears, yes, salty when he kissed her eyes, and her face too warm, like a sick person's.

"So you lost him," Stavros said. "Probably sooner or later it would happen anyhow. You're too strong for that man. Come on, enough those tears. Also, tell the truth, you're a beautiful woman and there are plenty more from where he comes. Where's that Hobe Sound?"

"Florida," she said.

"Go in Florida, you'll find another one like Paul, quick. Come on, come on, I'm not a man who suffers when you cry. I don't get fooled by that. Your brain is working already, I can see it; you're looking ahead again."

She laughed in spite of herself. "You're such a villain," she said.

"What you thinking now, adventurer? You want him back? Is that it? You want him, sooner or later he come back. Guarantee. If you want him."

"I don't. There's nothing to him."

"Except the money. You may want that again. He'll come begging, don't worry. Where's he going to find *mabl* as good as you, tell me that? All right, finish with that crying. I told you, I don't get fooled by that. You're tough baby, partner. You're a pirate—"

"Like you."

"Right. We're both hunters, looking for what we need to keep our bellies full. Hey! You listening?"

She turned her face to him and she was really beautiful. The tears had made her face moist and her eyes shine, and her lips were swollen and redder than Stavros had ever seen them. Her weight was soft against him and the white of her underclothing brought out the richness of her flesh. Oh yes, her body was soft and firm and pink, like lobster meat, like a *lokoum*, that Turkish candy, soft and sweet.

"Partner!" she said. "Bastard!" she said, smiling now in that wicked way she had when she wasn't pretending to be so damned sincere and pure. It was still there, thank God, that wicked smile. "Fuck them all," she said. "Right? Let's run away together, what do you say, partner? You adventurer, you pirate, hey, you hamal?"

"I'm going back to Anatolia," Stavros said.

"I'm going with you."

"I'm going to stay there; it's not a trip. I'm finished here, starting business there, rugs, so on." He kissed her. "In the interior. You'd last a week."

"Anything to get away from here. Anything!" She fell on top of Stavros and pushed him down. "Come on," she said. "You like me a lot, I can feel it. I still get to you, don't I? Oh yes, there it is. Come on, don't be so practical—now you're the one who's being practical. Come on, Greek! So it's for one week, maybe I wouldn't last longer, but what a week that would be! Come on, come on!"

"I'm going, business reasons," Stavros said, but he never got to say another word. She was after him, her face shining, and she pulled the top of her slip down and a minute later everything else, and she was crazy, as if Stavros meant everything to her, more than her own life.

"Am I interchangeable, hamal?" she said. "Am I? Come on, let's see. Am I?"

So he surrendered. He let go. What could he do? He'd been so controlled for so many weeks, like a good businessman, even in sex. But she'd brought the hamal back. And soon they both were crazy and all they knew was each other.

When her mother came into the room—once more without knocking —she saw them at their best. And Althea held Stavros where he was, her fingers digging into his soft parts behind, pulling him into her deeper. And he too, he held her harder, one hand under her neck, the other at the base of her spine, pulling her up to him even closer. Neither of them gave a

damn about her mother or could have said how long the woman watched
or when she shut the door behind her.

They laughed about it afterward. "Serves her right," Althea said. And
they slept.

When Stavros woke she was looking at him. Common sense had
returned, he could see it.

"Well, we did it," she said.

"What we did?"

"Broke it! No going back now."

"All roads travel two ways, old Turkish saying."

"Not this time." She smiled at him, but not like before. Cool. And
mean.

"Who knows the will of Allah?" Stavros said.

She made a sound like a horse. Patience gone! Then she sat up and
looked at her breasts. Carefully. Lifted one, let it drop. Was she thinking:
They used to be better?

"I've always known it about you," she said. "That's really why I never
trusted you, Mr. Greek Bastard."

"What you've always known?"

"That you were an adventurer. Paul had it right."

"He said it about you, not me. And your mother."

She picked up her brassiere and put it on. "Well, then, I say it about
you," she said. And again that cold smile, like a drunk trying to pick a fight.

"Return the compliment," Stavros said. "If that's what it was."

"It'll serve," she said. "It's the best we can say about each other now."

"I don't mind," Stavros said.

"Sure, because you're all out for yourself and nobody else, so naturally
you don't mind."

"No. Because I'm not afraid to say the truth I know about me, so what
the hell."

"When I first met you," she said, "it was everything for your family.
Now suddenly you drop them like a used condom."

"Why you angry at me?" Stavros said.

"I'm not angry." She leaned over and lay across his chest. "I was just
talking about your family. They're of no use to you now, are they? I've
noticed how you stopped talking about them, all of a sudden. Only Michaelis now. And if he's what he looks like, he's become a killer, so you
may need him someday. Bastard!" she said, getting altogether on top of
Stavros. "Coldhearted bastard!"

"No argument there," Stavros said. "Michaelis? He's good boy, but
also what you say. It's the only thing possible in his situation. Maybe mine
too. What do *you* know? Always safe all your life!"

She pressed down on Stavros's penis.

"You waiting for that?" he said.

"No. But I see it doesn't want me anymore. Not even a day and you've already had enough of me."

"What's the matter, you sorry?" he said. "About what happened?"

"Well, no—but I don't know what to do now."

"Want Paul back?"

"No."

"No?"

"It's just that I've got a big investment there—if you'll forgive my business lingo."

"Then you do want him back?"

"I didn't say that."

"First thing you got to understand in this situation is that Paul has pride too. Which was what you said your reason was for not signing that Mr. Wildberg's papers. Paul has his own reasons. If he thinks you were scheming and so on, well—"

"He does believe that. But I wasn't. Not consciously, anyway."

"Conscious, unconscious, what's the difference? He sees it one way—Mrs. Perry and sweet Miss Althea Perry after his money. And he's right."

"Then it's finished."

"Now I'm sure you want him back." She didn't answer. "If you do," Stavros said, "I have idea."

"Don't waste your ideas—you'll need them in Anatolia. You must be crazy to be going back there." She got up, went to the long mirror on the bathroom door and sucked in her belly. "I look terrible," she said.

"Because it's cold here and your body is covered with those little pin marks."

She let her belly out. "I'm getting old," she said.

"*Scada!* An old Greek word meaning you-know-what. Listen to me. You want him back, you can have him back."

"Come on, stop rubbing it in. Please. Stop."

"I have idea how. Guarantee! Take a little time, maybe two, three weeks, but—"

Stavros was watching her face in the mirror and she turned away. Then she admitted it, in her own way. "Paul, you know," she said, "hasn't a mean bone in his body. I'd always be able to trust Paul. Can't say the same about you. I can trust him to never do anything that hurts me. He'd never disappear, for instance, fuck and leave the next day. He's a gentle nice man and his only fault is a gentle nice fault. He's lazy. That's all I've got against him. The only one he'd ever hurt is himself."

"About that, you right. When we were playing *Tavli*, I saw his wrists," Stavros said. "Those lines there."

"He tried to kill himself. Twice. But he wouldn't if I was with him," she said.

"Listen, Miss Althea, stop looking at your behind in the mirror and come back here."

"I don't want you now," she said.

"Well, I'll get somebody else. Now listen. I'll make a deal with you. You help me, I'll help you."

"Doing what?"

"I'll get Paul back for you," Stavros said. "I'll get him back, absolutely, sure thing. Then you help me."

"What about what my mother just saw? You forgot that?"

"You think your mother such big damn fool she's going to tell that to Mr. Fernand Sarrafian? She's not crazy woman. About Paul, one thing sure: He can't live without his father's money, so he will always do what his father says. And that old man, he likes you. He thinks you can make a man out of his son, put some ambition into him. Or save him from killing himself someday when he's a little unhappy about some foolishness. That's what the old man is afraid, those lines across his son's wrist. That fear we can use. You see, you must understand your enemy's weak places. I have this idea. Not to go after Paul, but his father."

"That's just too damned scheming. And it wouldn't work."

"It would. But first you have to say something. To yourself, not to me."

"What's that? What horrible confession would that be?"

"That we're both what you called us before—adventurers—and both after same thing: you son's money, me old man's money."

"I'll never admit that."

"Then forget it," he said, and started to get up and dress.

"But suppose I did?"

"No 'suppose' business. You said it before. Admit it now. To yourself. You're like me, a hungry animal in bad trouble, yes, in fight for her life. Admit that to yourself."

She didn't say anything for a long minute. Then she said, "O.K., I did."

"Well, then, O.K. Now listen. You mean to tell me you still too humiliated at the idea of Mr. Wildberg's papers to sign them? What the hell's the matter with you? Is it a knife in your belly? Be smart, keep your honor like mine, safe inside you. No one can make me feel bad except myself. I know why I do certain things, so I—"

"That's pure shit, Stavros—and rather disgusting."

"Yeah, yeah, I know. So look at it another way. They scheme against you. They delayed this agreement on purpose until the day before the wedding, when they think it's impossible for you to say no. That old man, let me tell you, he is trickiest man in the world—maybe. We have to fight him same weapons he fights us, same tricks."

"What weapons, what tricks?"

"Sign the goddamn thing! If you do, I guarantee you have Paul back. Maybe also different terms agreement—leave that to me, better terms. After all, you never bargained yet, those terms, did you? But even the same terms—where the hell is your woman's confidence? You mean to tell me that you couldn't in a few months fix that Paul up—he's only a little boy —maneuver his brain around so he really believe he couldn't get along without you? That's what any wife supposed to do. Make that boy believe he's the world's greatest lover—but only with you, only with you, Miss Althea, you made him that—then you think you still must worry about a goddamn signature? Get his cock locked in your bureau drawer and give it back to him only when you want. Then you'll be boss. That's step number one. O.K. Now, what's step number two?"

"Something equally cynical and distasteful, I'm sure. What is it?"

"Jesus Christ, you're so dumb! Give him a kid. Or two, better. Name the first one after him. Paul. Pauline. Then what kind of agreement you need? If he ever gets the idea to leave you, Mr. Lawyer Wildberg, he move over your side—more money there."

"Are you aware that you are a thoroughly corrupt man?"

"Why? Because I tell the truth?"

"So what do you want me to do—fall on my knees and say, 'Please, dear Mr. Fernand, I'm so sorry. I agree to everything, I'll sign anything you want'?"

"Don't be an idiot. Really, you have a lot to learn from me."

"What do you want me to do?"

"Go to your room, take a bath, fix up your face—it looks terrible. Dress up in your best traveling outfit, load yourself with perfume, pack your bag, and come downstairs as if you're going back to the city with me. My girl, understand?"

"Jesus! Then?"

"Then? Follow me, what I do."

"What is that going to be?"

"I'm smarter than anybody living, always remember that. I'm smarter than Mr. Fernand, even him. I was born smart enough, but the rest I learned from my aching back. Sit there in your best dress with a cloud of perfume around you. Cross your legs, show them off. Keep your tits up! Say nothing, don't ask questions, don't answer them. The talking, I'll do. Above all, don't be a nice girl. Don't be apologetic. Don't be friendly. I tell you that old man looks feeble, but he's damn tiger. Show him weakness, he eat you alive. You run, he catch you. You must act like you don't give damn on anything. Only if you can slide in something quick, you worrying possibility suicide, that's good idea. Meantime you're leaving with me. Let's go, hamal. I'll be down there waiting for you when you come."

After she'd run down the hall to her room, holding the wedding dress up in front of her, Stavros dressed. He felt confident. He knew the old man's weakness—those lines across his son's wrists. When you know your enemy's weak place, that's the time to attack.

They were all there, sitting around the parlor like passengers in a railroad station where service has been discontinued. All the electric heaters had been brought into the room; Stavros could see the copper spheres glowing red as he came down the stairs. In the farthest corner, William Wildberg was on the telephone.

The Reverend Kenworthy, apparently having been summoned, was sitting at Morgan Perry's side, trying unsuccessfully to make him laugh. Mr. Fernand was pacing up and down, his hands clasped behind his back. Something had pumped energy into his spavined legs. Going to his chauffeur, who was looking out the window at the side of the front door, he asked, "What's it look like out there, Wynn?"

"Looks like snow, sir," Wynn said. "Sorry, sir."

Mr. Fernand made a peevish sound and returned to the parlor.

"Well, Mr. Fernand, what's going to happen now?" Maud asked. She was in a chair by the bookshelves, pretending to read a book bound in heavy embossed leather. "Are we going or are we staying?"

It was clear from Mr. Fernand's voice when he answered her that Maud had still not won his affection. "When I know, Freddie will inform you," he said.

"When he makes up his mind, Maud," Freddie said, "he'll let us know. Go on with your book. What are you reading?"

Maud crossed her legs in the masculine way, ankle over knee, and read the title on the spine of the book. " 'The Sonnets of Elizabeth Barrett Browning.' All I meant was that if he's not going, let's take the train."

"Let's be calm a little longer," Freddie said.

Freddie was sitting on a stool, looking up at his employer like an obedient dog.

"Look who's here," Mr. Fernand said when Stavros came into the room. "Hello, stranger. How have you been wasting your time?"

"Relaxing," Stavros said. "Sleeping, talking, relaxing."

"Talking with whom?" Mr. Fernand said. "Everybody's down here." He was more on edge than Stavros had ever seen him.

"Althea's not down here," Stavros said.

Mrs. Perry came into the room, followed by the maid, Agnes. "Cook has fixed you a nice plate, Ken," she said.

"Where is Althea?" Mr. Fernand asked Stavros.

"Upstairs dressing," Stavros said. "We're going back."

"Back where?" Mrs. Perry said as she placed a small side table in front of the Reverend Kenworthy.

"Ah," the Reverend Kenworthy said, "I believe I'm seeing lobster. Thank you, Agnes. Lobster meat, there's no meat sweeter."

"There's sweeter," Stavros said. And looked toward Mr. Fernand.

"Lobster newburg, Ken," Mrs. Perry said. Then she turned to Stavros. "What did you say? Just then?"

When Stavros smiled at her, she did an extraordinary thing. She blushed. "Back to the big city," Stavros said.

"Oh me, oh my," the Reverend Kenworthy said, his nose over the newburg.

"Would you like a glass of wine with that?" Mrs. Perry said.

"Well—perhaps just one. If it wouldn't disturb Mr. Perry," he said.

"Why should it disturb him? He's dozing. Agnes, a glass of the wine we had for lunch. There's half a bottle open on the pantry shelf."

"How is she going back?" Mr. Fernand asked Stavros. He was pacing faster and faster.

"With me," Stavros said. "We're going back together."

"Althea was always a damned fool," Maud said from behind the sonnets of Elizabeth Barrett Browning.

"I don't believe it," Mrs. Perry said.

"Sit down," Mr. Fernand said to Stavros. He always liked everyone else to sit while he stood or paced.

"I've been lying around all afternoon," Stavros said. He saw Mrs. Perry blush again, but she didn't say anything and it was clear that she hadn't informed Mr. Fernand of what she'd seen.

"Delicious," the reverend said. "There's no better way to fix lobster, is there, Morgan?"

Morgan Perry was asleep.

"Sit down," Mr. Fernand repeated. "Over here. I want to talk to you." He pointed to a corner of the room.

"Mr. Fernand," Stavros said, "I don't work for you anymore. If you want to say to me something you don't want people to hear, ask me to please walk with you to other room and if I feel like I will, maybe."

"This is the only warm room in the house," Mr. Fernand complained. "I cannot believe, Norma," he said to Mrs. Perry, "that this house could not have been heated. At least for this one weekend."

"I told you," she said, "it's not insulated. How many times must I repeat that?"

"There's no need to go into a corner," Stavros said. "I don't have secrets. Mr. Fernand, what's on your mind?"

"Have you thought it over?" he said. "I'd like to know."

"Thought what over?"

"My proposal to you. You said you were going to think it over."

"Didn't say that. I told you figure I want," Stavros said. "In Phoenix,

Arizona. Otherwise, satisfied where I am. If I move, I told you figure necessary."

"What was that?"

"Forty percent," Stavros said.

Mr. Fernand tried to laugh. "I think you're a madman," he said.

"He certainly is," Mrs. Perry said. Every time she looked at Stavros now, her cheeks colored.

"And without him," Stavros said, pointing to Freddie.

Maud stood up. "I've had all I'm going to take from you," she said. Freddie left the room.

"Without Freddie!" Stavros said to Maud.

"You're a vengeful, nasty little villain," she said. "And you've hurt Freddie's feelings." She sat down.

"What's the weather now, Wynn?" Mr. Fernand barked at his chauffeur.

" 'Fraid it's worse, sir," Wynn called from the hall. "Sleet, I'm afraid, sir."

"You think we can get through?"

"We can try," Wynn said. "But I'd advise against it."

"Sure we can get through," Mr. Fernand blustered. "What's the matter with you? You will drive slowly."

"Now, please, please Fernand, don't give up," Mrs. Perry said. "Stay tonight. We planned for you to stay tonight. I'll see that your room is warm as toast."

"There's nothing to wait for," Mr. Fernand said. "Nothing, I'm afraid, to wait for."

"For God's sake, give it a chance," Mrs. Perry said. "Leave in the morning. We must patch this up." She looked at the Reverend Kenworthy. "Ken!"

"Of course we can," Ken said.

"Fernand, we must not give up," Mrs. Perry said.

"But how?" Mr. Fernand said. "Without Paul, how?"

"I agree with Mr. Sarrafian," Stavros said. "I talked with Althea and I agree it's all over. We're going back to the city together and—"

Old Mrs. Murray and Michaelis came into the room, she looking excited and angry. "Michaelis has told me what's been going on here," she said to her daughter. "I have finally learned, Norma, what you've been up to. It's outrageous!" She approached Mr. Fernand, raising her cane and shaking it at him. "Unforgivable! There is no reason in the world why a grandchild of mine should be asked to do anything so humiliating. You—lawyer—you! Quiet!" Lawyer Wildberg was still at the small table in the corner, droning into the telephone. "You are a disgraceful man, bringing business papers into my home on this day."

Then she turned back to Mr. Fernand. "Who do you think is doing whom a favor in this matter? I must tell you, your son did not impress me favorably."

"Sit down, Mother," Mrs. Perry said. "Sit down and be quiet."

"This is my house, not yours, and I will not be quiet. You can all leave this minute. This minute!"

"Please, please," Mr. Fernand said in his most soothing voice. "Can I kindly ask you all to cooperate with me?"

"Cooperate in what?" Maud said. "I want to leave."

"In having a quiet civilized chat. If any one of you has anything to say, let him—or her—say it within the bounds of decent manners. After all, we're civilized, even cultured, people and—what are you doing out there?" he said, turning on Stavros.

Stavros was in the entrance hall with Michaelis, rolling up the nine-by-twelve silk Keshan. "I brought wedding present," he said, "but now no wedding, so—"

"Stop that. I want quiet here," Mr. Fernand barked. Then his voice softened. "Please, everybody, let's treat each other with respect despite whatever differences we may have. Look. I will sit, I will be quiet. Wildberg! Stop talking on the telephone. Immediately! Hang up."

Wildberg hung up.

"I want to go back to the city," Maud said, getting to her feet. "I hate this house. Freddie!" Freddie came hurrying back into the room.

"Well, then, go, get out of here," Mrs. Murray said. "Good riddance."

"Freddie, control her at once," Mr. Fernand said. "Be quiet!" he snapped at Maud. "Sit! Now! Everybody! Quiet!"

Such was Mr. Fernand's authority that everyone was silent. Stavros saw it was his chance. Before Mr. Fernand could continue, he said, "I like to say few words here." His tone was gentle. "O.K.? Please? Because I'm leaving your country for always, except maybe visit once in while, business reasons. But to live? No more. Going back where I came from. There I will start new business. Well, not your problem, right? I want to say goodbye now to all of you. Goodbye. I will soon forget you and as I forget you, I will forgive you for the bad things you done to me."

"What bad things?" Morgan Perry said. After all the turmoil, the relative quiet of Stavros's monotone had wakened him.

"Well, Mr. Morgan Perry, sure you remember, even in present condition, that you fire pistol at my head? You try to kill me. But, Mr. Morgan, don't carry that guilt on your soul."

"That's important," the Reverend Kenworthy said.

"Mrs. Perry, I forgive you too. You always treat me like I was what the donkey dropped, and you still doing it today—even when there is something you know about which no one else knows."

"What's that?" Mr. Fernand said. "Are you blushing, Norma? What is that?"

"And you, Mr. Fernand, I used to think of you as my model on everything. But that idea left me while ago. You remember you use me for immoral purposes, tried to humiliate me. Remember? I forgive you for that now. You also took advantage of me as employer, never pay me what I was worth. I stayed in your company only because I admire you—which now is finished. I could have done many things for you, Mr. Fernand, someday I tell you what I could have done for you."

"You've told me, time after time," Mr. Fernand said. "It's nonsense."

"Then why you trying to get me back? You know you need me, not other way 'round. But what I was talking about had nothing to do with business. I meant about your son, Paul, someday I tell you that, but not now, too late now."

Michaelis had come in from the entrance hall. "Time we go," he said.

"So we go," Stavros said. "That's that. Oh, yes, I see Maud looking very angry over there. I must help her and say that now I forgive Freddie, what he did. Freddie, I trusted you as friend but you give me the kiss of Judas. Now I forgive you that, I forget kiss of Judas."

He stopped. He'd spoken gently because Freddie was sensitive and Maud had been abusing him. Stavros could see what Freddie's life was going to be. "So now, my friends," he said, "I forgive you all. That's what I come down here to tell you. Don't have weight on your souls from me." He went to the bottom of the stairs and called up. "Althea! Come on!"

"I'm dressing, dear," she called down.

"Well, come on," Stavros said. "You're making me wait here." He spoke like a man from Anatolia, commanding his woman to heel. He could see that his manner displeased everyone, so he called up again, even more roughly. "Althea!"

"Yes, dear," she said, playing her part perfectly. "Just one more minute, please, dear."

"The weather, it's terrible," Stavros shouted. "Even Wynn doesn't want to drive. It's getting dark and it will be more dangerous if we have to drive through such weather at night! So hurry up!"

"We'll get through all right, dear," she called. "I'm coming."

The phone rang. Mr. Wildberg picked it up, but Mrs. Perry snatched it out of his hand.

"It's Paul," she whispered to everyone in the room. "Hello," Paul dear," she said into the phone. Everyone strained to listen. "He wants to talk to Althea," she whispered. Her eyes were bright with hope. "Just a minute, Paulie," she said, and gave the phone back to Lawyer Wildberg. "Hold this," she said. "I'll get her." Then she ran to the bottom of the stairs and called upstairs. "Althea dear, it's Paul. Paul wants to speak to you, honey. Hurry!"

"I don't want to speak to him," Althea called.

They could all hear the sounds of a party coming over the telephone, loud laughter, screams of exhilaration.

"You come down here this minute," Mrs. Perry said in what she hoped was a voice loud enough for Althea to heed but not for Paul to hear. "I said this minute!"

"No, Mother, never, not a chance. Hang up," Althea called.

At this, Mrs. Perry seemed to fly into pieces. "Hold him on that line!" she hissed at Wildberg, then charged up the stairs, a most desperate woman.

"Leave Althea alone," Mrs. Murray called after her. "She doesn't have to talk to anyone she doesn't want to talk to."

"Let me talk to him," Mr. Fernand said, taking the phone from Wildberg. "Hello. Who's this?" he said. "Miss who? Oh yes, of course, I remember you very well. Would you kindly ask Paul to come back on? I know, I know; I'll talk to Paul about that. Please put him on. Hello, Paul boy, how are you? Who? It's me, your father." Then he laughed. "You sound good," he said. "Have you had a couple of drinks? More than couple, maybe? You're what?" From above there came shouts and the sound of a slap. "Well, I'm glad you're having a good time, Paul boy," Mr. Fernand said. "Oh, we're just sitting around trying to decide whether to —I mean, we're going to have a little supper soon and then . . . Mrs. Perry has gone upstairs to get Althea—she'll be right here. Oh, here she comes."

Mrs. Perry was coming down the stairs, crying and cursing under her breath. "I don't care anymore," she said. "I give up. I just can't anymore, I just can't, I can't, I can't!"

"She'll be here in just a minute," Mr. Fernand said into the phone. "Don't go away now." Then he covered the mouthpiece and snapped at Stavros, "Go get her! Immediately. You, Stavros!"

"I will not," Stavros said.

"You're going where?" Mr. Fernand said into the phone. "But why don't you stay where you are now, Paul. The weather is quite ugly, Wynn says. He won't let me—and you know Wynn, he can get through anything. We'll be right here waiting for you. When are you coming back? You're not? Oh, Paul, come, don't be a child. Althea is here waiting for you."

"Like hell she is." Althea was coming down the stairs carrying her bag.

"Here," Mr. Fernand said, holding out the phone.

"Hang up," she said. "I don't want to talk to him."

She looked at the grandfather clock, which was striking the hour. "Four," she said. "It's getting very dark."

"Althea," Mr. Fernand pleaded. He was pathetic now.

"This is all your fault." Mrs. Perry came at Stavros. She was dangerously aroused now, her future at stake.

"I will not talk to him, not again, not ever!" Althea said to everyone in the room. "He and I are finished."

"Stop being a damned fool, Althea," Maud said.

"What's the matter with the weather!" Mr. Fernand shouted into the phone. He was losing his patience. "It's dangerous, that's what's the matter with the weather." He covered the mouthpiece and said, "Shshsh! I can't hear what the boy is saying." He looked as desperate as Mrs. Perry now.

"It's all your fault! You!" Mrs. Perry thrust her finger at Stavros. "You put her up to this. I saw you. I know what you did!"

"Well, be very careful, boy, won't you," Mr. Fernand said. "Don't do anything silly now, will you? Althea still loves you, hold that thought, don't forget that! Hold that dear thought, my boy. Whose house? Virginia's? Yes, of course, I know her very well—the one who eats caviar like marmalade. Ha-ha-ha! But why go there? For God's sake, stay where you are. Let me come there and join you. I'll have a couple of drinks with you, not more than two, and—"

Then everyone in the room could hear Paul shouting "No! Don't come here! You'll spoil *this* party too. You and that goddamn lawyer of yours—"

"Oh, Paul, Paul," the old man said. "Listen to me, Paul, please—"

Paul had hung up.

"I blame you," Mrs. Perry was screaming at Stavros.

"Blame yourself, Mother," Althea said. "You cooked up this whole thing."

"How did he sound?" Stavros said to Mr. Fernand. "Not so well?"

Mr. Fernand looked at Stavros as if he wanted to kill him on the spot. "Mr. Fernand," Stavros said, "I am talking to you. I think we—that is, you —ought to get where Paul is quick before he does something again." Stavros made a gesture across his wrist.

The old man, in a fury beyond control now, was bearing down on Stavros.

"She's right, Norma," Mrs. Murray said. "It's all your fault." She was leaning on Michaelis, who found the whole scene alternately funny and disgusting. He was shaking his head and suppressing laughter.

"Mr. Fernand," Stavros said, "you ought to get there soon as you— well, maybe too late already. But he really shouldn't drink anymore, you know how he gets—"

"Shut up!" Mr. Fernand shouted. "Go on, get out of here. I don't want to see you here again. Get out!"

"This is her house, Mr. Fernand," Stavros said, nodding at Mrs. Murray. "I go when she says, otherwise when I'm ready."

"That is right," Mrs. Murray said. "Mr. Fernand, I do wish you'd stop behaving as if you owned this place."

"*You* get out," Stavros said to Mr. Fernand. "Your son needs you. Or someone. Get into your car and—what's that smell?" He was standing next to Althea. "Is that you, dear?" he said to her.

"My perfume," she said. "Like it?" She smiled at him.

"Very nice," Stavros said. "Mr. Fernand, come smell Althea."

"Wynn," Mr. Fernand said, "put this man out!" He pointed at Stavros.

"Don't you dare," Mrs. Murray said. "Don't you take any such liberties here, Mr. Fernand Sarrafian, or I will call the police!"

Michaelis freed his arm, to be ready.

Wynn was coming toward Stavros. "Come on, mister," he said. "Mr. Fernand doesn't want you here anymore."

"But I think I stay," Stavros said.

"Chauffeur!" Mrs. Murray commanded. "Don't touch my guest."

"Come on, gentleman," Wynn said, taking Stavros's arm.

That was a mistake. Stavros was not a big man, but he'd learned to fight in gutters and under the docks against ruthless enemies. He kicked Wynn in one shin, bending him over, then smashed the point of his elbow into the chauffeur's face, straightening him up again. A foot behind Wynn and a push sent him crashing to the floor. All this was performed in what seemed to be one swift movement.

"Gangster! Gangster!" Mr. Fernand was yelling. "Freddie! Freddie!"

Stavros waited for Wynn to get up. Wynn was not eager to.

Freddie, feeling obliged to stand at his boss's side, moved forward but Michaelis showed him the knife he'd unsheathed, held it low, thrust it forward, then back, whereupon Maud screamed, "Freddie!" and when her fiancé turned his head, Michaelis settled him with a thrust of his shoulder into a chair. Freddie jumped to his feet, but Maud had him, pulling him to one side. "Stay out of this," she commanded. "It's revolting."

The excitement of combat was contagious. Mr. Fernand came at Stavros, screaming, "Criminal! Criminal!" like a baboon in a fury, teeth bared, nails (carefully manicured) ready to strike and tear. He leaped at Stavros, fixed his teeth in his neck, his nails clinging to Stavros's hair. The Anatolian was so surprised that he lost his balance and tumbled to the floor, Mr. Fernand on top of him, flailing at him with his nails and snapping at him with his dentures (which he kept pushing back in place).

"Stop that! Stop that!" Mrs. Murray commanded. "I will not tolerate this hooliganism in my home, especially from you, Mr. Fernand." She prodded him with her cane. "Stop this vulgar squabbling, sir. This instant!"

Stavros didn't want Michaelis to interfere—he might hurt someone—so he yelled in Greek, "Michaelis, do nothing, don't hurt these poor people."

It had all become too funny and Stavros began to laugh, laughed even louder when Mrs. Perry came running to where he lay on the floor to kick at him with the pointed toes and sharp French heels of her pumps. Doubled up, Stavros had one hand around his most vulnerable place and the other over his eyes while he laughed like a baby being tickled. When he lowered his hand for an instant, he saw Maud and Freddie standing apart, observing the action with cold indifference. Any regret he might have felt about being cruel to Freddie was relieved.

It was in the middle of this brawl that the phone rang again. Then Wildberg, who had never moved, was saying, calmly, "Mr. Fernand for you. It's about Paul, I think."

Mr. Fernand had trouble getting to his feet. In the end it was Stavros who helped him up and to the phone.

The old man couldn't have heard more than three or four words when he shouted, "That's impossible!" He was breathing with great difficulty. "We were—just talking—to him." Then he listened again and said, "Oh no! Oh my God—the driveway! Yes, yes—tell me where. Which hospital? Of course, of course—I'm coming!"

Wynn got the Rolls, holding Mr. Fernand, Mrs. Perry, and Lawyer Wildberg, to the hospital long before Stavros and Althea arrived in Althea's coupe. In the back seat was Michaelis, with the nine-by-twelve silk Keshan.

When Stavros and Althea found the others, Mr. Fernand was embroiled in an intense quarrel at the floor nurse's desk. Not receiving satisfaction there, he stormed to the admissions office, opposite the sun room where Mrs. Perry and William Wildberg were waiting.

"They put Paul in a ward," Mrs. Perry said to Althea.

"How can I talk to my son in a room full of strangers?" Mr. Fernand was shouting.

Stavros could see into the admissions office, where the old man was gesticulating violently. "I know Mr. Burgess very well," he heard him shout. Apparently, Mr. Fernand had insisted that they reach a Mr. Burgess, obviously someone of importance, on the phone. And in time they did. While he was talking to this figure of authority, Mr. Fernand's voice dropped to a wheedle. But he got what he wanted. "Outrageous," he said as he came back to the sun room. "They put the boy with six people!"

"But Paul, how is Paul now, poor dear?" Mrs. Perry said.

"Lucky to be alive," Mr. Fernand said. "His Packard, of course, is finished. He slid off the car he struck and smashed into a pole. His head hit the windshield and shattered it. The broken tibia is a trifle, but his face, they tell me, is badly swollen from splinters of glass. 'You may not recognize him,' the floor doctor told me."

"You mean you haven't seen him yet?" Stavros said in sympathetic outrage. "They didn't allow you to see your own son?"

"As soon as they move him into a private room," Mr. Fernand said. "They're doing it now."

They all sat and waited. After five minutes of silence, an intern came up and called, "Is there a Mr. Sar— something here?"

"Sarrafian!" Mr. Fernand said. "Here. What happened?"

"We've moved him to room 327," the intern said.

"About time." Mr. Fernand jumped up. "Didn't you realize I was waiting?" He hustled down the hall.

The rest of the group waited, but not for long. In a few minutes, Mr. Fernand was back, disconsolate.

"What's the matter, sir?" Stavros said. The old man looked so distraught that Stavros actually felt sorry for him.

"He won't see me. He gave orders that I'm not to be admitted."

"That's terrible," Stavros said. "I'm sorry, boss."

This refusal crushed Mr. Fernand. Paul, it seemed, would see only Althea. Mr. Fernand admitted that at last.

Coming down in Althea's car, Stavros and she had discussed things, and when Paul said he'd see only her, she refused—just as planned. This gave Stavros the chance to take her aside and force her to do it. He made sure they all saw how he overcame her resistance. Finally she obeyed him, her head down, the picture of acquiescence.

Stavros sat down next to Mr. Fernand as Althea took off her coat. "She'll go in now," he boasted.

"Good boy," Mr. Fernand said.

Althea had to pass Mr. Fernand's chair to get to Paul's room. As she went by, the father said to her, "Now be nice to him." She didn't respond.

"Didn't you hear what Mr. Fernand said?" Stavros scolded.

Althea behaved as he'd instructed her to—gave Mr. Fernand an obdurate, unyielding look, then pranced, defiant, down the hospital corridor.

Again they all waited.

"Mr. Fernand," Stavros said in a lighter tone, "I look in a mirror before and I notice you put teeth marks in my neck. Look! Here!"

"I'm terribly sorry about that," Mr. Fernand said. "I was not myself. Please forgive me. Can you possibly forgive me?"

"Of course," Stavros said.

"Thank you, dear boy. That's most generous of you," Mr. Fernand said.

"Don't talk to him," Mrs. Perry said. "He's the cause of all this."

"Dear lady," Mr. Fernand said, "kindly mind your business."

Althea didn't stay with Paul long. When she came out, she again did as Stavros had instructed—threw a cold goodbye at everyone, picked up her purse and coat, and walked away. Without Stavros.

He ran after her.

"I don't want to see you or any of these people again," she said, loudly enough for them all to hear.

"That's not nice," Stavros said.

At that, perfectly coached, she said, "You can go to hell too," walked off, and was gone. Mrs. Perry ran after her and apparently they reached some sort of truce, because Mrs. Perry didn't come back. They must have driven off in the coupe together.

Mr. Fernand tried to visit Paul again, but the boy would not see him. The old man was very broken up, the saddest Stavros had ever seen him. Stavros put his arm around Mr. Fernand's shoulder and said, "I'm sorry, boss. I know how painful all this has been for you." Then he said, "As you've often said, sir, time solves many things. He feel different in the morning."

"Do you think so?"

"Guarantee. Now may I have the privilege of riding into the city with you?"

"I wish you would," the old man said.

"I'm ashamed of myself," Mr. Fernand said when they were on the road to New York. "I'm thoroughly ashamed of myself." He was looking at Stavros's neck.

"You left your signature on me, all right," Stavros said.

"Don't tell anybody, I beg you, what those marks are. I hope and trust that in time they will disappear."

"If they don't, souvenir to remind me of you in Anatolia."

"At any rate, I humbly apologize."

"Not necessary second time, once is enough. But thank you. I accept."

"I don't know what got into me."

"Something very fine. Love for your son. Proof that you're human. It was worth the teeth marks on my neck, for me to see that."

Mr. Fernand looked so small and rickety—after all, he was a very old man and not in the best of health—and he suddenly looked so defeated, that Stavros put his arm around his shoulders and pulled him closer, as he might have a child.

"I understand how you feel," Stavros said.

"Do you?"

"Yes. I saw those lines on Paul's wrists. I know what they are and how you feel when you see them."

"Oh, God, oh, God, what did I do wrong, I ask myself. What mistakes did I make with that boy? Whatever they were, I am paying now."

"Sometimes children come out like that. I have brother— he's not what I would hope. There is inheritance too, such a thing, you realize. What was his mother?"

"Forgive me if I don't talk about that woman. Every fault that boy has is a reflection of her character. I don't know how I ever got mixed up with that woman. Please forgive me if I—"

"Of course, sure. Don't talk. Stay quiet, rest, you're all excited, relax." Gently Stavros pulled the old man's bald head against his shoulder. "If you promise don't fall asleep," Stavros said, "I tell you story."

"I won't sleep."

"When I was a boy, eighteen, nineteen, my best friend was Armenian fellow, he was always in trouble with the Turks and because I follow him everywhere he went, and made him my hero, many times I was in trouble too. Big problem for my father. My mother, she lost all hope that I would ever be anything. Tell you the truth, I never thought I'd be much myself.

"Those years the Turk was cutting the Armenians, *kess, kess,* cut, cut, more than us Greeks, but us too. My father got along by speaking nice always, bowing his head and saying, 'I know nothing,' and so on, very humble. But time came when that didn't work either. He was feeling frightened for himself and for his family. He loved his children more than his life, was like you that way. Time came when I learned he loved me too.

"One day, after the terrible slaughters of 'ninety-six—you remember? Terrible days! Then it happen. My father lock himself in his room for one week, seven days eating nothing, minimum. Minimum sleep, won't talk to his wife, my mother, or take food from her when she bring it. We were all frightened—never saw him like that before. Then one day he came out and who you think he ask for?"

"You."

"That's right. Alone. He took me in his room, close the door, and he told me he make up his mind that our family should leave that place. He put on me the job of getting us out. To provide me a little money for start, he collect everything family had of value—the blankets and rugs the girls had woven for their weddings, old family jewels, few pieces, sides of meat we had smoked ready for winter, some little money from his pocket, few bits lace and gold. He pile everything on the back of our donkey and told me make trip to Constantinople, sell these valuable things there and put what I get into business with his cousin, rug merchant with small place in closed bazaar. When our investment prosper, he said, and I establish myself in business, I should send money for passage, and bring the family out from interior to that safer place.

"My mother was very suspicious about this idea. She said to my father that even when she sent me to the baker for bread she wasn't sure I would come back. But my father, a gentle man, he was, and sometimes 'fraid of my mother, on this he didn't change his idea. We said our prayers together one night and the next morning they send me off with the donkey on whose back Father pile up everything our family had of value. Your eyes are closed. Are you awake?"

"Yes."

"Naturally, then, I made damn fool of myself, one disaster after another, last one a bandit who took everything my father had put on that donkey's back. And he was going to kill me too, in the end. So there I learned my lesson."

"Yes, that's when you learn—when your life's in danger."

"Don't fall asleep now."

"I'm very interested. Because I think you're speaking about me and Paul. What lesson did you learn?"

"Sometimes you have to kill man—if he's standing in the way of what you must have."

"I learned that with my mother's milk," the old man said. "So what happened?"

"I killed him, the bandit, stab him in the back while he was saying his prayers. I had enough money to reach Constantinople, no more; I got there, but without a penny. So my father's cousin didn't give me a big welcome. Soon I was on the streets. I became hamal and lived the life. That was my college. Coupla times I nearly starve to death, ate the garbage the palace kitchen threw out, fighting off dogs for this filthy food. Other time, I was shot by police and left for dead. But our cousin saved me. After that was a time when I did bad things to good people—a young woman, yes —I'm ashamed of that time, I can't talk about it.

"Through all this, I kept one thought close in my heart: that my father had trusted me. Which meant I must make good his trust. I saw that this place, Constantinople, was not what our family needed. I got the idea, America. I worked and I kept my hope and one day, from the deck of a ship, I saw the coast of America in the distance. When I land here I kiss the ground. Seven years I worked, seven years—you remember how I was when you first saw me—"

"Like a wild animal, ugly as a wolf."

"Ugly, yes, a wild animal, yes, but at last I put together the passage money, dollar by dollar, to make good my father's trust in me and bring my family here. I did it."

"I've never met your father, have I?"

"He died day before family sailed from Smyrna."

"They came without him?"

"It was his dying wish. That they come. So— That's the story of my life—what I went through and what helped me through it."

"You've been talking about me and Paul," Mr. Fernand said again.

"If you see it that way."

"I understand it that way."

"Have you ever shown faith in your son? Or trust?"

"I can't remember. I mean, I can't remember that I have."

"So why should he think you have any belief in him?"

"I don't know."

"How can he have faith in himself if you don't have faith in him?"

"I don't know. Don't say more. I understand what you've been saying very well."

"Just this last. You talk about Freddie and about me, but did you ever think to turn over Sarrafian Brothers to Paul?"

"He's not capable—I mean, he's always been indifferent to work. Even lazy."

"See how quickly you said that? You have boy who is ready any minute to cut his wrists and you complain about his laziness. You made him that way."

"It is his mother who spoiled him."

"Was it your place to make a man of him? You didn't. Not yet. It's still your place to do that! You act to the boy like he's weak, good for nothing. How you expect him to trust himself when you don't trust him? Don't you think he knows what you thinking of him? Damn fool! This is your last chance. The blood from your son's wrists will be on your hands, Mr. Fernand. But if you once give him your trust, as my father did me, he may live up to your hopes, as I believe I did to my father's." Stavros stopped. He was flooded with feeling. "Freddie nothing to you," he said. "Give the business to Paul."

"And you? To Paul and to you?" Mr. Fernand completed Stavros's thought.

"I have my own business," Stavros said.

"How much more do you want?"

"Mr. Fernand, you have a terrible mistake in your mind, the idea that every difference between men can be solved by *bazaarlik*—how much money, less, more, and so on."

"That's my experience. Everything is settled by where the money runs."

"Not in my case. I told you how much I wanted and you said no. Finish!"

"Now—how much now?"

"I can make man of your boy," Stavros said. "You have ruin him, but I can save him for you. And I can do something else. I can bring them together again."

"Althea?"

"Yes. I can bring them together."

"How do you know you can?"

"You have to have faith in me now. I not only do that, but I will make her sign the paper Lawyer Wildberg wrote. Maybe you give her little better terms but—"

"I thought that too. Why should we give all that to her mother and nothing to the girl?"

"Did you say 'we'?"

"Yes."

"You have some love in you, I know. You are something like my father. You would do anything for Paul. But you have let that love die. I told you again and again you need me. I can make your business grow. But you must stop trying to get me cheap. You must pay me what I'm worth. I can save your life with Paul which is more important than your business. Isn't it? Yes or no? Say!"

"Yes."

"I can make your son into a man. Which you fail to do. But you have to, in gratitude, pay me what that is worth. Which is your life. Right?"

"More."

"So?"

"And Althea—you can do that, what you said?"

"I have power over her."

"How much you want?" he said as they went over the bridge into the city.

"Forty percent," Stavros said. "And no Freddie."

"Poor Freddie," Mr. Fernand said, and he began to laugh. On and off, most of the way to his house on Sixty-eighth Street, he laughed.

The next morning Stavros saw him again. The old man had had a good night's sleep and seemed less sure he wanted to give up forty percent.

"You change your mind?" Stavros said. "It sounds to me—have you? Yes?"

"No," he said. "But forty percent! That's a lot of money!"

"I warn you, Mr. Sarrafian, if that's what you have on your mind, now or later, I will take Althea away and Paul will never see her again. I can do anything I want with her."

"I thought *I* was arrogant!"

"I was with her yesterday afternoon. You knew that, didn't you?"

"I thought I saw her going into your bedroom. So she stayed there?"

"Althea is not strong girl, morally."

"I know."

"So, once for all, settled? Forty!"

"Poor Freddie," Mr. Fernand said.

"Let's drink to celebrate," Stavros said.

The old man smiled at Stavros. "My partner," he said. "Who would have thought it possible?"

As soon as Paul's face had healed enough so that he could talk easily, father, son, and fiancée met at the hospital. Stavros waited in the hall outside, for the simple reason that he wasn't asked in. Naturally. It had to be an intimate talk. Although he couldn't hear the words, he understood the tone of their voices. Paul's had the ring of authority; he was giving the orders. What used to be petulance was now command. The accident had brought about a change in the man. Mr. Fernand sounded meek, ready to give his son anything he wanted.

"What happen?" Stavros asked Althea as she came out. Talking intently to Mr. Fernand, she gave Stavros a breezy smile and buzzed past. Later she didn't even say goodbye, but rode back to the city with Mr. Fernand; Stavros had to take a taxi, then the train.

It was Mr. Fernand who told Stavros that his son was going to be married the following Sunday. "How he's going to walk to the altar?" Stavros asked. "The ceremony will take place in his room at the hospital," Mr. Fernand said, as though this brilliant idea were his own. "That's the way he wanted it," he added. "He's the boss now. He's going to be a tough partner, Stavros. Remember I said it."

Later he told Stavros something else: Paul had insisted that Althea not sign "any goddamn letter"; he trusted her and a contract was a bad way to start a relationship. And so on. The old man had agreed. It was Althea, grateful for Paul's decision, who insisted that a letter be drawn up for her to sign. "I want your father to be comfortable and happy," she told Paul —all this according to Mr. Fernand. So he did what she wanted, took half away from the mother and gave it the daughter, plus another big bite. Everybody was happy—except Mrs. Perry.

The wedding was celebrated by the Armenian archbishop of that diocese who was carried out to the hospital in Mr. Fernand's Rolls. Another car followed with the paraphernalia for the ceremony. If there was the savor of incense in the hospital corridors that day, Stavros had to imagine it, because he was not invited.

FEBRUARY 1919

Ten days later, Paul was home, walking with a single crutch, and Mr. Fernand suggested they might have their first partnership conference. When Stavros entered Mr. Fernand's private office, Paul was waiting for him, sitting on the far end of the long banquette, and close beside him was his new wife, Althea, sitting, knees together, wearing a navy blue dress with white cuffs and collar. Before them on the small brass-top table was a yellow lined lawyer's pad, on which they had been writing. Well behind them, in a dark corner, was the now familiar figure of William Wildberg.

"I'm so happy to be here with you all," was how Mr. Fernand opened the meeting. He pulled his heavy gold watch out of his vest pocket and looked at it. "Well, let's start."

"What you doing here?" Stavros said to Althea.

"I'm Paul's wife and I'm interested," she said.

"You know something 'bout this business?"

"I want to learn. Do I make you uncomfortable?"

"Sure," Stavros said. He turned to Mr. Fernand. "She meeting here with us?" he asked.

"It's a family gathering," the old man said. "Everything nice. Instead of a regular business meeting."

"I want a regular business meeting first, then family gathering and so on. O.K.?"

"Oh, come, what's the difference? We can talk openly together," Mr. Fernand said.

"What she's writing there?" Stavros asked.

"Why you so touchy today?" Mr. Fernand said.

"Numbers," Althea said.

"Tell me, Mr. Fernand," Stavros said, "your idea. To let these two people here and Freddie run this end of the business? What's the matter —this girl got you soft in the head?"

"What's *your* idea?"

"I explain to you, but not here."

Stavros looked at Paul, expecting a quarrel, ready for one. But Paul seemed totally affable. "I asked her here," he said. "Please go along with it."

"Don't make a big thing of it, Joe," the old man said.

"What are those numbers you writing, Althea?" Stavros said. "Tell me that much."

"Some figures," Paul said.

"We're seeing how many different ways one hundred can be divided," Althea said.

"Paul can't do that without you?"

"He can, but—"

"I give you tip, make it easy. Take out forty percent for me, then divide up sixty any way you want."

"Paul is my husband," Althea said. "He's bighearted and he's innocent. All his life people have been taking advantage of him. I'm going to see to it that he's not taken again. Even by you."

"You're good wife," Stavros said.

"I hope so," she said.

Freddie came into the office. "Sorry," he said. "We got held up." In the doorway behind him, stood Maud.

"Hello, Maud," Stavros called out. "Bring her in, Freddie. This is family gathering, not business meeting."

"Oh, no. Maud—really? Mr. Fernand?"

"He's joking. Close the door, Freddie. This is a business meeting."

"That's right," Stavros said. "I see that now." He walked behind

Althea and leaned over and looked at the pad. "What's that number, that one there, Althea?"

"Twenty," she said.

"Who gets that?"

"Now, that's enough quizzing, Stavros. I was just speculating."

"Mr. Fernand," Stavros said, "you sitting there like a Buddha. What you say to that twenty? You speculating too? Is that for me, Althea? Says here twenty—whose idea is that, Mr. Fernand?"

"Well, I would really like to have it explained to me," Althea said, "why you should get forty percent and Paul, whose money it is—or is going to be one day—should get whatever, and Freddie, who's been here faithfully year after year, and especially these last years, when you—"

"All right, Mr. Fernand," Stavros said, "explain to the lady."

"She's just speculating," Mr. Fernand said.

"With my money," Stavros said. "Now come on, sir, Buddha, tell her that you agreed. Didn't you agree to forty?"

"Did I?" Mr. Fernand said. "I don't remember."

"What's the matter your memory—you getting old?"

"All I said was: 'Poor Freddie!'—excuse me, Freddie. That's all I said —'Poor Freddie.' "

"Now I got the situation," Stavros said, looking from one to the other. "Althea, she knows us all—well! She's Paul's wife. She knows me well. And, originally, Freddie. She knows what each of us is worth and what each of us can do. So she decides what the numbers will be, because of inside information—right, Althea?"

"Don't be insulting," she said. "There's no need for that."

"So now, along with everything else, she's our business partner, is that it, boys? Paul? Freddie? Is that it, Althea? Speak up!"

No one spoke up.

"We were going to have a civilized chat," Mr. Fernand said. "Why ruffle your feathers? We're all friends here. Let's come to an amicable agreement."

"Let's not," Stavros said. He got up. "Have your meeting without me," he said, and walked out of the office. On the way to the front of the store, he passed Maud, bent over a magazine, and said to her, "Why aren't you in there, protecting Freddie? Hurry up—he needs you."

On the corner of Twenty-fifth Street and Broadway was a bar the rug trade fancied. He had the first drink alone. Oh, how he wanted to go back home to Anatolia, where you could tell when a man wanted to rob you because he showed you his knife or pulled the pistol out of his belt! And where women stayed in the kitchen! He hadn't been home in twenty-two years. Well, soon he would be.

He had another drink. The younger merchants of the neighborhood

were getting in early for lunch—eleven-forty, the clock behind the bar said
—and to catch them, perhaps make a couple of bucks before the sun set,
there were some of the local girls. It was dark in the bar so they didn't look
bad, but Stavros knew them well and how they'd look in the light. He
counted four ass peddlers there and he'd sampled them all. The ugliest and
the oldest of them was called Caroline, but she was also the best-natured
and she got plenty of play because of that. Caroline! If you met her in a
nunnery, all decked out in black, you'd still know, instantly, what she was.

"Come on, Caroline," Stavros said. "You don't have to look further."

"Thanks, Joe. Buy me a drink," she said. "I had a bad night. Out-of-
towners, they're the worst. They come here for only one night away from
their wives, angry as hell, and they take it out on us. Look." She tipped
her head to a light and showed Stavros a black eye.

"Looks good on you, Caroline," Stavros said.

They had a drink, then another, and they both felt better.

"I have to meet my brother tonight and wanted to look good," she said.
"You'll take it easy on me, won't you, Joe?"

"Nothing but the best," Stavros said.

"He's back, my brother Willie. Remember I told you about him?"

"No," Stavros said.

"He was gassed in the Argonne. Spent seven months in a French
hospital, but they didn't do him any good. He still has terrible trouble
breathing. He's marching in the big parade Sunday. But I don't know how.
He keeps holding his chest, like this. How come you were never in the
army, Joe?"

"Anatolian people don't believe in fighting; we believe in running and
hiding."

She laughed. "Smart," she said. "Lousy Greeks are smart!"

Stavros ordered two more shots. The barware was made of thick glass
—but Stavros had had five and they were getting to him.

Caroline was silent now. Stavros looked at her and saw she was crying.
"Poor Willie," she said. "Coughs all the time."

"I realize," Stavros said, "I owe this country everything. Everything!"

"Same here," Caroline said. She leaned against him.

"You didn't have a bath this morning," Stavros said.

"Came right from the Bristol Hotel—that's where these men—how did
you know? Do I smell?"

"Yes," Stavros said.

A man was tapping his shoulder. It was Garabet, the Sarrafian repairman. "Big boss send me to get you," he said.

"Tell him to come down here," Stavros said. He ordered another
drink, and one for Caroline.

"Please, Joe, he'll fire me. He say don't come back without you."

"Have a drink, Garabet."

"No. Come on, please, they waiting for you. If he smells I been drinking . . . You can get away with that, not me."

"How did you know I was down here?"

"Mr. Fernand said he can read your face. Please, Joe, come on."

"All right." He put his drink down. "Drink up, Caroline. You're going with me."

"Where? Where we going?"

"To a board meeting."

"What the hell you doing?" Garabet said.

"Caroline is good businesswoman," Stavros said. "She'll protect me so they don't take advantage. Come on, Caroline, *embros!*"

"Let me go in there and fix up a little."

"No. I like you the way you are."

On the way, Stavros gave Caroline her orders. "All you got to do is, I nod my head like this, you say, 'Forty.' Forty! Got it?"

"Forty," she said. "Oh, Joe, you're so wonderful."

Stavros introduced her carefully around the room. "This is my old, good friend, Caroline," he said. "She going to advise me, business matters."

They looked at her as if she were carrying the plague.

"Sit down here, dear," Stavros said. "Move over, Althea."

"I get your idea," Althea said, moving over. "But I am not leaving this meeting." She looked at Paul.

"Now let's talk terms," Stavros said. Then, crossing his arms, he nodded at Caroline.

"Forty," she said.

"That your advice?" Stavros asked her. Then he nodded again.

"Forty," she said.

"You see, ladies and gentlemen, Caroline is here to advise me. We can meet with advisers or without. Whichever. If with—well, you heard what Caroline said. And that's her firm opinion." Stavros nodded.

"Forty," Caroline said. More confident now, she spoke firmly and boldly, then nodded back at Stavros.

Suddenly Althea got up and left the room. Maud followed her.

Stavros gave Caroline ten dollars and she went too.

"Now, Freddie, go out with the ladies," Stavros said. "Come on, Freddie, if you hope for anything good from me ever in the future. Freddie —go!"

Freddie left the room. Stavros stood up, swaying. He had to hold on to the table.

"Paul," he said, "I'm sorry I had to do this. Talk business with a woman? Can't do it. Mr. Fernand, forgive me. But I am only person here who has seen rug on a loom. No one else here knows anything 'bout this business. College education and so forth, but rugs? Nothing!" Abruptly, he sat down.

Stavros saw that Mr. Fernand had enjoyed the little drama he'd put on. The old Armenian smiled at him. Anyone could tell how much he liked him.

"Paul," Mr. Fernand said, "Mr. Topouzoglou and I came to an agreement a few days ago, the one he reminded us of. I agreed to forty percent. I think now that's high, but I also think he's worth it. He does know the business. That would leave you—once I take care of Freddie—maybe fifty percent. So you'd be boss—"

"Nobody's boss, sir. Sir! We agreed to that too. Paul and I equal! I'm drunk, right, but my memory doesn't go when I drink, only my legs. So I won't stand up again. Forty me, forty Paul. Now talk the other twenty." Stavros wanted that for his brother, Seraphim. "Half the time, next few years, I'll be in Asia Minor," he said. "Paul is fine man, I like Paul O.K., but he doesn't know the business. Adviser he has—what? Althea? She should make you grandson, Mr. Fernand, quick! Let's see if she can do that, not bother us here. Sorry, gentlemen, time to tell the truth. Freddie? Too nice! Has weak stomach, how can I trust him to fight for me—or for the business. Also, he has wife who is boss. So I want my brother Seraphim; I want him here. To be store manager. He knows this business perfect! Ten percent for Seraphim."

"Five!" Mr. Fernand said. "Fifteen for Freddie. Sounds better."

Later Stavros remembered how he'd felt that day. Nobody could deny him anything that day because he knew that everything he said was right. But when Mr. Fernand said that Freddie should have fifteen and Seraphim five, Stavros had agreed. He didn't have to, but he did.

Stavros was glad he wasn't the one who had to tell Althea. Or Maud.

"You are now business partner, Sarrafian Brothers," Stavros said to his brother Seraphim, who was sitting by the fire escape window in the dining room, reading the *Globe*. "Five percent profits."

He'd stolen into the house, as usual, approached the dining room unobserved, thrown the news at Seraphim casually, then proceeded to Vasso, who was clenched in her wooden armchair, a human knot. There was no medical explanation for her survival. It was simply willpower; she refused to die.

Seraphim lowered the evening paper, but otherwise didn't respond. Eleni, who was at the table composing her daily letter to Achilleas, quickly covered up what she'd been writing. Fofo appeared in the doorway from the kitchen, where she and Silo had been doing the supper dishes. Only Demo, who'd been enjoying a Havana in the chair at the window opposite his mother—it was one of his rare visits home—immediately understood the importance of the news. He bounded to his feet.

"Just Seraphim?" he demanded. "That the best you could do?"

Stavros bent over his mother and kissed her hands.

"For instance, what do I get out of this?" Demo said; he strode into the dining room to Seraphim.

"What happens to our store now?" Stavros heard Fofo ask.

There was a hush; they were consulting in whispers.

"Like I always told you, Mommah, now I'm going," Stavros said to the old woman. He sat on the stool in front of her and held her feet in his lap. "Anatolia, I'm coming!" Stavros said. "America, finished! I will make my life there now, get married—no girl yet, don't worry—find nice home looking on the harbor, like your father's place. Then I bring you over. You believe me now?"

The old woman gave this question some thought. "I have to," she said. Her voice was faint. "What else I got? But here's the problem. I can't go there until"—she thrust out her hand—"See! My teeth?" She was holding them. "Don't fit inside anymore."

"How many times I told them get Mother new teeth!"

"You know what they think." She gestured to him to lean close. "Dead woman don't need new teeth," she whispered.

"I tell them again."

"They don't pay attention. When you're not here, they have their own ideas."

There were sounds of conflict from the dining room.

"Why Seraphim yelling on Demo?" the old lady asked.

"Other way, Mommah. Demo hollering."

"Since you left here," the old lady said, *"chattr pattr, chattr pattr* all the time. Fighting every day. These people need Turkish *agha* with big stick."

Fofo stomped into the front room on her flat-heeled shoes. "We start business here together," she said, "put our lives inside. First you leave, now you take Seraphim?"

Demo came next, thrusting his hands toward the east. "You mean you will buy goods in Anatolia, that your idea, and then—" his hands swung to the west—"send them here to our competitors?" Turning to the dining room, he spoke with the voice of command he'd learned in the army. "Nothing doing, Seraphim. Absolutely not! Forget this idea!"

"So tell us who's going to look after the business now?" Fofo said. "What's your idea about that?"

"Not my problem," Stavros said.

"Not your problem!" Fofo screamed. "Are you our brother?"

"Talk to Demo," Stavros said. "He's boss now."

"Shame on you," Eleni said. "You forget your family! Shame! Shame!"

The old lady leaned forward from her crouched position and hissed at her children. "Ssssut! *Beerahk beezi!* Out from here!"

"How much you getting, leaving us like this?" Demo called from the dining room.

"Plenty!" Stavros said, smiling at his mother.

"If you take Seraphim—" Fofo started to say.

"That's up to him," Stavros said. "But he's not damn fool."

"You're trying to ruin us!" Fofo said.

Eleni came right up to Stavros. "Our father, watching in heaven, will not forgive you for this!" For some reason Eleni was the most venomous of them all.

The old lady spat at her—"Ptuh!"—then, *"Ghet burdan!* You, Eleni! Out! Go sit in toilet!"

Vasso looked so ferocious that they all retreated into the dining room and turned on Seraphim.

"You see damn woman like that Eleni?" the old lady said to Stavros. "Sure her husband leave her, she can't even make a good yogurt!"

"Her yogurt O.K., Mommah," Stavros said. "Her husband left her because he was far away and needed a woman there."

"He left her because she can't cook!" Vasso said. "Now listen to me." Anger had quickened her pulse. "You have to fix me up new teeth before I get on the boat. These teeth finished!"

"Sure thing, Mommah."

"When you going?"

"Three weeks."

"Take me to damn tooth doctor first. I can't go back like this."

"I promise."

"That's why I worry, because you promise. How many times you promise and nothing happen? I don't want to call you liar, boy, so never mind promise, bring out money here, then I believe you."

Stavros brought out a roll of bills and pulled free five twenties. "Here," he said. "Hundred dollars. Don't lose it."

Vasso took the money. Her hand, disappearing under her clothing, came out empty. "Where I put money," she said, "nobody looking nowdays."

Stavros, of course, had no plan to take her to a dentist; like the others, he believed it was too late for new teeth. But he was pleased to have made her happy, it was worth a hundred dollars to hear her snickering as she looked scornfully into the other room where her children were arguing angrily.

Now the sounds of contention quickened. Seraphim had told them he intended to take the job. "My share company," he said, "divide her up. For you!"

"I'm going to sue you!" Demo said. "You have a contract with us at the Anatolian Carpet Company."

"What kind contract I got?" Seraphim asked.

"Verbal!" Demo shouted. "You are destroying our business!"

"Traitor!" Fofo screamed. "Leaving your family for few dollars."

"I'm going to sue him!" Demo vowed. "Don't worry, Fofo!"

"Betrayer!" Fofo said. "Judas!"

"Shshsh! Fofo!" Silo was heard for the first time. "He's your brother, Fofo, God's sake!"

"You shshsh!" Fofo turned on her husband. "What the hell you know about this family?"

"You preferring those Armenians to your own family?" Eleni demanded of Seraphim. "Those Armenians with their whores? You will become like Stavros!"

"May disaster hit you and your Sarrafians!" Fofo said. "Anathema!"

"Don't worry! I will take away every customer he has, guarantee," Demo said to Fofo. "He'll be left with an empty store when I get through with him."

"Shame on all of you," Silo said. "Talking your brother that way. Tst-tst-tst!"

"Don't make that tst-tst-tst on me, Mr. Silo," Fofo said. "Shut your stupid mouth here!"

There was a sharp sound, a slap. Fofo screamed, then she was sobbing. The front door slammed.

"I think Silo left," Stavros said to his mother. "He hit Fofo and left."

"Good!" The old lady laughed her toothless laugh. "Eleni!" she called out. "Bring here piece your yogurt, let's see."

Stavros finally liberated Seraphim, leading him out of the apartment in search of a place where they might talk quietly. Eleni ran down the stairs after them. She held a package the size of a book in her hands. "Stavros! Stop!" she called, out of breath. "You do something for me, Stavros, eh? Maybe?" she asked, her voice angry despite the fact that she wanted a favor. "These are letters I wrote Achilleas, everything that happened last months." She bit her lip and went on. "Something's wrong with the postal service," she complained. "I wrote so many letters, and he's not receiving them. So please, will you"—she still hadn't looked at him—"put these new ones in his hands. Directly in his hands?"

"How you know he wasn't getting your letters?" Stavros asked.

"Because I don't get answers," she said. "Tell him I'm fine, true, and faithful, and that I'm waiting for him day and night." She thrust the package into Stavros's hands and turned to mount the stairs, her back erect and defiant.

True she was waiting, Stavros thought, and she certainly was faithful, but fine? Her chest now was as flat as her back and the lines around her eyes had deepened; they wouldn't soften again, nor would her turned-down mouth. He remembered the soft-skinned, soft-eyed girl who'd arrived in America ten years before. The prettiest of them all she'd been that day, her skin the most delicate olive, lightly brushed with rose; that day, she'd been a beauty.

MARCH 1919

It was now generally understood that the Greek army had been given the privilege by the Allies—the English, the French, and the Italians—of invading Anatolia, but the exact date was not yet known. Stavros planned his own invasion to come at exactly the same time—when the country was in a state of chaos. His plan was to send Michaelis as soon as possible to the island of Chios, to get the feel of the situation, organize their little expedition, and wait for him there. They'd go into Smyrna the day after the Greek army landed.

They were all so busy with new arrangements and alignments that Morgan Perry's death took them by surprise. He died in his sleep, alone in his house in Mount Ivy, on the maid's night out. Mrs. Perry was playing bridge with friends. Her husband's death, she assured Mr. Fernand the next day, had been comfortable; Morgan had been on the edge for weeks, and had simply slipped over.

Stavros decided to go to the funeral. No one wept, not Mrs. Perry, not Althea, not Mr. Fernand. They'd worn out their grief, waiting for the end. Stavros felt they should not have exhibited the body. Two hundred and twenty pounds had come down to one hundred and forty. As Stavros walked up to the casket, he remembered how Morgan Perry used to speak to him:

"You Greeks with olive oil in your veins instead of blood," he used to say, "you come here to see what you can get out of us, you and those other Mediterranean niggers. You grab what you can, then go back with our money. Make it here, spend it there; take everything, give nothing. Tell me what you've given this country? I know what you've taken—I pay you every Saturday. It's our generosity against your greed. Not just you, it's all the damn immigrants. But especially the Greeks, you're the worst. No wonder everybody in this country dislikes and distrusts you."

Stavros used to resent it, but now a strange thing happened. As he passed the open coffin, he looked at Morgan Perry's face and it was still accusing him. The eyelids were open a crack and Stavros thought he saw the scornful eyes underneath. And he felt that the man's accusation was justified.

Late that night, he decided to leave a token of thanks behind when he left America.

The next day was the victory parade of the Expeditionary Force. Stavros and Garabet put the nine-by-twelve silk Keshan into a taxi, took it to the arch through which the soldiers would be marching, and spread it out. Later they stood by, Michaelis and Stavros, Eleni and Fofo, Silo and Seraphim, even Vartan, the touch-up artist and Garabet the repairman— all Stavros could gather of his band of immigrants—reviewing the soldiers marching in their hobnail boots. Among the marchers was Demo, looking like what he was not, a soldier.

Stavros watched the Keshan being flailed apart, the tiny bits of bright silk ground loose and flying in the wind, and he felt no regret. When the parade was over, there was nothing there but a colorless web.

The next morning, Mr. Fernand told Stavros that they were stopping in England on their way to the Near East. "I want to make sure that if we invest what we are about to invest—I'm speaking about both Sarrafian Brothers and my other concerns—I want to make sure the British are behind us and will remain there."

"Last time I saw Aylesworth," Stavros said, "I ask him same question. He said absolutely not to worry; the British, he said, always keep their promises."

"He gave me that assurance too," Mr. Fernand said. "But I'd prefer to have it from a cabinet officer, someone near the top. You'll come with me. I think you'll be happier with what you're about to do if you're certain that the British navy is offshore with its sixteen-inchers, and their supplies are coming to the Greek army in a steady stream. Don't you think?"

"I'm here to say goodbye, Paul," Stavros said, coming through the door. The curtain of beads had been taken away; Mr. Fernand had surrendered his office to his son, and Paul, with Althea's help, was having it completely redone.

"My father, God save him," Paul said as Stavros was looking around at all the changes, "says he'd be content in a mud-brick hut in the Armenian district of Erzerum where he was born. But I know better. He prefers the Ritz Hotel. I also suspect that his origins were not humble, not at all, they were rather genteel, I'd guess. He hasn't known discomfort any more than I have. At any rate, as you see, we've let in the light and the air. Outside the windows he'd covered up with—what are they called?"

"Kilims."

"Thank you. Kilims. Outside, I found this remarkable view, this massive city of business, quite chaotic after London, but so dynamic. Althea came herself—you may have seen her—and ripped away the . . . kilims, right?" Stavros nodded. "The kilims off the walls. 'Replace these wire-glass windows,' she commanded, 'with clear panes.' " He laughed at the memory. "She also suggested that I replace Father's long banquettes—she's out buying new furnishings for me this minute. She did decide to keep these long tables covered with mosaic tiles; they are handsome, aren't they?"

"Very nice, very nice," Stavros said.

"Well, then—so goodbye," Paul said. "For a while. I've enjoyed our talks so much. But we'll be seeing each other in not too long. As soon as things are secure in Smyrna we'll be turning up. Father's partners in his oil interests have a yacht, and on our way to Beirut, where Father has some investment problems— He's such a busy old bugger, isn't he? Althea's finally taught me to appreciate his energy; it used to frighten me. Oh, yes, we'll be stopping off in Smyrna and see how you're getting along and if we might be of any help. I've had some good talks with your brother Sam —such a decent man! I believe I have him and Freddie organized to carry on here so I can leave for a while."

This sounded presumptuous to Stavros, coming from such a newcomer, but all he said was "Give my regards to Mrs. Sarrafian, your wife. She certainly got you looking good."

"I've never been so happy," Paul said. "That little problem you were witness to in Southampton has completely healed over just like my face. She's determined that we be close as the knots of a fine Kerman carpet. Notice what I said? And I know how many too: eighty knots to the square inch! Althea insists that I learn my new trade from loom to sales floor. She says—the little minx—that I've wasted my life until now and that it's about time I grew up and took my place as a man. Imagine that!" He laughed. "She's so full of energy and curiosity," Paul went on—and now he looked a little worried. "Besides helping me with this office, she's taking all kinds of lessons: watercolors and piano and Lord knows what else. She's out of the apartment all day, rushing somewhere or other. You saw her?"

"Here. She looks beautiful. You're lucky man."

"I know it! Confidentially—may I?—It seems we'll be producing a child—this is her estimate—in October."

"Congratulations! Every good wish."

"That has brought us so close. We go everywhere together. She has to know where I am every moment of the day. Against her doctor's advice, she insists she'll come to Beirut with me on the boat. Did she tell you that?"

"Haven't talked to her. Well, again, every good wish, and now goodbye."

"I'll walk you to the door. Althea says I can learn more about the rug trade—quality, prices, color, dyes, the competition—from you than from anybody. She has such respect for you. You must have had some very good talks."

"Nothing special."

"She has the highest respect. Knows all about your family."

"My brother Seraphim—Sam—you can learn more from him. And now, here's the door."

"Yes, your brother is a fine man. By the time we get to Smyrna, I assure you you'll find me much more knowledgeable. I must tell you, Stavros, that it's profoundly embarrassing to me, my position in this firm—the owner's son and so on, brought in as I was, being carried, so to speak, by Freddie and Sam and"—his face darkened—"above all by you. It's humiliating, it makes me quite crazy."

"Don't feel that way. No use."

"I must learn everything there is to know, Althea says, then I'll feel better about my place here."

"There's not so much to know. So here we are. Goodbye."

"Be patient with my ignorance, won't you?" Paul said. "And when I ask stupid questions. A kilim—I learned that, anyway!" He laughed nervously, then stretched out his hand. "Be my friend," he said. "Of course you are, I know you are, but . . ."

As Stavros walked away, he thought *October* and began to make a simple mathematical computation. Then he abandoned it all to fate. "As the Turks say," he advised himself, "it's all kismet. Whatever comes will come. Besides, it's too late now."

A week later Stavros sailed for Europe with Mr. Fernand on the *Berengaria.* First class. In London, Mr. Fernand made a date for them with an under secretary of the Admiralty.

The lunch meeting took place at a restaurant called the Buttery. Their guest was exhausted, yawned every half minute. Finally, over a gooseberry tart covered with thick dairy cream, Mr. Fernand asked the question. "Is your navy now definitely committed to oil-burning vessels?"

The guest said it was. "We are no longer building coal burners," he said.

"Which means that you have to secure the sources of oil, wherever they are in the world?" Mr. Fernand said.

"Yes."

"Which means that everything east of Constantinople until perhaps India has to be under the control of your land and sea forces?"

"Precisely," the man said.

"Which, by a final process of deduction," Mr. Fernand said, "would lead me to believe that you would require a friendly and, if possible, a Christian power to control the littoral of Asia Minor?"

"If you are referring to the Greeks, yes." He looked at Stavros, studied him for a moment. "I believe they are Christians," he said. It was an English joke, spoken without smiling.

"Which means," Mr. Fernand went on, "that you will cover their landing when it takes place?"

"That is our plan."

"When will it be?"

"Late spring."

"When?"

"The date is not being revealed. For obvious reasons."

"But you will cover it, the landing, with your sea power?"

"I said yes."

"Can I have assurance on these facts?"

"I gave you my word. Do you want more than that?"

Mr. Fernand hesitated just long enough to make the pause meaningful.

They spent a week in England and at the end of it, Mr. Fernand assured Stavros that he had in hand certain assurances executed in writing. "They're not worth the paper they're written on," he said. "No politician's word in a democracy is worth anything, since they are open to dismissal at any time. But I am convinced that our interests in that part of the world are identical with theirs, so I am satisfied."

Stavros said that he was too, and three days later they took the train to Dover, crossed a very rough sea to Calais, and from there took the train to another cold-damp city and moved into the Ritz Hotel on the Place Vendôme.

"The English are comparatively trustworthy," Mr. Fernand said. "The farther south you go, the less you should trust the governments or even the people. France is halfway to Italy," he continued. "And you know what the Italians are."

There was a series of legal meetings at which innumerable documents were signed. "The more papers you are asked to sign, the less the accord can be trusted," Mr. Fernand said.

Stavros got tired of the meetings and walked about the wonderful city of light. Mr. Fernand provided him with suitable companionship for evening entertainment and sometimes Stavros prolonged his pleasure into the morning and on until lunch. After ten days—a long weekend was lost, the French were not to be hurried—Mr. Fernand showed Stavros a portfolio of documents and again said he was satisfied.

The next morning he told Stavros they might as well go on to Italy, although a promise from an Italian was worthless. Stavros wondered what one was to think of Mr. Fernand's promises—his country was even farther south. "They've already moved into the Dodecanese," Mr. Fernand said. "And with the port of Antalya on the southern coast unprotected . . . You might as well trust an artist in love as an Italian in politics. By the way, who is that new friend of Althea's?"

"I don't know," Stavros said. "Has she a new friend?"

"So it would seem," Mr. Fernand said. "An Italian, a painter."

"How do you know?"

"Everything can be purchased, including information. I am going to have a very serious talk with that young woman next time I see her. Do you think, my expert in this field, that leopards change their spots?"

Stavros decided to defend his friend. "Althea is very sincere about Paul," he said.

Later, with another of the companions Mr. Fernand provided, Stavros grew bitterly melancholy. It was their last night in Paris and he was glad to be leaving. He drank too much, and was alternately disagreeable and silent with the woman. What was wrong? He knew. It was the hint that Althea might already be seeing someone not her husband. A painter? Watercolor lessons? Why hadn't he taken her up on her suggestion that they run off together? For a week, she'd said. A week!

And she'd said she would have married him—once. Did he want that? Marry her? Never!

Still, here he was with women who irritated him—heavy-limbed, flabby, oily, overused. He missed Althea's whiteness, her clean light skin, her clear green eyes, her light sweet smell.

And her. He missed Althea.

When should he have spoken? Should he have spoken?

No. Forget her!

He told the woman to leave.

"You don't want me again?" she said. "You don't fancy me?" It was all a whore's act.

"I prefer someone else," Stavros said, and paid her off.

Stavros liked Rome—when it stopped raining. Word came from Seraphim that the check from Mr. Fernand had cleared and they now had a great deal of money—$100,000—to invest in Anatolia. Seraphim said he was sending Stavros letters of credit and also, through Efstathis, who was on his way to join them in Chios, a great deal of cash—pounds, francs, lire —but also gold: Gold was the best, gold coins. They should be immediately lodged in Michaelis's belt. There were few places Stavros could imagine safer than Michaelis's belt.

In Rome Mr. Fernand and Stavros parted company. The old man's last words were: "Now tell me the truth. You haven't been suffering from *chagrin d'amour* because Althea Perry is married to your partner, have you?"

"They have my blessing," Stavros said. "Soon as I set up our office in Smyrna, and my looms in the interior, I will do the right thing myself."

"What would that be?" Mr. Fernand asked with a cynical smile, imply-
ing that if there was one thing Stavros was incapable of, it was doing the
right thing. "I didn't know you had any ethical impulses."

"I am going to marry one of ours," Stavros said. "A girl of my own
country."

"Are you sure that will be the solution to your life? Are you sure you
will be satisfied with the married life?"

"I'm sure," Stavros said.

He made the journey to Athens by slow stages. He'd found a North
Italian lady, a bottle blonde, who liked to travel by day and fuck by night.
And since there was no way he could move into Anatolia before the Greek
army landed in Smyrna in May—the date was now fixed—he had to find
ways to pass the time. *Kef!* Makes you forget! So Stavros moved slowly
and pleasurably rather than speedily and anxiously. Yes, perhaps the last
of *kef*.

The sun's first yellow glow woke him. The cabin window was to the
east and there, dark beneath the rising golden sphere, was the somber land.
On the deck a sailor told him it was not Anatolia but the small island of
Oinousai; they'd passed the northern point of Chios, Cape Vamvakas, and
were entering the strait between that island and the Bay of Smyrna.

Stavros headed for the prow. The weight of the ship lifted under him,
then dropped into a void of water. His body tensed as if alerting to danger.
The swagger with which he'd affronted the world for so many years was
gone now, the strut and the old flamboyance. Facing the unknown, he was
humbled.

When he reached the prow, the wind had freshened and the point of
the heaving ship was flinging up spray. Recalling a day twenty years
before, he did nothing to shield himself from the wet; it was the North
Atlantic then, kicking up sea, and he was coming into a new land. That
day he'd promised himself, his face and hair water-soaked, that America
would wash him clean.

Had it? Here he was again, seeking redemption, throwing himself at
the land where he'd been born and raised, to help redeem it and so redeem
himself. That was his hope and his faith.

The cool, clean spray made his skin tingle as if beads were striking
him, hard little pellets. It never occurred to Stavros that it might be too
late.

"For seven years I've been away from my country"—so went the old
song popular among the hamals in those years long gone. "I didn't look
for someone to share my worries. If one day you will follow me, ask only
your heart where I am."

Now there it was! He could see Anatolia, the dark land, huddled under the eastern sky. He turned to go down into his cabin and pack his bag. "Forget her," he said to himself. "Find yourself a woman here."

The steamer turned slowly in place, heavy in the water, until it faced the opening of the breakwater across the harbor of Chios. Stavros was back where his father had died, and where he'd been born.

Had he fulfilled his father's charges? He remembered only a few of the words, but all of the old man's severity. "In time you will bring your three sisters out. As the eldest, it is your responsibility to see that they marry well." His sisters? Yes, they were married, and considering everything, he'd fulfilled that charge reasonably well.

"Then, as your business prospers, you will bring your four brothers out and to your side. As the eldest, it is your responsibility to set them up in business." His brothers—two of them—were in business; yes, his father may have been satisfied with this too.

"Then it will be your mother's turn!" His father's last charge. "It is your responsibility to make her final days happy ones." Happy! Had they been? Hardly. Her wits were so scattered now, how could anyone tell what she felt? Still, there was a chance, however thin, that he'd be able to give that gnarled old stump of a woman the only thing left that she wanted, to die in Anatolia.

Seeing Michaelis waiting on the dock, Stavros waved, then picked up his bag—a handsome British steerhide valise with buckles of brass, a present from Mr. Fernand.

Yes, he'd come back in good form, with a plan and the money to carry it out, and—this certainly would have pleased his father—unencumbered by the wrong wife. All in all, he'd accomplished what he had been sent to accomplish. His father would have been proud of this model of a successful entrepreneur, elegantly dressed and in the full vigor of life, who walked down the gangplank.

The brothers strolled through the community of homes and kaffenions around the harbor. Stavros smelled the East. Parts of Athens had something of the same odor, but Athens was West. Here the pressure on the nostrils was heavier. The open fires browning lambs' entrails, the sewers opening into the harbor water, the corruption of rotting fish along the water's edge—all of it told Stavros that he was back in another part of the world. Asia.

Michaelis and Efstathis were housed in a narrow three-story house poised at the edge of the sea. From the terrace they could look across a great weight of water to the continent opposite. The land closest was a peninsula ending in a massive promontory whose face was shaded from the morning sun rising behind it. Receding away and down to the east, most of the peninsula caught rays of light, but the part directly opposite was the dark, forbidding cliff of Cesme. Stavros had reached his objective and it was awesome. Even now, with the sea softened by a blue haze, the mass before him—that long black cliff—was formidable, a true symbol of his task.

Then he had a vision. He saw his father's body lying in state under the great promontory—an immense figure it was, as long as the cliff above. The apparition, as he imagined it, seemed at ease, laid out in its ceremonial posture: Isaac Topouzoglou on his back, face to heaven, hands folded devoutly in front of him. He seemed to be saying, "Come! I've been waiting for you."

It was more, Stavros decided, than a single great figure; it represented every Anatolian Greek waiting to be redeemed. And it was time for him to do his small part. He felt strangely ennobled by the difficulty of the task, but he also felt fear. Would he be up to the charge he'd given himself?

Now the surface of the water between the island and the mainland stirred, the wind ruffling the water into tiny flashing triangles.

"It's the *melteme,*" Michaelis said. "Comes up every morning out of a sky without clouds, blows stronger as the day goes on, until at sunset it dies down and is still, waiting like us for morning."

He gestured toward a figure at the far end of the terrace, where the winter waves had undercut and collapsed the edge. A man in uniform was looking at the shore opposite through field glasses. "The army," Michaelis whispered, "they're here. In two weeks—two, or three, no one will say exactly when—we will be seeing great ships of war, flying the flags of many nations, steaming toward the harbor of Smyrna and, following them, troop transports carrying our army."

The officer walked up to them and Michaelis introduced his brother. The man in uniform bowed courteously. "Michaelis tells me you're going to follow us in," he said. "Here—want a look? They still have their soldiers there."

Stavros thanked him, took the glasses, and lifted them to his eyes.

And he saw Anatolia. Unredeemed.

A NOTE ON THE TYPE

This book was set via computer-driven cathode-ray tube
in Janson, a redrawing of type cast from matrices long
thought to have been made by the Dutchman Anton
Janson, who was a practicing type founder in Leipzig
during the years 1668–87. However, it has been
conclusively demonstrated that these types are actually
the work of Nicholas Kis (1650–1702), a Hungarian, who
most probably learned his trade from the master Dutch
type founder Dirk Voskens. The type is an excellent
example of the influential and sturdy Dutch types that
prevailed in England up to the time William Caslon
developed his own incomparable designs from them.

Composed, printed, and bound by
The Haddon Craftsmen, Inc., Scranton, Pennsylvania

Designed by Al Chiang